**Late Last Night
and the Night Before . . .**

THE TOMMYKNOCKERS

*. . . Tommyknockers, tommyknockers,
knocking at the door.*

Something was happening in Bobbi Anderson's idyllic small town of Haven, Maine. Something that gave every man, woman, and child in town powers far beyond ordinary mortals. Something that turned the town into a death trap for all outsiders. Something that came from a metal object, buried for millennia, that Bobbi stumbled across.

It wasn't that Bobbi and the other good folks of Haven had sold their souls to reap the rewards of the most deadly evil this side of hell. It was more like a diabolical takeover . . . and invasion of body and soul—and mind.

"King at his best."
—*San Francisco Chronicle*

WORKS BY STEPHEN KING

NOVELS

Carrie
'Salem's Lot
The Shining
The Stand
The Dead Zone
Firestarter
Cujo
THE DARK TOWER I:
The Gunslinger
Christine
Pet Sematary
Cycle of the Werewolf
The Talisman
(with Peter Straub)
It
The Eyes of the Dragon
Misery
The Tommyknockers
THE DARK TOWER II:
The Drawing of the Three
THE DARK TOWER III:
The Waste Lands
The Dark Half
Needful Things
Gerald's Game
Dolores Claiborne
Insomnia
Rose Madder
Desperation
The Green Mile
THE DARK TOWER IV:
Wizard and Glass
Bag of Bones
The Girl Who Loved Tom Gordon
Dreamcatcher
Black House
(with Peter Straub)
From a Buick 8
THE DARK TOWER V:
Wolves of the Calla
THE DARK TOWER VI:
Song of Susannah
THE DARK TOWER VII:
The Dark Tower

AS RICHARD BACHMAN

Rage
The Long Walk
Roadwork
The Running Man
Thinner
The Regulators

COLLECTIONS

Night Shift
Different Seasons
Skeleton Crew
Four Past Midnight
Nightmares and Dreamscapes
Hearts in Atlantis
Everything's Eventual

NONFICTION

Danse Macabre
On Writing

SCREENPLAYS

Creepshow
Cat's Eye
Silver Bullet
Maximum Overdrive
Pet Sematary
Golden Years
Sleepwalkers
The Stand
The Shining
Rose Red
Storm of the Century

The Tommyknockers

Stephen King

A SIGNET BOOK

SIGNET
Published by New American Library, a division of
Penguin Group (USA) Inc., 375 Hudson Street,
New York, New York 10014, USA
Penguin Group (Canada), 10 Alcorn Avenue, Toronto,
Ontario M4V 3B2, Canada (a division of Pearson Penguin Canada Inc.)
Penguin Books Ltd., 80 Strand, London WC2R 0RL, England
Penguin Ireland, 25 St. Stephen's Green, Dublin 2,
Ireland (a division of Penguin Books Ltd.)
Penguin Group (Australia), 250 Camberwell Road, Camberwell, Victoria 3124,
Australia (a division of Pearson Australia Group Pty. Ltd.)
Penguin Books India Pvt. Ltd., 11 Community Centre, Panchsheel Park,
New Delhi - 110 017, India
Penguin Group (NZ), Cnr Airborne and Rosedale Roads, Albany,
Auckland 1310, New Zealand (a division of Pearson New Zealand Ltd.)
Penguin Books (South Africa) (Pty.) Ltd., 24 Sturdee Avenue,
Rosebank, Johannesburg 2196, South Africa

Penguin Books Ltd., Registered Offices:
80 Strand, London WC2R 0RL, England

Published by Signet, an imprint of New American Library, a division of Penguin Group (USA) Inc. Previously published in a G. P. Putnam's Sons edition.

First Signet Printing, November 1988
50 49 48 47 46 45 44 43 42 41

(An extension of this copyright page is on page 749.)

Printed in the United States of America

PUBLISHER'S NOTE
This is a work of fiction. Names, characters, places, and incidents either are the product of the author's imagination or are used fictitiously, and any resemblance to actual persons, living or dead, business establishments, events, or locales is entirely coincidental.

For Tabitha King

". . . promises to keep."

LIKE MANY OF THE MOTHER GOOSE RHYMES, the verse about the Tommyknockers is deceptively simple. The origin of the word is difficult to trace. *Webster's Unabridged* says Tommyknockers are either (a) tunneling ogres or (b) ghosts which haunt deserted mines or caves. Because "tommy" is an archaic British slang term referring to army rations (leading to the term "tommies" as a word used to identify British conscripts, as in Kipling—"it's Tommy this, an' Tommy that . . ."), the *Oxford Unabridged Dictionary,* while not identifying the term itself, at least suggests that Tommyknockers are the ghosts of miners who died of starvation, but still go knocking for food and rescue.

The first verse ("Late last night and the night before," etc.) is common enough for my wife and myself to have heard it as children, although we were raised in different towns, different faiths, and came from different descendants—hers primarily French, mine Scots-Irish.

All other verses are products of the author's imagination.

That author—me, in other words—wishes to thank his spouse, Tabitha, who is an invaluable if sometimes maddening critic (if you get mad at critics, you almost always can be sure they are right), the editor, Alan Williams, for his kind and careful attention, Phyllis Grann for her patience (this book was not so much written as gutted out), and, in particular, George Everett McCutcheon, who has read each of my novels and vetted it carefully—primarily for weapons and ballistics reasons, but also for his attention to continuity. Mac died while this book was in rewrite. In fact, I was obediently making corrections suggested by one of his notes when I learned he had finally succumbed to the leukemia he had battled for nearly two years. I miss him terribly, not because he helped me fix things but because he was part of my heart's neighborhood.

Thanks are due to others, more than I could name: pilots, dentists, geologists, fellow writers, even my kids, who listened to the book aloud. I'm also grateful to Stephen Jay Gould. Although he is a Yankee fan and thus not entirely to be trusted, his comments on the possibilities of what I'd call "dumb evolution" helped to shape the redraft of this novel (e.g. *The Flamingo's Smile*).

Haven is not real. The characters are not real. This is a work of fiction, with one exception:

The *Tommyknockers* are real.

If you think I'm kidding, you missed the nightly news.

—STEPHEN KING

Late last night and the night before,
Tommyknockers, Tommyknockers,
knocking at the door.
I want to go out, don't know if I can,
'cause I'm so afraid
of the Tommyknocker man.

—TRADITIONAL

BOOK I

The Ship in the Earth

Well we picked up Harry Truman, floating down from Independence,
We said, "What about the war?"
He said, "Good riddance!"
We said, "What about the bomb? Are you sorry that you did it?"
He said, "Pass me that bottle and mind your own bidness."

—THE RAINMAKERS,
"Downstream"

1.

ANDERSON STUMBLES

1

For want of a nail the kingdom was lost—that's how the catechism goes when you boil it down. In the end, you can boil *everything* down to something similar—or so Roberta Anderson thought much later on. It's either all an accident . . . or all fate. Anderson literally stumbled over her destiny in the small town of Haven, Maine, on June 21, 1988. That stumble was the root of the matter; all the rest was nothing but history.

2

Anderson was out that afternoon with Peter, an aging beagle who was now blind in one eye. Peter had been given to her by Jim Gardener in 1976. Anderson had left college the year before with her degree only two months away to move onto her uncle's place in Haven. She hadn't realized how lonely she'd been until Gard brought the dog. He'd been a pup then, and Anderson sometimes found it difficult to believe he was now old—eighty-four in dog's years. It was a way of measuring her own age. Nineteen-seventy-six had receded. Yes indeed. When you were twenty-five, you could still indulge in the luxury of believing that, in *your* case, at least, growing up was a clerical error which would eventually be rectified. When you woke up one day and discovered your dog was eighty-four and you yourself were thirty-seven, that was a view that had to be reexamined. Yes indeed.

Anderson was looking for a place to cut some wood. She'd a cord and a half laid by, but wanted at least another three to take her through the winter. She had cut a lot since those early days when Peter had been a pup sharpening his teeth on an old slipper (and wetting all too often on the dining-room rug), but the place was still not short. The property (still, after thirteen years, mostly referred to by the townspeople as the old Garrick place) had only a hundred and eighty feet on Route 9, but the rock walls marking the north and south boundaries marched off at diverging angles. Another rock wall—this one so old it had degenerated into isolated rock middens furred with moss—marked the property's rear boundary about three miles into an unruly forest of first- and second-growth trees. The total acreage of this pie-shaped wedge was huge. Beyond the wall at the western edge of Bobbi Anderson's land were miles of wilderness owned by the New England Paper Company. Burning Woods, on the map.

In truth, Anderson didn't really need to hunt a place to do her cutting. The land her mother's brother had left her was valuable because most of the trees on it were good hardwood relatively untouched by the gypsy-moth infestation. But this day was lovely and warm after a rainy spring, the garden was in the ground (where most of it would rot, thanks to the rains), and it wasn't yet time to start the new book. So she had covered the typewriter and here she was with faithful old one-eyed Peter, rambling.

There was an old logging road behind the farm, and she followed this almost a mile before striking off to the left. She was wearing a pack (a sandwich and a book in it for her, dog biscuits for Peter, and lots of orange ribbon to tie around the trunks of the trees she would want to cut as September's heat ebbed toward October) and a canteen. She had a Silva compass in her pocket. She had gotten lost on the property only once, and once was enough to last her forever. She had spent a terrible night in the woods, simultaneously unable to believe she had actually gotten lost on property she for Christ's sweet sake *owned* and sure she would die out here—a possibility in those days, because only Jim would know she was missing, and Jim only came when you weren't expecting him. In the morning, Peter had led her to a stream, and the stream had led her back to Route 9, where it burbled cheerfully through a culvert under the tar only two miles from home. Nowadays she probably had enough woods savvy to find her way back to the road or to one of the rock walls bounding her land, but the key word was *probably*. So she carried a compass.

She found a good stand of maple around three o'clock. In fact, she had found several other good stands of wood, but this one was close to a path she knew, a path wide enough to accommodate the Tomcat. Come September 20th or so—if someone didn't blow the world up in the meantime—she would hook her sledge up to the Tomcat, drive in here, and do some cutting. Besides, she had walked enough for one day.

"Look good, Pete?"

Pete barked feebly, and Anderson looked at the beagle with a sadness so deep it surprised and disquieted her. Peter was done up. He seldom took after birds and squirrels and chipmunks and the occasional woodchuck these days; the thought of Peter running a deer was laughable. She would have to take a good many rest stops on the way back for him . . . and there had been a time, not that long ago (or so her mind stubbornly maintained), when Peter would always have been a quarter of a mile ahead of her, belling volleys of barks back through the woods. She thought there might come a day when she would decide enough was enough; she'd pat the seat on the passenger side of the Chevrolet pickup for the last time, and take Peter to the vet down in Augusta. But not this summer, please God. Or this fall or winter, please God. Or ever, please God.

Because without Peter, she would be alone. Except for Jim, and Jim Gardener had gotten more than just a trifle wiggy over the last eight years or so. Still a friend, but . . . wiggy.

"Glad you approve, Pete old man," she said, putting a ribbon or two around the trees, knowing perfectly well she might decide to cut another stand and the ribbons would rot here. "Your taste is only exceeded by your good looks."

Peter, knowing what was expected of him (he was old,

but not stupid), wagged his scraggy stub of a tail and barked.

"Be a Viet Cong!" Anderson ordered.

Peter obediently fell on his side—a little wheeze escaped him—and rolled on his back, legs splayed out. That almost always amused Anderson, but today the sight of her dog playing Viet Cong (Peter would also play dead at the words "hooch" or "My Lai") was too close to what she had been thinking about.

"Up, Pete."

Pete got up slowly, panting below his muzzle. His white muzzle.

"Let's go back." She tossed him a dog biscuit. Peter snapped at it and missed. He snuffed for it, missed it, then came back to it. He ate it slowly, without much relish. "Right," Anderson said. "Move out."

3

For want of a shoe, the kingdom was lost . . . for the choice of a path, the ship was found.

Anderson had been down here before in the thirteen years that the Garrick place hadn't become the Anderson place; she recognized the slope of land, a deadfall left by pulpers who had probably all died before the Korean War, a great pine with a split top. She had walked this land before and would have no trouble finding her way back to the path she would use with the Tomcat. She might have passed the spot where she stumbled once or twice or half a dozen times before, perhaps by yards, or feet, or bare inches.

This time she followed Peter as the dog moved slightly to the left, and with the path in sight, one of her elderly hiking boots fetched up against something . . . fetched up hard.

"Hey!" she yelled, but it was too late, in spite of her pinwheeling arms. She fell to the ground. The branch of a low bush scratched her cheek hard enough to bring blood.

"Shit!" she cried, and a bluejay scolded her.

Peter returned, first sniffing and then licking her nose.

"Christ, don't do that, your breath stinks!"

Peter wagged his tail. Anderson sat up. She rubbed her left cheek and saw blood on her palm and fingers. She grunted.

"Nice going," she said, and looked to see what she had tripped over—a fallen piece of tree, most likely, or a rock poking out of the ground. Lots of rock in Maine.

What she saw was a gleam of metal.

She touched it, running her finger along it and then blowing off black forest dirt.

"What's this?" she asked Peter.

Peter approached, sniffed at it, and then did a peculiar thing. The beagle backed off two dog-paces, sat down, and uttered a single low howl.

"Who got on your case?" Anderson asked, but Peter only sat there. Anderson hooked herself closer, still sitting down, sliding on the seat of her jeans. She examined the metal in the ground.

Roughly three inches stuck out of the mulchy earth—just enough to trip over. There was a slight rise here, and perhaps the runoff from the heavy spring rains had freed it. Anderson's first thought was that the skidders who had logged this land in the twenties and thirties must have buried a bunch of their leavings here—the cast-off swill of a three-day cutting, which in those days had been called a "loggers' weekend."

A tin can, she thought—B&M beans or Campbell's soup. She wiggled it the way you'd wiggle a tin can out of the earth. Then it occurred to her that no one except a toddler would be apt to trip over the leading edge of a can. The metal in the earth didn't wiggle. It was as solid as mother-rock. A piece of old logging equipment, maybe?

Intrigued, Anderson examined it more closely, not seeing that Peter had gotten to his feet, backed away another four paces, and sat down again.

The metal was a dull gray—not the bright color of tin or iron at all. And it was thicker than a can, maybe a quarter-inch at its top. Anderson placed the pad of her right index finger on this edge and felt a momentary odd tingling, like a vibration.

She took her finger away and looked at it quizzically.

Put it back.

Nothing. No buzz.

Now she pinched it between her thumb and finger and tried to draw it from the earth like a loose tooth from a gum. It didn't come. She was gripping the protrusion in the rough center. It sank back into the earth—or that was the impression she had then—on either side at a width of less than two inches. She would later tell Jim Gardener that she could have walked past it three times a day for forty years and never stumbled over it.

She brushed away loose soil, exposing a little more of it. She dug a channel along it about two inches deep with her fingers—the soil gave easily enough, as forest soil does . . . at least until you hit the webwork of roots. It continued smoothly down into the ground. Anderson got up on her knees and dug down along either side. She tried wiggling it again. Still no go.

She scraped away more soil with her fingers and quickly exposed more—now she saw six inches of gray metal, now nine, now a foot.

It's a car or a truck or a skidder, she thought suddenly. *Buried out here in the middle of nowhere. Or maybe a Hooverville kind of stove. But why here?*

No reason that she could think of; no reason at all. She found things in the woods from time to time—shell casings, beer cans (the oldest not with pop-tops but with triangle-shaped holes made by what they had called a "churchkey" back in those dim dead days of the 1960s), candy wrappers, other stuff. Haven was not on either of Maine's two major tourist tracks, one of which runs through the lake and mountain region to the extreme west of the state and the other of which runs up the coast to the extreme east, but it had not been the forest primeval for a long, long time. Once (she had been over the decayed stone wall at the back of her land and actually trespassing on New England Paper Company's land at the time) she had found the rusted hulk of a late-forties Hudson Hornet standing in what had once been a woods road and what was now, over twenty years after the cutting had stopped, a tangle of second growth—what the locals called shit-wood. No reason that hulk of a car should have been there, either . . . but it was easier to explain than a stove or a refrigerator or any other damn thing actually buried in the ground.

She had dug twin trenches a foot long on either side of the object without finding its end. She got down almost a foot before scraping her fingers on rock. She might have been able to pull the rock out—*that* at least had some wiggle—but there was no reason to do it. The object in the earth continued down past it.

Peter whined.

Anderson glanced at the dog, then stood up. Both knees popped. Her left foot tingled with pins and needles. She fished her pocket watch out of her pants—old and tarnished, the Simon watch was another part of her legacy from Uncle Frank—and was astonished to see that she had been here a long time: an hour and a quarter at least. It was past four.

"Come on, Pete," she said. "Let's bug out."

Peter whined again but still wouldn't move. And now, with real concern, Anderson saw that her old beagle was shivering all over, as if with ague. She had no idea if dogs could catch ague, but thought old ones might. She did recollect that the only time she had ever seen Peter shiver like that was in the fall of 1977 (or maybe it had been '78). There had been a catamount on the place. Over a series of perhaps nine nights it had screamed and squalled, very likely in unrequited heat. Each night Peter would go to the living-room window and jump up on the old church pew Anderson kept there by her bookcase. He never barked. He only looked out into the dark toward that unearthly, womanish squealing, nostrils flaring, ears up. And he shivered.

Anderson stepped over her little excavation and went to Peter. She knelt down and ran her hands along the sides of Peter's face, feeling the shiver in her palms.

"What's wrong, boy?" she murmured, but she knew what was wrong. Peter's good eye shifted past her, toward the thing in the earth, and then back to Anderson. The plea in the eye not veiled by the hateful, milky cataract was as clear as speech: *Let's get out of here, Bobbi, I like that thing almost as much as I like your sister.*

"Okay," Anderson said uneasily. It suddenly occurred to her that she could not remember ever having lost track of time as she had today, out here.

Peter doesn't like it. I don't either.

"Come on." She started up the slope to the path. Peter followed with alacrity.

They were almost to the path when Anderson, like Lot's wife, looked back. If not for that last glance, she might actually have let the whole thing go. Since leaving college before finals—in spite of her mother's tearful pleas and her sister's furious diatribes and baleful ultimatums—Anderson had gotten good at letting things go.

The look back from this middle distance showed her two things. First, the thing did not sink back into the earth as she had at first thought. The tongue of metal was sticking up in the middle of a fairly fresh declivity, not wide but fairly deep, and surely the result of late-winter runoff and the heavy spring rains that had followed it. So the ground to either side of the protruding metal was higher, and the metal simply disappeared back into it. Her first impression, that the thing in the ground was the corner of something, wasn't true after all—or not necessarily true. Second, it looked like a plate—not a plate you'd eat from, but a dull metal plate, like metal siding or—

Peter barked.

"Okay," Anderson said. "I hear you talking. Let's go."

Let's go . . . and let's let it go.

She walked up the center of the path, letting Peter lead them back toward the woods road at his own bumbling pace, enjoying the lush green of high summer . . . and this *was* the first day of summer, wasn't it? The solstice. Longest day of the year. She slapped a mosquito and grinned. Summer was a good time in Haven. The best of times. And if Haven wasn't the best of places, parked as it was well above Augusta in that central part of the state most tourists passed by, it was still a good place to come to rest. There had been a time when Anderson had honestly believed she would only be here a few years, long enough to recover from the traumas of adolescence, her sister, and her abrupt, confused withdrawal (surrender, Anne called it) from college, but a few years had become five, five had become ten, ten had become thirteen, and looky 'yere, Huck, Peter's old and you got a pretty good crop of gray coming up in what used to be hair as black as the River Styx (she'd tried cropping it close two years ago, almost a punk do, had been horrified to find it made the gray even more noticeable, and had let it grow ever since).

She now thought she might spend the rest of her life in Haven, with the sole exception of the duty trip she took to visit her publisher in New York every year or two. The town got you. The place got you. The *land* got you. And that wasn't so bad. It was as good as anything else, maybe.

Like a plate. A metal plate.

She broke off a short limber branch well plumed with fresh green leaves and waved it around her head. The mosquitoes had found her and seemed determined to have their high tea off her. Mosquitoes whirling around her head . . . and thoughts like mosquitoes inside her head. Those she couldn't wave off.

It vibrated under my finger for a second. I felt it. Like a tuning fork. But when I touched it, it stopped. Is it possible for something to vibrate in the earth like that? Surely not. Maybe . . .

Maybe it had been a *psychic* vibration. She did not absolutely disbelieve in such things. Maybe her mind had sensed something about that buried object and had told her about it in the only way it could, by giving her a tactile impression: one of vibration. Peter had certainly sensed something about it; the old beagle hadn't wanted to go near it.

Forget it. She did.

For a little while.

4

That night a high, mild wind arose and Anderson went out on her front porch to smoke and listen to the wind walk and talk. At one time—even a year earlier—Peter would have come out with her, but now he remained in the parlor, curled up on his small hooked rug by the stove, nose to tail.

Anderson found her mind replaying that last look back at the plate sticking out of the earth, and she later came to believe that there was a moment—perhaps when she flicked the cigarette into the gravel drive—when she decided she would have to dig it up and see what it was . . . although she didn't consciously recognize the decision then.

Her mind worried restlessly at what it might be, and this time she allowed it to run—she had learned that if your mind insisted on returning to a topic no matter how you tried to divert it, it was best to let it return. Only obsessives worried about obsession.

Part of some building, her mind hazarded, a prefab. But no one built Quonset huts out in the woods—why drag all that metal in when three men could throw up a cutter's lean-to with saws, axes, and a two-handed bucksaw in six hours? Not a car, either, or the protruding metal would have been flaked with rust. An engine-block seemed slightly more likely, but why?

And now, with dark drawing down, that memory of vibration returned with inarguable certainty. It *must* have been a psychic vibration, if she had felt it at all. It—

Suddenly a cold and terrible certainty rose in her: someone was buried there. Maybe she had uncovered the leading edge of a car or an old refrigerator or even some sort of steel trunk, but whatever it had been in its aboveground life, it was now a coffin. A murder victim? Who else would be buried in such a way, in such a box? Guys who happened to wander into the woods during hunting season and got lost there and died there didn't carry along metal caskets to pop themselves into when they died . . . and even given such an idiotic idea, who would shovel the dirt back in? Cut me a break, folks, as we used to say back in the glorious days of our youth.

The vibration. It had been the call of human bones.

Come on, Bobbi—don't be so fucking stupid.

A shudder worked through her nevertheless. The idea had a certain weird persuasiveness, like a Victorian ghost story that had no business working as the world hurtled down Microchip Alley toward the unknown wonders and horrors of the twenty-first century—but somehow produced the gooseflesh just the same. She could hear Anne laughing and saying *You're getting as funny in the head as Uncle Frank, Bobbi, and it's just what you deserve, living out there alone with your smelly dog.* Sure. Cabin fever. The hermit complex. Call the doctor, call the nurse, Bobbi's bad . . . and getting worse.

All the same, she suddenly wanted to talk to Jim Gardener—*needed* to talk to him. She went in to call his place up the road in Unity. She had dialed four numbers when she remembered he was off doing readings—those and the poetry workshops were the way he supported himself. For itinerant artists, summer was prime time. *All those menopausal matrons have to do something with their summers,* she could hear Jim saying ironically, *and I have to eat in the winter. One hand washes the other. You ought to thank God you're saved the reading circuit, anyway, Bobbi.*

Yes, she was saved that—although she thought Jim liked it more than he let on. Certainly did get laid enough.

Anderson put the phone back in the cradle and looked at the bookcase to the left of the stove. It wasn't a handsome bookcase—she was no one's carpenter, nor ever would be—but it served the purpose. The bottom two shelves were taken up by the Time-Life series of volumes on the old west. The two shelves above were filled with a mixture of fiction and fact on that same subject; Brian Garfield's early westerns jostled for place with Hubert Hampton's massive *Western Territories Examined,* Louis L'Amour's Sackett saga lay cheek by jowl with Richard Marius' wonderful two novels, *The Coming of Rain* and *Bound for the Promised Land.* Jay R. Nash's *Bloodletters and Badmen* and Richard F. K. Mudgett's *Westward Expansion* bracketed a riot of paperback westerns by Ray Hogan, Archie Joceylen, Max Brand, Ernest Haycox, and, of course, Zane Grey—Anderson's copy of *Riders of the Purple Sage* had been read nearly to tatters.

On the top shelf were her own books, eleven of them. Ten were westerns, beginning with *Hangtown,* published in 1975, and ending with *The Long Ride Back,* published in '86. *Massacre Canyon,* the new one, would be published in September, as all of her westerns had been since the beginning. It occurred to her now that she had been here, in Haven, when she had received her first copy of *Hangtown,* although she'd begun the novel in the room of a scuzzy Cleaves Mills apartment, on a thirties-vintage Underwood dying of old age. Still, she'd finished here, and it was here that she'd held the first actual copy of the book in her hands.

Here, in Haven. Her entire career as a publishing writer was here . . . except for the first book.

She took that down now and looked at it curiously, realizing it had been perhaps five years since she had last held this slim volume in her hands. It was not only depressing to realize how fast time got by; it was depressing to think of how often she thought about that lately.

This volume was a total contrast to the others, with

their jackets showing mesas and buttes, riders and cows and dusty trail-drive towns. This jacket was a nineteenth-century woodcut of a clipper ship quartering toward land. Its uncompromising blacks and whites were startling, almost shocking. *Boxing the Compass* was the title printed above the woodcut. And below it: *Poems by Roberta Anderson.*

She opened the book, paging past the title, musing for a moment over the copyright date, 1974, then pausing at the dedication page. It was as stark as the woodcut. *This book is for James Gardener.* The man she had been trying to call. The second of the only three men she had ever had sex with, and the only one who had ever been able to bring her to orgasm. Not that she attached any special importance to *that.* Or not much, anyway. Or so she thought. Or *thought* she thought. Or something. And it didn't matter anyway; those days were also old days.

She sighed and put the book back on the shelf without looking at the poems. Only one of them was much good. That one had been written in March of 1972, a month after her grandfather died of cancer. The rest of them were crap—the casual reader might have been fooled, because she *was* a talented writer . . . but the heart of her talent had been somewhere else. When she had published *Hangtown,* the circle of writers she had known had all denied her. All except Jim, who had published *Boxing the Compass* in the first place.

She had dropped Sherry Fenderson a long chatty letter not long after coming to Haven, and had received a curt postcard in return: *Please don't write me anymore. I don't know you.* Signed with a single slashed S. as curt as the message. She had been sitting on the porch, crying over that card, when Jim showed up. *Why are you crying over what that silly woman thinks?* he had asked her. *Do you really want to trust the judgment of a woman who goes around yelling "Power to the people" and smelling of Chanel Number Five?*

She just happens to be a very good poet, she had sniffled.

Jim gestured impatiently. *That doesn't make her any older,* he had said, *or any more able to recant the cant she's been taught and then taught herself. Get your mind right, Bobbi. If you want to go on doing what you like, get your fucking mind right and stop that fucking crying. That fucking crying makes me sick. That fucking crying makes me want to* puke. *You're not weak. I know weak when I'm with it. Why do you want to be something you're not? Your sister? Is that why? She's not here, and she's not you, and you don't have to let her in if you don't want to. Don't whine to me about your sister anymore. Grow up. Stop bitching.*

She'd looked at him, she remembered now, amazed.

There's a big difference between being good at what you DO *and being smart about what you* KNOW, he said. *Give Sherry some time to grow up. Give yourself some time to grow up. And stop being your own jury. It's boring, I don't want to listen to you snivel. Sniveling is for jerks. Quit being a jerk.*

She had felt herself hating him, loving him, wanting all of him and none of him. Did he say he knew weak when he was with it? Boy, he ought to. He was bent. She knew it even then.

Now, he had said, *you want to lay an ex-publisher or do you want to cry all over that stupid postcard?*

She had laid him. She didn't know now and hadn't known then if she *wanted* to lay him, but she had. And screamed when she came.

That had been near the end.

She remembered that too—how it had been near the end. He had gotten married not long after, but it would have been near the end anyway. He was weak, and he was bent.

Doesn't matter anyway, she thought, and gave herself the old, good advice: *Let it go.*

Advice easier given than followed. It was a long time before Anderson got over into sleep that night. Old ghosts had stirred when she moved her book of undergraduate poems . . . or perhaps it was that high, mild wind, hooting the eaves and whistling the trees.

She had almost made it when Peter woke her up. Peter was howling in his sleep.

Anderson got up in a hurry, scared—Peter had made a lot of noises in his sleep before this (not to mention some unbelievably noxious dogfarts), but he had never howled. It was like waking to the sound of a child screaming in the grip of a nightmare.

She went into the living room naked except for her socks and knelt by Peter, who was still on the rug by the stove.

"Pete," she muttered. "Hey, Pete, cool it."

She stroked the dog. Peter was shivering and jerked away when Anderson touched him, baring the eroded remains of his teeth. Then his eyes opened—the bad one and the good one—and he seemed to come back to himself. He whined weakly and thumped his tail against the floor.

"You all right?" Anderson asked.

Peter licked her hand.

"Then lie down again. Stop whining. It's boring. Stop fucking off."

Peter lay down and closed his eyes. Anderson knelt, looking at him, troubled.

He's dreaming of that thing.

Her rational mind rejected that, but the night insisted on its own imperative—it was true, and she knew it.

She went to bed at last, and sleep came sometime after two in the morning. She had a peculiar dream. In it she was groping in the dark . . . not trying to find something but to get away from something. She was in the woods. Branches whipped into her face and poked her arms. Sometimes she stumbled over roots and fallen trees. And then, ahead of her, a terrible green light shone out in a single pencillike ray. In her dream she thought of Poe's "The Tell-Tale Heart," the mad narrator's lantern, muffled up except for one tiny hole, which he used to direct a beam of light onto the evil eye he fancied his elderly benefactor possessed.

Bobbi Anderson felt her teeth fall out.

They went painlessly, all of them. The bottom ones tumbled, some outward, some back into her mouth, where they lay on her tongue or under it in hard little lumps. The top ones simply dropped down the front of her blouse. She felt one catch in her bra, which clasped in front, poking her skin.

The light. The green light. The light—

5

—was wrong.

It wasn't just that it was gray and pearly, that light; it was expected that such a wind as had blown up the night before would bring a change in the weather. But Anderson knew there was something more than that wrong even before she looked at the clock on the nightstand. She picked it up in both hands and drew it close to her face, although her vision was a perfect 20/20. It was quarter past three in the afternoon. She had gone to sleep late, given. But no matter how late she slept, either habit or the need to urinate always woke her up by nine o'clock, ten at the latest. But she had slept a full twelve hours . . . and she was ravenous.

She shuffled out into the living room, still wearing only her socks, and saw that Peter was lying limply on his side, head back, yellow stubs of teeth showing, legs splayed out.

Dead, she thought with a cold and absolute certainty. *Peter's dead. Died in the night.*

She went to her dog, already anticipating the feel of cold flesh and lifeless fur. Then Peter uttered a muzzy, lip-flapping sound—a blurry dog-snore. Anderson felt huge relief course through her. She spoke the dog's name aloud and Peter started up, almost guiltily, as if he was also aware of oversleeping. Anderson supposed he was—dogs seemed to have an acutely developed sense of time.

"We slept late, fella," she said.

Peter got up and stretched first one hind leg and then the other. He looked around, almost comically perplexed, and then went to the door. Anderson opened it. Peter stood there for a moment, not liking the rain. Then he went out to do his business.

Anderson stood in the living room a moment longer, still marveling over her certainty that Peter had been dead. Just what in hell was wrong with her lately? Everything was doom and gloom. Then she headed for the kitchen to fix a meal . . . whatever you called breakfast at three in the afternoon.

On the way she diverted into the bathroom to do her own business. Then she paused in front of her reflection in the toothpaste-spotted mirror. A woman pushing forty. Graying hair, otherwise not too bad—she didn't drink much, didn't smoke much, spent most of her time outside when she wasn't writing. Irish black hair—no romance-novel blaze of red for her—rather too long. Gray-blue eyes. Abruptly she bared her teeth, expecting for just a moment to see only smooth pink gums.

But her teeth were there—all of them. Thank the fluoridated water in Utica, New York, for that. She touched them, let her fingers prove their bony reality to her brain.

But something wasn't right.

Wetness.

There was wetness on her upper thighs.

Oh no, oh shit, this is almost a week early, I just put clean sheets on the bed yesterday—

But after she had showered, put a pad in a fresh pair of cotton panties, and pulled the whole works snug, she checked the sheets and saw them unmarked. Her period was early, but it had at least had the consideration to wait until she was almost awake. And there was no cause for alarm; she was fairly regular, but she had been both early and late from time to time; maybe diet, maybe subconscious stress, maybe some internal clock slipping a cog or two. She had no urge to grow old fast, but she often thought that having the whole inconvenient business of menstruation behind her would be a relief.

The last of her nightmare slipped away, and Bobbi Anderson went in to fix herself a very late breakfast.

2.

ANDERSON DIGS

1

It rained steadily for the next three days. Anderson wandered restlessly around the house, made a trip with Peter into Augusta in the pickup for supplies she didn't really need, drank beer, and listened to old Beach Boys tunes while she made repairs around the house. Trouble was, there weren't really that many repairs that needed to be done. By the third day she was circling the typewriter, thinking maybe she would start the new book. She knew what it was supposed to be about: a young schoolmarm and a buffalo-hunter caught up in a range war in Kansas during the early 1850s—a period when everyone in the midsection of the country seemed to be tuning up for the Civil War, whether they knew it or not. It would be a good book, she thought, but she didn't think it was quite "ready" yet, whatever that meant (a sardonic mimic awoke in her mind, doing an Orson Welles voice: *We will write no oater before its time)*. Still, her restlessness dug at her, and the signs were all there: an impatience with books, with the music, with herself. A tendency to drift off . . . and then she would be looking at the typewriter, wanting to wake it into some dream.

Peter also seemed restless, scratching at the door to go out and then scratching at it to come back in five minutes later, wandering around the place, lying down, then getting up again.

Low barometer, Anderson thought. That's all it is. *Makes us both restless, cranky.*

And her damned period. Usually she flowed heavy and then just stopped. Like turning off a faucet. This time she just went on leaking. *Bad washer, ha-ha,* she thought with no humor at all. She found herself sitting in front of the typewriter just after dark on the second rainy day, a blank sheet rolled into the carriage. She started to type and what came out was a bunch of X's and O's, like a kid's tic-tac-toe game, and then something that looked like a mathematical equation . . . which was stupid, since the last math she'd taken was Algebra II in high school. These days, x was for crossing out the wrong word, and that was all. She pulled the blank sheet out and tossed it away.

After lunch on the third rainy day, she called the English Department at the university. Jim no longer taught there, not for eight years, but he still had friends on the faculty and kept in touch. Muriel in the office usually knew where he was.

And did this time. Jim Gardener, she told Anderson, was doing a reading in Fall River that night, June 24th, followed by two in Boston over the next three nights, followed by readings and lectures in Providence and New Haven—all part of something called the New England Poetry Caravan. Must be Patricia McCardle, Anderson thought, smiling a little.

"So he'd be back . . . when? Fourth of July?"

"Gee, I don't know when he'll be back, Bobbi," Muriel said. "You know Jim. His last reading's June 30th. That's all I can say for sure."

Anderson thanked her and hung up. She looked at the phone thoughtfully, calling up Muriel fully in her mind—another Irish colleen (but Muriel had the expected red hair) just now reaching the far edge of her prime, round-faced, green-eyed, full-breasted. Had she slept with Jim? Probably. Anderson felt a spark of jealousy—but not much of a spark. Muriel was okay. Just speaking to Muriel made her feel better—someone who knew who she was, who could think of her as a real person, not just as a customer on the other side of the counter in an Augusta hardware store or as someone to say how-do to over the mailbox. She was solitary by nature, but not monastic . . . and sometimes simple human contact had a way of fulfilling her when she didn't even know she needed to be fulfilled.

And she supposed she knew now why she had wanted to get in contact with Jim—talking with Muriel had done that, at least. The thing in the woods had stayed on her mind, and the idea that it was some sort of clandestine coffin had grown to a certainty. It wasn't *writing* she was restless to do; it was *digging*. She just hadn't wanted to do it on her own.

"Looks like I'll have to, though, Pete," she said, sitting down in her rocker by the east window—her reading chair. Peter glanced at her briefly, as if to say, *Whatever you want, babe.* Anderson sat forward, suddenly looking at Pete—really *looking* at him. Peter looked back cheerfully enough, tail thumping on the floor. For a moment it seemed there was something different about Peter . . . something so obvious she should be seeing it.

If so, she wasn't.

She settled back, opening her book—a master's thesis from the University of Nebraska, the most exciting thing about it the title: *Range War and Civil War.* She remembered thinking a couple of nights ago as her sister Anne would think: *You're getting as funny in the head as Uncle Frank, Bobbi.* Well . . . maybe.

Shortly she was deep into the thesis, making an occasional note on the legal pad she kept near. Outside, the rain continued to fall.

2

The following day dawned clear and bright and flawless: a postcard summer day with just enough breeze to make the bugs keep their distance. Anderson pottered around the house until almost ten o'clock, conscious of the growing pressure her mind was putting on her to get out there and dig it up, already. She could feel herself consciously pushing back against that urge (Orson Welles again—*We will dig up no body before its* . . . oh, shut up, Orson). Her days of simply following the urge of the moment, a lifestyle that had once been catechized by the bald motto "If it feels good, do it," were over. It had never worked well for her, that philosophy—in fact, almost every bad thing that had happened to her had its roots in some impulsive action. She attached no moral stigma to people who did live their lives according to impulse; maybe her intuitions just hadn't been that good.

She ate a big breakfast, added a scrambled egg to Peter's Gravy Train (Peter ate with more appetite than usual, and Anderson put it down to the end of the rainy spell), and then did the washing-up.

If her dribbles would just stop, everything would be fine. Forget it; we will stop no period before its time. Right, Orson? You're fucking-A.

Bobbi went outside, clapped an old straw cowboy hat on her head, and spent the next hour in the garden. Things out there were looking better than they had any right to, given the rain. The peas were coming on and the corn was rearing up good, as Uncle Frank would have said.

She quit at eleven. Fuck it. She went around the house to the shed, got the spade and shovel, paused, and added a crowbar. She started out of the shed, went back, and took a screwdriver and an adjustable wrench from the toolbox.

Peter started out with her as he always did, but this time Anderson said, "No, Peter," and pointed back at the house. Peter stopped, looking wounded. He whined and took a tentative step toward Anderson.

"*No*, Peter."

Peter gave in and headed back, head down, tail drooping dispiritedly. Anderson was sorry to see him go that way, but Peter's previous reaction to the plate in the ground had been bad. She stood a moment longer on the path which would lead her to the woods road, spade in one hand, shovel and crowbar in the other, watching as Peter mounted the back steps, nosed open the back door, and went into the house.

She thought: *Something was different about him . . . is different about him. What is it?* She didn't know. But for a moment, almost subliminally, her dream flickered back to her—that arrow of poisonous green light . . . and her teeth all falling painlessly out of her gums.

Then it was gone and she set off toward the place where it was, that odd thing in the ground, listening to the crickets make their steady *ree-ree-ree* sound in this small back field which would soon be ready for its first cutting.

3

At three that afternoon it was Peter who raised her from the semidaze in which she had been working, making her aware she was two damn-nears: damn-near starving and damn-near exhausted.

Peter was howling.

The sound raised gooseflesh on Anderson's back and arms. She dropped the shovel she had been using and backed away from the thing in the earth—the thing that was no plate, no box, not anything she could understand. All she knew for sure was that she had fallen into a strange, thoughtless state she didn't like at all. This time she had done more than lose track of time; she felt as if she had lost track of *herself*. It was as if someone else had stepped into her head the way a man would step into a bulldozer or a payloader, simply firing her up and starting to yank the right levers.

Peter howled, nose pointing toward the sky—long, chilling, mournful sounds.

"Stop it, Peter!" Anderson yelled, and thankfully, Peter did. Any more of that and she might simply have turned and run.

Instead, she fought for control and got it. She backed up another step and cried out when something flapped loosely against her back. At her cry, Peter uttered one more short, yipping sound and fell silent again.

Anderson grabbed for whatever had touched her, thinking it might be . . . well, she didn't know what she thought it might be, but even before her hand closed on it, she remembered what it was. She had a hazy memory of stopping just long enough to hang her blouse on a bush; here it was.

She took it and put it on, getting the buttons wrong on the first try so that one tail hung down below the other. She rebuttoned it, looking at the dig she had begun—and now that archaeological word seemed to fit what she was doing exactly. Her memories of the four and a half hours she'd spent digging were like her memory of hanging her blouse on the bush—hazy and broken. They were not memories; they were fragments.

But now, looking at what she had done, she felt awe as well as fear . . . and a mounting sense of excitement.

Whatever it was, it was huge. Not just big, but *huge.*

The spade, shovel, and crowbar lay at intervals along a fifteen-foot trench in the forest floor. She had made neat piles of black earth and chunks of rock at regular intervals. Sticking up from this trench, which was about four feet deep at the point where Anderson had originally stumbled over three inches of protruding gray metal, was the leading edge of some titanic object. *Gray metal . . . some object . . .*

You'd ordinarily have a right to expect something better, more specific, from a writer, she thought, arming sweat from her forehead, but she was no longer sure the metal was steel. She thought now it might be a more exotic alloy, beryllium, magnesium, perhaps—and composition aside, she had absolutely no idea what it *was.*

She began to unbutton her jeans so she could tuck in her blouse, then paused.

The crotch of the faded Levi's was soaked with blood.

Jesus. Jesus Christ. This isn't a period. This is Niagara Falls.

She was momentarily frightened, really frightened, then told herself to quit being a ninny. She had gone into some sort of daze and done digging a crew of four husky men could have been proud of . . . her, a woman who went one-twenty-five, maybe one-thirty, tops. Of *course* she was flowing heavily. She was fine—in fact, should be grateful she wasn't cramping as well as gushing.

My, how poetic we are today, Bobbi, she thought, and uttered a harsh little laugh.

All she really needed was to clean herself up: a shower and a change would do fine. The jeans had been ready for either the trash or the ragbag anyway. Now there was one less worry in a troubled, confusing world, right? Right. No big deal.

She buttoned her pants again, not tucking the blouse in—no sense ruining that as well, although God knew it wasn't exactly a Dior original. The feel of the sticky wetness down there when she moved made her grimace. God, she wanted to get cleaned up. In a hurry.

But instead of starting up the slope to the path, she

walked back toward the thing in the earth, again driven to it. Peter howled, and the gooseflesh reappeared again. *"Peter, will you for Christ's sake shut UP!"* She hardly ever shouted at Pete—really *shouted* at him—but the goddam mutt was starting to make her feel like a behavioral-psychology subject. Gooseflesh when the dog howled instead of saliva at the sound of the bell, but the same principle.

Standing close to her find, she forgot about Peter and only stared wonderingly at it. After some moments she reached out and gripped it. Again she felt that curious sense of vibration—it sank into her hand and then disappeared. This time she thought of touching a hull beneath which very heavy machinery is hard at work. The metal itself was so smooth that it had an almost greasy texture—you expected some of it to come off on your hands.

She made a fist and rapped her knuckles on it. It made a dull sound, like a fist rapping on a thick chunk of mahogany. She stood a moment longer, then took the screwdriver from her back pocket, held it indecisively for a moment, and then, feeling oddly guilty—feeling like a vandal—she drew the blade down the exposed metal. It wouldn't scratch.

Her eyes suggested two further things, but either or both could have been an optical illusion. The first was that the metal seemed to grow slightly thicker as it went from its edge to the point where it disappeared into the earth. The second was that the edge was slightly curved. These two things—if true—suggested an idea that was at once exciting, ludicrous, frightening, impossible . . . and possessed of a certain mad logic.

She ran her palm over the smooth metal, then stepped away. What the hell was she doing, petting this goddam thing while the blood was running down her legs? And her period was the least of her concerns if what she was starting to think just might turn out to be the truth.

You better call somebody, Bobbi. Right now.

I'll call Jim. When he gets back.

Sure. Call a poet. Great idea. Then you can call the Reverend Moon. Maybe Edward Gorey and Gahan Wilson to draw pictures. Then you can hire a few rock bands and have fucking Woodstock 1988 out here. Get serious, Bobbi. Call the state police.

No. I want to talk to Jim first. Want him to see it. Want to talk to him about it. Meantime, I'll dig around it some more.

It could be dangerous.

Yes. Not only could be, probably was—hadn't she felt that? Hadn't Peter felt it? There was something else, too. Coming down the slope from the path this morning, she had found a dead woodchuck—had almost stepped on it. Although the smell when she bent over the animal told her it had been dead two days at least, there had been no buzz of flies to warn her. There were no flies at all around ole Chuck, and Anderson could not remember ever having seen such a thing. There was no obvious sign of what had killed it, either, but believing that thing in the ground had had anything to do with it was boolsheet of the purest ray serene. Ole Chuck had probably gotten some farmer's poison bait and stumbled out here to die.

Go home. Change your pants. You're bloody and you stink.

She backed away from the thing, then turned and climbed the slope back to the path, where Peter jumped clumsily on her and began to lick her hand with an eagerness that was a little pathetic. Even a year ago he would have been trying to nose at her crotch, attracted by the smell there, but not now. Now all he could do was shiver.

"Your own damn fault," Anderson said. "I *told* you to stay home." All the same, she was glad Peter had come. If he hadn't, Anderson might have worked right through until nightfall . . . and the idea of coming to in the dark, with that thing bulking close by . . . that idea didn't fetch her.

She looked back from the path. The height gave her a more complete view of the thing. It jutted from the ground at a slight angle, she saw. Her impression that the leading edge had a slight curve recurred.

A plate, that's what I thought when I first dug around it with my fingers. A steel plate, not a dinner-plate, I thought, but maybe even then, with so little of it sticking out of the ground, it was really a dinner-plate I was thinking of. Or a saucer.

A flying fucking saucer.

4

Back at the house, she showered and changed, using one of the Maxi-Pads even though the heavy menstrual flow already appeared to be lessening. Then she fixed herself a huge supper of canned baked beans and knockwurst. But she found herself too tired to do much more than pick at it. She put the remains—more than half—down for Peter and went over to her rocker by the window. The thesis she had been reading was still on the floor beside the chair, her place marked with a torn-off matchbook cover. Her notepad was beside it. She picked it up, turned to a fresh page, and began to sketch the thing in the woods as she had seen it when she took that last look back.

She was no great shakes with a pen unless it was words she was making, but she had some small sketching talent. This sketch went very slowly, however, not just because she wanted it to be as exact as she could make it but because she was so tired. To make matters worse, Peter came over and nuzzled her hand, wanting to be patted.

She stroked Peter's head absently, erasing a jag his nose had put into the horizon-line of her sketch. "Yeah, you're a good dog, great dog, go check the mail, why don't you?"

Peter trotted across the living room and nosed the screen door open. Anderson went back to work on her sketch, glancing up once to see Peter do his world-famous canine mail-retrieval trick. He put his left forepaw up on the mailbox post and then began to swipe at the door of the box. Joe Paulson, the postman, knew about Peter and always left it ajar. He got the door down, then lost his balance before he could hook the mail out with his paw. Anderson winced a little—until this year, Peter had *never* lost his balance. Getting the mail had been his *pièce de résistance,* better than playing dead Viet Cong and *much* better than anything mundane like sitting up or "speaking" for a dog biscuit. It wowed everyone who saw him do it, and Peter knew it . . . but these days it was a painful ritual to watch. It made Anderson feel the way she imagined she would feel if she saw Fred Astaire and Ginger Rogers as they were now, trying to do one of their old dance routines.

The dog managed to get up on the post again, and this time Peter hooked the mail—a catalogue and a letter (or a bill—yes, with the end of the month coming, it was more likely a bill)—out of the box with the first swipe of his paw. It fluttered to the road, and as Peter picked it up, Anderson dropped her eyes back to her sketch, telling herself to stop banging the goddam funeral bell for Peter every two minutes. The dog actually looked half-alive tonight; there *had* been nights recently when he'd had to totter up on his hind legs three or four times before he was able to get his mail—which usually came to no more than a free sample from Procter & Gamble or an advertising circular from K-Mart.

Anderson stared at her sketch closely, absently shading in the trunk of the big pine-tree with the split top. It wasn't a hundred-percent accurate . . . but it was pretty close. She'd gotten the angle of the thing right, anyway.

She drew a box around it, then turned the box into a cube . . . as if to isolate the thing. The curve was obvious enough in her sketch, but had it really been there?

Yes. And what she was calling a metal plate—it was really a hull, wasn't it? A glassy-smooth, rivetless hull.

You're losing your mind, Bobbi . . . you know that, don't you?

Peter scratched on the screen to be let in. Anderson went to the door, still looking at her sketch. Peter came in and dropped the mail on a chair in the hallway. Then he walked slowly down to the kitchen, presumably to see if there was anything he had overlooked on Anderson's plate.

Anderson picked up the two pieces of mail and wiped them on the leg of her jeans with a little grimace of disgust. It was a good trick, granted, but dog-spit on the mail was never going to be one of her favorite things. The catalogue was from Radio Shack—they wanted to sell her a word processor. The bill was from Central Maine Power. That made her think briefly of Jim Gardener again. She tossed both on the table in the hall, went back to her chair, sat down again, flipped to a fresh page, and quickly copied her original sketch.

She frowned at the mild arc, which was probably a bit of extrapolation—as if she had dug down maybe twelve or fourteen feet instead of just four. Well, so what? A little extrapolation didn't bother her; hell, that was part of a fiction writer's business, and people who thought it belonged solely to science fiction or fantasy writers had never looked through the other end of the telescope, had never been faced with the problem of filling in white spaces that no history could provide—things like what had happened to the people who had colonized Roanoke Island, off the North Carolina coast, and then simply disappeared, for example, leaving no mark but the inexplicable word CROATOAN carved on a tree, or the Easter Island monoliths, or why the citizens of a little town in Utah called Blessing had all suddenly gone crazy—or so it seemed—on the same day in the summer of 1884. If you didn't know for sure, it was okay to imagine—until and unless you found out different.

There was a formula by which circumference could be determined from an arc, she was quite sure of it. She had forgotten what the damned thing was, that was the only problem. But she could maybe get a rough idea—always assuming her impression of just how much the thing's edge curved was accurate—by estimating the thing's center point . . .

Bobbi went back to the hall table and opened its middle drawer, which was a sort of catchall. She rooted past untidy bundles of canceled checks, dead C, D, and nine-volt batteries (for some reason she had never been able to shitcan old batteries—what you did with old batteries was throw them in a drawer, God knew why, it was just the Battery Graveyard instead of the one the elephants were supposed to have), bunches of rubber bands and wide red canning-rubbers, unanswered fan letters (she could no more throw out an unanswered fan letter than a dead battery), and recipes jotted on file-cards. At the very bottom of the drawer was a litter of small tools, and among them she found what she was looking for—a compass with a yellow stub of pencil sleeved into the armature.

Sitting in the rocker again, Anderson turned to a fresh sheet and drew the leading edge of the thing in the earth for the third time. She tried to keep it in scale, but drew it a little bigger this time, not bothering with the surrounding trees and only suggesting the trench for the sake of perspective.

"Okay, guesswork," she said, and dug the point of the compass into the yellow legal pad below the curved edge.

She adjusted the compass's arc so it traced that edge fairly accurately—and then she swept the compass around in a complete circle. She looked at it, then wiped her mouth with the heel of her hand. Her lips suddenly felt too loose and too wet.

"Boolsheet," she whispered.

But it wasn't boolsheet. Unless her estimate of the edge's curvature and of midpoint were both wildly off the beam, she had unearthed the edge of an object which was at least three hundred yards in circumference.

Anderson dropped the compass and the pad on the floor and looked out the window. Her heart was beating too hard.

5

As the sun went down, Anderson sat on her back porch staring across her garden toward the woods, and listened to the voices in her head.

In her junior year at college she had taken a Psychology Department seminar on creativity. She had been amazed—and a little relieved—to discover that she was not concealing some private neurosis; almost all imaginative people heard voices. Not just thoughts but actual *voices* inside their heads, different personae, each as clearly defined as voices on an old-time radio show. They came from the right side of the brain, the teacher explained—the side which is most commonly associated with visions and telepathy and that striking human ability to create images by drawing comparisons and making metaphors.

There are no such things as flying saucers.

Oh yeah? Who says so?

The Air Force, for one. They closed the books on flying saucers twenty years ago. They were able to explain all but three percent of all verified sightings, and they said those last three were almost certainly caused by ephemeral atmospheric conditions—stuff like sun-dogs, clear-air turbulence, pockets of clear-air electricity. Hell, the Lubbock Lights were front-page news, and all they *turned out to be was . . . well, there were these traveling packs of moths, see? And the Lubbock streetlights hit their wings and reflected big light-colored moving shapes onto the low cloud masses that a stagnant weather pattern kept over the town for a week. Most of the country spent that week thinking someone dressed like Michael Rennie in* The Day the Earth Stood Still *was going to come walking up Lubbock's main drag with his pet robot Gort clanking along beside him, demanding to be taken to our leader. And they were moths. Do you like it? Don't you have to like it?*

This voice was so clear it was amusing—it was that of Dr. Klingerman, who had taught the seminar. It lectured her with good old Klingy's unfailing—if rather shrill—enthusiasm. Anderson smiled and lit a cigarette. Smoking a little too much tonight, but the damned things were going stale anyway.

In 1947 an Air Force captain named Mantell flew too high while he was chasing a flying saucer—what he thought *was a flying saucer. He blacked out. His plane crashed. Mantell was killed. He died chasing a reflection of Venus on a high scud of clouds—a sun-dog, in other words. So there are reflections of moths, reflections of Venus, and probably reflections in a golden eye as well, Bobbi, but there are no flying saucers.*

Then what is that in the ground?

The voice of the lecturer fell still. It didn't know. So in its place came Anne's voice, telling her for the third time that she was getting funny in the head, getting weird like Uncle Frank, saying they'd be measuring her for one of those canvas coats you wear backwards soon; they'd cart her up to the asylum in Bangor or the one in Juniper Hill, and she could rave about flying saucers in the woods while she wove baskets. It was Sissy's voice, all right; she could call her on the phone right now, tell her what had happened, and get that scripture by chapter and by verse. She knew it.

But was it right?

No. It wasn't. Anne would equate her sister's mostly solitary life with madness no matter what Bobbi did or said. And yes, the idea that the thing in the earth was some sort of spaceship certainly *was* mad . . . but was playing with the possibility, at least until it was disproven, mad? Anne would think so, but Anderson did not. Nothing wrong with keeping an open mind.

Yet the speed with which the possibility had occurred to her . . .

She got up and went inside. Last time she had fooled with that thing in the woods, she had slept for twelve hours. She wondered if she could expect a similar sleep marathon this time. She felt almost tired enough to sleep twelve hours, God knew.

Leave it alone, Bobbi. It's dangerous.

But she wouldn't, she thought, pulling off her OPUS FOR PRESIDENT T-shirt. Not just yet.

The trouble with living alone, she had discovered—and the reason why most people she knew didn't like to be alone even for a little while—was that the longer you lived alone, the louder those voices on the right side of your brain got. As the yardsticks of rationality began to shrink in the silence, those voices did not just request attention; they *demanded* it. It was easy to become frightened of them, to think they meant madness after all.

Anne would sure think they did, Bobbi thought, climbing into bed. The lamp cast a clean and comforting circle of light on the counterpane, but she left the thesis she'd been reading on the floor. She kept expecting the cramps that usually accompanied her occasional early and heavy menstrual flow, but so far they hadn't come. Not that she was anxious for them to put in an appearance, you should understand.

She crossed her hands behind her head and looked at the ceiling.

No, you're not crazy at all, Bobbi, she thought. *You think Gard's getting wiggy but you're perfectly all right—isn't that also a sign that you're wobbling? There's even a name for it . . . denial and substitution. "I'm all right, it's the world that's crazy."*

All true. But she still felt firmly in control of herself, and sure of one thing: she was saner in Haven than she had been in Cleaves Mills, and *much* saner than she had been in Utica. A few more years in Utica, a few more years around Sissy, and she would have been as mad as a hatter. Anderson believed Anne actually saw driving her close relatives crazy as part of her . . . her job? No, nothing so mundane. As part of her sacred mission in life.

She knew what was really troubling her, and it wasn't the speed with which the possibility had occurred. It was the feeling of *certainty*. She would keep an open mind, but the struggle would be to keep it open in favor of what Anne would call "sanity." Because she *knew* what she had found, and it filled her with fear and awe and a restless, moving excitement.

See, Anne, ole Bobbi didn't move up to Sticksville and go crazy; ole Bobbi moved up here and went sane. Insanity is limiting *possibilities, Anne, can you dig it? Insanity is refusing to go down certain paths of speculation even though the logic is there . . . like a token for the turnstile. See what I mean? No? Of course you don't. You don't and you never did. Then go away, Anne. Stay in Utica and grind your teeth in your sleep until there's nothing left of them, make whoever is mad enough to stay within range of your voice crazy, be my guest,* but stay out of my head.

The thing in the earth was a ship from space.

There. It was out. No more bullshit. Never mind Anne, never mind the Lubbock Lights or how the Air Force had closed its file on flying saucers. Never mind the chariots of the gods, or the Bermuda Triangle, or how Elijah was drawn up to heaven in a wheel of fire. Never mind any of it—her heart knew what her heart knew. It was a ship, and it had either landed or crash-landed a long time ago—maybe millions of years ago.

God!

She lay in bed, hands behind her head. She was calm enough, but her heart was beating fast, fast, fast.

Then another voice, and this was the voice of her dead grandfather, repeating something Anne's voice had said earlier.

Leave it alone, Bobbi. It's dangerous.

That momentary vibration. Her first premonition, suffocating and positive, that she had found the edge of some weird steel coffin. Peter's reaction. Starting her period early, only spotting here at the farm but bleeding like a stuck pig when she was close to it. Losing track of time, sleeping the clock all the way around. And don't forget ole Chuck the Woodchuck. Chuck had smelled gassy and decomposed, but there were no flies. No flies on Chuck, you might say.

None of that shit adds up to Shinola. I'll buy the possibility of a ship in the earth because no matter how crazy it sounds at first, the logic's still there. But there's no logic to the rest of this stuff; they're loose beads rolling around on the table. Thread them onto a string and maybe I'll buy it—I'll think about it, anyway. Okay?

Her grandfather's voice again, that slow, authoritative voice, the only one in the house that had even been able to strike Anne silent as a kid.

Those things all happened after *you found it, Bobbi. That's your string.*

No. Not enough.

Easy enough to talk back to her grandfather now; the man was sixteen years in his grave. But it was her grandfather's voice that followed her down to sleep, nevertheless.

Leave it alone, Bobbi. It's dangerous—

—and you know that, too.

3.

PETER SEES THE LIGHT

1

She thought she had seen something different about Peter, but hadn't been able to tell exactly what it was. When Anderson woke up the next morning (at a perfectly normal nine o'clock), she saw it almost at once.

She stood at the counter, pouring Gravy Train into Peter's old red dish. As always, Peter came strolling in at the sound. The Gravy Train was fairly new; up until this year the deal had always been Gaines Meal in the morning, half a can of Rival canned dogfood at night, and everything Pete could catch in the woods in between. Then Peter had stopped eating the Gaines Meal and it had taken Anderson almost a month to catch on—Peter wasn't bored; what remained of his teeth simply couldn't manage to crunch up the nuggets anymore. So now he got Gravy Train . . . the equivalent, she supposed, of an old man's poached egg for breakfast.

She ran warm water over the Gravy Train nuggets, then stirred them with the old battered spoon she kept for the purpose. Soon the softening nuggets floated in a muddy liquid that actually did look like gravy . . . *either that,* Anderson thought, *or something out of a backed-up septic tank.*

"Here you go," she said, turning away from the sink. Peter was now in his accustomed spot on the linoleum—a polite distance away so Anderson wouldn't trip over him when she turned around—and thumping his tail. "Hope you enjoy it. Myself, I think I'd ralph my g—"

That was where she stopped, bent over with Peter's red dish in her right hand, her hair falling over one eye. She brushed it away.

"Pete?" she heard herself say.

Peter looked at her quizzically for a moment and then padded forward to get his morning kip. A moment later he was slurping it up enthusiastically.

Anderson straightened, looking at her dog, rather glad she could no longer see Peter's face. In her head her grandfather's voice told her again to leave it alone, it was dangerous, and did she need any more string for her beads?

There are about a million people in this country alone who would come running if they got wind of this *kind of dangerous,* Anderson thought. *God knows how many in the rest of the world. And is that all it does? How is it on cancer, do you suppose?*

All the strength suddenly ran out of her legs. She felt her way backward until she touched one of the kitchen chairs. She sat down and watched Peter eat.

The milky cataract which had covered his left eye was now half gone.

2

"I don't have the slightest idea," the vet said that afternoon.

Anderson sat in the examining room's only chair while Peter sat obediently on the examining table. Anderson found herself remembering how she had dreaded the possibility of having to bring Peter to the vet's this summer . . . only now it didn't look as if Peter would have to be put down after all.

"But it isn't just my imagination?" Anderson asked, and she supposed that what she really wanted was for Dr. Etheridge to either confirm or confute the Anne in her head: *It's what you deserve, living out there alone with your smelly dog. . . .*

"Nope," Etheridge said, "although I can understand why you feel flummoxed. I feel a little flummoxed myself.

His cataract is in active remission. You can get down, Peter." Peter climbed down from the table, going first to Etheridge's stool and then to the floor and then to Anderson.

Anderson put her hand on Peter's head and looked closely at Etheridge, thinking: *Did you see that?* Not quite wanting to say it out loud. For a moment Etheridge met her eyes, and then he looked away. *I saw it, yes, but I'm not going to admit that I saw it.* Peter had gotten down carefully, in a descent that was miles from the devil-take-the-hindmost bounds of the puppy he had once been, but neither was it the trembling, tentative, wobbly descent Peter would have made even a week ago, cocking his head unnaturally to the right so he could see where he was going, his balance so vague that your heart stopped until he was down with no bones broken. Peter came down with the conservative yet solid confidence of the elder statesman he had been two or three years ago. Some of it, Anderson supposed, was the fact that the vision in his left eye was returning—Etheridge had confirmed that with a few simple perception tests. But the eye wasn't all of it. The rest was overall improved body coordination. Simple as that. Crazy, but simple.

And the shrinking cataract hadn't caused Pete's muzzle to return to salt-and-pepper from an almost solid white, had it? Anderson had noticed that in the pickup truck as they headed down to Augusta. She had almost driven off the road.

How much of this was Etheridge seeing and not being prepared to admit he was seeing? Quite a bit, Anderson guessed, but part of it was just that Etheridge wasn't Doc Daggett.

Daggett had seen Peter at least twice a year during the first ten years of Peter's life . . . and then there were the things that came up, like the time Pete had mixed in with a porcupine, for instance, and Daggett had removed the quills, one by one, whistling the theme music from *The Bridge on the River Kwai* as he did so, soothing the trembling year-old dog with one big kindly hand. On another occasion Peter had come limping home with a backside full of birdshot—a cruel present from a hunter either too stupid to look before he shot or perhaps sadistic enough to inflict misery on a dog because he couldn't find a partridge or pheasant to inflict it on. Dr. Daggett would have seen *all* the changes in Peter, and would not have been able to deny them even if he had wished to. Dr. Daggett would have taken off his pink-rimmed glasses, polished them on his white coat, and said something like: *We have to find out where he's been and what he's gotten into, Roberta. This is serious. Dogs don't just get younger, and that is what Peter appears to be doing.* That would have forced Anderson to reply: *I know where he's been, and I've got a pretty good idea of what did it.* And that would have taken a lot of the pressure off, wouldn't it? But old Doc Daggett had sold the practice to Etheridge, who seemed nice enough, but who was still something of a stranger, and retired to Florida. Etheridge had seen Peter more often than Daggett had done—four times in the last year, as it happened—because as Peter grew older he had grown steadily more infirm. But he still hadn't seen him as often as his predecessor . . . and, she suspected, he didn't have his predecessor's clear-eyed perceptions. Or his guts.

From the ward behind them, a German shepherd suddenly exploded a string of heavy barks that sounded like a string of canine curses. Other dogs picked it up. Peter's ears cocked forward and he began to tremble under Anderson's hand. The Benjamin Button routine apparently hadn't done a thing for the beagle's equanimity, Anderson thought; once through his puppyhood storms, Peter had been so laid-back he was damn near paralytic. This high-strung trembling was brand-new.

Etheridge was listening to the dogs with a slight frown—now almost all of them were barking.

"Thanks for seeing us on such short notice," Anderson said. She had to raise her voice to be heard. A dog in the waiting room also started to bark—the quick, nervous yappings of a very small animal . . . a Pom or a poodle, most likely. "It was very—" Her voice broke momentarily. She felt a vibration under her fingertips and her first thought

(the ship)

was of the thing in the woods. But she knew what this vibration was. Although she had felt it very, very seldom, there was no mystery about it.

This vibration was coming from Peter. Peter was growling, very low and deep in his throat.

"—kind of you, but I think we ought to split. It sounds

like you've got a mutiny on your hands." She meant it as a joke, but it no longer sounded like a joke. Suddenly the entire small complex—the cinderblock square that was Etheridge's waiting room and treatment room, plus the attached cinderblock rectangle that was his ward and operating theater—was in an uproar. All the dogs out back were barking, and in the waiting room the Pom had been joined by a couple of other dogs . . . and a feminine, wavering wail that was unmistakably feline.

Mrs. Alden popped in, looking distressed. "Dr. Etheridge—"

"All right," he said, sounding cross. "Excuse me, Ms. Anderson."

He left in a hurry, heading for the ward first. When he opened the door, the noise of the dogs seemed to double—*they're going bugshit,* Anderson thought, and that was all she had time to think, because Peter almost lunged out from under her hand. That idling growl deep in his throat suddenly roughened into a snarl. Etheridge, already hurrying down the ward's central corridor, dogs barking all around him and the door swinging slowly shut on its pneumatic elbow behind him, didn't hear, but Anderson did, and if she hadn't been lucky in her grab for Peter's collar, the beagle would have been across the room like a shot and into the ward after the doctor. The trembling and the deep growl . . . those hadn't been fear, she realized. They had been rage—it was inexplicable, completely unlike Peter, but that's what it had been.

Peter's snarl turned to a strangled sound—*yark!*—as Anderson pulled him back by the collar. He turned his head, and in Peter's rolling red-rimmed right eye Anderson saw what she would later characterize only as fury at being turned from the course he wanted to follow. She could acknowledge the possibility that there was a flying saucer three hundred yards around its outer rim buried on her property; the possibility that some emanation or vibration from this ship had killed a woodchuck that had the bad luck to get a little too close, killed it so completely and unpleasantly that even the flies seemingly wanted no part of it; she could deal with an anomalous menstrual period, a canine cataract in remission, even with the seeming certainty that her dog was somehow growing younger.

All this, yes.

But the idea that she had seen an insane hate for her, for Bobbi Anderson, in her good old dog Peter's eyes . . . no.

3

That moment was thankfully brief. The door to the ward shut, muffling the cacophony. Some of the tenseness seemed to go out of Peter. He was still trembling, but at least he sat down again.

"Come on, Pete, we're getting out of here," Anderson said. She was badly shaken—much more so than she would later admit to Jim Gardener. For to admit that would have perhaps led back to that furious leer of rage she had seen in Peter's good eye.

She fumbled for the unfamiliar leash which she had taken off Peter as soon as they got into the examination room (that dogs should be leashed when owners brought them in for examination was a requirement Anderson had always found annoying—until now), almost dropping it. At last she managed to attach it to Peter's collar.

She led Peter to the door of the waiting room and pushed it open with her foot. The noise was worse than ever. The yapper was indeed a Pomeranian, the property of a fat woman wearing bright yellow slacks and a yellow top. Fatso was trying to hold the Pom, telling it to "be a good boy, Eric, be a good boy for Mommy." Very little save the dog's bright and somehow ratty eyes were visible between Mommy's large and flabby arms.

"Ms. Anderson—" Mrs. Alden began. She looked bewildered and a little frightened, a woman trying to conduct business as usual in a place that had suddenly become a madhouse. Anderson understood how she felt.

The Pom spotted Peter—Anderson would later swear that was what set it off—and seemed to go crazy. It certainly had no problem choosing a target. It sank its sharp teeth into one of Mommy's arms.

"*Cocksucker!*" Mommy screamed, and dropped the Pom on the floor. Blood began to run down her arm.

At the same time, Peter lunged forward, barking and snarling, fetching up at the end of the short leash hard enough to jerk Anderson forward. Her right arm flagged out straight. With the clear eye of her writer's mind Anderson saw exactly what was going to happen next. Peter the beagle and Eric the Pom were going to meet in the middle of the room like David and Goliath. But the Pom had no brains, let alone a sling. Peter would tear its head off with one large chomp.

This was averted by a girl of perhaps eleven, who was sitting to Mommy's left. The girl had a Porta-Carry on her lap. Inside was a large blacksnake, its scales glowing with luxuriant good health. The little girl shot out one jeans-clad leg with the unearthly reflexes of the very young and stomped on the trailing end of Eric's leash. Eric did one complete snap-roll. The little girl reeled the Pom in. She was by far the calmest person in the waiting room.

"What if that little fucker gave me the rabies?" Mommy was screaming as she advanced across the room toward Mrs. Alden. Blood twinkled between the fingers clapped to her arm. Peter's head turned toward her as she passed, and Anderson pulled him back, heading toward the door. Fuck the little sign in Mrs. Alden's cubbyhole reading IT IS CUSTOMARY TO PAY CASH FOR PROFESSIONAL SERVICES UNLESS OTHER ARRANGEMENTS HAVE BEEN MADE IN ADVANCE. She wanted to get out of here and drive the speed limit all the way home and have a drink. Cutty. A double. On second thought, make that a triple.

From her left came a long, low, virulent hissing sound. Anderson turned in that direction and saw a cat that might have stepped out of a Halloween decoration. Black except for a single dab of white at the end of its tail, it had backed up as far as its carrying cage would allow. Its back was humped up; its fur stood straight up in hackles; its green eyes, fixed unwaveringly on Peter, glowed fantastically. Its pink mouth was jointed wide, ringed with teeth.

"Get your dog out, lady," the woman with the cat said in a voice cold as a cocking trigger. "Blacky don't like im."

Anderson wanted to tell her she didn't care if Blacky farted or blew a tin whistle, but she would not think of this obscure but somehow exquisitely apt expression until later—she rarely did in hot situations. Her characters always knew exactly the right things to say, and she rarely had to deliberate over them—they came easily and naturally. This was almost never the case in real life.

"Hold your water," was the best she could do, and she spoke in such a craven mutter that she doubted if Blacky's owner had the slightest idea what she had said, or maybe even that she had said anything at all. She really *was* pulling Peter now, using the leash to yank the dog along in a way she hated to see a dog pulled whenever she observed it being done on the street. Peter was making coughing noises in his throat and his tongue was a saliva-dripping runner hanging askew from one side of his mouth. He stared at a boxer whose right foreleg was in a cast. A big man in a blue mechanic's coverall was holding the boxer's rope leash with both hands; had, in fact, taken a double-twist of the hayrope around one big grease-stained fist and was still having trouble holding his dog, which could have killed Peter as quickly and efficiently as Peter himself could have the Pomeranian. The boxer was pulling mightily in spite of its broken leg, and Anderson had more faith in the mechanic's grip than she did the hayrope leash, which appeared to be fraying.

It seemed to Anderson that she fumbled for the knob of the outer door with her free hand for a hundred years. It was like having a nightmare where your hands are full and your pants start, slowly and inexorably, to slip down.

Peter did this. Somehow.

She turned the knob, then took one final hasty glance around the waiting room. It had become an absurd little no-man's-land. Mommy was demanding first aid of Mrs. Alden (and apparently really did need some; blood was now coursing down her arm in freshets, spotting her yellow slacks and white institutional shoes); Blacky the cat was still hissing; even Dr. Etheridge's gerbils were going mad in the complicated maze of plastic tubes and towers on the far shelf that made up their home; Eric the Crazed Pomeranian stood at the end of his leash barking at Peter in a strangled voice. Peter was snarling back.

Anderson's eye fell on the little girl's blacksnake and saw that it had reared up like a cobra inside its Porta-Carry and was also looking at Peter, its fangless mouth yawning, its narrow pink tongue shuttling at the air in stiff little jabs.

Blacksnakes don't do that, I never saw a blacksnake do that in my life.

Now in something very close to real horror, Anderson fled, dragging Peter after her.

4

Pete began to calm down almost as soon as the door sighed shut behind them. He stopped coughing and dragging on the leash and began to walk at Anderson's side, glancing at her occasionally in that way that said *I don't like this leash and I'm* never *going to like it, but okay, okay, if it's what you want.* By the time they were both in the cab of the pickup, Peter was entirely his old self again.

Anderson was not.

Her hands were shaking so badly that she had to try three times before she could get the ignition key into its slot. Then she popped the clutch and stalled the engine. The Chevy pickup gave a mighty jerk and Peter tumbled off the seat onto the floor. He gave Anderson a reproachful beagle look (although all dogs are capable of reproachful looks, only beagles seem to have mastered that long-suffering stare). *Where did you say you got your license, Bobbi?* that expression seemed to ask. *Sears and Roebuck?* Then he climbed up on the seat again. Anderson was already finding it hard to believe that only five minutes ago Peter had been growling and snarling, a bad-tempered dog she had never encountered before, apparently ready to bite anything that moved, *and that expression, that* . . . But her mind snapped shut on that before it could go any further.

She got the engine going again and then headed out of the parking lot. As she passed the side of the building—AUGUSTA VETERINARY CLINIC, the neat sign read—she rolled her window down. A few barks and yaps. Nothing out of the ordinary.

It had stopped.

And that wasn't all that had stopped, she thought. Although she couldn't be completely sure, she thought her period was over, too. If so, good riddance to bad rubbish.

To coin a phrase.

5

Bobbi didn't want to wait—or couldn't—to get back before having the drink she had promised herself. Just outside the Augusta city limits was a roadhouse that went by the charming name of the Big Lost Weekend Bar and Grille (Whopper Spareribs Our Specialty; The Nashville Kitty-Cats This Fri and Sad).

Anderson pulled in between an old station wagon and a John Deere tractor with a dirty harrow on the back with its blades kicked up. Further down was a big old Buick with a horse-trailer behind. Anderson had kept away from that on purpose.

"Stay," Anderson said, and Peter, now curled up on the seat, gave her a look as if to say, *Why would I want to go anywhere with you? So you can choke me some more with that stupid leash?*

The Big Lost Weekend was dark and nearly deserted on a Wednesday afternoon, its dance floor a cavern which glimmered faintly. The place reeked of sour beer. The bartender *cum* counterman strolled down and said, "Howdy, purty lady. The chili's on special. Also—"

"I'd like Cutty Sark," Anderson said. "Double. Water back."

"You always drink like a man?"

"Usually from a glass," Anderson said, a quip which made no sense at all, but she felt very tired . . . and harrowed to the bone. She went into the ladies' to change her pad and did slip one of the minis from her purse into the crotch of her panties as a precaution . . . but precaution was all it was, and that was a relief. It seemed that the cardinal had flown off for another month.

She returned to her stool in a better humor than she had left it, and felt better still when she had gotten half the drink inside her.

"Say, I sure didn't mean to offend you," the bartender said. "It gets lonely in here, afternoons. When a stranger comes in, my lip gets runny."

"My fault," Anderson said. "I haven't been having the best day of my life."

She finished the drink and sighed.

"You want another one, miss?"

I think I liked "purty lady" better, Anderson thought, and shook her head. "I'll take a glass of milk, though. Otherwise I'll have acid indigestion all afternoon."

The bartender brought her the milk. Anderson sipped it and thought about what had happened at the vet's. The answer was quick and simple: she didn't know.

But I'll tell you what happened when you brought him in, she thought. *Not a thing.*

Her mind seized on this. The waiting room had been almost as crowded when she brought Peter in as it had been when she dragged him back out, only there had been no bedlam scene the first time. The place had not been quiet—animals of different types and species, many of them ancient and instinctive antagonists, do not make for a library atmosphere when brought together—but it had been normal. Now, with the booze working in her, she recalled the man in the mechanic's coverall leading the boxer in. The boxer had looked at Peter. Peter had looked mildly back. No big deal.

So?

So drink your milk and get on home and forget it.

Okay. And what about that thing in the woods? Do I forget that, too?

Instead of an answer, her grandfather's voice came: *By the way, Bobbi, what's that thing doing to* you? *Have you thought about that?*

She hadn't.

Now that she had, she was tempted to order another drink . . . except another, even a single, would make her drunk, and did she really want to be sitting in this huge barn in the early afternoon, getting drunk alone, waiting for the inevitable someone (maybe the bartender himself) to cruise up and ask what a pretty place like this was doing around a girl like her?

She left a five on the counter and the bartender saluted her. On her way out she saw a pay phone. The phone-book was dirty and dog-eared and smelled of used bourbon, but at least it was still there. Anderson deposited twenty cents, crooked the handset between shoulder and ear while she hunted through the V's in the Yellow Pages, then called Etheridge's clinic. Mrs. Alden sounded quite composed. In the background she could hear one dog barking. One.

"I didn't want you to think I stiffed you," she said, "and I'll mail your leash back tomorrow."

"Not at all, Ms. Anderson," she said. "After all the years you've done business with us, you're the last person we'd worry about when it comes to deadbeats. As for leashes, we've got a closetful."

"Things seemed a little crazy there for a while."

"Boy, were they ever! We had to call Medix for Mrs. Perkins. I didn't think it was bad—she'll have needed stitches, of course, but lots of people who need stitches get to the doctor under their own power." She lowered her voice a little, offering Anderson a confidence that she probably wouldn't have offered a man. "Thank God it was her own dog that bit her. She's the sort of woman who starts shouting lawsuit at the drop of a hat."

"Any idea what might have caused it?"

"No—neither does Dr. Etheridge. The heat after the rain, maybe. Dr. Etheridge said he heard of something like it once at a convention. A vet from California said that all the animals in her clinic had what she called 'a savage spell' just before the last big quake out there."

"Is that so?"

"There was an earthquake in Maine last year," Mrs. Alden said. "I hope there won't be another one. That nuclear plant at Wiscasset is too close for comfort."

Just ask Gard, Bobbi thought. She said thanks again and hung up.

Anderson went back to the truck. Peter was sleeping. He opened his eyes when Anderson got in, then closed them again. His muzzle lay on his paws. The gray on that muzzle was fading away. No question about it; no question at all.

And by the way, Bobbi, what's that thing doing to you?

Shut up, Granddad.

She drove home. And after fortifying herself with a second Scotch—a weak one—she went into the bathroom and stood close to the mirror, first examining her face and then running her fingers through her hair, lifting it and then letting it drop.

The gray was still there—all of it that had so far come in, as far as she could tell.

She never would have thought she would be glad to see gray hair, but she was. Sort of.

6

By early evening, dark clouds had begun to build up in the west, and by dark it had commenced thundering. The rains were going to return, it seemed, at least for a one-night stand. Anderson knew she wouldn't get Peter outside that night to do more than the most pressing doggy business; since his puppyhood, the beagle had been utterly terrified of thunderstorms.

Anderson sat in her rocker by the window, and if someone had been there she supposed it would have looked like she was reading, but what she was really doing was grinding: grinding grimly away at the thesis *Range War and Civil War.* It was as dry as dust, but she thought it was going to be extremely useful when she finally got around to the new one . . . which should be fairly soon now.

Each time the thunder rolled, Peter edged a little closer to the rocker and Anderson, seeming almost to grin shamefacedly. *Yeah, it's not going to hurt me, I know, I know, but I'll just get a little closer to you, okay? And if there comes a real blast, I'll just about crowd you out of that fucking rocker, what do you say? You don't mind, do you, Bobbi?*

The storm held off until nine o'clock, and by then Anderson was pretty sure they were going to have a good one—what Havenites called "a real Jeezer." She went into the kitchen, rummaged in the walk-in closet that served as her pantry, and found her Coleman gas lantern on a high shelf. Peter followed directly behind her, tail between his legs, shamefaced grin on his face. Anderson almost fell over him coming out of the closet with the lantern.

"Do you mind, Peter?"

Peter gave a little ground . . . and then crowded up to Anderson's ankles again, when thunder cannonaded hard enough to rattle the windows. As Anderson got back to her chair, lightning sheeted blue-white and the phone tinged. The wind began to rise, making the trees rustle and sigh.

Peter sat hard by the rocker, looking up at Anderson pleadingly.

"Okay," she said with a sigh. "Come on up, jerk."

Peter didn't have to be asked twice. He sprang into Anderson's lap, getting her crotch a pretty good one with one forepaw. He always seemed to whang her there or on one boob; he didn't aim—it was just one of those mysterious things, like the way elevators invariably stopped at every floor when you were in a hurry. If there was a defense, Bobbi Anderson had yet to find it.

Thunder tore across the sky. Peter crowded against her. His smell—*Eau de Beagle*—filled Anderson's nose.

"Why don't you just jump down my throat and have done with it, Pete?"

Peter grinned his shamefaced grin, as if to say *I know it, I know it, don't rub it in.*

The wind rose. The lights began to flicker, a sure sign that Roberta Anderson and Central Maine Power were about to bid each other a fond adieu . . . at least until three or four in the morning. Anderson laid the thesis aside and put her arm around her dog. She didn't really mind the occasional summer storm, or the winter blizzards, for that matter. She liked their big power. She liked the sight and sound of that power working on the land in its crude and blindly positive way. She sensed insensate compassion in the workings of such storms. She could feel this one working inside her—the hair on her arms and the nape of her neck stirred, and a particularly close shot of lightning left her feeling almost galvanized with energy.

She remembered an odd conversation she'd once had with Jim Gardener. Gard had a steel plate in his skull, a souvenir of a skiing accident that had almost killed him at the age of seventeen. Gardener had told her that once, while changing a light bulb, he had gotten a hell of a shock by inadvertently sticking his forefinger into the socket. This was hardly uncommon; the peculiar part was that, for the next week, he had heard music and announcers and newscasts in his head. He told Anderson he had really believed for a while he was going crazy. On the fourth day of this, Gard had even identified the call letters of the station he was receiving: WZON, one of Bangor's three AM radio stations. He had written down the names of three songs in a row and then called the station to see if they had indeed played those songs—plus ads for Sing's Polynesian Restaurant, Village Subaru, and the Bird Museum in Bar Harbor. They had.

On the fifth day, he said, the signal started to fade, and two days later it was gone entirely.

"It was that damned skull plate," he had told her, rapping his fist gently on the scar by his left temple. "No doubt about it. I'm sure thousands would laugh, but in my own mind I'm completely sure."

If someone else had told her the story, Anderson would have believed she was having her leg pulled, but Jim hadn't been kidding—you looked in his eyes and you knew he wasn't.

Big storms had big power.

Lightning flared in a blue sheet, giving Anderson a shutter-click of what she had come to think of—as her neighbors did—as her dooryard. She saw the truck, with the first drops of rain on its windshield; the short dirt driveway; the mailbox with its flag down and tucked securely against its aluminum side; the writhing trees. Thunder exploded a bare moment later, and Peter jumped against her, whining. The lights went out. They didn't bother dimming or flickering or messing around; they went out all at once, completely. They went out with *authority*.

Anderson reached for the lantern—and then her hand stopped.

There was a green spot on the far wall, just to the right of Uncle Frank's Welsh dresser. It bobbed up two inches, moved left, then right. It disappeared for a moment and then came back. Anderson's dream recurred with all the eerie power of *déjà vu.* She thought again of the lantern in Poe's story, but mixed in this time was another memory: *The War of the Worlds.* The Martian heat-ray, raining green death on Hammersmith.

She turned toward Peter, hearing the tendons in her neck creak like dirty door hinges, knowing what she was going to see. The light was coming from Peter's eye. His left eye. It glared with the witchy green light of St. Elmo's fire drifting over a swamp after a still, muggy day.

No . . . not the *eye*. It was the *cataract* that was glowing . . . at least, what remained of the cataract. It had gone back noticeably even from that morning at the vet's office. That side of Peter's face was lit with a lurid green light, making him look like a comic-book monstrosity.

Her first impulse was to get away from Peter, dive out of the chair and simply run . . .

. . . but this *was* Peter, after all. And Peter was scared to death already. If she deserted him, Peter would be terrified.

Thunder cracked in the black. This time both of them jumped. Then the rain came in a great sighing sheetlike rush. Anderson looked back at the wall across the room again, at the green splotch bobbing and weaving there. She was reminded of times she had lain in bed as a child, using the watchband of her Timex to play a similar spot off the wall by moving her wrist.

And by the way, what's it doing to you, *Bobbi?*

Green sunken fire in Peter's eye, taking away the cataract. Eating it. She looked again, and had to restrain herself from jerking back when Peter licked her hand.

That night Bobbi Anderson slept hardly at all.

4.

THE DIG, CONTINUED

1

When Anderson finally woke up, it was almost ten A.M. and most of the lights in the place were on—Central Maine Power had gotten its shit together again, it seemed. She walked around the place in her socks, turning off lights, and then looked out the front window. Peter was on the porch. Anderson let him in and looked closely at his eye. She could remember her terror of the night before, but in this morning's bright summer daylight, terror had been supplanted by fascination. *Anyone* would have been scared, she thought, seeing something like that in the dark, with the power out, and a thunderstorm stomping the earth and the sky outside.

Why in hell didn't Etheridge see this?

But that was easy. The dials of radium watches glow in the day as well as in the dark; you just can't see the glow in bright light. She was a little surprised she had missed the green glow in Peter's eye on the previous nights, but hardly flabbergasted . . . after all, it had taken her a couple of days to even realize the cataract was shrinking. And yet . . . Etheridge had been *close,* hadn't he? Etheridge had been right in there with the old ophthalmoscope, looking into Peter's eye.

He had agreed with Anderson that the cataract was shrinking . . . but hadn't mentioned any glow, green or otherwise.

Maybe he saw it and decided to unsee it. The way he

saw Peter was looking younger and decided he didn't see that. Because he didn't want *to see that.*

There was a part of her that didn't like the new vet a whole hell of a lot; she supposed it was because she had liked old Doc Daggett so much and had made that foolish (but apparently unavoidable) assumption that Daggett would be around as long as she and Peter were. But it was a silly reason to feel hostility toward the old man's replacement, and even if Etheridge had failed (or refused) to see Peter's apparent age regression, that didn't change the fact that he seemed a perfectly competent vet.

A cataract that glowed green . . . she didn't think he would have ignored something like that.

Which led her to the conclusion that the green glow hadn't been there for Etheridge to see.

At least, not right away.

There hadn't been any big hooraw right away, either, had there? Not when they came in. Not during the exam. Only when they were getting ready to go out.

Had Peter's eye started to glow then?

Anderson poured Gravy Train into Peter's dish and stood with her left hand under the tap, waiting for the water to come in warm so she could wet it down. The wait kept getting longer and longer. Her water heater was slow, balky, sadly out of date. Anderson had been meaning to have it replaced—would certainly have to do so before cold weather—but the only plumber in either Haven or the rural towns to Haven's immediate north and south was a rather unpleasant fellow named Delbert Chiles, who always looked at her as if he knew *exactly* what she would look like with her clothes off *(not much,* his eyes said, *but I guess it'd do in a pinch*) and always wanted to know if Anderson was "writing any new books lately." Chiles liked to tell her that he could have been a damned good writer himself, but he had too much energy and "not enough glue on the seat of my pants, get me?" The last time she'd been forced to call him had been when the pipes burst in the minus-twenties cold snap winter before last. After he set things to rights, he had asked her if she would like "to go steppin" sometime. Anderson declined politely, and Chiles tipped her a wink that aspired to worldly wisdom and made it almost to informed vacuity. "You don't know what you're missin, sweetie," he said. *I'm pretty sure I do, which is why I said no* had come to her lips, but she said nothing—as little as she liked him, she had known she might need Chiles again sometime. Why was it the really good zingers only came immediately to mind in real life when you didn't dare use them?

You could do something about that hot-water heater, Bobbi, a voice in her mind spoke up, one that she couldn't identify. A *stranger's* voice in her head? Oh golly, should she call the cops? *But you could,* the voice insisted. *All you'd need to do would be—*

But then the water started to come in warm—tepid, anyway—and she forgot about the water heater. She stirred the Gravy Train, then set it down and watched Peter eat. He was showing a much better appetite these days.

Ought to check his teeth, she thought. *Maybe you can go back to Gaines Meal. A penny saved is a penny earned, and the American reading public is not exactly beating a path to your door, babe. And—*

And exactly when *had* the uproar in the clinic started?

Anderson thought about this carefully. She couldn't be completely sure, but the more she thought about it the more it seemed that it might have been—not for sure, but *might* have been—right after Dr. Etheridge finished examining Peter's cataract and put down the ophthalmoscope.

Attend, Watson, the voice of Sherlock Holmes suddenly spoke up in the quick, almost urgent speech rhythms of Basil Rathbone. *The eye glows. No . . . not the* eye; *the* cataract *glows. But Anderson does not observe it, although she should. Etheridge does not observe it, and he* definitely *should. May we say that the animals at the veterinary clinic do not become upset until Peter's cataract begins to glow . . . until, we might further theorize, the healing process has resumed? Possibly. That the glow is seen only when being seen is safe? Ah, Watson, that is an assumption as frightening as it is unwarranted. Because that would indicate some sort of—*

—some sort of intelligence.

Anderson didn't like where this was leading and tried to choke it off with the old reliable advice: Let it go.

This time it worked.

For a while.

2

Anderson wanted to go out and dig some more.

Her forebrain didn't like that idea at all.

Her forebrain thought that idea sucked.

Leave it alone, Bobbi. It's dangerous.

Right.

And by the way, what's it doing to you?

Nothing she could *see.* But you couldn't see what cigarette smoke did to your lungs, either; that's why people went on smoking. It could be that her liver was rotting, that the chambers of her heart were silting up with cholesterol or that she had rendered herself barren. For all she knew her bone marrow might be producing outlaw white cells like mad right this minute. Why settle for an early period when you could have something *really* interesting like leukemia, Bobbi?

But she wanted to dig it up just the same.

This urge, simple and elemental, had nothing to do with her forebrain. It came baking up from someplace deeper inside. It had all the earmarks of some physical craving—for salt, for some coke or heroin or cigarettes or coffee. Her forebrain supplied logic; this other part supplied an almost incoherent imperative: *Dig on it, Bobbi, it's okay, dig on it, dig on it, shit, why not dig on it awhile more, you know you want to know what it is, so dig on it till you* see *what it is, dig dig dig—*

She was able to turn the voice off by conscious effort and would then realize fifteen minutes later she had been listening to it again, as if to a Delphic oracle.

You've got to tell somebody what you've found.

Who? The police? Huh-uh. No way. Or—

Or who?

She was in her garden, madly weeding . . . a junkie in withdrawal.

—or anyone in authority, her mind finished.

Her right-brain supplied Anne's sarcastic laughter, as she had known it would . . . but the laughter didn't have as much force as she had feared. Like a good many of her generation, Anderson didn't put a great deal of stock in "let the authorities handle it." Her distrust in the way the authorities handled things had begun at the age of thirteen, in Utica. She had been sitting on the sofa in their living room with Anne on one side and her mother on the other. She had been eating a hamburger and watching the Dallas police escort Lee Harvey Oswald across an underground parking garage. There were lots of Dallas police. So many, in fact, that the TV announcer was telling the country that someone had shot Oswald before all those police—all those people in authority—seemed to have the slightest inkling something had gone wrong, let alone what it was.

So far as she could tell, the Dallas police had done such a good job protecting John F. Kennedy and Lee Harvey Oswald that they had been put in charge of the summer race riots two years later, and then the war in Viet Nam. Other assignments followed: handling the oil embargo ten years after the Kennedy assassination, the negotiations to secure the release of the American hostages at the embassy in Tehran, and, when it became clear that the ragheads were not going to listen to the voice of reason and authority, Jimmy Carter had sent the Dallas police in to rescue those pore fellers—after all, authorities who had handled that Kent State business with such coolheaded aplomb could surely be counted upon to perform the sort of job those *Mission: Impossible* guys did every week. Well, the old Dallas police had had a spot of tough luck on that one, but by and large, they had the situation under control. All you had to do was look at how damned *orderly* the world situation had become in the years since a man in a strappy T-shirt with Vitalis on his thinning hair and fried-chicken grease under his fingernails had blown out a President's brains as he sat in the back seat of a Lincoln rolling down the street of a Texas cow town.

I'll tell Jim Gardener. When he gets back. Gard'll know what to do, how to handle it. He'll have some ideas, anyway.

Anne's voice: *You're going to ask a certified loony for advice. Great.*

He's not a loony. Just a little bit weird.

Yeah, arrested at the last Seabrook demonstration with a loaded .45 in his backpack. That's weird, all right.

Anne, shut up.

She weeded. All that morning in the hot sun she weeded, the back of her T-shirt wet with sweat, last year's scarecrow wearing the hat she usually put on to keep the sun off.

After lunch she lay down to take a nap and couldn't sleep. Everything kept going through her mind, and that stranger's voice never shut up. *Dig on it, Bobbi, it's okay, dig on it—*

Until at last she *did* get up, grabbed the crowbar, spade, and shovel, and set out for the woods. At the far end of her field she paused, forehead grooved in thought, and came back for her pickax. Peter was on the porch. He looked up briefly but made no move to come with Anderson.

Anderson was not really surprised.

3

So about twenty minutes later she stood above it, looking down the forested slope to the trench she had begun in the ground, freeing what she now believed was a very tiny section of an extraterrestrial spacecraft. Its gray hull was as solid as a wrench or a screwdriver, denying dreams and vapors and supposings; it was *there.* The dirt she had thrown to either side, moist and black and forest-secret, was now a dark brown—still damp from last night's rain.

Going down the slope, her foot crunched on something that sounded like newspaper. It wasn't newspaper; it was a dead sparrow. Twenty feet further down was a dead crow, feet pointed comically skyward like a dead bird in a cartoon. Anderson paused, looked around, and saw the bodies of three other birds—another crow, a bluejay, and a scarlet tanager. No marks. Just dead. And no flies around any of them.

She reached the trench and dropped her tools on the bank. The trench was muddy. She stepped in nevertheless, her workshoes squashing in the mud. She bent down and could see smooth gray metal going into the earth, a puddle standing on one side.

What are you?

She put her hand on it. That vibration sank into her skin and seemed for a moment to go all through her. Then it stopped.

Anderson turned and put her hand on her shovel, feeling its smooth wood, slightly warmed by the sun. She was vaguely aware that she could hear no forest noises, none at all . . . no birds singing, no animals crashing through the undergrowth and away from the smell of a human being. She was more sharply aware of the smells: peaty earth, pine needles, bark and sap.

A voice inside her—very deep inside, not coming from the right of her brain but perhaps from the very root of her mind—screamed in terror.

Something's happening, Bobbi, something is happening right NOW. *Get out of here dead chuck dead birds Bobbi please please* PLEASE–

Her hand tightened on the shovel's handle and she saw it again as she had sketched it—the gray leading edge of something titanic in the earth.

Her period had started again, but that was all right; she had put a pad in the crotch of her panties even before she went out to weed the garden. A Maxi. And there were half a dozen more in her pack, weren't there? Or was it more like a dozen?

She didn't know, and it didn't matter. Not even discovering some part of her had known she would end up here in spite of whatever foolish conceptions of free will the rest of her mind might possess disturbed her. A shining sort of peace had filled her. Dead animals . . . periods that stopped and started again . . . arriving prepared even after you had assured yourself the decision had not yet been taken . . . these were small things, smaller than small, a whole lot of boolsheet. She would just dig for a while, dig on this sucker, see if there was anything but smooth metal skin to see. Because everything—

"Everything's fine," Bobbi Anderson said in the unnatural stillness, and then she began to dig.

5.

GARDENER TAKES A FALL

1

While Bobbi Anderson was tracing a titanic shape with a compass and thinking the unthinkable with a brain more numbed with exhaustion than she knew, Jim Gardener was doing the only work he could these days. This time he was doing it in Boston. The poetry reading on June 25th was at B.U. *That* went all right. The twenty-sixth was an off-day. It was also the day that Gardener stumbled—only "stumble" didn't really describe what happened, unfortunately. It was no minor matter like snagging your foot under a root while you were walking in the woods. It was a *fall* that he took, one long fucking *fall*, like taking a no-expenses-paid bone-smasher of a tumble down a long flight of stairs. *Stairs?* Shit, he had almost fallen off the face of the earth.

The fall started in his hotel room; it ended on the breakwater at Arcadia Beach, New Hampshire, eight days later.

Bobbi wanted to dig; Gard woke up on the morning of the twenty-sixth wanting to drink.

He knew there was no such thing as a "partially arrested alcoholic." You were either drinking or you weren't. He wasn't drinking now, and that was good, but there had always been long periods when he didn't even *think* about booze. Months, sometimes. He would drop into a meeting once in a while (if two weeks went by in which Gard didn't attend an AA meeting, he felt uneasy—the way he felt if he spilled the salt and didn't toss some over his shoulder) and stand up and say, "Hi, my name's Jim and I'm an alcoholic." But when the urge was absent, it didn't feel like the truth. During these periods, he wasn't actually dry; he could and did drink—*drink,* that was, as opposed to boozing. A couple of cocktails around five, if he was at a faculty function or a faculty dinner party. Just that and no more. Or he could call Bobbi Anderson and ask if she'd like to come over to go out for a couple of cold ones and it was fine. No sweat.

Then there would come a morning like this when he would wake up wanting all the booze in the world. This seemed to be an *actual* thirst, a physical thing—it made him think of those cartoons Virgil Partch used to do in the *Saturday Evening Post,* the ones where some funky old prospector is always crawling across the desert, his tongue hanging out, looking for a waterhole.

All he could do when the urge came on him was fight it off—stand it off, try to earn a draw. Sometimes it was actually better to be in a place like Boston when this happened, because you could go to a meeting every night—every four hours, if that was what it took. After three or four days, it would go away.

Usually.

He would, he thought, just wait it out. Sit in his room and watch movies on cable TV and charge them to room service. He had spent the eight years since his divorce and severance from college teaching as a Full-Time Poet . . . which meant he had come to live in an odd little subsociety where barter was usually more important than money.

He had traded poems for food: on one occasion a birthday sonnet for a farmer's wife in exchange for three shopping bags of new potatoes. "Goddam thing better rhyme, too," the farmer had said, fixing a stony eye upon Gardener. "*Real* poimes rhyme."

Gardener, who could take a hint (especially when his stomach was concerned), composed a sonnet so filled with exuberant masculine rhymes that he burst into gales of laughter after scanning the second draft. He called Bobbi, read it to her, and they both howled. It was even better out loud. Out loud it sounded like a love letter from Dr. Seuss. But he hadn't needed Bobbi to point out to him that it was still an honest piece of work, jangly but not condescending.

On another occasion, a small press in West Minot agreed to publish a book of his poems (this had been in early 1983 and was, in fact, the last book of poems Gardener had published), and offered half a cord of wood as an advance. Gardener took it.

"You should have held out for three-quarters of a cord," Bobbi told him that night as they sat in front of her stove, feet up on the fender, smoking cigarettes as a wind shrieked fresh snow across the fields and into the trees. "Those're good poems. There's a lot of them, too."

"I know," Gardener said, "but I was cold. Half a cord'll get me through until spring." He dropped her a wink. "Besides, the guy's from Connecticut. I don't think he knew most of it was ash."

She dropped her feet to the floor and stared at him. "You kidding?"

"Nope."

She began to giggle and he kissed her soundly and later took her to bed and they slept together like spoons. He remembered waking up once, listening to the wind, thinking of all the dark and rushing cold outside and all the warmth of this bed, filled with their peaceful heat under two quilts, and wishing it could be like this forever—only nothing ever was. He had been raised to believe God was love, but you had to wonder how loving a God could be when He made men and women smart enough to land on the moon but stupid enough to have to learn there was no such thing as forever over and over again.

The next day Bobbi had again offered money and Gardener again refused. He wasn't exactly rolling in dough, but he made out. And he couldn't help the little spark of anger he felt in spite of her matter-of-fact tone. "Don't you know who's supposed to get the money after a night in bed?" he asked.

She stuck out her chin. "You calling me a whore?"

He smiled. "You need a pimp? There's money in it, I hear."

"You want breakfast, Gard, or do you want to piss me off?"

"How about both?"

"No," she said, and he saw she was really mad—Christ,

he was getting worse and worse at seeing things like that, and it used to be so *easy*. He hugged her. *I was only kidding, couldn't she see that?* he thought. *She always* used *to be able to tell when I was kidding.* But of course she hadn't known he was kidding because he hadn't been. If he believed different, the only one getting kidded was himself. He had been trying to hurt her because she'd embarrassed him. And it wasn't her offer that had been stupid; it was his embarrassment. He had more or less chosen the life he was living, hadn't he?

And he didn't want to hurt Bobbi, didn't want to drive Bobbi away. The bed part was fine, but the bed part wasn't the really important part. The really important part was that Bobbi Anderson was a friend, and something scary seemed to be happening just lately. How fast he seemed to be running out of friends. That was pretty scary, all right.

Running out of friends? Or running them out? Which is it, Gard?

At first hugging her was like hugging an ironing board and he was afraid she would try to pull away and he would make the mistake of trying to hold on, but she finally softened.

"I want breakfast," he said. "And to say I'm sorry."

"It's all right," she said, and turned away before he could see her face—but her voice held that dry briskness that meant she was either crying or near it. "I keep forgetting it's bad manners to offer money to Yankees."

Well, he didn't know if it was bad manners or not, but he would not take money from Bobbi. Never had, never would.

The New England Poetry Caravan, however, was a different matter.

Grab that chicken, son, Ron Cummings, who needed money about as much as the pope needed a new hat, would have said. *The bitch is too slow to run and too fat to pass up.*

The New England Poetry Caravan paid cash. Coin of the realm for poetry—two hundred up front and two hundred at the end of the tour. The word made flesh, you might say. But hard cash, it was understood, was only part of the deal.

The rest was THE TAB.

While you were on tour, you took advantage of every

opportunity. You got your meals from room service, your hair cut in the hotel barbershop if there was one, brought your extra pair of shoes (if you had one) and put *them* out one night instead of your regulars so you could get the extras shined up.

There were the in-room movies, movies you never got a chance to see in a theater, because theaters persisted in wanting money for much the same thing poets, even the very good ones, were for some reason supposed to provide for free or next to it—three bags of spuds = one (1) sonnet, for instance. There was a room charge for the movies, of course, but what of that? You didn't even have to put them on THE TAB; some computer did it automatically, and all Gardener had to say on the subject was God bless and keep THE TAB, and bring those fuckers *on!* He watched *everything,* from *Emmanuelle in New York* (finding the part where the girl flogs the guy's doggy under a table at Windows on the World particularly artistic and uplifting; it certainly uplifted part of him, anyway) to *Indiana Jones and the Temple of Doom* to *Rainbow Brite and the Star-Stealer.*

And that's what I'm going to do now, he thought, rubbing his throat and thinking about the taste of good aged whiskey. EXACTLY *what I'm going to do. Just sit here and watch them* all *over again, even* Rainbow Brite. *And for lunch I'm going to order three bacon cheeseburgers and eat one cold at three o'clock. Maybe skip* Rainbow Brite *and take a nap. Stay in tonight. Go to bed early. And stand it off.*

Bobbi Anderson tripped over a three-inch tongue of metal protruding from the earth.

Jim Gardener tripped over Ron Cummings.

Different objects, same result.

For want of a nail.

Ron popped in around the same time that, some two hundred and ten miles away, Anderson and Peter were finally getting home from their less-than-normal trip to the vet's. Cummings suggested they go down to the hotel bar and have a drink or ten.

"Or," Ron continued brightly, "we could just skip the foreplay and get shitfaced."

If he had put it more delicately, Gard might have been okay. Instead, he found himself in the bar with Ron Cummings, raising a jolly Jack Daniel's to his lips and telling himself the old one about how he could choke it off when he really wanted to.

Ron Cummings was a good, serious poet who just happened to have money practically falling out of his asshole . . . or so he often told people. "I am my own de' Medici," he would say; "I have money practically falling out of my asshole." His family had been in textiles for roughly nine hundred years and owned most of southern New Hampshire. They thought Ron was crazy, but because he was the second son, and because the first one was *not* crazy (i.e., uninterested in textiles), they let Ron do what he wanted to do, which was write poems, read poems, and drink almost constantly. He was a narrow young man with a TB face. Gardener had never seen him eat anything but beer-nuts and Goldfish crackers. To his dubious credit, he had no idea of Gardener's own problem with booze . . . or the fact that he had once come very close to killing his wife while drunk.

"Okay," Gardener said. "I'm up for it. Let's get 'faced."

After a few in the hotel bar, Ron suggested that a couple of smart fellers like them could find a place with entertainment a tad more exciting than the piped-in Muzak drifting down from the overhead speakers. "I think my heart can take it," Ron said. "I mean, I'm not sure, but—"

"—God hates a coward," Gardener finished.

Ron cackled, clapped him on the back, and called for THE TAB. He signed it with a flourish and then added a generous tip from his money clip. "Let's boogie, m'man." And off they went.

The late-afternoon sun lanced Gardener's eyes like glass spears and it suddenly occurred to him that this might be a bad idea.

"Listen, Ron," he said, "I think maybe I'll just—"

Cummings clapped him on the shoulder, formerly pale cheeks flushed, formerly watery blue eyes blazing (to Gard, Cummings now looked rather like Toad of Toad Hall after the acquisition of his motor-car), and cajoled: "Don't crap out on me now, Jim! Boston lies before us, so various and new, glistening like the fresh ejaculate of a young boy's first wetdream—"

Gardener burst into helpless gales of laughter.

"That's more like the Gardener we've all come to know and love," Ron said, cackling himself.

"God hates a coward," Gard said. "Hail us a cab, Ronnie."

He saw it then: the funnel in the sky. Big and black and getting closer. Soon it was going to touch down and carry him away.

Not to Oz, though.

A cab pulled over to the curb. They got in. The driver asked them where they wanted to go.

"Oz," Gardener muttered.

Ron cackled. "What he means is someplace where they drink fast and dance faster. Think you can manage that?"

"Oh, I think so," the driver said, and pulled out.

Gardener draped an arm around Ron's shoulders and cried: *"Let the wild rumpus start!"*

"I'll drink to that," Ron said.

2

Gardener awoke the next morning fully dressed in a tubful of cold water. His best set of clothes—which he'd had the misfortune to be wearing when he and Ron Cummings set sail the day before—were bonding themselves slowly to his skin. He looked at his fingers and saw they were very white and very pruny. Fishfingers. He'd been here for a while, apparently. The water might even have been hot when he climbed in. He didn't remember.

He opened the tub drain. Saw a bottle of bourbon standing on the toilet seat. It was half-full, its surface bleary with some sort of grease. He picked it up. The grease smelled vaguely of fried chicken. Gardener was more interested in the aroma coming from *inside* the bottle. Don't do this, he thought, but the neck of the bottle was rapping against his teeth before the thought was even half-finished. He had a drink. Blacked out again.

When he came to, he was standing naked in his bedroom with the phone to his ear and the vague idea that he had just finished dialing a number. Whose? He had no idea until Cummings answered. Cummings sounded even worse than Gardener felt. Gardener would have sworn this was impossible.

"How bad was it?" Gardener heard himself ask. It was always this way when he was in the grip of the cyclone; even when he was conscious, everything seemed to have the gray grainy texture of a tabloid photograph, and he never seemed to exactly be *inside* of himself. A lot of the time he seemed to be floating above his own head, like a kid's silvery Puffer balloon. "How much trouble did we get into?"

"Trouble?" Cummings repeated, and then fell silent. At least Gardener *thought* he was thinking. *Hoped* he was thinking. Or maybe dreaded the idea. He waited, his hands very cold. "No trouble," Cummings said at last, and Gard relaxed a little. "Except for my head, that is. I got my head in *plenty* of trouble. Jee-*zus!*"

"You sure? *Nothing?* Nothing at *all?*"

He was thinking of Nora.

Shot your wife, uh? a voice spoke up suddenly in his mind—the voice of the deputy with the comic book. *Good fucking deal.*

"We-ell . . ." Cummings said reflectively, and then stopped.

Gardener's hand clenched tight on the phone again.

"Well *what?*" Suddenly the lights in the room were too bright. Like the sun when they had stepped out of the hotel late yesterday afternoon.

You did something. You had another fucking blackout and did another stupid thing. Or crazy thing. Or horrible thing. When are you going to learn to leave it alone? Or can *you learn?*

An exchange from an old movie clanged stupidly into his mind.

Evil *El Comandante:* Tomorrow before daybreak, *señor,* you will be dead! You have seen the sun for the last time!

Brave *Americano:* Yeah, but you'll be bald for the rest of your life.

"What was it?" he asked Ron. "What did I do?"

"You got into an argument with some guys at a place called the Stone Country Bar and Grille," Cummings said. He laughed a little. "Ow! Christ, when it hurts to laugh, you *know* you abused yourself. You remember the Stone Country Bar and Grille and them thar good ole boys, James, my dear?"

He said he didn't. Really straining, he could remember a place called Smith Brothers. The sun had just been going down in a kettle of blood, and this being late June, that meant it had been . . . what? eight-thirty? quarter of nine? about five hours after he and Ron had gotten started, give or take. He could remember the sign outside bore the likeness of the famous coughdrop siblings. He could remember arguing furiously about Wallace Stevens with Cummings, shouting to be heard over the juke, which had been thundering out something by John Fogerty. That was where the last jagged edges of memory came to a halt.

"It was the place with the WAYLON JENNINGS FOR PRESIDENT bumper-sticker over the bar," Cummings said. "That refresh the old noggin?"

"No," Gardener said miserably.

"Well, you got into an argument with a couple of the good ole boys. Words were passed. These words grew first warm and then hot. A punch was thrown."

"By me?" Gardener's voice was now only dull.

"By you," Cummings agreed cheerfully. "At which point we flew through the air with the greatest of ease, landing on the sidewalk. I thought we got off pretty cheap, to tell you the truth. You had them frothing, Jim."

"Was it about Seabrook or Chernobyl?"

"Shit, you *do* remember!"

"If I remembered, I wouldn't be asking you which one it was."

"As a matter of fact, it was both." Cummings hesitated. "Are you all right, Gard? You sound real low."

Yeah? Well, actually, Ron, I'm way up. *Up in the cyclone. Going around and around and up and down, and where it ends nobody knows.*

"I'm okay."

"That's good. One hopes you know who you have to thank for it."

"You, maybe?"

"None other. Man, I landed on that sidewalk like a kid hitting the ground the first time he comes off the end of a slide. I can't quite see my ass in the mirror, but that's probably a good thing. I bet it looks like a Day-Glo Grateful Dead poster from sixty-nine. But you wanted to go back in and talk about how all the kids around Chernobyl were gonna be dead of leukemia in five years. You wanted to talk about how some guys almost blew up

Arkansas looking for faulty wiring with a candle in a nuclear-power plant. You said they caught the place on fire. Me, I'd bet my watch—and it's a Rolex—that they were Snopeses from Em-Eye-Double-Ess-Eye-Pee-Pee-Eye. Only way I could get you into a cab was by telling you we'd come back later and bust heads. I sweet-talked you up to your room and started the tub for you. You said you were all right. You said you were going to take a bath and then call some guy named Bobby."

"The guy's a girl," Gardener said absently. He was rubbing at his right temple with his free hand.

"Good-looking?"

"Pretty. No knockout." An errant thought, nonsensical but perfectly concrete—*Bobbi's in trouble*—kicked across his mind the way an errant billiard ball will roll across the clean green felt of a pool table. Then it was gone.

3

He walked slowly over to a chair and sat down, now massaging both temples. The nukes. Of course it had been the nukes. What else? If it wasn't Chernobyl it was Seabrook, and if it wasn't Seabrook it was Three-Mile Island and if it wasn't Three-Mile Island it was Maine Yankee in Wiscasset or what could have happened at the Hanford Plant in Washington State if someone hadn't happened to notice, just in the nick of time, that their used core-rods, stored in an unlined ditch outside, were getting ready to blow sky-high.

How many nicks of time could there be?

Spent fuel rods that were stacking up in big hot piles. They thought the Curse of King Tut was bad? Brother! Wait until some twenty-fifth-century archaeologist dug up a load of *this* shit! You tried to tell people the whole thing was a *lie*, nothing but a baldfaced naked *lie*, that nuclear-generated power was eventually going to kill millions and render huge tracts of land sterile and unlivable. What you got back was a blank stare. You talked to people who had lived through one administration after another in which their elected officials told one lie after another, then lied about the *lies*, and when *those* lies were found out the liars said: Oh jeez, I forgot, sorry—

and since they *forgot,* the people who elected them behaved like Christians and *forgave.* You couldn't believe there were so fucking *many* of them willing to do that until you remembered what P. T. Barnum said about the extraordinarily high birth rate of suckers. They looked you square in the face when you tried to tell them the truth and informed you that you were full of shit, the American government didn't tell lies, not telling lies was what made America great, *Oh dear Father, here's the facts, I did it with my little ax, I can't keep silent for it was I, and come what may, I cannot tell a lie.* When you tried to talk to them, they looked at you as if you were babbling in a foreign language. It had been eight years since he had almost killed his wife, and three since he and Bobbi had been arrested at Seabrook, Bobbi on the general charge of illegal demonstration, Gard on a much more specific one—possession of a concealed and unlicensed handgun. The others paid a fine and got out. Gardener did two months. His lawyer told him he was lucky. Gardener asked his lawyer if he knew he was sitting on a time bomb and jerking his meat. His lawyer asked him if he had considered psychiatric help. Gardener asked his lawyer if he had ever considered getting stuffed.

But he had had sense enough not to attend any more demonstrations. That much, anyway. He kept away from them. They were poisoning him. When he got drunk, however, his mind—whatever the booze had left of it—returned obsessively to the subject of the reactors, the core-rods, the containments, the inability to slow down a runaway once it really got going—

To the nukes, in other words.

When he got drunk, his heart got hot. The nukes. The goddam nukes. It was symbolic, yeah, okay, you didn't have to be Freud to figure that what he was *really* protesting was the reactor in his own heart. When it came to matters of restraint, James Gardener had a bad containment system. There was some technician inside who should have long since been fired. He sat and played with all the wrong switches. That guy wouldn't be really happy until Jim Gardener went China Syndrome.

The goddam fucking nukes.

Forget it.

He tried. For a start, he tried thinking about tonight's reading at Northeastern—a fun-filled frolic that was being sponsored by a group that called itself the Friends of Poetry, a name which filled Gardener with fear and trembling. Groups with such names tended to be made up exclusively of women who called themselves ladies (most of them of a decidedly blue-haired persuasion). The ladies of the club tended to be a good deal more familiar with the works of Rod McKuen than those of John Berryman, Hart Crane, Ron Cummings, or that good old drunken blackout brawler and wife shooter James Eric Gardener.

Get out of here, Gard. Never mind the New England Poetry Caravan. Never mind Northeastern or the Friends of Poetry or the McCardle bitch. Get out of here right now before something bad happens. Something really bad. Because if you stay, something really bad will. There's blood on the moon.

But he was damned if he'd go running back to Maine with his tail between his legs. Not him.

Besides, there was the bitch.

Patricia McCardle was her name, and if she wasn't one strutting world-class bitch, Gard had never met one.

She had a contract, and it specified no play, no pay.

"Jesus," Gardener said, and put a hand over his eyes, trying to shut away the growing headache, knowing there was only one kind of medicine that would do that, and also knowing it was exactly the sort of medicine that could bring that really bad thing on.

And *also* knowing that knowing would do no good at all. So after a while the booze started to flow and the cyclone started to blow.

Jim Gardener, now in free fall.

4

Patricia McCardle was the New England Poetry Caravan's principal contributor and head ramrod. Her legs were long but skinny, her nose aristocratic but too bladelike to be considered attractive. Gard had once tried to imagine kissing her and had been horrified by the image which had risen, unbidden, in his mind: her nose not just sliding up his cheek but slicing it open like a razor blade. She had a high forehead, nonexistent breasts, and eyes as gray as a glacier on a cloudy day. She traced her ancestry back to the *Mayflower*.

Gardener had worked for her before and there had been trouble before. He had become part of the 1988 New England Poetry Caravan in rather grisly fashion . . . but the reason for his abrupt inclusion was no more unheard-of in the world of poetry than it was in those of jazz and rock and roll. Patricia McCardle had been left with a last-minute hole in her announced program because one of the six poets who had signed on for this summer's happy cruise had hung himself in his closet with his belt.

"Just like Phil Ochs," Ron Cummings had said to Gardener as they sat near the back of the bus on the first day of the tour. He said it with a nervous bad-boy-at-the-back-of-the-classroom giggle. "But then, Bill Claughtsworth always was a derivative son of a bitch."

Patricia McCardle had gotten twelve reading dates and fairly good advances on a deal which, when stripped of all the high-flown rhetoric, boiled down to six poets for the price of one. Following Claughtsworth's suicide, she found herself with three days to find a publishing poet in a season when most publishing poets were booked solid ("Or on permanent vacation like Silly Billy Claughtsworth," Cummings said, laughing rather uneasily).

Few if any of the booked groups would balk at paying the stipulated fee just because the Caravan happened to be short one poet—to do such a thing would be in rawther shitty taste, particularly when one considered the *reason* the Caravan was a poet short. All the same, it put Caravan, Inc., in a position of contractual default, at least technically, and Patricia McCardle was not a woman to brook loopholes.

After trying four poets, each more minor-league than the last, and with only thirty-six hours before the first reading, she had finally called Jim Gardener.

"Are you still drinking, Jimmy?" she asked bluntly. Jimmy—he hated that. Most people called him Jim. Jim was all right. No one called him Gard except himself . . . and Bobbi Anderson.

"Drinking a little," he said. "Not bingeing at all."

"I'm dubious," she said coldly.

"You always have been, Patty," he replied, knowing she hated that even more than he did Jimmy—her Puritan blood screamed against it. "Were you asking because you happen to be short a quart, or did you have a more pressing reason?"

Of course he knew, and of course she knew he knew, and of course she knew he was grinning, and of course she was infuriated, and of course all of this tickled him just about to death, and of course she knew he knew *that* too, and that was just the way he liked it.

They sparred a few more minutes, and then came to what was not a marriage of convenience but one of necessity. Gardener wanted to buy a good used wood furnace for the coming winter; he was tired of living like a slut, bundled up at night in front of the kitchen stove while the wind rattled the plastic stapled over the windows; Patricia McCardle wanted to buy a poet. There would be no handshake agreement, though, not with Patricia McCardle. She had driven down from Derry that afternoon with a contract (in triplicate) and a notary public. Gard was a little surprised she hadn't brought a second notary, just in case the first one happened to suffer a coronary or something.

Feelings and hunches aside, there was really no way he could leave the tour and get the wood furnace, because if he left the tour he would never see the second half of his fee. She'd haul him into court and spend a thousand dollars trying to get him to cough up the three hundred Caravan, Inc., had paid up front. She might be able to do it, too. He had done almost all the dates, but the contract he had signed was crystal clear on the subject: if he took off *for any reason unacceptable to the Tour Co-Ordinator, any and all fees unpaid shall be declared null and void, and any and all fees prepaid shall be refundable to Caravan, Inc., within thirty (30) days.*

And she *would* go after him. She might think she was doing it on principle, but it would really be because he had called her Patty in her hour of need.

Nor would that be the end of it. If he left, she would work with unflagging energy to get him blackballed. He would certainly never read again for another poetry tour with which she was associated, and that was a lot of poetry tours. Then there was the delicate matter of grants. Her husband had left her a lot of money (although he didn't think you could say, as Ron Cummings did, that she practically had money falling out of her asshole, because Gard didn't believe Patricia McCardle *had* anything so vulgar as an asshole, or even a rectum—when in need of relief, she probably performed an Act of Immaculate Excretion). Patricia McCardle had taken a great deal of this money and set up a number of grants-in-aid. This made her simultaneously a serious patron of the arts and an extremely smart businesswoman in regard to the nasty business of income taxes: the grants were write-offs. Some of them funded poets for specific time periods. Some funded cash poetry awards and prizes, and some underwrote magazines of modern poetry and fiction. The grants were administered by committees. Behind each of them moved the hand of Patricia McCardle, making sure that they meshed as neatly as the pieces of a Chinese puzzle . . . or the strands of a spider's web.

She could do a lot more to him than get back her lousy six hundred bucks. She could muzzle him. And it was just possible—unlikely, but possible—that he might write a few more good poems before the madmen who had stuffed a shotgun up the asshole of the world decided to pull the trigger.

So get through it, he thought. He had ordered a bottle of Johnnie Walker from room service (God bless THE TAB, forever and ever, amen), and now he poured his second drink with a hand that had become remarkably steady. *Get through it, that's all.*

But as the day wore on, he kept thinking about grabbing a Greyhound bus at the Stuart Street terminal and getting off five hours later in front of the dusty little drugstore in Unity. Thumbing a ride up to Troy from there. Calling Bobbi Anderson on the phone and saying: *I almost went up in the cyclone, Bobbi, but I found the storm cellar just in time. Lucky break, uh?*

Shit on that. You make your own luck. If you be strong, Gard, you be lucky. Get through it, that's all. That's what's to do.

He scrummed through his totebag, looking for the best clothes he had left, since his reading clothes appeared to be beyond salvage. He tossed a pair of faded jeans, a plain white shirt, a tattered pair of skivvies, and a pair of socks onto the bedspread (*thanks, ma'am, but there's no need to make up the room, I slept in the tub*). He got dressed, ate some Certs, ate some booze, ate some more Certs, and then went through the bag again, this time looking for the aspirin. He found it and ate some of those. He looked at the bottle. Looked away. The pulse of the headache was getting worse. He sat down by the window with his notebooks, trying to decide what he should read that night.

In this dreadful long afternoon light all his poems looked as if they had been written in Punic. Instead of doing anything positive about his headache, the aspirin seemed to actually be intensifying it: *slam, bam, thank you, ma'am.* His head whacked with each heartbeat. It was the same old headache, the one that felt like an auger made of dull steel being slowly driven into his head at a point slightly above and to the left of his left eye. He touched the tips of his fingers to the faint scar there and ran his fingers lightly along it. The steel plate buried under the skin there was the result of a skiing accident in his teens. He remembered the doctor saying, *You may suffer headaches from time to time, son. When they come, just thank God you can feel anything. You're lucky to be alive.*

But at times like this he wondered.

At times like this he wondered a lot.

He put the notebooks aside with a shaking hand and closed his eyes.

I can't get through it.

You can.

I can't. There's blood on the moon, I feel it, I can almost see *it.*

Don't give me any of your Irish willywags! Just get tough, you weak fucking sister! Tough!

"I'll try," he muttered, not opening his eyes, and fifteen minutes later, when his nose began to bleed slightly, he didn't notice. He had fallen asleep in the chair.

5

He always got stage fright before reading, even if the group was a small one (and groups which turned out to hear readings of modern poetry tended to be just that). On the night of June 27th, however, Jim Gardener's stage fright was intensified by his headache. When he woke from his nap in the hotel room chair the shakes and the fluttery stomach were gone, but the headache had gotten even worse: it had graduated to a Genuine Class-A Thumper & World-Beater, maybe the worst of all time.

When his turn to read finally came, he seemed to hear himself from a great distance. He felt a little like a man listening to a recording of himself on a shortwave broadcast coming in from Spain or Portugal. Then a wave of light-headedness coursed through him and for a few moments he could only pretend to be looking for a poem, some special poem, perhaps, that had been temporarily misplaced. He shuffled papers with dim and nerveless fingers, thinking: *I'm going to faint, I think. Right up here in front of everyone. Fall against this lectern and pitch both it and me into the front row. Maybe I can land on that blue-blooded cunt and kill her. That would almost make my whole life seem worthwhile.*

Get through it, that implacable inner voice responded. Sometimes that voice sounded like his father's; more often it sounded like the voice of Bobbi Anderson. *Get through it, that's all. That's what's to do.*

The audience that night was larger than usual, maybe a hundred people squeezed behind the desks of a North-eastern lecture hall. Their eyes seemed too big. *What big eyes you have, Gramma!* It was as if they would eat him up with their eyes. Suck out his soul, his *ka,* his whatever you wanted to call it. A snatch of old T. Rex occurred to him: *Girl, I'm just a vampire for your love . . . and I'm gonna* SUCK YA!

Of course there was no more T. Rex. Marc Bolan had wrapped his sports car around a tree and was lucky not to be alive. *Bang-a-Gong, Marc,* you *sure got it on. Or got it off. Or whatever. A group called Power Station is going to cover your tune in 1986 and it's going to be really bad, it . . . it . . .*

He raised an unsteady hand to his forehead, and a quiet murmur ran through the audience.

Better get going, Gard. Natives are getting restless.

Yeah, that was Bobbi's voice, all right.

The fluorescents, embedded in pebbled rectangles overhead, seemed to be pulsing in cycles which perfectly matched the cycles of pain driving into his head. He could see Patricia McCardle. She was wearing a little black dress that surely hadn't cost a penny more than three hundred dollars—distress-sale stuff from one of those tacky little shops on Newbury Street. Her face was as narrow and pallid and unforgiving as that of any of her Puritan forebears, those wonderful, fun-loving guys who had been more than happy to stick you in some stinking gaol for three or four weeks if you had the bad luck to be spied going out on the Sabbath Day without a snotrag in your pocket. Patricia's dark eyes lay upon him like dusty stones and Gard thought: *She sees what's happening and she couldn't be more pleased. Look at her. She's waiting for me to fall down. And when I do, you know what she'll be thinking, don't you?*

Of course he did.

That's what you get for calling me Patty, you drunken son of a bitch. That was what she would be thinking. *That's what you get for calling me Patty, that's what you get for doing everything but making me get down on my knees and beg. So go on, Gardener. Maybe I'll even let you keep the up-front money. Three hundred dollars seems a cheap-enough price to pay for the exquisite pleasure of watching you crack up in front of all these people. Go on. Go on and get it over with.*

Some members of the audience were becoming visibly uneasy now—the delay between poems had stretched out far beyond what might be considered normal. The murmur had become a muted buzz. Gardener heard Ron Cummings clear his throat uneasily behind him.

Get tough! Bobbi's voice yelled again, but the voice was fading now. Fading. Getting ready to high-side it. He looked at their faces and saw only pasty-pale blank circles, ciphers, big white holes in the universe.

The buzz was growing. He stood at the podium, swaying noticeably now, wetting his lips, looking at his audience with a kind of numb dismay. And then, suddenly, instead of *hearing* Bobbi, Gardener actually *saw* her. This image had all the force of vision.

Bobbi was up there in Haven, up there right now. He saw her sitting in her rocking chair, wearing a pair of shorts and a halter top over what boobs she had, which wasn't much. There was a pair of battered old mocs on her feet and Peter was curled before them, deeply asleep. She had a book but wasn't reading it. It lay open facedown in her lap (this fragment of vision was so perfect Gardener could even read the book's title—it was *Watchers,* by Dean Koontz) while Bobbi looked out the window into the dark, thinking her own thoughts—thoughts which would follow one after the other as sanely and rationally as you could want a train of thought to run. No derailments; no late freights; no head-ons. Bobbi knew how to run a railroad.

He even knew what she was thinking about, he discovered. Something in the woods. Something . . . it was something she had *found* in the woods. Yes. Bobbi was in Haven, trying to decide what that thing might be and why she felt so tired. She was not thinking about James Eric Gardener, the noted poet, protester, and Thanksgiving wifeshooter, who was currently standing in a lecture hall at Northeastern University under these lights with five other poets and some fat shit named Arberg or Arglebargle or something like that, and getting ready to faint. Here in this lecture hall stood the Master of Disaster. God bless Bobbi, who had somehow managed to keep her shit together while all about her people were losing theirs, Bobbi was up there in Haven, thinking the way people were *supposed* to think—

No she's not. She's not doing that at all.

Then, for the first time, the thought came through with no soundproofing around it; it came through as loud and urgent as a firebell in the night: *Bobbi's in trouble! Bobbi's in* REAL TROUBLE!

This surety struck him with the force of a roundhouse slap, and suddenly the light-headedness was gone. He fell back into himself with such a thud he almost seemed to feel his teeth rattle. A sickening bolt of pain ripped through his head, but even that was welcome—if he felt pain, then he was back here, *here,* not drifting around someplace in the ozone.

And for one puzzling moment he saw a new picture, very brief, very clear, and very ominous: it was Bobbi in the cellar of the farmhouse she'd inherited from her uncle. She was hunkered down in front of some piece of machinery, working on it . . . or was she? It seemed so dark, and Bobbi wasn't much of a hand with mechanical stuff. But she sure was doing *something,* because ghostly blue fire leapt and flickered between her fingers as she fiddled with tangled wires inside . . . inside . . . but it was too dark to see what that dark, cylindrical shape was. It was familiar, something he had seen before, but—

Then he could hear as well as see, although what he heard was even less comforting than that eldritch blue fire. It was Peter. Peter was howling. Bobbi took no notice, and that was *utterly* unlike her. She only went on fiddling with the wires, jiggering them so they would do something down there in the root-smelling dark of the cellar . . .

The vision broke apart on rising voices.

The faces which went with those voices were no longer white holes in the universe but the faces of real people: some were amused (but not many), a few more embarrassed, but most just seemed alarmed or worried. Most looked, in other words, the way he would have looked had his position been reversed with one of them. Had he been afraid of them? *Had* he? If so, why?

Only Patricia McCardle didn't fit. She was looking at him with a quiet, sure satisfaction that brought him all the way back.

Gardener suddenly spoke to the audience, surprised at how natural and pleasant his voice sounded. "I'm sorry. Please excuse me. I've got a batch of new poems here, and I went woolgathering among them, I'm afraid." Pause. Smile. Now he could see some of the worried ones settling back, looking relieved. There was a little laughter, but it was sympathetic. He could, however, see a flush of anger rising in Patricia McCardle's cheeks, and it did his headache a world of good.

"Actually," he went on, "even that's not the truth. Fact is, I was trying to decide whether or not to read some of this new stuff to you. After some furious sparring between those two thundering heavyweights Pride of Authorship and Prudence, Prudence has won a split decision. Pride of Authorship vows to appeal the decision—"

More laughter, heartier. Now old Patty's cheeks looked like his kitchen stove through its little isinglass windows on a cold winter night. Her hands were locked together, the knuckles white. Her teeth weren't quite bared, but almost, friends and neighbors, almost.

"In the meantime, I'm going to finish with a dangerous act: I'm going to read a fairly long poem from my first book, *Grimoire.*"

He winked in Patricia McCardle's direction, then took them all into his humorous confidence. "But God hates a coward, right?"

Ron snorted laughter behind him and then they were all laughing, and for a moment he actually *did* see a glint of her pearly-whites behind those stretched, furious lips, and oh boy howdy, that was just about as good as you'd want, wasn't it?

Watch out for her, Gard. You think you've got your boot on her neck now, and maybe you even do, for the moment, but watch out for her. She won't forget.

Or forgive.

But that was for later. Now he opened the battered copy of his first book of poems. He didn't need to look for "Leighton Street"; the book fell open to it of its own accord. His eyes found the subscript. *For Bobbi, who first smelled sage in New York.*

"Leighton Street" had been written the year he met her, the year Leighton Street was all she could talk about. It was, of course, the street in Utica where she had grown up, the street she'd needed to escape before she could even start being what she wanted to be—a simple writer of simple stories. She could do that; she could do that with flash and ease. Gard had known that almost at once. Later that year he had sensed that she might be able to do more: to surmount the careless, profligate ease with which she wrote, and do, if not great work, brave work. But first she had to get away from Leighton Street. Not the real one, but the Leighton Street which she carried with her in her mind, a demon geography populated by haunted tenements, her sick, loved father, her weak, loved mother, and her defiant crone of a sister, who rode over them all like a demon of endless power.

Once, that year, she had fallen asleep in class—Freshman Comp, that had been. He had been gentle with her, because he already loved her a little and he had seen the huge circles under her eyes.

"I've had problems sleeping at night," she said, when he held her after class for a moment. She had *still* been half-asleep, or she never would have gone on from there; that was how powerful Anne's hold—which was the hold of Leighton Street—had been over her. But she was like a person who has been drugged, and exists with one leg thrown over each side of the sleep's dark and stony wall. "I almost fall asleep and then I hear her."

"Who?" he asked gently.

"Sissy . . . my sister Anne, that is. She grinds her teeth and it sounds like b-b-b—"

Bones, she wanted to say, but then she woke into a fit of hysterical weeping that had frightened him very badly.

Anne.

More than anything else, Anne was Leighton Street.

Anne had been

(*knocking at the door*)

the gag of Bobbi's needs and ambitions.

Okay, Gard thought. *For you, Bobbi. Only for you.* And began to read "Leighton Street" as smoothly as if he had spent the afternoon rehearsing it in his room.

"These streets begin where the cobbles
surface through tar like the heads
of children buried badly in their textures,"

Gardener read.

"What myth is this?
we ask, but
the children who play stickball and
Johnny Jump-My-Pony round here just laugh.

No myth they tell us *no myth,*
just they say *hey motherfucker aint*
nothing but Leighton Street here,
aint nothing but all small houses
aint only but back porches where our mothers
wash there and they're and their.

Where days grow hot
and on Leighton Street they listen to the radio
while pterodactyls flow between the TV aerials
on the roof and they say *hey motherfucker* they say
Hey motherfucker!

No myth they tell us *no myth,*
just they say *hey motherfucker aint*
nothing but Leighton Street round here

This they say *is how you be silent in your silence*
of days. Motherfucker.

When we turned our back on these upstate roads,
warehouses with faces of blank brick,
when you say 'O, but I have reached the end

of all I know and still hear her grinding,
grinding in the night . . .' "

Because it had been so long since he had read the poem, even to himself, he did not just "perform" it (something, he had discovered, that was almost impossible not to do at the end of a tour such as this); he *rediscovered* it. Most of those who came to the reading at Northeastern that night—even those who witnessed the evening's sordid, creepy conclusion, agreed that Gardener's reading of "Leighton Street" had been the best of the night. A good many of them maintained it was the best they had ever heard.

Since it was the last reading Jim Gardener would ever give in his life, it was maybe not such a bad way to go out.

6

It took him nearly twenty minutes to read all of it, and when he finished he looked up uncertainly into a deep and perfect well of silence. He had time to think he had never read the damned thing at all, that it had just been a vivid hallucination in the moment or two before the faint.

Then someone stood up and began to clap steadily and hard. It was a young man with tears on his cheeks. The girl beside him also stood and began to clap and she was also crying. Then they were all standing and applauding, yeah, they were giving him a fucking standing O, and in their faces he saw what every poet or would-be poet hopes to see when he or she finished reading: the faces of people suddenly awakened from a dream brighter than any reality. They looked as dazed as Bobbi had on that day, not quite sure where they were.

But they weren't *all* standing and applauding, he saw; Patricia McCardle sat stiff and straight in her third-row seat, her hands clasped tightly together in her lap over her small evening bag. Her lips had closed. No sign of the old pearly-whites now; her mouth had become a small bloodless cut. Gard felt a weary amusement. *As far as you're concerned, Patty, the* real *Puritan ethic is no one who's a black sheep should dare rise above his designated level of mediocrity, correct? But there's no mediocrity clause in your contract, is there?*

"Thank you," he muttered into the mike, sweeping his books and papers together into an untidy pile with his shaking hands—and then almost dropping them all over the floor as he stepped away from the podium. He dropped into his seat next to Ron Cummings with a deep sigh.

"My God," Ron whispered, still applauding. "My *God!*"

"Stop clapping, you ass," Gardener whispered back.

"Damned if I will. I don't care when you wrote it, it was fucking *brilliant,*" Cummings said. "And I'll buy you a drink on it later on."

"I'm not drinking anything stronger than club soda tonight," Gardener said, and knew it was a lie. His headache was already creeping back. Aspirin wouldn't cure that, Percodan wouldn't, a 'lude wouldn't. Nothing would fix his head but a great big clout of booze. Fast, fast relief.

The applause was finally beginning to die away. Patricia McCardle looked acidly grateful.

7

The name of the fat shit who had introduced each of the poets was Arberg (although Gardener kept wanting to call him Arglebargle), and he was the assistant professor of English who headed the sponsoring group. He was the sort of man his father had called a "beefy sonofawhore."

The beefy sonofawhore threw a party for the Caravan, the Friends of Poetry, and most of the English Department faculty at his house after the reading. It began around eleven o'clock. It was stiffish at first—men and women standing in uncomfortable little groups with glasses and paper plates in their hands, talking your usual brand of cautious academic talk. This sort of bullshit had struck Gard as a stupid waste of time when he was teaching. It still did, but there was also something nostalgic and pleasing—in a melancholy way—about it now.

His Party Monster streak told him that, stiff or not, this was a Party with Possibilities. By midnight the Bach études would almost certainly be replaced by the Pretenders, and talk of classes, politics, and literature would be replaced by more interesting fare—the Red Sox, who on the faculty was drinking too much, and that all-time favorite, who was fucking whom.

There was a large buffet for which most of the poets made a beeline, reliably following Gardener's First Rule for Touring Poets: *If it's gratis, grab it.* As he watched, Ann Delaney, who wrote spare, haunting poems about rural working-class New England, stretched her jaws wide and ripped into the huge sandwich she was holding. Mayonnaise the color and texture of bull semen squirted between her fingers, and Ann licked it off her hand nonchalantly. She tipped Gardener a wink. To her left, last year's winner of Boston University's Hawthorne Prize (for his long poem *Harbor Dreams 1650—1980*) was cramming green olives into his mouth with blurry speed. This fellow, Jon Evard Symington by name, paused long enough to drop a handful of wrapped mini-wheels of Bonbel cheese into each pocket of his corduroy sport-coat (patched elbows, naturally), and then went back to the olives.

Ron Cummings strolled over to where Gardener was standing. As usual, he wasn't eating. He had a Waterford glass that looked full of straight whiskey in one hand. He nodded toward the buffet. "Great stuff. If you're a connoisseur of Kirschner's bologna and iceberg lettuce, you in like Flynn, bo."

"That Arglebargle really knows how to live," Gardener said.

Cummings, in the act of drinking, snorted so hard his eyes bulged. "You're on the hit-line tonight, Jim. Arglebargle. Jesus." He looked at the glass in Gardener's hand. It was a vodka and tonic—weak, but his second, just the same.

"Tonic water?" Cummings asked slyly.

"Well . . . mostly."

Cummings laughed again and walked away.

By the time someone pulled Bach and put on B. B. King, Gard was working on his fourth drink—on this one he'd asked the bartender, who had been at the reading, to go a little heavier on the vodka. He had begun to repeat two remarks that seemed wittier as he got drunker: first, that if you were a connoisseur of Kirschner's bologna and iceberg lettuce you were in like Flynn here, bo, and second, that all assistant professors were like T. S. Eliot's

Practical Cats in at least one way: they all had secret names. Gardener confided that he had intuited that of their host: Arglebargle. He went back for a fifth drink, and told the bartender just to wave the tonic bottle in that old drink's face—that would be fine. The bartender waggled the bottle of Schweppes solemnly in front of Gardener's glass of vodka. Gardener laughed until tears stood in his eyes and his stomach hurt. He really *was* feeling fine tonight . . . and who, sir or madam, deserved it more? He had read better than he had in years, maybe in his whole life.

"You know," he told the bartender, a needy postgrad hired especially for the occasion, "all assistant professors are like T. S. Eliot's Practical Cats in one way."

"Is that so, Mr. Gardener?"

"Jim. Just Jim." But he could see from the look in the kid's eyes that he was never going to be *just Jim* to this guy. Tonight he had seen Gardener blaze, and men who blazed could never be anything so mundane as *just Jim.*

"It is," he told the kid. "Each of them has a secret name. I have intuited that of our host. It's Arglebargle. Like the sound you make when you use the old Listerine." He paused, considering. "Of which the gentleman under discussion could use a good dose, now that I think of it." Gardener laughed quite loudly. It was a fine addition to the basic thrust. *Like adding a tasteful hood ornament to a fine car,* he thought, and laughed again. This time a few people glanced around before going back to their conversations.

Too loud, he thought. *Turn down your volume control, Gard, old buddy.* He grinned widely, thinking he was having one of those magic nights—even his damn *thoughts* were funny tonight.

The bartender was also smiling, but his smile had a slightly concerned edge to it. "You ought to be careful what you say about Professor Arberg," he said, "or who you say it to. He's . . . a bit of a bear."

"Oh *is* he!" Gardener popped his eyes round and waggled his eyebrows energetically up and down like Groucho Marx. "Well, he's got the build for it. Beefy sonofawhore, ain't he?" But he was careful to keep the old volume control down when he said it.

"Yeah," the bartender said. He looked around and then leaned over the makeshift bar toward Gardener. "There's a story that he happened to be passing by the grad assistants' lounge last year and heard one of them joking about how he'd always wanted to be associated with a school where *Moby Dick* wasn't just another dry classic but an actual member of the faculty. That guy was one of the most promising English students Northeastern has ever had, I heard, but he was gone before the semester was over. So was everyone who laughed. The ones who didn't laugh stayed."

"Jesus Christ," Gardener said. He had heard stories like it before—one or two that were even worse—but still felt disgusted. He followed the bartender's glance and saw Arglebargle at the buffet, standing next to Patricia McCardle. Arglebargle had a stein of beer in one hand and was gesturing with it. His other hand was plowing potato chips through a bowl of clam dip and then conveying them to his mouth, which went right on talking as it slobbered them chips in. Gardener could not remember ever having seen anything so quintessentially disgusting. Yet the McCardle bitch's rapt attention suggested that she might at any moment drop to her knees and give the man a blowjob out of sheer adoration. Gardener thought, *and the fat fuck would go right on eating while she did it, dropping potato-chip crumbs and globs of clam dip in her hair.*

"Jesus wept," he said, and slugged back half of his vodka-*sans*-tonic. It hardly burned at all . . . what burned was the evening's first real hostility—the first outrider of that mute and inexplicable rage that had plagued him almost since the time he began drinking. "Freshen this up, would you?"

The bartender dumped in more vodka and said shyly: "I thought your reading tonight was wonderful, Mr. Gardener."

Gardener was absurdly touched. "Leighton Street" had been dedicated to Bobbi Anderson, and this boy behind the bar—barely old enough to drink legally himself—reminded Gardener of Bobbi as she had been when she first came to the university.

"Thank you."

"You want to be a little careful of that vodka," the bartender said. "It has a way of blindsiding you."

"I'm in control," Gardener said, and gave the bartender a reassuring wink. "Visibility ten miles to unlimited."

He pushed off from the bar, glancing toward the beefy

sonofawhore and McCardle again. She caught him looking at her and gazed back, cool and unsmiling, her blue eyes chips of ice. *Bite my bag, you frigid bitch,* he thought, and raised his drink to her in a boorish barrelhouse salute, at the same time favoring her with an insultingly wide grin.

"Just tonic, right? Pure tonic."

He looked around. Ron Cummings had appeared at his side as suddenly as Satan. And his grin was properly satanic.

"Bugger off," Gardener said, and more people turned around to look.

"Jim, old buddy—"

"I know, I know, turn down the volume control." He smiled, but he could feel that pulse in his head getting harder, more insistent. It wasn't like the headaches the doctor had predicted following his accident; it didn't come from the front of his head but rather from someplace deep in the back. And it didn't hurt.

It was, in fact, rather pleasant.

"You got it." Cummings nodded almost imperceptibly toward McCardle. "She's got a heavy down on you, Jim. She'd love to dump you off the tour. Don't give her a reason."

"Fuck her."

"*You* fuck her," Cummings said. "Cancer, cirrhosis of the liver, and brain damage are all statistically proven results of heavy drinking, so I could reasonably expect any of them in my future, and if one of them were to come down on my head, I'd have no one to blame but myself. Diabetes, glaucoma, and premature senility all run in my family. But hypothermia of the penis? That I can do without. Excuse me."

Gardener stood still for a moment, puzzled, watching him go. Then he got it and brayed laughter. This time the tears did not just stand in his eyes; this time they actually rolled down his cheeks. For the third time that evening people were looking at him—a big man in rather shabby clothes with a glass full of what looked suspiciously like straight vodka, standing by himself and laughing at the top of his voice.

Put a lid on it, he thought. *Turn down the volume,* he thought. *Hypothermia of the penis,* he thought, and sprayed more laughter.

Little by little he managed to regain control. He headed for the stereo in the other room—that was where the most interesting people at a party were usually found. He grabbed a couple of canapés from a tray and swallowed them. He had a strong feeling that Arglebargle and McCarglebargle were looking at him still, and that McCarglebargle was giving Arglebargle a complete rundown on him in neat phrases, that cool, maddening little smile never leaving her face. *You didn't know? It's quite true—he shot her. Right through the face. She told him she wouldn't press charges if he would give her an uncontested divorce. Who knows if it was the right decision or not? He hasn't shot any more women . . . at least, not yet. But however well he might have read tonight—after that rather eccentric lapse, I mean—he is unstable, and as you can see, he's not able to control his drinking . . .*

Better watch it, Gard, he thought, and for the second time that night a thought came in a voice that was very much like Bobbi's. *Your paranoia's showing. They're not talking about you, for Chrissake.*

At the doorway he turned and looked back.

They were looking directly at him.

He felt nasty, dismayed shock race through him . . . and then he forced another big, insulting grin and tipped his glass toward both of them.

Get out of here, Gard. This could be bad. You're drunk.

I'm in control, don't worry. She wants me to leave, that's why she keeps looking at me, that's why she's telling that fat fuck all about me—that I shot my wife, that I was busted at Seabrook with a loaded gun in my packsack—she wants to get rid of me because she doesn't think drunken wifeshooting commiesymp nuclear protesters should get the biggest motherfucking hand of the night. But I can be cool. No problem, baby. I'm just going to hang out, taper off on the firewater, grab some coffee, and go home early. No problem.

And although he didn't drink any coffee, didn't go home early, and didn't taper off on the firewater, he was okay for the next hour or so. He turned down the volume control every time he heard it start going up, and made himself quit every time he heard himself doing what his wife had called *holding forth.* "When you get drunk, Jim," she had said, "not the least of your problems is a tendency to stop conversing and start *holding forth.*"

He stayed mostly in Arberg's living room, where the crowd was younger and not so cautiously pompous. Their conversation was lively, cheerful, and intelligent. The thought of the nukes rose in Gardener's mind—at hours such as this it always did, like a rotting body floating to the surface in response to cannonfire. At hours such as these—and at this stage of drunkenness—the certainty that he must alert these young men and women to the problem always floated up, trailing its heat of anger and irrationality like rotted waterweed. As always. The last six years of his life had been bad, and the last three had been a nightmare time in which he had become inexplicable to himself and scary to almost all the people who really knew him. When he drank, this rage, this terror, and most of all, this inability to explain whatever had happened to Jimmy Gardener, to explain even to himself—found outlet in the subject of the nukes.

But tonight he had hardly raised the subject when Ron Cummings staggered into the parlor, his narrow, gaunt face glowing with feverish color. Drunk or not, Cummings was still perfectly able to see how the wind was blowing. He adroitly turned the conversation back toward poetry. Gardener was weakly grateful but also angry. It was irrational, but it was there: he had been denied his fix.

So, partly thanks to the tight checkrein he had imposed on himself and partly due to Ron Cummings' timely intervention, Gardener avoided trouble until Arberg's party was almost over. Another half-hour and Gardener might have avoided trouble completely . . . at least, for *that* night.

But when Ron Cummings began to hold forth on the beat poets with his customary cutting wit, Gardener wandered back into the dining room to get another drink and perhaps something to nosh on from the buffet. What followed might have been arranged by a devil with a particularly malignant sense of humor.

"Once we've got Iroquois on line, you'll have the equivalent of three dozen full scholarships to give away," a voice on Gardener's left was saying. Gardener looked around so suddenly that he almost spilled his drink. Surely he must be imagining this conversation—it was too coincidental to be real.

Half a dozen people were grouped at one end of the buffet—three men and three women. One of the couples was that World-Famous Vaudeville Team of Arglebargle and McCarglebargle. The man speaking looked like a car salesman with better taste in clothes than most of the breed. His wife stood next to him. She was pretty in a strained way, her fading blue eyes magnified by thick spectacles. Gardener saw one thing at once. He might be an alky, and obsessive on this one subject, but he had always been a sharp observer and still was. The woman with the thick spectacles was aware that her husband was doing exactly that which Nora had accused Gard himself of doing at parties once he got drunk: *holding forth*. She wanted to get her husband out, but as yet couldn't see how to do it.

Gardener took a second look and guessed they had been married eight months. Maybe a year, but eight months was a better guess.

The man speaking had to be some sort of wheel with Bay State Electric. *Had* to be Bay State, because Bay State owned the boondoggle that was the Iroquois plant. This guy was making it sound like the greatest thing since sliced bread, and because he looked as though he really believed it, Gardener decided he must be a wheel of a rather small sort, maybe even a spare tire. He doubted if the big guys were so crazy about Iroquois. Even putting aside the insanity of nuclear power for a moment, there was the fact that Iroquois was five years late coming "on-line" and the fate of three interconnected New England bank chains depended on what would happen when—and if—it did. They were all standing chest-deep in radioactive quicksand and trading paper. It was like some crazy game of musical chairs.

Of course, the courts had finally given the company permission to begin loading hot rods the month before, and Gardener supposed that had the motherfuckers breathing a little easier.

Arberg was listening with solemn respect. He wasn't a trustee of the college, but anyone above the post of instructor would know enough to butter up an emissary from Bay State Electric, even a spare tire. Big private utilities like Bay State could do a lot for a school if they wanted to.

Was Reddy Kilowatt here a Friend of Poetry? About as much, Gard suspected, as he himself was a Friend of the Neutron Bomb. His *wife,* however—she of the thick glasses and the strained, pretty face—*she* looked like a Friend of Poetry.

Knowing it was a terrible mistake, Gardener drifted over. He was wearing a pleasant late-in-the-party-gotta-go-soon smile, but the pulse in his head was faster, centering on the left. The old helpless anger was rising in a red wave. *Don't you know what you're talking about?* was almost all that his heart could cry. There were logical arguments against nuclear power plants that he could muster, but at times like this he could only find the inarticulate cry of his heart.

Don't you know what you're talking about? Don't you know what the stakes are? Don't any of you remember what happened in Russia two years ago? They *haven't; they* can't. *They'll be burying the cancer victims far into the next century. Jesus-jumped-up-fiddling-Christ! Stick one of those used core-rods up your ass for half an hour or so and tell everyone how safe nuclear power is when your turds start to glow in the dark! Jesus!* JESUS! *You jerks are standing here listening to this man talk as if he was* sane!

He stood there, drink in hand, smiling pleasantly, listening to the spare tire spout his deadly nonsense.

The third man in the group was fifty or so and looked like a college dean. He wanted to know about the possibility of further organized protests in the fall. He called the spare tire Ted.

Ted the Power Man said he doubted there was much to worry about. Seabrook had had its vogue, and the Arrowhead installation in Maine—but since the federal judges had started to deal out some stiff sentences for what *they* saw as merely hell-raising, the protests had slowed down fast. "These groups go through targets almost as fast as they go through rock groups," he said. Arberg, McCardle, and the others laughed—all except the wife of Ted the Power Man. Her smile only frayed a little more.

Gardener's pleasant smile remained. It felt flash-frozen onto his face.

Ted the Power Man grew more expansive. He said it was time to show the Arabs once and for all that America and Americans didn't need them. He said that even the most modern coal-fired generators were too dirty to be acceptable by the EPA. He said that solar power was great . . . "as long as the sun shines." There was another burst of laughter.

Gardener's head thudded and whipped, whipped and thudded. His ears, tuned to an almost preternatural pitch, heard a faint crackling sound, like ice shifting, and he relaxed his hand a bare moment before it tightened enough to shatter the glass.

He blinked and Arberg had the head of a pig. This hallucination was utterly complete and utterly perfect, right down to the bristles on the fat man's snout. The buffet was in ruins, but Arberg was scavenging, finishing up the last few Triscuits, spearing a final slice of salami and chunk of cheese on the same plastic toothpick, chasing them with the last potato-chip crumbs. It all went into his snuffling snout, and he went on nodding all the while as Ted the Power Man explained that nuclear was the only alternative, really. "Thank God the American people are finally getting that Chernobyl business into some kind of perspective," he said. "Thirty-two people dead. It's horrible, of course, but there was an airplane crash just a month ago that killed a hundred and ninety-some. You don't hear people yelling for the government to shut down the airlines, though, do you? Thirty-two dead is horrible, but it's far from the Armageddon these nuke-freaks made it sound like." He lowered his voice a little. "They're as nuts as the LaRouche people you see in airports, but in a way, they're worse. They *sound* more rational. But if we gave them what they wanted, they'd turn around a month or so later and start whining about not being able to use their blow-dryers, or found out their Cuisinarts weren't going to work when they wanted to mix up a bunch of macrobiotic food."

To Gard he didn't look like a man anymore. The shaggy head of a wolf poked out of the collar of his white shirt with the narrow red pinstripes. It looked around, pink tongue lolling, greenish-yellow eyes sparkling. Arberg squealed some sort of approval and stuffed more odd lots into his pink pig's snout. Patricia McCardle now had the smooth sleek head of a whippet. The college dean and his wife were weasels. And the wife of the man from the electric company had become a frightened rabbit, pink eyes rolling behind thick glasses.

Oh, Gard, no, his mind moaned.

He blinked again and they were just people.

"And one thing these protesters never remember to mention at their protest rallies is just this," Ted the Power Man finished, looking around at them like a trial lawyer reaching the climax of his summation. "In thirty years of peaceful nuclear-power development, there has never been *one single fatality as the result of nuclear power in the United States of America.*" He smiled modestly and tossed off the rest of his Scotch.

"I'm sure we'll all rest easier knowing *that,*" the man who looked like a college dean said. "And now I think my wife and I—"

"Did you know that Marie Curie died of radiation poisoning?" Gardener asked conversationally. Heads turned. "Yeah. Leukemia induced by direct exposure to gamma rays. She was the first casualty along the death march with this guy's power plant at the end. She did a lot of research, and recorded it all."

Gardener looked around the suddenly silent room.

"Her notebooks are locked up in a vault," he said. "A vault in Paris. It's lead-lined. The notebooks are whole, but too radioactive to touch. As for who's died here, we don't really know. The AEC and the EPA keep a lid on it."

Patricia McCardle was frowning at him. With the dean temporarily forgotten, Arberg went back to scrounging along the denuded buffet table.

"On the fifth of October 1966," Gardener said, "there was a partial nuclear meltdown of the Enrico Fermi breeder reactor in Michigan."

"Nothing happened," Ted the Power Man said, and spread his hands to the assembled company as if to say, *You see? QED.*

"No," Gardener said. "Nothing did. God may know why, but my guess is no one else does. The chain reaction stopped on its own. No one knows why. One of the engineers the contractors called in took a look, smiled, and said, 'You guys almost lost Detroit.' Then he fainted."

"Oh, but Mr. Gardener! That was—"

Gardener held up a hand. "When you examine the cancer-death stats for the areas surrounding every nuclear-power facility in the country, you find anomalies, deaths that are way out of line with the norm."

"That is utterly untrue, and—"

"Let me finish, please. I don't think the facts make any

difference anymore, but let me finish anyway. Long before Chernobyl, the Russians had an accident at a reactor in a place called Kyshtym. But Khrushchev was Premier then, and the Soviets kept their lips a lot tighter. It looks like maybe they were storing used rods in a shallow ditch. Why not? As Madame Curie might have said, it seemed like a good idea at the time. Our best guess is that the core-rods oxidized, only instead of creating ferrous oxide, or rust, the way steel rods do, these rods rusted pure plutonium. It was like building a campfire next to a tank filled with LP gas, but they didn't know that. They assumed it would be all right. They *assumed.*" He could hear the rage filling his voice and was helpless to stop it. "They *assumed,* they played with the lives of living human beings as if they were . . . well, so many dolls . . . and guess what happened?"

The room was silent. Patty's mouth was a frozen red slash. Her complexion was milky with rage.

"It rained," Gardener said. "It rained *hard.* And that started a chain reaction that caused an explosion. It was like the eruption of a mud volcano. Thousands were evacuated. Every pregnant woman was given an abortion. There was no choice involved. The Russian equivalent of a turnpike in the Kyshtym area was closed for almost a year. Then, when word started to leak out that a very bad accident had happened on the edge of Siberia, the Russians opened the road again. But they put up some really hilarious signs. I've seen the photos. I don't read Russian, but I've asked four or five different people for a translation, and they all agree. It sounds like a bad ethnic joke. Imagine yourself driving along an American thruway—I-95 or I-70, maybe—and coming up on a sign that says PLEASE CLOSE ALL WINDOWS, TURN OFF ALL VENTILATION ACCESSORIES, AND DRIVE AS FAST AS YOUR CAR WILL GO FOR THE NEXT TWENTY MILES."

"Bullshit!" Ted the Power Man said loudly.

"Photographs available under the Freedom of Information Act," Gard said. "If this guy was only lying, maybe I could live with it. But he and the rest of the people like him are doing something worse. They're like salesmen telling the public that cigarettes not only don't cause lung cancer, they're full of vitamin C and keep you from having colds."

"Are you implying—"

"Thirty-two at Chernobyl we can *verify*. Hell, maybe it *is* only thirty-two. We've got photos taken by American doctors which suggest there must be well over two hundred already, but say thirty-two. It doesn't change what we've learned about high-rad exposure. The deaths don't all come at once. That's what's so deceiving. The deaths come in three waves. First, the people who get fried in the accident. Second, the leukemia victims, mostly kids. Third, the most lethal wave: cancer in adults forty and over. So much cancer you might as well go on and call it a plague. Skin cancer, breast cancer, liver cancer, melanoma, and bone cancer are the most common. But you also got your intestinal cancer, your bladder cancer, your brain tumors, your—"

"Stop, can't you please *stop?*" Ted's wife cried. Hysteria lent her voice a surprising power.

"I would if I could, dear," he said gently. "I can't. In 1964 the AEC commissioned a study on a worst-case scenario if an American reactor one-fifth the size of Chernobyl blew. The results were so scary the AEC buried the report. It suggested—"

"Shut up, Gardener," Patty said loudly. "You're drunk."

He ignored her, fixing his eyes on the power-man's wife. "It suggested that such an accident in a relatively rural area of the USA—the one they picked was midstate Pennsylvania, where Three-Mile Island is, by the way—would kill 45,000 folks, rad seventy percent of the state, and do seventeen million dollars' worth of damage."

"Holy fuck!" someone cried. "Are you *shitting?*"

"Nope," Gardener said, never taking his eyes from the woman, who now seemed hypnotized with terror. "If you multiply by five, you get 225,000 dead and eighty-five million dollars' worth of damage." He refilled his glass nonchalantly in the silent grave of the room, tipped it at Arberg, and drank two mouthfuls of straight vodka. *Uncontaminated* vodka, one hoped. "So!" he finished. "We're talking almost a quarter of a million people dead by the time the third wave dissipates, around 2040." He winked at Ted the Power Man, whose lips had pulled back from his teeth. "Be hard to get *that* many people even on a 767, wouldn't it?"

"Those figures came directly out of your butt," Ted the Power Man said angrily.

"Ted—" the man's wife said nervously. She had gone

dead pale except for tiny spots of red burning high up on her cheekbones.

"You expect me to stand here and listen to that . . . that party-line rhetoric?" he asked, approaching Gardener until they were almost chest to chest. "*Do* you?"

"At Chernobyl they killed the kids," Gardener said. "Don't you understand that? The ones ten years old, the ones *in utero*. Most may still be alive, but they are dying right now while we stand here with our drinks in our hands. Some can't even read yet. Most will never kiss a girl in passion. Right now while we're standing here with our drinks in our hands.

"They killed their children."

He looked at Ted's wife, and now his voice began to shake and to rise slightly, as if in a plea.

"We know from Hiroshima, Nagasaki, from our own tests at Trinity and on Bikini. *They killed their own children, do you dig what I'm saying? There are nine-year-olds in Pripyat who are going to die shitting out their own intestines! They killed the children!*"

Ted's wife took a step back, eyes wide behind her glasses, mouth twitching.

"We'll acknowledge that Mr. Gardener is a fine poet, I think," Ted the Power Man said, putting an arm around his wife and pulling her to his side again. It was like watching a cowboy rope a calf. "He's not very well-informed about nuclear power, however. We really have no idea what may or may not have happened at Kyshtym, and the Russian figures on the Chernobyl casualties are—"

"Cut the shit," Gardener said. "You know what I'm talking about. Bay State Electric has got all this stuff in its files, along with the elevated cancer rates in the areas surrounding American nuclear-power facilities, the water contaminated by nuclear waste—the water in deep aquifers, the water people wash their clothes and their dishes and themselves in, the water they drink. You *know*. You and every other private, municipal, state, and federal power company in America."

"Stop it, Gardener," McCardle warned, stepping forward. She flashed an overbrilliant smile around the group. "He's a little—"

"Ted, *did* you know?" Ted's wife asked suddenly.

"Sure, I've got some stats, but—"

He broke off. His jaw snapped shut so hard you could

almost hear it. It wasn't much . . . but it was enough. Suddenly they knew—all of them—that he had omitted a good deal of scripture from his sermon. Gardener felt a moment of sour, unexpected triumph.

There was a moment of awkward silence and then, quite deliberately, Ted's wife stepped away from him. He flushed. To Gard he looked like a man who has just whanged his thumb with a hammer.

"Oh, we have all kinds of reports," he said. "Most are nothing but a tissue of lies—Russian propaganda. People like this idiot are more than happy to swallow it hook, line, and sinker. For all we know, Chernobyl may have been no accident at all, but an effort to keep us from—"

"Jesus, next you'll be telling us the earth is flat," Gardener said. "Did you see the photographs of the Army guys in radiation suits walking around a power plant half an hour's drive from Harrisburg? Do you know how they tried to plug one of the leaks there? They stuffed a basketball wrapped with friction-tape into a busted waste-pipe. It worked for a while, then the pressure spit it out and busted a hole right through the containment wall."

"You spout some pretty goddam good propaganda." Ted grinned savagely. "The Russians *love* people like you! Do they pay you, or do you do it for free?"

"Who sounds like an airport Moonie now?" Gardener asked, laughing a little. He took a step closer to Ted. "Nuclear reactors are better built than Jane Fonda, right?"

"As far as I'm concerned, that's about the size of it, yes."

"Please," the dean's wife said, distressed. "We may discuss, but let's not *shout*, please—after all, we're *college* people—"

"*Somebody* better fucking shout about it!" Gardener shouted. She recoiled, blinking, and her husband stared at Gardener with eyes as bright as chips of ice. Stared as if he were marking Gard forever. Gard supposed he was. "Would you shout if your house was on fire and you were the only one in your family to wake up in the middle of the night and realize what was happening? Or just kinda tiptoe around and whisper, on account of you're a *college* person?"

"I just believe this has gone far en—"

Gardener dismissed her, turned to Mr. Bay State

Electric, and winked at him confidentially. "Tell me, Ted, how close is *your* house located to this nifty new nuclear facility you guys are building?"

"I don't have to stand here and—"

"Not too close, uh? That's what I thought." He looked at Mrs. Ted. She shrank away from him, clutching at her husband's arm. Gard thought, *What is it that she sees to make her shrink away from me like that? What, exactly?*

The voice of the booger-hooking, comic-book-reading deputy clanged back in dolorous answer: *Shot your wife, uh? Good fucking deal.*

"Are *you* planning to have children?" he asked her gently. "If so, I would hope for your sake that you and your husband really *are* located a safe distance from the plant . . . they keep goofing, you know. Like at Three-Mile Island. Not long before they opened the sucker, someone discovered the plumbers had somehow hooked up a 3,000-gallon tank for liquid radioactive waste to the drinking fountains instead of the scuts. In fact, they found out about a week before the place went on line. You like it?"

She was crying.

She was crying, but he couldn't stop.

"The guys investigating wrote in their report that hooking up radioactive waste-coolant pipes to the ones feeding water to the drinking fountains was 'a generally inadvisable practice.' If your hubby here invites you to take the company tour, I'd do the same thing they tell you to do in Mexico: don't drink the water. And if your hubby invites you after you're pregnant—or after you even *think* you might be—tell him . . ." Gardener smiled, first at her, then at Ted. "Tell him you've got a headache," he said.

"Shut up," Ted said. His wife had begun to moan.

"That's right," Arberg said. "I really do think it's time for you to shut up, Mr. Gardener."

Gard looked at them, then at the rest of the partygoers, who were staring at the tableau by the buffet, wide-eyed and silent, the young bartender among them.

"Shut up!" Gardener yelled. Pain drove a gleaming spike into the left side of his head. "Yeah! Shut up and let the goddam house burn! You can bet these fucking slumlords will be around to collect the fire insurance later on, after the ashes cool and they rake out what's left of

the bodies! *Shut up!* That's what all these guys want us to do! And if you don't shut up on your own, maybe you *get* shut up, like Karen Silkwood—"

"Quit it, Gardener," Patricia McCardle hissed. There were no sibilants in the words she spoke, making a hiss an impossibility, but she hissed just the same.

He bent toward Ted's wife, whose sallow cheeks were now wet with tears. "Also, you might check the IDS rates—infant-death syndrome, that is. They go up in plant areas. Birth defects, such as Down's syndrome—mongoloidism, in other words—and blindness, and—"

"I want you to get out of my house," Arberg said.

"You've got potato chips on your chin," Gardener said, and turned back to Mr. and Mr. Bay State Electric. His voice was coming from deeper and deeper inside him. It was like listening to a voice coming out of a well. Everything going critical. Red lines showing up all over the control panel.

"Ted here can lie about how vastly overrated it all was, nothing but a little fire and a lot of headline fodder, and all of you can even believe him . . . but the fact is, *what happened at the Chernobyl nuclear plant released more radioactive waste into the atmosphere of this planet than all the A-bombs set off aboveground since Trinity.*

"Chernobyl's hot.

"It's going to stay that way for a long time. How long? No one really knows, do they, Ted?"

He tipped his glass toward Ted and then looked around at the partygoers, all of them now standing silent and watching him, many looking just as dismayed as Mrs. Ted.

"And it'll happen again. Maybe in Washington State. They were storing core-rods in unlined ditches at the Hanford reactors just like they were at Kyshtym. California the next time there's a big quake? France? Poland? Or maybe right here in Massachusetts, if this fellow here has his way and the Iroquois plant goes on line in the spring. Just let one guy pull the wrong switch at the wrong time, and the next time the Red Sox open at Fenway will be around 2075."

Patricia McCardle was as white as a wax candle . . . except for her eyes, which were spitting blue sparks that looked freshly dropped from an arc-welder. Arberg had gone the other route: he was as red and dark as the bricks of his fine-old-family Back Bay home. Mrs. Ted was looking from Gardener to her husband and back again as if they were a pair of dogs that might bite. Ted saw the look; felt her trying to back out of his encircling, imprisoning arm. Gardener supposed it was her reaction to what he had been saying which provoked the final escalation. Ted had doubtless been instructed about how to handle hysterics like Gardener; the company taught their Teds to do that as routinely as the airlines taught stewardesses how to demonstrate the emergency oxygen system of the jets in which they flew.

But it was late, Gardener's drunken but eloquent rebuttal had blown up like a pocket thunderstorm . . . and now his wife was acting as though he might be the Butcher of Riga.

"God, I get tired of you guys and your simpering! There you were tonight, reading your incoherent poems into a microphone that runs on electricity, having your braying voice amplified by *speakers* that run on electricity, using electric lights to see by . . . where do you Luddites think that power comes from? The Wizard of Oz? Jesus!"

"It's late," McCardle said hurriedly, "and we all—"

"Leukemia," Gardener said, speaking directly to Ted's wide-eyed wife with dreadful confidentiality. "The children. The children are always the ones to go first after a meltdown. One good thing; if we lose Iroquois, it'll keep the Jimmy Fund busy."

"Ted?" she whimpered. "He's wrong, isn't he? I mean—" She was fumbling for a handkerchief or tissue in her purse and dropped it. There was the brittle sound of something breaking inside.

"Stop it," Ted said to Gardener. "We'll talk about it if you want, but stop deliberately upsetting my wife."

"I *want* her to be upset," Gardener said. He had embraced the darkness completely now. He belonged to it and it belonged to him and that was just fine. "There's so much she doesn't seem to know. Stuff she *ought* to know. Considering who she's married to, and all."

He turned the beautiful, wild grin on her. She looked into it without flinching this time, mesmerized like a doe in a pair of oncoming headlights.

"Used core-rods, now. Do you know where they go when they're no more good in the pile? Did he tell you that the Core Rod Fairy takes them? Not true. The power folks sort of squirrel them away. There are great big hot piles of core-rods here, there, and everywhere, sitting in nasty pools of shallow water. They're *really* hot, ma'am. And they're going to stay that way for a long time."

"Gardener, I want you out," Arberg said again.

Ignoring him, Gardener went on, speaking to Mrs. Ted and Mrs. Ted only: "They're already losing track of some of those piles of used rods, did you know that? Like little kids who play all day and go to bed tired and wake up the next day and can't remember where they left their toys. And then there's the stuff that just goes poof. The ultimate Mad Bomber stuff. Enough plutonium has already disappeared to blow up the eastern seaboard of the United States. But I've got to have a mike to read my incoherent poems into. God forbid I should have to raise my v—"

Arberg grabbed him suddenly. The man was big and flabby but quite powerful. Gardener's shirt pulled out of his pants. His glass tumbled out of his fingers and shattered on the floor. In a rolling, carrying voice—a voice which maybe only an indignant teacher who has spent many years in lecture halls could muster—Arberg announced to everyone present: "I'm throwing this bum out."

This declaration was greeted by spontaneous applause. Not everyone in the room applauded—maybe not even half of them did. But the power guy's wife was crying hard now, pressing against her husband, no longer trying to get away; until Arberg grabbed him, Gardener had been hulking over her, seeming to menace her.

Gardener felt his feet skim over the floor, then leave it entirely. He caught a glimpse of Patricia McCardle, her mouth compressed, her eyes glaring, her hands smacking together in the furious approval she had refused to accord him earlier. He saw Ron Cummings standing in the library door, a monstrous drink in one hand, his arm around a pretty blond girl, his hand pressed firmly against the sideswell of her breast. Cummings looked concerned but not exactly surprised. After all, it was only the argument in the Stone Country Bar and Grille continued to another night, wasn't it?

Are you going to let this swollen bag of shit just put you out on the doorstep like a stray cat?

Gardener decided he wasn't.

He drove his left elbow backward as hard as he could.

It slammed into Arberg's chest. Gardener thought that was what it would feel like to drive your elbow into a bowl of extremely firm Jell-O.

Arberg uttered a strangled cry and let go of Gardener, who turned, hands doubling into fists, ready to punch Arberg if Arberg tried to grab him again, tried to so much as touch him again. He rather hoped Arglebargle wanted to fight.

But the beefy sonofawhore showed no signs of wanting to fight. He had also lost interest in putting Gardener out. He was clutching his chest like a hammy actor preparing to sing a bad aria. Most of the bricklike color had left his face, although flaring strips stood out on each cheek. Arberg's thick lips flexed into an O; slacked; flexed into an O again; slacked again.

"—heart—" he wheezed.

"What heart?" Gardener asked. "You mean you *have* one?"

"—attack—" Arberg wheezed.

"Heart attack, bullshit," Gardener said. "The only thing getting attacked is your sense of propriety. And you deserve it, you son of a bitch."

He brushed past Arberg, still standing frozen in his about-to-sing pose, both hands clutched to the left side of his chest, where Gardener had connected with his elbow. The door between the dining room and the hallway had been crowded with people; they stepped back hurriedly as Gardener strode toward them and past them, heading for the front door.

From behind him a woman screamed: "Get out, do you hear me? Get out, you bastard! *Get out of here! I never want to see you again!*"

This shrewish, hysterical voice was so unlike Patricia McCardle's usual purr (steel claws buried somewhere inside pads of velvet) that Gardener stopped. He turned around . . . and was rocked by an eye-watering roundhouse slap. Her face was ill with rage.

"I should have known better," she breathed. "You're nothing but a worthless, drunken lout—a contentious, obsessive, bullying, ugly human being. But I'll fix you. I'll do it. You know I can."

"Why, Patty, I didn't know you cared," he said. "How sweet of you. I've been waiting to be fixed by you for years. Shall we go upstairs or give everyone a treat and do it on the rug?"

Ron Cummings, who had moved closer to the action, laughed. Patricia McCardle bared her teeth. Her hand flickered out again, this time connecting with Gardener's ear.

She spoke in a voice which was low but perfectly audible to everyone in the room: "I shouldn't have expected anything better from a man who would shoot his own wife."

Gardener looked around, saw Ron, and said: "Excuse me, would you?" and plucked the drink from Ron's hand. In a single quick, smooth gesture, he hooked two fingers into the bodice of McCardle's little black dress—it was elastic and pulled out easily—and dumped the whiskey inside.

"Cheers, dear," he said, and turned for the door. It was, he decided, the best exit line he could hope to manage under the circumstances.

Arberg was still frozen with his fists clutched to his chest, mouth flexing into an O and then relaxing.

"—heart—" he wheezed again to Gardener—Gardener or anyone who would listen to him. In the other room, Patricia McCardle was shrieking: *"I'm all right! Don't touch me! Leave me alone! I'm all right!"*

"Hey. You."

Gardener turned toward the voice and Ted's fist struck him high on one cheek. Gardener stumbled most of the way down the hall, clawing at the wall for balance. He struck the umbrella stand, knocked it over, then hit the front door hard enough to make the glass in the fanlight shiver.

Ted was walking down the hall toward him like a gunfighter.

"My wife's in the bathroom having hysterics because of you, and if you don't get out of here right now, I'm going to beat you silly."

The blackness exploded like a rotted, gas-filled pocket of guts.

Gardener seized one of the umbrellas. It was long, furled, and black—an English lord's umbrella if there had ever been one. He ran toward Ted, toward this fellow who knew exactly what the stakes were but who was going ahead anyway, why not, there were seven payments left on the Datsun Z and eighteen on the house, so why not, right? Ted who saw a six-hundred-percent increase in leukemia merely as a fact which might upset his wife. Ted, good old Ted, and it was just lucky for good old Ted that it had been umbrellas instead of hunting rifles at the end of the hall.

Ted stood looking at Gardener, eyes widening, jaw dropping. The look of flushed anger gave way to uncertainty and fear—the fear that comes when you decide you're dealing with an irrational being.

"Hey—!"

"Caramba, you asshole!" Gardener screamed. He waggled the umbrella and then poked Ted the power man in the belly with it.

"Hey!" Ted gasped, doubling over. *"Stop* it!"

"Andale, andale!" Gardener yelled, now beginning to whack Ted with the umbrella—back and forth, back and forth, back and forth. The strap which held the umbrella furled against its handle came loose. The umbrella, still closed but now loose, slopped around the handle. *"Arriba, arriba!"*

Ted was now too unnerved to think about renewing his attack or to think about anything but escape. He turned and ran. Gardener chased him, cackling, beating the back of his head and the nape of his neck with the umbrella. He was laughing . . . but nothing was funny. His earlier sense of victory was leaving fast. What victory was there in getting the best of a man like this in an argument, even temporarily? Or of making his wife cry? Or of beating him with a closed umbrella? Would any of those things keep the Iroquois plant from going on line next May? Would any of those things save what was left of his own miserable life, or kill those tapeworms inside him that kept digging and munching and growing, eating whatever was left inside that was sane?

No, of course not. But for now, senseless forward motion was all that mattered . . . because that was all there was left.

"Arriba, you bastard!" he cried, chasing Ted into the dining room.

Ted had his hands up to his head and was waving them about his ears; he looked like a man beset by bats. The umbrella *did* look a little batlike as it lashed up and down.

"Help me!" Ted squealed. "Help me, man's gone crazy!"

But they were all backing away, eyes wide and scared.

Ted's hip struck one corner of the buffet. The table rocked forward and upward, silverware sliding down the inclined plane of the wrinkling tablecloth, plates falling and shattering on the floor. Arberg's Waterford punch bowl detonated like a bomb, and a woman screamed. The table tottered for a moment and then went over.

"Help? Help? *Heellllp!*"

"*Andale!*" Gardener brought the umbrella down on Ted's head in a particularly hard swipe. Its trigger engaged and the umbrella popped open with a hollow *pwushhh!* Now Gardener looked like a mad Mary Poppins, chasing Ted the Power Man with an umbrella in one hand. Later it would occur to him that opening an umbrella in the house was supposed to be bad luck.

Hands grabbed him from behind.

He whirled, expecting that Arberg was over his impropriety attack and was back to have another go at giving him the bum's rush.

It wasn't Arberg. It was Ron. He still seemed calm—but there was something in his face, something dreadful. Was it compassion? Yes, Gardener saw, that was what it was.

Suddenly he didn't want the umbrella anymore. He threw it aside. The dining room was silent but for Gardener's rapid breathing and Ted's harsh, sobbing gasps. The overturned buffet table lay in a puddle of linen, broken crockery, shattered crystal. The odor of spilled rum punch rose in an eyewatering fog.

"Patricia McCardle is on the telephone, talking to the cops," Ron said, "and when it's Back Bay, they show up in a hurry. You want to bug out of here, Jim."

Gardener looked around and saw knots of partygoers standing against the walls and in the doorways, looking at him with those wide, frightened eyes. *By tomorrow they won't remember if it was about nuclear power or William Carlos Williams or how many angels can dance on the head of a pin,* he thought. *Half of them will tell the other half I made a pass at his wife. Just that good old funloving wife-shooting Jim Gardener, going crazy and beating the shit out of a guy with an umbrella. Also dumping about a pint of Chivas between the teeny tits of the woman who gave him a job when he had none. Nuclear power, what did that have to do with it?*

"What a Christless mess," he said hoarsely to Ron.

"Shit, they'll talk about it for years," Ron said. "The best reading they ever heard followed by the best party blowoff they ever saw. Now get going. Get your ass up to Maine. I'll call."

Ted the Power Man, eyes wide and teary, made a lunge for him. Two young men—one was the bartender—held him back.

"Goodbye," Gardener said to the huddled knots of people. "Thank you for a lovely time."

He went to the door, then turned back.

"And if you forget everything else, remember about the leukemia and the children. Remember—"

But what they'd remember was him whacking Ted with the umbrella. He saw it in their faces.

Gardener nodded and went down the hallway past Arberg, who was still standing with his hands clutched to his chest, lips flexing and closing. Gardener did not look back. He kicked aside the litter of umbrellas, opened the door, and stepped out into the night. He wanted a drink more than he ever had in his life, and he supposed he must have found one, because that was when he fell into the belly of the big fish and the blackout swallowed him.

6.

GARDENER ON THE ROCKS

1

Not long after dawn on the morning of July 4th, 1988, Gardener awoke—came to, anyway—near the end of the stone breakwater which extends out into the Atlantic not far from the Arcadia Funworld Amusement Park in Arcadia Beach, New Hampshire. Not that Gardener knew where he was then. He barely knew anything save for his own name, the fact that he was in what seemed to be total physical agony, and the somewhat less important fact that he had apparently almost drowned in the night.

He was lying on his side, feet trailing in the water. He supposed that he had been high and dry when he had waltzed out here the night before, but he had apparently rolled over in his sleep, slid a little way down the breakwater's sloped north side . . . and now the tide was coming in. If he had been half an hour later in waking up, he thought he very well might have simply floated off the rocks of the breakwater as a grounded ship may float off a sandbar.

One of his loafers was still on, but it was shriveled and useless. Gardener kicked it off and watched apathetically as it floated down into greeny darkness. *Something for the lobsters to shit in,* he thought, and sat up.

The bolt of pain which went through his head was so immense he thought for a moment that he was having a stroke, that he had survived his night on the breakwater only to die of an embolism the morning after.

The pain receded a little and the world came back from the gray mist into which it had receded. He was able to appreciate just how miserable he was. It was what Bobbi Anderson would undoubtedly have called "the whole body trip," as in *Savor the whole body trip, Jim. What can be better than the way you feel after a night in the eye of the cyclone?*

A *night? One* night?

No way, baby. This had been a *jag*. The real fucking thing.

His stomach felt sour and bloated. His throat and sinuses were caked with elderly puke. He looked to his left, and sure enough, there it was, a little above him in what must have been his original position, the drinker's signature—a great big splash of drying vomit.

Gardener wiped a shaking, dirty right hand under his nose and saw flakes of dried blood. He'd had a nosebleed. He'd had them off and on ever since the skiing accident at Sunday River when he was seventeen. He could almost count on the nosebleeds when he had been drinking.

At the end of all his previous binges—and this was the first time he had gone whole hog in almost three years—Gardener had felt what he was feeling now: a sickness that went deeper than the thudding head, the stomach curled up like a sponge filled with acid, the aches, the quivering muscles. That deep sickness couldn't even be called depression—it was a feeling of utter doom.

This was the worst ever, even worse than the depression that had followed the Famous Thanksgiving Jag of 1980, the one that had ended his teaching career and his marriage. It had also come close to ending Nora's life. He had come to that time in Penobscot County Jail. A deputy was sitting outside his cell reading a copy of *Crazy* magazine and picking his nose. Gardener learned later that all police departments are aware that jag-drinkers frequently come off their binges deeply depressed. So if there happens to be a man available, he keeps an eye on you, to make sure you don't highside it . . . at least not until you post bond and get off county property.

"Where am I?" Gardener had asked.

"Where do you think you are?" the deputy asked. He looked at the large green booger he had just scraped out of his nose and then wiped it slowly and with apparent enjoyment onto the sole of his shoe, squashing it down, smearing it along the dark dirt there. Gardener had been unable to take his eyes from this operation; a year later he would write a poem about it.

"What did I do?"

Save for occasional flashes, the previous two days had been totally black. The flashes were unrelated, like cloud-rifts which let through uncertain flickers of sunlight as a storm approaches. Bringing Nora a cup of tea and then starting to harangue her about the nukes. *Ave Nukea Eterna.* When he died, his final word on the whole fucking mess wouldn't be *Rosebud* but *Nukes.* He could remember falling down in the driveway beside his house. Getting a pizza and being so drunk runny clots of cheese went down inside his shirt, burning his chest. He could remember calling Bobbi. Calling and babbling something to her, something awful, and had Nora been screaming? *Screaming?*

"What did I do?" he asked, more urgently.

The deputy looked at him for a moment with a perfect clear-eyed contempt. "Shot your wife. That's what you did. Good fucking deal, uh?"

The deputy had gone back to his *Crazy* magazine.

That had been bad; this was worse. That depthless feeling of self-contempt, the grisly certainty *that you had done bad things you couldn't remember.* Not a few too many glasses of champagne at the New Year's Eve party where you put a lampshade on your head and boogied around the room with it slipping down over your eyes, everybody in attendance (with the exception of your wife) thinking it was just the funniest thing they'd ever seen in their *lives.* Not knowing you did fun things like punching department heads. Or shooting your wife.

It had been worse this time.

How *could* it be worse than Nora?

Something. For the time being his head hurt too badly to even try reconstructing the last unknown period of time.

Gardener looked down at the water, the waves bulging smoothly up toward where he sat, forearms on his knees, head sagging. When the troughs passed he could see barnacles and slick green seaweed. No . . . not really seaweed. Green slime. Like boogers.

Shot your wife . . . good fucking deal, uh?

Gardener closed his eyes against the sickening pulses of pain, then opened them again.

Jump in, a voice cajoled him softly. *I mean, what the fuck, you don't really need any more of this shit, do you? Game called in the bottom of the first. Not official. Rainout. To be rescheduled when the Great Wheel of Karma turns into the next life . . . or the one after that, if I have to spend the next making up for this one by being a dung beetle or something. Hang up your jock, Gard. Jump in. In your current state, both of your legs will cramp and it'll be over quick. Gotta beat a bedsheet in a jail cell, anyway. Go on, jump.*

He got up and stood swaying on the rocks, looking at the water. Just one big step, that's all it would take. He could do it in his sleep. Shit, almost had.

Not yet. Want to talk to Bobbi first.

The part of his mind which still wanted a little to live grasped at this idea. Bobbi. Bobbi was the only part of his old life that still seemed somehow whole and good. Bobbi was living down there in Haven, writing her westerns, still sane, still his friend if no longer his lover. His last friend.

Want to talk to Bobbi first, okay?

Why? So you can make a last stab at fucking her up too? God knows you've tried hard enough. She's got a police record because of you, and undoubtedly her own FBI folder as well. Leave Bobbi out of this. Jump and stop fucking around.

He swayed forward, very close to doing it. The part of him that still wanted to live seemed to have no arguments left, no delaying tactics. It could have said that he had stayed sober—more or less—for the last three years, there had been no blackouts since he and Bobbi had been arrested at Seabrook in 1985. But that was a hollow argument. Except for Bobbi he was now completely alone. His mind was in turmoil almost all of the time, returning again and again—even sober—to the subject of the nukes. He recognized that his original concern and anger had rotted into obsession . . . but recognition and rehabilitation were not the same things at all. His poetry had deteriorated. His *mind* had deteriorated. Worst of all, when he wasn't drinking he wished he was. *It's just that the hurting's all the time now. I'm like a bomb walking around and looking for a place to go off. Time to defuse.*

Okay, then. Okay. He closed his eyes and got ready.

As he did, an odd certainty came to him, an intuition so strong that it was nearly precognitive. He felt that Bobbi needed to talk to *him,* rather than the other way around. That it was no mind trick. She really was in some kind of trouble. *Bad* trouble.

He opened his eyes and looked around, like a man coming out of a deep daze. He would find a phone and call her. He wouldn't say "Hey Bobbi I had another blackout" and he wouldn't say "I don't know where I am Bobbi but this time there's no nose-picking deputy to stop me." He would say "Hey, Bobbi, how you doin?" and when she told him she was doin okay, never better, shooting it out with the James gang in Northfield, or lighting out for the territories with Butch Cassidy and the Sundance Kid, and by the way, Gard, how's your own bad self, Gard would tell her he was fine, writing some good stuff for a change, thinking of going over Vermont way for a bit, see some friends. Then he would go back out to the end of the breakwater and jump off. Nothing fancy; he would just bellyflop into the dead zone. That seemed to fit; after all, it was the way he had mostly gotten through the live one. The ocean had been here for a billion years or so. It would wait another five minutes while he did that.

But no laying it off on her, you hear me? Promise, Gard. No breaking down and blubbering. You're supposed to be her friend, not the male equivalent of her slimebucket sister. None of that shit.

He had broken promises in his life, God knew—a few thousand of them to himself. But this one he would keep.

He climbed clumsily up to the top of the breakwater. It was rough and rocky, a really fine place to break an ankle. He looked around apathetically for his scuffed brown totebag, the one he always took with him when he went off to read, or just to ramble, thinking it might be lodged in one of the holes between the rocks. It wasn't. It was an old campaigner, scuffed and battered, going back to the last troubled years of his marriage, something he had managed to hold onto while all the valuable things got lost. Well, now the tote was finally gone too. Clothes, toothbrush, bar of soap in a plastic dish, a bunch of jerky meat-sticks (it amused Bobbi to cure jerky in her shed, sometimes), a twenty-dollar bill under the tote's bottom . . . and all his unpublished poems, of course.

The poems were the least of his worries. The ones he had written over the last couple of years, and to which he had given the wonderfully witty and upbeat title "The Radiation Cycle," had been submitted to five different publishers and rejected by all five. One anonymous editor had scribbled: "Poetry and politics rarely mix; poetry and propaganda, never." This little homily was perfectly true, he knew it . . . and still hadn't been able to stop.

Well, the tide had administered the Ultimate Blue Pencil to them. *Go and do thou likewise,* he thought, and lurched slowly along the breakwater toward the beach, thinking that his walk out to where he had awakened must have been better than a death-defying circus act. He walked with the summer sun rising up red and bloated from the Atlantic behind him, his shadow trailing out in front of him, and on the beach a kid in jeans and a T-shirt set off a string of firecrackers.

2

A marvel: his totebag wasn't lost after all. It was lying upside-down on the beach just above the high-tide line, unzipped, looking to Gardener like a big leather mouth biting at the sand. He picked it up and looked inside. Everything was gone. Even his frayed undies. He pulled up the tote's imitation leather bottom. The twenty was gone too. Fond hope, too quickly banish'd.

Gardener dropped the tote. His notebooks, all three of them, lay a little further along the beach. One was resting on its covers in a tent shape, one lay soggily just below the high-tide line, swelled up to the size of a telephone book, and the wind was leafing through the third idly. *Don't bother,* Gardener thought. *Lees of an ass.*

The kid with the firecrackers came toward him . . . but not too close. *Wants to be able to take off in a hurry if I turn out to be as weird as I undoubtedly look,* Gardener thought. *Smart kid.*

"That your stuff?" the kid asked. His T-shirt showed a guy blowing his groceries. SCHOOL-LUNCH VICTIM, the shirt said.

"Yeah," Gardener said. He bent down and picked up the soggy notebook, looked at it for a moment, and then tossed it down again.

The kid handed him the other two. What could he say? *Don't bother, kid? The poems suck, kid? Poetry and politics rarely mix, kid, poetry and propaganda* never?

"Thanks," he said.

"Sure." The kid held the bag so Gardener could drop the two dry notebooks back inside. "Surprised you got anything left at all. This place is full of ripoff artists in the summer. The park, I guess."

The kid gestured with his thumb and Gardener saw the roller coaster silhouetted against the sky. Gard's first thought was that he had somehow managed to roister all the way north to Old Orchard Beach before collapsing. A second look changed his mind. No pier.

"Where am I?" Gardener asked, and his mind harked back with an eerie totality to the jail cell and the nose-picking deputy. For a moment he was sure the kid would say, *Where do you think you are?*

"Arcadia Beach." The kid looked half-amused, half-contemptuous. "You must have really hung one on last night, mister."

"Last night, and the night before," Gardener chanted, his voice a little rusty, a little eerie. "Tommyknockers, Tommyknockers, knocking at the door."

The boy blinked at Gardener in surprise . . . and then delighted him by unexpectedly adding a couplet Gardener had never heard: "Wanna go out, dunno if I can, cause I'm so afraid of the Tommyknocker man."

Gardener grinned . . . but the grin turned into a wince of fresh pain. "Where'd you hear that, kid?"

"My mom. When I was a baby."

"I heard about the Tommyknockers from my mother too," Gardener said, "but never that part."

The kid shrugged as if the topic had lost whatever marginal interest it might have had for him. "She used to make all kinds of stuff up." He appraised Gardener. "Don't you ache?"

"Kid," Gardener said, leaning forward solemnly, "in the immortal words of Ed Sanders and Tuli Kupferberg, I feel like homemade shit."

"You look like you been drunk a long time."

"Yeah? How would you know?"

"My mom. With her it was always funny stuff like the Tommyknockers or too hung-over to talk."

"She give it up?"

"Yeah. Car crash," the kid said.

Gardener was suddenly racked with shivers. The boy appeared not to notice; he studied the sky, tracing the path of a gull. It coursed a morning sky of blue delicately shelled with mackerel scales, turning black for a moment as it flew in front of the sun's rising red eye. It landed on the breakwater, where it began to pick at something which gulls presumably found tasty.

Gardener looked from the gull to the kid. All of this was taking on decidedly omenish tones. The kid knew about the fabled Tommyknockers. How many kids in the world knew about them, and what were the odds that Gardener would happen to stumble on one who both (a) knew about them and (b) had lost his mother because of drink?

The kid reached in his pocket and brought out a small tangle of firecrackers. *Sweet bird of youth,* Gard thought, and smiled.

"Want to light a couple? Celebrate the Fourth? Might cheer you up."

"The Fourth? The Fourth of *July?* Is that what this is?"

The kid gave him a dry smile. "It ain't Arbor Day."

The twenty-sixth of June had been . . . he counted backwards. Good Christ. He had eight days which were painted black. Well . . . not quite. That actually would have been better. Patches of light, not at all welcome, were beginning to illuminate parts of that blackness. The idea that he had hurt someone—*again*—arose now in his mind as a certainty. Did he want to know who that

(arglebargle)

was, or what he had done to him or her? Probably not. Best to call Bobbi and finish himself before he remembered.

"Mister, how'd you get that scar on your forehead?"

"Ran into a tree while I was skiing."

"Bet it hurt."

"Yeah, even worse than this, but not by much. Do you know where there's a pay phone?"

The kid pointed to an eccentric green-roofed manse which stood perhaps a mile down the beach. It topped a crumbling granite headland and looked like the cover of a paperback gothic. It had to be a resort. After a moment's fumbling, Gard came up with the name.

"That's the Alhambra, isn't it?"

"The one and only."

"Thanks," he said, and started off.

"Mister?"

He turned.

"Don't you want that last book?" The kid pointed to the wet notebook lying on the high-tide line. "You could dry it out."

Gardener shook his head. "Kid," he said, "I can't even dry *me* out."

"You sure you don't want to light off some firecrackers?"

Gardener shook his head, smiling. "Be careful with 'em, okay? People hurt themselves with things that go bang."

"Okay." He smiled, a little shyly. "My mother did for a long time before the, you know—"

"I know. What's your name?"

"Jack. What's yours?"

"Gard."

"Happy Fourth of July, Gard."

"Happy Fourth, Jack. And watch out for the Tommy-knockers."

"Knocking at my door," the kid agreed solemnly, and looked at Gardener with eyes which seemed queerly knowing.

For a moment Gardener seemed to feel a second premonition (*whoever would have guessed a hangover was so conducive to the psychic emanations of the universe?* a bitterly sarcastic voice inside asked). He didn't know what of, exactly, but it filled him with urgency about Bobbi again. He tipped the kid a wave and set off up the beach. He walked at a fast, steady pace, although the sand drew at his feet, clinging, pulling. Soon his heart was racing and his head was thudding so hard his eyeballs seemed to pulse.

The Alhambra did not seem to be drawing appreciably closer.

Slow down or you'll have a heart attack. Or a stroke. Or both.

He did slow down . . . and then doing so struck him as palpably absurd. Here he was, planning to drown himself in fifteen minutes or so, but minding his heart in the meantime. It was like the old joke about the condemned man turning down the cigarette offered by the captain of the firing squad. "I'm trying to quit," the guy says.

Gardener picked up his pace again, and now the bolts of pain began to beat out steady pulses of jingle-jangle verse:

Late last night and the night before,
Tommyknockers, Tommyknockers,
Knocking at the door.
I was crazy and Bobbi was sane
But that was before the Tommyknockers came.

He stopped. *What is this Tommyknocker shit?*

Instead of an answer, that deep voice, as terrifying and yet as sure as the voice of a loon crying out on an empty lake came back: *Bobbi's in trouble!*

He began to walk again, getting up to his former brisk pace . . . and then moving even faster. *Wanna go out,* he thought. *Dunno if I can, cause I'm so afraid of the Tommy-knocker man.*

He was climbing the weather-whitened stairs which led up the side of the granite headland from the beach to the hotel when he wiped his hand across his nose and saw that it was bleeding again.

3

Gardener lasted exactly eleven seconds in the lobby of the Alhambra—long enough for the desk clerk to see he had no shoes on. The clerk nodded to a husky bellman when Gardener began to protest, and the two of them gave him the bum's rush.

They would have booted me even if I had *been wearing shoes,* Gard reflected. *Shit,* I *would have booted me.*

He had gotten a good look at himself in the glass of the lobby door. Too good. He had managed to mop most of the blood off his face with his sleeve, but there were still traces. His eyes were bloodshot and starey. His week's growth of beard made him look like a porcupine about six weeks after a shearing. In the genteel summer world of the Alhambra, where men were men and women wore tennis skirts, he looked like a male bag-lady.

Because only the earliest risers had begun to stir, the bellman took the time to inform him there was a pay phone at the Mobil station.

"Intersection of U.S. 1 and Route 26. Now get the hell out before I call the cops."

If he had needed to know any more about himself than he already did, it was in the husky bellman's disgusted eyes.

Gardener trudged slowly down the hill toward the gas station. His socks flapped and flailed against the tar. His heart knocked like a wheezy Model T engine that's experienced too much hard traveling and too little maintenance. He could feel the headache moving to the left, where it would eventually center in a brilliant pinpoint . . . if he'd had plans to live that long, anyway. And suddenly he was seventeen again.

He was seventeen, and his obsession wasn't nukes but nooky. The girl's name was Annmarie and he thought he was going to make it with her pretty soon, maybe, if he didn't lose his nerve. If he kept his cool. Maybe even tonight. But part of keeping his cool was doing okay today. Today, right here, here being Straight Arrow, an intermediate ski trail at Victory Mountain in Vermont. He was looking down at his skis, mentally reviewing the steps necessary to come to your basic snowplow stop, reviewing as he would study for a test, wanting to pass, knowing he was still pretty new at this and Annmarie wasn't, and he somehow didn't think she would be so apt to come across if he ended up looking like Frosty the Snowman his first day off the beginners' slopes; he didn't mind looking a little *inexperienced* as long as he didn't look downright *stupid,* so there he had been, looking stupidly down at his feet instead of where he was going, which was directly at a gnarled old pine with the warning red stripe painted on its bark, and the only sounds were the wind in his ears and the snow sliding dryly under his skis, and they were the same soothing hush-a-bye sound: *Shhhhhh . . .*

It was the rhyme that broke into the memory, making him stop near the Mobil station. The rhyme came back and it stayed, beating in time with his throbbing head. *Late last night and the night before, Tommyknockers, Tommyknockers, knocking at the door.*

Gard hawked, tasted the coppery, unpleasant flavor of

his own blood, and spat a reddish glob of phlegm into the trash-littered dirt of the soft shoulder. He remembered asking his mother who or what Tommyknockers were. He couldn't remember what, if anything, she had replied, but he'd always thought they must be highwaymen, robbers who stole by moonlight, killed in shadow, and buried in the darkest part of the night. And hadn't he spent one tortured, endless half-hour in the darkness of his bedroom before sleep finally decided to be merciful and claim him, thinking they might be cannibals as well as robbers? That instead of burying their victims in the dark of the night, they might have cooked them and . . . well . . .

Gardener wrapped his thin arms (there didn't seem to be any restaurants up in the cyclone) around his chest and shuddered.

He crossed to the Mobil station, which was hung with bunting but not yet open. The signs out front read SUPERUNLEADED .99 and GOD BLESS AMERICA and WE LUV WINNEBAGOS! The pay phone was on the side of the building. Gardener was grateful to find it was one of the new ones; you could dial long distance without depositing any money. That at least spared him the indignity of spending part of his last morning on earth panhandling.

He punched zero, then had to stop. His hand was shaking wildly, it was all over the place. He cocked the phone between head and shoulder this time, leaving both hands free. Grasped his right wrist with his left hand to hold the hand steady . . . as steady as possible, anyway. Now, looking like a shooter on a target range, he used his forefinger to punch the buttons with slow and horrible deliberation. The robot voice told him to punch in either his telephone credit-card number (a task Gard thought he would have been utterly incapable of performing, even if he'd had such a card) or zero for an operator. Gardener hit zero.

"Hi, happy holiday, this is Eileen," a voice chirruped. "May I have your billing, please?"

"Hi, Eileen, happy holiday to you too," Gard said. "I'd like to bill the call collect to anyone from Jim Gardener."

"Thank you, Jim."

"You're welcome," he said, and then, suddenly: "No, change that. Tell her it's Gard calling."

As Bobbi's telephone began to ring up there in Haven,

Gardener turned and looked toward the rising sun. It was even redder than before, rising toward the scud of thickening mackerel scales like a great round blister in the sky. The sun and the clouds together brought another childhood rhyme to mind: *Red sky at night, sailor's delight. Red sky at morning, sailor, take warning.* Gard didn't know about red sky at morning *or* at night, but he knew those delicate scales of cloud were a reliable harbinger of rain.

Too goddam many rhymes for a man's last morning on earth, he thought irritably, and then: *I'm going to wake you up, Bobbi. Going to wake you up, but I promise you I'll never do it again.*

But there was no Bobbi to wake up. The phone rang, that was all. Rang . . . and rang . . . and rang.

"Your party doesn't answer," the operator told him, just in case he was deaf or had maybe forgotten what he was doing for a few seconds and had been holding the phone against his asshole instead of his ear. "Would you like to try again later?"

Yeah, maybe. But it'd have to be by Ouija board, Eileen.

"Okay," he said. "You have a good one."

"Thank you, Gard!"

He pulled the phone away from his ear as if it had bitten him and stared at it. For a moment she had sounded so *much* like Bobbi . . . so goddam *much* . . .

He put the phone back and got as far as, "Why did you—" before realizing that cheerful Eileen had clicked off.

Eileen. Eileen, not Bobbi. But—

She had called him Gard. *Bobbi* was the only one who—

No, change that, he'd said. *Tell her it's Gard calling.*

There. Perfectly reasonable explanation.

Then why didn't it *seem* that way?

He hung up slowly. He stood at the side of the Mobil station in wet socks and shrunken pants and untucked shirt, his shadow long and long. A phalanx of motorcycles went by on Route 1, headed for Maine.

Bobbi's in trouble.

Will you please just let that go? It's boolsheet, as Bobbi herself would say. Somebody tell you the only holiday you could go home for was Christmas? She went back to Utica for the Glorious Fourth, that's all.

Yeah, sure. Bobbi was as likely to go back to Utica for the Fourth as Gard was to apply as an intern at the new Bay State nuclear plant. Sister Anne would probably celebrate the holiday by ramming a few M-80s up Bobbi's cooze and lighting them.

Well, maybe she got invited to be parade marshal—or sheriff marshal, ha-ha—in one of those cow towns she's always writing about. Deadwood, Abilene, Dodge City, someplace like that. You did what you could. Now finish what you started.

His mind made no effort to argue; he could have dealt with that. Instead it only reiterated its original thesis: *Bobbi's in trouble.*

Just an excuse, you chickenshit bastard.

He didn't think so. Intuition was solidifying into certainty. And whether it was boolsheet or not, that voice continued to insist that Bobbi was in a jam. Until he knew one way or the other for sure, he supposed he could table his personal business. As he had told himself not long ago, the ocean wasn't going anywhere.

"Maybe the Tommyknockers got her," he said out loud, and then laughed—a scared, husky little laugh. He was going crazy, all right.

7.

GARDENER ARRIVES

1

Shushhhhh . . .

He's staring down at his skis, plain brown wood strips racing over the snow. He started looking down just to make sure he was keeping the skis nice and parallel, not trying to look like a snowbunny with no business here after all. Now he's almost hypnotized by the liquid speed of his skis, by the crystal flicker of snow passing in a steady white strip, six inches wide, between the skis. He doesn't realize his state of semihypnosis until Annmarie screams: "Gard, watch out! Watch out!"

It's like being roused from a light doze. That's when he realizes he's been in a semitrance, that he has been looking down at that shiny, flowing strip far too long.

Annmarie screams: "Stem christie! Gard! Stem christie!"

She screams again, and this time is she telling him to fall down, just fall down? Christ, you could break a leg that way!

In these last few seconds before the crunching impact, he still can't comprehend how things got serious so fast.

He has somehow managed to drift far off to the left side of the trail. Pines and spruces, their blue-gray branches heavy with snow, are blurring past less than three yards from him. A rock poking out of the snow blips by; his left ski has missed it by inches. He realizes with cold horror that he has lost all control, has forgotten everything Annmarie has taught him, maneuvers that seemed so easy on the kiddie slopes.

And now he's going . . . what? Twenty miles an hour? Thirty? Forty? Cold air cuts against his face and he sees the line of trees at the edge of the Straight Arrow trail getting ever closer. His own straight arrow has become a mild diagonal. Mild, but enough to be deadly, just the same. He sees his path will soon take him off the trail completely and then *he will stop, you bet, then he will stop very quickly.*

She shrieks again and he thinks: Stem christie? Did she really say that? I can't even *snowplow* for beans and she wants me to do a *stem christie?*

He tries to turn right but his skis remain stubbornly on course. Now he can see the tree he'll hit, a big, hoary old pine. A red stripe has been painted around its gnarly trunk—a wholly unnecessary danger signal.

He tries again to turn but he's forgotten how to do it.

The tree swells, seeming to rush toward him while he himself remains still; he can see jagged knobs, splintery groping butts of branches on which he may impale himself, he can see nicks in the old bark, he can see drips where the red paint has run.

Annmarie shrieks again and he's aware he himself is screaming.

Shusshhhhhh . . .

2

"Mister? Mister, are you all right?"

Gardener sat up suddenly, startled, expecting to pay for the movement with a whacking thud of pain through his head. There was none. He experienced a moment of nauseous vertigo that might have come from hunger, but his head was clear. The headache had passed in its sudden way while he slept—perhaps even while he was dreaming of his accident.

"I'm okay," he said, looking around. His head thudded now—but against a drum. A girl in cutoff denim jeans laughed. "You're supposed to use sticks on those, man, not your head. You were mumbling in your sleep."

He saw he was in a van—and now everything fell into place. "Was I?"

"Yeah. Not good mumbles."

"It wasn't a good dream," Gardener said.

"Have a hit off this," the girl said, and handed him a joint. The roachclip it was in, he saw, was a golden oldie: Richard Nixon in a blue suit, fingers thrust up in the characteristic double-V gesture that probably not even the oldest of the five other people in this van remembered. "Guaranteed to cure all bad dreams," the girl added solemnly.

That's what they told me about the booze, Lady Day. But sometimes they lie. Take it from me. Sometimes they lie.

He took a small hit off the joint for politeness' sake and felt his head begin to swim almost at once. He handed it back to the girl, who was sitting against the van's sliding door, and said: "I'd rather have something to eat."

"Got a box of crackers," the driver said, and handed it back. "We ate everything else. Beaver even ate the fucking *prunes*. Sorry."

"Beaver'd eat anything," the girl in the cutoffs said.

The kid in the van's shotgun seat looked back. He was a plump boy with a wide, pleasant face. "Untrue," he said. "*Un*true. I'd *never* eat my mother."

At that they were all laughing wildly, Gardener included. When he was able, he said: "The crackers are fine. Really." And they were. He ate slowly at first, tentatively, monitoring his works closely for signs of rebellion. There were none and he began to eat faster and faster, until he was gobbling the crackers in big handfuls, his stomach snarling and yapping.

When had he last eaten? He didn't know. It was lost in the blackout. He did know from previous experience that he never ate much when he was busy trying to drink up the world—and a lot of what he tried to eat either ended up in his lap or ran down his shirt. That made him think of the big greasy pizza he had eaten—*tried* to eat—Thanksgiving evening, 1980. The night he had shot Nora through the cheeks.

—or you could have severed one or both optic nerves! Nora's lawyer suddenly shouted furiously at him inside his head. *Partial or total blindness! Paralysis! Death! All that bullet had to do was chip one tooth to go flying off in any direction, any damned direction at all! Just* one! *And don't sit there and try any bullshit like how you didn't*

mean to kill her, either. You shoot a person in the head, what else are you trying to do?

The depression came rolling back—big, black, and a mile high. *Should have killed yourself, Gard. Shouldn't have waited.*

Bobbi's in trouble.

Well, maybe so. But getting help from a guy like you is like hiring a pyromaniac to fix the oil-burner.

Shut up.

You're wasted, Gard. Fried. What that kid back there on the beach would undoubtedly call a burnout.

"Mister, you sure you're all right?" the girl asked. Her hair was red, cut punkily short. Her legs went approximately up to her chin.

"Yeah," he said. "Did I look not all right?"

"For a minute there you looked terrible," she answered gravely. That made him grin—not what she'd said but the solemnity with which she'd said it—and she grinned back, relieved.

He looked out the window and saw they were headed north on the Maine Turnpike—only up to mile thirty-six, so he couldn't have slept too long. The feathery mackerel scales of two hours ago were beginning to merge into a toneless gray that promised rain by afternoon—before he got to Haven, it would probably be dark and he would be soaked.

After hanging up the telephone at the Mobil station, he had stripped off his socks and tossed them into the wastecan on one of the gasoline islands. Then he walked over to Route 1 northbound in his bare feet and stood on the shoulder, old totebag in one hand, the thumb of his other out and cocked north.

Twenty minutes later this van had come along—a fairly new Dodge Caravel with Delaware plates. A pair of electric guitars, their necks crossed like swords, were painted on the side, along with the name of the group inside: THE EDDIE PARKER BAND. It pulled over and Gardener had run to it, panting, totebag banging his leg, headache pulsing white-hot pain into the left side of his head. In spite of the pain, he had been amused by the slogan carefully lettered across the van's doors: IF EDDIE'S ROCKIN', DON'T COME KNOCKIN'.

Now, sitting on the floor in back and reminding himself not to turn around quickly and thump the snare drum again, Gardener saw the Old Orchard exit coming up. At the same time, the first drops of rain hit the windshield.

"Listen," Eddie said, pulling over, "I hate to leave you off like this. It's starting to rain and you don't even have any fuckin shoes."

"I'll be all right."

"You don't look so all right," the girl in the cutoffs said softly.

Eddie whipped off his hat (DON'T BLAME ME; I VOTED FOR HOWARD THE DUCK written over the visor) and said: "Cough up, you guys." Wallets appeared; change jingled in jeans pockets.

"No! Hey, thanks, but no!" Gardener felt hot blood rush into his cheeks and burn there. Not embarrassment but outright shame. Somewhere inside him he felt a strong painful thud—it didn't rattle his teeth or bones. It was, he thought, his soul taking some final fall. It *sounded* melodramatic as hell. As for how it felt . . . well, it just felt real. That was the horrible part about it. Just . . . real. *Okay,* he thought. *That's what it feels like. All your life you've heard people talk about hitting bottom, this is what it feels like. Here it is. James Eric Gardener, who was going to be the Ezra Pound of his generation, taking spare change from a Delaware bar band.*

"Really . . . no—"

Eddie Parker went on passing the hat just the same. There was a bunch of change and a few one-dollar bills in it. Beaver got the hat last. He tossed in a couple of quarters.

"Look," Gardener said, "I appreciate it, but—"

"C'mon, Beaver," Eddie said. "Cough up, you fuckin Scrooge."

"Really, I have friends in Portland, I'll just call a few up . . . and I think I might have left my checkbook with this one guy I know in Falmouth," Gardener added wildly.

"*Bea*-ver's a *Scrooge,*" the girl in the cutoffs began to chant gleefully. "*Bea*-ver's a Scrooge, *Bea*-ver's a *Scrooge!*" The others picked it up until Beaver, laughing and rolling his eyes, added another quarter and a New York lottery ticket.

"There, I'm tapped," he said, "unless you want to wait around for the prunes to work." The guys in the band and the girl in the cutoffs were laughing wildly again. Looking resignedly at Gardener, as if to say, *You see the morons I have to deal with? You dig it?,* Beaver handed the hat to Gardener, who had to take it; if he hadn't, the change would have rolled all over the van floor.

"Really," he said, trying to give the hat back to Beaver. "I'm perfectly okay—"

"You *ain't,*" Eddie Parker said. "So cut the bullshit, what do you say?"

"I guess I say thanks. It's all I can think of right now."

"Well, it ain't so much you'll have to declare it on your income taxes," Eddie said. "But it'll buy you some burgers and a pair of those rubber sandals."

The girl slid open the door in the Caravel's sidewall. "Get better, understand?" she said. Then, before he could reply, she hugged him and gave him a kiss, her mouth moist, friendly, half-open, and redolent of pot. "Take care, big guy."

"I'll try." On the verge of getting out he suddenly hugged her again, fiercely. "Thank you. Thank you all."

He stood at the end of the ramp, the rain falling a little harder now, watching as the van's sidewall door rumbled shut on its track. The girl waved. Gardener waved back and then the van was rolling down the breakdown lane, gathering speed, finally sliding over into the travel lane. Gardener watched them go, one hand still raised in a wave in case they might be looking back. Tears were running freely down his cheeks now, to mix with the rain.

3

He never did get a chance to buy a pair of rubber sandals, but he got to Haven before dark and he didn't have to walk the last ten or so miles to Bobbi's house, as he'd thought he might; you'd think people would be more apt to pick up a guy hitching in the rain, but that was just when they were most likely to pass you by. Who needed a human puddle in the passenger seat?

But he got a ride outside of Augusta with a farmer who complained constantly and bitterly about the government all the way up to the China town line, where he let Gard out. Gard walked a couple of miles, thumbing the few cars that passed, wondering if his feet were turning to ice or if it was just his imagination, when a pulp truck pulled to a rackety halt beside him.

Gardener climbed into the cab as fast as he could. It smelled of old woodchips and sour loggers' sweat . . . but it was warm.

"Thanks," he said.

"Don't mention it," the driver said. "Name's Freeman Moss." He stuck out a hand. Gardener, who had no idea that he would meet this man in the not-too-distant future under far less cheery circumstances, took it and shook it.

"Jim Gardener. Thanks again."

"Shoot a pickle," Freeman Moss scoffed. He got the truck moving. It shuddered along the edge of the road, picking up speed, Gard thought, not just grudgingly but with actual pain. *Everything* shook. The universal moaned beneath them like a hag in a chimney corner. The world's oldest toothbrush, its eroded bristles dark with the grease it had been employed to coax out of some clotted gear- or cog-tooth, chittered along the dashboard, passing an old air freshener of a naked woman with very large breasts on its way. Moss punched the clutch, managed to find second after an endless time spent grinding gears, and wrestled the pulp truck back onto the road. "Y'look half-drownded. Got half a thermos of coffee from the Drunken Donuts in Augusta left over from my dinner . . . you want it?"

Gardener drank it gratefully. It was strong, hot, and heavily laced with sugar. He also accepted a cigarette from the driver, dragging deeply and with pleasure, although it hurt his throat, which was getting steadily sorer.

Moss dropped him off just over the Haven town line at quarter to seven. The rain had slacked off, and the sky was lightening up in the west. "Do believe God's gonna let through some sunset," Freeman Moss said. "I wish like hell I had a pair of shoes I could give you, mister—I usually carry an old pair behind the seat, but it was so rainy today I never brought nothin but m'gumrubbers."

"Thanks, but I'll be fine. My friend is less than a mile up the road." Actually Bobbi's place was still three miles away, but if he told Moss that, nothing would do but that he drive Gardener up there. Gardener was tired, increasingly feverish, still damp even after forty-five minutes of the heater's dry, blasting air . . . but he couldn't stand any more kindness today. In his present state of mind it could well drive him crazy.

"Okay. Good luck."

"Thank you."

He got down and waved as the truck turned off on a side road and rumbled away toward home.

Even after Moss and his museum piece of a truck had disappeared, Gardener stood where he was for a moment longer, his wet totebag in one hand, his bare feet, white as Easter lilies, planted in the dirt of the soft shoulder, looking at the marker some two hundred feet back the way he had come. *Home is the place where, when you have to go there, they have to take you in,* Frost had said. But he'd do well to remember he wasn't home. Maybe the worst mistake a man could make was to get to the idea that his friend's home was his own, especially when the friend was a woman whose bed you had once shared.

Not home, not at all—but he *was* in Haven.

He started to walk up the road toward Bobbi's house.

4

About fifteen minutes later, when the clouds in the west finally broke open to let through the westering sun, something strange happened: a burst of music, clear and brief, went through his head.

He stopped, looking at the sunlight as it spilled across rolling miles of wet woods and hayfields in the west, the rays beaming down like the dramatic sunrays in a DeMille Bible epic. Route 9 began to rise here, and the western view was long and gorgeous and solemn, the evening's light somehow English and pastoral in its clear beauty. The rain had given the landscape a sleek, washed look, deepening colors, seeming to fulfill the texture of things. Gardener was suddenly very glad he had not committed suicide—not in any corny Art Linkletter way, but because he had been allowed this moment of beauty and perceptual glow. Standing here, now almost at the end of his energy, feverish and sick, he felt a child's simple wonder.

All was still and silent in the final sunshine of evening. He could see no sign of industry or technology. Humanity, yes; a big red barn attached to a white farmhouse, sheds, a trailer or two, but that was all.

The light. It was the light that struck him so strongly.

Its sweet clarity, so old and deep—those rays of sun slanting almost horizontally through the unraveling clouds as this long, confusing, exhausting day neared its end. That ancient light seemed to deny time itself, and Gardener almost expected to hear a huntsman winding his horn, announcing "All Assemble." He would hear dogs, and horses' hooves, and—

—and that was when the music, jarring and modern, blasted through his head, scattering all thought. His hands flew to his temples in a startled gesture. The burst lasted at least five seconds, perhaps as long as ten, and what he heard was perfectly identifiable; it was Dr. Hook singing "Baby Makes Her Blue Jeans Talk."

The lyric was tinny but clear enough—as if he were listening to a small transistor radio, the kind that people used to take to the beach with them before that punk-rock group Walkman and the Ghetto-Blasters had taken over the world. But it wasn't pouring into his ears, that lyric; it was coming from the front of his head . . . from the place where the doctors had filled a hole in his skull with a piece of metal.

The queen of all the nightbirds,
A player in the dark,
She don't say nothing
But baby makes her blue jeans talk.

The volume was so loud it was almost unbearable. It had happened once before, this music in his head, after he'd stuck his finger into a light socket—and was he drunk at the time? My dear, does a dog piss on a fireplug?

He had discovered such musical visitations were neither hallucinatory nor all that rare—people had gotten radio transmissions on the lawn flamingos in their yards; on teeth fillings; on the steel rims of their spectacles. For a week and a half in 1957 a family in Charlotte, North Carolina, had received signals from a classical-music station in Florida. They first heard them coming from the bathroom water-glass. Soon other glasses in the house began to pick up the sound. Before it ended, the whole house was filled with the eerie sound of glassware broadcasting Bach and Beethoven, the music broken only by an occasional time-check. Finally, with a dozen violins holding one long, high note, almost all the glasses in the house shattered spontaneously and the phenomenon ceased.

So Gardener had known he wasn't alone, and had been sure he wasn't going crazy—but that wasn't much comfort, and never had been as loud as this after the light-socket incident.

The sound of Dr. Hook faded as quickly as it had come. Gardener stood tensely, waiting for it to come back. It didn't. What came instead, louder and more urgent than before, was a repetition of what had gotten him going in the first place: *Bobbi's in trouble!*

He turned away from the western view and started up Route 9 again. And although he was feverish and very tired, he walked fast—in fact, before long he was almost running.

5

It was seven-thirty when Gardener finally arrived at Bobbi's—what the locals still called the old Garrick place even after all these years. Gardener came swinging up the road, puffing, his color high and unhealthy. Here was the Rural Free Delivery box, its door slightly ajar, the way both Bobbi and Joe Paulson, the mailman, left it so it would be easier for Peter to paw open. There was the driveway, with Bobbi's blue pickup truck parked in it. The stuff in the truck bed had been covered with a tarp to protect it from the rain. And there was the house itself, with a light shining through the east window, the one where Bobbi kept her rocker and did her reading.

Everything *looked* all right; not a single sour note. Five years ago—even three—Peter would have barked at the arrival of a stranger outside, but Peter had gotten older. Hell, they all had.

Standing out here, Bobbi's place held the sort of quiet, pastoral loveliness that the western view at the town line had held for him—it represented all the things Gardener wished he had for himself. A sense of peace, or maybe just a sense of place. Certainly he could see nothing odd as he stood here by the mailbox. It looked—*felt*—like the house of a person who is content with herself. Not completely at rest, exactly, or retired, or checked out from the world's concerns . . . but rocking steady. This was the house of a sane, relatively happy woman. It had not been built in the tornado belt.

All the same, something was wrong.

He stood there, the stranger out here in the dark,

(but I'm not a stranger I'm a friend her friend Bobbi's friend . . . aren't I?)

and a sudden frightening impulse rose within him: to leave. Just turn on one bare heel and bug out. Because he suddenly doubted if he wanted to find out what was going on inside that house, what kind of trouble Bobbi had gotten herself into.

(Tommyknockers Gard that's what kind Tommyknockers)

He shivered.

(late last night and the night before Tommyknockers Tommyknockers at Bobbi's door and I don't know if you can)

Stop it

(because Gard's so afraid of the Tommyknocker man)

He licked his lips, trying to tell himself it was just the fever that made them feel so dry.

Get out, Gard! Blood on the moon!

The fear was now very deep indeed, and if it had been anyone but Bobbi—anyone but his last real friend—he would have split, all right. The farmhouse looked rustic and pleasant, the light spilling from the east window was cozy, and all looked well . . . but the boards and the glass, the stones in the driveway, the very air pressing against his face . . . all these things screamed at him to leave, get out, that things inside that house were bad, dangerous, perhaps even evil.

(Tommyknockers)

But whatever else was in there, Bobbi was too. He hadn't come all these miles, most in the pouring rain, to turn and run at the last second. So, in spite of the dread, he left the mailbox and started up the driveway, moving slowly, wincing as the sharp stones dug at the tender soles of his feet.

Then the front door jerked open, startling his heart up into his throat in a single nimble bound and he thought *It's one of them, one of the Tommyknockers, it's going to rush down here and grab me and eat me up!* He was barely able to stifle a scream.

The silhouette in the doorway was thin—much too thin, he thought, to be Bobbi Anderson, who had never been beefy but who was solidly built and pleasantly round in all the right places. But the voice, shrill and wavering though it was, was unmistakably Bobbi's . . . and Gardener relaxed a little, because Bobbi sounded even more terrified than he felt, standing by the mailbox and looking at the house.

"Who is it? Who's there?"

"It's Gard, Bobbi."

There was a long pause. There were footfalls on the porch.

Cautiously: "Gard? Is it really you?"

"Yeah." He worked his way over the hard, biting stones of the driveway to the lawn. And he asked the question he had come all this way and deferred his own suicide to ask: "Bobbi, are you all right?"

The quaver left Bobbi's voice, but Gardener could still not see her clearly—the sun had long since gone behind the trees, and the shadows were thick. He wondered where Peter was.

"I'm fine," Bobbi said, just as if she had always looked so terribly thin, just as though she had always greeted arrivals in her dooryard with a shrill voice full of fear.

She came down the porch steps and passed out of the shadow of the overhanging porch roof. As she did, Gardener got his first good look at her in the ashy twilight. He was struck by horror and wonder.

Bobbi was coming toward him, smiling, obviously delighted to see him. Her jeans fluttered and flapped on her, and so did her shirt; her face was gaunt, her eyes deep in their sockets, her forehead pale and somehow too wide, the skin taut and shiny. Bobbi's uncombed hair flopped against the nape of her neck and lay over her shoulders like waterweed cast up on a beach. The shirt was buttoned wrong. The fly of her jeans was three-quarters of the way down. She smelled dirty and sweaty and . . . well, as if she might have had an accident in her pants and then forgotten to change them.

A picture suddenly flashed into Gardener's mind: a photo of Karen Carpenter taken shortly before her death, which had allegedly resulted from *anorexia nervosa*. It had seemed to him the picture of a woman already dead but somehow alive, a woman who was all smiling teeth and shrieking feverish eyes. Bobbi looked like that now.

Surely she had lost no more than twenty pounds—that was all she could *afford* to lose and stay on her feet—but Gard's shocked mind kept insisting it was more like thirty, had to be.

She seemed to be on the last raggedy end of exhaustion. Her eyes, like the eyes of that poor lost woman on the magazine cover, were huge and glittery, her smile the huge brainless grin of a KO'd fighter just before his knees come unhinged.

"Fine!" this shambling, dirty, stumbling skeleton reiterated, and as Bobbi approached, Gardener could hear the waver in her voice again—not fear, as he'd thought, but utter exhaustion. "Thought you'd given up on me! Good to see you, man!"

"Bobbi . . . Bobbi, Jesus Christ, what . . ."

Bobbi was holding out a hand for Gardener to take. It trembled wildly in the air, and Gardener saw how thin, how woefully, incredibly thin Bobbi's arm had become.

"A lot of stuff going on," Bobbi croaked in her wavering voice. "A lot of work done, a hell of a lot more left to do, but I'm getting there, getting there, wait'll you see—"

"Bobbi, what—"

"Fine, I'm fine," Bobbi repeated, and she fell forward, semiconscious, into Gardener's arms. She tried to say something else but only a loose gargle and a little spit came out. Her breasts were small, wasted pads against his forearm.

Gardener picked her up, shocked by how light she was. Yes, it was thirty, at *least* thirty. It was incredible, but not, unfortunately, deniable. He felt recognition that was both shocking and miserable: *This isn't Bobbi at all. It's me. Me at the end of a jag.*

He carried Bobbi swiftly up the steps and into the house.

8.

MODIFICATIONS

1

He put Bobbi on the couch and went quickly to the telephone. He picked it up, meaning to dial 0 and ask the operator what number he should dial to get the nearest rescue unit. Bobbi needed a trip to Derry Home Hospital, and right away. A breakdown, Gardener supposed (although in truth he was so tired and confused that he hardly knew what to think). Some kind of breakdown. Bobbi Anderson seemed like the last person in the world to go over the top, but apparently she had.

Bobbi said something from the couch. Gardener didn't catch it at first; Bobbi's voice was little more than a harsh croak.

"What, Bobbi?"

"Don't call anybody," Bobbi said. She managed a little more volume this time, but even that much effort seemed to nearly exhaust her. Her cheeks were flushed, the rest of her face waxen, and her eyes were as bright and feverish as blue gemstones—diamonds, or sapphires, perhaps. "Don't . . . Gard, not *anybody!*"

Anderson fell back against the couch, panting rapidly. Gardener hung up the telephone and went to her, alarmed. Bobbi needed a doctor, that was obvious, and Gardener meant to get her one . . . but right now her agitation seemed more important.

"I'll stay right with you," he said, taking her hand, "if

that's what's worrying you. God knows you stuck with me through enough sh—"

But Anderson had been shaking her head with mounting vehemence. "Just need sleep," she whispered. "Sleep . . . and food in the morning. Mostly sleep. Haven't had any . . . three days. Four, maybe."

Gardener looked at her, shocked again. He put together what Bobbi had just said with the way she looked.

"What rocket have you been riding?"—*and why?* his mind added. "Bennies? Reds?" He thought of coke and then rejected it. Bobbi could undoubtedly afford coke if she wanted it, but Gardener didn't think even 'basing could keep a man or woman awake for three or four days and melt better than thirty pounds off in—Gardener calculated the time since he had last seen Anderson—in three weeks.

"No dope," Bobbi said. "No drugs." Her eyes rolled and glittered. Spit drizzled helplessly from the corners of her mouth and she sucked it back. For an instant Gardener saw an expression in Bobbi's face he didn't like . . . one that scared him a little. It was an *Anne* expression. Old and crafty. Then Bobbi's eyes slipped closed, revealing lids stained the delicate purplish color of total exhaustion. When she opened her eyes again it was just Bobbi lying there . . . and Bobbi needed help.

"I'm going to phone for the rescue unit," Gardener said, getting up again. "You look really unwell, B—"

Bobbi's thin hand reached out and caught his wrist as Gardener turned to the phone. It held him with surprising strength. He looked down at Bobbi, and although she still looked terribly exhausted and almost desperately wasted, that feverish glitter was gone from her eyes. Now her gaze was straight and clear and sane.

"If you call anybody," she said, her voice still wavering a little but almost normal, "we're done being friends, Gard. I mean it. Call the rescue unit, or Derry Home, even old Doc Warwick in town, and that's the end of the line for us. You'll never see the inside of my house again. The door will be closed to you."

Gardener looked at Bobbi with mounting dismay and horror. If he could have persuaded himself in that moment that Bobbi was delirious, he would gladly have done so . . . but she obviously wasn't.

"Bobbi you—" *—don't know what you're saying?* But she did; that was the horror of it. She was threatening to end their friendship if Gardener didn't do what she wanted, using their friendship as a club for the first time in all the years Gardener had known her. And there was something else in Bobbi Anderson's eyes: the knowledge that her friendship was maybe the last thing on earth that Gardener valued.

Would it make any difference if I told you how much you look like your sister, Bobbi?

No—he saw in her face nothing would make any difference.

"—don't know how bad you look," he finished lamely.

"No," Anderson agreed, and a ghost of a smile surfaced on her face. "I got an idea, though, believe me. Your face . . . better than any mirror. But, Gard—sleep is all I need. Sleep and . . ." Her eyes slipped shut again, and she opened them with an obvious effort. "Breakfast," she finished. "Sleep and breakfast."

"Bobbi, that isn't all you need."

"No." Bobbi's hand had not left Gardener's wrist and now it tightened again. "I need *you.* I called for you. And you heard, didn't you?"

"Yes," Gardener said uncomfortably. "I guess I did."

"Gard . . ." Bobbi's voice slipped off. Gard waited, his mind in a turmoil. Bobbi needed medical help . . . but what she had said about ending their friendship if Gardener called anyone . . .

The soft kiss she put in the middle of his dirty palm surprised him. He looked at her, startled, and looked at her huge eyes. The fevered glitter had left them; all he saw in them now was pleading.

"Wait until tomorrow," Bobbi said. "If I'm not better tomorrow . . . a thousand times better . . . I'll go. All right?"

"Bobbi—"

"All right?" The hand tightened, demanding Gardener to say it was.

"Well . . . I guess . . ."

"Promise me."

"I promise." *Maybe,* Gardener added mentally. *If you don't go to sleep and then start to breathe funny. If I don't come over and check you around midnight and see your lips look like you've been eating blueberries. If you don't pitch a fit.*

This was silly. Dangerous, cowardly . . . but most of all just silly. He had come out of the big black tornado convinced that killing himself would be the best way to end all of his misery and ensure that he caused no more misery in others. He had meant to do it; he knew that was so. He had been on the edge of jumping into that cold water. Then his conviction that Bobbi was in trouble

(I called and you heard didn't you)

had come and he was here. *Now, ladies and gentlemen,* he seemed to hear Allen Ludden saying in his quick light quizmaster's voice, *here is your toss-up question. Ten points if you can tell me why Jim Gardener cares about Bobbi Anderson's threat to end their friendship, when Gardener himself means to end it by committing suicide? What? No one? Well, here's a surprise! I don't know, either!*

"Okay," Bobbi was saying. "Okay, great."

The agitation which was nearly terror slipped away—the fast gasping for breath slowed and some of the color faded from her cheeks. So the promise had been worth something, at least.

"Sleep, Bobbi." He would sit up and watch for any change. He was tired, but he could drink coffee (and maybe take one or two of whatever Bobbi'd been taking, if he came across them). He owed Bobbi a night's watching. There were nights when she had watched over him. "Sleep now." He gently disengaged his wrist from Bobbi's hand.

Her eyes closed, then slowly opened one last time. She smiled, a smile so sweet that he was in love with her again. She had that power over him. "Just . . . like old times, Gard."

"Yeah, Bobbi. Like old times."

". . . love you . . ."

"I love you too. Sleep."

Her breathing deepened. Gard sat beside her for three minutes, then five, watching that Madonna smile, becoming more and more convinced she was asleep. Then, very slowly, Bobbi's eyes struggled open again.

"Fabulous," she whispered.

"What?" Gardener leaned forward. He wasn't sure what she'd said.

"What it *is* . . . what it can *do* . . .what it *will* do . . ."

She's talking in her sleep, Gard thought, but he felt a recurrence of the chill. That crafty expression was back in Bobbi's face. Not on it but *in* it, as if it had grown under the skin.

"You should have found it . . . I think it was for you, Gard . . ."

"What was?"

"Look around the place," Bobbi said. Her voice was fading. "You'll see. We'll finish digging it up together. You'll see it solves the . . . problems . . . all the problems . . ."

Gardener had to lean forward now to hear anything. "What does, Bobbi?"

"Look around the place," Bobbi repeated, and the last word drew out, deepening, and became a snore. She was asleep.

2

Gardener almost went to the phone again. It was close. He got up, but halfway across the living room he diverted, going to Bobbi's rocking chair instead. He would watch for a while first, he thought. Watch for a while and try to think what all this might mean.

He swallowed and winced at the pain in his throat. He was feverish, and he suspected the fever was no little one-degree job, either. He felt more than unwell; he felt *unreal.*

Fabulous . . . what it is . . . *what it can* do . . .

He would sit here for a while and think some more. Then he would make a pot of strong coffee and dump about six aspirin into it. That would take care of the aches and fever, at least temporarily. Might help keep him awake too.

. . . *what it* will *do* . . .

Gard closed his eyes, dozing himself. That was okay. He might doze, but not for long; he'd never been able to sleep sitting up. And Peter was apt to appear at any time; he would see his old friend Gard, jump into his lap, and get his balls. *Always.* When it came to jumping into the chair with you and getting your balls, Peter never failed. Hell of an alarm clock, if you happened to be sleeping. Five minutes, that's all. Forty winks. No harm, no foul.

You should have found it. I think it was for you, Gard . . .

He drifted, and his doze quickly deepened into sleep so deep it was close to coma.

3

shusshhhhh . . .

He's looking down at his skis, plain brown wood strips racing over the snow, hypnotized by their liquid speed. He doesn't realize this state of near-hypnosis until a voice on his left says: "One thing you bastards never remember to mention at your fucking Communist antipower rallies is just this: in thirty years of peaceful nuclear-power development, we've never been caught once."

Ted is wearing a reindeer sweater and faded jeans. He skis fast and well. Gardener, on the other hand, is completely out of control.

"You're going to crash," a voice on his right says. He looks over and it is Arglebargle. Arglebargle has begun to rot. His fat face, which had been flushed with alcohol on the night of the party, is now the yellow-gray of old curtains hanging in dirty windows. His flesh has begun to slough downward, pulling and splitting. Arglebargle sees his shock and terror. His gray lips spread in a grin.

"That's right," he says. "I'm dead. It really was *a heart attack. Not indigestion, not my gall-bladder. I collapsed five minutes after you were gone. They called an ambulance and the kid I hired to tend bar got my heart started again with CPR, but I died for good in the ambulance."*

The grin stretches; becomes as moony as the grin of a dead trout lying on the deserted beach of a poisoned lake.

"I died at a stoplight on Storrow Drive," Arglebargle says.

"No," Gardener whispers. This . . . this is what he has always feared. The final, irrevocable drunken act.

"Yes," the dead man insists as they speed down the hill, drifting closer to the trees. "I invited you into my house,

gave you food and drink, and you repaid me by killing me in a drunken argument.”

“Please . . . I . . .”

“You what? *You* what?” *from his left again. The reindeer on Ted’s sweater have disappeared. They have been replaced by yellow radiation warning symbols. “You* nothing, *that’s what! Where do you latter-day Luddites think all that power comes from?”*

“You killed me,” Arberg drones from his right, “but you’ll pay. You’re going to crash, Gardener.”

“Do you think we get it from the Wizard of Oz?” Ted screams. Weeping sores suddenly erupt on his face. His lips bubble, peel, crack, begin to suppurate. One of his eyes shimmers into the milkiness of cataract. Gardener realizes with mounting horror that he is looking into a face exhibiting symptoms of a man in the last, advanced stages of radiation sickness.

The radiation symbols on Ted’s shirt are turning black.

“You’ll crash, you bet,” Arglebargle drones on. “Crash.”

He is weeping with terror now, as he wept after shooting his wife, hearing the unbelievable report of the gun in his hand, watching as she staggered backward against the kitchen counter, one hand clapped to her cheek like a woman uttering a shocked “My land! I NEVER!” *And then the blood squirting through her fingers and his mind in a last desperate effort to deny it all had thought* Ketchup, relax, that’s just ketchup. *Then beginning to weep as he was now.*

“As far as you guys are concerned, all your responsibility ends at the wall plate where you plug in.” Pus runs and dribbles down Ted’s face. His hair has fallen out. The sores cover his skull. His mouth spreads in a grin as moony as Arberg’s. Now in a last extremity of terror Gardener realizes he is skiing out of control down Straight Arrow flanked by dead men. “But you’ll never stop us, you know. No one will. The pile is out of control, you see. Has been since . . . oh, around 1939, I’d reckon. We reached critical mass along about 1965. It’s out of control. The explosion will come soon.”

“No . . . no . . .”

“You’ve been riding high, but those who ride highest fall hardest,” Arberg drones. “Murder of a host is the foulest murder of all. You’re going to crash . . . crash . . . crash!”

How true it is! He tries to turn but his skis remain stubbornly on course. Now he can see the hoary old pine. Arglebargle and Ted the Power Man are gone and he thinks: Were they Tommyknockers, Bobbi?

He can see a red swatch of paint around the pine's gnarly trunk . . . and then it begins to flake and split. As he slides helplessly toward the tree he sees that it has come alive, that it has split open to swallow him. The yawning tree grows and swells, seems to rush toward him, grows tentacles, and there is a horrible rotten blackness in its center, with red paint around it like the lipstick of some sinister whore, and he can hear dark winds howling in that black, squirming mouth and

4

he doesn't wake up then, as much as it seems he has— everyone knows that even the most outlandish dreams feel *real, that they may even have their own spurious logic, but this is* not *real, cannot be. He has simply exchanged one dream for another. Happens all the time.*

In this dream he has been dreaming about his old skiing accident—for the second time that day, can you believe it? Only this time the tree he struck, the one which almost killed him, grows a rotted mouth like a squirming knothole. He snaps awake and finds himself sitting in Bobbi's rocking chair, too relieved by simple waking to care that he's stiff all over and that his throat is now so sore that it feels like it's been lined with barbed wire.

He thinks: I'm going to get up and make myself a dose of coffee and aspirin. Wasn't I going to do that before? He starts to get up, and that's when Bobbi opens her eyes. That's also when he knows he is dreaming, must be, because green rays of light shoot from Bobbi's eyes— Gardener is reminded of Superman's X-ray vision in the comic-books, the way the artist drew it in lime-colored beams. But the light which comes from Bobbi's eyes is swamplike and somehow dreadful . . . there is something rotted about it, like the drifting glow of St. Elmo's fire in a swamp on a hot night.

Bobbi sits up slowly and looks around . . . looks toward

Gardener. He tries to tell her no . . . Please don't put that light on me.

No words come out and as that green light hits him he sees that Bobbi's eyes are blazing with it—at its source it is as green as emeralds, as bright as sun-fire. He cannot look at it, has to avert his eyes. He tries to bring an arm up to shield his face but he can't, his arm is too heavy. It'll burn, *he thinks,* it'll burn, and then in a few days the first sores will show up, you'll think they're pimples at first because that's what radiation sickness looks like when it starts, just a bunch of pimples, only *these* pimples never heal, they only get worse . . . and worse . . .

He hears Arberg's voice, a disembodied holdover from the previous dream, and now there seems to be triumph in his drone: "I knew *you were going to crash, Gardener!"*

The light touches him . . . washes over him. Even with his eyes squeezed shut it lights the darkness as green as radium watch-dials. But there's no real pain in dreams, and there is none here. The bright green light is neither hot nor cold. It is nothing. Except . . .

His throat.

His throat is no longer sore.

And he hears this, clearly and unmistakably: "—percent off! This is the sort of price reduction that may never be repeated! EVERYONE gets credit! Recliners! Waterbeds! Living-room s—"

The plate in his skull, talking again. Gone almost before it was fairly begun.

Like his sore throat.

And that green light was gone too.

Gardener opens his eyes . . . cautiously.

Bobbi is lying on the couch, eyes shut, deeply asleep . . . just as she was. What's all this about rays shooting out of eyes? Good God!

He sits in the rocking chair again. Swallows. No pain. The fever has gone down a lot, too.

Coffee and aspirin, *he thinks.* You were going to get up for coffee and aspirin, remember?

Sure, *he thinks, settling more comfortably into the rocking chair and closing his eyes.* But no one gets coffee and aspirin in a dream. I'll do it just as soon as I wake up.

Gard, you are *awake.*

But that, of course, could not be. In the waking world,

people don't shoot green beams from their eyes, beams that cure fevers and sore throats. Dreams sí, *reality* no.

He crosses his arms over his chest and drifts away. He knows no more—either sleeping or waking—for the rest of that night.

5

When Gardener woke up, bright light was streaming into his face through the western window. His back hurt like a bastard, and when he stood up his neck gave a wretched arthritic creak that made him wince. It was quarter of nine.

He looked at Bobbi and felt a moment of suffocating fear—in that moment he was sure Bobbi was dead. Then he saw she was just so deeply, movelessly asleep that she gave a good impression of being dead. It was a mistake anyone might have made. Bobbi's chest rose in slow, steady pulls with long but even pauses in between. Gardener timed her and saw she was breathing no more than six times a minute.

But she looked better this morning—not great, but better than the haggard scarecrow who had reeled out to greet him last night.

Doubt if I looked much better, he thought, and went into Bobbi's bathroom to shave.

The face looking back from the mirror wasn't as bad as he had feared, but he noted with some dismay that his nose had bled again in the night—not a lot, but enough to have covered his philtrum and most of his upper lip. He got a facecloth out of the cupboard to the right of the sink and turned on the hot water to wet it down.

He put the facecloth under the water flowing from the hot tap with all the absentmindedness of long habit—with Bobbi's water heater, you just about had time for a cup of coffee and a smoke before you got a lukewarm stream—and that was on a good d—

"Youch!"

He pulled his hand back from water so hot it was steaming. Okay, that was what he got for assuming Bobbi was just going to go clipclopping down the road of life without ever getting her damned water heater fixed.

Gardener put his scalded palm to his mouth and looked at the water coming out of the tap. It had already fogged the lower edge of the shaving mirror on the back of the medicine cabinet. He reached out, found the tap's handle almost too hot to touch, and used the facecloth to turn it off. Then he put in the rubber plug, drew a little more hot water—cautiously!—and added a generous dollop of cold. The pad of flesh below his left thumb had reddened a little.

He opened the medicine cabinet and moved things around until he came to the prescription bottle of Valium with his own name on the label. *If that stuff improves with age, it ought to be great,* he thought. Still almost full. Well, what did he expect? Whatever Bobbi had been using, it sure as hell had been the opposite of Valium.

Gardener didn't want it either. He wanted what was behind it, if it was still—

Ah! Success!

He pulled out a double-edge razor and a package of blades. He looked a little sadly at the layer of dust on the razor—it had been a long time since he'd shaved in the morning here at Bobbi's—and then rinsed it off. *At least she didn't throw it out,* he thought. *That would have been worse than the dust.*

A shave made him feel better. He concentrated on it, drawing it out while his thoughts ran their own course.

He finished, replaced the shaving stuff behind the Valium, and cleaned up. Then he looked thoughtfully at the tap with the H on its handle, and decided to go down cellar and see what sort of magnificent water heater Bobbi had put in. The only other thing to do was watch Bobbi sleep, which she seemed to be doing well on her own.

He crossed into the kitchen thinking that he really did feel well, especially now that the aches from a night in Bobbi's rocking chair were starting to work out of his back and neck. *You're the guy who's never been able to sleep sitting up, right?* he jeered softly at himself. *Crashing out on breakwaters is more your style, right?* But this ribbing was nothing like the harsh, barely coherent self-mockery of the day before. The one thing he always forgot in the grip of the hangovers and the terrible post-jag depressions was the feeling of regeneration that sometimes came later. You could wake up one day realizing you hadn't put any poison in your system the night before . . . the week before . . . maybe the whole *month* before . . . and you felt really good.

As for what he had been afraid must be the onset of the flu, maybe even pneumonia—that was gone too. No sore throat. No plugged nose. No fever. God knew he had been a perfect target for a germ, after eight days drinking, sleeping rough, and finally hitching back to Maine in his bare feet during a rainstorm. But it had passed off in the night. Sometimes God was good.

He paused in the middle of the kitchen, his smile drifting away into a momentary expression that was puzzled and a little disquieted. A fragment of his dream—or dreams—came slipping back

(radio ads in the night . . . does that have something to do with feeling well this morning?)

and then it faded again. He dismissed it, content with the fact that he felt well and Bobbi looked well—better, anyway. If Bobbi wasn't awake by ten o'clock, ten-thirty at the latest, he would wake her up. If Bobbi felt better and spoke rationally, fine. They could discuss whatever had happened to her (SOMETHING *sure did,* Gardener thought, and wondered absently if she had gotten some terrible news report from home . . . a bulletin that would undoubtedly have been served up by Sister Anne). They would go on from there. If she still even slightly resembled the spaced-out and rather creepy Bobbi Anderson who had greeted him the night before, Gardener was going to call a doctor whether Bobbi liked it or not.

He opened the cellar door and fumbled for the old-fashioned toggle switch on the wall. He found it. The switch was the same. The light wasn't. Instead of the feeble flow from two sixty-watt bulbs—the only illumination in Bobbi's cellar since time out of mind—the cellar lit up with a brisk white glare. It looked as bright as a discount department store down there. Gardener started down, hand reaching for the rickety old banister. He found a thick and solid new one instead. It was held firmly against the wall with new brass fittings. Some of the stair treads, which had been definitely queasy, had also been replaced.

Gardener reached the bottom of the steps and stood looking around, his surprise now bordering on some stronger emotion—it was almost shock. That slightly moldy root-cellar smell was gone, too.

She looked like a woman running on empty, no joke. Right out on the ragged edge. She couldn't even remember how many days it had been since she'd gotten any sleep. No wonder. I've heard of home improvement, but this is ridiculous. She couldn't *have done it all herself, though. Could she? Of course not.*

But Gardener suspected that, somehow, Bobbi had.

If Gardener had awakened here instead of on the breakwater at Arcadia Point, with no memory of the immediate past, he wouldn't have known he was in Bobbi's cellar, although he had been here countless times before. The only reason he was sure of it now was because he had gotten here from Bobbi's kitchen.

That rooty smell *wasn't* entirely gone, but it was diminished. The cellar's dirt floor had been neatly raked—no, not *just* raked, Gardener saw. Cellar dirt got old and sour after a while; you had to do something about it if you planned to be spending much time belowground. Anderson had apparently brought in a fresh load of dirt and had spread it around to dry before raking. Gardener supposed that was what had sweetened the atmosphere of the place.

Fluorescents were racked in overhead rows, each hooded fixture hung from the old beams by chains and more brass fittings. They shed an even white glow. All the fixtures were single tubes except for those over the worktable; those each had a pair, so here the glow was so bright that it made Gardener think of operating theaters. He walked over to Bobbi's worktable. Bobbi's *new* worktable.

Anderson had had an ordinary kitchen table covered with dirty Con-Tact paper before. It had been lit with a gooseneck study lamp and littered with a few tools, most of them not in very good condition, and a few plastic boxes of nails, screws, bolts, and the like. It was the small-repairs workplace of a woman who is neither very good nor very interested in small repairs.

The old kitchen table was gone, replaced by three long, light tables, the sort on which bake-sale goods are placed at church sales. They had been placed end to end along the left side of the cellar to make one long table. It was littered with hardware, tools, spools of insulated wire both thin and thick, coffee cans full of brads and staples and fasteners . . . dozens of other items. Or hundreds.

Then there were the batteries.

There was a carton of them under the table, a huge loose collection of long-life batteries still in their blister-packs: C-cells, D-cells, double-A's, triple-A's, nine-volts. *Must be two hundred dollars' worth in there,* Gardener thought, *and more rolling around on the table. What in the blue hell—?*

Dazed, he walked along the table like a man checking out the merchandise and deciding whether or not to buy. It looked as though Bobbi was making several different things at once . . . and Gardener was not sure what any of them were. Here, standing halfway along the table, was a large square box with its front panel slid aside to reveal eighteen different buttons. Beside each button was the title of a popular song—"Raindrops Keep Fallin' on My Head," "New York, New York," "Lara's Theme," and so on. Next to it, an instruction sheet tacked neatly to the table identified it as the one-and-only SilverChime Digital Doorbell (Made in Taiwan).

Gardener couldn't imagine why Bobbi would want a doorbell with a built-in microchip that would allow the user to program a different song whenever she wanted to—did she think Joe Paulson would dig hearing "Lara's Theme" when he had to come to the door with a package? But that wasn't all. Gardener could at least have understood the *use* of the SilverChime Digital Doorbell, if not Bobbi's motivation in installing one. But she seemed to be in the process of *modifying* the thing somehow—hooking it, in fact, into the workings of a boom-box radio the size of a small suitcase.

Half a dozen wires—four thin, two moderately thick—snaked between the radio (*its* instruction sheet also tacked neatly to the table) and the opened gut of the SilverChime.

Gardener looked at this for some time and then passed on.

Breakdown. She's had a very odd sort of mental breakdown. The kind Pat Summerall would love.

Here was something else he recognized—a furnace accessory called a rebreather. You attached it to the flue and it was supposed to recirculate some of the heat that ordinarily got wasted. It was the sort of gadget Bobbi would see in a catalogue, or maybe in the Augusta Trustworthy Hardware Store, and talk about buying. She never actually would, though, because if she bought it she would have to install it.

But now she apparently *had* bought it . . . and installed it.

You can't say she's having a breakdown and "that's all," because when someone who's really creative highsides it, it's rarely a case of "that's all." Crackups are never pretty, but when someone like Bobbi tips over, it can be sort of amazing. Just look at this shit.

Do you believe that?

Yeah, I do. I don't mean that creative people are somehow finer, or more sensitive, and thus have finer, more sensitive nervous breakdowns—you can save that horseshit for the Sylvia Plath worshipers. It's just that creative people have creative breakdowns. If you don't believe it, I repeat: look *at this shit.*

Over there was the water heater, a white cylindrical bulk to the right of the root-cellar door. It *looked* the same, but . . .

Gardener went over, wanting to see how Bobbi had souped it up so radically.

She's gone on a mad home-improvement kick. And the nuttiest thing is that she doesn't seem to have differentiated between things like fixing the water heater and customizing doorbells. New banister. Fresh dirt brought in and raked over the floor of the root cellar. Christ knows what else. No wonder she's exhausted. And just by the bye, Gard, where did Bobbi come by the know-how *to do all this stuff? If it was a correspondence course from* Popular Mechanix, *she must have really crammed.*

His first dazed surprise at coming on this nutty workshop in Bobbi's basement was becoming deepening unease. It wasn't just the evidences of obsessive behavior that he saw along that table—heaps of equipment too neatly organized, all four corners of the instruction sheets tacked down—that bothered him. Nor was it the evidence of mania in Bobbi's apparent failure to discriminate between worthwhile renovations and nonsensical (*apparently* nonsensical, Gardener amended) ones.

What gave Gardener the creeps was thinking about—*trying* to think about—the huge, the *profligate* amounts of energy that had been expended here. To have done just those things he had seen so far, Bobbi must have blazed like a torch. There were projects like the fluorescent lights which had already been completed. There were the ones still pending. There were the trips to Augusta she must have needed to make to get all the equipment, hardware, and batteries. *Plus getting sweet dirt to replace the sour, don't forget that.*

What could have driven her to it?

Gardener didn't know, but he didn't like to imagine Bobbi here, racing back and forth, working on two different do-it-yourself projects at once, or five, or ten. The image was too clear. Bobbi with the sleeves of her shirt rolled up and the top three buttons undone, beads of sweat trickling down between her small breasts, her hair pulled back in a rough horsetail, eyes burning, face pale except for two hectic red patches, one in each cheek. Bobbi looking like Ms. Wizard gone insane, growing more haggard as she screwed screws, bolted bolts, soldered wires, trucked in dirt, and stood on her stepladder, bent backward like a ballet dancer, sweat running down her face, cords standing out in her neck as she hung up the new lights. Oh, and while you're at it, don't forget Bobbi putting in the new wiring and fixing the hot-water tank.

Gardener touched the tank's enamel side and pulled his hand back fast. It *looked* the same, but it wasn't. It was hot as hell. He squatted and opened the hatch at the bottom of the tank.

That was when Gardener *really* sailed off the edge of the world.

6

Before, the water heater had run on LP gas. The small-bore copper tubes which fed gas to the tank's burner ran from tanks in a hook-up behind the house. The delivery truck from Dead River Gas in Derry came once a month and replaced the tanks if they needed replacing—usually they did, because the tank was wasteful as well as inefficient . . . two things that went together more often than not, now that Gard thought about it. The first thing Gardener noticed was that the copper tubes were no longer hooked into the tank. They hung free behind it, their ends stuffed with cloth.

Holy shit, how's she heating her water? he thought, and then he *did* look into the hatch, and then for a little while he froze completely.

His mind seemed clear enough, yes, but that disconnected, floating sensation had come back—that feeling of separation. Ole Gard was going up again, up like a child's silver Puffer balloon. He knew he felt afraid, but this knowledge was dim, hardly important, compared to that dismal feeling of coming untethered from himself. *No, Gard, Jesus!* a mournful voice cried from deep inside him.

He remembered going to the Fryeburg Fair when he was a little kid, no more than ten. He went into the Mirror Maze with his mother, and the two of them had gotten separated. That was the first time he had felt this odd sensation of separation from self, of drifting away, or above, his physical body and his physical (if there was such a thing) mind. He could *see* his mother, oh yes—five mothers, a dozen, a *hundred* mothers, some short, some tall, some fat, some scrawny. At the same time he saw five, a dozen, a hundred Gards. Sometimes he'd see one of his reflections join one of hers and he would reach out, almost absently, expecting to touch her slacks. Instead, there was only empty air . . . or another mirror.

He had wandered for a long time, and he supposed he had panicked, but it hadn't *felt* like panic, and so far as he could remember, no one had *acted* like he had been in a panic when he finally floundered his way out—this only after fifteen minutes of twisting, turning, doubling back, and running into barriers of clear glass. His mother's brow had furrowed slightly for a moment, then cleared. That was all. But he *had* felt panic, just as he was feeling it now: that sensation of feeling your mind coming unbolted from itself, like a piece of machinery falling apart in zero-g.

It comes . . . but it goes. Wait, Gard. Just wait for it to be over.

He squatted on his hunkers, looking into the open hatch at the base of Anderson's water tank, and waited for it to be over, as he had once waited for his feet to lead him down the correct passage and out of that terrible Mirror Maze at the Fryeburg Fair.

The removal of the gas ring had left a round hollow area at the base of the tank. This area had been filled with a wild tangle of wires—red, green, blue, yellow. In the center of the tangle was a cardboard egg carton. HILLCREST FARMS, the blue printing read. GRADE A JUMBO. Sitting in each of the egg cradles was an Eveready alkaline D-cell battery, + terminals up. A tiny funnel-shaped gadget capped the terminals, and all of the wires seemed to either start—or end—in these caps. As he looked longer, in a state that did not precisely *feel* like panic, Gardener saw that his original impression—that the wires were in a wild jumble—was no more true than his original impression that the stuff on Bobbi's worktable was in a litter. No, there was order in the way the wires came out of or went into those twelve funnel-shaped caps—as few as two wires coming in or going out of some, as many as six coming in or going out of others. There was even order in the shape they made—it was a small arch. Some of the wires bent back into the funnels capped over other batteries, but most went to circuit boards propped against the sides of the water tank's heating compartment. They were from electronic toys made in Korea, Gardener surmised—too much cheap silvery solder on corrugated fiberboard. A weird Gyro Gearloose conglomeration if ever there had been one . . . but this weird conglomeration of components was doing something. Oh yes. It was heating water fast enough to raise blisters, for one thing.

In the center of the compartment, directly over the egg carton, in the arch formed by the wires, glowed a bright ball of light, no larger than a quarter but seemingly as bright as the sun.

Gardener had automatically put his fist up to block out that savage glow, which shone out of the hatch in a solid white bar of light that cast his shadow long behind him on the dirt floor. He could look at it only by wincing his eyes down to the barest slits and then opening his fingers a little.

As bright as the sun.

Yes—only instead of yellow, it was a dazzling bluish-white, like a sapphire. Its glow pulsated and shifted slightly, then remained constant, then pulsated and shifted again: it was cycling.

But where is the heat? Gardener thought, and that began to bring him back to himself. *Where is the* heat?

He reached one hand up and laid it on the smooth, enameled side of the tank again—but only for a second. He snatched it away, thinking of the way the water had smoked coming out of the tap in the bathroom. There was hot water in the tank, all right, and plenty of it—by all rights it should boil away to steam and blow Bobbi Anderson's tank all over the basement. It wasn't doing that, obviously, and that was a mystery . . . but it was a minor mystery compared to the fact that he wasn't feeling any heat coming out of the hatch—none at all. He should have burned his fingers on the little knob you pulled to open the hatch, and when it was open, that coin-size sun should have burned the skin right off his face. So . . . ?

Slowly, hesitantly, Gardener reached toward the opening with his left hand, keeping his right fisted before his eyes to block out the worst of the glow. His mouth was pulled down in a wince as he anticipated a burn.

His splayed fingers slipped into the hatchway . . . and then struck something yielding. He thought later it was a little like pushing your fingers into a stretched nylon stocking—only this gave just so much and then stopped. Your fingers never punched through, as they would have punched through a nylon stocking.

But there was no barrier. None, at least, that he could see.

He stopped pressing and the invisible membrane gently pushed his fingers back out of the hatchway. He looked at his fingers and saw they were shaking.

It's a force field. Some sort of a force field that damps heat. Dear God, I've walked into a science-fiction story from Startling Stories. *Right around 1947, I'd guess. I wonder if I made the cover? If I did, who drew me? Virgil Finlay? Hannes Bok?*

His hand was beginning to shake harder. He groped for the little door, missed it, found it again, and slammed it shut, cutting out that dazzling flood of white light. He lowered his right hand slowly but he could still see an afterimage of that tiny sun, the way one can see a flashbulb after it has gone off in one's face. Only what Gardener saw was a large green fist floating in the air, with bright, ectoplasmic blue between the fingers.

The afterimage faded. The shakes didn't.

Gardener had never wanted a drink so badly in his life.

7

He got one in Anderson's kitchen.

Bobbi didn't drink much, but she kept what she called "the staples" in a cabinet behind the pots and pans: bottle of gin, bottle of Scotch, bottle of bourbon, bottle of vodka. Gardener pulled out the bourbon—some cut-rate brand, but beggars couldn't be choosers—poured an inch into a plastic tumbler, and downed it.

Better watch your step, Gard. You're tempting fate.

Except he wasn't. Right now he almost would have welcomed a jag, but the cyclone had gone somewhere else to blow . . . at least for the time being. He poured another two inches of whiskey into the glass, contemplated it for a moment, then poured most of it down the sink. He put the bottle back, and added water and ice cubes, converting what had been liquid dynamite into a civilized drink.

He thought the kid on the beach would have approved.

He supposed the dreamlike calm that had surrounded him when he came out of the Mirror Maze, and felt again now, was a defense against just lying down on the floor and screaming until he lost consciousness. The calm was all right. What scared him was how fast his mind had gone to work trying to convince him that none of it was true—that he had hallucinated the whole thing. Incredibly, his mind was suggesting that what he had seen when he opened the hatch in the heater's base was a very bright light bulb—two hundred watts, say.

It wasn't a light bulb and it wasn't hallucination. It was something like a sun, very small and hot and bright, floating in an arch of wires, over an egg carton filled with D-cells. Now you can go crazy if you want, or get Jesus, or get drunk but you saw what you saw and leave us not gild the lily, all right? All right.

He checked on Anderson and saw she was still sleeping like a stone. Gardener had decided to wake Bobbi up by ten-thirty if she hadn't awakened on her own; he looked at his watch now, and was astonished to see it was twenty minutes past nine. He had been in the cellar much longer than he had thought.

Thinking of the cellar called up the surreal vision of

that miniature sun hanging suspended in its arch of wires, glowing like a superhot tennis ball . . . and thinking about that brought back the unpleasant sense that his mind was uncoupling itself. He pushed it away. It didn't want to go. He pushed harder, telling himself he was simply not going to think about it anymore until Bobbi woke up and told him what was going on around here.

He looked down at his arms and saw that he was sweating.

8

Gardener took his drink out back, where he found more evidence of Bobbi's almost supernatural burst of activity.

Her Tomcat tractor was standing in front of the large shed to the left of the garden—nothing unusual about that, it was where she most commonly left it when the weatherman said it wasn't going to get rained on. But even from twenty feet away Gardener could see that Anderson had done something radical to the Tomcat's motor.

No. No more. Forget this shit, Gard. Go home.

There was nothing dreamy or disconnected about *that* voice—it was harsh, vital with panic and scared dismay. For a moment Gardener felt himself on the verge of giving in to it . . . and then he thought what an abysmal betrayal *that* would be—of Bobbi, of himself. The thought of Bobbi had kept him from killing himself yesterday. And by not killing himself, he thought he had kept her from doing the same thing. The Chinese had a proverb: "If you save a life, you are responsible for it." But if Bobbi needed help, how was he supposed to give it? Didn't finding out begin with trying to find out just what had been going on out here?

(but you know who did all the work don't you Gard?)

He knocked back the last of the drink, set the empty glass on the top back step, and walked toward the Tomcat. He was distantly aware of the crickets singing in the high grass. He wasn't drunk, not squiffy, as far as he could tell; the booze seemed to have shot past his entire nervous system. Gave it a miss, as the British said.

(like the leprechauns that made the shoes tap-tap-tappety-tap while the cobbler slept)

But Bobbi hadn't been sleeping, had she? Bobbi had been driven until she dropped—literally dropped—into Gardener's arms.

(tap-tap-tappety-tap knock-knock-knockety-knock late last night and the night before Tommyknockers Tommyknockers knocking at the door)

Standing by the Tomcat, looking into the open engine compartment, Gardener didn't just shiver—he shuddered like a man dying of cold, his upper teeth biting into his lower lip, his face pale, his temples and forehead covered with sweat.

(they fixed the water heater and the Tomcat too there's lots of things the Tommyknockers do)

The Tomcat was a small working vehicle which would have been almost useless on a big spread where farming was the main work. It was bigger than a riding lawnmower, smaller than the smallest tractor Deere or Farmall had ever made, but just right for someone who kept a garden that was a little too big to be called a plot—and that was the case here. Bobbi had a garden of about an acre and a half— beans, cukes, peas, corn, radishes, and potatoes. No carrots, no cabbages, no zucchini, no squash. "I don't grow what I don't like," she had told Gardener once. "Life's too short."

The Tomcat was fairly versatile; it had to be. Even a well-off gentleman farmer would have trouble justifying the purchase of a $2,500 mini-tractor on the basis of a one-acre garden. It could roto-till, mow grass with one attachment and cut hay with another; it could haul stuff over rough terrain (she used it as a skidder in the fall, and so far as Gardener knew, Bobbi had gotten stuck only once), and in the winter she attached a snow-blower unit and cleared her driveway in half an hour. It was powered by a sturdy four-cc engine.

Or had been.

The engine was still in there, but now it was tarted up with the weirdest array of gadgets and attachments imaginable—Gardener found himself thinking of the doorbell/radio thing on the table in Anderson's basement, and wondering if Bobbi meant to put it on the Tomcat soon . . . maybe it was radar or something. A single bewildered bark of laughter escaped him.

A mayonnaise jar jutted from one side of the engine. It was filled with a fluid too colorless to be gasoline and screwed into a brass fitting on the engine head. Sitting on the cowling was something that would have looked more at home on a Chevy Nova or SuperSport: the air scoop of a supercharger.

The modest carb had been replaced with a scrounged four-barrel. Bobbi had had to cut a hole through the cowling to make room for it.

And there were wires—wires everywhere, snaking in and out and up and down and all around, making connections that made absolutely no sense . . . at least, not as far as Gardener could see.

He looked at the Tomcat's rudimentary instrument panel, started to look away . . . and then his gaze snapped back, his eyes widening.

The Tomcat had a stick shift, and the gearing pattern had been printed on a square of metal bolted to the dashboard above the oil-pressure gauge. Gardener had seen that square of metal often enough; he had driven the Tomcat frequently over the years. Before, it had always been:

1 3
N 4
2 R

Now, something new had been added—something which was just simple enough to be terrifying:

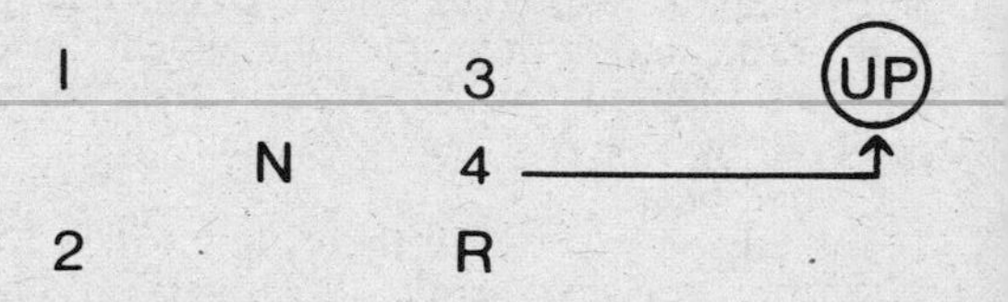

You don't believe that, do you?
I don't know.
Come on, Gard—flying tractors? Give me a break!
She's got a miniature sun in her water heater.

Bullshit. I *think it might have been a light bulb, a bright one, like a two-hundred-watt—*

It was *not* a light bulb!

Okay, all right, calm down. It just sounds like an ad for a really E.T. *ripoff, that's all. "You'll believe a tractor can fly."*

Shut up.

Or "John Deere, 'phone home." How's that?

He stood in Anderson's kitchen again, looking longingly at the cabinet where the booze was. He shifted his eyes away—it was not easy because they felt as if they had gained weight—and walked back into the living room. He saw that Bobbi had changed positions and that her respiration was moving along a bit more rapidly. First signs of waking up. Gardener glanced at his watch again and saw it was nearly ten o'clock. He went over to the bookcase by Bobbi's desk, wanting to find something to read until she came around, something that would take his mind off this whole business for a little while.

What he saw on Bobbi's desk, beside the battered old typewriter, was in some ways the worst shock of all. Shocking enough, anyway, so that he barely noticed another change: a roll of perforated computer paper hung on the wall above and behind the desk and typewriter like a giant roll of paper towels.

9

THE BUFFALO SOLDIERS
a novel by Roberta Anderson

Gardener put the top sheet aside, facedown, and saw his own name—or rather, the nickname only he and Bobbi used.

For Gard, who's always there when I need him.

Another shudder worked through him. He put the second sheet aside facedown on the first.

1

In those days, just before Kansas began to bleed, the buffalo were still plentiful on the plains—plentiful enough, anyway, for poor men, white and Indian alike, to be buried in buffalo skins rather than in coffins.

"Once you get a taste of buffaler meat, you'll never want what come off'n a cow again," the old-timers said, and they must have believed what they said, because these hunters of the plains, these buffalo soldiers, seemed to exist in a world of hairy, humpbacked ghosts—all about them they carried the memory of the buffalo, the smell of the buffalo—the smell, yes, because many of them smeared buff-tallow on their necks and faces and hands to keep the prairie sun from burning them black. They wore buffalo teeth in necklaces and sometimes in their ears; their chaps were of buffalo hide; and more than one of these nomads carried a buffalo penis as a good-luck charm or guarantee of continued potency.

Ghosts themselves, following herds that crossed the short-wire grass like the great clouds which cover the prairie with their shadows; the clouds remain but the great herds are gone . . . and so are the buffalo soldiers, madmen from wastes that had as yet never known a fence, men who came striding out of nowhere and went striding back into that same place, men with buffalo-hide moccasins on their feet and bones clicking about their necks; ghosts out of time, out of a place that existed just before the whole country began to bleed.

Late in the afternoon, of August 24th, 1848, Robert Howell, who would die at Gettysburg not quite fifteen years later, made camp near a small stream far out along the Nebraska panhandle, in that eerie section known as the Sand Hill Country. The stream was small but the water smelled sweet enough . . .

Gardener was forty pages into the story and utterly absorbed when he heard Bobbi Anderson call sleepily:

"Gard? Gard, are you still around?"

"I'm here, Bobbi," he said, and stood up, dreading what would come next and already half-believing he had gone insane. That had to be it, of course. There could not be a tiny sun in the bottom of Bobbi's hot-water tank, nor a new gear on her Tomcat which suggested levitation . . . but it would have been easier for him to believe either of those things than to believe that Bobbi had written a four-hundred-page novel called *The Buffalo Soldiers* in the three weeks or so since Gard had last seen her—a novel that was, just incidentally, the best thing she had ever written. Impossible, yeah. Easier—hell, *saner*—to believe he had gone crazy and simply leave it at that.

If only he could.

9.

ANDERSON SPINS A TALE

1

Bobbi was getting off the couch slowly, wincing like an old woman.

"Bobbi—" Gardener began.

"Christ, I ache all over," Anderson said. "And I've got to change my—never mind. How long did I sleep?"

Gardener glanced at his watch. "Fourteen hours, I guess. A little more. Bobbi, your new book—"

"Yeah. Hold that until I get back." She walked slowly across the floor toward the bathroom, unbuttoning the shirt she'd slept in. As she hobbled toward the bathroom, Gardener got a good look—a better one than he wanted, actually—of just how much weight Bobbi had lost. This went beyond scrawniness to the point of emaciation.

She stopped, as if aware Gardener was looking at her, and without looking around she said: "I can explain everything, you know."

"Can you?" Gardener asked.

2

Anderson was in the bathroom a long time—much longer than it should have taken her to use the toilet and change her pad—Gardener was pretty sure that was what she'd gone to do. Her face just had that I-got-the-curse look.

He listened for the shower but it wasn't running, and he began to feel uneasy. Bobbi had seemed perfectly lucid when she woke up, but did that necessarily mean she *was?* Gardener began to have uncomfortable visions of Bobbi wriggling out the bathroom window and then running off into the woods in nothing but blue jeans, cackling wildly.

He put his right hand to the left side of his forehead, where the scar was. His head had started to throb a little. He let another minute or two slip by, and then he got up and walked toward the bathroom, making an effort to step quietly that was not quite unconscious. Visions of Bobbi escaping through the bathroom window to avoid explanations had been replaced by one of Bobbi serenely cutting her throat with one of Gard's own razor blades to avoid explanations permanently.

He decided he would just listen. If he heard normal-sounding movements, he would go on out to the kitchen and put on coffee, maybe scramble a few eggs. If he didn't hear anything—

His worries were needless. The bathroom door hadn't latched when she closed it, and other improvements aside, the unlatched doors in the place apparently still had their old way of swinging open. She'd probably have to shim up the whole north side of the house to do that. *Maybe that was* next *week's project,* he thought.

The door had swung open enough for him to see Bobbi standing at the mirror where Gardener had stood himself not long ago. She had her toothbrush in one hand and a tube of toothpaste in the other . . . but she hadn't uncapped the tube yet. She was looking into the mirror with an intensity that was almost hypnotic. Her lips were pulled back, her teeth bared.

She caught movement in the mirror and turned around, making no particular effort to cover her wasted breasts.

"Gard, do my teeth look all right to you?"

Gardener looked at them. They looked to him about as they always had, although he couldn't remember ever having seen quite this much of them—he was reminded of that terrible photo of Karen Carpenter again.

"Sure." He kept trying not to look at her stacked ribs, the painful jut of her pelvic bones above the waist of her jeans, which were drooping in spite of a belt cinched so tight it looked like a hobo's length of clothesline. "I guess so." He smiled cautiously. "Look, ma, no cavities."

Anderson tried to return Gardener's smile with her lips still pulled back to the gums; the result of this experiment was mildly grotesque. She put a forefinger on a molar and pressed.

"Oes it iggle en I ooo at?"

"What?"

"Does it wiggle when I do that?"

"No. Not that I can see, anyway. Why?"

"It's just this dream I keep having. It—" She looked down at herself. "Get out of here, Gard, I'm in dishabilly."

Don't worry, Bobbi. I wasn't going to jump your bones. Mostly because that'd be too close to what I'd really be doing.

"Sorry," he said. "Door was open. I thought you'd gone out."

He closed the door, latching it firmly.

Through it she said clearly: "I know what you're wondering."

He said nothing—only stood there. But he had a feeling she knew—*knew*—he was still there. As if she could see through the door.

"You're wondering if I'm losing my mind."

"No," he said then. "No, Bobbi. But—"

"I'm as sane as you are," Anderson said through the door. "I'm so stiff I can hardly walk and I've got an Ace bandage wrapped around my right knee for some reason I can't quite remember and I'm hungry as a bear and I know I've lost too much weight . . . but I *am* sane, Gard. I think you may have times before the day's over when you wonder if *you* are. The answer is, we both are."

"Bobbi, what's happening here?" Gardener asked. It came out in a helpless sort of cry.

"I want to unwrap the goddam Ace bandage and see what's under it," Anderson said through the door. "Feels like I jobbed my knee pretty good. Out in the woods, probably. Then I want to take a hot shower and put on some clean clothes. While I do that, you could make us some breakfast. And I'll tell you everything."

"Will you?"

"Yes."

"Okay, Bobbi."

"I'm glad to have you here, Gard," she said. "I had a

bad feeling once or twice. Like maybe you weren't doing so good."

Gardener felt his vision double, treble, then float away in prisms. He wiped an arm across his face. "No pain, no strain," he said. "I'll make some breakfast."

"Thanks, Gard."

He walked away, but he had to walk slow, because no matter how often he wiped his eyes, his vision kept trying to break up on him.

3

He stopped just inside the kitchen and went back to the closed bathroom door as a new thought occurred to him. Water was running in there now.

"Where's Peter?"

"What?" she called over the drumming shower.

"I said, where's Peter?" he called, raising his voice.

"Dead," Bobbi called back over the drumming water. "I cried, Gard. But he was . . . you know . . ."

"Old," Gardener muttered, then remembered and raised his voice again. "It was old age, then?"

"Yes," Anderson called back over the drumming water.

Gardener stood there for just a moment before going back to the kitchen, wondering why he believed Bobbi was lying about Peter and how he had died.

4

Gard scrambled eggs and fried bacon on Bobbi's grill. He noticed that a microwave oven had been installed over the conventional one since he'd last been here, and there was now track lighting over the main work areas and the kitchen table, where Bobbi was in the habit of eating most of her meals—usually with a book in her free hand.

He made coffee, strong and black, and was just bringing everything to the table when Bobbi came in, wearing a fresh pair of cords and a T-shirt with a picture of a blackfly on it and the legend MAINE STATE BIRD. Her wet hair was wrapped in a towel.

Anderson surveyed the table. "No toast?" she asked.
"Make your own frigging toast," Gardener said amiably. "I didn't hitchhike two hundred miles to buttle your breakfast."

Anderson stared. "You did *what?* Yesterday? In the rain?"

"Yeah."

"What in God's name happened? Muriel said you were doing a reading tour and your last one was June 30th."

"You called Muriel?" He was absurdly touched. "When?"

Anderson flapped a hand as if that didn't matter—probably it didn't. "What happened?" she asked again.

Gardener thought about telling her—*wanted* to tell her, he realized, dismayed. Was that what Bobbi was for, then? Was Bobbi Anderson really no more than the wall he wailed to? He hesitated, wanting to tell her . . . and didn't. There would be time for that later.

Maybe.

"Later," he said. "I want to know what happened here."

"Breakfast first," Anderson said, "and that's an order."

5

Gard gave Bobbi most of the eggs and bacon, and Bobbi didn't waste time—she went to them like a woman who hasn't eaten well for a long time. Watching her eat, Gardener remembered a biography of Thomas Edison he had read when he was quite young—no more than ten or eleven. Edison had gone on wild work-jags in which idea had followed idea, invention had followed invention. During these spurts, he had ignored wife, children, baths, even food. If his wife hadn't brought him his meals on a tray, the man might literally have starved to death between the light bulb and the phonograph. There had been a picture of him, hands plunged into hair that was wildly awry—as if it had been actually trying to get at the brain beneath hair and skull, the brain which would not let him rest—and Gardener remembered thinking that the man looked quite insane.

And, he thought, touching the left side of his forehead,

Edison had been subject to migraines. Migraines and deep depressions.

He saw no sign of depression in Bobbi, however. She gobbled eggs, ate seven or eight slices of bacon wrapped in a slice of toast slathered with oleo, and swallowed two large glasses of orange juice. When she had finished, she uttered a resounding belch.

"Gross, Bobbi."

"In Portugal, a good belch is considered a compliment to the cook."

"What do they do after a good lay? Fart?"

Anderson threw her head back and roared with laughter. The towel fell off her hair, and all at once Gard wanted to take her to bed, bag of bones or not.

Smiling a little, Gardener said: "Okay, it was good. Thanks. Some Sunday I'll make you some swell eggs Benedict. Now give."

Anderson reached behind him and brought down a half-full package of Camels. She lit one and pushed the pack toward Gardener.

"No thanks. It's the only bad habit I ever succeeded in mostly giving up."

But before Bobbi was done, Gardener had smoked four of them.

6

"You looked around," Anderson said. "I remember telling you to do that—just barely—and I know you did. You look like I felt after I found the thing in the woods."

"What thing?"

"If I told you now you'd think I was crazy. Later on I'll show you, but right now I think we'd better just talk. Tell me what you saw around the place. What changes."

So Gardener ticked them off: the cellar improvements, the litter of projects, the weird little sun in the water heater. The strange job of customizing on the Tomcat's engine. He hesitated for a moment, thinking of the addition to the shifting diagram, and let that go. He supposed Bobbi knew he had seen it, anyway.

"And somewhere in the middle of all that," he said, "you found time to write another book. A long one. I read the first forty pages or so while I was waiting for you to wake up, and I think it's good as well as long. The best novel you've ever written, probably . . . and you've written some good ones."

Anderson was nodding, pleased. "Thank you. I think it is too." She pointed to the last slice of bacon on the platter. "You want that?"

"No."

"Sure?"

"Yes."

She took it and made it gone.

"How long did it take you to write it?"

"I'm not completely sure," Anderson said. "Maybe three days. No more than a week, anyway. Did most of it in my sleep."

Gard smiled.

"I'm not joking, you know," Anderson smiled.

Gardener stopped smiling.

"My time sense is pretty fucked up," she admitted. "I do know I wasn't working on it the twenty-seventh. That's the last day when time—sequential time—seemed completely clear to me. You got here last night, July 4th, and it was done. So . . . a week, max. But I really don't think it was more than three days."

Gardener gaped. Anderson looked back calmly, wiping her fingers on a napkin. "Bobbi, that's impossible," Gardener said finally.

"If you think so, you missed my typewriter."

Gardener had glanced at Bobbi's old machine when he sat down, but that was all—his attention had been riveted immediately by the manuscript. He had seen the old black Underwood thousands of times. The manuscript, on the other hand, was new.

"If you'd looked closely, you would have seen the roll of computer paper on the wall behind it and another of those gadgets behind it. Egg crate, heavy-duty batteries, and all. What? These?"

She pushed the cigarettes across to Gardener, who took one.

"I don't know how it works, but then, I don't really know how any of them work—including the one that's running *all* the juice in this place." She smiled at Gardener's expression. "I'm off the Central Maine Power tit, Gard. I had them interrupt service . . . that's how they put it, as if they know damned well you'll want it back before too long . . . let's see . . . four days ago. That I *do* remember."

"Bobbi—"

"There's a gadget like the thing in the water heater and the one behind my typewriter in the junction box out back, only that one's the granddaddy of them all." Anderson laughed—the laugh of a woman in the grip of pleasant reminiscences. "There's twenty or thirty D-cells in that one. I think Poley Andrews down at Cooder's Market thinks I've gone nuts—I bought every battery he had in stock, and then I went to Augusta for more.

"Was that the day I got the dirt for the cellar?" She addressed this last to herself, frowning. Then her face cleared. "I think so, yeah. The Historic Battery Run of 1988. Hit about seven different stores, came back with *hundreds* of batteries, and then I stopped in Albion and got a truckload of loam to sweeten the cellar. I'm almost positive I did both of those things the same day."

The troubled frown resurfaced, and for a moment Gardener thought Bobbi looked scared and exhausted again—of *course* she was still exhausted. Exhaustion of the sort Gardener had seen last night went bone-deep. A single night's sleep, no matter how long and deep, wouldn't erase it. And then there was this wild, hallucinatory talk—books written in her sleep; all the AC current in the house being run by D-cells, runs to Augusta on crazy errands—

Except that the proof was here, all around him. He had *seen* it.

"—*that* one," Anderson said, and laughed.

"What, Bobbi?"

"I said I had a devil of a job setting up the one that generates the juice here in the house, and out at the dig."

"What dig? Is it the thing in the woods you want to show me?"

"Yes. Soon. Just give me a few more minutes." Anderson's face again assumed that look of pleasure in telling, and Gardener suddenly thought it must be the expression on the faces of all those who have tales they don't just *want* to tell but tales they *must* tell—from the lecture-hall bore who was part of an Antarctic expedition in 1937 and who still has his fading slides to prove it, to

Ishmael the Sailor-Man, late of the ill-fated *Pequod,* who finishes his tale with a sentence that seems a desperate cry only thinly and perfunctorily disguised as information: "Only I am left to tell you." Was it desperation and madness that Gardener detected beneath Bobbi's cheerful, disjointed remembrances of Ten Wacky Days in Haven? Gardener thought so . . . *knew* so. Who was better equipped to see the signs? Whatever Bobbi had faced here while Gardener was reading poetry to overweight matrons and their bored husbands, it had nearly broken her mind.

Anderson lit another cigarette with a hand that trembled slightly, making the matchflame quiver momentarily. It was the sort of thing you would have seen only if you were looking for it.

"I was out of egg cartons by then, and the thing was going to have too many batteries for just one or two anyway. So I got one of Uncle Frank's cigar boxes—there must be a dozen old wooden ones up in the attic, probably even Mabel Noyes down at Junque-a-Torium would pay a few bucks for them, and you know what a skinflint *she* is—and I stuffed them with toilet paper and tried to make nests in the paper for the batteries to stand up in. You know . . . nests?"

Anderson made quick poking gestures with her right index finger and then looked, bright-eyed, at Gard, to see if he got it. Gardener nodded. That feeling of unreality was stealing back, that feeling of his mind getting ready to seep through the top of his skull and float up to the ceiling. *A drunk would fix that,* he thought, and the pulse in his head sharpened.

"But the batteries kept falling over anyway." She snuffed her cigarette and immediately lit another one. "They were wild, just wild. I was wild, too. Then I got an idea."

They?

"I went down to Chip McCausland's. Down on the Dugout Road?"

Gardener shook his head. He had never been down the Dugout Road.

"Well, he lives out there with this woman—she's his common-law wife, I guess—and about ten kids. Man, you talk about sluts . . . the dirt on her neck, Gard . . . you couldn't wash it off unless you used a jackhammer on it first. I guess he was married before, and . . . doesn't matter . . . it's just . . . I haven't had anyone to talk to . . . I mean, *they* don't talk, not the way a couple of people do, and I keep mixing up the stuff that's not important with the stuff that is—"

Anderson's words had started to come out quicker and quicker, until now they were almost tripping over each other. *She's speed-rapping,* Gardener thought with some alarm, *and pretty soon she's going to start either yelling or crying.* He didn't know which he dreaded more and thought again of Ishmael, Ishmael rambling through the streets of Bedford, Massachusetts, stinking more of madness than whale oil, finally grabbing some unlucky passerby and screaming: *Listen! I'm the only fucking one left to tell you and so you better listen, damn you! You better listen if you don't want to be using this harpoon for a fucking suppository! I got a tale to tell, it's about this white fucking whale and* YOU'RE GOING TO LISTEN!

He reached across the table and touched her hand. "You tell it any old way you want to. I'm here and I'm going to listen. We've got time; like you said, it's your day off. So slow down. If I fall asleep, you'll know you got too far from the point. Okay?"

Anderson smiled and relaxed visibly. Gardener wanted to ask again what was going on in the woods. More than that, who *they* were. But it would be best to wait. *All bad things come to him who waits,* he thought, and after a pause to collect herself, Bobbi went on.

"Chip McCausland's got three or four henhouses, that's all I started to say. For a couple of bucks I was able to get all the egg cartons I wanted . . . even a few of the big egg-crate sheets. Those sheets each have ten dozen cradles."

Anderson laughed cheerfully and added something that brought gooseflesh out on Gardener's skin.

"Haven't used one of those yet, but when I do I guess we'll have enough zap for the whole town of Haven to let go of the CMP tit. With enough left over for Albion and most of Troy as well.

"So I got the power going here—Jesus, I'm rambling—and I already had the gadget hooked up to the typewriter—and I really did sleep—napped, anyway—and that's about where we came in, isn't it?"

Gardener nodded, still trying to cope with the idea that there might be fact as well as hallucination in Bobbi's casual statement that she could build a "gadget" which could power three small towns from a source consisting of one hundred and twenty D-cell batteries.

"What the gadget on the typewriter does is . . ." Anderson frowned. Her head cocked a little, as if she were listening to a voice Gardener could not hear. "It might be easier to show you. Go on over there and roll in a sheet of paper, would you?"

"Okay." He headed for the door into the living room, then looked back at Anderson. "Aren't you coming?"

Bobbi smiled. "I'll stay here," she said, and then Gardener got it. He got it, and even understood on some mental level where only pure logic was allowed that it might be so—hadn't the immortal Holmes himself said that when you eliminated the impossible, you had to believe whatever was left, no matter how improbable? And there *was* a new novel sitting in there on the table by what Bobbi sometimes called her word-accordion.

Yeah, except typewriters don't write books by themselves, Gard old buddy. You know what the immortal Holmes probably would *say? That the fact that there is a novel sitting next to Bobbi's typewriter, and the* added *fact that this is a novel you never saw before does not mean it is a* new *novel. Holmes would say Bobbi wrote that book at some time in the past. Then, while you were gone and Bobbi was losing her marbles, she brought it out and set it beside the typewriter. She may believe what she's telling you, but that doesn't make it so.*

Gardener walked into the cluttered corner of the living room that served as Bobbi's writing quarters. It was handy enough to the bookshelf so she could simply rock back on the legs of her chair and grab almost anything she wanted. *It's too good to be a trunk novel.*

He knew what the immortal Holmes would say about *that* too: he would agree that *The Buffalo Soldiers'* being a trunk novel was improbable; he would argue, however, that writing a novel in three days—and not at the typewriter but while taking catnaps between repeated frenzies of activity—was im-fucking-possible.

Except that novel hadn't come out of any trunk. Gardener knew it, because he knew *Bobbi.* Bobbi would have been just as incapable of sticking a novel that good in her trunk as Gard was of remaining rational in a discussion on the subject of nuclear power.

Fuck you, Sherlock, and the hansom cab you and Dr. W. rode in on. Christ I want a drink.

The urge—the *need*—to drink had come back in full, frightening force.

"You there, Gard?" Anderson called.

"Yes."

This time he consciously saw the roll of computer paper. It hung down loosely. He looked behind the typewriter and did indeed see another of Bobbi's "gadgets." This one was smaller—half an egg carton with the last two egg cradles standing empty. D-cells stood in the other four, each neatly capped with one of those little funnels (looking at them more closely, Gard decided they were scraps of tin can carefully cut to shape with tin snips), each with a wire coming out of the funnel over the + post . . . one red, one blue, one yellow, one green. These went to another circuit board. This one, which looked as if it might have come from a radio, was held vertical by two short flat pieces of wood that had been glued to the desk with the board sandwiched in between. Those pieces of wood, each looking a little like the chalk gutter at the foot of a blackboard, were so absurdly familiar to Gardener that for a moment he was unable to identify them. Then it came. They were the tile-holders you put your letters on when you were playing Scrabble.

One single wire, almost as thick as an AC cord, ran from the circuit board into the typewriter.

"Put in some paper!" Anderson called. She laughed. "*That* was the part I almost forgot, isn't that stupid? They were no help there and I almost went crazy before I saw the answer. I was sitting on the jakes one day, wishing I'd gotten one of those damned word-crunchers after all, and when I reached for the toilet paper . . . *eureka!* Boy, did I feel dumb! Just roll it in, Gard!"

No. I'm getting out of here right now, and then I'm going to hitch a ride up to the Purple Cow in Hampden and get so fucking drunk I'll never *remember this stuff. I don't* ever *want to know who "they" are.*

Instead, he pulled on the roll, slipped the perforated end of the first sheet under the roller, and turned the knob on the side of the old machine until he could snap the bar down. His heart was beating hard and fast. "Okay!" he called. "Do you want me to . . . uh, turn something on?" He didn't see any switch, and even if he had, he wouldn't have wanted to touch it.

"Don't need to!" she called back. Gard heard a click. It was followed by a hum—the sound of a kid's electric train transformer.

Green light began to spill out of Anderson's typewriter.

Gardener took an involuntary, shambling step backward on legs that felt like stilts. That light rayed out between the keys in weird, diverging strokes. There were glass panels set into the Underwood's sides and now they glowed like the walls of an aquarium.

Suddenly the keys of the typewriter began to depress themselves, moving up and down like the keys of a player piano. The carriage moved rapidly and letters spilled across the page:

Full fathom five my father lies

Ding! Bang!

The carriage returned.

No. I'm not seeing this. I don't believe I'm seeing this.

These are the pearls that were his eyes.

Sickly green light spilling up through the keyboard and over the words like radium.

Ding! Bang!

My beer is Rheingold the dry beer

The line appeared in the space of a second, it seemed. The keys were a hammering blur of speed. It was like watching a news ticker.

Think of Rheingold whenever you buy beer!

Dear God, is she really doing this? Or is it a trick?

With his mind tottering again in the face of this new wonder, he found himself grasping eagerly for Sherlock Holmes—a trick, of course it was a trick, all a part of poor old Bobbi's nervous breakdown . . . her very *creative* nervous breakdown.

Ding! Bang! The carriage shot back.

No trick, Gard.

The carriage returned, and the hammering keys typed this before his wide, staring eyes.

You were right the first time. I'm doing it from the kitchen. The gadget behind the typewriter is thought-sensitive, the way a photoelectric cell is light-sensitive. This thing seems to pick up my thoughts clearly up to a distance of five miles. If I'm further away than that, things start to get garbled. Beyond ten or so, it doesn't work at all.

Ding! Bang! The big silver lever to the left of the carriage worked itself twice, cranking the paper—which now held three perfectly typed messages—up a few lines. Then it resumed.

So you see I didn't have to be sitting at the typewriter to work on my novel—look, ma, no hands! This poor old Underwood ran like a bastard for those two or three days, Gard, and all the time it was running I was in the woods, working around the place, or down cellar. But as I say, mostly I was sleeping. It's funny . . . even if someone could have convinced me such a gadget existed, I wouldn't have believed it would work for me, because I've always been lousy at dictating. I have to write my own letters, I always said, because I have to see the words on paper. It was impossible for me to imagine how someone could dictate a whole novel into a tape recorder, for instance, although some writers apparently do just that. But this isn't like dictating, Gard—it's like a direct tap into the subconscious, more like dreaming than writing . . . but what comes out is unlike dreams, which are often surreal and disconnected. This really isn't a typewriter at all anymore. It's a dream machine. One that dreams rationally. There's something cosmically funny about them giving it to me, so I could write The Buffalo Soldiers. *You're right, it really is the best thing I've ever written, but it's still your basic oat opera. It's like inventing a perpetual-motion machine so your little kid won't pester you anymore about changing*

> *the batteries in his toy car! But can you imagine what the results might have been if F. Scott Fitzgerald had had one of these gadgets? Or Hemingway? Faulkner? Salinger?*

After each question mark the typewriter fell momentarily silent and then burst out with another name. After Salinger's, it stopped completely. Gardener had read the material as it came out, but in a mechanical, almost uncomprehending way. His eyes went back to the beginning of the passage. *I was thinking that it was a trick, that she might have hoked the typewriter up somehow to write those two little snatches of verse. And it wrote—*

It had written: *No trick, Gard.*

He thought suddenly: *Can you read my mind, Bobbi?*

Ding! Bang! The carriage returned suddenly, making him jump and almost cry out.

Yes. But only a little.

What did we do on the fourth of July the year I quit teaching?

> *Drove up to Derry. You said you knew a guy who'd sell us some cherry bombs. He sold us the cherry bombs but they were all duds. You were pretty drunk. You wanted to go back and knock his block off. I couldn't talk you out of it, so we went back, and damned if his house wasn't on fire. He had a lot of real stuff in the basement, and he'd dropped a cigarette butt into a box of it. You saw the fire and the fire-trucks and got laughing so hard you fell down in the street.*

That feeling of unreality had never been as strong as it was now. He fought it, keeping it at arm's length while his eyes searched through the previous passage for something else. After a second or two he found it: *There's something almost cosmically funny about them giving it to me, you know . . .*

And earlier Bobbi had said: *The batteries kept falling over and they were wild, just wild . . .*

His cheeks felt hotly flushed, as if with fever, but his forehead felt as cold as an icepack—even the steady pulse of pain from above his left eye seemed cold . . . shallow stabs hitting with metronomelike regularity.

Looking at the typewriter, which was filled with that somehow ghastly green light, Gardener thought: *Bobbi, who are "they"?*

Ding! Bang!

The keys rattled off a burst, letters forming words, the words forming a child's couplet:

> Late last night and the night before
> Tommyknockers, Tommyknockers, knocking at the door.

Jim Gardener screamed.

7

At last his hands stopped shaking—enough so he could get the hot coffee to his mouth without slopping it all over himself, thus finishing the morning's lunatic festivities with a few more burns.

Anderson kept watching him from the other side of the kitchen table with concerned eyes. She kept a bottle of very good brandy in the darkest depths of the pantry, far away from the "alcoholic staples," and she had offered to spike Gard's coffee with a wallop of it. He had declined, not just with regret but with real pain. He *needed* that brandy—it would dull the ache in his head, maybe kill it entirely. More important, it would bring his mind back into focus. It would get rid of that I-just-sailed-off-the-edge-of-the-world feeling.

Only problem was, he'd finally gotten to "that" point, hadn't he? Correct. The point where it wouldn't stop with a single wallop of brandy in his coffee. There had been entirely too much input since he had opened the hatch at the bottom of Bobbi's water heater and then gone upstairs for a belt of whiskey. It had been safe then; now the air was the unsteady sort that spawned tornadoes.

So: no more drinks. Not so much as an Irish sweetener in his coffee until he understood what was happening here. Including what was happening to Bobbi. That, most of all.

"I'm sorry that last bit happened," Anderson said, "but I'm not sure I could have stopped it. I told you it was a dream machine; it's also a 'subconscious machine.' I'm really not getting much of your thoughts at all, Gard—I've tried this with other people, and in most cases it's as easy as sinking your thumb into fresh dough. You can core all the way down to what I guess you'd call the id . . . although it's awful down there, full of the most monstrous . . . you can't even call them ideas . . . *images,* I guess you'd say. Simple as a child's scrawl, but they're alive. Like those fish they find down deep in the ocean, the ones that explode if you bring them up." Bobbi suddenly shuddered. "They're *alive,*" she repeated.

For a second there was no sound but the birds singing outside.

"Anyway, all I get from you is surface stuff, and most of *that* is all broken up and garbled. If you were like anyone else, I'd know what's been going on with you, and why you look so crappy—"

"Thanks, Bobbi. I knew there was a reason I keep coming here, and since it's not the cooking, it must be the flattery." He grinned, but it was a nervous grin, and he lit another cigarette.

"As it is," Bobbi went on as if he hadn't spoken, "I can make some educated guesses on the basis of what's happened to you before, but you'd have to tell me the details . . . I couldn't snoop even if I wanted to. I'm not sure I could get it clear even if you shoved it all up to the front of your mind and put out a Welcome mat. But when you asked who 'they' were, that little rhyme about the Tommyknockers came up like a big bubble. And it ran itself off on the typewriter."

"All right," Gardener said, although it wasn't all right . . . nothing was all right. "But who are they besides the Tommyknockers? Are they pixies? Leprechauns? Grem—"

"I asked you to look around because I wanted you to get an idea of how big all of this is," Anderson said. "How far-reaching the implications could be."

"I realize that, all right," Gardener said, and a smile ghosted around the corners of his mouth. "A few more far-reaching implications and I'll be ready for a strait-waistcoat."

"Your Tommyknockers came from space," Anderson said, "as I think you must have deduced by now."

Gardener supposed the thought had done more than cross his mind—but his mouth was dry, his hands frozen around the coffee cup.

"Are they around?" he asked, and his voice seemed to come from far, far away. He was suddenly afraid to turn around, afraid he might see some gnarled thing with three eyes and a horn where its mouth should have been come waltzing out of the pantry, something that belonged only on a movie screen, maybe in a *Star Wars* epic.

"I think they—the actual physical they—have been dead for a long time," Anderson said calmly. "They probably died long before men existed on earth. But then . . . Caruso's dead, but he's still singing on a hell of a lot of records, isn't he?"

"Bobbi," Gardener said, "tell me what happened. I want you to begin at the beginning and end by saying, 'Then you came up the road just in time to grab me when I passed out.' Can you do that?"

"Not entirely," she said, and grinned. "But I'll do my best."

8

Anderson talked for a long time. When she finished, it was past noon. Gard sat across the kitchen table, smoking, excusing himself only once to go into the bathroom, where he took three more aspirin.

Anderson began with her stumble, told of coming back and digging out more of the ship—enough to realize she had found something utterly unique—and then going back a third time. She did not tell Gardener about Chuck the Woodchuck, who had been dead but not flyblown; nor about Peter's shrinking cataract; nor about the visit to Etheridge, the vet. She passed over those things smoothly, saying only that when she came back from her first whole day of work on the thing, she had found Peter dead on the front porch.

"It was as if he'd gone to sleep," Anderson said, and there was a note of schmaltz in her voice so unlike the Bobbi he knew that Gardener looked up sharply . . . and then looked down at his hands quickly. Anderson was crying a little.

After a few moments Gardener asked: "What then?"

"Then you came up the road just in time to grab me when I passed out," Anderson said, smiling.

"I don't understand what you mean."

"Peter died on the twenty-eighth of June," Anderson said. She had never had much practice as a liar, but thought this one came out sounding smooth and natural. "That's the last day I remember clearly and sequentially. Until you showed up last night, that is." She smiled openly and guilelessly at Gardener, but this was also a lie—her clear, sequential, unjumbled memories ended the day before, on June 27th, with her standing above that titantic thing buried in the earth, gripping the handle of the shovel. They ended with her whispering, "Everything's fine," and then beginning to dig. There was more to the tale, all right, all kinds of more, but she couldn't remember it sequentially and what she could remember would have to be edited . . . carefully edited. For instance, she couldn't really tell Gard about Peter. Not yet. *They* had told her she couldn't, but on that one she didn't need any telling.

They had also told her Jim Gardener would have to be watched very, very closely. Not for long, of course—soon Gard would be

(part of us)

on the team. Yes. And it would be *great* to have him on the team, because if there was anyone in the world Anderson loved, it was Jim Gardener.

Bobbi, who are "they"?

The Tommyknockers. That word, which had risen out of the queer opaqueness in Gard's mind like a silvery bubble, was as good a name as any, wasn't it? Sure. Better than some.

"So what now?" Gardener asked, lighting her last cigarette. He looked both dazed and wary. "I'm not saying I can swallow all this . . ." He laughed a bit wildly. "Or maybe it's just that my throat's not big enough for it all to go down at once."

"I understand," Anderson said. "I think the main reason I remember so little about the last week or so is that it's all so . . . weird. It's like having your mind strapped to a rocket-sled."

She didn't like lying to Gard; it made her uneasy. But

all the lying would be done soon enough. Gard would be . . . would be . . .

Well . . . persuaded.

When he saw the ship. When he *felt* the ship.

"No matter how much I do or don't believe, I'm forced to believe most of it, I guess."

" 'When you remove the impossible, whatever remains is the truth, no matter how improbable.' "

"You got that too, did you?"

"The shape of it. I might not have even known what it was if I hadn't heard you say it once or twice."

Gardener nodded. "Well, I guess it fits the situation we have here. If I don't believe the evidence of my senses, I have to believe I'm crazy. Although God knows there are enough people in the world who would be more than happy to testify that's just what I am."

"You're not crazy, Gard," Anderson said quietly, and put her hand over his. He turned his own over and squeezed it.

"Well . . . you know, a man who shot his wife . . . there are people who'd say that's pretty persuasive evidence of insanity. You know?"

"Gard, that was eight years ago."

"Sure. And that guy I elbowed in the tit, that was eight *days* ago. I also chased a guy down Arberg's hall and across his dining room, with an umbrella, did I tell you that? My behavior over the last five years has been increasingly self-destructive—"

"Hi, folks, and welcome once more to the National Self-Pity Hour!" Bobbi Anderson chirruped brightly. "Tonight's guest is—"

"I was going to kill myself yesterday morning," Gardener said quietly. "If I hadn't gotten the idea—really *strong* idea—that you were in trouble, I'd be fishfood now."

Anderson looked at him closely. Her hand slowly tightened down on his until it was hurting. "You mean it, don't you? Christ!"

"Sure. You want to know how bad it's gotten? It seemed like the sanest thing I could do under the circumstances."

"Come off it."

"I'm serious. Then this idea came. The idea you were in trouble. So I put it off long enough to call you. But you weren't here."

"I was probably in the woods," Anderson said. "And you came running." She lifted his hand to her mouth and kissed it gently. "If this whole crazy business doesn't mean anything else, at least it means you're still alive, you asshole."

"As always, I'm impressed by the almost Gallic range of your compliments, Bobbi."

"If you ever *do* do it, I'll see it's written on your tombstone, Gard. ASSHOLE in letters carved deep enough so they won't wear off for at least a century."

"Well, thanks," Gardener said, "but you won't have to worry about it for a while. Because I still got it."

"What?"

"That feeling that you're in trouble."

She tried to look away, tried to take her hand away.

"Look at me, Bobbi, goddammit."

At last, reluctantly, she did, her lower lip slightly pushed out in that stubborn expression he knew so well—but didn't she also look just the tiniest bit uneasy? He thought so.

"All of this seems so wonderful—house-power from D-cells, books that write themselves, God knows what else—so why should I feel that you're in trouble?"

"I don't know," she said softly, and got up to do the dishes.

9

"Of course I worked until I damn near dropped, that's one thing," Anderson said. Her back was to him now, and he had a feeling she liked it that way fine. Dishes rattled in hot, soapy water. "And I didn't just say 'Aliens from space, ho-hum, cheap clean electric power and mental telepathy, big deal,' you know. My mailman's cheating on his wife, I know about it—I don't *want* to know about it, hell, I'm no snoop, but it was just there, Gard, right there in the front of his head. Not seeing it would be like not seeing a neon sign a hundred feet high. Christ, I've been rocking and reeling."

"I see," he said, and thought: *She's not telling the truth, at least not all of it, and I don't think she even knows it.* "The question remains: what do we do now?"

"I don't know." She glanced around, saw Gardener's raised eyebrows, and said, "Did you think I was going to give you the answer in a neat little essay, five hundred words or less? I can't. I've got some ideas, but that's all. Maybe not even very good ones. I suppose the first thing is to take you out so you can

(be persuaded)

have a look at it. Afterward . . . well . . ."

Gardener looked at her for a long time. Bobbi did not drop her eyes this time; they were open and guileless. But things were wrong here, off-note and off-key. Things like that note of fake schmaltz in Bobbi's voice when she spoke of Peter. Maybe the tears had been real, but that tone . . . it had been all wrong.

"All right. Let's go take a look at your ship in the earth."

"But let's have lunch first," Anderson said placidly.

"You're hungry *again?*"

"Sure. Aren't you?"

"Christ, no!"

"Then I'll eat for both of us," Anderson said, and she did.

10.

GARDENER DECIDES

1

"Good God." Gardener sat down heavily on a fresh stump. It felt like a case of sit down or fall down. Like being punched hard in the stomach. No; it was stranger and more radical than that. It was more like someone had slammed the hose of an industrial vacuum cleaner into his mouth and turned it on, sucking all the wind out of his lungs in a second's time. "Good God," he repeated in a tiny breathless voice. It seemed to be all of which he was capable.

"It's something, isn't it?"

They were halfway down the slope, not far from where Anderson had found the dead chuck. Before, the slope had been pretty heavily wooded. Now a lane had been cut through the trees to admit a strange vehicle which Gardener almost recognized. It stood at the edge of Anderson's dig, and it was dwarfed both by the excavation and by the thing which was being unearthed.

The trench was now two hundred feet long and twenty feet wide at either end. The cut bulged to thirty feet or so in width for perhaps forty feet of the slit's total length—that bulge made a shape like a woman's hips seen in silhouette. The gray leading edge of the ship, its curvature now triumphantly revealed, rose out of this bulge like the edge of a giant steel tea saucer.

"Good God," Gardener gasped again. "Look at that thing."

"I *have* been," Bobbi said, a distant little smile playing over her lips. "For over a week I've been looking at it. It's the most beautiful thing I've ever seen. And it's going to solve a lot of problems, Gard. 'There came a man on horseback, riding and riding—' "

That cut through the fog. Gardener looked around at Anderson, who might have been drifting in the dark places from which that incredible thing had come. The look on her face chilled Gardener. Bobbi's eyes were not just far-off. They were vacant windows.

"What do you mean?"

"Hmmm?" Anderson looked around as if coming out of a deep daze.

"What do you mean, a man on horseback?"

"I mean you, Gard. I mean me. But I think . . . I think I mostly mean you. Come on down here and take a look."

Anderson started down the slope quickly, with the casual grace of previous experience. She got maybe twenty feet before she realized Gardener wasn't with her. She looked back. He had gotten up from the stump, but that was all.

"It won't bite you," Anderson said.

"No? What *will* it do to me, Bobbi?"

"Nothing! They're *dead,* Gard! Your Tommyknockers *were* real enough, but they were *mortal,* and this ship has been here for at least fifty million years. The glacier broke around it! It covered it but it couldn't move it. Not even all those tons of ice could move it. So the glacier broke around it. You can look into the cut and *see* it, like a frozen wave. Dr. Borns from the university would go batshit over this . . . but they're dead enough, Gard."

"Have you been inside?" Gardener asked, not moving.

"No. The hatch—I think, I *feel,* there is one—is still buried. But that doesn't change what I *know.* They're dead, Gard. *Dead."*

"They're dead, you haven't been in the ship, but you're inventing like Thomas Edison on a speed trip and you can read minds. So I repeat: what's it going to do to *me?"*

So she told the biggest lie of all—told it calmly, with no regret at all. She said: "Nothing you don't want it to."

And started down again, without looking back to see if he was following.

Gardener hesitated, his head throbbing miserably, and then he started down after her.

2

The vehicle by the trench was Bobbi's old truck—only before that, it had been a Country Squire station wagon. Anderson had driven it from New York when she came to college. That had been thirteen years ago, and it had not been new then. She had run it on the road until 1984, when even Elt Barker down at the Shell station, Haven's only garage and gas stop, would no longer slap an inspection sticker on it. Then, in one weekend of frenzied work—they had been drunk for most of it, and Gardener still thought it something of a miracle that they hadn't blown themselves up with Frank Garrick's old blowtorch rig—they had cut off the roof of the wagon from above the front seat on back, turning it into a half-assed truck.

"Lookit that, Gard-ole-Gard," Bobbi Anderson had proclaimed solemnly, staring at the remains of the wagon. "We done made ourselves an honest-to-God fiel'-bomber." Then she leaned over and threw up. Gardener had picked her up and carried her onto the porch (Peter twining anxiously around his feet the whole way). By the time he got her there, she had passed out. He put her down carefully, and then passed out himself.

The half-assed truck had been a tough old Detroit rod-bucket, but it had finally gone toes-up. Anderson had put it on blocks at one end of the garden, claiming no one would want to buy it even for parts. Gardener thought she just felt sentimental.

Now the truck had been resurrected—although it hardly looked like the same vehicle, except for the blue paint and the remains of fake wood siding that had been one of the Country Squire's trademarks. The driver's door and most of the front end were gone entirely. The latter had been replaced with a weird conglomeration of digging and earth-moving equipment. To Gardener's disturbed eye, Anderson's truck now looked like a deranged child's bulldozer. Something which looked like a giant screwdriver blade protruded from the place where the grille had been. The engine looked like something which had been yanked whole from an old D-9 Caterpillar.

Bobbi, where did you get that engine? How did you move it from where it was then to where it is now? Good Jesus!

Yet all this, remarkable as it was, could hold his eye for only a moment or two. He walked across the ripped earth to where Bobbi was standing, hands in pockets, looking into the slash in the earth.

"What do you think, Gard?"

He didn't know what he thought, and was speechless anyway.

The excavation went down to an amazing depth: thirty or forty feet, he guessed. If the angle of the sun hadn't been exactly right, he wouldn't have been able to see the bottom of the trench at all. There was a space of about three feet between the side of the excavation and the smooth hull of the ship. That hull was utterly unbroken. There were no numbers, symbols, pictures, or hieroglyphs on it.

At the bottom of the cut, the thing disappeared into the earth. Gardener shook his head. Opened his mouth, found he still had no words, and shut it again.

The part of the hull Anderson had first tripped over and then tried to wriggle with her hand—thinking it might be a tin can left over from a loggers' weekend—was now directly in front of Gardener's nose. He could easily have reached across the three-foot space and grasped it as Anderson herself had just two weeks ago . . . with this difference: when Anderson first grasped the edge of the ship in the earth, she had been on her knees. Gardener was standing. He had vaguely noted the going-over this slope had taken—rough, muddy terrain, trees that had been cut and moved aside, stumps that had been pulled like rotten teeth—but beyond that momentary observation, he had dismissed it. He would have taken a closer look if Anderson had told him how much of the slope she had simply cut away. The hill had made the thing harder to get out . . . so she had simply removed half the hillside to make it easier.

Flying saucer, Gardener thought faintly, and then: *I* did *jump. This is a death fantasy. Any second now I'll come to and find myself trying to breathe salt water. Any second now. Just any old second.*

Except that nothing of the sort did or would happen, because all this was *real.* It was a flying saucer.

And that, somehow, was the worst. Not a spaceship, or an alien craft, or an extraterrestrial vehicle. It was a *flying saucer.* They had been debunked by the Air Force, by thinking scientists, by psychologists. No self-respecting science-fiction writer would put one in his story, and if he did, no self-respecting editor would touch it with a ten-foot pole. Flying saucers had gone out of vogue in the genre at roughly the same time as Edgar Rice Burroughs and Otis Adelbert Kline. It was the oldest wheeze in the book. Flying saucers were more than *passé;* the idea itself was a joke, given mental house-room these days only by crackpots, religious eccentrics, and, of course, the tabloid newspapers, where any week's budget of news had to include at least one saucer story, such as SIX-YEAR-OLD PREGNANT BY SAUCER ALIEN, TEARFUL MOTHER REVEALS.

These stories, for some odd reason, all seemed to originate in either Brazil or New Hampshire.

And yet here was such a thing—it had been here all the while, as centuries passed above it like minutes. A line from Genesis suddenly occurred to him, making him shiver as if a cold wind had blown past: *There were giants in the earth in those days.*

He turned toward Anderson, his eyes almost pleading.

"Is it real?" he could no more than whisper.

"It's real. Touch it." She knocked on it, producing that dull fist-on-mahogany sound again. Gardener reached out . . . then pulled his hand back.

A look of annoyance passed over Anderson's face like a shadow. "I told you, Gard—it won't bite you."

"It won't do anything to me I don't want it to."

"Absolutely not."

Gardener reflected—as much as he was able to reflect in his current state of roaring confusion—that he had once believed that about booze. Come to think of it, he had heard people—most of them his college students in the early seventies—say the same thing about various drugs. Many of them had ended up in clinics or drug-counseling sessions with severe nose-candy problems.

Tell me, Bobbi, did you want to work until you dropped? Did you want to lose so much weight that you looked like an anorexic? I guess all I really want to know is, Did you drive or was you driven? Why did you lie about Peter? Why don't I hear birds in these woods?

"Go on," Anderson said patiently. "We've got some talking to do and some hard decisions to make, and I don't want you breaking in halfway through to say you've decided the whole thing was just a hallucination that came out of a liquor bottle."

"That's a shitty thing to say."

"So are most of the things people really have to say. You've had the DTs before. You know it and so do I."

Yeah, but the old Bobbi never would have brought it up . . . or at least not in that way.

"You touch it, you'll believe it. That's all I'm saying."

"You make it sound important to you."

Anderson shifted her feet restlessly.

"All right," Gardener said. "All right, Bobbi."

He reached out and grasped the edge of the ship, much as Anderson had that first day. He was aware—too aware—that an expression of naked eagerness had spread over Bobbi's face. It was the face of a someone who is waiting for a firecracker to go off.

Several things happened almost simultaneously.

The first was a sense of vibration settling into his hand—the sort of vibration one might feel when one lays a hand on a power pole carrying high-voltage wires. For a moment it seemed to numb his flesh, as if the vibration was moving at an incredibly high speed. Then the feeling was gone. As it went, Gardener's head filled with music, but it was so loud it was more like a scream than music. It made what he had heard the night before sound like a whisper in comparison—it was like being inside a stereo speaker turned all the way up.

Daytime turns me off and I don't mean maybe,
Nine-to-five ain't takin' me where I'm bound,
When it's done I come home to s—

He was opening his mouth to scream when it cut off, all at once. Gardener knew the song, which had been popular when he was in grade school, and later he sang the snatch of lyrics he had heard, looking at his watch as he did so. The sequence seemed to have been a second or two of high-speed vibration; a burst of ear-splitting music which had lasted roughly twelve seconds; then the bloody nose.

Except *ear*-splitting was wrong. It had been *head*-splitting. It had never come through his ears at all. It arrowed into his head from that damned piece of steel in his forehead.

He saw Anderson go staggering backward, her hands thrown out in what seemed to be a warding-off gesture. Her look of eagerness became one of surprised fear, bewilderment, and pain.

The last thing was that his headache was gone.

Utterly and completely gone.

But his nose was not just bleeding; it was *spouting*.

3

"Here, take it. Christ, Gard, are you all right?"

"I'll be fine," Gardener said, his voice slightly muffled by her handkerchief. He doubled it and settled it over his nose, pressing down firmly on the bridge. He tilted his head up, and the slimy taste of blood began to fill his throat. "I've had worse ones than this." So he had . . . but not for a long time.

They had moved back about ten paces from the edge of the cut and seated themselves on a felled tree. Bobbi was looking at him anxiously.

"Christ, Gard, I didn't know anything like *that* was going to happen. You believe me, don't you?"

"Yes," Gardener said. He didn't know precisely *what* Bobbi had been expecting . . . but not that. "Did you hear the music?"

"I didn't exactly *hear* it," Anderson said, "I got it secondhand from your head. It just about ruptured me."

"Did it?"

"Yeah." Bobbi laughed a little shakily. "When I'm around a lot of people, I turn 'em off—"

"You can do that?" He took the handkerchief off his nose. It was sopping with blood—Gardener could have twisted it between his fingers and wrung blood out of it in a gory little stream. But the flow was finally slowing down . . . thank God. He dropped the handkerchief and tore the tail off his shirt.

"Yes," Anderson said. "Well . . . not entirely. I can't turn the thoughts completely *off,* but I can dial them way down, so it's like . . . well, like a faint whisper at the bottom of my mind."

"That's incredible."

"That's *necessary,*" Anderson said grimly. "If I couldn't, I don't think I'd ever leave this goddam house again. I was in Augusta on Saturday and I opened my mind up to see what it'd be like."

"And you found out."

"Yeah, I found out. It was like having a hurricane in your head. And the scary thing was how hard it was to get the door shut again."

"This door . . . barrier . . . whatever . . . how do you put it up?"

Anderson shook her head. "Can't explain, anymore than a guy who can wiggle his ears can explain how *he* does it." She cleared her throat and looked down at her shoes for a moment—muddy workboots, Gardener saw. They looked as if they hadn't been off her feet much in the last couple of weeks.

Bobbi grinned a little. The grin was embarrassed and painfully humorous at the same time—and in that moment she looked completely like the old Bobbi. The one who had been his friend after nobody else wanted to be. It was Bobbi's *aw-shucks* look—Gardener had seen it the very first time he met her, when Bobbi was a freshman English student and Gardener a freshman English instructor banging apathetically away at a PhD thesis he probably knew even then he was never going to finish. Hung-over and feeling bilious, Gardener had asked the class of new freshmen what the dative case was. No one offered an answer. Gardener had been about to take great pleasure in blowing them all out of the water when Anderson, Roberta, Row 5, Seat 3, raised her hand and took a shot at it. Her answer was diffident . . . but correct. Not surprisingly, she turned out to be the only one of them who'd had Latin in high school. The same *aw-shucks* grin he was seeing now had been on Bobbi's face then, and Gard felt a wave of affection sweep over him. Shit, Bobbi had been through a tough time . . . but this *was* Bobbi. No question about it.

"I keep the barriers up most of the time anyway," she was saying. "Otherwise it's like peeking in windows. You remember me telling you my mailman, Paulson, has got something going on the side?"

Gardener nodded.

"That isn't anything I want to know. Or if some poor slob is a klepto, or if some guy's a secret drinker . . . how's your nose?"

"Bleeding's stopped." Gardener put down the bloody piece of shirting beside Bobbi's handkerchief. "So you keep the blocks up."

"Yes. For whatever reasons—moral, ethical, or just to keep from going batshit with the noise, I keep them up. With you I let them down because I wasn't getting squat even when I tried. I *did* try a couple of times, and if that makes you mad I understand, but it was only curiosity, because no one else is . . . blank . . . like that."

"No one?"

"Nope. There must be some reason for it, something like having a really rare blood type. Maybe that even *is* it."

"Sorry, I'm type O."

Anderson laughed and got up. "You feel up to going back, Gard?"

It's the plate in my head, Bobbi. He almost said it, and then, for some reason, decided not to. *The plate in my head is keeping you out. I don't know how I know that, but I do.*

"Yeah, I'm fine," he said. "I could use

(a drink)

a cup of coffee, that's all."

"You got it. Come on."

4

While part of her had been reacting to Gard with the warmth and genuine good feeling she had always felt for him, even during the worst times, another part of her (a part that was not, strictly speaking, Bobbi Anderson at all anymore) had stood coldly off to one side, watching everything carefully. Assessing. Questioning. And the first question was whether

(they)

she really wanted Gardener around at all. She

(they)

had thought at first that all her problems would now be

solved, Gard would join her on the dig and she would no longer have to do this . . . well, this first part . . . all alone. He was right about one thing: trying to do it all by herself had nearly killed her. But the change she had expected in him hadn't happened. Only that distressing nosebleed.

He won't touch it again if it makes his nose bleed like that. He won't touch it and he certainly won't go inside it.

It may not come to that. After all, Peter never touched it. Peter didn't want to go near it, but his eye . . . and the age reversal . . .

It's not the same. He's a man, not an old beagle dog. And, face it, Bobbi, except for the nosebleed and that blast of music, there was absolutely no change.

No immediate *change.*

Is it the steel plate in his skull?

Maybe . . . but why should something like that make any difference?

That cold part of Bobbi didn't know; she only knew that it could have. The ship itself broadcast some kind of tremendous, almost animate force; whatever had come in it was dead, she was sure she hadn't lied about that, but *the ship itself* was almost alive, broadcasting that enormous energy pattern through its metal skin . . . and, she knew, the broadcast area widened its umbrella a little with every inch of its surface she dug free. That energy *had* communicated itself to Gard. But then it had . . . what?

Been converted somehow. First converted and then blow off in a short, ferociously powerful radio transmission.

So what do I do?

She didn't know, but she knew it didn't matter.

They would tell her.

When the time came, *they* would tell her.

In the meantime, he would bear watching. But if only she could *read* him! It would be so much simpler if she could fucking *read* him!

A voice responded coldly: *Get him drunk. Then you'll be able to read him. Then you'll be able to read him just fine.*

5

They had come out on the Tomcat, which did not fly at all but rolled along the ground just as it always had—but instead of the former racket and roar of its engine, it now rolled in a complete silence that was somehow ghastly.

They came out of the woods and bumped along the edge of the garden. Anderson parked the Tomcat where it had been that morning.

Gardener glanced up at the sky, which was beginning to cloud over again, and said: "You better put it in the shed, Bobbi."

"It'll be all right," she said shortly. She pocketed the key and started toward the house. Gardener glanced toward the shed, started after Bobbi, then looked back. There was a big Kreig padlock on the shed door. Another new addition. The woods, you should pardon the pun, seemed to be full of them.

What have you got in there? A time machine that runs on Penlites? What's the New Improved Bobbi got in there?

6

When he came into the house, Bobbi was rummaging in the fridge. She came up with a couple of beers.

"Were you serious about coffee, or do you want one of these?"

"How about a Coke?" Gardener asked. "Flying saucers go better with Coke, that's my motto." He laughed rather wildly.

"Sure," Bobbi said, then stopped in the act of returning the cans of beer and grabbing two cans of Coke. "I did, didn't I?"

"Huh?"

"I took you out there and showed it to you. The ship. Didn't I?"

Jesus, Gardener thought. *Jesus Christ.*

For a moment, standing there with the bottles in her hands, she looked like someone with Alzheimer's disease.

"Yes," Gardener said, feeling his skin grow cold. "You did."

"Good," Bobbi said, relieved. "I thought I did."

"Bobbi? You all right?"

"Sure," Anderson said, and then added offhandedly, as if it were a thing of little or no importance: "It's just that I can't remember much from when we left the house until now. But I guess it doesn't really matter, does it? Here's your Coke, Gard. Let's drink to life on other worlds, what do you say?"

7

So they drank to other worlds and then Anderson asked him what they should do with the spaceship she had stumbled on in the woods behind her house.

"*We're* not going to do anything. *You're* going to do something."

"I already am, Gard," she said gently.

"Of course you are," he said a little testily, "but I'm talking about some final disposition. I'll be happy to give you all the advice you want—us drunken, bröken-down poets are great at giving advice—but in the end, *you're* going to do something. Something a little more far-reaching than just digging it up. Because it's yours. It's down on your land and it's yours."

Anderson looked shocked. "You don't really think that thing *belongs* to anyone, do you? Why, because Uncle Frank left me this place in his will? Because he had a clear title going back to part of a crown parcel that King George III swiped from the French after the French had swiped it from the Indians? Good Christ, Gard, that thing was fifty million years old when the forebears of the whole damned human race were squatting on their hunkers in caves and picking their noses!"

"I'm sure that's very true," Gardener said dryly, "but it doesn't change the law. And anyway, are you going to sit there and try to tell me you're not possessive of it?"

Anderson looked both upset and thoughtful.

"Possessive? No—I wouldn't say that. It's responsibility I feel, not possessiveness."

"Well, whatever. But since you asked my opinion, I'll give it to you. Call Limestone Air Force Base. Tell whoever answers that you've found an unidentified object down on your land that looks like an advanced flying machine of some sort. You might have some trouble at first, but you'll convince them. Then—"

Bobbi Anderson laughed. She laughed long and hard and loud. It was genuine laughter, and there was nothing mean about it, but it made Gardener feel acutely uncomfortable all the same. She laughed until tears streamed down her face. He felt himself stiffening.

"I'm sorry," she said, seeing his expression. "It's just that I can't believe I'm hearing this from you, of all people. You know . . . it's just . . ." She snorted laughter again. "Well, it's a shock. Like having a Baptist preacher advise drinking as a cure for lust."

"I don't understand what you mean."

"Sure you do. I'm listening to the guy who got arrested at Seabrook with a gun in his pack, the guy who thinks the government won't really be happy until we all glow in the dark like radium watches, tell me to just call up the Air Force so they can come down here and take charge of an interstellar spacecraft."

"It's your land—"

"Shit, Gard! My land is as vulnerable to the U.S. government's right of eminent domain as anyone else's. Eminent domain's what gets turnpikes built.

"And sometimes nuclear reactors."

Bobbi sat down again and looked at Gardener in level silence.

"Think about what you're saying," she said softly. "Three days after I made a call like that, neither the land nor the ship would be 'mine' anymore. Six days after, they'd have barbed wire strung around the whole place and sentries posted every fifty feet. Six *weeks* after, I think you'd probably find eighty percent of Haven's population bought out, kicked out . . . or simply lost. They could do it, Gard. You know they could. What it comes down to is this: you want me to pick up the phone and call the Dallas police."

"Bobbi—"

"Yes. That's what it boils down to. I've found an alien spacecraft and you want me to turn it over to the Dallas police. Do you think they're going to come down here and say, 'Please come to Washington with us, Ms. Anderson, the Joint Chiefs of Staff are very anxious to hear your ideas on this matter, not only because you own—well, *used* to own—the land the thing is on, but because the Joint Chiefs *always* poll western writers before they decide what they should do about such things. Also, the President wants you to pop around to the White

House so he can get your thinking. In addition, he wants to tell you how much he liked *Rimfire Christmas.*' "

Anderson threw back her head and this time the laughter she uttered was wild, hysterical, and quite creepy. Gardener barely noticed. *Did* he really think they were going to come down here and be polite? With something as potentially enormous as this on the line? The answer was no. They would take the land. They would gag him and Bobbi . . . but even that might not be enough to make them feel comfortable. Could be they'd wind up someplace like a weird cross between a Russian gulag and a posh Club Med resort. All the beads are free, and the only catch is you never get out.

Or even *that* might not be enough . . . so mourners please omit flowers. Then and only then could the ship's new caretakers sleep easy at night.

After all, it wasn't exactly an artifact, like an Etruscan vase or minié balls dug out of the ground at the site of some long-ago Civil War battle, was it? The woman who had found it had subsequently managed to power her entire house on D-cells . . . and he was now ready to believe that, even if the new gear on the Tomcat didn't work yet, it soon would.

And what, exactly, would *make* it work? Microchips? Semiconductors? No. *Bobbi* was the extra added ingredient, the New Improved Bobbi Anderson. *Bobbi.* Or maybe it was anybody who got close to the thing. And a thing like that . . . well, you couldn't let an ordinary private citizen hold on to it, now could you?

"Whatever else it is," he muttered, "the goddam thing must be one hell of a brain booster. It's turned you into a genius."

"No. An idiot savant," Anderson said quietly.

"What?"

"Idiot savant. They've got maybe half a dozen of them down at Pineland—that's the state facility for the severely retarded. I was there for two summers on a work-study program while I was in college. There was a guy who could multiply two six-digit numbers in his head and give you a correct answer in less than five seconds . . . and he was just as apt to piss in his pants while he was doing it as not. There was a twelve-year-old kid who was hydrocephalic. His head was as big as a prize pumpkin. But he could set perfectly justified type at the rate of a hundred and sixty words a minute. Couldn't talk, couldn't read, couldn't *think,* but he could set type like a hurricane."

Anderson pawed a cigarette out of the pack and lit it. Her eyes looked steadily at Gardener out of her thin, haggard face.

"That's what I am. An idiot savant. That's *all* I am, and they'd know it. Those things—customizing the typewriter, fixing the water heater—I only remember them in bits and pieces. When I'm *doing* them, everything seems as clear as a bell. But later—" She looked pleadingly at Gardener. "Do you get it?"

Gardener nodded.

"It's coming from the ship, like radio transmissions from a broadcast tower. But just because a radio can pick up transmissions and send them to a human ear, it's not *talking*. The government would be happy to take me, lock me up somewhere, and then to cut me into little pieces to see if there had been any physical changes . . . just as soon as my unfortunate accident gave them a reason to do an autopsy, that is."

"Are you sure you're not reading my mind, Bobbi?"

"No. But do you really think they'd scruple at wasting some people over a thing like this?"

Gardener slowly shook his head.

"So taking your advice would amount to this," Anderson said. "First, call the Dallas police; then get taken into custody by the Dallas police; then get killed by the Dallas police."

Gard looked at her, troubled, and then said, "All right. I cry uncle. But what's the alternative? You have to do *something*. Christ, the thing is *killing* you."

"What?"

"You've lost thirty pounds, how's that for a start?"

"Thir—" Anderson looked startled and uneasy. "No, Gard, no way. *Fifteen,* maybe, but I was getting love handles anyway, and—"

"Go weigh yourself," Gardener said. "If you can get the needle over ninety-five, even with your boots on, I'll eat the scale. Lose a few more pounds and you'll get sick. The state you're in, you could go into heartbeat arrhythmia and die in two days."

"I needed to lose some weight. And I was—"

"—too busy to eat, was that what you were going to say?"

"Well, not exactly in those w—"

"When I saw you last night, you looked like a survivor of the Bataan death march. You knew who I was, and that was *all* you knew. You're still not tracking. Five minutes after we got back in here from looking at your admittedly amazing find, you were asking me if you'd taken me to see it yet."

Bobbi's eyes were still on the table, but he could see her expression: it was set and sullen.

He touched her gently. "All I'm saying is that no matter how wonderful that thing in the woods is, it's done things to your body and mind that have been terrible for you."

Bobbi drew away from him. "If you're saying I'm crazy—"

"No, I'm not saying you're crazy, for God's sake! But you could *get* crazy if you don't slow down. Do you deny you've been having blackouts?"

"You're cross-examining me, Gard."

"And for a woman who was asking my advice fifteen minutes ago, you're being a pretty fucking hostile witness."

They glared at each other across the table for a moment.

Anderson gave first. "Blackouts isn't the right word. Don't try to equate what happens to you when you drink too much with what's been happening to me. They're not the same."

"I'm not going to argue semantics with you, Bobbi. That's a sidetrack and you know it. The thing out there is dangerous. That's what seems important to me."

Anderson looked up at him. Her face was unreadable. "You think it is," she said, the words making neither a question nor a declarative sentence—they came out perfectly flat and inflectionless.

"You haven't just been getting or receiving ideas," Gardener said. "You've been *driven.*"

"Driven." Anderson's expression did not change.

Gardener rubbed at his forehead. "Driven, yes. Driven the way a bad, stupid man will drive a horse until it drops dead in the traces . . . then stand over it and whip the carcass because the damned nag had the nerve to die. A man like that is dangerous to horses, and whatever there is in that ship . . . I think it's dangerous to Bobbi Anderson. If I hadn't shown up . . ."

"What? If you hadn't shown up, what?"

"I think you'd still be at it right now, working day and night, not eating . . . and that by this coming weekend you'd have been dead."

"I think not," Bobbi said coolly, "but just for the sake of argument, let's say you're right. I'm on track again now."

"You're *not* on track again, and you're *not* all right."

That mulish look was back on her face, that look which said Gard was talking trash Bobbi would just as soon not hear.

"Look," Gardener said, "I'm with you on at least one thing, all the way. This is the biggest, most important, utterly mind-blowing thing that's ever happened. When it comes out, the headlines in the New York *Times* are going to make it look like the *National Enquirer.* People are going to change their fucking *religions* over this, do you know it?"

"Yes."

"This isn't a powder keg; it's an A-bomb. Do you know *that?"*

"Yes," Anderson said again.

"Then get that pissed-off look off your face. If we're going to talk about it, let's fucking *talk* about it."

Anderson sighed. "Yeah. Okay. Sorry."

"I admit I was wrong about calling the Air Force."

They spoke together, then laughed together, and that was good.

Still smiling, Gard said: *"Something* has to be done."

"I'll buy that," Anderson said.

"But, Bobbi, Jesus! I flunked chemistry and barely got through funnybook physics. I don't know exactly, but I do know it's got to be . . . well . . . damped out, or something."

"We need some experts."

"That's right!" Gardener said, seizing on it. "Experts."

"Gard, all the experts work for the Dallas police."

Gardener threw his hands up in disgust.

"Now that you're here, I'll be all right. I know it."

"It's more likely to go the other way. Next thing, *I'll* start having blackouts."

Anderson said: "I think the risk might be worth it."

"You've decided already, haven't you?"

"I've decided what I *want* to do, yeah. What I want to do is keep quiet about it and finish the dig. Digging it all the way out shouldn't even be necessary. I think that once I—once *we,* I hope—can free it to a depth of another forty or fifty feet, we could come to a hatchway. If we can get inside . . ." Bobbi's eyes gleamed and Gardener felt an answering excitement rise in his own chest at the thought. All the doubts in the world could not hold back that excitement.

"If we can get inside?" Gardener repeated.

"If we can get inside, we can get at the controls. And if we can do that, I'm going to fly that fucker right out of the ground."

"You think you can do that?"

"I *know* I can."

"And then?"

"Then I don't know," Bobbi said, shrugging. It was the best, most efficient lie she had told so far . . . but Gardener thought it *was* a lie. "The next thing will happen, that's all I know."

"But you say it's my decision to make."

"Yes, I do. As far as the outside world goes, all I can do is continue to *not* tell. If you decide you *will,* well, what could I do to stop you? Shoot you with Uncle Frank's shotgun? I couldn't. Maybe a character in one of my books could, but *I* couldn't. This, unfortunately, is real life, where there are no real answers. I guess in real life I'd just stand here watching you go.

"But whoever you called, Gard—scientists from the university up in Orono, biologists from Jennings Labs, physicists from MIT—whoever you called, it would turn out you'd *actually* called the Dallas Police. You'd have people coming in here with trucks full of barbed wire and men with guns." She smiled a little. "At least I wouldn't have to go to that police-state Club Med alone."

"No?"

"No. You're in it now too. When they flew me out there, you'd be right beside me in the next seat." The wan smile broadened, but there still wasn't much humor in it. "Welcome to the monkey-house, my friend. Aren't you glad you came?"

"Charmed," Gardener said, and suddenly they were both laughing.

8

When the laughter passed, Gardener found that the atmosphere in Bobbi's kitchen had eased considerably.

Anderson asked: "What do you think would happen to the ship if the Dallas Police got hold of it?"

"Have you ever heard of Hangar 18?" Gard asked.

"No."

"According to the stories, Hangar 18's supposed to be part of an Air Force base outside of Dayton. Or Dearborn. Or somewhere. Anywhere, USA. It's where they're supposed to have the bodies of about five little men with fishy faces and gills on their necks. Saucerians. It's just one of those stories you hear, like how somebody found a rat head in his fast-food burger, or how there are alligators in the New York sewers. Only now I sort of wonder if it *is* a fairy tale. But I think that would be the end."

"Can I tell *you* one of those modern fairy tales, Gard?"

"Lay it on me."

"Have you ever heard the one," she asked, "about the guy who invented a pill to take the place of gasoline?"

9

The sun was going down in a bright blaze of reds and yellows and purples. Gardener sat on a big stump in Bobbi Anderson's back yard, watching it go. They had talked most of the afternoon, sometimes discussing, sometimes reasoning, sometimes arguing. Bobbi had ended the palaver by declaring herself ravenous again. She made a huge pot of spaghetti and broiled thick pork chops. Gardener had followed her out into the kitchen, wanting to reopen the discussion—thoughts were rolling around in his mind like balls on a pooltable. Anderson wouldn't allow it. She offered Gardener a drink, which Gardener, after a long, thoughtful pause, took. The whiskey went down good, and felt good, but he seemed to have no need for a second—well, no *great* need. Now, sitting here full of food and drink and looking at the sky, he supposed Bobbi had been right. They'd done all the constructive talking there was to do.

It was decision time.

Bobbi had eaten a tremendous supper. "You're gonna puke, Bobbi," Gardener said. He was serious but still couldn't help laughing.

"Nope," Bobbi said placidly. "Never felt better." She burped. "In Portugal, that's a compliment to the cook."

"And after a good lay—" Gard lifted one leg and broke wind. Bobbi laughed gustily.

They did the dishes ("Haven't invented anything to do this yet, Bobbi?" "It'll come, give me time.") and then they went into the small drab living room, which hadn't changed much since the time of Bobbi's uncle, to watch the evening news. None of it was very good. The Middle East was smoldering again, with Israel flying air strikes against Syrian ground forces in Lebanon (and hitting a school by accident—Gardener winced at the pictures of burned, screaming children), the Russians driving against the mountain strongholds of the Afghan rebels, a coup in South America.

In Washington, the NRC had issued a list of ninety nuclear facilities in thirty-seven states with safety problems ranging from "moderate to serious."

Moderate to serious, great, Gardener thought, feeling the old impotent rage stir and twist, biting into him like acid. *If we lose Topeka, that's moderate. If we lose New York, that's serious.*

He became aware that Bobby was looking at him a little sadly. "The beat goes on, right?" she said.

"Right."

When the news was over, Anderson told Gardener she was going to bed.

"At seven-thirty?"

"I'm still bushed." And she looked it.

"Okay. I'll sack out myself pretty soon. I'm tired too. It's been a crazy couple of days, but I'm not completely sure I'd sleep, the way this stuff is whizzing around in my head."

"You want a Valium?"

He smiled. "I saw they were still there. I'll pass. You were the one who could have used a trank or two, last couple of weeks."

The State of Maine's price for going along with Nora's decision not to press charges was that Gardener should go into a counseling program. The program had lasted six months; the Valium was apparently going to go on forever. Gardener hadn't actually taken any in almost three years, but every now and then—usually when he was going traveling—he filled the prescription. Otherwise, some computer might burp up his name and a psychologist picking up a few extra bucks courtesy of the State of Maine might drop by to make sure his head was staying shrunk to a suitable size.

After she was in bed, Gardener had turned off the TV and sat awhile in Bobbi's rocker, reading *The Buffalo Soldiers*. In a short time, he heard her snoring away. Gardener supposed Bobbi's snores would also be part of a conspiracy to keep him awake, but he didn't really mind—Bobbi had always snored, the price of a deviated septum, and that had always annoyed Gardener, but he had discovered last night that some things were worse. The ghastly silence in which she had slept on the couch, for instance. That was *much* worse.

Gardener had poked his head in for a moment, had seen Bobbi in a much more typical Bobbi Anderson sleeping posture, naked except pajama bottoms, small breasts bare, blankets kicked into disarray between her legs, one hand curled under her cheek, the other by her face, her thumb almost in her mouth. Bobbi was okay.

So Gardener had come out here to make his decision.

Bobbi's patch of garden was going great guns—the corn was taller than any Gardener had seen on his way north from Arcadia Beach, and her tomatoes were going to be blue-ribbon winners. Some of them would have come to the chest of a man walking down the row. In the middle of it all was a cluster of giant sunflowers, ominous as triffids, nodding in the slight breeze.

When Bobbi asked him earlier if he'd ever heard of the so-called "gasoline pill," Gardener had smiled and nodded. More twentieth-century fairy tales, all right. She'd then asked him if he believed it. Gardener, still smiling, said no. Bobbi reminded him about Hangar 18.

"Are you saying you *do* believe there's such a pill? Or *was?* Something you'd just drop into your gas tank and run on all day?"

"No," Bobbi said quietly. "Nothing I've ever read suggests the possibility of such a pill." She leaned forward, forearms on her thighs. "But I'll tell you what I *do* believe: if there *was*, it wouldn't be on the market. Some big cartel, or maybe the government itself, would buy it . . . or steal it."

"Yeah," Gard said. He had thought more than once about the crazy ironies inherent in every status quo: open the U.S. borders and put all those customs people out of work? Legalize dope and destroy the DEA? You might as well try to shoot the man in the moon with a BB gun.

Gard burst out laughing.

Bobbi looked at him, puzzled but also smiling a little. "So? Share."

"I was just thinking that if there *was* a pill like that, the Dallas Police would shoot the guy who invented it and then put it next to the green guys in Hangar 18."

"Not to mention his whole family," Bobbi agreed.

Gard didn't laugh this time. This time it didn't seem quite so hilarious.

"In that light," Anderson had said, "look at what I've done here. I'm not even a good handyman, let alone anyone's scientist, and so the force that worked through me produced a bunch of stuff that looks more like stuff from *Boy's Life* plans than anything else—built by a fairly incompetent boy, at that."

"They work," Gardener replied.

Yes, Anderson had agreed. They did. She even had a vague idea of *how* they worked—on a principle which could be called "collapsing-molecule fusion." It was nonatomic, totally clean. The telepathic typewriter, she said, depended on collapsing-molecule fusion for juice, but the actual *principle* of that one was much different, and she *didn't* understand it. There was a powerpack inside that had begun life as a fuzz-buster, but beyond that she was blank.

"You get a bunch of scientists in here from the NSA or the Shop, and they'd probably have this stuff down pat in six hours," Anderson said. "They'd go around looking like somebody just kicked them in the balls, asking each other how the hell they could have missed such elementary concepts for so long. And do you know what would happen next?"

Gardener thought about it hard, his head down, one hand gripping the can of beer Bobbi had given him, the other gripping his forehead, and suddenly he was back at that terrible party listening to Ted the Power Man defend the Iroquois plant, which even now was loading hot rods:

If we gave these nuke-freaks what they wanted, they'd turn around a month or so later and start whining about not being able to use their blow-dryers, or found out their Cuisinarts weren't going to work when they wanted to mix up a bunch of macrobiotic food. He saw himself leading Ted the Power Man over to Arberg's buffet—he saw this as clearly as if it had happened . . . shit, as if it was happening *right then.* On the table, between the chips and the bowl of raw veggies, was one of Bobbi's contraptions. The batteries were hooked up to a circuit board; that was in turn hooked up to an ordinary wall switch, the sort available in any hardware store for a buck or so. Gardener saw himself turn this switch, and suddenly everything on the table—chips, raw veggies, the lazy Susan with its five different kinds of dip, the remains of the cold cuts and the carcass of the chicken, the ashtrays, the drinks—rose six inches into the air and then simply held there, their shadows pooling decorously beneath them on the linen. Ted the Power Man looked at this for a moment, mildly annoyed. Then he swept the contraption off the table. The wires snapped. Batteries rolled hither and yon. Everything fell back to the table with a crash, glasses spilling, ashtrays overturning and scattering butts. Ted took off his sport coat and covered the remains of the gadget, the way you might cover the corpse of an animal hit and killed in the road. That done, he turned back to his small captive audience and resumed speaking. *These people think they can go on having their cake and eating it too forever. These people assume that there is always going to be a fallback position. They are wrong. There is no fallback position. It's simple: nukes or nothing.* Gardener heard himself screaming in a rage that was, for a change, totally sober: *What about the thing you just broke? What about* that? Ted bent and picked up his sport coat as gracefully as a magician waving his cape before a bedazzled audience. The floor beneath was bare except for a few potato chips. No sign of the gadget. No sign at all. *What about* what *thing?* Ted the Power Man asked, looking straight at Gardener with an expression of sympathy into which a liberal helping of contempt had been mixed. He turned to his audience. *Does anybody here see anything? . . . No,* they were answering in unison, like children reciting: Arberg, Patricia McCardle, all the rest; even the young bartender and Ron Cummings were reciting it. *No, we don't see anything, we don't see anything at all, Ted, not a thing, you're right, Ted, it's the nukes or nothing*. Ted was smiling. *Next thing you know, he'll be telling us that old wheeze about the itty-bitty pill you can put in your gas tank and run your car on all day*. Ted the Power Man began to laugh. All the others joined in. All of them were laughing at him.

Gardener raised his head and turned agonized eyes on Bobbi Anderson. "You think they'd . . . what? Classify all this?"

"Don't you?" And, after a moment, in a very gentle voice, Anderson prompted: "Gard?"

"Yes," Gardener said after a long time, and for a moment he was very close to bursting into tears. "Yeah, sure. Sure they would."

10

Now he sat on a stump in Bobbi's back yard without the slightest idea there was a loaded shotgun pointed at the back of his head.

He sat thinking of his mental replay of the party. It was so horrifying and so utterly obvious that he supposed he could be forgiven the time it had taken him to see it and grasp it. The ship in the earth could not be dealt with just on the basis of Bobbi's welfare, or Haven's welfare. Regardless of what it was or what it was doing to Bobbi or anyone else in the immediate area, the ultimate disposition of the ship in the earth would have to be made on the basis of the *world's* welfare. Gardener had served on dozens of committees whose goals ranged from the possible to the wildly crazed. He had marched; had given more than he could afford to help pay for newspaper ads in two unsuccessful campaigns to close Maine Yankee by referendum; as a college student he had marched against the U.S. involvement in Vietnam; he belonged to Greenpeace; he supported NARAL. In half a dozen muddled ways he had tried to deal with the world's welfare, but his efforts, although growing out of individual thought, had always been expressed as part of a group. Now . . .

Up to you, Gard-ole-Gard. Just you. He sighed. It was

like a sob. *Ring those funky changes, white boy . . . sure. But first ask yourself who* wants *the world to change? The unfed, the unwell, the unhomed, right? The parents of those kids in Africa with the big bellies and the dying eyes. The blacks in South Africa. The PLO. Does Ted the Power Man want a big helping of funky changes? Bite your tongue! Not Ted, not the Russian Politburo, not the Knesset, not the President of the United States, not the Seven Sisters, not Xerox, not Barry Manilow.*

Oh no, not the big boys, not the ones with the real power, the ones who drove the Status Quo Machine. Their motto was "Get the funk outta my face."

There was a time when he would not have hesitated for a moment, and that time was not so long past. Bobbi wouldn't have needed any arguments; Gard himself would have been the guy flogging the horse until its heart burst . . . only he would have been right there in harness too, pulling alongside. Here, at last, was a source of clean power, so abundant and easy to produce it might as well be free. Within six months, every nuclear reactor in the United States could be brought to a cold stop. Within a year, every reactor in the world. Cheap power. Cheap transport. Travel to other planets, even other star-systems seemed possible—after all, Bobbi's ship had not gotten to Haven, Maine, on the good ship *Lollypop*. It was, in fact—give us a drumroll, please, maestro—THE ANSWER TO EVERYTHING.

Are there weapons on board that ship, do you think?

He had started to ask Bobbi that and something had stopped his mouth. Weapons? Maybe. And if Bobbi could receive enough of that residual "force" to create a telepathic typewriter, could she also create something that would look like a *Flash Gordon* stun-gun but which might actually work? Or a disintegrator? A tractor-beam? Something which would, instead of just going *Brummmmmmm* or *Wacka-Wacka-Wacka,* would actually turn people into piles of smoldering ash? Possibly. And if not, wouldn't some of Bobbi's hypothetical scientists *adapt* things like the water-heater gadget or the customized Tomcat motor to something that would put a radical hurt on people? Sure. After all, long before toasters and hair dryers and baseboard heaters were ever thought of, the State of New York was using electricity to fry murderers at Sing-Sing.

What scared Gardener was that the idea of weapons held a certain attractiveness. Part of it, he supposed, was just self-interest. If the order came down to put a sport coat over the mess, then surely he and Bobbi would be part of what was to be covered. But beyond that were other possibilities. One of them, wild but not unattractive, was the idea that he and Bobbi might be able to kick a lot of asses that deserved kicking. The idea of sending happy-time folks like the Ayatollah into the Phantom Zone was so delightful that it almost made Gardener chuckle. Why wait for the Israelis and the Arabs to sort out their problems? And terrorists of all stripes . . . goodbye, fellas. Catch you on the flip-flop.

Wonderful, Gard! I love it! We'll put it on network TV! It'll be better than Miami Vice! *Instead of two fearless drug-busters, we got Gard and Bobbi, cruising the planet in their flying saucer! Gimme the phone, someone! I got to call CBS!*

You're not funny, Gardener thought.

Who's laughing? Isn't that what you're talking about? You and Bobbi playing the Lone Ranger and Tonto?

So what if it is? How long does it take before that option starts looking good? How many suitcase bombs? How many women shot in embassy toilets? How many dead kids? How long do we let it all go on?

Love it, Gard. "Okay, everyone on Planet Earth, sing along with Gard and Bobbi—just follow the bouncing ball: 'The aaanswer, my friend, is blooowin' in the wind . . .' "

You're disgusting.

And you're starting to sound downright dangerous. You remember how scared you were when that state trooper found the pistol in your pack? How scared you were because you didn't even remember putting it in there? *This is it all over again. The only difference is that now you're talking about a bigger caliber. Dear Christ, are you ever.*

As a younger man, these questions never would have occurred to him . . . and if they had, he would simply have brushed them aside. Apparently Bobbi already had. She was, after all, the one who had mentioned the man on horseback.

What do you mean, a man on horseback?

I mean us, Gard. But I think . . . I think I mostly mean you.

Bobbi, when I was twenty-five I burned all the time. When I was thirty, I burned some of the time. But the oxygen in here must be getting thin, because now I only burn when I'm drunk. I'm scared to climb up on that horse, Bobbi. If history ever taught me anything, it taught me that horses like to bolt.

He shifted on the stump again, and the shotgun followed him. Anderson sat in the kitchen on a stool, the barrels swiveling a bit on the window-sill with every move Gardener made. She was getting very little of his thoughts; it was frustrating, maddening. But she was getting enough to know that Gardener was approaching a decision . . . and when he made it, Anderson thought she would know what it was.

If it was the wrong one, she was going to blow off the back of his head and bury the body in the soft soil at the foot of the garden. She would hate to do that, but if she had to, she would.

Anderson waited calmly for the moment, her mind tuned to the faint run of Gardener's thoughts, making the tenuous connection.

It would not be long now.

11

What really scares you is the chance to deal from a position of strength for the first time in your miserable, confused life.

He sat up straighter, an expression of dismay on his face. It wasn't true, was it? *Surely* it wasn't.

Oh, but Gard, it is. You even root for baseball teams that are cataclysmic underdogs. That way you never have to worry about being depressed if one of them blows it in the World Series. It's the same with the candidates and the causes you support, isn't it? Because if your politics never get the chance to be tried out, you never have to worry about finding out that the new boss is the same as the old boss, do you?

I'm not scared. Not of that.

The fuck you're not. A man on horseback? You? *Man, that's a laugh. You'd have a heart attack if someone asked you to be a man on* a tricycle. *Your own personal life has been nothing but a constant effort to destroy every power base you have. Take marriage. Nora was tough, you finally had to shoot her to get rid of her, but when the chips were down, you didn't stick at it, did you? You're a man who manages to rise to every occasion, I'll give you that. You got yourself fired from your teaching job, thus eliminating another power base. You've spent twelve years pouring enough booze onto the little spark of talent God gave you to put it out. Now this. You better run, Gard.*

That's not fair! Honest to God, it's not!

No? Isn't there enough truth in it to make a comeuppance?

Maybe. Maybe not. Either way, he discovered that the decision had already been made. He would stick with Bobbi, at least for a while, do it her way.

Bobbi's blithe assurance that everything was just ducky didn't jibe very well with her exhaustion and weight loss. What the ship in the earth could do to Bobbi it would probably do to him. What had happened—or failed to happen—today proved nothing; he would not have expected all the changes to come at once. Yet the ship—and whatever force emanated from it—had a great capacity to do good. That was the main thing, and . . . well, *fuck* the Tommyknocker man.

Gardener got up and walked toward the house. The sun had gone down, and the twilight was turning ashy. His back was stiff. He stretched, standing on his toes, and grimaced as his spine crackled. He looked past the dark, silent shape of the Tomcat to the shed door with its new padlock. He thought of going to it, trying to look through one of the dirt-grimed windows . . . and decided not to. Perhaps he was afraid a white face would pop up inside the dark window, its grin showing a mouthful of filed cannibal teeth in a deadly ring. *Hello, Gard, you want to meet some* genuine *Tommyknockers? Come on in! There's lots of us in here!*

Gardener shivered—he could almost hear thin, evil fingers scrabbling on the panes. Too much had happened today and yesterday. His imagination had gotten out. Tonight it would walk and talk. He didn't know if he should hope for sleep or for it to stay away.

12

Once he was back inside, his uneasiness began to fade. With it went some of his craving for drink. He took off his shirt and then peered into Anderson's room. Bobbi lay just as she had lain before, blankets caught between her dreadfully thin legs, one hand thrown out, snoring.

Hasn't even moved. Christ, she must be tired.

He took a long shower, turning the water up as hot as he dared (with Bobbi Anderson's new water heater, that meant barely jogging the knob five degrees west of dead cold). When his skin began to turn red, he stepped out into a bathroom as steamy as London in the grip of a late-Victorian-era fog. He toweled, brushed his teeth with a finger—*got to do something about getting some supplies here,* he thought—and went to bed.

Drifting off, he found himself thinking again about the last thing Bobbi had said during their discussion. She believed the ship in the earth had begun to affect the townspeople. When he asked for specifics, she grew vague, then changed the subject. Gardener supposed anything was possible in this crazy business. Although the old Frank Garrick place was in the boonies, it was almost exactly in the geographic center of the township itself. There *was* a Haven Village, but that was five miles further north.

"You make it sound as if it was throwing off poison gas," he had said, hoping he didn't sound as uneasy as he felt. "Paraquat from Space. They Came from Agent Orange."

"Poison gas?" Bobbi repeated. She had gone off by herself again. Her face, so thin now, was closed and distant. "No, not poison gas. Call it *fumes* if you want to call it anything. But it's more than just the vibration when a person touches it."

Gardener said nothing, not wanting to break her mood.

"Fumes? Not that either. But *like* fumes. If EPA came in here with sniffers, I don't think they'd find any pollutants at all. If there's any actual, physical residue in the air, it's nothing but the tiniest trace."

"Do you think that's possible, Bobbi?" Gardener asked quietly.

"Yes. I'm not telling you I *know* that's what's happening,

because I don't. I have no inside information. But I think that a very thin layer of the ship's hull—and I mean *thin*, maybe no more than a single molecule or two in depth—could be oxidizing as I uncover it and the air hits it. That means I'd get the first, heaviest dose . . . and then it would go with the wind, like fallout. The people in town would get most of it . . . but 'most' would really mean 'damn little' in this case."

Bobbi shifted in her rocker and reached down with her right hand. It was a gesture Gardener had seen her make many times before, and his heart went out to his friend when he saw the look of sorrow cross Bobbi's face. Bobbi put her hand back into her lap.

"But I'm not sure that's what's going on at all, you know. There's a novel by a man named Peter Straub called *Floating Dragon*—have you read it?"

Gardener had shaken his head.

"Well, it postulates something similar to your Agent Orange from Space or Paraquat of the Gods or whatever you called it."

Gardener smiled.

"In the story, an experimental chemical is sucked out into the atmosphere and falls on a piece of suburban Connecticut. This stuff really *is* poison—a kind of insanity gas. People get in fights for no reason, some fellow decides to paint his whole house—including the windows—bright pink, a woman jogs until she drops dead of a massive coronary, and so on.

"There's another novel—this one is called *Brain Wave*, and it was written by . . ." Anderson wrinkled her brow, thinking. Her hand stole down to the right of the rocker again, then came back. "Same name as mine. Anderson. Poul Anderson. In that one, the earth passes through the tail of a comet and some of the fallout makes animals smarter. The book starts with a rabbit literally reasoning its way out of a trap."

"Smarter," Gardener echoed.

"Yes. If you had an IQ of 120 before the earth went through the comet, you'd end up with an IQ of 180. Get it?"

"Well-rounded intelligence?"

"Yes."

"But the term you used before was idiot savant. That's the exact opposite of well-rounded intelligence, isn't it? It's a kind of . . . of *bump*."

Anderson waved this aside. "Doesn't matter," she said.
Now, lying here in bed, drifting off to sleep, Gardener wondered.

13

That night he had a dream. It was simple enough. He was standing in darkness outside of the shed between the farmhouse and the garden. To his left, the Tomcat was a dark shape. He was thinking exactly what he had been thinking tonight—that he would go over and look in one of the windows. And what would he see? Why, the Tommyknockers, of course. But he wasn't afraid. Instead of fear he felt delighted, relieved joy. Because the Tommyknockers weren't monsters or cannibals; they were like the elves in that story about the good shoemaker. He would look in through the dirty shed window like a delighted child looking out a bedroom window in an illustration from "The Night Before Christmas" (and what was Santa Claus, that right jolly old elf, but a big old Tommyknocker in a red suit?), and he would see *them,* laughing and chattering as they sat at a long table, cobbling together power generators and levitating skateboards and televisions which showed mind-movies instead of regular ones.

He drifted toward the shed, and suddenly it was lighted by the same glare he had seen coming out of Bobbi's modified typewriter—it was as if the shed had turned into some weird jack-o'-lantern, only this light was not a warm yellow but an awful, rotten green. It spilled out between the boards; it spilled rays through knotholes and tattooed evil cats' eyes on the ground, it filled the windows. And *now* he was afraid, because no friendly little aliens from space made *that* light; if cancer had a color, it would be the one that spilled from every chink and crack and knothole and window of Bobbi Anderson's shed.

But he drew closer, because in dreams you can't always help yourself. He drew closer, no longer wanting to see, no more than a kid would want to look out his bedroom window on Christmas Eve and see Santa Claus striding along the snow-covered slope of roof across the way with a severed head in each gloved hand, the blood from the ragged necks steaming in the cold.

Please no, please no—

But he drew closer and as he entered that haze of green, rock music spilled into his head in a paralyzing, mind-splitting flood. It was George Thorogood and the Destroyers, and he knew that when George started to play that slide guitar, his skull would vibrate for a moment with killing harmonics and then simply explode like the water glasses in the house he had once told Bobbi about.

None of it mattered. The fear mattered, that was all—the fear of the Tommyknockers in Bobbi's shed. He sensed them, could almost *smell* them, a rich, electric smell like ozone and blood.

And . . . the weird liquid sloshing sounds. He could hear those even over the music in his head. It sounded like an old-fashioned washing machine, except that sound wasn't water, and that sound was wrong, wrong, *wrong*.

As he stood on his tiptoes to look into the shed, his face as green as the face of a corpse pulled out of quicksand, George Thorogood started to play that slide blues guitar, and Gardener began screaming with pain—and *that* was when his head exploded and he woke sitting bolt upright in the old double bed in the guestroom, his chest covered with sweat, his hands trembling.

He lay down again, thinking: *God! If you're going to have nightmares about it, take a look in tomorrow. Get your mind easy.*

He had expected nightmares in the wake of his decision; he lay back down again, thinking that this was only the first. But there were no more dreams.

That night.

The next day he joined Bobbi on the dig.

BOOK II

Tales of Haven

The terrorist got bombed!
The President got hit!
Security was tight!
The Secret Service got lit!
And everybody's drunk,
Everybody's wasted,
Everybody's stoned,
And there's nothin gonna change it,
Cause everybody's drunk,
Everybody's wasted,
Everybody's drinkin on the job.

—THE RAINMAKERS,
"Drinkin' on the Job"

Then he ran all the way to town, screamin
"It came out of the sky!"

—CREEDENCE CLEARWATER REVIVAL,
"It Came Out of the Sky"

1.

THE TOWN

1

The town had four other names before it became Haven.

It began municipal existence in 1816 as Montville Plantation. It was owned, lock, stock, and barrel, by a man named Hugh Crane. Crane purchased it in 1813 from the Commonwealth of Massachusetts, of which Maine was then a province. He had been a lieutenant in the Revolutionary War.

The Montville Plantation name was a gibe. Crane's father had never ventured east of Dover in his life, and remained a loyal Tory when the break with the colonies came. He ended life as a peer of the realm, the twelfth Earl of Montville. As his eldest son, Hugh Crane would have been the thirteenth Earl of Montville. Instead, his enraged father disinherited him. Not put out of countenance in the slightest, Crane went about cheerfully calling himself the first earl of Central Maine and sometimes the Duke of Nowhere at All.

The tract of land which Crane called Montville Plantation consisted of about twenty-two thousand acres. When Crane petitioned and was granted incorporated status, Montville Plantation became the one hundred and ninety-third town to be so incorporated in the Massachusetts Province of Maine. Crane bought the land because good timber was plentiful, and Derry, where timber could be floated downriver to the sea, was only twenty miles away.

How cheap was the area of land which eventually became Haven?

Hugh Crane had bought the whole shebang for the equivalent of eighteen hundred pounds.

Of course, a pound went a lot further in those days.

2

When Hugh Crane died in 1826, there were a hundred and three residents of Montville Plantation. Loggers swelled the population to twice that for six or seven months of the year, but they didn't really count, because they took their little bit of money into Derry, and it was in Derry that they usually settled when they grew too old to work the woods anymore. In those days, "too old to work the woods anymore" usually meant about twenty-five.

Nevertheless, by 1826 the settlement which would eventually become Haven Village had begun to grow up along the muddy road leading north toward Derry and Bangor.

Whatever you called it (and eventually it became, except in the memory of the oldest old-timers, like Dave Rutledge, plain old Route 9), that road was the one the loggers had to take when they went to Derry at the end of each month to spend their pay drinking and whoring. They saved their serious spending for the big town, but most were willing to bide long enough at Cooder's Tavern and Lodging-House to lay the dust with a beer or two on the way. This wasn't much, but it was enough to make the place a successful little business. The General Mercantile across the road (owned and operated by Hiram Cooder's nephew) was less successful but still a marginally profitable business. In 1828, a Barber Shop and Small Surgery (owned and operated by Hiram Cooder's cousin) opened next to the General Mercantile. In those days it was not unusual to stroll into this lively, growing establishment and see a logger reclining in one of the three chairs, having the hair on his head cut, the cut in his arm stitched, and a couple of large bloodsuckers from the jar by the cigar-box reposing above each closed eye, turning from gray to red as they swelled, simultaneously protecting against any infection from the cut and taking away that malady which was then known as "achin' brains." In 1830, a hostelry and feed store (owned by Hiram Cooder's brother George) opened at the south end of the village.

In 1831, Montville Plantation became Coodersville.

No one was very surprised.

Coodersville it remained until 1864, when the name was changed to Montgomery, in honor of Ellis Montgomery, a local boy who had fallen at Gettysburg, where, some say, the 20th Maine preserved the Union all by itself. The change seemed a fine idea. After all, the town's one remaining Cooder, crazy old Albion, had gone bankrupt and committed suicide two years before.

In the years following the end of the Civil War, a craze, as inexplicable as most crazes, swept the state. This craze was not for hoop skirts or sideburns; it was a craze for giving small towns classical names. Hence, there is a Sparta, Maine; a Carthage; an Athens; and, of course, there was Troy right next door. In 1878, the residents of the town voted to change the town's name yet *again,* this time from Montgomery to Ilium. This provoked a tearful tirade at town meeting from the mother of Ellis Montgomery. In truth, the tirade was more senile than ringing, the hero's mother being by then full of years—seventy-five of them, to be exact. Town legend has it that the townsfolk listened patiently, a little guiltily, and that the decision might even have been recanted (Mrs. Montgomery was surely right, some thought, when she said that fourteen years was hardly the "immortal memory" her dead son had been promised at the name-changing ceremonies which had taken place on July 4th, 1864) if the good lady's bladder hadn't picked that particular moment to let go. She was helped from the town-meeting hall, still ranting about ungrateful Philistines who would rue the day.

Montgomery became Ilium, just the same.

Twenty-two years passed.

3

Came a fast-talking revival preacher who for some reason bypassed Derry and elected instead to spread his tent in Ilium. He went by the name of Colson, but Myrtle Duplissey, Haven's self-appointed historian, eventually became convinced that Colson's real name was Cooder, and that he was the illegitimate son of Albion Cooder.

Whoever he was, he won most of the Christians in town over to his own lively version of the faith by the time the corn was ready for picking—much to the despair of Mr. Hartley, who ministered to the Methodists of Ilium and Troy, and Mr. Crowell, who looked after the spiritual welfare of Baptists in Ilium, Troy, Etna, and Unity (the joke in those days was that Emory Crowell's parsonage belonged to the town of Troy, but his piles belonged to God). Nevertheless, their exhortations were voices crying in the wilderness. Preacher Colson's congregation continued to grow as that well-nigh perfect summer of 1900 drew toward its conclusion. To call the crops of that year "bumpers" was to poor-mouth them; the thin northern New England earth, usually as stingy as Scrooge, that year poured forth a bounty which seemed never-ending. Mr. Crowell, the Baptist whose piles belonged to God, grew depressed and silent and, three years later, hung himself in the cellar of the Troy parsonage.

Mr. Hartley, the Methodist minister, grew ever more alarmed by the evangelical fervor which was sweeping Ilium like a cholera epidemic. Perhaps this was because Methodists are, under ordinary circumstances, the most undemonstrative worshipers of God; they listen not to sermons but to "messages," pray mostly in decorous silence, and consider the only proper places for congregation-spoken amens to be at the end of the Lord's Prayer and those few hymns not sung by the choir. But now these previously undemonstrative people were doing everything from speaking in tongues to holy rolling. Next, Mr. Hartley sometimes said, they will be handling snakes. The Tuesday, Thursday, and Sunday meetings in the revival tent beside Derry Road became steadily louder, wilder, and more emotionally explosive. "If it was happening in a carnival tent, they'd call it hysteria," he told Fred Perry, a church deacon and his only close friend, one night over glasses of sherry in the church rectory. "Because it's happening in a revival tent, they can get away with calling it Pentecostal Fire."

Rev. Hartley's suspicions of Colson were amply justified in the course of time, but before then Colson fled, having harvested a goodly crop of cold cash and warm women instead of punkins and taters. And before then he put his lasting stamp on the town by changing its name for the final time.

His sermon on that hot August night began with the subject of the harvest as a symbol of God's great reward, and then moved on to the subject of this very town. By this time, Colson had stripped off his frock coat. His sweatsoaked hair had tumbled in his eyes. The sisters had commenced getting down in the amen corner, although it would be yet a while before the speaking in tongues and the holy rolling got going.

"I consider this town sanctified," Colson told his audience, gripping the sides of his pulpit with his big hands—he might have considered it sanctified for some reason other than the fact that his honored self had chosen it in which to spread his tent (not to mention his seed), but if so, he didn't say so. "I consider it a *haven.* Yes! I have found a haven here that reminds me of my haven-home, a lovely land maybe not so different from the one Adam and Eve knew before they went picking fruit from that tree they should have left alone. *Sanctified!*" Preacher Colson bellowed. Years after, there were members of his congregation who still spoke admiringly of how that man could shout for Jesus, scoundrel or not.

"Amen!" the congregation cried back. The night, though warm, was perhaps not quite warm enough to completely explain the blushes on so many feminine cheeks and brows; such flushes had become common since Preacher Colson came to town.

"This town is nothing short of a glory to *God!*"

"Hallelujah!" the congregation yelled jubilantly. Breasts heaved. Eyes sparkled. Tongues slipped out and wetted lips.

"This town has got a *promise!*" Preacher Colson shouted, now striding rapidly back and forth, occasionally flicking his black locks back from his forehead with a quick snap that showed his cleanly corded neck to good advantage. "This town has got a *promise* and that *promise* is the fullness of the *harvest,* and *that promise shall be fulfilled!*"

"Praise Jesus!"

Colson came back to the pulpit, grasped it, and looked out at them forbiddingly. "So why you want to have a town which promises the *harvest* of God and the *haven* of God—why you want to have a town that speaks of those things named after some dago is more than I can figure out, brethern. Must have been the devil working somewhere in the last generation is all I can figure."

Talk about changing the town's name from Ilium to Haven began the very next day. The Rev. Mr. Crowell protested the change listlessly, the Rev. Mr. Hartley much more strongly. Ilium's selectmen were neutral, except to point out that it would cost the town twenty dollars to change the Papers of Incorporation on file in Augusta, and probably another twenty to change the municipal road signs. Not to mention the letterheads on town documents and stationery.

Long before the March town meeting at which Article 14, "To see if the town will approve changing the name of Incorporated Maine Town #193 from ILIUM to HAVEN," was discussed and voted on, Preacher Colson had literally folded his tent and stolen into the night. Said folding and stealing took place on the night of September 7th, following what Colson had for weeks been calling the great Harvest Home Revival of 1900. He'd been making it clear for at least a month that he considered it the most important meeting he would hold in town this year; perhaps the most important meeting he *ever* held, even if he should settle here, something he felt more and more often that God was calling him to do—and didn't *that* news just make the ladies' hearts go pitty-pat! It was, he said, to be a great love-offering to the loving God who had provided the town with such a wonderful growing season and harvest.

Colson did some harvesting of his own. He began by cajoling the attendees to give the largest "love-offering" of his stay, and finished by plowing and planting not two, not four, but *six* young maidens in the field behind the tent after the meeting.

"Men love to talk big, but I guess most of em pack derringers in their pants no matter how big they *talk,*" old Duke Barfield said in the barbershop one evening. If there had been a Stinkiest Man in Town contest, old Duke would have won hands down. He smelled like a pickled egg that has spent a month in a mud puddle. He was listened to, but at a distance, and upwind, if there was a wind to make this possible. "I *heerd* o men with double-barrel shotguns in their pants, and I reckon it's so every once n agin, and once't I even heerd tell o some fella had him a three-shot pistol, but that fucker Colson's the *only* man I ever heerd of who come packin a six-shooter."

Three of Preacher Colson's conquests were virgins before the invasion of the Pentecostal pecker.

The love-offering that night in the late summer of 1900 was indeed generous, although the barbershop gossips differed on just how generous the *monetary* part of it had been. All agreed that, even before the great Harvest Home Revival, where the preaching had gone on until ten, the gospel-singing until midnight, and the field-fucking until well past two, there had been a great outpouring of hard cash. Some also pointed out that Colson hadn't had many expenses during his stay, either. The women damn near fought for the privilege of bringing him his meals, the fellow who now owned the hostelry made him the long-term loan of a buggy . . . and, of course, no one at all charged him for his nightly entertainments.

On the morning of September 8th, tent and preacher were gone. He had harvested well . . . and seeded with equal success. Between January lst and town meeting in late March 1901, nine illegitimate children, three girls and six boys, were born in the area. All nine of these "love-children" bore a remarkable resemblance each to the other—six had blue eyes, and all were born with lusty crops of black hair. The barbershop gossips (and no group of men on earth can so successfully marry logic and prurience as these idlers farting into wicker chairs as they roll cigarettes or drive brown bullets of tobacco-juice into tin spittoons) also pointed out that it was hard telling just how many young girls had left "to visit relatives" downstate, in New Hampshire, or even all the way down to Massachusetts. It was also pointed out that quite a few *married* women in the area had given birth between January and March. About those women, who knew for sure? But the barbershop gossips of course knew what had happened on March 29th, after Faith Clarendon gave birth to a bouncing eight-pound baby boy. A wild wet norther was whooping around the eaves of the Clarendon house, dropping 1901's last large budget of snow until November. Cora Simard, the midwife who had delivered the baby, was in a half-doze by the kitchen stove, waiting for her husband Irwin to finally make his way through the storm and take her home. She saw Paul Clarendon approach the crib where his new son lay—it was on the other side of the stove, in the corner which was warmest—and stand looking fixedly down at the new baby for over an hour. Cora made the dreadful error of mistaking Paul Clarendon's fixed stare for wonder and love. Her eyes drifted closed. When she awoke from her doze, Paul Clarendon was standing over the crib with his straight-razor in his hand. He seized the baby by its thick crop of blue-black hair, and before Cora could unlock her throat to scream, he had cut its throat. He left the room without a word. A moment later she heard wet gargling sounds coming from the bedroom. When a terrified Irwin Simard finally found the courage to enter the Clarendon bedroom, he found man and wife on the bed, hands joined. Clarendon had cut his wife's throat, laid down beside her, grasped her right hand with his left, and then cut his own. All this happened two days after the town had voted to change its name.

4

The Rev. Mr. Hartley was dead-set against changing the town's name to one suggested by a man who had proved to be a thief, fornicator, false prophet, and all-around snake in the grass. He had said as much from his pulpit and had noted the agreeing nods from his parishioners with an almost vindictive pleasure that was really not much like him. He came to the town meeting held on March 27th, 1901, confident that Article 14 would be resoundingly voted down. He was not even troubled by the brevity of discussion between the Town Clerk's reading of the article and Head Selectman Luther Ruvall's laconic, "What's y'pleasure, people?" If he had had the slightest inkling, Hartley would have spoken vehemently, even furiously, for the only time in his life. But he never had so much as an inkling.

"Those in favor signify by sayin aye," Luther Ruvall said, and at the solid—if not very passionate—*Aye!* that shook the roof-beams, Hartley felt as if he had been punched in the gut. He stared around wildly, but it was too late. The strength of the *Aye!* had taken him so totally by surprise that he had no idea how many from his own congregation had turned on him and voted the other way.

"Wait—" he said aloud in a strangled voice that nobody heard.

"Those opposed?"

A scattered straggle of *Nays.* Hartley tried to scream his, but the only sound to escape his throat was a nonsense syllable—*Nik!*

"Motion's carried," Luther Ruvall said. "Now, Article 15—"

The Rev. Mr. Hartley suddenly felt warm—much *too* warm. He felt, in fact, as though he might faint. He pushed his way through standing throngs of men in red-and-black-checked shirts and muddy flannel pants, through clouds of acrid smoke puffed from corncobs and cheap cigars. He still felt faint, but now he felt that he might also vomit *before* he fainted. A week later he would not be able to understand the depth of his shock, so deep it was really horror. A year later he would not even acknowledge that he had felt such an emotion.

He stood on the top town-hall step, snatching great swoops of forty-degree air, clutching the handrail in a death-grip, and looked out across fields of melting snow. In places it had now drawn back enough to show the muddy earth beneath, and he thought with vicious crudity that was *also* unlike him that the fields looked like splotches of shit on the tail of a nightshirt. For the first and only time, he felt a bitter envy for Bradley Colson—or Cooder, if that was his real name. Colson had run away from Ilium . . . oh, beg your pardon, from *Haven.* He had run, and now Donald Hartley found himself wishing *he* could do the same. *Why did they do it?* Why? *They knew what he was, they* knew! *So why did they—*

A strong, warm hand fell on his back. He turned and saw his good friend Fred Perry. Fred's long, homely face looked distressed and concerned, and Hartley felt an unwilling smile cross his face.

"Don, are you all right?" Fred Perry asked.

"Yes. I had a moment in there when I felt light-headed. It was the vote. I didn't expect it."

"Nor I," Fred replied.

"My parishioners were part of it," Hartley said. "They had to have been. It was so loud, they had to have been, don't you think?"

"Well . . ."

The Rev. Mr. Hartley smiled a little. "I apparently do not know as much about human nature as I thought I did."

"Come back in, Don. They're going to take up paving Ridge Road."

"I think I'll stay out awhile longer," Hartley said, "and think about human nature." He paused, and just as Fred Perry was turning to go back, the Rev. Mr. Donald Hartley asked, almost appealed: "Do *you* understand, Fred? Do you understand why they did it? You're almost ten years older than I. Do you understand it?"

And Fred Perry, who had shouted out his own *Aye!* from behind a curled fist, shook his head and said no; he didn't understand at all. He *did* like the Rev. Mr. Hartley. He *did* respect the Rev. Mr. Hartley. But in spite of those things (or maybe—just maybe—because of them), he had taken a mean and spiteful pleasure in voting for a name suggested by Colson: Colson the false prophet, Colson the confidence man, Colson the thief, Colson the seducer.

No, Fred Perry did not understand human nature at all.

2.

'BECKA PAULSON

1

Rebecca Bouchard Paulson was married to Joe Paulson, one of Haven's two mail carriers and one-third of Haven's postal staff. Joe was cheating on his wife, something Bobbi Anderson knew already. Now 'Becka Paulson knew it as well. She had known it for the last three days. Jesus told her. In the last three days or so, Jesus had told her the most amazing, terrible, distressing things imaginable. They sickened her, they destroyed her sleep, they were destroying her sanity . . . but weren't they also sort of wonderful? Boy howdy! And would she stop listening, maybe just tip Jesus over on His face, or scream at Him to shut up? Absolutely not. For one thing, there was a grisly sort of compulsion in knowing the things Jesus told her. For another, He was the Savior.

Jesus was on top of the Paulsons' Sony TV. He had been there for just six years. Before that, He had rested atop two Zeniths. 'Becka estimated that Jesus had been in roughly the same spot for about sixteen years. Jesus was represented in lifelike 3-D. This was a picture of Him that 'Becka's older sister, Corinne, who lived in Portsmouth, had given them as a wedding present. When Joe commented that 'Becka's sister was a little on the cheap side, wa'ant she, 'Becka told him to hush up. Not that she was terribly surprised; you couldn't expect a man like Joe to understand the fact that you couldn't put a price-tag on true Beauty.

In the picture, Jesus was dressed in a simple white robe and holding a shepherd's staff. The Christ on 'Becka's TV combed His hair a little bit like Elvis after Elvis got out of the Army. Yes; he looked quite a bit like Elvis in *G.I. Blues.* His eyes were brown and mild. Behind Him, in perfect perspective, sheep as white as the linens in TV soap commercials trailed off and over the horizon. 'Becka and Corinne had grown up on a sheep farm in New Gloucester, and 'Becka knew from personal experience that sheep were *never* that white and uniformly woolly, like little fair-weather clouds fallen to earth. But, she reasoned, if Jesus could turn water into wine and bring the dead back to life, there was no reason at all why He couldn't make the shit caked around a bunch of lambs' rumps disappear if He wanted to.

A couple of times Joe had tried to move that picture off the TV, and she supposed that now she knew why, oh yessirree! Boy howdy! Joe, of course, had his trumped-up tales. "It doesn't seem right to have Jesus on top of the television while we're watching *Magnum* or *Miami Vice,*" he'd say. "Why not put it up on your bureau, 'Becka? Or . . . I'll tell you what! Why not put it up on your bureau until *Sunday,* then you can bring it down and put it back while you watch Jimmy Swaggart and Jack van Impe? I'll bet Jesus likes Jimmy Swaggart a helluva lot better than He likes *Miami Vice.*"

She refused.

Another time he said, "When it's my turn to have the Thursday-night poker game, the guys don't like it. No one wants to have Jesus Christ looking at him while he tries to draw to an inside straight."

"Maybe they feel uncomfortable because they know gambling's the devil's work," 'Becka said.

Joe, a good poker player, bridled. "Then it was the devil's work bought you your blow-dryer and that garnet ring you like s'well," he said. "Better take 'em back for refunds and give the money to the Salvation Army. I think I got the receipts in my den."

So she allowed Joe to turn the 3-D picture of Jesus around on the one Thursday night a month that he had his dirty-talking, beer-swilling friends in to play poker . . . but that was all.

And now she knew the *real* reason he had wanted to get rid of that picture. He must have had the idea all along that that picture might be a *magic* picture. Oh, she supposed "sacred" was a better word, magic was for pagans, headhunters and cannibals and Catholics and people like that, but they almost came to the same thing, didn't they? Anyway, Joe must have sensed that picture was special, that it would be the means by which his sin would be found out.

Oh, she supposed she had known *something* was going on. He was never after her at night anymore, and while that was something of a relief (sex was just as her mother had told her it would be, nasty, brutish, sometimes painful, always humiliating), she had also smelled perfume on his collar from time to time, and *that* was not a relief at all. She supposed she could have ignored the connection—the fact that the pawings had stopped at the same time that occasional smell of perfume started showing up in his collars—indefinitely if the picture of Jesus on top of the Sony hadn't begun to speak on July 7th. She could even have ignored a third factor: at about the same time the pawings had stopped and the perfume smells had begun, old Charlie Estabrooke had retired from the post office and a woman named Nancy Voss had come up from the Augusta post office to take his place. She guessed that the Voss woman (whom 'Becka now thought of simply as The Hussy) was perhaps five years older than she and Joe, which would make her around fifty, but she was a trim, well-kept fifty. 'Becka would admit she herself had put on a little weight, going from one hundred and twenty-six to two hundred and three, most of that since Byron, their only chick, had left home.

She could have ignored it, *would* have ignored it, perhaps even have come to tolerate it with relief; if The Hussy enjoyed the animalism of sexual congress, with its gruntings and thrustings and that final squirt of sticky stuff that smelled faintly like codfish and looked like cheap dish detergent, then it only proved The Hussy was little more than an animal herself. Also, it freed 'Becka of a tiresome, if ever-more-occasional, obligation. She could have ignored it, that was, if the picture of Jesus hadn't spoken up.

It happened for the first time at just past three in the afternoon on Thursday. 'Becka was coming back into the living room from the kitchen with a little snack (half a coffee cake and a beer stein filled with cherry Za-Rex) to watch *General Hospital.* She could no longer really believe that Luke and Laura would ever come back, but she was not able to *completely* give up hope.

She was bending down to turn on the TV when Jesus said, " 'Becka, Joe is putting it to that Hussy down at the pee-oh just about every lunch-hour and sometimes after quitting time, too. Once he was so randy he put it to her while he was supposed to be helping her sort the mail. And do you know what? She never even said 'At least wait until I get the first-class took care of.'

"And that's not all," Jesus said. He walked halfway across the picture, His robe fluttering around His ankles, and sat down on a rock that jutted from the ground. He held His staff between his knees and looked at her grimly. "There's a lot going on in Haven. You won't believe the half of it."

'Becka screamed again and fell on her knees. "My Lord!" she shrieked. One of her knees landed squarely on her piece of coffee cake (which was roughly the size and thickness of the family Bible), squirting raspberry filling into the face of Ozzie, the cat, who had crept out from under the stove to see what was going on. "My Lord! My Lord!" 'Becka continued to shriek. Ozzie ran, hissing, for the kitchen, where he crawled under the stove again with red goo dripping from his whiskers. He stayed there the rest of the day.

"Well, none of the Paulsons was ever good for much," Jesus said. A sheep wandered toward Him and He whacked it away, using His staff with an absentminded impatience that reminded 'Becka, even in her current frozen state, of her late father. The sheep went, rippling slightly because of the 3-D effect. It disappeared, actually seeming to *curve* as it went off the edge of the picture . . . but that was just an optical illusion, she felt sure. "Nossir!" Jesus declared. "Joe's great-uncle was a murderer, as you well know, 'Becka. Murdered his son, his wife, and then himself. And when he came up here, do you know what We said? 'No room!' that's what We said." Jesus leaned forward, propped on His staff. " 'Go see Mr. Splitfoot down below,' We said. 'You'll find your Haven-home, all right. But you may find your new landlord asks a hell of a high rent and never turns down the heat,' We said." Incredibly, Jesus winked at her . . . and that was when 'Becka fled, shrieking, from the house.

2

She stopped in the back yard, panting, her mousy blond hair hanging in her face, her heart beating so fast that it frightened her. No one had heard her shriekings and carryings-on, thank the Lord; she and Joe lived far out on the Nista Road, and their nearest neighbors were the Brodskys, who lived in that slutty trailer. The Brodskys were half a mile away. That was good. Anyone who *had* heard her would have thought there was a crazywoman down at the Paulsons'.

Well there is, *isn't there? If you think that picture started to talk, why, you* must *be crazy. Daddy'd beat you three shades of blue for saying such a thing—one for lying, another for believing it, and a third for raising your voice. 'Becka, pictures don't talk.*

No . . . nor did it, another voice spoke up suddenly. *That voice came out of your own head, 'Becka. I don't know how it could be . . . how you could know such things . . . but that's what happened. You made that picture of Jesus talk your own self, like Edgar Bergen used to make Charlie McCarthy talk on the Ed Sullivan show.*

But somehow that idea seemed more frightening, more downright *crazy,* than the idea that the picture itself had spoken, and she refused to allow it mental house-room. After all, miracles happened every day. There was that Mexican fellow who had found a picture of the Virgin Mary baked into an enchilada, or something. There were those miracles at Lourdes. Not to mention those children that had made the headlines of one of the tabloids—they had cried rocks. These were bona fide *miracles* (the children who wept rocks was, admittedly, a rather gritty one), as uplifting as a Pat Robertson sermon. Hearing voices was just nuts.

But that's what happened. And you've been hearing voices for quite a while now, haven't you? You've been hearing his *voice. Joe's. And that's where it came from. Not from Jesus but from Joe—*

"No," 'Becka whimpered. "I ain't heard any voices in my *head.*"

She stood by her clothesline in the back yard, looking blankly off toward the woods on the other side of the

Nista Road. They were hazy in the heat. Less than half a mile into those woods, as the crow flew, Bobbi Anderson and Jim Gardener were steadily unearthing more and more of a titanic fossil in the earth.

Crazy, her dead father's implacable voice tolled in her head. *Crazy with the heat. You come on over here, 'Becka Bouchard, I'm gonna beat you three shades of blister-blue for that crazy talk.*

"I ain't heard no voices in my *head*," 'Becka moaned. "That picture really *did* talk, I swear, I can't *do* ventriloquism!"

Better the picture. If it was the picture, it was a miracle, and miracles came from God. A miracle could drive you nuts—and dear God knew she felt like she was going nuts right now—but it didn't mean you were crazy to *start* with. Hearing voices in your head, however, or believing that you could hear other people's thoughts . . .

'Becka looked down, and saw blood gushing from her left knee. She shrieked again and ran back into the house to call the doctor, Medix, somebody, anybody. She was in the living room again, pawing at the dial with the phone to her ear, when Jesus said:

"That's just raspberry filling from your coffee cake, 'Becka, Why don't you just cool it before you have a heart attack?"

She looked at the Sony, the telephone receiver falling to the table with a clunk. Jesus was still sitting on the rock outcropping. It looked as though He had crossed His legs. It was really surprising how much He looked like her father . . . only He didn't seem forbidding, ready to be angry at a moment's notice. He was looking at her with a kind of exasperated patience.

"Try it and see if I'm not right," Jesus said.

She touched her knee gently, wincing, anticipating pain. There was none. She saw the seeds in the red stuff and relaxed. She licked the raspberry filling off her fingers.

"Also," Jesus said, "you have got to get these ideas about hearing voices and going crazy out of your head. It's just Me, and I can talk to anyone I want to, any *way* I want to."

"Because you're the Savior," 'Becka whispered.

"Right," Jesus said. He looked down. Below Him, on the screen, a couple of animated salad bowls were dancing in appreciation of the Hidden Valley Ranch Dressing which they were about to receive. "And I'd like you to please turn that crap off, if you don't mind. We can't talk with that thing running. Also, it makes My feet tingle."

'Becka approached the Sony and turned it off.

"My Lord," she whispered.

3

The following Sunday afternoon, Joe Paulson was lying fast asleep in the back yard hammock with Ozzie the cat zonked out on Joe's ample stomach. 'Becka stood in the living room, holding the curtain back and looking at Joe. Sleeping in the hammock. Dreaming of his Hussy, no doubt—dreaming of throwing her down in a great big pile of catalogues and Woolco circulars and then—how would Joe and his piggy poker buddies put it?—"putting the shoes to her."

She was holding the curtain with her left hand because she had a handful of square nine-volt batteries in her right. She took the batteries into the kitchen, where she was assembling something on the kitchen table. Jesus had told her to make it. She told Jesus she couldn't make things. She was clumsy. Her daddy had always told her so. She thought of adding how he sometimes told her he was surprised she could wipe her own butt without an instruction manual, and then decided that wasn't the sort of thing you told the Savior.

Jesus told her not to be a fool; if she could follow a recipe, she could build this little thing. She was delighted to find that He was absolutely right. It was not only easy, it was fun! More fun than cooking, certainly; she had never really had the knack for that, either. Her cakes fell and her breads never rose. She had begun this little thing yesterday, working with the toaster, the motor from her old Hamilton Beach blender, and a funny board full of electronics things which had come from the back of an old radio in the shed. She thought she would be done long before Joe woke up and came in to watch the Red Sox game on TV at two o'clock.

She picked up his little blowtorch and lit it deftly with a kitchen match. She would have laughed a week ago if you'd told her she would be working with a propane torch now. But it was easy. Jesus told her exactly how and where to solder the wires to the electronics board from the old radio.

That wasn't all Jesus had told her during the last three days. He had told her things that murdered her sleep, that made her afraid to go into the village and do her shopping, lest her guilty knowledge show on her face *(I'll always know when you done something wrong, 'Becka,* her father had told her, *because you ain't got the kind of face can keep a secret)*; that had, for the first time in her life, made her lose her appetite. Joe, totally bound up in his work, the Red Sox, and his Hussy, noticed hardly anything amiss . . . although he *had* seen 'Becka gnawing her fingernails the other night as they watched *Hill Street Blues,* and nail-biting was something she had never done before—was, in fact, one of the things *she* nagged *him* about. Joe Paulson considered this for all of twelve seconds before looking back at the Sony TV and losing himself in dreams of Nancy Voss's heaving white breasts.

Among others, these were a few of the things Jesus told her, causing 'Becka to sleep poorly and to begin biting her fingernails at the advanced age of forty-five:

In 1973, Moss Harlingen, one of Joe's poker buddies, had murdered his father. They had been hunting deer up in Greenville and it had supposedly been one of those tragic accidents, but the shooting of Abel Harlingen had been no accident. Moss simply laid up behind a fallen tree with his rifle and waited until his father splashed across a small stream about fifty yards down the hill from where Moss was. Moss potted his father as easily as a clay duck in a shooting gallery. He *thought* he had killed his father for money. Moss's business, Big Ditch Construction, had two notes falling due with two different banks within six weeks' time, and neither would extend because of the other. Moss went to Abel, but his dad refused to help, although he could afford to. So Moss shot his father and inherited a pot of money after the county coroner handed down a verdict of death by misadventure. The notes were paid and Moss Harlingen really believed (except perhaps in his deepest dreams) that he had committed murder for gain. The *real* motive had been something else. Far in the past, when Moss was ten and his brother Emory seven, Abel's wife went south to Rhode Island for one whole winter. Her brother had died suddenly, and his wife needed help getting on her feet. While their mother was gone, there were several incidents of buggery at the Harlingen place. The buggery stopped when the boys' mother came back, and the incidents were never repeated. Moss had forgotten all about them. He never remembered lying awake in the dark anymore, lying awake in mortal terror and watching the doorway for the shadow of his father. He had absolutely no recollection of lying with his mouth pressed against his forearm, salty tears of shame and rage squeezing out of his hot eyes and coursing down his cold face to his mouth as Abel Harlingen slathered lard onto his cock and slid it up his son's back door with a grunt and a sigh. It had all made so little impression on Moss that he could not remember biting his arm until it bled to keep from crying out, and he certainly could not remember Emory's breathless bird-cries from the next bed—"Please, Daddy, no, Daddy, please not me tonight, please, Daddy." Children, of course, forget very easily. But *some* memory might have lingered, because when Moss Harlingen actually pulled the trigger on the buggering son of a whore, as the echoes first rolled away and then rolled back, finally disappearing into the great forested silence of the up-Maine wilderness, Moss whispered: "Not you, Em, not tonight."

Alice Kimball, who taught at the Haven Grammar School, was a lesbian. Jesus told 'Becka this on Friday, not long after the lady herself, looking large and solid and respectable in a green pantsuit, had stopped by, collecting for the American Cancer Society.

Darla Gaines, the pretty seventeen-year-old girl who brought the Sunday paper, had half an ounce of "bitchin reefer" between the mattress and box spring of her bed. Jesus told 'Becka this right after Darla had come on Saturday to collect for the last five weeks (three dollars plus a fifty-cent tip 'Becka now wished she had withheld), and that she and her boyfriend smoked the reefer in Darla's bed before having intercourse, only they called having intercourse "doing the horizontal bop." They smoked reefer and "did the horizontal bop" almost every weekday afternoon from two-thirty until three or so. Darla's parents both worked at Splendid Shoe in Derry and they didn't get home until well past four.

Hank Buck, another of Joe's poker cronies, worked at

a large supermarket in Bangor and hated his boss so much that a year ago he had put half a box of Ex-Lax in the man's chocolate shake when the boss had sent Hank out to get his lunch at McDonald's one day. The boss had had something rather more spectacular than a bowel movement; at three-fifteen that day he had done something in his pants that was the equivalent of a shit A-bomb. The A-bomb—or S-bomb, if you preferred—had gone off as he was slicing lunchmeat in the deli of Paul's Down-East SuperMart. Hank managed to keep a straight face until quitting time, but by the time he got into his car to go home, he was laughing so hard he almost shit his *own* pants. Twice he had to pull off the road, he got laughing so hard.

"Laughed," Jesus told 'Becka. "What do you think of *that?"*

'Becka thought it was a low-down mean trick. And such things were only the beginning, it seemed. Jesus knew something unpleasant or upsetting about everyone 'Becka came in contact with, it seemed.

She couldn't live with such an awful outpouring.

She couldn't live *without* it, either.

One thing was certain: she had to do something *about* it.

"You *are,"* Jesus said. He spoke from behind her, from the picture on top of the Sony. Of *course* He did. The idea that His voice was coming *from inside her own head*—that she was somehow . . . well . . . somehow *reading people's thoughts* . . . that was only a dreadful passing illusion. It *must* be. That alternative was horrifying.

Satan. *Witchcraft.*

"In fact," Jesus said, confirming His existence with that dry, no-nonsense voice so like her father's, "you're almost done with this part. Just solder that red wire to that point to the left of the long doohickey . . . no, not there . . . *there.* Good girl! Not too much solder, mind! It's like Brylcreem, 'Becka. A little dab'll do ya."

Strange, hearing Jesus Christ talk about Brylcreem.

4

Joe woke up at a quarter to two, tossed Ozzie off his lap, strolled to the back of his lawn, brushing cat hairs off his T-shirt, and had a comfortable whiz into the poison ivy back there. Then he headed into the house. Yankees and Red Sox. Great. He opened the fridge, glancing briefly at the snippets of wire on the counter and wondering just what in the hell that dimbulb 'Becka had been up to. But mostly he dismissed it. He was thinking of Nancy Voss. He was wondering what it would feel like to squirt off between Nancy's tits. He thought maybe Monday he'd find out. He squabbled with her; Christ, sometimes they squabbled like a couple of dogs in August. Seemed like it wasn't just them; everyone seemed short-fused lately. But when it came to fucking . . . son of a bitch! He hadn't been so randy since he was eighteen, and she was the same way. Seemed like neither of them could get enough. He'd even squirted in the night a couple of times. It was like he was sixteen again. He grabbed a quart of Bud and headed toward the living room. Boston was almost certainly going to win today. He had the odds figured at 8–5. Lately he seemed to have an amazing head for odds. There was a guy down in Augusta who'd take bets, and Joe had made almost five hundred bucks in the last three weeks . . . not that 'Becka knew. He'd ratholed it. It was funny; he'd know exactly who was going to win and why, and then he'd get down to Augusta and forget the *why* and only remember the *who*. But that was the important thing, wasn't it? Last time the guy in Augusta had grumbled, paying off at three to one on a twenty-dollar bet. Mets against the Pirates, Gooden on the mound, looked like a cinch for the Mets, but Joe had taken the Pirates and they'd won, 5–2. Joe didn't know how much longer the guy in Augusta would take his bets, but if he stopped, so what? There was always Portland. There were two or three books there. It seemed like lately he got a headache whenever he left Haven—needed glasses, maybe—but when you were rolling hot, a headache was a small price to pay. Enough money and the two of them could go away. Leave 'Becka with Jesus. That was who 'Becka wanted to be married to anyway.

Cold as ice, she was. But that Nancy? One hot ticket! And smart! Why, just today she'd taken him out back at the P.O. to show him something. "Look! Look what I thought of! I think I ought to patent it, Joe! I really do!"

"What idear?" Joe asked. The truth was, he felt a little mad with her. The truth *was,* he was more interested in her *tits* than her *idears,* and mad or not, he was already getting a blue-steeler. It really *was* like being a kid again. But what she showed him was enough to make him forget all about his blue-steeler. For at least four minutes, anyway.

Nancy Voss had taken a kid's Lionel train transformer and hooked it somehow to a bunch of D-cell batteries. This gadget was wired to seven flour sifters with their screens knocked out. The sifters were lying on their sides. When Nancy turned on the transformer, a number of filament-thin wires hooked to something that looked like a blender began to scoop first-class mail from a pile on the floor into the sifters, seemingly at random.

"What's it doing?" Joe asked.

"Sorting the first-class," she said. She pointed at one sifter after another. "That one's Haven Village . . . that's RFD 1, Derry Road, you know . . . that one's Ridge Road . . . that one's Nista Road . . . that one's . . ."

He didn't believe it at first. He thought it was a joke, and he wondered how she'd like a slap upside the head. *Why'd you do that?* she'd whine. *Some men can take a joke,* he'd answer like Sylvester Stallone in that movie *Cobra, but I ain't one of em.* Except then he saw it was really working. It was quite a gadget, all right, but the sound of the wires scraping across the floor was a little creepy. Harsh and whispery, like big old spiders' legs. It was working, all right; damned if he knew how, but it *was.* He saw one of the wires snag a letter for Roscoe Thibault and push it into the correct sifter—RFD 2, which was the Hammer Cut Road—even though it had been misaddressed to Haven Village.

He wanted to ask her how it worked, but he didn't want to look like a goddam dummy, so he asked her where she got the wires instead.

"Out of these telephones I bought at Radio Shack," she said. "The one at the Bangor Mall. They were on sale! There's some other stuff from the phones in it too. I had to change everything around, but it was easy. It just, you know . . . come to me. You know?"

"Yeah," Joe said slowly, thinking about the bookie's face when Joe had come in to collect his sixty bucks after the Pirates beat Gooden and the Mets. "Not bad. For a woman."

For a moment her brow darkened and he thought: *You*

want to say something? You want to fight? Come on. That's okay. That's just about as okay as the other.

Then her brow cleared and she smiled. "Now we can do *it* even longer." Her fingers slid down the hard ridge in his pants. "You do want to do it don't you, Joe?"

And Joe did. They slipped to the floor and he forgot all about being mad at her, and how all of a sudden he seemed to be able to figure the odds on everything from baseball games to horse races to golf matches in the wink of an eye. He slid into her and she moaned and Joe even forgot the tenebrous whispering sound those wires made as they sifted the first-class mail into the row of flour sifters.

5

When Joe entered the living room, 'Becka was sitting in her rocker, pretending to read the latest issue of *The Upper Room*. Just ten minutes before Joe came in, she had finished wiring the gadget Jesus had shown her how to make into the back of the Sony TV. She followed His instructions to the letter, because He said you had to be careful when you were fooling around inside the back of a television.

"You could fry yourself," Jesus advised. "More juice back there than there is in a Birds Eye warehouse, even when it's turned off."

The TV was off now and Joe said ill-temperedly, "I thought you'd have this all wa'amed up for me."

"I guess you know how to turn on the damned TV," 'Becka said, speaking to her husband for the last time.

Joe raised his eyebrows. *Damned* anything was damned odd, coming from 'Becka. He thought about calling her on it, and decided to let it ride. Could be there was one fat old mare who'd find herself keeping house by herself before much of a longer went by.

"Guess I do," Joe said, speaking to his *wife* for the last time.

He pushed the button that turned the Sony on, and better than two thousand volts of current slammed into him, AC which had been boosted, switched over to lethal DC, and then boosted again. His eyes popped wide open, bulged, and then burst like grapes in a microwave. He had started to set the quart of beer on top of the TV next to Jesus. When the electricity hit, his hand clenched tightly enough to break the bottle. Spears of brown glass drove into his fingers and palm. Beer foamed and ran. It hit the top of the TV (its plastic casing already blistering) and turned to steam that smelled like yeast.

"EEEEEOOOOOOARRRRHMMMMMMM!" Joe Paulson screamed. His face began to turn black: Blue smoke poured out of his hair and his ears. His finger was nailed to the Sony's On button.

A picture popped on the TV. It was Dwight Gooden throwing the wild pitch that let in two runs and chased him, making Joe Paulson forty dollars richer. It flipped and showed him and Nancy Voss screwing on the post-office floor in a litter of catalogues and *Congressional Newsletters* and ads from insurance companies saying you could get all the coverage you needed even if you were over sixty-five, no salesman would call at your door, no physical examination would be required, your loved ones would be protected at a cost of pennies a day.

"No!" 'Becka screamed, and the picture flipped again. Now she saw Moss Harlingen behind a fallen pine, notching his father in the sight of his .30-.30 and murmuring *Not you, Em, not tonight.* It flipped and she saw a man and a woman digging in the woods, the woman behind the controls of something that looked a little bit like a payloader and a little bit like something out of a Rube Goldberg cartoon, the man looping a chain around a stump. Beyond them, a vast dish-shaped object jutted out of the earth. It was silvery, but dull; the sun struck it in places but did not twinkle.

Joe Paulson's clothes burst into flame.

The living room was filled with the smell of cooking beer. The 3-D picture of Jesus jittered around and then exploded.

'Becka shrieked, understanding that, like it or not, it had been her all along, her, her, her, *and she was murdering her husband.*

She ran to him, seized his looping, spasming hand . . . and was herself galvanized.

Jesus oh Jesus save him, save me, save us both, she thought as the current slammed into her, driving her up on her toes like the world's heftiest ballerina *en pointe.*

And a mad, cackling voice, the voice of her father, rose in her brain: *Fooled you, 'Becka, didn't I? Fooled you good! Teach you to lie! Teach you for good and all!*

The rear of the television, which she had screwed back on after she had finished adding her alterations, blew back against the wall with a mighty blue flash of light. 'Becka tumbled to the carpet, pulling Joe with her. Joe was already dead.

By the time the smoldering wallpaper behind the TV had ignited the chintz curtains, 'Becka Paulson was dead too.

3.

HILLY BROWN

1

The day Hillman Brown did the most spectacular trick of his career as an amateur magician—the *only* spectacular trick of his career as an amateur magician, actually—was Sunday, July 17th, exactly one week before the Haven town hall blew up. That Hillman Brown had never managed a really spectacular trick before was not so surprising. He was only ten, after all.

His given name had been his mother's maiden name. There had been Hillmans in Haven going back to the time when it had been Montgomery, and although Marie Hillman had no regrets about becoming Marie Brown—after all, she loved the guy!—she had wanted to preserve the name, and Bryant had agreed. The new baby wasn't home a week before everyone was calling him Hilly.

Hilly grew up nervous. Marie's father, Ev, said he had cat whiskers for nerves and would spend his whole life on the jump. It wasn't news Bryant and Marie Brown wanted to hear, but after their first year with Hilly, it wasn't really news at all; just a fact of life. Some babies attempt to comfort themselves by rocking in their cribs or cradles; some by sucking a thumb. Hilly rocked in his crib almost constantly (crying angrily at the same time, more often than not), and sucked *both* thumbs—sucked them so hard that he had painful blisters on them by the time he was eight months old.

"He'll stop now," Dr. Lester in Derry told them confidently, after examining the nasty blisters that ringed

Hilly's thumbs . . . blisters Marie had wept over as if they had been her own. But Hilly hadn't stopped. His need for comfort was apparently greater than whatever pain his hurt thumbs gave him. Eventually the blisters turned to hard calluses.

"He'll always be on the jump," the boy's grandfather prophesied whenever anyone asked him (and even when no one did; at sixty-three, Ev Hillman was garrulous-going-on-tiresome). "Cat whiskers for nerves, ayuh! He'll keep his mom n dad on the hop, Hilly will."

Hilly kept them hopping, all right. Lining both sides of the Brown driveway were stumps, placed there by Bryant, at Marie's instigation. Upon each she put a planter, and in each planter was a different sort of plant or bunch of flowers. At age three, Hilly one day climbed out of his crib where he was supposed to be taking a nap ("Why do I have to have a nap, Mom?" Hilly asked. "Because I need the rest, Hilly," his exhausted mother replied), wriggled out the window, and knocked over all twelve of the planters, stumps and all. When Marie saw what Hilly had done, she wept as inconsolably as she had wept over her boy's poor thumbs. Seeing her cry, Hilly had also burst into tears (around his thumbs; he was attempting to suck both of them at once). He hadn't knocked over the stumps and the planters to be mean; it had just seemed a good idea at the time.

"You don't count the cost, Hilly," his father said on that occasion. He would say it a good many times before Sunday, July 17th, 1988.

At the age of five, Hilly got on his sled and shot down the ice-coated Brown driveway one December day and out into the road. It never occurred to him, he told his ashy-faced mother later, to wonder if something might be coming down Derry Road; he had gotten up, seen the glaze of ice that had fallen, and had only wondered how fast his Flexible Flyer would go down their driveway. Marie saw him, saw the fuel tanker lumbering down Route 9, and shrieked Hilly's name so loudly that she could barely talk above a whisper for the next two days. That night, trembling in Bryant's arms, she told him she had seen the boy's tombstone in Homeland—had actually *seen* it: *Hillman Richard Brown, 1978—1983, Taken Too Soon.*

"Hiiillyyyyyyyy!"

Hilly's head snapped around at the sound of his mother's scream, which sounded to him as loud as a jet plane. As a result, he fell off his sled just before it reached the foot of the driveway. The driveway was asphalted, the glaze of sleet was really quite thin, and Hilly Brown never had that knack with which a kind God blesses most squirmy, active children—the knack of falling lucky. He broke his left arm just above the elbow and fetched his forehead such a dreadful crack that he knocked himself out.

His Flexible Flyer shot into the road. The driver of the Webber Fuel truck reacted before he had a chance to see there was no one on the sled. He spun the wheel and the tanker-truck waltzed into a low embankment of snow with the huge grace of the elephant ballet dancers in *Fantasia*. It crashed through and landed in the ditch, canted alarmingly to one side. Less than five minutes after the driver wriggled out of the passenger door and ran to Marie Brown, the truck tipped over on its side and lay in the frozen grass like a dead mastodon, expensive No. 2 fuel oil gurgling out of its three overflow vents.

Marie was running down the road with her unconscious child in her arms, screaming. In her terror and confusion she felt sure that Hilly must have been run over, even though she had quite clearly seen him fall off his sled at the bottom of the driveway.

"Is he dead?" the tanker driver screamed. His eyes were wide, his face pale as paper, his hair standing on end. There was a dark spot spreading on the crotch of his pants. "Oh sufferin Jesus lady, is he dead?"

"I think so," Marie wept. "I think he is, oh I think he's dead."

"Who's dead?" Hilly asked, opening his eyes.

"Oh, Hilly, thank God!" Marie screamed, and hugged him. Hilly screamed back with great enthusiasm. She was grinding together the splintered ends of the broken bone in his left arm.

Hilly spent the next three days in Derry Home Hospital.

"It'll slow him down, at least," Bryant Brown said the next evening over a dinner of baked beans and hot dogs.

Ev Hillman happened to be taking dinner with them that evening; since his wife had died, Ev Hillman did that every now and again; about five evenings out of every seven on the average. "Want to bet?" Ev said now, cackling through a mouthful of cornbread.

Bryant cocked a sour eye at his father-in-law and said nothing.

As usual, Ev was right—that was one of the reasons Bryant so often felt sour about him. On his second night in the hospital, long after the other children in Pediatrics were asleep, Hilly decided to go exploring. How he got past the duty nurse was a mystery, but get past he did. He was discovered missing at three in the morning. An initial search of the pediatrics ward did not turn him up. Neither did a floor-wide search. Security was called in. A search of the whole hospital was then mounted—administrators who had at first only been mildly annoyed were now becoming worried—and discovered nothing. Hilly's father and mother were called and came in at once, looking shell-shocked. Marie was weeping, but because of her swollen larynx, she could only do so in a breathy croak.

"We think he may have wandered out of the building somehow," the Head of Administrative Services told them.

"How the hell could a five-year-old just *wander out of the building?*" Bryant shouted. "What kind of a place you guys *running* here?"

"Well . . . well . . . you understand it's hardly a prison, Mr. Brown—"

Marie cut them both off. "You've got to find him," she whispered. "It's only twenty-two degrees out there. Hilly was in his pj's. He could be . . . be . . ."

"Oh, Mrs. Brown, I really think such worries are premature," the Head of Administrative Services broke in, smiling sincerely. He did not, in fact, think they were premature at all. The first thing he had done after ascertaining that the boy *might* have been gone ever since the eleven-o'clock bedcheck was to find out how cold the night had been. The answer had occasioned a call to Dr. Elfman, who specialized in cases of hypothermia—there were a lot of those in Maine winters. Dr. Elfman's prognosis was grave. "If he got out, he's probably dead," Elfman said.

Another hospital-wide search, this one augmented by Derry police and firemen, turned up nothing. Marie Brown was given a sedative and put to bed. The only good news was of a negative sort; so far no one had found Hilly's frozen pajama-clad body. Of course, the Head of Administrative Services thought, the Penobscot River was close to the hospital. Its surface had frozen. It was just possible that the boy had tried to cross the ice and had plunged through. Oh, how he wished the Browns had taken their little brat to Eastern Maine Medical.

At two that afternoon, Bryant Brown sat numbly in a chair beside his sleeping wife, wondering how he could tell her their only child was dead, if it became necessary to do so. At about that same time, a janitor who was in the basement to check on the laundry boilers saw an amazing sight: a small boy wearing nothing but pajama bottoms and a plaster cast on one arm strolling nonchalantly between two of the hospital's giant furnaces in his bare feet.

"Hey!" the janitor yelled. "Hey, kid!"

"Hi," Hilly said, coming over. His feet were black with dirt; his pajama bottoms were swatched with grease. "Boy, this is a big place! I think I'm lost."

The janitor carried Hilly upstairs to the administration office. The Head sat Hilly down in a large wing chair (after prudently putting down a double spread of the Bangor *Daily News)* and sent his secretary out to fetch back a Pepsi-Cola and a bag of Reese's Pieces for the brat. Under other circumstances the Head would have gone himself, thereby impressing the boy with his grandfatherly kindness. Under other circumstances—*by which I mean,* the Head thought grimly to himself, *with a different boy*. He was afraid to leave Hilly alone.

When the secretary came back with the candy and the soft drink, the Head sent her away again . . . after Bryant Brown this time. Bryant was a strong man, but when he saw Hilly sitting in the Head's wing chair, his dirty feet swinging four inches off the rug and the papers crackling under his butt as he ate candy and drank Pepsi, he was unable to hold back his tears of relief and thanksgiving. This of course made Hilly—who never in his life had ever done anything *consciously* bad—also burst into tears.

"Christ, Hilly, where you been?"

Hilly told the story as best he could, leaving Bryant and the Head to parse objective truth out of it as best *they* could. He had gotten lost, wandered into the basement ("I was followin a pixie," Hilly told them), and had crawled *under* one of the furnaces to sleep. It had been very warm there, he told them, so warm he had taken off his pajama shirt, working it carefully over the new cast.

"I liked the pups, too," he said. "Can we have a puppy, Daddy?"

The janitor who had spotted Hilly also found Hilly's shirt. It was under the No. 2 furnace. Getting the shirt out, he saw the "puppies" too, although they skittered away from his light. He did not mention them to Mr. and Mrs. Brown, who looked like folks who would just fall apart if faced with one more shock. The janitor, a kindly man, thought they would do just as well not knowing that their son had spent the night with a pack of basement rats, some of which had indeed looked as large as puppies as they fled from his flashlight beam.

2

Asked for *his* perceptions of these things—and the similar (if less spectacular) incidents that occurred over the next five years of his life—Hilly would have shrugged and said, "I'm always getting in trouble, I guess." Hilly meant he was accident-prone, but no one had taught him this valuable phrase yet.

When he was eight—two years after David was born—he brought home a note from Mrs. Underhill, his third-grade teacher, asking if Mr. and Mrs. Brown could come in for a brief conference. The Browns went, not without some trepidation. They knew that during the previous week, Haven's third-graders had been given IQ tests. Bryant was secretly convinced that Mrs. Underhill was going to tell them Hilly had tested far below normal and would have to be put in remedial classes. Marie was convinced (and just as secretly) that Hilly was dyslexic. Neither had slept very well the night before.

What Mrs. Underhill told them was that Hilly was completely off the scale—bluntly put, the lad was a genius. "You'll have to take him to Bangor and have him take the Wechsler Test if you want to know how high his IQ actually is," Mrs. Underhill told them. "Giving Hilly the Tompall IQ Test is like trying to determine a human's IQ by giving him an intelligence test designed for goats."

Marie and Bryant discussed it . . . and decided against pursuing the matter any further. They didn't really want to know how bright Hilly was. It was enough to know he was not disadvantaged . . . and, as Marie said that night in bed, it explained so much: Hilly's restlessness, his apparent inability to sleep much more than six hours a night, his fierce interests which blew in like hurricanes, then blew out again with the same rapidity. One day when Hilly was almost nine, she had come back from the post office with baby David to find the kitchen, which had been spotless when she left only fifteen minutes before, a complete shambles. The sink was full of flour-clotted bowls. There was a puddle of melting butter on the counter. And something was cooking in the oven. Marie popped David quickly in his playpen and had pulled the oven open, expecting to be greeted by billows of smoke and the smell of burning. Instead, she found a tray of Bisquick rolls which, while misshapen, were quite tasty. They had had them for supper that night . . . but before then, Marie had paddled Hilly's bottom and sent him, wailing apologies, to his room. Then she had sat down at the kitchen table and cried until she laughed, while David—a placid, happy-go-lucky baby who was a sunny Tahiti to Hilly's Cape of Storms—sat holding the bars of the playpen, staring at her comically.

One mark very much in Hilly's favor was his frank love for his brother. And although Marie and Bryant hesitated to let Hilly hold the new baby, or even to leave Hilly alone in the same room with David for more than, say, thirty seconds at a time, they gradually relaxed.

"Hell, you could send Hilly and David off for two weeks campin up in the Allagash together and they'd come back fine," Ev Hillman said. "He loves that kid. And he's *good* with him."

This proved to be so. Most—if not quite all—of Hilly's "in-troubles" stemmed from either an honest desire to help his parents or to better himself. They simply went wrong, that was all. But with David, who worshiped the ground on which his older brother walked, Hilly always seemed to go right. . . .

Until the seventeenth of July, that was, when Hilly did *the* trick.

3

Mr. Robertson Davies (may his death be postponed a thousand years) has suggested in his *Deptford Trilogy* that our attitude toward magic and magicians in large part indicates our attitude toward reality, and that our attitudes on the matter of reality indicate our attitudes toward the whole world of wonders in which we find ourselves—nothing but babes in the woods, even the oldest of us (even Mr. Davies himself, one must believe), where some of the trees bite and some confer great mystic favors—a property in their bark, no doubt.

Hilly Brown very much felt he *did* exist in a world of wonders. This had always been his attitude, and it never changed, no matter how many "in-troubles" he had. The world was as mystically beautiful as the glass balls his mother and father hung on the Christmas tree each year (Hilly longed to hang some too, but experience had taught him—as it had his parents—that to hand a glass ball to Hilly was to issue that glass ball's death warrant). To Hilly the world was as gorgeously perplexing as the Rubik's Cube he had gotten for his ninth birthday (the cube was gorgeously perplexing for two weeks, anyway, and then Hilly began to solve it routinely). His attitude toward magic was thus predictable—he loved it. Magic was made for Hilly Brown. Unfortunately, Hilly Brown, like Dunstable Ramsey in Davies' *Deptford Trilogy*, was not made for magic.

On the occasion of Hilly's tenth birthday, Bryant Brown had to stop at the Derry Mall to pick up another present for his son. Marie had called him on his coffee break. "My dad forgot to get Hilly anything, Bryant. He wanted to know if you'd stop at the mall and buy him a toy or something. He'll pay you when his check comes in."

"Sure," Bryant said, thinking: *And pigs will ride broomsticks.*

"Thanks, honey," she said gratefully. She knew perfectly well that her father—who now took dinner with them six and seven nights a week instead of just five—was the sandpaper on her husband's soul. But he had never complained, and for this Marie loved him dearly.

"What did he think Hilly might like?"

"He said he'd trust your judgment," she said.

Typical, Bryant thought. So he had found himself in one of the mall's two toy stores that afternoon, looking at games, dolls (the dolls for boys going under the euphemism "action-figures"), models, and kits (Bryant saw a large chemistry set, thought of Hilly mixing things up in test-tubes, and shuddered). Nothing seemed quite right; at ten his eldest son had reached an age when he was too old for baby toys and too young for such sophisticated items as box kites or gas-powered model planes. *Nothing* seemed quite right, and he was pressed for time. Hilly's birthday party was scheduled for five, and it was a quarter past four now. That barely left him time to get home.

He grabbed the magic set almost at random. *Thirty New Tricks!,* the box said. Good. *Hours of Fun for the Young Prestidigitator!,* the box said. Also good. *Ages 8–12,* the box said. Fine. *Safety-Tested for the Young Conjurer,* the box said, and that was best of all. Bryant bought it and smuggled it into the house under his jacket while Ev Hillman was leading Hilly, David, and three of Hilly's friends in a rousing off-key chorus of "Sweet Betsy from Pike."

"You're just in time for birthday cake," Marie said, kissing him.

"Wrap this first, will you?" He handed her the magic kit. She gave it a quick glance and nodded. "How's it going?"

"Fine," she said. "When it was Hilly's turn to pin the tail on the donkey, he tripped on a table leg and stuck the pin into Stanley Jernigan's arm, but that's all so far."

Bryant cheered up at once. Things really *were* going well. The year before, while wriggling into Hilly's "neatest all-time hiding place" during a game of hide-and-go-seek, Eddie Golden had torn his leg open on a strand of rusty barbed wire Hilly had always managed to miss (Hilly had, in fact, never even seen that old piece of sticker-wire at all). Eddie had to go to the doctor, who treated him to three stitches and a tetanus shot. Poor Eddie had had a bad reaction to the shot and had spent the two days following Hilly's ninth birthday in the hospital.

Now Marie smiled and kissed Bryant again. "Dad thanks you," she said. "And so do I."

Hilly opened all his presents with pleasure, but when he opened the magic set, he was transported with joy. He rushed to his grandfather (who had by that time managed to wolf down half of Hilly's devil's food birthday cake and was even then cutting himself another slice) and hugged him fiercely.

"Thanks, Grampy! Thanks! Just what I wanted! How did you know?"

Ev Hillman smiled warmly at his grandson. "I guess I ain't forgot everythin about being a boy," he said.

"It's boss, Grampy! Wow! Thirty tricks! Look, Barney—"

Whirling to show Barney Applegate, he whacked the corner of the box into Marie's coffee-cup, breaking it. Coffee sprayed and scalded Barney's arm. Barney screamed.

"Sorry, Barney," Hilly said, still dancing. His eyes were so bright they seemed almost afire. "But look! Neat-o, huh! *Awesome!*"

With the three or four gifts for which Bryant and Marie had saved and then ordered far in advance from an FAO Schwarz catalogue to make sure they would arrive on time thus relegated to the status of spear-carriers in a jungle epic, Bryant and Marie exchanged a telepathic glance.

Gee, honey, I'm sorry, her eyes said.

Well, what the hell . . . that's life with Hilly, his replied.

They both burst out laughing.

The partygoers turned to look at them for a moment—Marie never forgot David's round, solemn eyes—and then turned back to watch Hilly open his magic set.

"I wonder if there's any of that maple-walnut ice cream left," Ev wondered aloud. And Hilly, who that afternoon believed his grandfather to be the greatest man on earth, ran to get it.

4

Mr. Robertson Davies has *also* suggested in his *Deptford Trilogy* that the same great truism which applies to writing, painting, picking horses at the track, and telling lies in a sincerely believable way, also applies to magic: some people got the knack, and some people don't.

Hilly didn't.

In Davies' *Fifth Business*, the first of the *Deptford* books, the narrator, enchanted by magic (he is a boy of about Hilly's age), does any number of tricks—badly—for an approving, uncritical audience of one (a much younger boy of about David's age), with this ironic result: the older boy discovers the younger has the great natural talent for prestidigitation he himself lacks. This younger boy puts the narrator completely to shame, in fact, the first time he ever tries to palm a shilling.

On this last point, the similarity broke down; David had no more talent for magic than Hilly did. But David adored his brother, and would have sat in patient, attentive, loving silence if, instead of trying to make the Jacks run from the burning house, or Victor, the family cat, pop out of his magician's hat (said hat was thrown out in June, when Victor shat in it), he had lectured to David on the thermodynamics of steam or read him all the begats from the Gospel According to Matthew.

Not that Hilly was an utter failure as a magician; he wasn't. In fact, HILLY BROWN'S FIRST GALA MAGIC SHOW, which was held on the Browns' back lawn on the day Jim Gardener left Troy to join the New England Poetry Caravan, was considered a great success. A dozen children—mostly Hilly's friends, but with a few of David's from nursery school thrown in for good measure—and four or five adults showed up and watched Hilly do almost a dozen tricks, give or take. Most of these tricks worked, not because of any talent or real flair, but because of the sheer determination with which Hilly had rehearsed. All the intelligence and determination in the world cannot create art without a bit of talent, but intelligence and determination *can* create some great forgeries.

Besides, there was this to be said for the magic set Bryant had picked up almost at random: its creators, knowing that most of the aspiring magicians into whose hands their creation would fall were apt to be clumsy and untalented, had relied mostly upon mechanical devices. You had to *work* to screw up the Multiplying Coins, for instance. The same went for the Magic Guillotine, a tiny model (with MADE IN TAIWAN stamped discreetly on its plastic base) loaded with a razor-blade. When a nervous member of the audience (or a perfectly blasé David) put his finger into the guillotine's cradle, above a hole which held a cigarette, Hilly would slam the blade down, cut the cigarette in two . . . but leave the finger miraculously whole.

Not all of the tricks depended on mechanical devices for their effect. Hilly spent hours practicing a two-handed shuffle which allowed him to "float" a card on the bottom of a deck to the top. He actually got quite good at it, not knowing that a good float is much more useful to a card-weasel like "Pits" Barfield than to a magician. In an audience of more than twenty, the atmosphere of living-room intimacy is lost, and even the most spectacular card-tricks usually fall flat. Hilly's audience was small enough, however, so he was able to charm them—adults as well as children—by nonchalantly peeling cards that had been stuck into the middle of the deck from the top, by causing Rosalie Skehan to find a card which she had looked at and then pushed back into the deck residing in her purse, and, of course, by making the Jacks run from the burning house, which may be the best card-trick ever invented.

There *were* failures, of course. Hilly without screw-ups, Bryant said that night in bed, would be like McDonald's without hamburgers. When he attempted to pour a pitcher of water into a handkerchief he had borrowed from Joe Paulson, the postman who would be electrocuted about a month later, he succeeded in doing no more than wetting both the handkerchief and the front of his pants. Victor refused to pop out of the hat. Most embarrassing, the Disappearing Coins, a trick Hilly had sweat blood to master, went wrong. He palmed the coins (actually cartwheel-size rounds of chocolate wrapped in gold foil and marketed under the trade name Munchie Money) with no trouble, but as he was turning around, they all fell out of his sleeve, to the general hilarity and wild applause of his friends.

Still, the round of applause at the end of Hilly's show was genuine. Everyone agreed that Hilly Brown was quite a magician, "for only ten." Only three people disagreed with this judgment: Marie Brown, Bryant Brown, and Hilly himself.

"He still hasn't found *it,* has he?" Marie asked her husband that night in bed. Both of them understood that *it* was whatever God had for Hilly to do with the searchlight He had put in Hilly's brain.

"No," Bryant said after a long, thinking pause. "I don't think so. But he worked hard, didn't he? Worked like a carthorse."

"Yes," she said. "I was glad to see him do it. It's good to know he *can,* instead of just jumping from pillar to post. But it made me a little sad, too. He worked at those tricks the way a college kid studies for his finals."

"I know."

Marie sighed. "He's had his show. I suppose now he'll drop it and go on to something else. He'll find *it* eventually."

5

At first it seemed that Marie was right; that Hilly's interest in magic would go the way of Hilly's interest in ant farms, moon rocks, and ventriloquism. The magic set had moved from under his bed, where it was handy in case Hilly woke up in the middle of the night with an idea, to the top of his cluttered desk. Marie recognized this as the opening scene in an old play. The denouement would come when the magic set was finally relegated to the dusty recesses of the attic.

But Hilly's mind *hadn't* moved on—it was nothing as simple as that. The two weeks following his magic show were periods of fairly deep depression for Hilly. This was something his parents didn't sense and never knew. David knew, but at four there was nothing he could do about it, other than to hope Hilly would cheer up.

Hilly Brown was trying to cope with the idea that for the first time in his life he had failed at something he *really wanted to do*. He had been pleased with the applause and congratulations, and he was not so self-deprecating as to mistake honest praise for politeness . . . but there was a stony part of him—the part, which, under other circumstances, might have made him a great artist—which was not satisfied with honest praise. Honest praise, this stony part insisted, was what the bunglers of the world heaped on the heads of the barely competent.

In short, honest praise was not enough.

Hilly did not think all this in such adult terms, of course . . . but he *did* think it. If his mother had known his thoughts, she would have been very angry with him for his pride . . . which, her Bible taught her, went before a fall. Certainly she would have been angrier with him than she'd been the time he slid into the road in front of the Webber Oil truck, or the time he tried to give Victor a bubble bath in the toilet bowl. *What do you want, Hilly?* she would have cried, throwing up her hands. Dis*honest praise?*

Ev, who saw much, and David, who saw more, could have told her.

He wanted to make their eyes get so big they looked like they were going to fall out. He wanted to make the girls scream and the boys yell. He wanted to make everyone laugh when Victor came out of that hat with a ribbon in his tail and a chocolate coin in his mouth. He would have traded all the honest praise and genuine applause in the world for just one scream, one belly-laugh, one woman fainting dead away like the booklet says they did when Harry Houdini did his famous milk-can escape. Because honest praise means you only got good. When they scream and laugh and faint, that means you got great.

But he suspected—no, he *knew*—that he was never going to get great, and all the want in the world would not change that fact. It was a bitter blow. Not the failure itself so much as the knowing it couldn't be changed. It was like the end of Santa Claus, in a way.

So, while his parents believed his lapse of interest to be just another shift in the capricious spring wind that blows through most childhoods, it was, in fact, the result of Hilly's first adult conclusion: if he was never going to get great at magic, he ought to put the set away. He couldn't leave it around and just do a trick now and then as a hobby. His failure hurt too badly for that. It was a bad equation. Best erase it and try a new one.

If adults could put aside their obsessions with such firmness, the world would undoubtedly be a better place. Robertson Davies does not say that in his *Deptford Trilogy* . . . but he strongly hints at it.

6

It was on the Fourth of July that David came into Hilly's room and saw Hilly had gotten the magic kit out again. He had a lot of the tricks spread out in front of him . . . and something else, as well. Batteries. The batteries from Daddy's big radio, David thought.

"Watcha doon, Hilly?" David asked, companionably enough.

Hilly's brow darkened. He sprang to his feet and shoved David out of the room so hard that David fell to the carpet. This behavior was so unusual that David was too surprised to cry.

"Get out!" Hilly shouted. "Can't look at new tricks! The Medici princes used to have people *executed* if they caught them looking at tricks that belonged to their favorite magicians!"

Having uttered this pronouncement, Hilly slammed the door in David's face. David howled for admittance, but to no avail. This unaccustomed stoniness in his harum-scarum but usually sweet-natured brother was so unusual that David went downstairs, turned on the TV, and cried himself to sleep in front of *Sesame Street.*

7

Hilly's interest in magic had abruptly been rekindled at about the same time the picture of Jesus had begun speaking to 'Becka Paulson.

A single powerful thought had seized his mind: if mechanical tricks like the Multiplying Coins were the best he could do, he would invent his own mechanical tricks. The best anyone had ever seen! Better than Thurston's clockwork or Blackstone's hinged mirrors! If what it took to elicit gasps and screams and belly-laughs was invention rather than manipulation, so be it.

Lately he felt very capable of inventing things.

Lately his mind seemed almost *stuffed* with ideas for inventions.

This was not the first time the idea of *inventing* had crossed his mind, but his previous ideas had been vague, powered by daydreams rather than scientific principles—rocket ships made out of cardboard boxes, ray-guns that looked suspiciously like small tree-branches with pieces of Styrofoam packing pushed onto the barrels, things like that. He had had *good* ideas from time to time, ideas that were almost practical, but he had always dropped them before because he had no idea how to proceed with them—he could pound a nail straight and saw a board, but that was all.

Now, however, the methods seemed as clear as crystal.

Great tricks, he thought, wiring and bolting and screwing things together. When his mother told him, on July 8th, that she was going to Augusta to shop (she spoke in a distracted sort of way; for the last week or so Marie had had a headache, and the news that Joe and 'Becka Paulson had both been killed in a house fire had not helped it one little bit), Hilly asked her if she would stop at Radio Shack in the Capitol Mall and pick him up a couple of things. He gave her his list, the eight surviving dollars of his birthday money, and asked her if she could "kinda loan him" the rest.

Ten (10) spring-type contact points @ $.70 ea (No. 1334567)
Three (3) "T" contacts (spring-type) @ $1.00 ea (No. 1334709)
One (1) coaxial cable "barrier" plug @ $2.40 ea (No. 19776-C)

If it hadn't been for her headache and general feeling of listlessness, Marie would have doubtless wondered what this stuff was *for*. She would have doubtless wondered how Hilly could have gotten his information so exactly—right down to the inventory numbers—without making a long-distance call to the Augusta Radio Shack. She might even have suspected that Hilly had finally found *it*.

In a terrible sense, this was exactly what had happened.

Instead, she simply agreed to pick the stuff up and "kinda loan him" the extra four dollars or so.

By the time she and David came back from Augusta, some of these questions *had* occurred to her. The trip had made her feel much better; her headache had blown completely away. And David, who had been silent and introspective—not at all his usual bouncy, babbly, bubbly self—ever since Hilly had pushed him out of his room, also seemed to cheer up. He talked her ear off, and it was from David that she learned Hilly had scheduled his SECOND GALA MAGIC SHOW for the back yard nine days hence.

"He's gonna do lots of new tricks," David said, looking glum.

"Is he?"

"Yes," David said.

"Do you think they'll be good?"

"I don't know," David said, thinking of the way Hilly had pushed him from the room. He was on the verge of tears, but Marie didn't notice. Ten minutes before, they had passed from Albion back into Haven, and her headache was coming back . . . and with it, that previous sense—now a little stronger—that her thoughts were somehow not under control as they should be. There seemed to be too *many,* for one thing. For another, she couldn't even tell what a lot of them *were.* They were like . . . She thought carefully, and finally came up with it. In high school she had been in the dramatics society (she thought Hilly must get much of his love of dramatics from her), and the thoughts in her mind now were like the murmur of an audience heard through the curtain before the show starts. You didn't know what they were saying, but you knew they were there.

"I don't think they'll be so hot," David finally said. He was looking out through the window, and his eyes were suddenly prisoner's eyes, lonely and trapped. David saw Justin Hurd out in his field, chugging along on his tractor, harrowing. Harrowing even though it was already the second week of July. For a moment forty-two-year-old Justin Hurd's mind was totally open to four-year-old David Brown's, and David understood that Justin was ripping his entire garden to pieces, plowing the unripened corn back under, tearing up the pea-patch, squashing the new melons to pulp under the wheels of his tractor. Justin Hurd thought it was May. May of 1951, in fact. Justin Hurd had gone crazy.

"I don't think they'll be good at all," David said.

8

There had been roughly twenty people at Hilly's FIRST GALA MAGIC SHOW. There were only seven at the second: his mother, his father, his grandfather, David, Barney Applegate (who was, like Hilly, ten), Mrs. Crenshaw from the village (Mrs. Crenshaw had dropped by in hopes of selling Marie some Avon), and Hilly himself. This drastic drop in attendance was not the only contrast with the first show.

The audience at that first one had been lively—even a little cheeky (the sarcastic applause which greeted the Munchie Money when it fell from Hilly's sleeve, for instance). The audience at the second was glum and listless, sitting like department-store mannequins on the camp chairs that Hilly and his "assistant" (a pale and silent David) had set up. Hilly's dad, who had laughed and applauded and raised hell at the first show, interrupted Hilly's opening speech about "the mysteries of the Orient" by saying that he couldn't spare a whole lot of time for those mysteries, if Hilly didn't mind; he had just finished mowing the lawn, and he wanted a shower and a beer.

The weather had changed too. The day of THE FIRST GALA MAGIC SHOW had been clear and warm and green, the most gorgeous sort of late-spring day northern New England can offer. This day in July was hot and sullenly humid, with hazy sun beating down from a sky the color of chrome. Mrs. Crenshaw sat fanning herself with one of her own Avon catalogues and waited for this to be over. A person could faint, sitting out here in the hot sun. And that little kid up there on a stage made of orange crates, wearing a black suit and a shoepolish mustache . . . spoiled . . . showing off . . . Mrs. Crenshaw suddenly felt like killing him.

The magic this time was much better—startling, really—but Hilly was stunned and infuriated to find he was nonetheless boring his audience to tears. He could see his father shifting around, getting ready to leave, and this made Hilly feel frantic, because he wanted to impress his father above all others.

Well, what do they want? he asked himself angrily, sweating just as freely as Mrs. Crenshaw under his black wool Sunday suit. *I'm doing great—better than Houdini, even—but they're not screaming or laughing or gasping. Why not? What the heck's wrong?*

At the center of Hilly's orange-crate stage was a small platform (another orange crate, this one covered with a sheet). Hidden inside this was a device that Hilly had invented, using the batteries David had seen in his room and the guts of an old Texas Instruments calculator that he had stolen (with no compunctions at all) from the bottom of his mother's desk in the front hall. The sheet covering the orange crate was pooled around its edges, and concealed in one of these pools of cloth was another of Hilly's out-of-character thefts—the foot-pedal of his mother's sewing machine. Hilly had connected the pedal to his gadget. He used the spring-connectors his mother had bought him in Augusta to do it.

The device he had invented first made things disappear, then brought them back again.

Hilly found this spectacular, mind-boggling. The reaction of his audience, however, started low and went downhill from there.

"For my first trick, the Disappearing Tomato!" Hilly trumpeted. He pulled a tomato out of his box of "magic supplies" and held it up. "I would like a volunteer from the audience to verify this is a real tomato and not just a fake or something. You, sir! Thanks!" He pointed at his father, who just waved wearily and said, "It's a tomato, Hilly, I can see that."

"Okay! Now watch as the Mysteries of the Orient . . . *take hold!*"

Hilly stooped, put the tomato in the center of the white sheet covering the crate, and then covered it with one of his mother's silk scarves. He waved his magic wand over the circular hump in the blue scarf. *"Presto-majesto!"* he yelled, and stepped surreptitiously on the concealed sewing-machine pedal. There was a brief low hum.

The hump in the scarf disappeared. The scarf itself settled flat. He removed the scarf to show them the top of the platform was bare, and then waited complacently for the gasps and shouts of amazement. What he got was applause.

Polite applause, no more.

Clearly, from Mrs. Crenshaw's mind, this came: *A trapdoor. Nothing to* that. *I can't believe I'm sitting out here in the sun watching this spoiled brat put tomatoes through trapdoors just so I can sell a bottle of perfume to his mother. Really!*

Hilly began to get mad.

"Now another Mystery of the Orient! The *Return* of the Disappearing Tomato!" He frowned formidably at Mrs. Crenshaw. "And for those of you who're thinking about anything stupid like trapdoors, well, I guess even stupid people must know that a person could make a tomato go *down* through a trapdoor, but he'd have a pretty hard time trying to make it come back *up*, wouldn't he?"

Mrs. Crenshaw just sat there, buttocks shlomping over the edges of the lawn chair she was slowly driving into the sod, smiling pleasantly. Her thoughts had faded from Hilly's head like a bad radio signal.

He put the scarf on top of the platform again. Waved his wand. Stepped on the pedal. The blue scarf pushed up in a sphere. Hilly whipped it triumphantly off to reveal the tomato again.

"Ta-*daaa!*" he shouted. *Now* the gasps and shouts would come.

More polite applause.

Barney Applegate yawned.

Hilly could have cheerfully shot him.

Hilly had planned to work his way up from the tomato trick to his Grand Finale, and it was a good plan, as far as it went. It just didn't go far enough. In his forgivable excitement at having invented a machine that actually made things disappear (he thought he might give it to the Pentagon or something after he had gotten his picture on the cover of *Newsweek* as the greatest magician in history), Hilly overlooked two things. First, that no one but infants and morons at *any* magic show believe the tricks are real, and second, he was doing essentially the same trick over and over again. Each fresh instance differed from the last only in degree.

From the Disappearing Tomato and the Return of the Disappearing Tomato, Hilly pushed grimly on to the Disappearing Radio (his father's, considerably lighter with its eight D-cell batteries now in the guts of the gadget under the platform) and the Return of Same.

Polite applause.

The Disappearing Lawn Chair, followed by the Return of the You-Guessed-It.

His audience sat lumpishly, as if sun-stunned . . . or perhaps stunned by whatever was now in the air of Haven. If anything *was* oxidizing from the ship's hull and entering the atmosphere, it was surely heavy that day, which was without even a slight stir of wind.

Got to do something, Hilly thought, panicked.

He decided on the spur of the moment to skip the Disappearing Bookcase, the Disappearing Exer-Cycle (Mom's), and the Disappearing Motorcycle (Dad's, and in his dad's present mood, Hilly doubted if he would volunteer to drive it up onto the platform anyway). He would go right to the Grand Finale:

The Disappearing Little Brother.

"And now—"

"Hilly, I'm sorry, but—" his father began.

"—for my *final* trick," Hilly added quickly, and saw his father settle back reluctantly, "I need a volunteer from the audience. C'mere, David."

David came forward with an expression in which fear and resignation were perfectly balanced. Although he had not been precisely told, David knew what the final trick was. He knew too well.

"I don't wanna," he whispered.

"You're *gonna,*" Hilly said grimly.

"Hilly, I'm scared." David was pleading, his eyes filled with tears. "What if I don't come back?"

"You *will,*" Hilly whispered. "Everything *else* did, didn't it?"

"Yeah, but you didn't disappear nothin that was *alive,*" David said. Now the tears overspilled and ran down his face.

Looking at his brother, whom he had loved so well and so successfully (he'd had more success loving David than he had doing anything else he had set his hand to, including magic), Hilly felt a moment of horrible doubt. It was like waking temporarily from a nightmare before it sucked you back down. *You aren't going to do this, are you? You wouldn't push him out into a busy street just because you thought all the cars would stop in time, would you? You don't even know where those things go when they stop being here!*

Then he looked out at the audience—bored and inattentive, the only one who looked half-alive being Barney Applegate, who was carefully picking a scab off his elbow—and the resentment rose up again. He stopped seeing the frightened tears in David's eyes.

"Get up on the platform, David!" Hilly whispered grimly.

David's small face began to quiver all over . . . but he walked toward the platform. He had never disobeyed Hilly, whom he had idolized all the fifteen-hundred-odd days of his life, and he did not disobey him now. Nevertheless, his pudgy legs could barely hold him as he stepped onto the sheet-covered orange crate with the nutty machine underneath.

David faced the audience, a small round boy in blue shorts and a faded T-shirt that said THEY CALL ME DR. LOVE. Tears streamed down his face.

"*Smile,* dammit," Hilly hissed, putting his foot on the sewing-machine pedal.

Weeping harder, David nevertheless managed a hideous parody of a smile. Marie Brown did not see her younger son's tears of terror. Mrs. Crenshaw had changed seats (half the aluminum legs of the one she had been in had now submerged in the lawn) and prepared to go. She didn't care if she sold the stupid cunt any Avon or not. This torture wasn't worth it.

"And *NOW!*" Hilly blared at his dazed audience. "The biggest secret the Orient holds! Known to few and practiced by fewer! The Disappearing Human! Watch closely!"

He threw the sheet over David's quivering form. As it billowed down to David's feet, an audible sob came from beneath. Hilly felt another quiver of what might have been fear or sanity struggling feebly to reassert itself.

"Hilly, please . . . please, I'm scared . . ." The muffled whisper drifted out.

Hilly hesitated. And suddenly thought: *Off you go! Know that you can! Cause I learned this trick . . . from the Tommyknocker Man!*

It was shortly after that when Hilly Brown really and truly lost his mind.

"Presto-majesto!" he shouted, and waved his hand at the quivering sheet-covered form on the platform, and stomped the pedal.

Hummmmmmmmmmmm.

The sheet puffed down lazily, as a sheet will do when a man or a woman tosses it over a bed and allows it to settle.

Hilly whipped it away.

"Ta-*daaaaa!*" he shrieked. He was half-delirious with a mixture of triumph and fear, the two of them for the moment perfectly balanced, like children of equal weights on a teeter-totter.

David was gone.

9

For a moment the general apathy was broken. Barney Applegate stopped picking his scab. Bryant Brown sat up in his chair, his mouth open. Marie and Mrs. Crenshaw broke off their whispered conversation, and Ev Hillman frowned and looked worried . . . although this expression was not exactly new. Ev had looked and felt worried for some days now.

Ahhh, Hilly thought, and balm flowed over his soul. *Success!*

Both the audience's interest and Hilly's triumph were short-lived. Tricks involving *people* are always more interesting than tricks involving things or animals (pulling a rabbit from a hat is all perfectly well, but no magician worth his salt ever decided on that basis that an audience would rather watch a horse be sawed in half than a pretty girl with a generous figure packed into a small costume) . . . but it was still, after all, the same trick. The applause was louder this time (and Barney Applegate let out a hearty *"Yayyyyy, Hilly!"),* but it died quickly. Hilly saw that his mother was whispering with Mrs. Crenshaw again. His father got up.

"Gonna take a shower, Hilly," he mumbled. "Damn good show."

"But—"

A horn honked from the driveway.

"That's my mom," Barney said, jumping up so fast he almost knocked Mrs. Crenshaw over. "Seeya, Hilly! Good trick!"

"But—" Now Hilly felt tears sting his own eyes.

Barney dropped to his knees and waved, as if underneath the platform. "Bye, Davey! Good job!"

"He's not under there, dammit!" Hilly yelled.

But Barney was already scampering away. Hilly's mother and Mrs. Crenshaw were walking toward the back door, examining an Avon catalogue. It was all happening so *fast.* "Don't swear, Hilly," his mom called without looking back. "And make David wash his hands when you come into the house. It's dirty under there."

Only David's grandfather, Ev Hillman, was left. Ev was looking at Hilly with that same worried expression.

"Why don't you go away, too?" Hilly asked with a bitter fierceness that was spoiled only by the blurriness of his voice.

"Hilly, if your brother *isn't* under there," Ev said in a slow voice that was totally unlike his usual one, "then just where *is* he?"

I don't know, Hilly thought, and that was when the teeter-totter began to shift. Anger went down. Way down. And fear went way, way up. With fear came guilt. A snapshot of David's weeping, terrified face. A snapshot of his own (courtesy of a good imagination), looking angry and almost vicious—bullying for sure. *Smile, dammit.* David trying to smile through his tears.

"Oh, he's under there, all right," Hilly said. He burst into loud sobs and sat down on his stage, pulling his knees up and leaning his hot face against them. "He's under there, yeah, everybody guessed my tricks and nobody liked them, I hate magic, I wish you'd never given me that stupid magic set in the first place—"

"Hilly—" Ev came forward, looking distressed as well as worried now. Something was wrong here . . . here and all over Haven. He *felt* it. "What's wrong?"

"Get out of here!" Hilly sobbed. *"I hate you! I HATE you!"*

Grandfathers are every bit as subject to hurt, shame, and confusion as anyone else. Ev Hillman felt all three now. It hurt to hear Hilly say he hated him—it hurt even though the boy was obviously emotionally exhausted. Ev felt shamed that it was his gift that had provoked Hilly's tears . . . and never mind the fact that his son-in-law had picked out the magic set. Ev had accepted it as his gift when it had pleased Hilly; he supposed he must also accept it now that it was making Hilly weep with his face against his dirty knees. He felt confused because something *else* was going on here . . . but what? He did not know. He did know that he had just begun to get used to the idea that he was becoming senile—oh, the effects were still quite small, but the condition seemed to accelerate a little every year—when this summer came along. And this summer *everybody* seemed to be getting senile . . . but what exactly did he mean by that? A look in the eyes? Odd lapses, gropings for names that should have come quickly and easily? Those things, yes. But there was more. He just couldn't put his finger on what that more might be.

This confusion, so unlike the vacuity which had afflicted the others who had attended the SECOND GALA MAGIC SHOW, caused Ev Hillman, who had been the only person there whose *mentis* was really *compos* (he was, in fact, the only person in Haven these days whose *mentis* was really *compos*—Jim Gardener was also relatively unaffected by the ship in the earth, but by the seventeenth, Gardener had begun drinking heavily again), to do something he regretted bitterly later. Instead of getting down on his arthritis-creaky knees and peering under Hilly's makeshift stage to see if David Brown really *was* under there, he retreated. He retreated as much from the idea that his birthday gift had caused Hilly's present grief as from anything else. He left Hilly alone, thinking he would come back "when the boy got hold of himself."

10

As he watched his grampy shuffle away, Hilly's guilt and misery doubled . . . then trebled. He waited until Ev was gone, then scrambled to his feet and walked back to the platform. He put his foot on the concealed sewing-machine pedal and stepped on it.

Hummmmmmmmm.

He waited for the sheet to plump up in David's shape. He would whip the sheet off him and say, *There, ya baby, see? That wasn't* NOTHING, *was it?* He might even swat David a good one for scaring him and making him feel so lousy. Or maybe he'd just—

Nothing was happening.

Fear began to swell in Hilly's throat. Began . . . or had it really been there all the time? All the time, he thought. Only now it was . . . swelling, yeah, that was just the right word! *Swelling* in there, as if someone had stuck a balloon down his throat and was now inflating it. This new fear made misery look good and guilt absolutely peachy in comparison. He tried to swallow and couldn't get any spit past that swelling.

"David?" he whispered, and pushed the pedal again.

Hummmmmmm.

He decided he wouldn't swat David. He would *hug* David. When David got back, Hilly would fall down on his knees and hug David and tell David he could have *all* the G.I. Joe guys (except maybe for Snake-Eyes and Crystal Ball) for a whole week.

Nothing was *still* happening.

The sheet that had covered David lay crumpled on the one which covered the crate over his machine. It didn't plump up in a David-shape at all. Hilly stood all by himself in his back yard with the hot July sun beating down on him, his heart racing faster and faster in his chest, that balloon swelling in his throat. *When it finally gets big enough to pop,* he thought, *I'll probably scream.*

Quit it! He'll come back! Sure he will! The tomato came back, and the radio, and the lawn chair. Also, all the things I experimented on in my room came back. He . . . he . . .

"You and David come in and wash up, Hilly!" his mother called.

"Yeah, Mom!" Hilly called back in a wavering, insanely cheerful voice. "Pretty soon!"

And thought: *Please God let him come back, I'm sorry God, I'll do anything, he can have all the G.I. Joe guys forever, I swear he can, he can have the* MOBAT *and even the Terrordome, only God dear God,* PLEASE LET IT WORK THIS TIME LET HIM COME BACK!

He pressed on the pedal again.

Hummmmmm . . .

He looked at the crumpled sheet through tear-blurred eyes. For a moment he thought something was happening, but it was only a puff of wind stirring the crumpled sheet.

Panic as bright as metal shavings began to twist through Hilly's mind. Shortly he *would* begin to scream, drawing his mother from the kitchen and his dripping father, naked except for a towel around his waist and shampoo running down his cheeks, both of them wondering what Hilly had done this time. The panic would be merciful in one way: when it came, it would obliterate thought.

But things had not gone that far yet, unfortunately. Two thoughts occurred to Hilly's bright mind in rapid succession.

The first: *I never disappeared anything that was alive. Even the tomato was picked, and Daddy said once you pick something it's not really alive anymore.*

The second thought: *What if David can't breathe wherever he is? What if he can't BREATHE?*

He had wondered very little about what happened to the things he "disappeared" until this moment. But now . . .

His last coherent thought before the panic descended like a pall—or a mourning veil—was actually a mental image. He saw David lying in the middle of some weird, inimical landscape. It looked like the surface of a harsh, dead world. The gray earth was dry and cold; cracks gaped like dead reptilian mouths. They went zigzagging away in every direction. Overhead was a sky blacker than jewelers' velvet, and a billion stars screamed down—they were brighter than the stars anyone on the surface of the earth had ever seen, because the place Hilly was looking at with the wide, horrified eye of his imagination was almost or totally airless.

And in the middle of this alien desolation lay his chubby four-year-old brother in a pair of shorts and a T-shirt reading THEY CALL ME DR. LOVE. David was clutching at his throat, trying to breathe the no-air of a world that was maybe a trillion light-years from home. David was gagging, turning purple. Frost was tracing death-patterns across his lips and fingernails. He—

Ah, but then the merciful panic finally took over.

He raked back the sheet he had used to cover David and overturned the crate that had concealed the machine. He stomped the sewing-machine pedal again and again, and began to scream. It was not until his mother reached him that she realized he was not *just* screaming; there were actually *words* in all that noise.

"*All* the G.I. Joes!" Hilly shrieked. "All the G.I. Joes! *All* the G.I. Joes! Forever and ever! *All* the G.I. Joes!"

And then, infinitely more chilling:

"Come back, David! Come back, David! Come back!"

"Dear God, what does he mean?" Marie cried.

Bryant took his son by the shoulders and turned him around so they were face-to-face.

"Where's David? Where did he go?"

But Hilly had fainted, and he never really came to. Not long after, over a hundred men and women, Bobbi and Gard among them, were in the woods across the road, beating the bushes for Hilly's brother David.

If he could have been asked, Hilly would have told them that, in his opinion, they were looking too close to home.

Far too close.

4.

BENT AND JINGLES

1

On the evening of July 24th, a week after the disappearance of David Brown, Trooper Benton Rhodes was driving a state police cruiser out of Haven around eight o'clock. Peter Gabbons, known to his fellow officers as Jingles, was riding shotgun. Twilight lay in ashes. These were *metaphorical* ashes, of course, as opposed to the ones on the hands and faces of the two state cops. *Those* ashes were real. Rhodes's mind kept returning to the severed hand and arm, and to the fact that he had known instantly to whom they had once belonged. Jesus!

Stop thinking about it! he ordered his mind.

Okay, his mind agreed, and went right on thinking about it. "Try the radio again," he said. "I bet we're getting interference from that damn microwave dish they put up in Troy."

"All right." Jingles grabbed the mike. "This is Unit 16 to Base. Do you copy, Tug? Over."

He let go of the button and they both listened. What they heard was a peculiar screaming static, with ghostly voices buried deep inside it.

"Want me to try again?" Jingles asked.

"No. We'll be clear soon enough."

Bent was running with the flashers on, doing seventy along Route 3 toward Derry. Where the hell were the backup units? There hadn't been a communications problem to and from Haven Village; radio transmissions so clear they were almost eerie. Nor had the radio been the only eerie thing about Haven tonight.

Right! his mind agreed. *And by the way, you recognized the ring right away, didn't you? No mistaking a trooper's ring, even on a woman's hand, is there? And did you see the way her tendons were hanging down in flaps? Looked like a cut of meat in a butcher shop, didn't it? Leg of lamb, or something. Tore her arm right off! It—*

Stop it, I said! Goddammit, JUST QUIT!

Okay, yeah, right. Forgot for a sec that you didn't want to think about it. Or like a rolled roast, huh? And all that blood!

Stop it, please stop it, he moaned.

Right, okay, I know I'll drive me crazy if I keep thinking about it but I think I'll just keep thinking about it anyway because I just can't seem to stop. Her hand, her arm, they were bad, worse than any traffic accident I ever saw, but what about all those other pieces? The severed heads? The eyes? The feet? Yessir, that must have been a wowser of a furnace explosion, all right!

"Where's our backup?" Jingles asked restlessly.

"I don't know."

But when he saw them, he could really stump them, couldn't he?

Got a riddle for you, he could say. *You'll never get it. How can you have mangled bodies all over the place after an explosion, but only one dead? And just by the way, how come the only real damage a* furnace *explosion did was to tear off the* steeple *of the town hall? For that matter, how come the head selectman, that guy Berringer, wasn't able to ID the body, when even* I *knew who it was? Give up, guys?*

He had covered the arm with a blanket. There was nothing to be done about all the other body parts, and he supposed it didn't matter anyway. But he had covered Ruth's arm.

On the sidewalk in Haven Village's town square he had done that. He had done it while that idiot volunteer fire chief, Allison, stood grinning as if it was a bean supper instead of an explosion that had killed a fine woman. It was all crazy. Crazy to the max.

Peter Gabbons was nicknamed Jingles because of his gravelly Andy Devine voice—Jingles was a character Devine had played in an old TV western series. When

Gabbons came up from Georgia, Tug Ellender, the dispatcher, had started calling him that and it had stuck. Now, speaking in a high, strangled voice completely unlike his usual Jingles voice, Gabbons said: "Pull over, Bent. I'm sick."

Rhodes pulled over in a hurry, on the very edge of a skid that almost dumped the cruiser in the ditch. At least Gabbons had been the first to call it; that was something.

Jingles dove from the cruiser on the right. Bent Rhodes dove out on the left. In the blue strobe of the state police cruiser's lights, they both threw up everything available. Bent staggered back against the side of the car, pawing his mouth with one hand, hearing the retching noises still coming from the weeds beyond the edge of the road. He rolled his head skyward, dimly grateful for the breeze.

"That's better," Jingles said at last. "Thanks, Bent."

Benton turned toward his partner. Jingles' eyes were dark, shocked holes in his face. It was the look of a man who is processing all his information and reaching no sane conclusions at all.

"What happened back there?" Bent asked.

"You blind, hoss? Town-hall steeple took off like a rocket."

"So how did a furnace explosion blow off the steeple?"

"Dunno."

"Spit on that." Bent tried to spit. He couldn't. "You believe it? A July furnace explosion that blows the *steeple* off the town hall?"

"No. It stinks."

"Right, pard. It stinks to high heaven." Bent paused. "Jingles, what did you *feel?* Did you feel anything weird back there?"

Jingles said cautiously: "Maybe. Maybe I did feel something."

"What?"

"I don't *know,*" Jingles said. His voice had begun to climb, to take on the uneven, warbling inflections of a small child near tears. Above them, a galaxy of stars shone down. Crickets sang in fragrant summer silence. "I'm just so damn glad to be out of there—"

Then Jingles, who knew he would be going back to Haven the next day to assist in the cleanup and investigation, *did* begin to cry.

2

After a while they drove on. Any remaining trace of daylight had by then left the sky. Bent was glad. He didn't really want to look at Jingles . . . and didn't really want Jingles looking at him.

By the way, Bent, his mind now spoke up, *it was pretty goddam startling, wasn't it? Pretty goddam weird. The severed heads and the legs with the little shoes still on most of the little feet? And the torsos! Did you see the torsos? The eye! That one blue eye? Did you see that? Must have! You kicked it into the gutter when you bent over to pick up Ruth McCausland's arm. All those severed arms and legs and heads and torsos, but Ruth was the only person who died. It's a riddle for a champeen riddle contest, all right.*

The body parts had been bad. The shredded remains of the bats—an almighty lot of them—had *also* been bad. But neither had been as bad as Ruth's arm with her husband's ring on the third finger of the right hand, because Ruth's hand and arm had been *real.*

The severed heads and legs and torsos had given him a hell of a shock at first—for a numb instant he had wondered, summer vacation or not, if a class had been touring the town hall when it blew. Then his numbed mind realized that not even kindergarten kids possessed limbs so small, and that *no* children possessed arms and legs which did not bleed when they were ripped from their bodies.

He had looked around and seen Jingles holding a small, smoking head in one hand and a partially melted leg in the other.

"Dolls," Jingles had said. "Fucking *dolls.* Where did all the fucking dolls come from, Bent?"

He had been about to answer, to say he didn't know (although even then something about those dolls had tugged at him; it would come to him in time), when he noticed that there were people still eating in the Haven Lunch. People still shopping in the market. A deep chill had touched his heart like a finger made of ice. This was a woman most of them had known all their lives—known, respected, and in many cases loved—but they were going on about their business.

Going on about their business as if nothing at all had happened.

That was when Bent Rhodes started wanting—*seriously* wanting—to be out of Haven.

Now, turning down the radio that was still grinding out nothing but meaningless static, Bent remembered what had tugged at his mind earlier. *"She* had dolls. Mrs. McCausland." *Ruth,* Bent thought. *I wish I'd known her well enough to call her Ruth, like Monster does. Did. Everyone liked her, s'far as I know. Which is why it seemed so wrong to see them just going about their business—*

"I guess I heard that," Jingles said. "Hobby of hers, right? I guess I might've heard that at the Haven Lunch. Or maybe at Cooder's, having a pop with the oldtimers."

A beer with the oldtimers, more like it, Rhodes thought, but he only nodded. "Yeah. And that's what they were, I reckon. Her dolls. I was talking about Mrs. McCausland one day last spring, I guess it was, with Monster, and—"

"Monster?" Jingles asked. "Monster Dugan knew Mrs. McCausland?"

"Pretty well, I guess. Monster and her husband were partners before her husband died. Anyway, he said she had a hundred dolls, maybe two hundred. He said they were her only hobby, and they were exhibited once in Augusta. He said she was prouder of that exhibit than she was of any of the things she'd done for the town—and I guess she did a lot of things for Haven."

I wish I could have called her Ruth, he thought again.

"Monster said except for her dolls, she worked all the time." Bent considered, then added: "The way Monster talked, I got an idea he was . . . uh, sweet on her." That sounded as old-fucking-fashioned as a Roy Rogers western, but that was just how Butch "Monster" Dugan had always seemed about Ruth McCausland. "Most likely you won't be the one gets stuck breaking the news to him, but if you should, lemme give you some advice: don't crack wise."

"Yeah, okay, duly noted. Monster Dugan on my case, that's all I'd need to round the day off, you know?"

Bent smiled with no humor.

"Her doll collection," Jingles said. He nodded. "Course

I knew they were dolls—" He saw Bent's wry glance, and smiled a little. "Okay, I had a second or two there when . . . but soon's I saw the way the sun was shinin on them, and how there was no blood, I knew what they were. Just couldn't figure out how come there was so many."

"You *still* don't know that. That, or much else. We don't know what they were doing there. Hell, what was *she* doing there?"

Jingles looked miserable. "Who would have killed her, Bent? She was such a nice lady. Goddam!"

"I think she was murdered," Bent said. His voice sounded like breaking sticks in his ears. "Did it look like an accident to you?"

"No. That wasn't no furnace explosion. And the fumes that kept us from going down in the basement—that smell like oil to you?"

Bent shook his head. Whatever it was, he'd never before smelled anything like it in his life. Maybe the only thing that nit Berringer had been right about was his opinion that breathing those fumes could be dangerous and it might be best to stay upstairs until the air in the town-hall basement cleared. Now he had to wonder if they'd been kept away on purpose—maybe so they wouldn't see a furnace that was completely unwounded.

"After we file our reports on this fucker," Jingles said, "the local yokels are gonna have a lot of explaining to do. Allison, Berringer, those guys. And they may have to do some of it to Dugan."

Bent nodded thoughtfully. "Whole fucking thing was crazy. The place *felt* crazy. I mean, I actually started to get dizzy. Did you?"

"The fumes—" Jingles began doubtfully.

"Fuck the fumes. I was dizzy in the *street.*"

"Her dolls, Bent. What were her dolls doing there?"

"I don't know."

"Me either. But it's another thing that doesn't fit for shit. Try this on: if somebody hated her enough to murder her, maybe they hated her enough to blow her dolls up with her. You think?"

"Not really," Benton Rhodes said.

"But it *could* be," Jingles said, as if saying so proved it. Bent began to understand that Jingles was striving to create sanity out of insanity. He told Jingles to try the radio again.

Their reception was a little better but still nothing to write home about. Bent couldn't remember ever getting deep interference from the Troy microwave dish this close to Derry before.

3

According to the witnesses they spoke to, the explosion had occurred at 3:05 P.M., give or take half a minute. The town-hall clock struck three as it always did. Five minutes later, KA-BAM! And now, riding back to Derry in the dark, an oddly persuasive picture occurred to Benton Rhodes, one that brought gooseflesh to attention all over his body. He saw the clock in the town-hall tower standing at four minutes past three on that hot and windless late-July afternoon. And suddenly, a look passes among those in the Haven Lunch; those in Cooder's General Store; those in Haven Hardware; the ladies in the Junque-A-Torium; the children on the swings or hanging listlessly in the summer heat from the bars of the jungle gym in the playyard beside the school; it goes from the eyes of one of the overweight ladies playing doubles on the town tennis courts behind the town hall to her partner, and then to their overweight opponents on the other side of the net. The game-ball goes rolling slowly into a far corner of the court as they lie down and put their hands over their ears . . . and wait. As they wait for the explosion.

Everyone in town, lying down and waiting for that KA-BLAM to drill into the day like the stroke of a sledgehammer on thick wood.

Bent suddenly shuddered behind the wheel of the cruiser.

The checkout girls at Cooder's. The customers in the aisles. The people in the Haven Lunch by the stools or behind the counter. At 3:04 P.M. they laid down, the whole fucking bunch of them. And at 3:06 they got up and went about their business. All of 'em except for the Designated Gawkers. Also Allison and Berringer, who told everybody it was a furnace explosion, which it wasn't, and that they didn't know who the victim was, which they fucking well did.

You don't believe they all knew it was going to happen, do you?

A part of him believed *just* that. Because if the good folks of Haven *hadn't* known, how come the only casualties had been Ruth McCausland and her dolls? How come there hadn't been so much as a single cut arm when a shower of glass had flown across Main Street at a speed of roughly one hundred and ten miles an hour?

"I think we ought to be clear of that fucking dish by now," Bent said. "Try it again."

Jingles took the mike. "I still don't understand where the goddam backups are."

"Maybe something happened somewhere else. It never rains—"

"Yeah, it pours. Dolly arms and legs, among other things." As Jingles depressed the mike button, Bent piloted the cruiser around a curve. The headlights and flashers splashed over a pickup truck that was slewed diagonally in the middle of the road.

"Jesus Chr—" Then reflexes took over and he hit the brakes. Firestone rubber screamed and smoked; for a moment Bent thought he was going to lose it. Then the cruiser came to a halt with its nose three yards from the body of the mongrel truck sitting silent in the road.

"Please pass the toilet paper," Jingles said in a low, trembling voice.

They got out, both unstrapping the handles of their guns without thinking. The smell of cooked rubber hung in the summer air.

"What's *this* shit?" Jingles cried, and Bent thought: *He feels it too. This isn't right, this is part of what was going on back in that creepy little town, and he feels it too.*

The breeze stirred, and Bent heard canvas flap stiffly for a moment, and a tarp slid off something in the bed of the pickup with a dry rattlesnake sound. Bent felt his balls climb north in a hurry. It looked like the barrel of a bazooka. He started to crouch, then realized with bewilderment that the bazooka was only a length of corrugated culvert-pipe in some sort of wooden cradle. Nothing to be afraid of. But he *was* afraid. He was *terrified*.

"I saw that truck back in Haven, Bent. Parked in front of the restaurant."

"Who's there?" Bent shouted.

No answer.

He looked at Jingles. Jingles, eyes wide and dark in his white face, looked back at him.

Bent thought suddenly: *Microwave interference? Was that really what was keeping us from getting through?*

"If someone's in that truck, you better speak up!" Bent called. "You—"

A shrill, crazed titter came from the truck-bed, then drifted into silence.

"Oh Christ, I don't like this," Jingles Gabbons moaned.

Bent started forward, raising his gun, and then the world was filled with green light.

5.

RUTH McCAUSLAND

1

Ruth Arlene Merrill McCausland was fifty but looked ten years younger—fifteen on a good day. Everyone in Haven agreed that, woman or not, she was just about the best damned constable the town had ever had. It was because her husband had been a state trooper, some said. Others said it was simply because Ruth was Ruth. Either way, they agreed Haven was lucky to have her. She was firm but fair. She was able to keep her wits in an emergency. Haven folk said these things about her, and more besides. In a small Maine town run by the men since there had been a town to run, such testimonials were of some note. That was fair enough; she was a noteworthy woman.

She was born and raised in Haven; she was, in fact, the great-niece of the Rev. Mr. Donald Hartley, who had been so cruelly surprised by the town's vote to change its name back in '01. In 1955 she had been granted early admittance to the University of Maine—only the third female student in the history of the university to be granted full-time-student status at the tender age of seventeen. She enrolled in the college's pre-law program.

The following year she fell in love with Ralph McCausland, who was also in pre-law. He was tall; at six-five he was still three inches shorter than his friend Anthony Dugan (known as Butch by his friends, as Monster only by his two or three *close* friends), but he towered a full foot over Ruth. He was oddly—almost absurdly—graceful for such a big man, and good-natured. He wanted to be a state trooper. When Ruth asked him why, he said it was because his father had been one. He didn't need a law degree to join the fuzz, he explained to her; to become a state trooper he needed only a high-school education, good eyes, good reflexes, and a clean record. But Ralph McCausland had wanted something more than to do his father the honor of following in his footsteps. "Any man who gets into a job and doesn't plan a way to get ahead is either lazy or crazy," he told Ruth one night over Cokes in the Bear's Den. What he didn't tell her, because he was shy about his ambition, was that he hoped to be Maine's top cop someday. Ruth knew anyway, of course.

She accepted Ralph's proposal of marriage the following year on condition that he would wait until she had her own degree. She did not want to practice law, she said, but she *did* want to help him all she could. Ralph agreed. Any sane man confronted with Ruth Merrill's clear-eyed, intelligent beauty would have agreed. When Ralph married her in 1959, she was a lawyer.

She came to their marriage bed a virgin. She had been a little worried about this, although only a deep part of her mind—a part over which even she could not exert her usual iron control—dared to wonder in a murky way if *that* part of him was as big as the rest of him; it felt that way sometimes when they danced, and petted. But he was gentle, and there was only a momentary discomfort that quickly turned to pleasure. "Make me pregnant," she whispered in his ear as he began to move above her, in her.

"My pleasure, lady," Ralph said a little breathlessly.

But Ruth never quickened.

Ruth, the only child of John and Holly Merrill, had inherited a fairish sum of money and a fine old house in Haven Village when her father died in 1962. She and Ralph sold their small postwar tract home in Derry and moved back to Haven in 1963. And although neither of them would admit anything less than perfect happiness to the other, both were aware that there were too many empty rooms in the old Victorian house. Perhaps, Ruth sometimes thought, perfect happiness occurs only in a context of small discordancies: the shattering crash of an overturned vase or fishbowl, an exultant, laughing yell just as you are drifting into a pleasant late-afternoon doze, the child who gets pregnant with Halloween candy and who must perforce give birth to a nightmare in the early-morning hours of November lst. In her wistful moments (she saw to it that there were damned few of them) Ruth sometimes thought of the Mohammedan rugmakers, who always included a deliberate error in their work to honor the perfect Deity who had made them, more fallible creatures. It occurred to her more than once that, in the tapestry of an honestly lived life, a child guaranteed such a respectful error.

But, for the most part, they *were* happy. They prepared Ralph's most difficult cases together, and his court testimony was always quiet, respectful, and devastating. It mattered little if you were a drunk driver, an arsonist, or a fellow who'd broken a beer bottle over another fellow's head in a drunken roadhouse argument. If you were arrested by Ralph McCausland, your chances of beating the rap were roughly the chances of a guy standing at ground-zero of a nuclear test site receiving only minor flesh-wounds.

During the years when Ralph was making his slow but steady climb up the ladder of the Maine State Police bureaucracy, Ruth began her career of town service—not that she ever thought of it as a "career," and certainly she never thought of it in the context of "politics." Not town politics, but town service. That was a small but crucial difference. She was not as calmly happy about her work as she seemed to the people she was working for. It would have taken a child to completely fulfill her. There was nothing surprising or demeaning in this. She was, after all, a child of her own time, and even the very intelligent are not immune to a steady barrage of propaganda. She and Ralph had been to a doctor in Boston, and after extensive tests, he assured them that they were both fertile. His advice was for them to relax. In a way, this was cruel news. If one of them had proved to be sterile, they would have adopted. As it was, they decided to wait awhile and take the doctor's advice . . . or try. And although neither knew or even intuited it, Ralph didn't have long to live by the time they had begun to discuss adoption again.

In those last years of her marriage, Ruth had performed a sort of adoption of her own—she adopted Haven.

The library, for instance. The Methodist parsonage had been full of books since time out of mind—some were Detective Book Club and Reader's Digest Condensed Books from which a clear scent of mold arose when you opened them; others had bloated to the size of telephone books when the pipes in the parsonage burst in 1947, but most were in surprisingly good condition. Ruth patiently winnowed them, keeping the good ones, selling the bad ones to be repulped, throwing away only those completely beyond salvage. The Haven Community Library had officially opened in the repainted and refurbished Methodist parsonage in December of 1968, with Ruth McCausland as volunteer librarian, a post she held until 1973. On the day she retired, the trustees hung a photograph of her over the mantel in the reading room. Ruth protested, then gave in when she saw they meant to honor her whether she wanted the honor or not. She could hurt their feelings, she saw, but not alter their purpose. They *needed* to honor her. The library, which she had begun single-handed, sitting on the cold parsonage floor, bundled up in one of Ralph's old red-checked hunting jackets, her breath smoking from her mouth and nose, sorting patiently through boxes of books until her hands went numb, was in 1972 voted Maine's Small Town Library of the Year.

Ruth would have taken at least some pleasure at this under other circumstances, but she took little pleasure in anything during 1972 and '73. Nineteen seventy-two was the year Ralph McCausland died. In the late spring, he began to complain of bad headaches. In June, a large firespot appeared in his right eye. X-rays revealed a brain tumor. He died in October, two days short of his thirty-seventh birthday.

In the funeral parlor, Ruth stood looking down into his open coffin for a long time. She had wept almost steadily over the last week, and she suspected that there would be more tears to shed—oceans, perhaps—in the weeks and months ahead. But she would no more have wept in public than she would have appeared there naked. To those watching (which was damned near everyone), she seemed as sweetly composed as always.

"Goodbye, dear," she said at last, and kissed the corner of his mouth. She slipped his trooper's ring from the third finger of his right hand and onto the third finger of her own. The next day she drove to G. M. Pollock's in

Bangor and had it sized. She wore it until the day she died, and although in the violence of her dying her arm would be ripped from her shoulder, neither Bent nor Jingles had any trouble ID'ing that ring.

2

The library was not Ruth's only service to the town. Each fall she collected for the Cancer Society, and for each of the seven years she did this, she collected the largest total donation in the Maine Cancer Society's small-town category. The secret of her success was simple: Ruth went *everywhere.* She spoke pleasantly and fearlessly to thick-browed, sunken-eyed backroad dwellers who often looked almost as mongrelized as the snarling dogs they kept in back yards filled with the dead and decaying bodies of old cars and farm implements. And in most cases she got a donation. Perhaps some were surprised into it simply because it had been so long since they'd had company.

She was dog-bit only once. It was, however, a memorable occasion. The dog itself wasn't big, but it had *lots* of teeth.

MORAN, the mailbox said. No one home but the dog. The dog came around the side of the house, growling, as she stood knocking on the unpainted porch door. She held out a hand to it, and Mr. Moran's dog immediately bit it and then stepped away from Ruth and piddled on the porch in its excitement. Ruth started down the steps, taking a handkerchief from her purse and wrapping it around her bleeding hand. The dog bounded after her and bit her again, this time on the leg. She kicked at it and it shied away, but as she limped on toward her Dart, it came up behind her and bit her a third time. This was the only serious bite. Mr. Moran's dog removed a sizable chunk of meat from Ruth's left calf (she was wearing a skirt that day; she never went out collecting for the Cancer Society in a skirt again) and then retired to the center of Mr. Moran's weedy front lawn, where it sat snarling and slobbering, Ruth's blood dripping from its lolling tongue. Instead of getting behind the wheel of her car, she opened the Dart's trunk. She did not hurry. She felt if she did, the dog would almost certainly attack her again. She took the Remington .30-06 she'd had ever since she was sixteen. She shot the dog dead just as it began trotting toward her again. She picked up the corpse and laid it on spread newspapers in her trunk and drove it to Dr. Daggett, the Augusta vet who had cared for Bobbi's dog, Peter, before selling the practice and moving to Florida. "If this bitch was rabid, I am in a good deal of trouble," she told Daggett. The vet peered from the dog, which had a bullet directly between its glazed eyes and very little left to the back of its skull, to Ruth McCausland, who, although bitten and bleeding, was as pleasant as ever. "I know I haven't left as much of the brain for examination as you'd probably like, but that was unavoidable. Would you take a look, Dr. Daggett?" He told her she needed to see a doctor; the wounds had to be flushed, and she'd need stitches in her calf. Daggett was as close to flustered as Daggett ever got. Ruth told him he was perfectly capable of flushing the wounds. As for what she called "the crocheting," she would go to the emergency room at Derry Home as soon as she made a few telephone calls. She told him to work on the dog while she made them, and asked if she could use his private office so as not to upset the clientele. A woman had screamed when Ruth came in, which was not really surprising. One of Ruth's legs was bloody and torn open. In her blood-streaked arms she bore the stiffening, blanket-wrapped corpse of Moran's dog. Daggett said she was welcome to use his phone. She did so (being careful to reverse the charges the first time and billing the call to her home telephone the second time; she somehow doubted if Mr. Moran would accept a collect call). Ralph was at Monster Dugan's house, going over crime photos for an upcoming manslaughter trial. Monster's wife detected nothing amiss in Ruth's voice and neither did Ralph; he told her later that she would have made a great criminal. She said she had taken a delay while canvassing for the Cancer Society. She told him if he got home before she did, he should warm up the meatloaf and make himself some of those stir-fried vegetables that he liked; there were six or seven packages in the freezer. Also, she said, there was a coffee cake in the breadbox if he fancied something sweet. By now, Daggett had come into the office and was disinfecting her wounds and Ruth was very pale. Ralph wanted to know what kind of delay she had taken. She said she'd tell him about it when she got home. Ralph said he looked forward to it and said he loved her. Ruth said she felt exactly the same way about him. Then, as Daggett finished with the bite behind her knee (he'd done her hand while she spoke to Ralph) and went on to the deep wound in her calf (she could actually *feel* her wounded flesh trying to pull away from the alcohol), she called Mr. Moran. Ruth told him his dog had bitten her three times and that was one time too many so she had shot and killed it and that she had left his pledge card in his mailbox and the American Cancer Society would be very grateful for any donation he felt he could make. There was a brief silence. Then Mr. Moran began to speak. Soon Mr. Moran began to shout. Finally Mr. Moran began to scream. Mr. Moran was so enraged he attained a vulgar fluency of expression that neared not just poetry but Homeric verse. He would never equal it again in his life, although when he sometimes tried and failed, he would remember that conversation with a sad, almost fond nostalgia. She'd brought out the best in him, no denying *that.* Mr. Moran said she could expect to get sued for every town dollar she had, and a few country ones in the bargain. Mr. Moran said he was going to law, and he was poker-buddies with the best lawyer in the county. Mr. Moran opined that Ruth was going to find the cartridge she had used to kill his good old dog the most expensive one she had ever jacked into a breech. Mr. Moran said when he got done with her she would curse her mother for ever having opened her legs to her father. Mr. Moran said that even though her mother *had* been stupid enough to do that, he could tell, just talking to her, that the best part of her had squirted out'n her father's unquestionably substandard pecker and run down the chunk of lard her mother called a thigh. Mr. Moran informed her that, while Mrs. High and Mighty Ruth McCausland might currently feel she was Queen Turd of Shit Hill, she would shortly find out she was just another little turd floating in the Great Toilet Bowl of Life. Mr. Moran added that, in this particular case, he had his hand on the lever of that great disposal unit and fully intended to push it. Mr. Moran said a great deal more. Mr. Moran did more than speak; Mr. Moran *sermonized.* Preacher Colson (or was it Cooder?) at the height of his powers could not have equaled Moran on that day. Ruth waited patiently until he had at least temporarily run dry. Then, speaking in a low and pleasant voice that did not at all suggest that her calf now felt as if it was burning in a furnace, she told Mr. Moran that while the law was not entirely clear on the point, damages had more often been awarded to the caller, even if uninvited, rather than the owner, in cases of animal assault. The real question was whether or not the owner had taken all reasonable care to ensure . . .

"What the fuck are you talking about?" Moran screamed.

"I'm trying to tell you that the courts take a dim view of a man leaving his dog untied so it can bite a woman soliciting for a charitable organization like the American Cancer Society. Put another way, I'm trying to make you see that in court, they make you *pay* for acting like an asshole."

Stunned silence from the other end of the line. Mr. Moran's muse had fled forever.

Ruth paused briefly and fought off a wave of faintness as Daggett finished the disinfecting process and put a light sterile bandage on the wound. "If you took me to court, Mr. Moran, could my lawyer find someone to testify that your dog had bitten before?"

Silence from the other end of the line.

"Perhaps *two* someones?"

More silence.

"Perhaps *three—*"

"Fuck you, you highbrow cunt," Moran said suddenly.

"Well," Ruth said, "I can't say it's been pleasant talking with you, but listening to you air your views has certainly been instructive. A person sometimes believes she's seen all the way to the bottom of the well of human stupidity, and a reminder that that well apparently has no bottom is sometimes useful. I'm afraid I'll have to hang up now. I'd hoped to canvass six more houses today, but I'm afraid I'll have to put them off. I have to go up to Derry Home Hospital and get some stitches, I'm afraid."

"I hope they fucking kill you," Moran said.

"I understand. But *do* try to help the Cancer Society if you can. We need all the help we can get if we're going to stop cancer in our lifetime. Even ill-tempered, foul-mouthed, idiotic, misbegotten sons of bitches such as yourself can do their part."

Mr. Moran did not sue her. A week later she received a Cancer Society pledge envelope from him, however. He had not stamped it, on purpose, she suspected, so it would be delivered postage-due. Inside was a note and a one-dollar bill with a large brown stain on it. I WIPED MY ASS ON THIS, YOU BITCH! the note cried triumphantly. It was written in the large straggling letters of a first-grader with motor-control problems. Ruth held the bill by the corner and put it in with the rest of the morning wash. When it came out (clean; among the many other things Mr. Moran did not seem to know was that shit washes off), she ironed it. Then it was not only clean, it was crisp—it might have come from the bank only yesterday. She put it in the canvas bank bag where she kept all her collection money. In her record book she noted: *B. Moran, Amount Contributed: $1.00.*

3

The Haven Town Library. The Cancer Society. The New England Conference of Small Towns. Ruth served Haven in all of them. She was also active in the Methodist church; it was a rare church supper at which there wasn't a Ruth McCausland casserole or a bake-sale at which there wasn't a Ruth McCausland pie or loaf of raisin bread. She had served on the school board and on the school textbook committee.

People said they didn't know how she did it all. When asked directly, she would smile and say she believed busy hands were happy hands. With all of this going on in her life, you would have thought she'd have had no time for hobbies . . . but she did in fact have two. She loved to read (she particularly enjoyed Bobbi Anderson's westerns; she had all of them, each signed) and she collected dolls.

A psychiatrist would have equated Ruth's doll collection with her unfulfilled wish for children. Ruth, although she did not much hold with psychiatrists, would have agreed. Up to a point, anyway. *Whatever the reason, they make me happy,* she might have said if this psychiatric viewpoint had been brought to her attention. *And I believe that happiness is the exact opposite of sadness, bitterness, and hatred: happiness should remain unexamined as long as possible.*

In the early Haven years she and Ralph shared a study upstairs. The house was big enough so each could have had one to him- or herself, but they liked to be together in the evenings. The big study *had* been two rooms before Ralph had knocked out the wall between, creating a space even bigger than the living room downstairs. Ralph had his coin and matchbook collections, a wall of bookshelves (all of Ralph's books were nonfiction, most military history), and an old rolltop desk which Ruth had refinished herself.

For Ruth he made what both came to call "the schoolroom."

About two years before the headaches began, Ralph saw that Ruth was fast running out of space for her dolls (now there was even a row of them atop her own desk, and they sometimes fell off when she typed). They sat on the stool in the corner, they dangled their small legs nonchalantly from the window-ledges, and still visitors usually had to hold three or four on their laps when they took a chair. She had a lot of visitors, too: Ruth was also a notary public, and there was always someone dropping by to have her notarize a bill of sale or frank a promissory note.

So for Christmas that year, Ralph had constructed a dozen small pewlike benches for her dolls. Ruth was delighted. They reminded her of the one-room schoolhouse she had attended at Crosman Corner. She arranged them in neat rows and set the dolls upon them. Ever after, that part of Ruth's study was called the schoolroom.

The following Christmas—his last, although at that point he felt fine, the brain tumor that would kill him no more than a microscopic dot in his head—Ralph gave her another four benches, three new dolls, and a blackboard in scale with the benches. It was all that was needed to complete the amiable schoolroom illusion.

Written on the blackboard were the words *"Dear Teacher, I love you truly*—A SECRET ADMIRER.

Adults were charmed by Ruth's schoolroom. Most children were equally charmed, and Ruth was always happy to see the kids—boys as well as girls—play with the dolls, although some were quite valuable and many of the old ones delicate. Some parents became very nervous when they realized their children were playing with a doll from pre-Communist China or one that had belonged to the daughter of Chief Justice John Marshall. Ruth was a kind woman; if she sensed that a child's enjoyment of her dolls was making a parent *really* uncomfortable, she would take out a Barbie and Ken she kept for such occasions. The children played with them, but listlessly, as if they realized the really *good* dolls had for some reason been put off-limits. If, however, Ruth sensed that parents were saying no because they felt it was somehow impolite for their kids to play with the grownup lady's toys, she would make it clear that she really didn't mind.

"Ain't you afraid some kid'll break a bunch of them?" Mabel Noyes asked her once. Mabel's Junque-A-Torium was well-supplied with signs such as LOVELY TO LOOK AT, DELIGHTFUL TO HOLD, BUT IF YOU BREAK IT, THEN IT'S SOLD. Mabel knew that the doll which had belonged to Justice Marshall's little girl was worth at least six hundred dollars—she had shown a picture of it to a dealer in rare dolls in Boston and he had told her four hundred, so Mabel guessed six as a fair price. Then there was a doll that had belonged to Anna Roosevelt . . . a genuine Haitian voodoo doll . . . God knew what else, sitting cheek to cheek and thigh to thigh with such common old things as Raggedy Ann and Andy.

"Not a bit," Ruth responded. She found Mabel's attitude as puzzling as Mabel found hers. "If God means one of these dolls to be broken, He may break it Himself, or He may send a child to do it. But so far, no child has ever broken one. Oh, a few heads have rolled, and Joe Pell did something to the pull-ring in Mrs. Beasley's back, and now all she'll say is something like 'Do you want to have a shower?', but that's about all the damage that's been done."

"Well, you'll pardon me if I still think it's an awfully big risk to take with such fragile, irreplaceable things," Mabel said. She sniffed. "Sometimes I believe the only thing I've ever learned in my whole life is that children break things."

"Well, perhaps I've just been lucky. But they *are* careful with them, you know. Because they love them, I think." Ruth paused, frowning slightly. "*Most* of them do," she amended after a moment.

That not all children wanted to play with "the kids in the schoolroom"—that some actually seemed to *fear* them—was a fact which puzzled and grieved her. Little

Edwina Thurlow, for instance. Edwina had burst into a shrill spate of screams when her mother took her by the hand and actually *pulled* her over to the dolls on their rows of benches, looking attentively at their blackboard. Mrs. Thurlow thought Ruth's dolls were *just the dearest things, cunning as a cat a-running, sweet as a lick of cream;* if there are other country clichés for "fascinating," Mrs. Thurlow had undoubtedly applied them to Ruth's dolls, and she was totally unable to credit her daughter's fear of them. She thought Edwina was "just being shy." Ruth, who had seen the flat unmistakable glitter of fear in the child's eyes, had been unable to dissuade the mother (who, Ruth thought, was a stupid, pigheaded woman) from almost physically *pushing* the child at the dolls.

So Norma Thurlow had dragged little Edwina over to the schoolroom and little Edwina's screams had been so loud they had brought Ralph all the way up from the cellar, where he had been caning chairs. It took twenty minutes to coax Edwina out of her hysterics, and of course she had to be brought downstairs, away from the dolls. Norma Thurlow was ill with embarrassment, and every time she threw a black look Edwina's way, her daughter was overcome again by hysterical weeping.

Later that evening, Ruth went upstairs and looked sorrowfully at her schoolroom full of silent children (the "children" included such grandmotherly figures as Mrs. Beasley and Old Gammar Hood, which, when turned over and slightly rearranged, became the Big Bad Wolf), wondering how they could have scared Edwina so badly. Edwina herself certainly hadn't been able to explain; even the most gentle inquiry brought on fresh shrieks of terror.

"You made that kid really unhappy," Ruth said at last, speaking softly to the dolls. "What did you *do* to her?"

The dolls only looked back at her with their glass eyes, their shoebutton eyes, their sewn eyes.

"And Hilly Brown wouldn't go near them the time his mother came over to have you notarize that bill of sale," Ralph said from behind her. She looked around, startled, then smiled at him.

"Yes, Hilly too," she said. And there had been others. Not many, but enough to trouble her.

"Come on," Ralph said, slipping an arm around her

waist. "Give, you guys. Which one of youse mugs scared the little goil?"

The dolls looked back silently.

And for a moment . . . just a moment . . . Ruth felt a stir of fright uncoil in her stomach and chase up her spine, rattling vertebrae like a bony xylophone . . . and then it was gone.

"Don't worry about it, Ruthie," Ralph said, leaning closer. As always, the smell of him made her feel a bit giddy. He kissed her hard. Nor was his kiss the only thing hard about him at that moment.

"Please," she said a little breathlessly, breaking the kiss. "Not in front of the children."

He laughed and swept her into his arms. "How about in front of the collected works of Henry Steele Commager?"

"Wonderful," she gasped, aware that she was already half . . . no, three-quarters . . . no, four-fifths . . . out of her dress.

He made love to her urgently, and with tremendous satisfaction on both their parts. *All* their parts. The brief chill was forgotten.

But this year she remembered on the night of July 19th. The picture of Jesus had begun to speak to 'Becka Paulson on July 7th. On July 19th, Ruth McCausland's dolls began to speak to her.

4

The townsfolk were surprised but pleased when, two years after Ralph McCausland's death in 1972, his widow ran for the position of Haven town constable. A young fellow named Mumphry ran against her. This fellow was foolish, most people agreed, but they also agreed that he probably couldn't help it; he was new in town and did not know how to behave. Those who discussed the matter at the Haven Lunch agreed Mumphry was more to be pitied than disliked. He ran as a partisan Democrat, and the gist of his platform seemed to be that when it came to a position such as constable, the elected official would have to arrest drunks, speeders, and hooligans; he might even be called upon to arrest a dangerous criminal from time to time and run him up to the county jail. Surely the citizens of Haven weren't going to elect a *woman* to do such a job, law degree or not, were they?

They were and did. The vote was McCausland 407, Mumphry 9. Of his nine votes, it would be fair to assume he had gotten those of his wife, his brother, his twenty-three-year-old son, and himself. That left five unaccounted for. No one ever 'fessed up, but Ruth herself always had an idea that Mr. Moran out there on the south end of town had had four more friends than she would have credited him with. Three weeks after the election, Mumphry and his wife left Haven. His son, a nice-enough fellow named John, elected to stay, and although he was still, after fourteen years, often referred to as "the new fella," as in "That new fella, Mumphry, come by to get his hair cut this mawnin; member when his daddy ran against Ruth and got whipped s'bad?" And since then, Ruth had never been opposed.

The townsfolk had rightly seen her candidacy as a public announcement that her period of mourning was over. One of the things (one among many) the unfortunate Mumphry had failed to understand was that the lopsided vote had been, in part, at least, Haven's way of crying: "Hooray, Ruthie! Welcome back!"

Ralph's death had been sudden and shocking, and it came close—too very damn close—to killing the part of her which was outward and giving. That part softened and complimented the dominant side of her personality, she felt. The dominant side was smart, canny, logical, and—although she hated to admit this last, she knew it was true—sometimes uncharitable.

She came to feel that if that outward and giving side of her nature were to lapse, it would be something like killing Ralph a second time. And so she came back to Haven. Came back to service.

In a small town, even one such person can make a crucial difference in how things are and in what jargon-meisters are pleased to call "the quality of life"; that person can become, in fact, something very like the heart of the town. Ruth had been well on her way to becoming such a valuable person when her husband died. Two years later—after what seemed in retrospect to be a long, bleak season in hell—she had rediscovered that valuable person, as one might rediscover something moderately wonderful in a dark attic corner—a piece of carnival glass, or a bentwood rocking chair that was still serviceable. She held it up to the light, made sure it was unbroken, dusted it, polished it, and then returned it to her life. Running for town constable had only been the first step. She could not have said why this seemed so right, but it did—it seemed the perfect way to at the same time remember Ralph and get on with the work of being herself. She thought she would probably find the job both boring and unpleasant . . . but that had also been true of canvassing for the Cancer Society and serving on the Textbook Selection Committee. Boring and unpleasant did not mean a task was *unfruitful,* a fact a lot of people seemed not to know, or to willfully ignore. And, she told herself, if she really didn't like it, there was no law to make her stand for reelection. She wanted to serve, not to martyr herself. If she hated it, she would let Mumphry or someone like him have a turn.

But Ruth discovered she *liked* the job. Among other things, it gave her a chance to put a stop to some nasty goings-ons that old John Harley had allowed to continue . . . and grow.

Del Cullum, for instance. The Cullums had been in Haven since time out of mind, and Delbert—a thick-browed mechanic who worked at Elt Barker's Shell—was probably not the first of them to engage in sexual congress with his daughters. The Cullum line was incredibly twisted and interbred; there were at least two cataclysmically retarded Cullums in Pineland that Ruth knew of (according to town gossip, one had been born with webs between its fingers and toes).

Incest is one of those time-honored country traditions of which the romantic poets rarely write. Its traditional aspect might have been the reason John Harley had never seriously tried to put an end to it, but the idea of "tradition" in such a grotesque matter cut no ice with Ruth. She went out to the Cullum place. There was shouting. Albion Thurlow heard it clearly, although Albion lived a quarter of a mile down the road and was deaf in one ear. Following the shouting there was a sound of a chainsaw cranking up, followed by a gunshot and a scream. Then the chainsaw stopped and Albion, standing out in the middle of the road now, one hand shading his eyes as he looked toward the Cullum place, heard girls' voices (Delbert had been cursed with girls, six of them, and of course they literally *were* his curse, and he theirs) raised in cries of distress.

Later, in the Haven Lunch, recounting his tale to a fascinated audience, old Albion said that he thought about going back into his house and calling the constable . . . and then he realized the constable had probably been the one fired the shot.

Albion only stood by his mailbox instead, awaiting developments. About five minutes after the sound of the chainsaw died, Ruth McCausland drove back toward town. Five minutes after *that,* Del Cullum drove by in his pickup. His washed-out wife was in the shotgun seat. A mattress and some cardboard boxes filled with clothes and dishes sat in the truck's bed. Delbert and Maggie Cullum were seen no more in Haven. The three Cullum girls over eighteen went to work in Derry and in Bangor. The three minors were placed in foster homes. Most of Haven was glad to see the Cullum family broken up. They had festered out there at the end of the Ridge Road like a rash of poison toadstools growing in a dark cellar. Folks speculated about what Ruth had done and how she did it, but Ruth never told.

Nor were the Cullums the only people Ruth McCausland, graying, trim, five-feet-five, and one hundred and twenty-five pounds, either ran out of town or had jailed over the years. There were the dope-smoking hippies that moved in a mile east of the old Frank Garrick farm, for instance. Those worthless, crab-raddled excuses for human beings came in one month and went out on the toe of Ruth's dainty size-five shoe the next. Frank's niece, who wrote those books, probably smoked some rope from time to time, the town thought (the town thought that all writers must smoke dope, drink to excess, or spend their evenings having sex in odd positions), but she didn't sell it, and the hippies half a mile down from her had been doing just that.

Then there were the Jorgensons out on the Miller Bog Road. Benny Jorgenson died of a stroke, and Iva remarried three years later, becoming Iva Haney. Not long after, her seven-year-old son and five-year-old daughter started having household mishaps. The boy fell getting out of the tub; the girl burned her arm on the stove. Then the boy slipped on the wet kitchen floor and broke his arm and the girl stepped on a rake half-buried in fallen leaves and the handle spanged her upside the head. Last but hardly least, the boy stumbled on the basement stairs while going after some kindling and fractured his skull. For a while it looked as if he wasn't going to pull through. It was a real run of bad luck, all right.

Ruth decided there had been enough bad luck at the Haney place.

She went out, driving her old Dodge Dart, and found Elmer Haney sitting on the porch drinking a quart of Miller Lite, picking his nose, and reading *Soldier of Fortune* magazine. Ruth suggested to Elmer Haney that *he* was bad luck around Iva's place, particularly for Bethie and Richard Jorgenson. She had noticed, she said, that some stepfathers were *very* bad luck for their stepchildren. She said she thought their luck might improve if Elmer Haney left town. Very soon. Before the end of the week.

"You are not scaring me," Elmer Haney said serenely. "This is *my* place now. You want to get off it before I brain you with a stick of stovewood, you meddling bitch."

"Think it over," Ruth said, smiling.

Joe Paulson had been parked out by the mailbox at the time. He heard the whole thing—Elmer Haney's voice had been slightly raised, and there was nothing wrong with Joe's hearing. The way Joe told it down at the Haven Lunch later that day, he had been sorting mail while the two of them argued it up and down, and he couldn't seem to get it sorted just right until that conversation was over.

"Then how'dya know she was *smiling?*" Elt Barker asked.

"Heard it in her voice," Joe replied.

Later that same day, Ruth had taken a ride up to the Derry state-police barracks and spoke with Butch "Monster" Dugan. At six-feet-eight and two hundred and eighty pounds, Monster was the largest state cop in New England. Monster would have done anything short of murder (maybe that, too) for Ralph's widow.

Two days later, they went back to the Haney place. It was Monster's day off and he was in civvies. Iva Haney was at work. Bethie was in school. Richard was, of course, still in the hospital. Elmer Haney, who was *still* unemployed, sat on the porch with a quart of Miller Lite in one hand and the latest issue of *Hot Talk* in the other. Ruth and Monster Dugan visited with him for an hour or so. During that hour, Elmer Haney had an extraordinary run of bad luck. Those who saw him leaving town that night said he looked like someone ran him through a potato grader, but the only one with nerve enough to ask just what had happened was old John Harley himself.

"Well, I swan," Ruth said, smiling. "It was the darnedest thing I ever saw. While we were trying to persuade him his stepkids might live luckier if he left, he decided he wanted to take a shower. Right while we were talking to him! And do you know, he fell down in the tub! Then he burned his arm on the stove and slipped on the linoleum while he was backing away from it! Then he decided he wanted some fresh air and he went outside and stepped on the same rake little Bethie Jorgenson stepped on two months ago, and that was when he decided he ought to just pack up and go. I think he was right to do it, poor man. He'll live luckier himself somewhere else."

5

She really was the person who came closest to being the heart of the town, and that may have been why she was one of the first to feel the change.

It began with a headache and bad dreams.

The headache came in with the month of July. Sometimes it was so faint she barely noticed it. Then, without warning, it would swell to a thick, throbbing beat behind her forehead. It was so bad on the night of July 4th that she called Christina McKeen, with whom she had planned to go see the fireworks in Bangor, and begged off.

She went to bed that night with light still lingering in the sky outside, but it was dark before she was finally able to drift off to sleep. She supposed the heat and humidity were keeping her awake—they would keep people awake all over New England that night, she reckoned, and this wasn't the first night that had been like this. It had been one of the stillest, hottest summers in her memory.

She dreamed of fireworks.

Only these fireworks were not red and white and coruscating orange; they were all a dull and terrible green. They burst across the sky in starbursts of light . . . only instead of going out, the starfish shapes in the sky oozed together and became huge sores.

Looking around, she saw people she had lived with all her life—Harleys and Crenshaws and Browns and Duplisseys and Andersons and Clarendons—staring up at the sky, their faces rotted swampfire green. They stood in front of the post office, the drugstore, the Junque-A-Torium, the Haven Lunch, the Northern National Bank; they stood in front of the school and the Shell station, eyes filled with green fire, mouths hanging stupidly agape.

Their teeth were falling out.

Justin Hurd turned to her and grinned, lips pulling back to show bare pink gums. In the crazy light of her dream, the saliva streaking those gums looked like snot.

"Feelth *good,*" Justin lisped, and she thought: *Get out of here! They all have to get out of here right now! If they don't, they are going to die the same way Ralph did!*

Now Justin was walking toward her and she saw with mounting horror that his face was shriveling and changing —it was becoming the bulging, stitched face of Lumpkin, her scarecrow doll. She looked around wildly and saw that they had all become dolls. Mabel Noyes turned and stared at her and Mabel's blue eyes were as calculating and avaricious as ever, but her lips were plumped up in the Cupid's-bow smile of a china doll.

"Tommyknockerth," Mabel lisped in a chiming, echoing voice, and Ruth woke up with a gasp, wide-eyed in the dark.

Her headache was gone, at least for the time being. She came out of the dream directly into wakefulness with the thought: *Ruth, you have to leave right now. Don't even take time to pack a bag—just pull on some clothes, get in the Dart, and* GO!

But she could not do that.

Instead, she lay down again. After a long time, she slept.

6

When the report came in that the Paulsons' house was burning, the Haven Volunteer Fire Department turned out . . . but they were surprisingly slow about it. Ruth was there ten minutes before the first pumper showed up. She would have torn Dick Allison's head off when he finally showed up, except she had known both of the Paulsons were dead . . . and, of course, Dick Allison had known too. That was why he hadn't bothered to hurry, but that did not make Ruth feel a bit better. Quite the opposite.

That knowing, now. What exactly was that?

Ruth didn't know *what* it was.

Even grasping the *fact* of the knowing was almost impossible. On the day the Paulsons' house burned, Ruth realized that she had been knowing things she had no right to know for a week or more. But it seemed so *natural!* It didn't come with trumpets and bells. The knowing was as much a part of her—*of everyone* in Haven now—as the beat of her heart. She no more thought about it than she thought about her heartbeat thudding softly and steadily in her ears.

Only she *had* to think about it, didn't she? Because it was changing Haven . . . and the changes were not good.

7

Some few days before David Brown disappeared, Ruth realized with dull, dawning dismay that she had been ostracized by the town. No one spat at her when she walked down the street in the morning from her house to her office in the town hall . . . no one threw stones . . . she sensed much of the old kindness in their thoughts . . . but she knew people were turning to follow her progress as she walked. She did this with her head up, her face serene, just as if her head wasn't throbbing and pounding like a rotted tooth, just as if she hadn't spent the previous night (and the one before that, and the one before *that,* and . . .) tossing and turning, dozing into horrible, half-remembered dreams and then clawing her way out again.

They were watching her . . . watching and waiting for . . .

For what?

But she knew: they were waiting for her to "become."

8

In the week between the fire at the Paulsons' and Hilly's SECOND GALA MAGIC SHOW, things began to go wrong for Ruth.

The mail, now. That was one thing.

She kept on getting bills and circulars and catalogues, but there were no letters. No personal mail of *any* kind. After three days of this, she took a stroll down to the post office. Nancy Voss only stood behind the counter like a lump, looking at her expressionlessly. By the time Ruth finished speaking, she thought she could actually feel the *weight* of the Voss woman's stare. It felt like two small dusty stones were lying on her face.

In the silence, she could hear something in the office humming and making spiderlike scritching noises. She had no idea what it

(except it sorts the mail for her)

might be but she didn't like the sound of it. And she didn't like being here with this woman, because she had been sleeping with Joe Paulson, and she had hated 'Becka, and—

Hot outside. Hotter still in here. Ruth felt sweat break out over her body.

"Have to fill out a mail complaint form," Nancy Voss said in a slow, inflectionless voice. She slid a white card across the counter. "Here you go, Ruth." Her lips pulled back in a cheerless grin.

Ruth saw half the woman's teeth were gone.

From behind them, in the silence: *Scratch-scratch, scritchy-scratch, scratch-scratch, scritchy-scratch.*

Ruth began to fill out the form. Sweat darkened big circles around the armpits of her dress. Outside, the sun beat steadily down on the post-office parking lot. It was ninety in the shade, had to be, and not a breath of wind stirring, and Ruth knew the paving in that lot would be so soft that you could tear off a chunk with your fingers if you wanted and begin to chew it. . . .

State the Nature of Your Problem, the form read.

I'm going crazy, she thought, *that is the nature of my problem. Also, I am having my first menstrual period in three years.*

In a firm hand she began to write that she had gotten

no first-class mail for a week and wished for the matter to be looked into.

Scratch-scratch, scritchy-scratch.

"What's that noise?" she asked, without looking up from the form. She was afraid to look up.

"Mail-sorting gadget," Nancy droned. "I thought it up." She paused. "But you know that, don't you, Ruth?"

"How could I know a thing like that unless you told me?" Ruth asked, and with a tremendous effort she made her voice pleasant. The pen she was using trembled and blotted the form—not that it mattered; her mail wasn't coming because Nancy Voss was throwing it out. That was part of the knowing, too. But Ruth was tough; her face remained clear and firm. She met Nancy's eyes directly, although she was afraid of that dusty black gaze, afraid of its weight.

Go on and speak up, Ruth's gaze said. *I am not afraid of the likes of you. Speak up . . . but if you expect me to scutter away, squeaking like a mouse, get ready for a surprise.*

Nancy's gaze wavered and dropped. She turned away. "Call me when you get the card filled out," she said. "I've got too much work to do to just stand around shooting the breeze. Since Joe died, the work's piled up out of all season. That's probably why your mail isn't

(GET OUT OF TOWN YOU BITCH GET OUT WHILE WE'LL STILL LET YOU GO)

coming just on time, Missus McCausland."

"Do you think so?" Keeping her voice light and pleasant now required a superhuman effort. Nancy's last thought had slammed into her like an uppercut. It had been as bright and clear as a lightning stroke. She looked down at the complaint form and saw a large black

(tumor)

blot spreading over it. She crumpled it and threw it away.

Scritch-scritch-scratch.

The door opened behind her. She turned and saw Bobbi Anderson come in.

"Hello, Bobbi," she said.

"Hello, Ruth."

(go on she's right get out while you still can while you're still allowed please Ruth I we most of us bear you no ill will)

"Are you working on a new novel, Bobbi?" Ruth could now barely keep the tremor out of her voice. Hearing thoughts was bad—it made you think you were insane and hallucinating it. Hearing such a thing from Bobbi Anderson

(while you're still allowed)

of all people, Bobbi Anderson who was just about the *kindest—*

I didn't hear anything like that, she thought, and grasped the idea with a sort of tired eagerness. *I was mistaken, that's all.*

Bobbi opened her post-box and took out a bundle of mail. She looked at her and smiled. Ruth saw she had lost a molar on the bottom left and a canine on the top right. "Better go now, Ruth," she said gently. "Just get in your car and go. Don't you think so?"

Then she felt herself steady—in spite of her fear and her throbbing head, she steadied.

"Never," she said. "This is my town. And if you know what's going on, tell the others that know what's going on not to push me. I have friends outside of Haven, friends that will listen to me seriously no matter how crazy what I'm saying might sound. They would listen for my late husband's sake, if not for my own. As for you, you ought to be ashamed of yourself. This is your town too. It *used* to be, anyway."

For a moment she thought Bobbi looked confused and a little ashamed. Then she smiled sunnily, and there was something in that girlish, gap-toothed grin that scared Ruth more than anything else. It was no more human than a trout's grin. She saw Bobbi in this woman's eyes, and had certainly felt her in her thoughts . . . but there was nothing of Bobbi in the grin.

"Whatever you want, Ruth," she said. "Everyone in Haven loves you, you know. I think in a week or two . . . three, at the outside . . . you'll stop fighting. I just thought I'd offer you the option. If you decide to stay, though, that's fine. In a little while you'll be . . . just fine."

9

She stopped in Cooder's for Tampax. There were none. No Tampax, no Modess, no Stayfree maxis or minis, no generic pads or tampons.

A hand-lettered sign read: NEW SHIPMENT ARRIVES TOMORROW. SORRY FOR ANY INCONVENIENCE.

10

On July 15th, a Friday, she began having problems with her office phone.

In the morning it was just an annoyingly loud hum which she and the person she was talking to had to shout over. By noon a crackling noise had been added. By two P.M. it had gotten so bad that the phone was useless.

When she got home she found that the phone there wasn't noisy at all. It was just smoothly and completely dead. She went next door to the Fannins' to call the phone company's repair number. Wendy Fannin was making bread in her kitchen, kneading one batch of dough while her mixer worked a second batch.

Ruth saw with a weary lack of surprise that the mixer wasn't plugged into the wall but into what looked like an electronic game with its cover off. It was generating a strong glow as Wendy mixed her bread.

"Sure, go ahead and use the phone," Wendy said. "You know

(get out Ruth get out of Haven)

where it is, don't you?"

"Yes," she said. She started toward the hall, then paused. "I stopped at Cooder's market. I needed sanitary napkins, but they're all out."

"I know." Wendy smiled, showing three gaps in a smile which had been flawless a week before. "I got the second-to-last box. It will be over soon. We'll 'become' a little more and that part will end."

"Is that so?" Ruth said.

"Oh, yes," Wendy said, and turned back to her bread.

The Fannins' phone was working just fine. Ruth was not surprised. The office girl at New England Contel said they would send a man right out. Ruth thanked her, and on her way out she thanked Wendy Fannin.

"Sure," Wendy said, smiling. "Whatever you want, Ruth. Everyone in Haven loves you, you know."

Ruth shuddered in spite of the heat.

The telephone repair crew came and did something to the connection on the side of Ruth's house. Then they ran a test. The phone worked perfectly. They drove away. An hour later, the phone stopped working again.

On the street that evening, she felt a rising whisper of voices in her brain—thoughts as light as leaves kicked into a momentary rustle by a breath of October wind.

(our Ruth we love you all Haven loves)

(but go if you go or change)

(if you stay no one wants to hurt you Ruth so get out or stay)

(yes get out or stay but leave us)

(yes leave us alone Ruth don't interfere let us be let us)

(be be "become" yes let us "become" let us alone to "become")

She walked slowly, head throbbing with voices.

She glanced into the Haven Lunch. Beach Jernigan, the short-order cook, raised a hand to her. Ruth raised one in return. She saw Beach's mouth move, clearly forming the words *There she goes.* Several men at the counter turned around and waved. They smiled. She saw empty gaps where teeth had been not long ago. She passed Cooder's market. She passed the United Methodist Church. Ahead of her now was the town hall with its square brick clock tower. The hands of the clock stood at 7:15—7:15 of a summer night, and all over Haven men would be opening cold beers and turning radios to the voice of Ned Martin and the sound of *Red Sox Warmup.* She could see Bobby Tremain and Stephanie Colson walking slowly toward the edge of town along Route 9, hand in hand. They had been going together for four years and it really was a wonder Stephanie wasn't pregnant yet, Ruth thought.

Just a July evening with twilight coming on—everything normal.

Nothing was normal.

Hilly Brown and Barney Applegate came out of the library, Hilly's little brother David trailing behind them like the tail of a kite. She asked to see what books the boys had gotten and they showed her readily enough. Only in little David Brown's eyes had she seen a hesitant acknowledgment of the panic she felt . . . and felt it in his mind. That she felt his fear and did nothing about it was the main reason she drove herself so hard when the little boy disappeared two days later. Someone else might have justified it, might have said: *Look, I had enough on my own plate without worrying about what was dished onto David Brown's.* But she wasn't the sort of woman who could find any comfort in such loud defensiveness. She had felt that boy's low terror. Worse, she had felt his resignation—his sureness that nothing could stop events—that they would simply wind along their preordained course from bad to worse. And as if to prove him right, hey, presto! David was gone. And like the boy's grandfather, Ruth shouldered her share of the guilt.

At the town hall she turned and walked back to her house, keeping her face pleasant in spite of her drilling headache, in spite of her dismay. The thoughts swirled and rustled and danced.

(love you Ruth)

(we can wait Ruth)

(shhhh shhhh go to sleep)

(yes go to sleep and dream)

(dream of things dream of ways)

(to "become" ways to "become" ways to)

She went into her house and locked the door behind her and went upstairs and pressed her face into her pillow.

Dream of ways to "become."

Oh God she wished she knew exactly what that meant.

If you go you go if you stay you change.

She wished she knew because, whatever it meant, whether she wanted it or not, it *was* happening to her. No matter how much she resisted, she was also "becoming."

(yes Ruth yes)

(sleep . . . dream . . . think . . . "become")

(yes Ruth yes)

These thoughts, rustling and alien, followed her down into sleep and then funneled away into darkness. She lay crosswise on the big bed, fully dressed, and slept deeply.

When she woke, her body was stiff but her mind felt clear and refreshed. Her headache had blown away like smoke. Her period, so oddly undignified and shameful after she had thought *that* was finally over for good, had stopped. For the first time in almost two weeks she felt herself. She would have a long cool shower and then set about getting to the bottom of this. If what it took was outside help, okay. If she had to spend a few days or a few weeks with people thinking she was off her rocker, so be it. She had spent her life building a reputation for sanity and trustworthiness. And what good would such a reputation be if it couldn't convince people to take you seriously when you sounded nuts?

As she began to take off her sleep-rumpled dress, her fingers suddenly froze on the buttons.

Her tongue had found an empty place in the line of her bottom teeth—there was a dull, distant pain there. Her eyes dropped to the coverlet of the bed. On it, where her head had been, she saw the tooth that had fallen out in the night. Suddenly nothing seemed simple anymore—nothing at all.

Ruth was aware that her headache had returned.

11

There was even hotter weather in store for Haven—in August there would be a week when temperatures would crack the hundred-degree mark every single day—but in the meantime, the July stretch of hot-and-muggy which ran from the twelfth through the nineteenth was more than enough for everyone in town, thank you very much.

The streets shimmered. The leaves on the trees hung limp and dusty. Sounds carried in the still air; Bobbi Anderson's old truck, now rebuilt into a digging machine, could be heard clearly in Haven Village for most of that eight-day hot spell. People knew something important was going on out there at the old Frank Garrick place—important for the whole town—but no one mentioned it out loud, any more than they mentioned the fact that it had driven Justin Hurd, Bobbi's nearest neighbor, quite mad. Justin was building things—it was part of his "becoming"—but because he had gone crazy, some of the stuff he built was potentially dangerous. One of them was a thing that set up harmonic waves in the earth's crust—waves which could possibly trigger an earthquake big enough to tear the state wide open and send the eastern half sliding into the Atlantic.

Justin had made this harmonic-wave machine to get the goddam rabbits and woodchucks out of their burrows. They were eating all his fucking lettuces. *I'll* shake *the little bastards out,* he thought.

Beach Jernigan went out to Justin's place one day while Justin was out harrowing up the crops in his west field (he plowed under twelve acres of corn that day, sweating profusely, lips pulled back in a constant maniacal grimace as he worried about saving three rows of lettuces) and dismantled the gadget, which consisted of cannibalized stereo components. When Justin returned, he would find his gadget gone, perhaps assume the goddam chucks and rabbits had stolen it, and maybe set about rebuilding it . . . in which case Beach or someone else would dismantle it again. Or, maybe, if they were lucky, he would feel called upon to build something less dangerous.

The sun rose each day in a sky the color of pallid china and then seemed to hang at the roof of the world. Behind the Haven Lunch, a line of dogs lay in the scant shade of the overhanging eave, panting, even too hot to scratch fleas. The streets were mostly deserted. Every now and then someone would travel through Haven on his way up to or back from Derry and Bangor. Not too many, though, because the turnpike was so much quicker.

Those who did pass through noticed an odd and sudden improvement in radio reception—one startled truck-driver, on Route 9 because he had gotten bored with I-95, tuned in a rock station which turned out to be broadcasting from Chicago. Two old folks bound for Bar Harbor found a classical-music station from Florida. This eerie, bell-clear reception faded when they were clear of Haven again.

Some through travelers experienced more unpleasant side effects: headaches and nausea, mostly—sometimes severe nausea. This was most commonly blamed on road-food gone punky in the heat.

A little boy from Quebec, headed for Old Orchard Beach with his parents, lost four baby teeth in the ten minutes it took for the family station wagon to pass from one side of Haven to the other. The little boy's mother swore in French that she had never seen anything like it in her life. That night, in an Old Orchard Beach motel, the tooth fairy took them (and only one had been loose, the little boy's mother declared) and replaced them with a dollar.

A mathematician from MIT, headed up to UMO for a two-day conference on semilogical numbers, suddenly realized that he was on the verge of grasping an entirely new way of looking at mathematics and mathematical philosophy. His face went gray, his perspiring skin suddenly cold as he grasped with perfect clarity how such a concept could quickly produce proof that every even number over two is the sum of two prime numbers; how the concept could be used to trisect the angle; how it could—

He pulled over, scrambled out of his car, and threw up in the ditch. He stood trembling and weak-kneed over the mess (which contained one of his canines, although he was just then much too excited to realize he'd lost a tooth), his fingers itching to hold a piece of chalk, to cover a blackboard with sines and cosines. Visions of the Nobel Prize jittered in his overheated brain. He threw himself back into his car and began to drive toward Orono again, punching his rusty Subaru up to eighty. But by the time he got to Hampden, his glorious vision had clouded over, and by the time he reached Orono there was nothing left but a glimmer. He supposed it had been a momentary heat-stroke. Only the vomiting had been real; that he could smell on his clothes. During the first day of the conference he was pale and silent, offering little, mourning his glorious ephemeral vision.

That was also the morning Mabel Noyes became an unperson while puttering in the basement of the Junque-A-Torium. It would not have been correct to say that she "killed herself by accident" or "died by misadventure." Neither of those phrases exactly explained what had happened to her. Mabel didn't put a bullet in her head while cleaning a gun or stick a finger in an electrical socket; she simply collapsed her own molecules and winked out of existence. It was quick and not a bit messy. There was a flash of blue light and she was gone. Nothing was left but one smoldering bra strap and a gadget that looked like a silver polisher. That, in fact, was exactly what the gadget was supposed to be. Mabel thought it would make a dirty, tiresome job much easier and wondered why she had never made such a gadget before—or why, for goodness' sake, there weren't places where you could *buy* them, since it was a perfectly easy thing to make and those gooks over there in Korea could probably turn them out by the ton. God knew the Korea gooks turned enough other things out by the ton, although she supposed she ought to just be grateful, since the Jap gooks had apparently gotten too uppity to do the *little* stuff. She had begun to see all sorts of things she could make from the used appliances in her shop. *Wonderful* things. She kept looking in the catalogues and kept being amazed to find they weren't there. My God, she thought, I think I am going to be *rich!* Only she had made some sort of cross-connection on the silver polisher, and quarked off into the Twilight Zone in just under .0006 of a nanosecond.

She was not, in truth, greatly missed in Haven.

The town lay limp at the bottom of a stagnant bowl of air. From the woods behind the Garrick place came the sounds of engines as Bobbi and Gardener went on digging.

Otherwise, the whole town seemed to doze.

12

Ruth wasn't dozing that afternoon.

She was thinking about those sounds coming from Bobbi Anderson's place (she, at least, no longer thought of it as the old Garrick farm), and about Bobbi Anderson herself.

There was a communal well of knowledge in town now, a pool of thought they all shared. A month ago Ruth would have found such an idea insane. Now it was undeniable. Like the rising, whispering voices, the knowledge was *there.*

Part of it was knowing that Bobbi had started all this.

It had been inadvertent, but she had set it in motion. Now she and her friend (the friend was a perfect blank to Ruth; she knew about him only because she had seen him out there, sitting on the porch with Bobbi, evenings) were working twelve and fourteen hours a day, making it worse. She didn't think the friend had any real idea what he was doing. He was somehow outside of the communal net.

How were they making it worse?

She didn't know, didn't even know for sure what they were doing. That was also blocked, not just from Ruth but from everyone in Haven. They would know in time; they would not come to knowledge but *be*come to it, as the town-wide menstruation of every female between the ages of about eight and sixty had stopped at about the same time. It had something to do with digging; that was all Ruth could tell. One afternoon she napped lightly and dreamed Bobbi and her friend from Troy were unearthing a great silver cylinder some two hundred feet across. As they uncovered more and more of it, she could see a much smaller cylinder, this one steel, perhaps ten feet across and five feet high, protruding, nipplelike, from the center of the thing. Etched on this nipple was a + symbol, and as she awoke, Ruth understood: she had dreamed of a gigantic alkaline battery entombed in the earth and granite of the land behind Bobbi's house, a battery bigger than Frank Spruce's dairy barn.

Ruth knew that, whatever Bobbi and her friend were digging up in the woods, it certainly wasn't a gigantic Eveready Long-Life D-cell battery. Except . . . in a way, she thought that was *exactly* what it was. Bobbi had discovered some huge power source and had become its prisoner. That same force was simultaneously galvanizing and imprisoning the whole town. And it was growing steadily stronger.

Her mind whispered: *You've got to let it go. You've just got to stand back and let it run its course. They have loved you, Ruth; that much is true. You hear their voices in your head like a rising wind lifting October leaves, now not just puffing them and letting them drop but whipping them into a cyclone; you hear their mind-voices, and although they are sometimes garbled and confused, I don't think they can lie. And when these rising voices say they have loved you, still do love you, they are telling the truth. But if you meddle into what's going on here, I think they'll kill you, Ruth. Not Bobbi's friend—he's immune, somehow. He doesn't hear voices. He doesn't "become." Except drunk. That's what Bobbi's voice says: "Gard becomes drunk." But as for the rest of them . . . if you meddle into their business . . . they'll kill you, Ruth. Gently. With love. So just stand back. Let it happen.*

But if she did, her town would be destroyed . . . not changed, the way its name had been changed again and again, not hurt, as that sweet-talking preacher had hurt it, but *destroyed.* And she would be destroyed with it, because the force was already nibbling away at the core of her. She felt it.

All right, then . . . what do you do?

For the time being, nothing. Things might get better on their own. In the meantime, was there any way she could guard her thoughts?

She began to experiment with tongue-twisters: *She sells seashells down by the seashore. Betty Bitter bought some butter. Peter Piper picked a peck of pickled peppers.* With a little practice she found she could keep one of them playing constantly in the back of her mind. She walked downtown to the market, got some ground meat and two ears of fresh corn for her dinner, and spoke pleasantly with Madge Tilletts at the checkout counter and Dave Rutledge, who was sitting in his accustomed place at the front of the store, caning a chair slowly with his old, bunched, and arthritic hands. Except old Dave wasn't looking as old as he used to these days. Nowhere near.

Both of them looked at her, wary, surprised . . . puzzled.

They hear me . . . but not very well. I'm jamming them! I really am!

She didn't know how successfully, and it wouldn't do to bank on her ability to do it—but it *worked.* That didn't mean they couldn't read her if several of them linked up and worked together at picking her brain. She sensed that might be possible. But it was *something,* at least, one arrow in a previously empty quiver.

That night, Saturday night, she decided she would wait until Tuesday noon—roughly sixty hours. If things continued to deteriorate, she would go to the state-police barracks in Derry, seek out some of her husband's old friends—Monster Dugan for a start—and tell them what was going on forty miles or so downstate on Route 9.

It was maybe not the best of plans, but it would have to do.

Ruth McCausland fell asleep.

And dreamed of batteries in the earth.

6.

RUTH McCAUSLAND CONCLUDED

1

The disappearance of David Brown rendered Ruth's plan obsolete. After David disappeared, she found herself unable to leave town. Because David was gone and they all knew it . . . but they also knew that David was somehow still in Haven.

Always during the becoming came a time which might have been called "the dance of untruth." For Haven, this time commenced with the disappearance of David Brown and unfolded itself during the subsequent search.

Ruth was just sitting down to the local news when the phone rang. Marie Brown was hysterical, barely coherent.

"Calm down, Marie," Ruth said, and thought it was good she had eaten an early supper. She might not get another chance to eat for quite a while. At first the only clear fact she seemed able to get from Marie was that her boy David was in some kind of trouble, trouble that had started at a back yard magic show, and Hilly had gotten hysterical—

"Put Bryant on," Ruth said.

"But you'll come, won't you?" Marie wept. "Please, Ruth, before dark. We can still find him, I know we can."

"Of course I'll come," Ruth said. "Now put Bryant on."

Bryant was dazed but able to give a clearer picture of what had happened. It still sounded crazy, but then, what else was new in Haven these days? After the magic show, the audience had wandered away, leaving Hilly and David to clean up. Now David was gone. Hilly had fainted, and now had no memory of what had happened that afternoon at all. All he knew for sure was that when he saw David, he had to give him all the G.I. Joes. But he didn't remember why.

"You better come over quick as you can," Bryant said.

Going out, she paused for a moment on her way to her Dart and looked at Haven Village's Main Street with real hate. *What have you done now?* she thought. *Goddam you, what have you done now?*

2

With only two hours of good daylight left, Ruth wasted no time. She gathered Bryant, Ev Hillman, John Golden from just down the road, and Henry Applegate, Barney's father, in the Browns' back yard. Marie wanted to join the search party, but Ruth insisted she stay with Hilly. In her current frame of mind, Marie would be more hindrance than help. They had already searched, of course, but they had gone at it in a distracted, half-assed way. Eventually, as the boy's parents became convinced that David must have wandered across the road and into the woods, they had really ceased to search at all, although they had continued to move aimlessly around.

Ruth got some from what they said; some from the oddly distracted, oddly frightened way they looked; most from their minds.

Their *two* minds: the human one and the alien one. Always there came a point where the becoming might degenerate into madness—the madness of schizophrenia as the target minds tried to fight the alien group mind slowly welding them together . . . and then eclipsing them. This was the time of necessary acceptance. Thus, it was the time of the dance of untruth.

Mabel Noyes might have set it going, but she was not loved enough to make people dance. The Hillmans and the Browns were. They went far back in Haven's history, were well-loved and well-respected.

And, of course, David Brown was only a little boy.

The human net-mind, its "Ruth-mind," one might say, thought: *He could have wandered into the high grass of the Browns' back field and fallen asleep. More likely than Marie's idea that he went into the woods—he'd have to cross the road to do that, and he was well-behaved. Marie and Bryant both say so. More important, so do the others. He'd been told again and again and again that he was never to cross the road without a grown-up, so the woods don't seem likely.*

"We're going to cover the lawn and back field section by section," Ruth said. "And we're *not* just going to walk around; we're going to *look.*"

"But if we don't find him?" Bryant's eyes were scared and pleading. "If we don't find him, Ruth?"

She didn't really have to tell him; she only had to think it at him. If they didn't find David quickly, she would begin making calls. There would be a much larger search party—men with lights and bullhorns moving through the woods. If David wasn't found by morning, she would call Orval Davidson up in Unity and have him bring his bloodhounds. This was a familiar enough procedure to most of them. They knew about search parties, and most had been on them before; they were common enough during hunting season, when the woods filled up with out-of-staters carrying their heavy-caliber weapons and wearing their new orange flannel duds from L. L. Bean's. Usually these lost were found alive, suffering from nothing but mild exposure and severe embarrassment.

But sometimes they found them dead.

And sometimes they never found them at all.

They would not find David Brown, and they knew it long before the search began. Their minds had netted together as soon as Ruth arrived. This was an act of instinct as involuntary as a blink. They linked minds and searched for David's. Their mental voices united in a chorus so strong that if David had been in a radius of seventy miles, he would have clapped his hands to his head and screamed in pain. He would have heard and known they were looking for him at five times that distance.

No, David Brown was not lost. He was just . . . *not-there.*

The search they were preparing to make was totally useless.

But because it was the Tommyknocker-mind which knew this, and because they still thought of themselves as "human beings," they would begin the dance of untruth.

The becoming would demand many lies.

This one, the one they told themselves, the one that insisted they were really the same as ever, was the most important lie of all.

They all knew that, too. Even Ruth McCausland.

3

By eight-thirty, with dusk growing too thick to be much different from night, the five searchers had grown to a dozen. The news traveled quickly—a little *too* quickly to be normal. They covered all the yards and fields on the Browns' side, beginning at Hilly's stage (Ruth herself had crawled under there with a powerful flashlight, thinking that if David Brown was anywhere close by it should be here, fast asleep—but there was only flattened grass and a queer electrical smell that made her wrinkle her nose) and expanding the hunt outward in a beam shape from there.

"You think he's in the woods, Ruth?" Casey Tremain asked.

"He must be," she answered tiredly. Her head ached again. David was

(not-there)

no more in the woods than the President of the United States was. All the same . . .

In the back of her mind, tongue-twisters chased each other as restlessly as squirrels running on wire exercise wheels.

The dusk was not so thick she couldn't see Bryant Brown put a hand to his face and turn away from the others. There was a moment of awkward silence which Ruth finally broke.

"We need more men."

"State cops, Ruth?" Casey asked.

She saw them all looking at her, their faces still and sober.

(no Ruth no)

(outsiders no outsiders we'll take care)

(take care of this business we don't need outsiders while)
(while we shed our old skins put on our new skins while)
(we "become")
(if he's in the woods we'll hear him he'll call)
(call with his mind)
(no outsiders Ruth shhhh shhhh for your life Ruth we)
(we all love you but no outsiders)

These voices, rising in her mind, rising in the still, humid dark: she looked and saw only dark shapes and white faces, shapes and faces that for a moment barely seemed human. *How many of you still have your teeth?* Ruth McCausland thought hysterically.

She opened her mouth, thinking she might scream, but her voice sounded—at least to her own ears—normal and natural. In her mind, the tongue-twisters

(pretty Patsy picked some Betty Bitter bought some)

turned faster than ever.

"I don't think we need them just now, Casey, do you?"

Casey looked at her, a little puzzled.

"Well, I guess that'd be up to you, Ruth."

"Fine," she said. "Henry . . . John . . . you others. Make some calls. I want fifty woods-wise men and women here before we go in. Everyone who shows up at the Browns' has got to have a flashlight with him or he's not going *near* those woods. We've got a little boy lost; we don't need to add any grown men or women."

As she spoke, authority grew in her voice; the shaky fear lessened. They looked at her respectfully.

"I'll call Adley McKeen and Dick Allison. Bryant, go back and tell Marie to put on lots of coffee. It's going to be a long night."

They moved off in different directions; the men who had calls to make headed in the direction of Henry Applegate's house. The Browns' was nearer, but the situation had become worse and none of them wanted to go there just now. Not while Bryant was telling his wife that Ruth McCausland had decided their four-year-old son was probably lost in the

(not-there)

big woods after all.

Ruth was overwhelmed with weariness. She wished she

could believe she was just going mad; if she could believe that, everything would be easier.

"Ruth?"

She looked up. Ev Hillman was standing there, his thin white hair flying around his skull. He looked troubled and afraid.

"Hilly's doped off again. His eyes are open, but—" He shrugged.

"I'm very sorry," Ruth said.

"I'm takin him to Derry. Bryant n Marie want to stay here, o course."

"Why not Doc Warwick to start with?"

"Derry seems a better idea, that's all." Ev looked at Ruth unwinkingly. His eyes were old man's eyes, red-rimmed, rheumy, their blue faded to something which was almost no color at all. Faded but not stupid. And Ruth suddenly realized, with a wallop of excitement that nearly rocked her head back on her neck, that *she could barely read him at all!* Whatever was happening here in Haven, Ev, like Bobbi's friend, was exempt. It was going on around him, and he knew about it—some—but he was not a part of it.

She felt an excitement which was followed by bitter envy.

"I think he'll be better off out of town. Don't you, Ruthie?"

"Yes," she said slowly, thinking of those rising voices, thinking for the last time of how David was *not-there* and then pushing the lunatic idea away forever. Of *course* he was. Were they not human? They were. *Were.* But . . .

"Yes, I suppose he will."

"You could come with us, Ruthie."

She looked at him for a long time. "Did Hilly do something, Ev? I see his name in your head. I can't see anything else—just that. Winking on and off like a neon sign."

He looked at her, seemingly unsurprised by her tacit admission that she—sensible Ruth McCausland—was either reading his mind or believed she was.

"Maybe. He *acts* like he did. This . . . this half-swoon he's in . . . if that's what it is . . . could be he did something he's sorry for now. If so, it wasn't his fault, Ruthie. Whatever's going on here in Haven . . . that was what *really* did it."

A screen door banged. She looked over toward the Applegates' and saw several of the men on their way back.

Ev glanced around and then looked back at Ruth.

"Come with us, Ruth."

"And leave my town? Ev, I can't."

"All right. If Hilly should remember . . ."

"Get in touch with me," she said.

"If I can," Ev muttered. "They can make it tough, Ruthie."

"Yes," Ruth said. "I know they can."

"They're coming, Ruth," Henry Applegate said, and fixed Ev Hillman with a cold, appraising look. "Lots of *good* folks."

"Fine," Ruth said.

Ev looked unwinkingly back at Applegate for a moment and then moved away. An hour or so later, while Ruth was organizing the searchers and getting them ready for their first sweep, she saw Ev's old Valiant back down the Browns' driveway and turn toward Bangor. A small, dark shape—Hilly—was propped up in the passenger seat like a department-store mannequin.

Good luck, you two, Ruth thought. She wished—achingly! —that she was also on her way out of this feverish nightmare.

When the old man's car disappeared over the first hill, Ruth looked around and saw some twenty-five men and half a dozen women, some on this side of the road, some on the other. They were all standing motionless, simply watching

(loving)

her. Again she thought their shapes were changing, twisting, becoming inhuman; they were "becoming," all right, they were becoming something she didn't even dare think of . . . and so was she.

"What are you gawking at?" she called out, too shrilly. "Come on! Let's try to find David Brown!"

4

They didn't find him that night, nor on Monday, which was a hot white beating silence. Bobbi Anderson and her friend were part of the search; the roar of the digging machinery behind the old Garrick farm had stopped for a while. The friend, Gardener, looked pale, ill, and hung-over. Ruth doubted if he'd make it through the day when she first saw him. If he showed signs of dropping out of his place in the sweep, leaving a hole which could conceivably cause them to overlook the lost boy, Ruth would send him back to Bobbi's right away . . . but he kept up, hung-over or not.

By then, Ruth herself had already suffered a minor collapse, laboring under the double strain of trying to find David and resist the creeping changes in her own mind.

She had snatched two hours of uneasy sleep before dawn on Monday morning, then went back out, drinking cup after cup of coffee and bumming more and more cigarettes. There was no question in her mind of bringing in outside help. If she did, the outsiders would become aware very quickly—within hours, she thought—that Haven had changed its name to Weirdsville. The Haven lifestyle —so to speak—rather than the missing boy, would rapidly become the source of their attention. And then David would be lost for good.

The heat continued long after sundown. There was distant thunder but no breeze, no rain. Heat lightning flickered. In the thickets and blowdowns and choked second growth, mosquitoes hummed and buzzed. Branches crackled. Men cursed as they stumbled through wet places or clambered over deadfalls. Flashlight beams zigzagged aimlessly. There was a sense of urgency but not of cooperation; there were, in fact, several fistfights before Sunday midnight. Mental communication had not fostered a sense of peace and harmony in Haven; in fact, it seemed to have done exactly the opposite. Ruth kept them moving as best she could.

Then, shortly after midnight—early Monday morning, that would have been—the world simply swam away from her. It went fast, like a big fish that looks lazy until it gives a sudden powerful flick of its tail and disappears. She saw the flashlight tumble out of her fingers. It was like watching something happen in a movie. She felt the hot sweat on her cheeks and forehead suddenly turn chilly. The increasingly vicious headache that had racked her all day broke with a sudden painless pop. She *heard* this, as if, in the center of her brain, someone had pulled the string on a noisemaker. For a moment she could actually see brightly colored crepe streamers drifting down through the twisted gray channels of her cerebellum. Then her knees buckled. Ruth fell forward into a tangle of shrubs. She could see thorns in the slanted glow of her flashlight, long and cruel-looking, but the bushes felt as comfy as goosedown pillows.

She tried to call out and could not.

They heard anyway.

Feet approaching. Beams crissing and crossing. Someone

(Jud Tarkington)

bumped into someone else

(Hank Buck)

and a momentary hateful exchange flared between them

(you stay out of my way, strawfoot)

(I'll thump you with this light Buck swear to God I will)

then the thoughts focused on her with real and undeniable

(we all love you Ruth)

sweetness—but oh, it was a grasping sweetness, and it frightened her. Hands touched her, turned her over, and

(we all love you and we'll help you "become")

lifted her gently.

(And I love you too . . . now please, find him. Concentrate on that, concentrate on David Brown. Don't fight, don't argue.)

(we all love you Ruth . . .)

She saw that some of them were weeping, just as she saw (although she didn't want to) that others were snarling, lifting and dropping their lips, then lifting them again, like dogs about to fight.

5

Ad McKeen took her home and Hazel McCready put her to bed. She drifted off into wild, confused dreams. The only one she could remember when she woke up Tuesday morning was an image of David Brown gasping out the last of his life in an almost airless void—he was lying on black earth beneath a black sky filled with glaring stars, earth that was hard and parched and cracked. She saw blood burst from the membranes of his mouth and nose, saw his eyes burst, and that was when she came awake, sitting up in bed, gasping.

She called the town hall. Hazel answered. Just about every other able-bodied man and woman in town was out in the woods, Hazel said, searching. But if they didn't find him by tomorrow . . . Hazel didn't finish.

Ruth rejoined the search, which had now moved ten miles into the woods, at ten o'clock on Tuesday morning.

Newt Berringer took a look at her and said, "You got

(no business being out, Ruth)

"and you know it," he finished aloud.

"It *is* my business, Newt," she said with uncharacteristic curtness. "Now leave me alone to get about it."

She stayed with it all that long, sweltering afternoon, calling until she was too hoarse to speak. When twilight began to come down again, she allowed Beach Jernigan to ferry her back to town. There was something under a tarp in the back of Beach's truck. She had no idea what it was, and didn't want to know. She wanted desperately to stay in the woods, but her strength was failing and she was afraid that if she collapsed again, they wouldn't let her come back. She would force herself to eat, then sleep six hours or so.

She made herself a ham sandwich and passed up the coffee she really wanted for a glass of milk. She went up to the schoolroom, sat down, and put her small meal on her desk. She sat looking at her dolls. They looked back at her with their glassy eyes.

No more laughing, no more fun, she thought. *Quaker meeting has begun. If you show your teeth or tongue . . .*

The thought drifted away.

She blinked—not awake, precisely, but back to reality—some time later and looked at her watch. Her eyes widened. She had brought her small meal up here at eight-thirty. There they still were, near at hand, but it was now a quarter past eleven.

And—

—and some of the dolls had been moved around.

The German boy in his alpine shorts—*Lederhosen*—was leaning against the Effanbee lady-doll instead of sitting between the Japanese doll in her kimono and the Indian doll in her sari. Ruth got up, her heart beating too fast and too hard. The Hopi kachina doll was sitting on the lap of a burlap Haitian *vudun* doll with white crosses for eyes. And the Russian moss-man was lying on the floor, staring at the ceiling, his head wrenched to one side like the head of a gallows-corpse.

Who's been moving my dolls around? Who's been in here?

She looked around wildly and for a moment her frightened, confused mind fully expected to see the child-beater Elmer Haney standing in the shadowy space of the big upstairs room that had been Ralph's study, smiling his sunken, stupid grin. *I told you, woman: you are nothing but a meddling cunt.*

Nothing. No one.

Who's been in here? Who's been moving—

We move ourselves, dear.

A sly, tittering voice.

One hand went to her mouth. Her eyes widened. And then she saw the jagged letters sprawling and lurching across the blackboard. They had been made with so much force that that chalk had broken several times; untidy chunks of it lay in the chalk-gutter.

DAVID BROWN IS ON ALTAIR-4

What? What? What does that—

It means he's gone too far, the kachina doll said, and suddenly green light seemed to sweat out of its cottonwood pores. As she looked at it, numb with terror, its wooden face split open in a sinister, yawning grin. A dead cricket fell out of it and struck the floor with a dry desert click. *Gone too far, too far, too far . . .*

No, I don't believe that! Ruth screamed.

The whole town, Ruth . . . gone too far . . . too far . . . too far . . .

No!

Lost . . . lost. . . .

The eyes of the Greiner *papier-mâché* doll suddenly filled with that liquid green fire. *You're lost too,* it said. *You're just as crazy as the rest now. David Brown's just an excuse to stay here . . .*

No—

But all of her dolls were stirring now, that green fire moving from one to the other until her schoolroom flared with that light. It was waxing and waning, and she thought with sick horror that it was like being inside some ghastly emerald heart.

They stared at her with their glazey eyes and at last she understood why the dolls had frightened Edwina Thurlow so badly.

Now it was the voices of her dolls rising in that autumn-leafy swirl, whispering slyly, rattling among themselves, rattling to her . . . but these were the voices of the town, too, and Ruth McCausland knew it.

She thought they were perhaps the last of the town's sanity . . . and of her own.

Something has to be done, Ruth. It was the china bisque doll, fire dripping from its mouth; it was the voice of Beach Jernigan.

Have to warn someone. It was the French *poupée* with its rubbery gutta-percha body; it was the voice of Hazel McCready.

But they'll never let you out now, Ruth. It was the Nixon doll, his stuffed fingers raised in twin V's, speaking in the voice of John Enders down at the grammar school. *They could, but that would be wrong.*

They love you, Ruth, but if you try to leave now they'll kill you. You know that, don't you? Her 1910 Kewpie doll with its rubber head like an inverted teardrop; this voice was Justin Hurd's.

Have to send a signal.

Signal, Ruth, yes, and you know how—

Use us, we can show you how, we know—

She took a shambling step backward, her hands going to her ears, as if she could shut out the voices that way. Her mouth twisted. She was terrified, and what frightened her most was how she ever could have mistaken these voices, with their twisted truths, for sanity. All of Haven's concentrated madness was here, right now.

Signal, use us, we can show you how, we know and you WANT *to know, the town hall, Ruth, the clock tower—*

The rustling voices took up the chant: *The town hall, Ruth! Yes! Yes, that's it! The town hall! The town hall! Yes!*

Stop it! she screamed. *Stop it, stop it, oh please won't you—*

And then, for the first time since she was eleven and had passed out after winning the Girls' Mile Race at the Methodist Summer Picnic, Ruth McCausland fainted dead away.

6

Sometime early during the night she regained a soupy version of consciousness and stumbled downstairs to her bedroom without looking back. She was, in fact, afraid to look back. She was dully aware that her head was throbbing, as it had on the few occasions when she had drunk too much and awakened with a hangover. She was also aware that the old Victorian house was rocking and creaking like an old schooner in heavy weather. While Ruth had lain senseless on the schoolroom floor, terrible thunderstorms racked central and eastern Maine. A cold front from the Midwest had finally bulled its way into New England, pushing out the still sink of heat and humidity that had covered the area for the last week and a half. The change in the weather was accompanied by terrible thunderstorms in some places. Haven was spared the worst of these, but the power was out again and would remain so for several days this time.

But the fact of the power outage wasn't the important thing; Haven had its own unique power sources now. The important thing was simply that the weather had changed. When that happened, Ruth wasn't the only person in Haven to wake up with a horrible hangover sort of headache.

Everyone in town, from the oldest to the youngest, woke up feeling the same way as the strong winds blew the tainted air east, sending it out over the ocean, fragmenting it into harmless tatters.

7

Ruth slept until one o'clock Wednesday afternoon. She got up with the lingering remains of her headache, but two Anacin took care of that. By five she felt better than she had for a long time. Her body ached and her muscles were stiff, but these were minor matters compared with the things that had troubled her since the beginning of July, and they could not cut into her sense of well-being at all. Even her fear for David Brown couldn't spoil it completely.

On Main Street, everyone she passed had a peculiar dazed look in his or her eye, as though they had all just awakened from a spell cast by a fairy-tale witch.

Ruth went to her office in the town hall, enjoying the way the wind lifted her hair from her temples, the way the clouds moved across a sky that was a deep, crisp blue: a sky that looked almost autumnal. She saw a couple of kids flying a box kite in the big field behind the grammar school and actually laughed aloud.

But there was no laughing later as she spoke to a small group she quickly gathered—Haven's three selectmen, the town manager, and, of course, Bryant and Marie Brown. Ruth began by apologizing for not having called the state police and wardens before now, or even reporting the boy's disappearance. She had believed, she said, that they would find David quickly, probably the first night, certainly the next day. She knew that was no excuse, but it was why she had allowed it to happen. It had been, she said, the worst mistake she had made in her years as Haven's constable, and if David Brown had suffered for it . . . she would never forgive herself.

Bryant just nodded, dazed and distant and ill-looking. Marie, however, reached across the table and took her hand.

"You're not to blame yourself," she said softly. "There were other circumstances. We all know that." The others nodded.

I can't hear their minds anymore, Ruth realized suddenly, and her mind responded: *Could you ever, Ruth? Really? Or was that a hallucination brought on by your worry over David Brown?*

Yes. Yes, I could.

It would be easier to believe it had been a hallucination, but that wasn't the truth. And realizing that, she realized something else: *she could still do it.* It was like hearing a faint roaring sound in a conch shell, that sound children mistake for the ocean. She had no idea what their thoughts *were,* but she was still hearing them. Were they hearing her?

ARE YOU STILL THERE? she shouted as loudly as she could.

Marie Brown's hand went to her temple, as if she had felt a sudden stab of pain. Newt Berringer frowned deeply. Hazel McCready, who had been doodling on the pad in front of her, looked up as if Ruth had spoken aloud.

Oh yes, they still hear me.

"Whatever happened, right or wrong, is done now," Ruth said. "It's time—and overtime—that I contacted the state police about David. Do I have your approval to take this step?"

Under normal circumstances, it never would have crossed her mind that she should ask them a question like that. After all, they paid her pittance of a salary to *answer* questions, not ask them.

But things were different in Haven now. Fresh breeze and clear air or not, things were still different in Haven now.

They looked at her, surprised and a little shocked.

Now the voices came back to her clearly: *No, Ruth, no . . . no outsiders . . . we'll take care . . . we don't need any outsiders while we "become" . . . shhh . . . for your life, Ruth . . . shhh . . .*

Outside, the wind blew a particularly hard gust, rattling the windows of Ruth's office. Adley McKeen looked toward the sound . . . they all did. Then Adley smiled a puzzled, peculiar little smile.

"O' course, Ruth," he said. "If you think it's time to notify the staties, you got to go ahead. We trust your judgment, don't we?"

The others agreed.

The weather had changed, the wind was blowing, and by Wednesday afternoon, the state police were in charge of the search for David Brown.

8

By Friday, Ruth McCausland understood that Wednesday and Thursday had been an untrustworthy respite in an ongoing process. She was being driven steadily toward some alien madness.

A dim part of her mind recognized the fact, bemoaned it . . . but was unable to stop it. It could only hope that the voices of her dolls held some truth as well as madness.

Watching as if from outside herself, she saw her hands take her sharpest kitchen knife—the one she used for boning fish—from the drawer. She took it upstairs, into the schoolroom.

The schoolroom glowed, rotten with green light. Tommyknocker-light. That was what everyone in town was calling them now, and it was a good name, wasn't it? Yes. As good as any. The Tommyknockers.

Send a signal. That's all you can do now. They want to get rid of you, Ruth. They love you, but their love has turned homicidal. I suppose you can find a twisted sort of respect in that. Because they're still afraid of you. Even now, now when you're almost as nutty as the rest of them, they're afraid of you. Maybe someone will hear the signal . . . hear it . . . see it . . . understand it.

9

Now there was a shaky drawing of the town-hall clock tower on her board . . . the scrawled work of a first-grader.

Ruth could not stand to work on the dolls in the schoolroom . . . not in that terrible light that waxed and pulsed. She took them, one by one, into her husband's study, and slit their bellies open like a surgeon—the French *madame,* the nineteenth-century clown, the Kewpie, all of them—one by one. And into each she put a small gadget made of C-cells, wires, electronic-calculator circuit boards, and the cardboard cores from toilet-paper rolls. She sewed the incisions up quickly, using a coarse black thread. As the line of naked dolls grew longer on her husband's desk, they began to look like dead children, victims of some grisly mass poisoning, perhaps, who had been stripped and robbed after death.

Each sewn incision parted in the middle so that one of the toilet-paper rolls could poke out like the barrel of some odd telescope. Only cardboard, the rolls would still serve to channel the force when it was generated. She didn't know how she knew this, or how she had known to build the gadgets in the first place . . . the knowledge seemed to have come shimmering out of the air. The same air into which David Brown

(is on Altair-4)

had disappeared.

As she plunged the knife into their plump, defenseless bellies, green light puffed out.

I'm

(sending a signal)
murdering the only children I ever had.

The signal. Think of the signal, not the children.

She used extension cords to wire the dolls neatly together in a chain. She had stripped the insulation from the last four inches of these cords and slipped the gleaming copper into an M-16 firecracker she had confiscated from Beach Jernigan's fourteen-year-old son Hump (thus known because one shoulder rode slightly higher than the other) about a week before all this madness began. She looked back, doubtful for a moment, into her schoolroom with its empty benches. Enough light fell through the archway for her to be able to see the drawing of the town-hall clock tower. She had done it in one of those blank periods that seemed to be getting longer and longer.

The hands of the clock in the drawing were set at three.

Ruth set her work aside and went to bed. She slept, but her sleep was not easy; she twisted and turned and moaned. Even in her sleep the voices ran through her head—thoughts of revenge planned, of cakes to be baked, sexual fantasies, worries about irregularity, ideas for strange gadgets and machines, dreams of power. And below them all, a thin, irrational yammer like a polluted stream, thoughts coming from the heads of her fellow townspeople but not *human* thoughts, and in her nightmarish sleep, that part of Ruth McCausland which clung stubbornly to sanity knew the truth: these were *not* the rising voices of the people she had lived with all these years, but those of outsiders. They were the voices of the Tommyknockers.

10

Ruth understood by Thursday noon that the change in the weather hadn't solved anything.

The state police came, but they did not institute a widespread search; Ruth's report, detailed and complete, as always, made it clear that David Brown, four, could hardly have wandered outside their search area unless he'd been abducted—a possibility they would now have to consider. Her report was accompanied by topographical maps. These were annotated in her careful, no-nonsense handwriting, and made it clear she had conducted the search thoroughly.

"Careful and thorough you were, Ruthie," Monster Dugan told her that evening. His brow was furrowed in a frown so huge each line looked like an earthquake fissure. "You always have been. But I never knew you to pull a John Wayne stunt like *this* before."

"Butch, I'm sorry."

"Yeah, well . . ." He shrugged. "Done is done, huh?"

"Yes," she said, and smiled wanly. It had been one of Ralph's favorite sayings.

Butch asked a lot of questions, but not the one she needed to answer: *Ruth, what's wrong in Haven?* The high winds had cleansed the town's atmosphere; none of the outsiders sensed anything *was* wrong.

But the winds hadn't ended the trouble. The bad magic was still going on. Whatever it was, it seemed to continue by itself after a certain point. Ruth guessed that point had been reached. She wondered what a team of doctors, conducting mass physicals in Haven, might find. Iron shortages in the women? Men with suddenly receding hairlines? Improved visual acuity (especially peripheral vision) matched by a surprisingly high loss of teeth? People who seemed so bright they were spooky, so in tune with you they almost seemed to be—ha-ha—reading your mind?

Ruth herself had lost two more teeth Wednesday night. One she found on her pillow Thursday morning, a grotesquely middle-aged offering to the tooth fairy. The other was nowhere to be found. She supposed she had swallowed it. Not that it mattered.

11

The compulsion to blow up the town hall became maddening mental poison ivy, itching at her brain all the time. The doll-voices whispered and whispered. On Friday she made a final effort to save herself.

She decided to leave town after all—it was *not* hers anymore. She guessed that staying even this long had been one of the traps the Tommyknockers had laid for her . . . and, like the David Brown trap, she had blundered into it, as confused as a rabbit in a snare.

She thought her old Dodge wouldn't start. They would have fixed it. But it did.

Then she thought she would not be allowed out of Haven Village, that they would stop her, smiling like Moonies and sending their endless rustly *we-all-love-you-Ruth* thoughts. She wasn't.

She rolled down Main Street and out into the country, Ruth sitting bolt upright and white-knuckled, a graven smile on her face, tongue-twisters

(she sells pickled peppers bitter butter)

flying through her head. She felt her gaze being pulled toward the town-hall clock tower

(a signal Ruth send)

(yes the explosion the lovely)

(bang blow it blow it all the way to Altair-4 Ruth)

and resisted with all her might. This compulsion to blow up the town hall to call attention to what was going on here was insane. It was like setting your house on fire to roast a chicken.

She felt better when the brick tower was out of sight.

Once on Derry Road, she had to resist an urge to get the Dart moving as fast as it would go (which, considering its years, was still surprisingly fast). She felt like a lucky escapee from a den of lions—one who has escaped more by good luck than good sense. As the village dropped behind and those rustling voices fell away, she began to feel that someone *must* be giving belated chase.

She glanced again and again into the rearview mirror, expecting to see vehicles chasing after her, wanting to bring her back. They would *insist* that she come back.

They loved her too much to let her go.

But the road had remained clear. No Dick Allison screaming after her in one of the town's three fire engines. No Newt Berringer in his big old mint-green Olds-88. No Bobby Tremain in his yellow Challenger.

As she approached the Haven-Albion town line, she put the Dart up to fifty. The closer she got to the town line—which she had begun to think of, rightly or not, as the point at which her escape would become irrevocable, the more she found the last two weeks seeming like some black, twisted nightmare.

Can't go back. Can't.

Her foot on the Dart's accelerator pedal kept growing heavier.

At the end, something warned her—perhaps it was something the voices had said and her subconscious had filed away. She was, after all, receiving all sorts of information now, in her sleep as well as when she was awake. As the town-line marker came up—

A
L
B
I
O
N

—her foot left the Dart's gas pedal and stepped on the brake. It went down mushily and much too far, as it had for the last four years or so. Ruth allowed the car to roll off the tar and onto the shoulder. Dust, as white and dry as bone meal, plumed up behind her. The wind had died. The air of Haven was deadly still again. The dust she had raised, Ruth thought, would hang for a long time.

She sat with her hands curled tightly on the wheel, wondering why she had stopped.

Wondering. Almost knowing. Beginning

(to "become")

to know. Or guess.

A barrier? Is that what you think? That they've put up a barrier? That they've managed to turn all of Haven into a . . . an ant-farm, or something under a bowl? Ruth, that's ridiculous!

And so it was, not only according to logic and experience but also according to the evidence of her senses. As she sat behind the wheel, listening to the radio (soft jazz which was coming from a low-power college station in Bergenfield, New Jersey), a Hillcrest chicken truck, probably bound for Derry, rumbled past her. A few seconds later, a Chevy Vega went by in the other direction. Nancy Voss was behind the wheel. The sticker on the rear bumper read: POSTAL WORKERS DO IT BY EXPRESS MAIL.

Nancy Voss did not look at Ruth, simply went along her way—which in this case probably meant Augusta.

See? Nothing stopping them, Ruth thought.

No, her mind whispered back. *Not them, Ruth, just*

*you. It would stop you, and it would stop Bobbi Anderson's friend, maybe one or two others. Go on! Drive right into it at fifty miles an hour or so, if you don't believe it! We all love you, and we would hate to see it happen to you . . . but we wouldn't—*couldn't—*stop it from happening.*

Instead of driving, she got out and walked up to the Haven-Albion line. Her shadow trailed long behind her; the hot July sun beat down on her head. She could hear the dim but steady rumble of machinery from the woods behind Bobbi's place. Digging again. The David Brown vacation was over. And she sensed that they were getting close to . . . well, to *something.* This brought a sense of panic and urgency.

She approached the marker . . . passed it . . . kept walking . . . and began to feel a wild, rising hope. *She was out of Haven! She was in Albion!* In a moment she would run, screaming, to the nearest house, the nearest telephone. She—

—slowed.

A puzzled look settled upon her face . . . and then deepened into a dawning, horrified certainty.

It was getting hard to walk. The air was becoming tough, springy. She could feel it stretching her cheeks, the skin of her forehead; she could feel it flattening her breasts.

Ruth lowered her head and continued to walk, her mouth drawn down in a grimace of effort, cords standing out on her neck. She looked like a woman trying to walk into a gale-force wind, although the trees on either side of the road were barely swaying their leaves. The image which came to her now and the one which had come to Gardener when he tried to reach into the bottom of Anderson's customized water heater were exactly the same; they differed only in degree. Ruth felt as if the entire *road* had been blocked by an invisible nylon stocking, one large enough to fit a female Titan. *I've heard about nude-look hose,* she thought hysterically, *but really, this is ridiculous.*

Her breasts began to ache from the pressure. And suddenly her feet began to slip in the dirt. Panic slapped at her. She had reached, then passed the point where her ability to generate forward motion surpassed the elastic give of the invisible barrier. Now it was shoving her back out.

She struggled to turn, to get out on her own before that could happen, but she lost her footing and was snapped rudely back the way she had come, her feet scraping, her eyes wide and shocked. It was like being pushed by the expanding side of a large, rubbery balloon.

For a moment her feet left the ground entirely. Then she landed on her knees, scraping them both badly, tearing her dress. She got up and backed toward her car, crying a little with the pain.

She sat behind the wheel of her car for almost twenty minutes, waiting for the throbbing in her knees to subside. Cars and trucks passed occasionally along Derry Road in both directions, and once as she sat there, Ashley Ruvall came along on his bike. He had his fishing pole. He saw her and raised a hand to her.

"Hi, Mitsuths McCauthland!" he cried chirpily, and grinned. The lisp wasn't really surprising, she thought dully, considering that all of the boy's teeth were gone. Not some; *all.*

Still, she felt coldness rush through her as Ashley called: "We all love you, Mithuth McCauthland. . . ."

After a long time she backed the Dart up, U-turned, and went back through the hot silence to Haven Village. As she drove up Main Street to her house, it seemed that a great many people looked at her, their eyes full of a knowledge more sly than wise.

Ruth looked up into the Dart's rearview mirror and saw the clock tower at the other end of the village's short Main Street.

The hands were approaching three P.M.

She pulled to a stop in front of the Fannins', bumping carelessly up over the curb and stalling the engine. She didn't bother to turn off the key. She only sat behind the wheel, red idiot-lights glowing on the instrument panel, looking into the rearview mirror as her mind floated gently away. When she came back to herself, the town-hall clock was chiming six. She had lost three hours . . . and another tooth. The hours were nowhere to be found, but the tooth, an incisor, lay on the lap of her dress.

12

All that night her dolls talked to her. And she thought that none of what they said was precisely a lie . . . that was the most horrible thing of all. She sat in the green, diseased heart of their influence and listened to them tell their lunatic fairy-tales.

They told her she was right to believe she was going crazy; an X-ray of her brain, they said, one of anyone in Haven, for that matter, would make a neurologist run screaming for cover. Her brain was changing. It was . . . "becoming."

Her brain, her teeth—oh, excuse me, make that *ex*-teeth—both "becoming." And her eyes . . . they were changing color, weren't they? Yes. Their deep brown was fading toward hazel . . . and the other day, in the Haven Lunch, hadn't she noticed that Beach Jernigan's bright blue eyes were also changing color? Deepening toward hazel?

Hazel eyes . . . no teeth . . . oh dear God what's happening to us?

The dolls looked at her glassily, and smiled.

Don't worry, Ruth, it's only the invasion from space they've made cheap movies about for years. You see that, don't you? The Invasion of the Tommyknockers. *If you want to see the invaders from space the B movies and the science-fiction stories were always going on about, look in Beach Jernigan's eyes. Or Wendy's. Or your own.*

"What you mean is that I'm being eaten up," she whispered in the summer darkness as Friday night became Saturday morning.

Why, Ruth! What did you think "becoming" was? The dolls laughed, and Ruth's mind mercifully floated away once again.

13

When she woke on Saturday morning the sun was up, the shaky child's drawing of the town-hall clock tower was on the schoolroom blackboard, and there were better than two dozen calculators on Ralph's sheeted study desk.

They were in the canvas shoulder-bag she used when she went out collecting for the Cancer Society. There were Dymotapes on some on the calculators. BERRINGER. MCCREADY. SELECTMAN'S OFFICE DO NOT REMOVE. DEPT. OF TAXES. She hadn't gone to sleep after all. Instead, she had drifted into one of those blank periods . . . and looted all the town offices' calculators, it looked like.

Why?

Yours not to reason why, Ruth, the dolls whispered, and she understood better and better each day, better and better each *minute,* each *second,* in fact, what had frightened little Edwina Thurlow so badly. *Yours is but to send a signal . . . and die.*

How much of that idea is mine? And how much is them, driving me?

Doesn't matter, Ruth. It's going to happen anyway, so make it happen as fast and hard and soon as you can. Stop thinking. Let it happen . . . because part of you wants *it to happen, doesn't it?*

Yes. *Most* of her, in fact. And not to send a signal to the outside world, or any silly bullshit like that; that was just the sane icing on a rich devil's food cake of irrationality.

She wanted to be a part of it as it all went up.

The cardboard tubes would channel the force, send it up into the clock tower in a bright river of destructive power, and the tower would lift off like a rocket; the shockwave would hammer the street of this fouled Haven with destruction, and destruction was what she wanted; that want was part of *her* "becoming."

14

That night, Butch Dugan called her to update her on the David Brown case. Some of the developments were unusual. The boy's brother, Hillman, was in the hospital, in a state which closely resembled catatonia. The kid's grandfather wasn't much better. He had begun telling people that David Brown hadn't just gotten lost, but had actually disappeared. That the magic trick, in other words, had been real. And, Butch said, he was telling anyone who would listen that half the people in Haven were going crazy and the rest were already there.

"He went up to Bangor and talked to a fellow named Bright on the *News,*" Monster said. "They wanted human interest and got nut stuff instead. Old man's turning into a real quasar, Ruth."

"Better tell him to stay away," Ruth said. "They'll let him in, but he'll never get out again."

"What?" Monster shouted. His voice was suddenly becoming faint. "This connection's going to hell, Ruth."

"I said there may be something new tomorrow. I still haven't given up hope." She rubbed her temples steadily and looked at the dolls, in a row on Ralph's desk and wired up like a terrorist's bomb. "Look for a signal tomorrow."

"What?" Monster's voice was almost lost in the rising surf of the worsening connection.

"Goodbye, Butch. You're a hell of a sport. Listen for it. You'll hear it all the way up in Derry, I think. Three on the nose."

"Ruth I'm losing you . . . call back . . . soon . . ."

She hung up the useless telephone, looked at her dolls, listened to the rising voices, and waited for it to be time.

15

That Sunday was a picture-book summer day in Maine: clear, bright, warm. At a quarter to one, Ruth McCausland, dressed in a pretty blue summer frock, left her house for the last time. She locked the front door, and stood on tiptoe to hang the key on the little hook there. Ralph had argued that any burglar worth his salt would look over the door for a key first thing of all, but Ruth had gone on doing it, and the house had never been burgled. She supposed, at bottom, it came down to trust . . . and Haven had never let her down. She had put the dolls in Ralph's old canvas duffel. She dragged it down the porch steps.

Bobby Tremain was walking by, whistling. "Help you with that, Missus McCausland?"

"No thank you, Bobby."

"All right." He smiled at her. A few teeth were left in his smile—not many, but a few, like the last remaining pickets in a fence surrounding a haunted house. "We all love you."

"Yes," she said, hoisting the duffel into the passenger seat. A bolt of pain ripped through her head. "Oh how well I know it."

(what are you thinking Ruth where are you going)

(she sells seashells she sells seashells)

(tell us Ruth tell us what the dolls told you to do)

(Betty Bitter bought some butter)

(give Ruth tell is it what we want or are you holding out)

(wouldn't you like to know Peter Piper Peter Piper)

(it's what we want, isn't it? there are no changes, are there?)

She looked at Bobby for a moment and then smiled. Bobby Tremain's own smile faltered a little.

(love me? yes . . . but you are all still afraid of me. and are right to be)

"Go on, Bobby," she said softly, and Bobby went. He looked back over his shoulder once, his young face troubled, mistrusting.

Ruth drove to the town hall.

It was Sunday-silent, a dusty church of administration. Her footfalls clicked and echoed. The duffel was too heavy to carry so she dragged it along the waxed hall floor. It made a dry snakelike hiss. She hauled it up three flights of stairs, one riser at a time, her hands fisted around the cord that shut the duffel's mouth. Her head pumped and ached. She bit her lip and two teeth heeled over sideways with soft rottenness and she spat them out. Her breath was harsh straw in her throat. Dusty sunlight fell through the high third-floor windows.

She dragged the bag down the short, explosively hot corridor—there were only two rooms up here, one on each side. All the town's records were stored in them. If the town hall was Haven's brain, then here, in this still attic heat, was its paper memory, stretching back through the times the town had been Ilium, Montgomery, Coodersville, Montville Plantation.

The voices whispered and rustled around her.

For a moment she stood looking out of the last window, looking down on the short length of Main Street. There were maybe fifteen cars parked in front of Cooder's market, which was open from noon until six on Sundays—it was doing a brisk business. People sauntering into the Haven Lunch for coffee. A few cars passing back and forth.

It looks so normal . . . it all looks so damned normal!

She felt a giddy moment of doubt . . . and then Moose Richardson looked up and waved, as if he could see her, looking out of this dirty third-floor window.

And Moose wasn't the only one. Lots of them were looking at her.

She ducked back, turned, and got the window pole which stood in the far corner, where the hallway dead-ended. She used the pole to hook a ring in the middle of the ceiling and pull down the folding stairs. That done, she set the pole aside and bent back, looking up into the tower. She could hear the mechanical rattle and whir of clockwork, and below that, the dim rustle of sleeping bats. There were a lot of them up there. The town should have cleaned them out years ago, but the fumigation was apt to be nasty . . . and expensive. When the clock machinery broke down again, the bats would have to be cleared out before it could be fixed. That would surely be soon enough. As far as the selectmen were concerned, as long as someone else was in office when the clock rang twelve noon some night at three in the morning and then just stopped, all would be well.

Ruth wound the duffel's cotton cord around her arm three times and began to climb slowly up the ladder, dragging the bag between her legs. It bumped and rose in jerks, like a body in a canvas sack. The cord bit into her arm ever more deeply, and soon her hand had gone purple and numb. She breathed in long, tearing gasps that hurt something deep inside her chest.

At last, shadows enveloped her. She stepped off the ladder and into the town hall's *real* attic and pulled the duffel bag up, hand over hand. Ruth was dimly aware that her gums and ears had started to bleed and her mouth was full of the sour, coppery taste of blood.

All around her she could smell the crypt-stink of old brick fuming in dry, dark, pent-up summer heat. To her left was a vast dim circle: the back side of the clock-face which overlooked Main Street. In a more prosperous town, no doubt all four sides would have had a face; Haven's town-hall tower had only the one. It was twelve feet in diameter. Behind it, dimmer yet, she could see wheels and cogs slowly turning. She could see where the hammer would come down and strike the bell. The dent there was deep and ancient. The clock's works were very loud.

Working swiftly, jerkily—she was like a clock herself now, a clock that was running down, and her belfry was certainly full of bats, wasn't it?—Ruth unwound the cotton cord from her arm, actually peeling it out of a deep, spiraling groove in her flesh, and opened the mouth of the duffel. She began taking the dolls out one by one, moving as fast as she could. She laid them in a circle, legs out so that the feet maintained contact all around the circle, hands the same way. In the darkness they looked like dolls conducting a séance.

She attached the M-16 to the center of the dented place on the great bell. When the hour struck and the hammer fell—

Boom.

So I will just sit here, she thought. *Sit here and wait for the hammer to fall.*

Droning weariness suddenly washed over her. Ruth drifted away.

16

She came back slowly. At first she thought she must be in her bed at home with her face pressed into the pillow. She was in bed and all this had just been a terrible nightmare. Except her pillow was not this bristly, this hot; her blankets did not pulse and breathe.

She brought her hands up and touched a hot, leathery body, bones covered with scant flesh. The bat had roosted just above her right breast, in the hollow of her shoulder . . . she realized suddenly that she had called it . . . *that somehow she had called all of them.* She could hear its rodentine, scabrous mind, its thoughts dark and instinctual and insane. It thought only of blood and bugs and cruising in blind darkness.

"Oh God no!" she screamed . . . the rugose, alien crawl of its thoughts was maddening, not to be borne. "Oh *no,* oh please God *no—"*

She tightened her hands, not meaning to, and the

papery bones in its wings snapped under her fingers. It squealed, and she felt sharp, needling pain in her cheek as it bit her.

Now they were all squealing, *all,* and she realized that there were dozens of them on her—maybe hundreds. On her other shoulder, on her shoes, in her hair. As she looked, the lap of her dress began to squirm and twist.

"Oh *no!*" she shrieked again into the dusty dimness of the clock tower. Bats flew all around her. They squeaked. The whisper of their wings was a soft rising thunder, like the rising whisper of Haven's voices. "Oh *no!* Oh *no!* Oh *no!*"

A bat fluttered in her hair, caught, squealing.

Another flew into her face, and its breath was the stink of a dead henhouse.

The world spun and swung. Somehow she blundered to her feet. She beat her hands about her head, the bats were everywhere, all around her in a black cloud, and now there was no difference between the soft fluttery explosion of their wings and the voices

(we all love you, Ruth!)

the voices

(we hate you Ruth don't you meddle don't you dare meddle)

the voices of Haven.

She had forgotten where she was. She had forgotten the trapdoor which yawned almost at her feet, and as she stumbled toward it she heard the clock strike—but the sound was muffled, not true, because the hammer had struck her detonator and—

—and nothing was happening.

She turned, bats flying all about her, and now her incredulous eyes were also bleeding, but through a reddish haze she saw the hammer fall again, and then yet a third time, and still the world remained.

A dud, Ruth McCausland thought. *It was a dud.*

And fell through the trapdoor.

The bats flew up from her body, her dress flew up from her body, one loafer flew up from her foot. She struck the ladder, half-turned, and landed on her left side with a crunch that broke all her ribs. She struggled to turn over and somehow managed to do it. Most of the bats had found their way back through the trapdoor into the welcoming darkness of the clock-tower, but half a dozen or so were still circling, confused, below the roof of the third-floor corridor. The sound of their voices so alien and insectile, so hivelike and warm with insanity. *These* were the voices she had been hearing in her head ever since July 4th or so. The town was not just going mad. That would have been bad, but this was worse . . . oh God, it was much, much worse.

And it had all been for nothing. Hump Jernigan's M-16 had been nothing but a dud after all. She grayed out and came back some four minutes later with a bat roosting on the bridge of her nose, lapping bloody tears from her cheek.

"No you dirty FUCK!" she screamed, and tore it in two, her revulsion an agony. It made a sound like thick, tearing paper. Its alien guts dribbled onto her upturned, cobweb-smeared face. She could not open her mouth to scream—*Let me die, God, please, don't let me be like them, don't let me "become"*—because it would dribble its dying self into her and then Hump's M-16 exploded under the striker with an undramatic wet bang. Green light lit first the square of the trapdoor . . . and then the whole world. For one moment Ruth could see the bones of the bats standing out clearly, as if in an X-ray picture.

Then all the green turned black.

It was 3:05 P.M.

17

All over Haven, people were lying down. Some had gone to their cellars with a vague notion that now would be a good time to get preserves, some with just an idea that it would be cooler there. Beach Jernigan lay behind the counter of the Haven Lunch with his hands laced behind his neck. He was thinking of the thing in the back of his truck, the thing under the tarp.

At 3:05 the base of the clock-tower burst open, spraying powdered brick everywhere. A huge, explosive bellow chased off across the fields; it broke almost every window in Haven, and a good many in Troy and Albion as well.

Green fire spilled out through the jagged rent in the bricks, and the town-hall tower began to rise, a surreal brick missile, a Magritte rocket with a clock in its side. It rose on a pillar of cold green fire—surely cold, else the dolls would have been consumed, and Ruth McCausland's arm as well . . . the entire village, for that matter.

The clock-tower rose on this green torch, its sides now beginning to bulge outward—yet for an instant the illusion held: a brick rocket rising into the afternoon sky . . . and through the roar of the explosion, the clock could be heard, belling out hour after hour. On the twelfth stroke—noon? midnight?—it exploded like the ill-fated *Challenger*. Bricks flew everywhere—Benton Rhodes would later see some of the damage, but the worst of it was quickly covered up.

Flying bricks punched through the sides of houses, cellar windows, board fences. Bricks fell from the sky like bombs. The clock's long hand, lacy wrought iron, whickered through the air like a deadly boomerang and buried itself in one of the ancient oaks which stood outside the Haven Library.

Masonry and splintered boards rumbled back to earth.

Then, silence.

After a while, people all over Haven began to get cautiously to their feet, to look around . . . to begin sweeping up glass or examining damage. Destruction had swept the town, but no one had been hurt. And in the entire town, only one person had actually *seen* that brick rocket rising into the air, like a madman's grandiose dream.

That one person was Jim Gardener. Bobbi was taking a little nap—Gardener had coaxed her into it. Neither of them had any business working in the heat of the afternoon—especially not Bobbi. She had come back a little from the terrible state in which Gardener had found her, but she was still pushing herself much too hard, and she had abruptly begun to menstruate heavily again.

I wonder, he thought morbidly, *when she's going to need a blood transfusion instead of just a couple of extra iron pills a day?* But that was unlikely, he knew. His ex-wife had suffered horrible menstrual problems, possibly because her mother had been given the drug known as DES. So Gardener had gotten a crash course in a body function his own body would never perform, and he knew the layman's idea of menstruation—a monthly flow of blood from the vagina—simply wasn't true. Most of the material which made up the menses wasn't blood at all, but useless tissue. Menstruation was an efficient waste-removal process on behalf of a woman capable of bearing children but not currently doing so.

No, he doubted if Bobbi would bleed to death . . . barring a uterine rupture, which was highly unlikely.

Bullshit. You don't know what's likely in this situation and what isn't.

Okay. Fair enough. And he knew that women weren't built to menstruate day after day and week after week, no matter what. At bottom, blood and tissue were both the same thing: the stuff of which Bobbi Anderson was made. It was like cannibalism, but—

No. No it wasn't. It was as if someone had turned her thermostat all the way to the end of the dial and she was burning herself up. She had nearly keeled over a couple of times during the hot spell of the week before, and Gardener knew that, although it sounded grotesque, the hunt for the little Brown boy had actually been a kind of rest for Bobbi.

Gardener hadn't really believed he would get her to take a nap. Then, at around a quarter to three, Bobbi had said that she *was* sorta tired, and that maybe she *could* use a nap. She asked Gardener if he wasn't going to catch an hour of rack time as well.

"Yes," he said. "I'll sit out on the porch and read a few minutes first." *And finish this little drinky-poo, while I'm at it.*

"Well, don't hang out too long," Bobbi said. "A siesta wouldn't hurt you, either."

But he had hung out long enough, stretching the drink, to still be there when the roar crossed the fields and hills between here and the village—roughly five miles.

"What the *fuck*—"

The roar grew louder . . . and suddenly he saw it, something out of a nightmare, it was DTs setting in, *had* to be, fucking *had* to be. This was no telepathic typewriter or water heater from space—*this was a motherfucking brick rocket taking off from Haven Village,* and that was it, everybody out of the pool, friends and neighbors, I have definitely blown my wheels.

Just before it exploded, splashing the sky with green fire, he recognized it and knew it was no hallucination.

There was Bobbi Anderson's power; *there* was what they were going to use to stop the nukes, the arms race, the bloody tide of worldwide madness; there it was, rising into the sky on a pillar of flame: one of the crazies in town had somehow laid a fuse under the town hall and struck a match to it and had just sent the Haven clock-tower into the sky like a fucking Roman candle.

"Holy *shit,*" Gardener whispered in a tiny, horrified voice.

There it is, Gard! Behold the future! Is it what you want? Because that woman in there is going bughouse, and you know it . . . the signs are just all too clear. Do you want to put that kind of power in her hands? Do you?

She's not crazy, Gardener responded, scared. *Not crazy at all, and do you think what you just saw changes the equation? It doesn't, it only underlines it. If not me and Bobbi, who? The Dallas Police, that's who. It's going to be all right, I'll keep an eye on her, keep a checkrein on her—*

Oh, you're doing great at that, you fucking lush, just great.

The incredible thing in the sky exploded, splashing green fire everywhere. Gardener shielded his eyes. He had gotten to his feet.

Anderson came out on the run.

"What in hell was *that?*" she asked, but she knew . . . she knew, and Gardener, with cold, sudden certainty, *knew* that she knew.

Gardener threw a barrier across his mind—in the last two weeks he had learned how to do that with complete success. The barrier consisted of nothing more than a random recitation of old addresses, bits of poems, snatches of songs . . . but it worked. It was not at all difficult to run such jamming interference, he had discovered; it wasn't much different from the random run of thoughts that went through almost everyone's head most of the time (he might have changed his mind if he had been aware of Ruth McCausland's tortured efforts to hide her thoughts—Gardener had no idea of how much trouble the plate in his head was saving him). He had seen Bobbi looking at him in a queer, puzzled way a couple of times, and although she looked away whenever she saw Gardener observing her, he knew that she was trying to read his thoughts . . . trying hard . . . and still failing.

He used the barrier to cover his first lie to Bobbi since

he had thrown in with her on July 5th, almost three weeks ago.

"I don't know, exactly," he said. "I dozed off in the chair. I heard an explosion and saw a big flash of light. Looked green. That's all."

Bobbi's eyes searched his face, and then she nodded. "Well, I guess we better go into the village and see."

Gardener relaxed slightly. He wasn't sure why he had lied, only that it seemed safer to do so . . . and she had believed him. Nor did he want to endanger that belief. "Would you mind going alone? I mean, if you want company—"

"No, that's fine," she said almost eagerly, and went.

Walking back to the porch after seeing the truck down the road, he kicked over his glass. The drinking was getting out of hand, and it was time to stop. Because something really weird was happening here. It would bear watching, and when you got drunk you went blind.

It was a pledge he had made before. Sometimes it even took for a while. This time it didn't. Gardener was sitting drunk and asleep on the porch that night when Bobbi returned.

Ruth's signal had been received, nevertheless. The receiver was troubled in mind, still committed to Bobbi's project, yet uneasy enough about it to be boozing more and more. But it *had* been received, and at least partially understood: Gardener's lie was an indication of that, if nothing else. But Ruth would perhaps have been happier with her other accomplishment.

Voices or no voices, the lady died sane.

7.

BEACH JERNIGAN AND DICK ALLISON

1

No one in Haven was more delighted about the "becoming" than Beach Jernigan. If Gard's Tommyknockers had appeared to Beach in person, carrying nuclear weapons and proposing that he plant one in each of the world's seven largest cities, Beach would have immediately started phoning for plane tickets. Even in Haven, where quiet zealotry was becoming a way of life, Beach's partisanship was extreme. If he had had any idea at all about Gardener's growing doubts, he would have removed him. Permanently. And at once, if not sooner.

There was a good reason for Beach's feelings. In May—not long after Hilly Brown's birthday, in fact—Beach developed a hacking cough that wouldn't go away. It was worrisome because he didn't have a fever or the sniffles to go with it. It became *more* worrisome when he began to cough up a little blood. When you run a restaurant, you don't want to be coughing *at all*. The customers don't like it. It makes them nervous. Sooner or later someone tells the Board of Health and maybe they shut you up for a week or so while they wait to see how your tine test comes out. The Haven Lunch was a marginally profitable business at best (Beach put in twelve hours a day short-ordering so he could clear sixty-five dollars a week—if the place hadn't been his free and clear, he would have starved), and Beach couldn't afford to be shut up for a week in the summer. Summer wasn't here yet, but it was coming on apace. So he went to see old Doc Warwick, and Doc Warwick sent him up to Derry Home for a chest X-ray, and when the X-ray came back Doc Warwick studied it for all of twenty seconds and then called Beach and when Beach got there, Doc Warwick said: "I've got hard news for you, Beach. Sit down."

Beach sat down. He felt that if there hadn't been a chair, he would have fallen on the floor. All the strength had run out of his legs. There was no telepathy going on in Haven back in May—no more than the ordinary kind that people use all the time, anyway—but that ordinary kind was all Beach needed. He knew what Doc Warwick was going to say before he said it. Not TB; big C. Lung cancer.

But that was in May. Now, in July, Beach was fit as a fiddle. Doc Warwick had told him he could expect to be in the hospital by July 15th, but here he was, eating like a horse, randy as a bear most of the time, and feeling like he could outrun Bobby Tremain in a footrace. He hadn't been back to the hospital for another chest X-ray. He didn't need one to know the large dark stain on his left lung had disappeared. Far as that went, if he had wanted an X-ray, he would have taken the afternoon off and built an X-ray machine himself. He knew just how it could be done.

But now, in the wake of the explosion, there were other things to be built, other things to do . . . and quickly.

They had a meeting. Everyone in town. Not that they gathered, as at a town meeting; that was quite unnecessary. Beach went on frying hamburgers in the Haven Lunch, Nancy Voss went on sorting stamps at the post office (now that Joe was dead, it was at least a place to come to, Sunday or not), Bobby Tremain stayed under his *Challenger*, putting on a backflow rebreather that would allow him to get roughly seventy miles to the gallon. Not Anderson's gasoline pill—not quite—but close. Newt Berringer, who knew goddamned well there was no time to waste, was driving out to the Applegate place as fast as he dared. But no matter what they were doing or where they were, they were together, a network of silent voices—the voices that had frightened Ruth so badly.

Less than forty-five minutes after the explosion, some seventy people had gathered at Henry Applegate's. Henry had the largest, best-equipped workshop in town now that the Shell station had mostly gone out of the engine-repair and tune-up business. Christina Lindley, who was only seventeen but had still taken second prize in the Fourteenth Annual State O' Maine Photography Competition the year before, arrived back almost two hours later, scared, out of breath (and feeling rather sexy, if the truth was to be told) from riding in from town with Bobby Tremain at speeds which sometimes topped a hundred and ten. When Bobby made the Dodge walk and talk, it was nothing but a yellow streak.

She had been dispatched to take two photographs of the clock-tower. This was delicate work, because, with the tower now reduced to scattered chunks of brick, masonry, and clockwork, it meant taking a photograph of a photograph.

Working fast, Christina had thumbed through a scrapbook of town photographs. Newt had told her mentally where to find this—in Ruth McCausland's own office. She rejected two shots because although both were quite good, both were also in black and white. The intention was to build an illusion—a clock-tower that people could look at . . . but one you could fly a plane through, if it came to that.

In other words, they intended to project a gigantic magic-lantern slide in the sky.

A good trick.

Once upon a time, Hilly Brown would have envied it.

Just as Christina was beginning to lose hope, she found it: a gorgeous photo of the Haven Village town hall with the tower prominently displayed . . . and from an angle that clearly showed two sides. Great. That would give them the depth of field they would need. Ruth's careful notation beneath the photograph said it came from *Yankee* magazine, 5/87.

We gotta go, Chris, Bobby had said, speaking to her without bothering to use his mouth. He was shifting impatiently from foot to foot like a small boy in need of the bathroom.

Yes, all right. This will—

She broke off.

Oh, she said. Oh dear.

Bobby Tremain came forward quickly. What the hell's wrong?

She pointed at the photograph.

"Oh, *SHIT!*" Bobby Tremain yelled out loud, and Christina nodded.

2

By seven that evening, working fast and silently (except for the occasional ill-tempered snarl of someone who felt someone else was not working fast enough), they had constructed a device that looked like a huge slide-projector on top of an industrial vacuum cleaner.

They tested it, and a woman's face, huge and stony, appeared in Henry's field. The people who had gathered stared at this stereopticon of Henry Applegate's grandmother silently but approvingly. The machine worked. Now, as soon as the girl brought the photograph—*photographs,* actually, because a stereopticon image was of course exactly what they had to create—of the town hall, they could—

Then her voice, faint, but boosted by Bobby Tremain's mind, came to them.

It was bad news.

"What was it?" Kyle Archinbourg asked Newt. "I didn't catch all of it."

"Are you fucking deaf?" Andy Baker snarled. "Jesus Christ, people in *three counties* heard the bang when that bitch blew the roof off. For two cents—" He balled his fists.

"Quit it, both of you," Hazel McCready said. She turned to Kyle. "That girl has done a hell of a job." She was deliberately projecting as hard as she could, hoping to reach Christina Lindley as well as explain the situation to Kyle Archinbourg . . . to buck her up. The girl had

(thought)

sounded distraught, nearly hysterical, and she wouldn't do them any good that way. In such a state she would fuck up for sure, and they just didn't have the time for fuck-ups.

"It's not her fault you can read the clock in the photo."

"What do you mean?" Kyle asked.

"She's found a color photo with an angle that couldn't be more perfect," Hazel said. "It'll look exactly right from the church and the cemetery, and only a little distorted from the road. We'll have to keep outsiders from going around to the back for a couple of days, until Chris finds a rough matching angle, but since they're going to be interested in the furnace . . . and in Ruth . . . I think we can get away with that. Close some roads?" she looked at Newt.

"Sewer work," he said promptly. "Easy as pie."

"I still don't understand the nature of the problem," Kyle said.

"Might be you, y'fuckin ijit," Andy Baker said.

Kyle swung truculently toward the mechanic and Newt said, "Stop it, both of you." And, to Kyle: "The *problem* is that Ruth blew the tower off the town hall at 3:05 this afternoon. In the only good picture Christina could find, you can read the clock-face.

"It says a quarter to ten."

"Oh," Kyle said. Sweat suddenly turned his face oily. He took out his handkerchief and mopped it. "Oh *shit.* What do we do now?"

"Ad-lib," Hazel said calmly.

"Bitch!" Andy cried. "I'd kill her if she wadn't already dead!"

"Everyone in town loved her, and you know it, Andy," Hazel said.

"Yeah. And I hope the devil's toasting her with a long fork down in hell." Andy switched the gadget off.

Henry's grandmother disappeared. Hazel was relieved. There was something a little ghastly about seeing that hatchet-faced woman floating in perfect 3-D above Henry's field, with the cows—which should have been stabled long ago—sometimes wandering through her as they grazed, or disappearing casually through the large old-fashioned brooch the woman wore at her high-necked collar.

"It's going to be fine," Bobbi Anderson said suddenly in the quiet, and everyone—including Christina Lindley back in town—heard, and was relieved.

3

"Take me to my house," she said to Bobby Tremain. "Quick. I know what to do."

"You're there." He took her arm and began pulling her toward the door.

"Hold it," she said.

"Huh?"

"Don't you think I better"

bring the photograph? she finished.

Oh shit! Bobby said, and slapped his forehead.

4

Dick Allison, meanwhile, who was chief of Haven's volunteer fire department, was sitting in his office sweating bullets in spite of the air-conditioning, fielding telephone calls. The first was from the Troy constable, the second from the Unity chief of police, the third from the state police, the fourth from AP.

He probably would have been sweating anyway, but one of the reasons the air-conditioning wasn't doing him any good was his door had been blown off its hinges by the force of the blast. Most of the plaster had fallen off the walls, revealing lathing like decayed ribs. He sat in the middle of the wreckage and told his callers that it sure *had* been a hell of a bang, and it looked as if they probably *had* had one fatality, but it was *nowhere near* as bad as it had probably sounded. While he was rolling out this bullshit for the guy from the Bangor *Daily News* named John Leandro, a cork ceiling panel fell on his head. Dick slashed it aside with a wolfish snarl, listened, laughed, and said it was just the bulletin board. Goddam thing had fallen over again. It just had those sucker things on the back, you know, well, if you bought cheap you got cheap, his mother had always told him, and . . .

It took another five minutes, but he finally bored Leandro off the phone. As he put his own telephone back in the cradle, most of the hallway ceiling outside his door fell with a powdery *crrrumpp!*

"MOTHER-FUCKING-COCK-SUCKING-SON-OF-

A-FUCKING BITCH!" Dick Allison screamed, and brought his left fist down on his desk as hard as he could. Although he broke all four fingers, he didn't even notice in his raving fury. If, at that moment, anyone had come into his office, Allison would have ripped that person's throat open, filled his mouth with hot blood, and then sprayed it back into the dying person's face. He screamed and swore and even drummed his feet up and down on the floor like a child doing a tantrum because he has been denied an outing.

He *looked* childish.

He also looked extremely *dangerous.*

Tommyknockers, Tommyknockers, knocking at the door.

5

In between phone calls, Dick went into Hazel's office, found the Midol in her drawer, and took six. Then he wrapped his throbbing, swelling hand tightly and forgot it. If he had still been human, this would have been impossible; one does not simply forget four broken fingers. But since then he had "become." One of the things that included was becoming able to exercise conscious will over pain.

It came in handy.

In between his conversations with the outside—and sometimes during them—Dick spoke to the men and women working furiously at Henry Applegate's. He told them he expected a couple of state cops by four-thirty, five o'clock at the latest. Could they have the slide-projector ready by then? When Hazel explained the problem, Dick began to rave again, this time with fear as well as anger. When Hazel explained what Christina Lindley was up to, he calmed . . . a little. She had a home darkroom. There she would carefully make a negative of the *Yankee* picture and enlarge it slightly, not because *it* needed to be bigger for the slide-projector device to work (and too much enlarging would give their clock-tower illusion an odd, grainy look), but because *she* needed a slightly bigger image to work with.

She's going to turn a negative, Hazel said in his mind,

then airbrush out the hands on the clock-face. Bobby Tremain is going to put them back in with an X-acto knife, so they say 3:05. He's got a steady hand and a little talent. Right now a steady hand seems more important.

I thought if you made a negative from a positive, it came out blurry, Dick Allison said. Specially if the positive's color.

She's improved her developing equipment, Hazel said. She didn't need to add that seventeen-year-old Christina Lindley now had what was probably the most advanced darkroom on earth.

So how long?

Midnight, she thinks, Hazel said.

Christ on a pony! Dick shouted, loud enough to make the people in Henry's field wince.

We'll need about thirty D-cells, Bobbi Anderson's voice cut in calmly. Be a love and see to that, Dick. And we understand about the police. Play *Hee-Haw* for them, you understand?

He paused. Yes, he said. Buck and Roy, Junior Samples.

Exactly. And *hold* them. It's their radio I'm really worried about, not them—they'll only send one unit, two at most, to start with. But if they see . . . if they radio it in . . .

There was a murmur of assent like the sound of the ocean in a conch shell.

Is there a way you can damp out their transmissions from town? Bobbi asked.

I—

Andy Baker suddenly cut in, gleeful: I got a better idea. Get Buck Peters to shuck his fat ass over to the gas station right now.

Yes! Bobbi overrode him, her thought shrill with excitement. Good! Great! And when they leave town, someone . . . Beach, I think . . .

Beach was honored to be chosen.

6

Bent Rhodes and Jingles Gabbons of the Maine State Police arrived in Haven at five-fifteen. They came expecting to find the smoky, uninteresting aftermath of a furnace explosion—one old pumper-truck idling at the curb, twenty or thirty onlookers idling on the sidewalk. Instead, they found the entire Haven town-hall clock-tower blown off like a Roman candle. Bricks littered the street, windows were blown out, there were dismembered dolls everywhere . . . and too damned many people going about their business.

Dick Allison greeted them with weird cordiality, as if this was a Republican bean supper instead of what now looked like a disaster of real magnitude.

"Christ Almighty, man, what happened here?" Bent asked him.

"Well, I guess maybe it was a little worse than I made out over the phone," Dick said, surveying the brick-littered street and then giving the two troopers an incongruous *ain't-I-a-bad-boy?* smile. "Guess I didn't think anyone would believe it unless they saw it."

Jingles muttered, "I'm *seeing* it and I don't believe it." They had both dismissed Dick Allison as a small-town bumbler, probably crazy in the bargain. That was all right. He stood behind them, watching them stare at the wreckage. The smile faded gradually from his face and his expression became cold.

Rhodes spotted the human arm amid all the tiny make-believe limbs. When he turned back to Dick, his face was whiter than it had been, and he looked considerably younger.

"Where's Mrs. McCausland?" he asked. His voice rose uncontrollably and broke on the last syllable.

"Well, you know, I think that might be part of our problem," Dick began. "You see—"

7

Dick *did* hold them in town as long as he could without being conspicuous about it. It was a quarter to eight before they left, and by then twilight was drawing down. Also, Dick knew, if they didn't leave soon, they would start wondering how come none of the backup units they had requested were arriving.

They had both talked on their cruiser's radio to Derry Base, and both hung the mike up again looking puzzled and distracted. The responses they were getting from the other end were right; it was the *voice* that seemed a little off. But neither of them could be bothered with such a minor matter, at least not for the time being. There were too many other things to cope with. The magnitude of the accident, for one thing. The fact that they had known the victim, for another. Trying to lay the groundwork of a potentially big case without committing any of the procedural fuckups that would muddy the waters later on, for a third.

Also, they were beginning to feel the effects of being in Haven.

They were like men applying vinyl seal to a big wooden floor in a room with no ventilation, getting stoned without even knowing it. They weren't healing thoughts—it was too early for that and they would be gone before it could happen—but they were feeling very strange. It was slowing them down, making ordinary routine something they had to fight their way through.

Dick Allison got all this from their minds as he sat across the street drinking a cup of coffee in the Haven Lunch. Ayuh, they were too busy and too screwed-up to think about the fact that

(Tug Ellender)

their dispatcher didn't exactly sound like himself tonight. The reason why was very simple. They weren't talking to Tug Ellender. They were talking to Buck Peters; their radio transmissions were not going to and coming from Derry but to and from the garage of Elt Barker's Shell, where Buck Peters was hunched, sweating, over a microphone, with Andy Baker beside him. Buck sent out fresh instructions and information on Andy's radio (a little something he had scrambled together in his spare time, a little something that could have contacted life on Uranus, had there been any goodbuddies up there to send back a big ten-four). Several townspeople were concentrating hard on the minds of Bent Rhodes and Jingles Gabbons. They relayed to Buck everything they were able to pick up about Ellender, from whom the cops just naturally *expected* to hear. Buck Peters had some natural mimicry (he was a great hit doing whoever happened to be President that year, plus such favorites as Jimmy Cagney and John Wayne, at each year's Grange Stage Spectacular). He was not Rich Little, never would be, but when he "did" somebody, you knew who it was. Usually.

More important, the listeners were able to relay to Buck how he should respond to each transmission, since almost every speaker knows in his own mind what response he expects to get from his questions or statements. If Bent and Jingles bought the impersonation—and to a large extent they really did—it wasn't so much due to Buck's talents as to their own fulfilled expectations in "Tug's" replies. Andy had further been able to blur Buck's voice by overlaying some static—not as much as they would hear on their way back to Derry, but enough so that "Tug's" voice grew a little blurred whenever that oddness

(Jesus that doesn't sound like Tug much at all I wonder does he have a cold)

surfaced in one of their minds.

At a quarter past seven, when Beach brought him a fresh cup of coffee, Dick asked: "You all set?"

"Sure am."

"And you're sure that gadget will work?"

"It works fine . . . want to see it?" Beach was almost fawning.

"No. There isn't time. What about the deer? You got that?"

"Ayuh. Bill Elderly kilt it and Dave Rutledge dressed it out."

"That's good. Get going."

"Okay, Dick." Beach took off his apron and hung it on a nail behind the counter. He turned over the sign which hung above the door, from OPEN to CLOSED. Ordinarily it would just have hung there, but tonight, because the glass was broken, it stirred and twisted in the mild breeze.

Beach paused and looked back at Dick with narrow, sunken anger.

"She wasn't supposed to do *nothing* like that," he said.

Dick shrugged. It didn't matter; it was done. "She's gone. That's the important thing. The kids are doing fine with that picture. As for Ruth . . . there's no one else like her in town."

"There's that fellow out at the old Garrick place."

"He's drunk all the time. And he *wants* to dig it up. Go on, Beach. They'll be leaving soon, and we want it to happen as far out of the village as you can *make* it happen."

"Okay, Dick. Be careful."

Dick smiled. "We all got to be careful now. This is touchy."

He watched Beach get into his truck and back out of the space in front of the Haven Lunch that had been that old Chevy's home for the last twelve years. As the truck started up the street, Beach driving slowly and weaving to avoid the litters of broken glass, Dick could see the shape under the tarp in the truck's bed, and, near the back, something else, wrapped in a sheet of heavy plastic. The biggest deer Bill Elderly had been able to find on such short notice. Deer hunting was most definitely against the law during July in the State of Maine.

When Beach's pickup was out of sight (MAKE LOVE NOT WAR BE READY FOR BOTH NRA, the bumper sticker on the tailgate read), Dick turned back to the counter and picked up his coffee cup. As always Beach's coffee was strong and good. He needed that. Dick was more than tired; he was worn out. Although there was still good light left in the sky and although he had always been the sort of person who found it impossible to go to sleep until the National Anthem had played on the last available TV channel, all he wanted now was his own bed. This had been a tense, frightening day, and it wouldn't be over until Beach reported in. Nor would the mess Ruth McCausland had succeeded in making be cleaned up when the two cops were erased. They could hide a lot of things, but not the simple fact that those cops had been on their way back from Haven, where another cop (just a town constable, true, but a cop was a cop, and this one had once been married to a State Bear, just to add to the fun) had been erased from the equation.

All of which meant that the fun was just beginning.

"If you call it fun," Dick said sourly to no one in particular. "Be dogfucked if *I* do." The coffee began to burn with acid indigestion in Dick's stomach. He went on drinking it anyway.

Outside, a powerful motor roared. Dick swiveled around on his stool and watched the cops drive out of town, the flashers on top of their cruiser swinging blue light and black shadow on the wreckage.

8

Christina Lindley and Bobby Tremain stood side by side, watching the blank sheet in the developing bath, neither of them breathing as they waited for the image to come or not come.

Little by little, it did.

There was the Haven town-hall clock-tower. In living, true color. And the hands of the clock stood at 3:05.

Bobby let out his breath in a low, slow exhalation. Perfect, he said.

Not quite, Christina said. There's one more thing.

He turned to her, apprehensive. What? What's wrong?

Nothing. Everything's right. It's just that there's one more thing we have to do.

She was not ugly, but because she wore glasses and her hair was mouse-brown, she had always *considered* herself ugly. She was seventeen and had never been on a date. Now none of that seemed to matter. She unzipped her skirt and pushed it, her rayon half-slip, and her cotton panties, both bought at the discount store in Derry, down. She stepped out of them and carefully took the wet photograph from the developing bath. She stood on tiptoe to hang it up, smooth buttocks flexing. Then she turned to him, legs spread.

I need doing.

He took her standing up. Against the wall. When her hymen burst, she bit his shoulder hard enough to bring blood from him, as well. And when they came together, they did it snarling and clawing and it was very, very good.

Just like old times, Bobby thought as he drove them out to the Applegate place, and wondered exactly what he meant by that.

Then he decided it really didn't matter anyway.

9

Beach got his Chevy pickup to a creaky sixty-five—as fast as it would go. One of the few things he hadn't gotten around to overhauling with his fantastic new knowledge was the old bomber. But he hoped it would get him as far as he needed to go tonight, and Old Betsy came through for him again.

When he had gotten over the Troy town line without hearing them or seeing any sign of their flashers behind him, he eased the truck back to fifty-five (with some relief; it had been on the edge of overheating), and when he got into Newport he dropped back to forty-five. Dark was coming on hard by then.

He was over the Derry town line and just starting to worry that the frigging cops had gone back some other way—it seemed unlikely, since this was the quickest way, but Jesus, where *were* they?—when he heard the low mutter of their thoughts.

He pulled over and sat quietly for a moment, head cocked, eyes half-closed, listening, making sure. His mouth, oddly infirm and puckered with most of the teeth gone, was the mouth of a much older man. It was something about

(freckles)

Ruth. It was them, all right. The thought came clearer

(you could see the freckles right through the blood)

and Beach nodded. It was them, all right. They were coming along fast. He'd have time, but only if he hustled.

Beach drove another quarter of a mile up the road, rounded a curve, and saw the last long stretch of Route 3 between here and Derry. He turned his pickup sideways, blocking the road. Then he removed the tarp from the rifle-thing in back, fingers plucking nervously at hayrope knots as their voices grew stronger, stronger, stronger in his head.

When their lights splashed the trees on this side of the curve, Beach got his head down. He reached for the train transformers, six of them, that had been nailed to a board (and the board had been bolted to the truck-bed so it wouldn't slide around) and turned them on, one after another. He heard the hum as they powered up . . . then that sound, every sound, was lost in the shriek of brakes and tires. Now light that was flashbulb-white and shot through with strobing blue flashes filled the bed of the pickup truck and Beach pressed himself against the bottom, hands laced over his head, thinking he had blown it, parked too close to a blind turn, and they were going to crash into his truck, and they might only be injured but he would be killed, and they would find the ruins of his "rifle" and say *Well now, what's this?* And . . . and . . .

You fucked up, Beach, they saved your life and you fucked up . . . oh, damn you . . . damn you . . . damn you . . .

Then the shrieking tires stopped. The smell of cooked rubber was strong and sickening, but the crash for which he had been braced hadn't come. Blue lights strobed. A microphone crackled static.

Dimly he heard the hoarse-voiced cop say, "What's *this* shit?"

Shakily Beach did a girly-pushup and peered over the edge of the truckbed with just his eyes. He saw their cruiser halted at the end of a long pair of black skid-marks. Even by starlight those marks were clearly visible. The cruiser was sitting at a cockeyed angle not nine feet away. *If they had been going just five miles an hour faster . . .*

Yeah, but they weren't.

Sounds. The double-clunk of their doors closing as they got out of their car. The faint, dull hum of the transformers which powered his gadget—a gadget that was not all that different from the ones Ruth had planted in the bellies of her dolls. And a low buzzing sound. Flies. They smelled the blood under the plastic sheet but couldn't get at the deer's carcass.

You'll get your chance soon enough, Beach thought, and grinned. *Too bad you won't get a taste of those old boys out there.*

"I saw that truck back in Haven, Bent," the hoarse-voiced one said. "Parked in front of the restaurant."

Beach swiveled the culvert pipe slightly in its cradle. Looking through it, he could see them both. And if one of them moved out of the actual power axis of the gadget, that was okay; there was a slight flare effect.

Get away from the car, boys, Beach thought, picking up the doorbell from Western Auto and settling a thumb on it. His grin showed pink gums. *Don't want to get none of the car. Move away, all right?*

"Who's there?" the other cop shouted.

Tommyknockers here, knocking at your door, you meddling shithead, he thought, and began to giggle. He couldn't help it. He tried to stifle it as best he could.

"If someone's in that truck, you better speak up!"

He began to giggle louder; just couldn't help it. And maybe that was just as well, because they took a look at each other and then began to move toward the truck, unholstering their guns. Toward the truck and away from their cruiser.

Beach waited until he was sure the cruiser wouldn't be touched by the flare—they had told him not to harm the police car, and he intended not to take so much as a layer of chrome off the bumper. When the cops were clear, Beach pushed the doorbell. *Avon calling, shitheads,* he thought, and this time he didn't just giggle; he *whooped.* A thick branch of green fire shot out in the dark, catching both of the policemen and enveloping them. Beach saw several bright yellow sparks inside that green glare, and understood that one of the cops was triggering his pistol off again and again.

Beach could smell the thick aroma of cooking train transformers. There was a sudden *pop!* and a twisting skyrocket of sparks from one of them. Some of the sparks landed on his arm, stinging, and he brushed them off. The green fire coming from the end of the culvert winked out. The policemen were gone. Well . . . *almost* gone.

Beach jumped over the tailgate of the truck, moving just as fast as he could. This wasn't the turnpike, God knew, and no one from the country headed into Derry to go shopping this late, but *someone* would be along sooner or later. He should—

Sitting on the pavement was a single smoking shoe. He picked it up, almost dropped it. He hadn't expected it to be so heavy. Looking inside, he saw why. A sock-encased foot was still inside it.

Beach carried it back to his truck and tossed it into the cab. When he got back to town he would get rid of it. No need to bury it; there were more efficient ways of getting rid of things in Haven. *If the Mayfia knew what us Yankee hicks got up here, I guess they'd want to buy them the franchise,* Beach thought, and tittered again.

He pulled the pins on the tailgate. It fell flat open with a rusty crash. He grabbed the plastic-wrapped carcass of the deer. Whose idea had this been? he wondered. Old Dave's? Didn't really matter. In Haven all ideas were now becoming one.

The plastic-wrapped bundle was heavy and awkward.

Beach got his arms around the buck's rear legs and pulled. It came out of the truck, its head thudding onto the tarvy. Beach looked around again for brightening headlights on either horizon, saw none, and dragged the deer across the road as fast as he could. He put it down with a grunt and flipped the carcass over so he could free the plastic. Now he got the deer, which had been neatly gutted and cleaned, in both arms and picked it up. Cords stood out in his neck like cables; his skinned-back lips would have shown his teeth, had any been left in his gums. The deer's head with its half-grown antlers hung down below his right forearm. Its dusty eyes stared off into the night.

Beach staggered three steps down the sloping soft shoulder and threw the deer's body into the ditch, where it landed with a thud. He stepped away and picked up the plastic. He carried it back to the truck and bundled it into the passenger side of the cab. He would have liked it better in back—it stank—but there was always a chance it would blow out and be found. He hurried around to the driver's side of the truck, plucking his blood-dampened shirt away from his chest with a little grimace as he did. He'd change as soon as he got home.

He got in and started Betsy's motor. He backed and filled until he was pointed back toward Haven and then paused for just a moment, surveying the scene, trying to see if the story it told was the one it was supposed to tell. He thought it did. Here was a Bearmobile sitting dead-empty in the middle of the road at the end of a long skid. Engine off, flashers going. There was the gutted carcass of a good-size buck in the ditch. That wouldn't go unnoticed long, not in July.

Was there anything in this story that whispered Haven?

Beach didn't think so. This story was about two cops returning to barracks after investigating a single-fatality accident. They just happened to run on a gang of men jacklighting deer. What happened to the cops? Ah, that was the question, wasn't it? And the possible answers would look more and more ominous as the days passed. There were jacklighters in the story, jacklighters who'd perhaps panicked, shot a couple of cops, and then buried them in the woods. But Haven? Beach really believed they would think that was a completely different story, one nowhere near as interesting.

Now, in his rearview mirror, he could see approaching headlights. He put his truck in low and skirted the police cruiser. Its flashers bathed him in half a dozen blue pulsebeats, and then it was behind him. Beach glanced to his right, saw the regulation-issue black shoe with its runner of regulation-blue sock poking out like the tail of a kite, and cackled. *Bet when you put that shoe on this mornin, Mr. Smartass State Bear, you didn't have no idea where it would finish up tonight.*

Beach Jernigan cackled again and fetched second gear with a ram and a jerk. He was headed home and he had never felt doodly-damn better in his whole life.

8.

EV HILLMAN

1

Lead story, Bangor Daily News, *July 25th, 1988:*

TWO STATE POLICE DISAPPEAR IN DERRY
Area-wide Manhunt Begins
by David Bright

The discovery of an abandoned state-police cruiser in Derry last night shortly after 9:30 has touched off the second major search of the summer in eastern and central Maine. The first was for four-year-old David Brown of Haven, who is still missing. Ironically, the officers, Benton Rhodes and Peter Gabbons, were returning from that same town at the time of their disappearance, having just completed their preliminary investigation of a furnace fire which took one life (see related story this page).

In a late development which one police insider described as "the worst possible news we could have at this time," the body of a deer which had been shot, gutted, and cleaned was found near the cruiser, leading to speculations that . . .

2

"There, looka that," Beach said to Dick Allison and Newt Berringer over coffee the next morning. They were in the Haven Lunch, looking at the paper, which had just come in. "We all thought nobody would make a connection. Damn!"

"Relax," Newt said, and Dick nodded. "No one is going to connect the disappearance of a four-year-old boy who prob'ly just wandered off into the woods or got picked up and driven away by a sex pervert with the disappearance of two big strong State Bears. Right, Dick?"

"As rain."

3

Wrong.

4

Page one, Bangor Daily News, *below the fold:*

HAVEN CONSTABLE KILLED IN FREAK ACCIDENT
WAS COMMUNITY LEADER
by John Leandro

Ruth McCausland, one of only three women constables in Maine, died yesterday in her home town of Haven. She was fifty. Richard Allison, head of Haven's volunteer fire department, says that Mrs. McCausland appears to have been killed when oil fumes which had collected in the town-hall basement as the result of a faulty valve ignited. Allison said that the lighting in the basement, where a lot of town records are stored, is not very good. "She may have struck a match," Allison said. "At least, that is the theory we are going on now."

Asked if any evidence of arson had been found, Allison said there had not, but admitted that the disappearance of the two state troopers sent to investigate the mishap (see story above) made that more difficult to determine. "Since neither of the investigating officers has been able to file a report, I imagine we'll have the state fire inspectors up here. Right now I'm more concerned that the investigating officers turn up safe and sound."

Newton Barringer, Haven's head selectman, said that the entire town was in deep mourning for Mrs. McCausland. "She was a great woman," Berringer said, "and we all loved her." Other Haven townspeople echoed the sentiment, not a few of them in tears as they spoke of Mrs. McCausland.

Her public service in the small town of Haven began in . . .

5

It was, of course, Hilly's grandfather, Ev, who made the connection. Ev Hillman, who could have rightly been called the town in exile, Ev Hillman, who had come back from Big II with two small steel plates in his head as a result of a German potato-masher which had exploded near him during the Battle of the Bulge.

He spent the Monday morning after Haven's explosive Sunday where he had been spending all of his mornings—in Room 371 of the Derry Home Hospital, watching over Hilly. He had taken a furnished room down on Lower Main Street, and spent his nights—his largely *sleepless* nights—there after the nurses finally turned him out.

Sometimes he would lie in the dark and think he heard chuckling noises coming from the drains and he would think: *You're going nuts, old-timer.* Except he wasn't. Sometimes he wished he were.

He had tried to talk to some of the nurses about what he believed had happened to David—what he *knew* had happened to David. They pitied him. He did not see their pity at first; his eyes were only opened after he had made the mistake of talking to the reporter. That had opened his eyes. He thought the nurses admired him for his loyalty to Hilly, and felt sorry for him because Hilly seemed to be slipping away . . . but they also thought him mad. Little boys did not disappear during tricks performed in back yard magic shows. You didn't even have to go to nursing school to know that.

After a while in Derry alone, half out of his mind with worry for Hilly and David and contempt for what he now saw as cowardice on his part and fear for Ruth McCausland and the others in Haven, Ev had done some drinking at the little bar halfway down Lower Main. In the course of a conversation with the bartender, he heard the story of a fellow named John Smith, who had taught in the nearby town of Cleaves Mills for a while. Smith had been in a coma for years, had awakened with some sort of psychic gift. He went nuts a few years ago—had tried to assassinate a fellow named Stillson, who was a U.S. representative from New Hampshire.

"Dunno if there was ever any truth to the psychic part of it or not," the bartender said, drawing Ev a fresh beer. "B'lieve most of that stuff is just eyewash, myself. But if you've got some wild-ass tale to tell"—Ev had hinted he had a story to tell that would make *The Amityville Horror* look tame—"then Bright at the Bangor *Daily News* is the guy you ought to tell it to. He wrote up the Smith guy for the paper. He drops in here for a beer every once in a while, and I'll tell you, mister, *he* believed Smith had the sight."

Ev had had three beers, rapidly, one after another—just enough, in other words, to believe that simple solutions might be possible. He went to the pay phone, laid out his change on the shelf, and called the Bangor *Daily News*. David Bright was in, and Ev spoke to him. He didn't tell him the story, not over the phone, but said that he had a tale to tell, and he didn't understand what it all meant, but he thought people ought to know about it, fast.

Bright sounded interested. More, he sounded sympathetic. He asked Ev when he could come up to Bangor (that Bright did not speak of coming to Derry to interview the old man should have tipped Ev to the idea that he might have overestimated both Bright's belief and his sympathy), and Ev had asked if that very night would be okay.

"Well, I'll be here another two hours," Bright said. "Can you be here before midnight, Mr. Hillman?"

"Bet your buns," the old man snapped, and hung up. When he walked out of Wally's Spa on Lower Main, there was fire in his eye and a spring in his step. He looked twenty years younger than the man who had shuffled in.

But it was twenty-five miles up to Bangor, and the three beers wore off. By the time Ev got to the *News* building he was sober again. Worse, his head was fuzzy and confused. He was aware of telling the story badly, of circling around again and again to the magic show, to the way Hilly had looked, to his certainty that David Brown had really disappeared.

At last he stopped . . . only it was not so much a stopping as a drying up of an increasingly sluggish flow.

Bright was tapping a pencil against the side of his desk, not looking at Ev.

"You never actually looked under the platform at the time, Mr. Hillman?"

"No . . . no. But . . ."

Now Bright did look at him, and he had a kind face, but in it Ev saw the expression which had opened his eyes—the man thought he was just as mad as a March hare.

"Mr. Hillman, all of this is very interesting—"

"Never mind," Ev said, getting up. The chair he had been sitting in bumped back so rapidly it almost fell over. He was dimly aware of word-processer terminals tapping, phones ringing, people walking back and forth in the city room with papers in their hands. Mostly he was aware that it was midnight, he was tired and sick with fear, and this fellow thought he was crazy. "Never mind, it's late, you'll be wanting to get home to y'family, I guess."

"Mr. Hillman, if you'd just see it from my perspective, you'd understand that—"

"I *do* see it from your side," Ev said. "For the first time, I guess. I have to go too, Mr. Bright. I got a long drive ahead of me and visitin hours start at nine. Sorry to've wasted y'time."

He got out of there fast, furiously reminding himself what he should have remembered in the first place, that there was no fool like an old fool, and he guessed tonight's work showed him off as just about the biggest old fool of all. Well, so much for trying to tell people what was happening in Haven. He was old, but he was damned if he'd ever put up with another look like that.

Ever, in his life.

6

That resolution lasted exactly fifty-six hours—until he got a look at the headlines on Monday's papers. Looking at them, he found himself wanting to go and see the man in charge of investigating the disappearance of the two state cops. The *News* said his name was Dugan, and mentioned that he had also known Ruth McCausland well—would, in fact, take time off from an extremely hot case to speak briefly at the lady's funeral. Must have known her pretty *damned* well, it seemed to Ev.

But when he searched for any of the previous night's fire and excitement, he found only sour dread and hopelessness. The two stories on the front page had taken most of the guts he had left. *Haven's turning into a nest of snakes and now they are starting to bite. I have to convince someone of that, and how am I going to do it? How am I going to convince anyone that there's telepathy going on in that town, and Christ knows what else? How, when I can barely remember how I knew things were going on? How, when I never really saw nothing myself? How? Most of all, how'm I supposed to do it when the whole goddam thing is staring them in the face and they don't even see it? There's a whole town going loony just down the road and no one has got the slightest idea it's happening.*

He turned to the obituary page again. Ruth's clear eyes looked up at him from one of those strange newsprint pictures that are nothing but densely packed dots. Her eyes, so clear and straightforward and beautiful, looked calmly back at him. Ev guessed that there had been at least five and maybe as many as a dozen men in Haven who had been in love with her, and she had never even known it. Her eyes seemed to deny the very idea of death, to declare it ridiculous. But dead she was.

He remembered taking Hilly out while the search party gathered.

You could come with us, Ruthie.

Ev, I can't . . . Get in touch with me.

He had tried just once, thinking that if Ruth joined him in Derry, she would be out of danger . . . and she could backstop his story. In his state of confusion and misery and, yes, even homesickness, Ev wasn't even sure which was more important to him. In the end it didn't matter. He had tried three times to dial Haven direct, the last one after speaking to Bright, and none of the calls took. He tried once with operator assistance, and she told him there must be lines down. Would he try later?

Ev said he would, but hadn't. He had lain down in the dark instead, and listened to the drains chuckle.

Now, less than three days later, Ruth had gotten in touch with him. Via the obituary page.

He looked up at Hilly. Hilly was sleeping. The doctors refused to call it a coma—his brain patterns were not the brain patterns of a comatose patient, they said; they were the brain patterns of a person in deep sleep. Ev didn't care what they called it. He knew Hilly was slipping away, and whether it was into a state called autism—Ev didn't know what the word meant, but he had heard one of the doctors mutter it to another in a low voice he hadn't been meant to overhear—or one called coma didn't make any difference at all. They were just words. Slipping away was what it came down to, and that was quite terrible enough.

On the ride to Derry, the boy had acted like a person in deep shock. Ev had had a vague idea that getting him out of Haven would improve matters, and in their frantic concern over David, neither Bryant nor Marie seemed to notice how odd their older boy seemed.

Getting out of Derry hadn't helped. Hilly's awareness and coherence had continued to decline. The first day in the hospital he had slept eleven hours out of twenty-four. He could answer simple questions, but more complicated ones confused him. He complained of a headache. He didn't remember the magic show at all, and seemed to think his birthday had been only the week before. That night, sleeping deeply, he had spoken one phrase quite clearly: "*All* the G.I. Joes." Ev's back had crawled. It was what he had been screaming over and over when they had all rushed out of the house to find David gone and Hilly in hysterics.

The following day, Hilly had slept for fourteen hours, and seemed even more confused in his mind during the time he spent in a soupy waking state. When the child psychologist detailed to his case asked him his middle name, he responded, "Jonathan." It was *David's* middle name.

Now he was sleeping, for all practical purposes, around the clock. Sometimes he opened his eyes, seemed even to be looking at Ev or one of the nurses, but when they spoke, he would only smile his sweet Hilly Brown smile and drift off again.

Slipping away. He lay like an enchanted boy in a fairy-tale castle, only the IV bottle over his head and the occasional P.A. announcements from the hospital corridor spoiling the illusion.

There had been a great deal of excitement on the neurological front at first; a dark, nonspecific shadow in the area of Hilly's cerebral cortex had suggested that the boy's strange dopiness might have been caused by a brain tumor. But when they got Hilly down to X-ray again, two day later (his plates had been slow-tracked, the X-ray technician explained to Ev, because no one *expects* to find a brain tumor in the head of a ten-year-old and there had been no previous symptoms to suggest one), the shadow had been gone. The neurologist had conferred with the X-ray technician, and Ev guessed from the technician's defensiveness that feathers must have flown. The neurologist told him that one more set of plates would be taken, but he believed they would show negative. The first set, he said, must have been defective.

"I suspected something must have been wacky," he told Ev.

"Why was that?"

The neurologist, a big man with a fierce red beard, smiled. "Because that shadow was *huge*. To be perfectly blunt, a kid with a brain tumor that big would have been an extremely sick child for an extremely long time . . . if he was still alive at all."

"I see. Then you still don't know what's wrong with Hilly."

"We're working on two or three lines of inquiry," the neurologist said, but his smile grew vague, his eyes shifted away from Ev's, and the next day the child psychologist showed up again. The child psychologist was a very fat woman with very dark black hair. She wanted to know where Hilly's parents were.

"Trying to find their other son." Ev expected that would squash her.

It didn't. "Call them up and tell them I'd like some help finding this one."

They came but were no help. They had changed; they were strange. The child psychologist felt it too, and after her initial run of questions, she started to pull away from them—Ev could actually *feel* her doing it. Ev himself had to work hard to keep from getting up and leaving the room. He didn't want to feel their strange eyes resting on him: their gaze made him feel as if he had been marked for something. The woman in the plaid blouse and the faded jeans had been his daughter, and she still *looked* like his daughter, but she wasn't, not anymore. Most of Marie was dead, and what was left was dying rapidly.

The child psychologist hadn't asked for them again.

She had been in to examine Hilly twice since then. The second occasion had been Saturday afternoon, the day before the Haven town hall blew up.

"What were they feeding him?" she asked abruptly.

Ev had been sitting by the window, the hot sun falling on him, almost dozing. The fat woman's question startled him awake. "What?"

"What were they *feeding* him?"

"Why, just regular food," he said.

"I doubt that."

"You needn't," he said. "I took enough meals with 'em to know. Why do you ask?"

"Because ten of his teeth are gone," she said curtly.

7

Ev clenched a fist tightly in spite of the dull throb of arthritis and brought it down on one leg, hard.

What are you going to do, old man? David's gone and it would be easier if you could convince yourself he was really dead, wouldn't it?

Yes. That would make things simpler. Sadder, but simpler. But he couldn't believe that. Part of him was still convinced that David was alive. Perhaps it was only wishful thinking, but somehow Ev didn't think so—he had done plenty of that in his time, and this didn't feel like it. This was a strong, pulsing intuition in his mind: *David is alive. He is lost, and he is in danger of dying, oh, most certainly . . . but he can still be saved. If. If you can make up your mind to do something. And if what you make up your mind to do is the right thing. Long odds for an old fart like you, who pisses a dark spot on his pants every once in a while these days when he can't get to the john in time. Long, long odds.*

Late Monday evening he had awakened from a dozing

sleep, trembling in Hilly's hospital room—the nurses often turned a leniently blind eye to him and allowed him to stay far past regular visiting hours. He'd had a dreadful nightmare. He had dreamed he was in some dark and stony place—needle-tipped mountains sawed at a black sky strewn with cold stars, and a wind as sharp as an icepick whined in narrow, rocky defiles. Below him, by starlight, he could see a huge flat plain. It looked dry and cold and lifeless. Great cracks zigzagged across it, giving it the look of crazy-paving. And from somewhere, he could hear David's thin voice: *"Help me, Grandpa, it hurts to breathe! Help me, Grandpa, it hurts to breathe! Help me! I'm scared! I didn't want to do the trick but Hilly made me and now I can't find my way home!"*

He sat looking at Hilly, his body bathed in sweat. It ran down his face like tears.

He got up, went over to Hilly, and bent close to him. "Hilly," he said, not for the first time. "Where's your brother? *Where is David?"*

Only this time Hilly's eyes opened. His watery, unseeing stare chilled Everett—it was the stare of a blind sibyl.

"Altair-4," Hilly said calmly, and with perfect clarity. "David is on Altair-4 and there's Tommyknockers, Tommyknockers, knocking at the door."

His eyes slipped shut and he slept deeply again.

Ev stood over him, perfectly motionless, his skin the color of putty.

After a while, he began to shudder.

8

He was the town in exile.

If Ruth McCausland had been Haven's heart and conscience, then Ev Hillman at seventy-three (and not nearly so senile as he had lately come to fear) was its memory. He had seen much of the town in his long life there, and had heard more; he had always been a good listener.

Leaving the hospital that Monday evening, he detoured by the Derry Mr. Paperback, where he invested nine dollars in a Maine Atlas—a compendium of large maps which showed the state in neat pieces, six hundred square miles in each piece. Turning to Map 23, he found the town of Haven. He had also bought a compass at the book-and-magazine shop, and now, without wondering why he was doing it, he drew a circle around the town. He did not plant the compass's anchor in Haven Village to do this, of course, because the village was actually on the edge of the township.

David is on Altair-4.

David is on Altair-4 and there's Tommyknockers, Tommyknockers knocking at the door.

Ev sat frowning over the map and the circle he had drawn, wondering if what Hilly had said had any significance.

Should have gotten a red pencil, old man. Haven ought to be circled in red now. On this map . . . on every *map.*

He bent closer. His far vision was still so perfect that he could have told a bean from a kernel of corn if you set both on a fencepost forty yards away, but his near vision was going to hell fast now, and he had left his reading glasses back at Marie and Bryant's—and he had an idea that if he went back to get them, he might find he had more to worry about than reading small print. For the time being it was better—safer—to just get along without them.

With his nose almost on the page, he examined the place where the compass-point had gone in. It was spang on the Derry Road, just a bit north of Preston Stream, and a bit east of what he and his friends had called Big Injun Woods when they were kids. This map identified them as Burning Woods, and Ev had heard that name once or twice, too.

He closed the compass to a quarter of the radius he had needed to put a circle around all of Haven and drew a second circle. He saw that Bryant and Marie's house lay just inside that circle. To the west was the short length of Nista Road, which ran from Route 9—Derry Road—to a gravel-pit dead-end on the edge of those same woods—call them Big Injun Woods or Burning Woods, it was the same thing, the same woods.

Nista Road . . . Nista Road . . . something about Nista Road, but what? Something that had happened before he himself was born but something that had still been worth talking of for years and years . . .

Ev closed his eyes and looked as if he was asleep sitting up, a skinny old man, mostly bald, in a neat khaki shirt and neat khaki pants with creases up the legs.

In a moment it came, and when it did he wondered how it could have taken him so long to get it. The Clarendons. The Clarendons, of course. They had lived at the junction of Nista Road and the Old Derry Road. Paul and Faith Clarendon. Faith, who had been so taken with that sweety-sugar preacher, and who had birthed a child with black hair and sweety-sugar blue eyes about nine months after the preacher blew town. Paul Clarendon, who had studied the baby as it lay in its crib, and who had then gotten his straight razor . . .

Some people had shaken their heads and blamed the preacher—Colson, his name was. He said it was, anyway.

Some people shook their heads and blamed Paul Clarendon; they said he'd always been crazy, and Faith should never have married him.

Some people had of course blamed Faith. Ev remembered some old man in the barbershop—this was years after, but towns like Haven have long memories—calling her "nothing but a titty-bump hoor born to make trouble."

And some people had—in low voices, to be sure—blamed the woods.

Ev's eyes flashed open.

Yes; yes, they had. His mother called such people ignorant and superstitious, but his father only shook his head slowly and puffed his pipe and said that sometimes old stories had a grain or two of truth in them and it was best not to take chances. It was why, he said, he crossed himself whenever a black cat crossed his path.

"Humpf!" Ev's mother had sniffed—Ev himself had then been nine or so, he recollected now.

"And I guess it's why your ma there tosses some salt over her shoulder when she spills the cellar," Ev's dad said mildly to Ev.

"Humpf!" she said again, and went inside to leave her husband smoking on the porch and her son sitting beside him, listening intently as his father yarned. Ev had always been a good listener . . . except for that one crucial moment when someone had so badly needed him to listen, that one unregainable moment when he had allowed Hilly's tears to drive him away in confusion.

Ev listened now. He listened to his memory . . . the town's memory.

9

They had been called Big Injun Woods because it was there that Chief Atlantic had died. It was the whites who called him Chief Atlantic—his proper Micmac name had been Wahwayvokah, which means "by tall waters." "Chief Atlantic" was a contemptuous translation of this. The tribe had originally covered much of what was now Penobscot County, with large groups centered in Oldtown, Skowhegan, and the Great Woods, which began in Ludlow—it was in Ludlow that they buried their dead when they were decimated by influenza in the 1880s and drifted south with Wahwayvokah, who had presided over their further decline. Wahwayvokah died in 1885, and on his deathbed he declared that the woods to which he had brought his dying people were cursed. That was known and reported by the two white men who had been present when he died—one an anthropologist from Boston College, the other from the Smithsonian Institution—who had come to the area in search of Indian artifacts from the tribes of the Northeast, which were degenerating rapidly and would soon be gone. What was less sure was whether Chief Atlantic was laying the curse himself or only making note of an existing condition.

Either way, his only monument was the name Big Injun Woods—even the site of his grave was no longer known. The name for that large piece of forest was, so far as Ev knew, still the one most commonly used in Haven and the other towns which were a part of it, but he could understand how the cartographers responsible for the Maine atlas might not have wanted to put a word like "Injun" in their book of maps. People had gotten touchy about such casual slurs.

Old tales sometimes have a grain of truth, his dad had said. . . .

Ev, who also crossed himself when black cats crossed his path (and, truth to tell, when one looked likely to, just to be safe), thought that his dad was right, and that grain was usually there. And, cursed or not, Big Injun Woods had never been very lucky.

Not lucky for Wahwayvokah, not lucky for the Clarendons. It had never been very lucky for the hunters who tried their hand in there, either, he recalled. Over the years there had been two . . . no, three . . . wait a minute . . .

Ev's eyes widened and he made a silent whistle as he thumbed through a mental card-file labeled HUNTING ACCIDENTS, HAVEN. He could just offhand think of a dozen accidents, most of them shootings, which had taken place in Big Injun Woods, a dozen hunters who had been lugged out bleeding and cursing, bleeding and unconscious, or just plain dead. Some had shot themselves, using loaded guns for crutches to help them climb over fallen trees, or dropping them, or some damn thing. One was a reputed suicide. But Ev now remembered that on two occasions murder had been done during November in Big Injun Woods—it had been done in hot blood both times, once in an argument over a card game at someone's camp, once because of a squabble between two friends over whose bullet had taken down a buck of record-breaking size.

And hunters got lost there. Christ! Did they ever! Every year it seemed there was at least one search party sent out to find some poor scared slob from Massachusetts or New Jersey or New York, and some years there were two or three. Not all of them were found.

Most were city people who had no business in the woods to start with, but that wasn't always the case. Veteran hunters said compasses worked poorly or not at all in Big Injun Woods. Ev's dad said he guessed there must be a helluva chunk of magnetic rock buried somewhere out there, and it foozled a compass needle to hell and gone. The difference between city folks and those who were veterans of the woods was that the city folks learned how to read a compass and then put all their trust in it. So when it packed up and said east was north and west was east or just spun around and around like a milk bottle in a kissing game, they were like men stuck in the shithouse with diarrhea and no corncobs. Wiser men just cursed their compasses, put them away, and tried another of the half-dozen ways there were of finding a direction. Lacking all else, you looked for a stream to lead you out. Sooner or later, if you held a straight course, you'd either hit a road or a set of CMP power pylons.

But Ev had known a few fellows who had lived and hunted all their lives in Maine and who *still* had to be pulled by a search party or who finally made it out on their own only by dumb luck. Delbert McCready, whom Ev had known since childhood, had been one of these. Del had gone into Big Injun Woods with his twelve-gauge on Tuesday, November 10th, 1947. When forty-eight hours had passed and he still hadn't shown up, Mrs. McCready called Alf Tremain, who in those days had been the constable. A search party of twenty went into the woods where the Nista Road petered out at the Diamond Gravel Pit and by the end of the week it had swelled to two hundred.

They were just about to give Del—whose daughter was, of course, Hazel McCready—up for lost when he stumbled out of the woods along the course of Preston Stream, pale and dazed and twenty pounds lighter than he had been when he went in.

Ev visited him in the hospital. "How'd it happen, Del? Night was clear. Stars were out. You can read the stars, can't you?"

"Ayuh." Del looked deeply ashamed. "Always could, anyway."

"And the moss. 'Twas you who told me about how to read north by the moss on the trees when we was kids."

"Ayuh," Del repeated. Just that. Ev gave him time, then pressed.

"Well, what happened?"

For a long time Del still said nothing. Then, in a voice which was almost inaudible, he said: "I got turned around."

Ev let the silence spin out, as difficult as that was.

"Everything was all right for a while," Del resumed at last. "I hunted most of the morning but didn't see no fresh sign. I sat down and ate m'dinner and had a bottle of my ma's beer. Made me sleepy and I napped. I had some funny dreams . . . can't remember em, but I know they was funny. And, look! This happened while I was sleepin."

Del McCready raised his upper lip and showed Ev a hole there.

"Lost a tooth?"

"Ayuh . . . it was layin in the crotch of m'pants when I woke up. Fell out when I was sleepin, I guess, but I ain't hardly ever had any trouble with my teeth, at least not since that one wisdom tooth got impacted and damn near killed me. By then it coming on dark—"

"Dark!"

"I know how it sounds, don't you worry," Del said crossly—but it was the crossness of someone who is deeply ashamed. "I just slept all the afternoon away, and when I got up, Ev—"

His eyes rolled up to meet Ev's for one miserable second and then shifted away, as if he could not bear to look his old friend in the eye for longer than that one second.

"It was like somethin stole m'brains. The tooth fairy, mayhap."

Del laughed, but there hadn't been much humor in the sound. "I wandered around for a while, thinking I was following the polestar, and when I still hadn't come out on the Hammer Cut Road by nine o'clock or so, I kinda rubbed my eyes and saw it wasn't Polaris at all, but one of the planets—Mars or Sat'n, I guess. I laid down to sleep, and until I came out along Preston Stream a week later, I don't remember nothing but little bits and pieces."

"Well . . ." Ev halted. It sounded entirely unlike Del, whose head was as level as a carpenter's plane. "Well, was you panicked, Del?"

Del's eyes rolled up to meet Ev's, and they were still ashamed, but there was also a leaven of real humor in them now. "A man can't stay in a panic for a whole week, I don't b'lieve," he said dryly. "It's *awful* tirin."

"So you just . . ."

"I just," Del agreed, "but just *what,* I don't know. I know that when I woke up from that nap my feet and my ass was both asleep and all numb, and I know that in one of those dreams it seemed like I heard somethin hummin—the way you can hear power lines hum on a still day, you know—and that's all. I forgot all m'woodcraft and wandered around in the woods like somebody who'd never even *seen* the woods before. When I hit Preston Stream I knew enough to follow it out, and I woke up in here, and I guess I'm a laughingstock in town, but I'm grateful to be alive. It's God's mercy that I am."

"You ain't a laughingstock, Del," Ev said, and of course that was a lie, because that was exactly what Del was. He worked at overcoming it for nearly five years, and when he saw for sure that the barbershop wits were never going to let him live it down, he moved up to East Eddington and opened a combination garage and small engine-repair shop. Ev still got up to see him once in a while, but Del didn't come down to Haven much anymore. Ev guessed he knew why.

10

Sitting in his rented room, Ev closed the compass up as tight as it would go and drew the tiniest circle yet, the smallest the compass would make. There was only one house inside this marble-sized circle, and he thought: *That house is the closest one there is to the center of Haven. Funny I never thought about it before.*

It was the old Garrick place, sitting there on Derry Road with Big Injun Woods widening out behind it.

Should have drawn this last circle in red, if no other.

Frank's niece, Bobbi Anderson, lived on the Garrick place now—not that she farmed, of course; she wrote books. Ev hadn't passed many words with Bobbi, but she had a good reputation in town. She paid her bills on time, folks said, and didn't gossip. Also, she wrote good old western stories that you could really sink your teeth into, not all full of make-believe monsters and a bunch of dirty words, like the ones that fellow who lived up Bangor wrote. Goddam good westerns, people said.

Especially for a girl.

People in Haven felt good about Bobbi Anderson, but of course she'd just been in town for thirteen years and people would have to wait and see. Garrick, most agreed, had been as crazy as a shithouse rat. He always brought in a good garden, but that didn't change his mental state. He was always trying to tell someone about his dreams. They were usually about the Second Coming. After a while it got so that even Arlene Cullum, who sold Amway with the zeal of a Christian martyr, would make herself scarce when she saw Frank Garrick's truck (plastered with bumper-stickers which said things like IF THE RAPTURE'S TODAY SOMEBODY GRAB MY STEERING WHEEL) driving down the village's Main Street.

In the late sixties, the old man had gotten a bee in his bonnet about flying saucers. Something about Elijah seeing a wheel within a wheel, and being taken up to heaven by angels driving chariots of fire powered by electromagnetism. He had been crazy, and he had died of a heart attack in 1975.

But before he died, Ev thought with rising coldness, *he lost all his teeth. I noticed it, and I remember Justin Hurd just down the road commenting on it, and . . . and now Justin's the closest, except for Bobbi herself, that is, and Justin also wasn't what you'd call a model of sanity and reason. Few times I saw him before I left, he even* reminded *me of old Frank.*

It was odd, he thought at first, that he had never put together the run of peculiar things that had happened within those two inner circles before, that no one had. Further reflection made him decide it really wasn't so strange, after all. A life—particularly a long one—was composed of millions of events; they made a crowded tapestry with many patterns woven into it. Such a pattern as this—the deaths, the murders, the lost hunters, crazy Frank Garrick, maybe even that queer fire at the Paulsons'—only showed up if you were looking for it. Once seen, you wondered how you could have missed it. But if you weren't—

And now a new thought dawned: Bobbi Anderson was perhaps *not* all right. He remembered that since the beginning of July, perhaps even *before,* there had been sounds of heavy machinery coming from Big Injun Woods. Ev had heard the sounds and dismissed them—Maine was heavily forested, and the sounds were all too familiar. New England Paper doing a spot of logging on its land, most likely.

Except, now that he thought about it—now that he had seen the pattern—Ev realized that the sounds weren't deep enough in the woods to be on NEP's land—those sounds were coming from the Garrick place. And he also realized that the earlier sounds—the cycling, waspy whine of a chainsaw, the crackle-crunch of falling trees, the coughing roar of a gas-powered chipper—had given way to sounds he didn't associate with woods work at all. The later sounds had been . . . what? Earth-moving machinery, perhaps.

Once you saw the pattern, things fell into place like the last dozen pieces going effortlessly into a big jigsaw puzzle.

Ev sat looking down at the map and the circles. A

numbing horror seemed to be filling his veins, freezing him from the inside out.

Once you saw the pattern, you couldn't *help* seeing it.

Ev slammed the atlas shut and went to bed.

11

Where he was unable to sleep.

What are they doing down there tonight? Building things? Making people disappear? What?

Every time he drifted near sleep, an image came: everyone in Haven Village standing in Main Street with drugged, dreamy expressions on their faces, all of them looking southwest, toward those sounds, like Muslims facing Mecca to pray.

Heavy machinery . . . earth-moving machinery.

As the pieces went into the puzzle, you began to see what it was, even if there was no picture on the box to help you. Lying in this narrow bed not far from where Hilly lay in his coma, Ev Hillman thought he saw the picture pretty well. Not all of it, mind you, but a lot. He saw it and knew perfectly well no one would believe him. Not without proof. And he dared not go back, dared not put himself in their reach. They would not let him go a second time.

Something. Something out in Big Injun Woods. Something in the ground, something on the land Frank Garrick had willed to his niece, who wrote those western books. Something that knocked compasses and human minds galley-west if you got too close. For all Ev knew, there might be such strange deposits all over the earth. If it did nothing else, it might explain why people in some places seemed so goddam pissed off all the time. Something bad. Haunted. Maybe even accursed.

Ev stirred restlessly, rolled over, looked at the ceiling.

Something *had* been in the earth. Bobbi Anderson had found it and she was digging it up, her and that fellow who was staying out at the farm with her. That fellow's name was . . . was . . .

Ev groped, but couldn't come up with it. He remembered the way Beach Jernigan's mouth had thinned when the subject of Bobbi's friend came up one day in the Haven

Lunch. The regulars on coffee break had just observed the man coming out of the market with a bag of groceries. He had a place over in Troy, Beach said; a shacky little place with a woodstove and plastic over the windows.

Someone said he'd heard the fella was educated.

Beach said an education never kept anyone from being no-account.

No one in the Lunch had argued the point, Ev remembered.

Nancy Voss had been equally disapproving. She said Bobbi's friend had shot his wife but had been let off because he was a college professor. "If you got a sheepskin written in Latin words in this country, you can get away with *anything,"* she had said.

They had watched the fellow get into Bobbi's truck and drive back toward the old Garrick place.

"I heard he done majored in drinkin," old Dave Rutledge said from the end stool that was his special place. "Everyone goes out there says he's most allus drunk as a coon on stump-likker."

There had been a burst of mean, gossipy country laughter at that. They hadn't liked Bobbi's friend; none had. Why? Because he had shot his wife? Because he drank? Because he was living with a woman he wasn't married to? Ev knew better. There had been men in the Lunch that day who had not just *beaten* their wives but beaten them into entirely new *shapes*. Out here it was part of the code: you were obligated to put one upside the old woman's head if she "got sma'at." Out here were men who lived on beer from eleven in the morning until six at night and cheap greenfront whiskey from six to midnight and would drink Old Woodsman flydope strained through a snotrag if they couldn't afford whiskey. Men who had the sex lives of rabbits, jumping from hole to hole. . . . And what had his name been?

Ev drifted toward sleep. Saw them standing on the sidewalks, on the lawn of the public library, over by the little park, staring dreamily toward those sounds. Snapped awake again.

What did you find out, Ruth? Why did they murder you?

He tossed onto his left side.

David's alive . . . but to bring him back I have to start in Haven.

He tossed onto his right side.

They'll kill me if I go back. There was once a time when I was almost as well-liked there as Ruth herself . . . least, I always liked to think so. Now they hate me. I saw it in their eyes the night they started looking for David. I took Hilly out because he was sick and needed the doctor, yes . . . but it was damned good to have a reason to go. Maybe they only let me go because David distracted them. Maybe they just wanted to be rid of me. Either way, I was lucky to get out. I'd never get out again. So how can I go back? I can't.

Ev tossed and turned, caught on the horns of two imperatives—he would have to go back to Haven if he wanted to rescue David before David died, but if he went back to Haven he would be killed and buried quickly in someone's back field.

Sometime shortly before midnight, he fell into a troubled doze which quickly deepened into the dreamless sleep of utter exhaustion.

12

He slept later than he had in years, awakening on Tuesday at a quarter past ten. He felt refreshed and whole for the first time in a long while. The sleep had done him a power of good, too: during it he had thought of how he could maybe get back into Haven and out again. *Maybe.* For David's sake, and Hilly's, that was a risk he would take.

He thought he could get in and out of Haven on the day of Ruth McCausland's funeral.

13

Butch "Monster" Dugan was the biggest man Ev had ever seen. Ev believed that Justin Hurd's father Henry might have been within a shout—Henry had stood six-six, weighed three hundred and eighty pounds, and had shoulders so broad he had to go through most doors sideways—but Ev thought this fellow was a tad bigger. Twenty or thirty pounds lighter, maybe, but that was all.

When Ev shook his hand, he saw that word on him had been getting around. It was in Dugan's face.

"Sit down, Mr. Hillman," Dugan said, and seated himself in a swivel chair that looked as if it might have been rammed out of a huge oak. "What can I do for you?"

He expects me to start raving, Ev thought calmly, *just the way we always expected Frank Garrick to start when he caught up to one of us on the street. And I guess I ain't going to disappoint him. But if you step careful, Ev, you may still get your way. You know now where you want to go, anyway.*

"Well, maybe you could do something, at that," Ev said. At least he hadn't been drinking; trying to talk to that reporter after those beers had been a bad mistake. "Paper says you'll be going to Ruth McCausland's funeral tomorrow."

Dugan nodded. "I'm going. Ruth was a personal friend."

"And there are others from Derry barracks that'll be going? Paper said her husband was a trooper, and *she* was in the line of policework herself—oh, bein a town constable's no great shakes, I know, but you get what I mean. There *will* be others, won't there?"

Dugan was frowning now, and he had a lot of face to frown with.

"Mr. Hillman, if you have a point to make, I'm not getting it." *And I'm a busy man this morning, in case you didn't know it,* his face added. *I've got two cops missing, it's starting to look more and more like they ran into some guys jacking deer and the jackers panicked and shot them; I'm in the hot-seat on that one, and on top of it all my old friend Ruth McCausland has died, and I don't have either the time or the patience for bullshit.*

"I know you're not. But you will. *Did* she have other friends who'll be going?"

"Yes. Half a dozen or more. I'm going by myself, starting a little early, so I can talk to some people about a related case."

Ev nodded. "I know about the related case," he said, "and I guess you know about me. Or think you do."

"Mr. Hillman—"

"I have talked foolishly, and to the wrong people, and at the wrong times," Ev said in that same calm voice. "Under other circumstances I would have known better, but I've been upset. One of my grandsons is missing. The other is in a sort of coma."

"Yes. I know."

"I've been so confused I haven't really known if I was comin or goin. So I blabbed to some of the nurses, and then I went up to Bangor and talked to a reporter. Bright. I kind of got the idea you'd heard most of the things I had to say to him."

"I understand you believe there was some sort of . . . of conspiracy in the matter of David Brown's disappearance—"

Ev had to struggle to keep from laughing. The word was both bizarre and apt. He never would have thought of it himself. Oh, there was a conspiracy going on, all right. One *hell* of a conspiracy.

"Yessir. I believe there was a conspiracy, and I think you've got three cases that are a lot more related than you understand—the disappearance of my grandson, the disappearance of those two troopers, and the death of Ruth McCausland—my friend as well as yours."

Dugan looked a bit startled . . . and for the first time that dismissive look went out of his eyes. For the first time Ev felt that Dugan was really seeing *him,* Everett Hillman, instead of just some crazy old rip who had blown in to fart away part of his morning.

"Perhaps you'd better give me the gist of what you believe," Dugan said, and took out a pad of paper.

"No. You can just put that pad away."

Dugan looked at him silently for a moment. He didn't put the pad away, but he put down the pencil.

"Bright thought I was crazy, and I didn't tell him half of what I thought," Ev said, "so I ain't going to tell you any. But here's the thing—I think David's still alive. I don't think he's in Haven anymore, but I think if I went back there I might be able to get an idea on where he *is*. Now, I have reasons—pretty good ones, I think—to believe that I'm not wanted in Haven. I have reasons to think that if I went back there under most circumstances, I'd most likely disappear like David Brown. Or have an accident like Ruth."

Butch Dugan's face changed. "I think," he said, "I got to ask you to explain that, Mr. Hillman."

"I ain't going to. I can't. I know what I know, and believe what I believe, but I ain't got a speck of proof. I know how crazy I must sound, but if you look into my face, you'll know one thing, at least: *I* believe what I'm saying."

Dugan sighed. "Mr. Hillman, if you were in this business, you'd know how sincere most liars look." Ev started to say something and Dugan shook his head. "Forget that. Cheap shot. I've only had about six hours' sleep since Sunday night. I'm getting too old for these marathons. Fact is, I *do* believe you're sincere. But you're only making ominous sounds, talking around the edges of things. Sometimes people do that when they're scared, but mostly they do it when edges are all they have. Either way, I haven't got time to woo you. I answered your questions; maybe you'd better state your business."

"Glad to. I came here for two reasons, Trooper Dugan. First one was to make sure there was going to be a lot of cops in Haven tomorrow. Things are less likely to happen when there are a lot of cops around, don't you agree?"

Dugan said nothing, only looked at Ev expressionlessly.

"Second was to tell you I'll be in Haven tomorrow too. I won't be at Ruth's funeral, though. I'm going to have a Very pistol with me, and if, during that funeral, you or any of your men should see a big old star-shell go off in the sky, you'll know I have run afoul of some of that craziness no one will believe. Do you follow me?"

"You said going back to Haven might be . . . uh, unhealthy for you." Dugan's face was still blank, but that didn't matter; Ev knew he had gone back to his original idea: Ev was crazy, after all.

"*Under most circumstances,* I said. Under *these* circumstances, I think I can get away with it. Ruth was loved in Haven, which is a fact I don't think I have to tell you. Most of the town will turn out to see her into the ground. I don't know if they still loved her when she died, but that don't matter—they'll turn out anyway."

"How do you figure that?" Dugan asked. "Or is that another one of those things you don't want to talk about?"

"No, I don't mind. It would look *wrong* if they didn't turn out."

"To who?"

"To you. To the other policemen who were friends to her and her husband. To the pols from the Penobscot County Democratic Committee. Why, 'twouldn't surprise me if Congressman Brennan sent someone up from

Augusta—she worked *awful* hard for him when he run for office in Washington. She wasn't just local, y'see, and that's part of what they got to deal with. They're like people who don't want to throw a party but who are stuck doing it just the same. I'm hoping they'll be so busy making things look right—with putting on a good show—that they'll not even know I've been in Haven until I'm gone."

Butch Dugan crossed his arms over his chest. Ev had been close to the truth—at first, Dugan had indulged himself in the fancy that David Bright, who was usually an accurate interpreter of human behavior, had been wrong this time; Hillman was as sane as *he* was. Now he was mildly disturbed, not because Hillman had turned out to be crazy after all, but because he had turned out to be *really* crazy. And yet . . . there was something oddly persuasive in the old man's calm, reasonable voice and his steady gaze.

"You speak as if everyone in Haven was in on something," Dugan said, "and I think that's impossible. I want you to know that."

"Yes, any normal person would say that. That's how they've been able to get away with it this long. Fifty years ago, people felt like the atomic bomb was impossible, and they would have laughed at the idea of TV, let alone a video recorder. Not much changes, Trooper Dugan. Most people see as far as the horizon, and that's all. If someone says there's something over it, people don't listen."

Ev stood up and extended his hand over Dugan's desk, as if he had every right in the world to expect Dugan to shake it. Which surprised Butch into doing just that.

"Well, I knew when I looked at you that you thought I was nuts," Ev said with a rueful little smile, "and I guess I've said enough to double the idear. But I've found out what I needed to know, and said what I needed to say. Do an old man a favor, and peek at the sky once in a while. If you see a purple star-shell . . ."

"The woods are dry this summer," Dugan said, and even as the words came out of his mouth they seemed helpless and oddly unimportant; almost frivolous. He realized he was being drawn helplessly toward belief again.

Dugan cleared his throat and pushed on.

"If you've really got a flare-gun, using it could start a

hell of a forest fire. If you don't have a permit to use such a thing—and I know goddam well you don't—it could get you thrown into jail."

Ev's grin widened a little, but there was still no humor in it. "If you see the star-shell," he said, "I got a feeling that being thrown into the pokey up to Bangor is gonna be the least of my worries. Good day to you, Trooper Dugan."

Ev stepped out and closed the door neatly behind him. Dugan stood for a moment, as perplexed and uneasy as he had ever been in his life. *Let him go,* he thought, and then got moving.

Something had been troubling Butch Dugan. The disappearance of the two troopers, both of whom he had known and liked, had temporarily driven it out of his mind. Hillman's visit had brought it back, and that was what sent him after the old man.

It was the memory of his last conversation with Ruth. He had been worried about her even before then; her handling of the David Brown search hadn't been like the Ruth McCausland he knew at all. For the only time he could remember, she had been unprofessional.

Then, the night before she died, he had called her about the investigation, to get information and to give it; to kibitz, in short. He knew neither of them had anything, but sometimes you could spin something out of plain speculation, like straw into gold. In the course of that conversation, the subject of the boy's grandfather had come up. By then Butch had spoken to David Bright of the *News*—had had a beer with him, in fact—and he passed on to Ruth Ev's idea that the whole town had gone crazy in some strange way.

Ruth hadn't laughed at the story, or clucked over the failure of Ev Hillman's mind, as he had expected she would do. He wasn't sure just *what* she had said, because just about then the connection had begun to get bad—not that there was anything very unusual in *that;* most of the lines going into small towns like Haven were still on poles, and the connections regularly went to hell—all it took was a high wind to make you feel like you and the other person were holding tomato-soup cans connected by a length of waxed string.

Better tell him to stay away, Ruth had said—he was sure of that much. And then, just before he lost her altogether, it seemed to him that she had said something about—of all things—nylon stockings. He must have heard her wrong, but there was no mistaking the tone—sadness and great weariness, as if her failure to find David Brown had taken all the heart out of her. A moment later the connection had broken down completely. He hadn't bothered to call her back because he had given her all the information he had . . . precious little, really.

The next day she was dead.

Better tell him to stay away. That much he was sure of.

Now, I have reasons . . . to believe that I'm not wanted in Haven.

Tell him to stay away.

I might disappear like David Brown.

Stay away.

Or have an accident like Ruth McCausland.

Away.

He caught up to the old man in the parking lot.

14

Hillman had an old purple Valiant with badly rusted rocker panels. He looked up, driver's-side door open, as Dugan loomed over him.

"I'm coming with you tomorrow."

Ev's eyes widened. "You don't even know where I'm going!"

"No. But if I'm with you I won't have to worry that you're going to set half the woods in eastern Maine on fire trying to send me a message like Double-O-Seven."

Ev looked at him consideringly and then shook his head. "I'd feel better having someone with me," he said, "especially a guy as big as Gorilla Monsoon who packs a gun. But they ain't stupid in Haven, Officer Dugan. They never were, and I got a feeling that they're a lot less stupid just lately. They expect to see you at her funeral. If they don't, they're going to be suspicious."

"Christ! I'd like to know how the hell you can stand there babbling all that crazy shit and sound so fucking *sane!*"

"Maybe because you know too," Ev said. "How funny it is. How funny all of these things started in Haven."

Then with a prescience that was startling, he added: "Or maybe you knew Ruth well enough yourself to sense she'd gotten off-kilter."

The two men stood looking at each other in the graveled parking lot of the Derry barracks, the sun beating down on them, their shadows, clear and black, slanting out neatly at two o'clock.

"I'll let on tonight that I'm sick," Dugan said. "That I've got stomach flu. It's been going around the barracks. What do you think?"

Ev nodded with sudden relief—that relief was so great it was startling. The idea of sneaking back into Haven had frightened him more than he had been willing to let on, especially to himself. He had half-convinced this big cop that something might be going on there; he could see it in his face. Half-convinced wasn't much, maybe, but it was still a giant step forward from where he had been. And of course, he hadn't done it alone; Ruth McCausland had helped.

"All right," he said, "but listen to me, Trooper Dugan, and listen good, because our lives could depend on it tomorrow. Don't you call up any of the men who'll be going to the funeral tomorrow and tell them the reason you're not going to be there is just a gag you're running. Call up a few people tonight and tell them you really are just as sick as a dog, that you hope you are going to be able to make it, but you doubt it."

Dugan frowned. "Why would you want me to say—" But suddenly he knew, and his mouth dropped open. The old man stared back at him calmly enough.

"Christ Jesus, are you telling me that you think the people in Haven are *mind-readers?* That if my men knew I really wasn't sick, the people in town could pick the news right out of their heads?"

"I ain't telling you a thing, Trooper Dugan," Ev said. "You are telling me."

"Mr. Hillman, I really think that you must be imagining—"

"I never expected you'd want to come with me when I came to see you. I wasn't angling for it, either. The most I hoped for was that you'd keep an eye out and see my flare if I got in trouble, and that would at least keep the heat on that nest of snakes down there awhile longer. But if you offer a man more, he wants more. Trust me a little further. Please. For Ruth's sake . . . if that's what it takes to convince you to come with me, I'm willing to use it. Something else: no matter what, you're going to feel some peculiar things tomorrow."

"I've felt some pretty peculiar ones today," Dugan said.

"Ayuh," Ev said, and waited for Dugan to decide.

"Do you have some actual place to go in mind?" Dugan asked after a moment. "Or are you just going to ramble around the town until you get tired of it?"

"I've got a place in mind," Ev said quietly. He thought: *Oh yes. Yessirree Bob. Up behind the old Garrick place, on the outskirts of Big Injun Woods, where compasses have never worked worth a tin shit in a goldmine. And I believe we'll strike on a pretty good path through the woods to it—whatever "it" is—because equipment like the stuff Bobbi Anderson and her friend have been using leaves a backtrail as wide as a freeway. No, I don't believe there will be any trouble finding it at all.*

"Okay. Give me the address of the place you're staying in Derry, and I'll pick you up at nine in my personal car. We'll get to Haven just about the time the service starts."

"The car's my treat," Ev said quietly. "Not this one; it's known in Haven. I'll have a rental. And you'll want to show up at eight, because we'll be doing a bit of backroading."

"I can get us into Haven and still keep clear of the village," Dugan said. "You don't have to worry about that."

"I ain't. But I want us to skirt the whole town and come in from the Albion side, and I think I know just the way to do it."

"Why the hell does it have to be that end of town?"

"Because it's the furthest from where they'll be, and that's where I want to come back into Haven. As far from em as I can get."

"You're really scared, aren't you?"

Ev nodded.

"Why a rental car?"

"Criminy, don't you ask a lot of questions!" And Ev rolled his eyes in such a comical way that Butch Dugan grinned.

"It's my job," he said. "Why *do* you want to go in a rental? No one in Haven is going to know my personal car." He paused, thinking. "At least, not now that Ruth's dead."

"Because it's my obsession," Ev Hillman said. His face suddenly cracked into a smile of startling sweetness. "And a person ought to pay the freight on his own obsession."

"All right," Butch said. "I give up. Eight o'clock. Your route, your car, your obsession. I must be crazy. I really must be."

"By tomorrow at this time, I think you're going to have a much better idea of what crazy is," Ev said, and climbed into his old purple Valiant before Dugan could ask him any more questions.

Butch, in fact, had no more questions to ask. He felt glum, as if he had bought the Brooklyn Bridge his first day in New York City, shelling out even though he knew a thing that big probably couldn't be for sale. *No one gets taken who doesn't want to get taken,* he thought. He had worked Fraud and Bunco out of Augusta for three years, and that was the first thing they taught you. The old man had been queerly persuasive, but Butch Dugan knew that he had not been *persuaded* into this; he had jumped. Because he had loved Ruth McCausland, and in another year or so he probably would have plucked up sufficient nerve to propose to her. Because when someone you love dies, it leaves a black hole in the middle of your heart, and one way to plug such a hole is to refuse to admit that he or she was taken away by a stupid mischance. Better if you can believe—even for a little while—that someone or something you can get hold of was responsible. It makes the hole a little smaller. Even a rube knows that much.

Sighing, suddenly feeling much older than his age, Dugan trudged back to the barracks.

Ev went to the hospital and sat for most of that day's remainder with Hilly. Around three o'clock, he wrote two notes. One he put on Hilly's night table, anchored against the breeze that pawed with occasional playfulness through the open window with a little pot of flowers. The other note was longer, and when he was done with it, he folded it and put it in his pocket. Then he left the hospital.

He drove to a small building in the Derry Industrial Park. MAINE MED SUPPLIES, the sign over the door read. And below that: Specializing in Respiration Supplies and Respiration Therapy Since 1946.

He told the man inside what he wanted. The man told him it sounded as if he really ought to take a ride up to Bangor and talk to the folks at Downeast ScubaDive. Ev explained that a scuba tank was the last thing he wanted; he was interested in as much dry-land portability as he could get. He and the fellow talked awhile longer, and Ev left, after signing a thirty-six-hour rental agreement, with a rather specialized piece of equipment. The fellow at Maine Med Supplies stood at the door watching him go, scratching his head.

15

The nurse read the note by Hilly's bed.

Hilly—
I may not see you for a while now, but I just wanted to tell you I think you'll get over this bad patch, and if I can help you do it, I guess I will be just about the happiest grampa in the world. I believe David is still alive and I don't think it's your fault that he got lost in the first place. I love you. Hilly, and I hope to see you soon.

Gramp

But he never saw Hilly Brown again.

9.

THE FUNERAL

1

From nine o'clock on, out-of-towners who had known or worked with Ruth McCausland began to come into Haven Village. Soon almost every parking space along Main Street was taken. The Haven Lunch did a brisk business. Beach kept busy short-ordering eggs, bacon, sausages, and home-fries. He brewed pot after pot of coffee. Representative Brennan hadn't come, but he had sent a close aide. *Should have come y'self, Joe,* Beach thought with a little sunken smile. *Might have got a whole slew of new ideas 'bout how to run the gov'mint.*

The day dawned brisk and clear, more like late September than late July. The sky was bright blue, the temperature a moderate sixty-eight degrees, the wind out of the west at about twenty miles an hour. Once more there were outsiders in Haven, and once more Haven had gotten lucky weather for them. And soon it wouldn't matter whether they were lucky or not, the townsfolk told each other without speaking; soon they would be in charge of their own luck.

A good day, you would have said; the best kind of New England summer's day, the sort the tourists come for. A day to prick the appetite fully alive. Those who came to Haven from out of town ordered hearty breakfasts, as people with lively appetites are apt to do, but Beach noted that most of those breakfasts came back only half-eaten. The newcomers lost their appetites quickly; the light went out of their eyes, and they began to look, for the most part, shallow and a little sick.

The Lunch was crowded, but conversation lagged.

Must be that the air here in our little town don't quite agree with you folks, Beach thought. He imagined going into the storeroom, where the device he had used to get rid of the two nosy cops was hidden under a pile of tablecloths. He imagined bringing it out here, a great big deadly bazooka, and just washing his lunchroom clean of all these outsiders with a purifying blast of green fire.

No; not now. Not yet. Soon it wouldn't matter. Next month. But for now . . .

He looked down at the plate he was scraping and saw a tooth in someone's scrambled eggs.

Tommyknockers coming, my friends, Beach thought. *Only when they finally get here, I don't think they'll even bother knocking; I think they'll just blow the fucking door right down.*

Beach's grin widened. He scraped the tooth off the plate with the rest of the garbage.

2

Dugan could be silent when he wanted, and this morning that was what he wanted. Apparently it was what the old man wanted, too. Dugan had gotten to Ev Hillman's apartment building on Lower Main promptly at eight, and had found a Jeep Cherokee standing at the curb behind the old party's Valiant. There was a big gunnysack in the back, its top tied with hayrope.

"Did you rent this in Bangor?"

"Leased it at Derry AMC," Ev said.

"Must have been expensive."

" 'Twasn't too dear."

That ended the conversation. They arrived somewhere near the Albion-Haven town line an hour and forty minutes later. *We'll be doing a bit of backroading,* the old man had said, and if that wasn't a classic understatement, Butch didn't know what was. He had been driving in this part of Maine for almost twenty years, and before today had thought he knew it like the back of his hand. Now he knew better. *Hillman* knew it like the back of his hand;

by comparison, Butch Dugan had a general working knowledge of the area, no more.

They went from the turnpike to Route 69; from 69 to two-lane blacktop; then to gravel in western Troy; then to hardpan; then to rutted dirt with grass growing up the middle; finally to an overgrown logging track that looked as if it might have last been seriously used around 1950.

"Do you know where the fuck you're going?" Butch shouted as the Cherokee crashed through rotted corduroy, then hauled itself out, engine howling, all four wheels spinning up mud and chewed splinters.

Ev only nodded. He clung to the Cherokee's big wheel like an old balding monkey.

One woods road led into another, and finally they crashed out of a scree of foliage and onto a dirt road Butch recognized as Albion Town Road # 5. Butch had thought it impossible, but the old man had done exactly what he promised: brought them all the way around Haven without ever once going in.

Now Ev brought the Cherokee to a stop just a hundred feet short of the marker announcing the Haven town line. He turned off the engine and unrolled his window. There was no sound but the tick of the engine. There was no birdsong, and Butch thought this odd.

"What's in that gunnysack back there?" Butch asked.

"All kinds of things. No need to worry about it now."

"What are you waiting for?"

"Churchbells," Ev said.

3

It was not the Methodist churchbells that Ev had grown up with and expected which rang out at a quarter to ten, calling Ruth's mourners—both the real ones and those prepared to shed copious floods of crocodile tears—to the Methodist church, where the first act of the three-act festivities was to be played out (Act II: Graveside Ceremonies; Act III: Refreshments in the Town Library).

Reverend Goohringer, a shy man who usually had not the fortitude to say boo to a goose, had gone around town a few weeks ago telling people he was getting damned tired of all that gonging.

"Then why don't you do something about it, Gooey?" Pamela Sargent asked him.

Rev. Lester Goohringer had never been called "Gooey" in his entire life, but in his current state of rancor he barely noticed.

"Maybe I will," he said, looking at her through his thick glasses grimly. "Just maybe I will."

"Got any ideas?"

"I might," he said slyly. "Time'll tell, won't it?"

"It always does, Gooey," she said. "Always does."

The Reverend Goohringer in fact had a fine idea about those bells—he could hardly believe it had never occurred to him before, it was so simple and beautiful. And the best thing about it was that he wouldn't have to take it up with the deacons, or with the Ladies' Aid (an organization which apparently attracted only two types of women—fat slobs with boobs the size of barrels and skinny-assed, flat-chested sluts like Pamela Sargent, with her fake ivory cigarette holder and her raspy smoker's cough), or with the few well-to-do members of his congregation . . . going to them always gave him a week's worth of acid indigestion. He did not like to beg. No, this was something the Rev. Lester Goohringer could do all by himself, and so he did it. Fuck 'em all if they couldn't take a joke.

"And if you ever call me Gooey again, Pam," he had whispered as he rewired the fuse box in the church basement so it could handle the heavy voltage his idea would require, "I'll jam the plumber's friend in the parsonage *pissoir* up your twat and plunge out your brains . . . if you haven't pissed 'em all away."

He cackled and went on rewiring. Rev. Lester Goohringer had never had such blunt thoughts or said such blunt things in his life, and he found the experience liberating and exhilarating. He was, in fact, prepared to tell anyone in Haven who didn't like his new carillon that they could take a flying fuck at a rolling doughnut.

But everyone in town had thought the change nothing short of magnificent. It was, too. And today the Rev. Goohringer felt a real heart swell of pride as he flicked the new switch in the vestry and the sound of the bells floated out over Haven, playing a medley of hymns. The carillon was programmable, and today Lester Goohringer plugged in the hymns which had been particular favorites of Ruth's. They included such old Methodist and Baptist standbys as "What a Friend We Have in Jesus" and "This Is My Father's World."

The Rev. Goohringer stood back, rubbing his hands together, and watched as people began to move toward the church in groups and twos and threes, drawn by the bells, the bells, the calling of the bells.

"Hot damn!" the Rev. Goohringer exclaimed. He had never felt better in his life, and he meant to send Ruth McCausland off in style. He intended to preach one *pie*-cutter of a eulogy.

After all, they had all loved her.

4

The bells.

Dave Rutledge, Haven's oldest citizen, tipped an ear toward them and smiled toothlessly—even if the bells had jangled discordantly he would have smiled, because he could *hear* them. Until early July, Dave had been almost completely deaf, and his lower limbs were always cold as his circulation steadily failed. He was, after all, ninety, and that made him an old dog. But this month, his hearing and circulation had magically improved. People told him he looked ten years younger, and by Christ, he felt *twenty* years younger. And my, wasn't the sound of those bells playing just the sweetest thing? Dave got up and started toward the church.

5

The calling of the bells.

In January, the aide U.S. Representative Brennan had sent to Haven had been in D.C., and there he had met a beautiful young woman named Annabelle. This summer she had come to Maine to be with him, and had come to Haven with him this morning to keep him company. He had promised her they would overnight in Bar Harbor before going back to Augusta. At first she thought it had been a bad idea, because she began to feel a little nauseated in the restaurant and hadn't been able to finish her breakfast. For one thing, the short-order cook looked like an older, fatter version of Charles Manson. He kept smiling the strangest little smile when he thought no one was looking—it was enough to make you wonder if he had powdered the scrambled eggs with arsenic. But the sound of the bells chiming hymns she hadn't heard since her Nebraska childhood charmed her with wonder.

"My God, Marty, how can a little wide-place-in-the-road town like this afford a *gorgeous* carillon like that?"

"Maybe some rich summer tourist died and left it to them," Marty said vaguely. He had no interest in the carillon. He'd had a headache ever since they got here, and was getting worse. Also, one of his gums was bleeding. Pyorrhea ran in his family; he hoped to God it wasn't that. "Come on, let's go over to the church." *So we can get it done and go up to Bar Harbor and screw our brains out,* he thought. *This is one creepy little town.*

They started across the street together, she in a black suit (but, she had told him archly on their way up, her underwear was all white silk . . . what little of it there was), he in a governmental charcoal gray. The people of Haven, dressed in their soberest finery, walked with them. Marty saw a surprising number of powder-blue state police uniforms.

"Look, Marty! The clock!"

She was pointing at the tower of the town hall. It was good solid red brick, but for a moment it seemed to swim and waver before Marty's eyes. His headache was instantly worse. Maybe it was eyestrain. He'd had a checkup three months ago and the guy had said his vision was good enough to fly a jet, but maybe he'd been wrong. Half the professional people in America were on coke these days. He had read all about it in *Time* . . . and why was his mind wandering like this, anyway? It was the bells. They seemed to be echoing and multiplying in his head. Ten, a hundred, a thousand, a million, all playing "When We Meet at Jesus' Feet."

"What about the clock?" he asked irritably.

"The hands are funny," she said. "They look almost . . . drawn on."

6

The calling of the bells.

Eddie Stampnell of the Derry barracks crossed the street with Andy Rideout from Orono—both of them had known Ruth, liked her.

"Pretty, ain't it?" Eddie asked dubiously.

"Maybe," Andy said. "I just keep thinking of Bent and Jingles getting blown away by a couple of numbnut rubes out here, probably buried in some farmer's potato field, and it just sounds like a bone-phone to me. Seems like Haven's bad luck now. I know that's stupid, but that's how I feel."

"It's bad luck for my head," Eddie replied. "It aches like a bastard."

"Well, let's get it over and get out," Andy said. "She was a good woman, but she's gone. And between you and me, I don't care if I never spend another fifteen minutes in Haven now that she is."

They stepped into the Methodist church together, neither of them looking at Rev. Lester Goohringer, who stood beside the switch which controlled his lovely carillon, smiling and rubbing his dry hands together and accepting the compliments of all and sundry.

7

The crying of the bells.

Bobbi Anderson got out of her blue Chevrolet truck, slamming the door, smoothing her dark blue dress over her hips, and checking her makeup in the truck's outside mirror before walking slowly down the sidewalk to the church. She walked with her head down and her shoulders slumped. She was trying hard to get the rest she needed to go on, and Gard had helped to put a brake on her obsession

(and that's what it is, an obsession, no use kidding yourself)

but Gard was a brake that was slowly wearing out. He wasn't at the funeral because he was sleeping off a monumental drunk, his grizzled, worn face pillowed on one arm, his breath a sour cloud around him. Anderson was tired, all right, but it was more than just that—a great unfocused grief seemed to fill her this morning. It was partly for Ruth, partly for David Brown, partly for the whole town. Yet mostly, she suspected, it was for herself. The "becoming" continued—for everyone in Haven except Gard, that was—and it was good, but she mourned her own unique identity, which was now fading like a morning mist. She knew now that *The Buffalo Soldiers* was her last book . . . and the irony was that she now suspected the Tommyknockers had written most of that, as well.

8

The bells, bells, bells.

Haven answered them. It was Act I of a charade titled *The Burial of Ruth McCausland,* or, *How We Loved That Woman.* Nancy Voss had closed the post office to come. The government would not have approved, but what the government didn't know wouldn't hurt them. They would know *plenty* soon enough, she thought. They would get a big old express-mail delivery from Haven very soon. Them and every other government on this flying mudball.

Frank Spruce, Haven's biggest dairy farmer, answered the bells. John Mumphry, whose father had run against Ruth for the position of town constable, answered them. Ashley Ruvall, who had passed her out by the town line two days before her death, answered them with his parents. Ashley was crying. Doc Warwick was there, and Jud Tarkington; Adley McKeen came with Hazel McCready on his arm; Newt Berringer and Dick Allison answered them, walking slowly and supporting Ruth's predecessor, John Harley, between them. John was feeble and nearly transparent. Maggie, his wife, was not well enough to attend.

They came, answering the summons of the bells—Tremains and Thurlows, Applegates and Goldmans, Duplisseys and Archinbourgs. Good Maine people, you would have said, drawn from a healthy stockpot that was mostly French, Irish, Scots, and Canadian. But they were different now; as they drew together at the church, so did their minds draw together and become one mind, watching the outsiders, listening for the slightest wrong note in their thoughts . . . they came together, they listened, and the bells rang in their strange blood.

9

Ev Hillman sat up behind the wheel of the Cherokee, eyes opening wide at the dim sound of the carillon. "What in the *hell—*"

"Churchbells, what else?" Butch Dugan said. "It sounds very pretty. They're getting ready to start the funeral, I suppose." *They're burying Ruth over in the village . . . what in God's name am I doing out here by the town line with this crazy old man?*

He wasn't sure, but it was too late to change his course now.

"The bells in the Methodist church never made a sound like that before in *my* time," Ev said. "Someone's changed them over."

"So what?"

"So nothing. So *everything*. I dunno. Come on, Trooper Dugan." He turned the key, and the Cherokee's engine roared.

"I'll ask you again," Dugan said with what he thought was extraordinary patience. "What are we looking *for?*"

"I don't rightly know." The Cherokee passed the town-line marker. They had left Albion now and entered Haven. Ev had a sudden sickening premonition that in spite of all his precautions and care, he was never going to leave it again. "We'll know it when we see it."

Dugan didn't reply, only held on for dear life and wondered again how he had gotten into this—he had to be as crazy as the old fart he was riding with, and then some. He raised one hand to his forehead and began rubbing, just above the eyebrows.

A headache was forming there.

10

There were sniffles, red eyes, and some sobbing as the Rev. Goohringer, his bald head gleaming mellowly and in a soft variety of colors courtesy of the summer sunshine falling through the stained-glass windows, launched into his funeral eulogy following a hymn, a prayer, another hymn, a reading of Ruth's favorite Scripture (the Beatitudes), and yet another hymn. Below him, foaming around the lectern in a semicircle, were great bunches of summer flowers. Even with the upper windows of the church thrown open and a good breeze blowing through, their smell was suffocatingly sweet.

"We have come here to praise Ruth McCausland and to celebrate her passing," Goohringer began.

The townsfolk sat with hands either folded or gripping handkerchiefs; their eyes—most wet—regarded Goohringer with sober, studious attention. They looked healthy, these folk—their color was good, their skin for the most part unblemished. And even someone who had never been in Haven before could have seen that the congregation here fell naturally into two groups. The outsiders *didn't* look healthy. They were pale. Their eyes were dazed. Twice during the eulogy, people left hurriedly, dashed around the corner of the church, and were quietly sick. For others, the nausea was a lower complaint—an uneasy rolling in the bowels not quite serious enough to cause an exit but simply going on and on.

Several outsiders would lose teeth before that day was over.

Several developed headaches which would dissolve almost as soon as they left town—the aspirin finally working, they would surmise.

And more than a few of them had the most *amazing* ideas as they sat on the hard pews and listened to Goohringer preach Ruth McCausland's eulogy. In some cases these ideas came so suddenly and seemed so huge, so *fundamental,* that the persons to whom they occurred would feel as if they had been shot in the head. Such persons had to fight down an urge to bolt out of their pews and run into the street screaming *"Eureka!"* at full volume.

The people of Haven saw this happening and were

amused. All of a sudden the apathetic, puddinglike expression on someone's face would be shocked away. The eyes would widen, the mouth flop open, and the Havenites would recognize the expression of a person in the throes of a Grand Idea.

Eddie Stampnell of the Derry barracks, for instance, conceived of a nationwide police band on which every cop in the land could communicate. And he saw how a cloak could easily be thrown over such a band; all those nosy civilians with their police-band radios would be shit out of luck. Ramifications and modifications poured into his mind faster than he could deal with them; if ideas had been water, he would have drowned. *I'm gonna be famous for this,* he thought feverishly. Rev. Goohringer was forgotten; Andy Rideout, his partner, was forgotten; his dislike of this goofy little town was forgotten; Ruth was forgotten. The idea had swallowed his mind. *I'm gonna be famous, and I'm gonna revolutionize policework in America . . . maybe in the whole world. Holy shit! Hoo-oly SHIT!*

The Havenites, who knew Eddie's great idea would be foggy by noon and gone by three, smiled and listened and waited. Waited for it to be over, so they could get back to their real business.

So they could get back to "becoming."

11

They rolled down a dirt track—Town Road # 5 in Albion, which became Fire Road # 16 here in Haven. Twice logging roads branched off into the woods, and each time one of these came up, Dugan braced himself for an even more bone-wrenching ride. But Hillman didn't take either. He reached Route 9 and swung right. He cranked the Cherokee up to fifty and headed deeper into Haven.

Dugan was skittery. He didn't know exactly why. The old man was crazy, of course; the idea that Haven had turned into a nest of snakes was pure paranoia. All the same, Monster felt a steady, pulsing nervousness growing inside him. It was vague, a low grassfire in his nerves.

"You keep rubbing your forehead," Hillman said.

"I've got a headache."

"It'd ache a lot worse if the wind wasn't blowin, I guess."

Another lapse into utter nonsense. What in God's name was he doing here? And why did he feel so goddam jumpy?

"I feel like somebody slipped me a couple of sleeping pills."

"Ayuh."

Dugan looked at him. "But you don't feel that way, do you? You're as cool as a goddam cucumber."

"I'm scared, but I don't have the jitters, and I don't have a headache, neither."

"Why *would* you have a headache?" Dugan asked crossly. The conversation had gotten decidedly *Alice in Wonderland*-ish. "Headaches aren't catching."

"If you and six other guys are painting a closed room, you are all apt to end up with headaches. Ain't that a true fact?"

"Yeah, I guess so. But this isn't—"

"No. It ain't. And we got lucky with the weather. Just the same, I guess that thing is putting out a powerful stink, because you feel it. I can see you do." Hillman paused and then said another *Alice in Wonderland* thing. "Had any good ideas yet, Trooper?"

"What do you mean?"

Hillman nodded, satisfied. "Good. If you do, tell me. I got something in that sack for you."

"This is crazy," Dugan said. His voice wasn't quite steady. "I mean, utterly nuts. Turn this thing around, Hillman. I want to go back."

Ev suddenly focused a single phrase in his mind, as sharply and as clearly as he could. He knew from his last three days in Haven that Bryant, Marie, Hilly, and David were routinely reading each other's minds. He could sense it even though he couldn't pick it up. By the same token, he had come to realize they couldn't get into *his* head unless he let them. He had begun to wonder if it had something to do with the steel in his skull, a souvenir of that German grenade. He had seen the potato-masher with dreadful, ineluctable clarity, a gray-black thing spinning in the snow. He'd thought, *Well, I'm dead. That's it for me.* After, he remembered nothing until he'd awakened in a French hospital. He remembered how his head had hurt; he remembered the nurse who had kissed him, and how her breath had smelled like anise, and how she kept saying, shaping her words as if speaking to a very small child, "*Je t'aime, mon amour. La guerre est fini. Je t'aime. Je t'aime les Etats-Unis.*"

La guerre est fini, he thought now. *La guerre est fini.*

"What is it?" he asked Dugan sharply.

"What do you m—"

Ev swerved the Cherokee over to the side of the road, kicking up a spume of dust. They were a mile and a half over the town line now; it was another three or four miles to the old Garrick farm.

"Don't *think*, don't *talk, just tell me what I was thinkin!*"

"Tout fini, you're thinking *la guerre est fini,* but you're crazy, people can't read minds, they c—"

Dugan stopped. He turned his head slowly and stared at Ev. Ev could hear the tendons in the man's neck creak. His eyes were huge.

"La guerre est fini," he whispered. "That's what you were thinking, and that she smelled like licorice—"

"Anise," Ev said, and smiled. Her thighs had been white, her cunt so tight.

"—and I saw a grenade in the snow, oh Jesus, what's going on?"

Ev pictured a red old-fashioned tractor in his mind. "What now?"

"Tractor," Dugan husked. "Farmall. But you got the wrong tires on it. My dad had a Farmall. Those are Dixie Field-Boss tires. They wouldn't fit a Far—"

Dugan suddenly turned around, grappled for the Cherokee's door handle, leaned out, and threw up.

12

"Ruth once asked me if I would read the Beatitudes at her funeral if it should fall to me to preside over it," the Rev. Goohringer was saying in a mellow Methodist voice the Rev. Donald Hartley would have completely approved of, "and I have honored her wishes. Yet—"

(la guerre you were thinking la guerre est)

Goohringer paused, a little expression of surprise and concern touching his face. A close observer might have thought a little gas had bubbled up, and he had paused to stifle an unseemly burp.

"—I think there is another set of verses she merits. They—"

(tractor Farmall tractor)

There was another small hitch in Goohringer's delivery, and that frown touched his face again.

"—are not the sort of verses, I suppose, that any Christian woman would dare ask for, knowing that a Christian woman must earn them. Listen as I read from the Book of Proverbs and see if you, who knew her, do not agree that this is the case with Ruth McCausland."

(those are Dixie Field-Boss tires)

Dick Allison glanced to his left and caught Newt's eye across the aisle. Newt looked dismayed. John Harley's mouth had dropped open; his faded blue eyes shifted back and forth in bewilderment.

Goohringer found his place, lost it, almost dropped his Bible. Suddenly he was flustered, no longer the master of ceremonies but a divinity student with stage-fright. As it happened, no one noticed; the outsiders were occupied either with physical distress or with mind-boggling ideas. The people of Haven drew together as an alarm went off, jumping from one mind to the next until their heads rang with it—this was a new carillon, one that jangled with discord.

(someone's looking where they have)

(have no business)

Bobby Tremain took Stephanie Colson's hand and squeezed it. She squeezed back, looking at him with wide brown eyes—the alarmed eyes of a doe who hears the slide and click of the bolt in a hunter's gun.

(out on Route 9)

(too close to the ship)

(one's a cop)

(cop, yes, but a special cop—Ruth's cop, he loved)

Ruth would have known these rising voices. And now even some of the outsiders began to feel them, although they were relatively new to Haven's infection. A few of them looked around like people coming out of thin dozes. One of these was the lady-friend of Representative Brennan's aide. She had been miles from here, it seemed—she was a minor bureaucrat in Washington, but she had just conceived of a filing system that might well get her a fat promotion. Then a random thought, a thought she would have sworn was not her own

(somebody has got to stop them quick!)
slashed across her mind and she looked around to see if someone had actually called out aloud in the church.

But it was quiet except for the preacher, who had found his place again. She looked at Marty, but Marty was sitting in a glassy daze, looking at one of the stained-glass windows with the fixed gaze of one deeply hypnotized. She supposed this to be boredom and went back to her own thoughts.

" 'Who can find a virtuous woman?' " Goohringer read, his voice a trifle uneven. He hesitated in the wrong places and stumbled a few times. " 'For her price is far above rubies. The heart of her husband doth safely trust in her, and he shall have no lack of gain. She doeth him good and not evil all the days of her life. She seeketh wool—' "

Now another burst of those alien thoughts came to the single sensitized ear in the church:

(sorry about that I just couldn't)

(. . .)

(what?)

(. . .)

(holy Christ that's Wheeling! how—)

(. . .)

There are two voices speaking but we are only hearing one, the mind-net thought, and eyes began to focus on Bobbi. There was only one person in Haven who could make his mind opaque to them, and that person wasn't here now. *Two voices—is the one we don't hear the voice of your drunken friend?*

Bobbi got up suddenly and worked her way along the pew, horribly aware that people were looking at her. Goohringer, the ass, had paused again.

"Excuse me," Bobbi muttered. "Excuse me . . . excuse me."

At last she escaped into the vestibule and the street. Others—Bobby Tremain, Newt, Dick, and Bryant Brown among them—began to follow. None of the outsiders noticed. They had lapsed back into their strange dreams.

13

"Sorry about that," Butch Dugan said. He pulled the door closed, got a handkerchief out of his back pocket, and began to rub his mouth. "I couldn't seem to help it. I feel better now."

Ev nodded. "I ain't going to explain. There isn't time. But I want you to listen to something."

"What?"

Ev snapped on the Cherokee's radio and dialed across the band. Dugan started. He had never heard so many stations, not even at night when they jumped all over each other, wavering in and out in a sea of voices. Nothing wavery about these; most were bellclear.

Ev stopped at a C&W station. A song by the Judds was just ending. When it did, there was a station ID. Butch Dugan could hardly believe what he was hearing: *"Doubleya-Doubleya-Vee-AYYYY!"* a perky girl group sang, to an accompaniment of fiddles and banjos.

"Holy Christ, that's Wheeling!" Dugan cried. "How—"

Ev snapped off the radio. "Now I want you to listen to my head."

Dugan stared at him for a moment, utterly flummoxed. Not even *Alice in Wonderland* had been *this* mad.

"What in the name of God are you talking about?"

"Don't argue with me, just do it." Ev turned his face away from Dugan, presenting him with the back of his head. "I got two pieces of steel plate in my head. War souvenir. Bigger one's back there. See the place where the hair don't grow?"

"Yes, but—"

"Time is short! Put your ear up close to that scar and *listen!*"

He *did* . . . and felt unreality wash over him. The back of the old man's head was playing music. It was tinny and distant but perfectly identifiable. It was Frank Sinatra singing "New York, New York."

Butch Dugan began to giggle. Soon he was laughing. Then he was roaring, arms wrapped around his stomach. He was out here in the back of the beyond with an old man whose head had just turned into a music-box. By God, this was better than Ripley's *Believe It or Not.*

Butch laughed and gasped and wept and roared and—

The old man's callused palm slammed across his face. The shock of being slapped like a small child surprised Butch out of his hysteria as much as the pain had done. He blinked at Ev, one hand going to his cheek.

"It started a week and a half before I left town," Ev

said grimly. "Blasts of music in my head. They were stronger when I got out this way, and I should have thought about that before now, but I didn't. They're stronger now. *Everything* is. So I got no time for you to get the screaming yaw-haws. Are you going to be all right?"

The flush spreading over Dugan's face mostly hid the red mark Ev's hand had made. *The screaming yaw-haws.* That pretty well described it. First he had puked, and then he had had a fit of hysterics like a teenage girl. This old man wasn't just showing him up; he was pulling past him in second gear.

"I'll be fine," he said.

"You believe now that something's going on here? That something in Haven has changed?"

"Yes. I . . ." He swallowed. "Yes," he repeated.

"Good." Ev stepped on the gas and roared back onto the road. "This . . . thing . . . it's changing everyone in town, Trooper Dugan. Everyone but me. I get music in my head, but that's all. I don't read minds . . . and I don't get ideas."

"What do you mean, 'ideas'? What kind of ideas?"

"All kinds." The Cherokee's speedometer touched sixty, then began to edge past it. "Thing is, I have no *proof* of what's going on. None at all. You thought I was right off'n my head, didn't you?"

Dugan nodded. He was holding on tight to the dashboard in front of him. He felt sick to his stomach again. The sun was too bright, dazzling on the windshield and the chrome.

"The reporter and the nurses did too. But there's something in the woods, and I'm going to find it, and I'm going to take some pitchers of it, and I'm going to take you out, and we're going to do some loud talking, and maybe we'll find a way to get my grandson David back and maybe we won't, but either way we ought to be able to shut down whatever's going on here before it's too late. *Ought* to? We *got* to."

Now the speedometer needle hung just below seventy.

"How far?" Dugan managed through closed teeth. He was going to puke again, and soon; he just hoped he could hold on until they got to wherever they were going.

"The old Garrick farm," Ev said. "Less than a mile."

Thank God, Dugan thought.

14

"It's not Gard," Bobbi said. "Gard's passed out on the porch of the house."

"How do you know?" Adley McKeen asked. "You can't read him."

"I can, though," Bobbi said. "A little more every day. He's still on the porch, I tell you. He's dreaming about skiing."

They looked at Bobbi silently for a moment—about a dozen men standing across the street from the Methodist church, in front of the Haven Lunch.

"Who is it, then?" Joe Summerfield asked at last.

"I don't know," Bobbi said. "Only that it's not Gard." Bobbi was swaying mildly on her feet. Her face was that of a woman who was fifty, not thirty-seven. There were brown circles of exhaustion under her eyes. The men seemed not to notice.

From the church, voices were raised in "Holy, Holy, We Adore Thee."

"I know who it is," Dick Allison said suddenly. His eyes had gone strange and dull with hate. "Only one other person it *could* be. Only one other person I know of in town with metal in his head."

"Ev Hillman!" Newt cried. "Christ!"

"We've got to get moving," Jud Tarkington said. "The bastards are getting close. Adley, get some guns from the hardware store."

"Okay."

"Get 'em, but don't use 'em," Bobbi said. Her eyes swept the men. "Not on Hillman, if it's him, and not on the cop. *Particularly* not on the cop. We can't afford another mess in Haven. Not before

(the "becoming")

it's all finished."

"I'll get my tube," Beach said. His face was vacant with eagerness.

Bobbi grabbed his shoulder. "No, you won't," she said. "No more messes includes no more cops disappearing."

She looked at them all again, then at Dick Allison, who nodded.

"*Hillman's* got to disappear," he said. "No way around

it. But that's maybe all right. Ev's crazy. A crazy old man might decide to do just about anything. A crazy old man might just decide to haul stakes and drive off to Zion, Utah, or Grand Forks, Idaho, to wait for the end of the world. The cop's going to make a mess, but he's going to make it in Derry, and it's going to be a mess everyone understands. No one else is going to shit in our nest. Go on, Jud. Get the guns. Bobbi, you pull in back of the Lunch with your pickup truck. Newt, Adley, Joe, you ride with me. You go with Bobbi, Jud. Rest of you go in Kyle's Caddy. Come on, hoss y'freight!"

They got moving.

15

Sushhhhh . . .

Same old dream, a few new wrinkles. Damned strange ones. The snow had gone pink. It was soaked with blood. Was it coming from *him?* Holy hell! *Who would have believed how much blood the old tosspot had in him?*

They are skiing the intermediate slope. He knows that he should have stayed on the beginners' slopes for at least one more session, this is too fast for him, and furthermore, all this bloody snow is very distracting, particularly when it's all your *blood.*

Now he looks up, sending a rip of pain through his head—and his eyes widen. There's a Jeep on the goddam slope!

Annmarie screams: "Stem Bobbi, Gard! STEM BOBBI!"

But he doesn't need to stem Bobbi because this is just a dream, it's become an old friend in the last few weeks, like the erratic bursts of music in his head; this is a dream and that isn't a Jeep and this isn't the Straight Arrow slope, it's—

—turning into Bobbi's driveway.

Is this a dream? Or is it real?

No, he realized; that was the wrong question. A better question would have been *How* much *of this is real?*

The chrome winked blinding arrows of light into Gardener's eyes. He winced and groped for

(ski poles? no, not a dream, it's summer you're in Haven)

the porch railing. He could remember almost everything. It was hazy, but he could remember. No blackouts since he had come back to Bobbi's. Music in his head but no blackouts. Bobbi had gone to a funeral. Later on, she'd come back and they would start digging again. He remembered it all, just as he remembered the town-hall clock tower lifting off into the afternoon sky like a big-ass bird. All present and accounted for, sir. Except this.

He stood with his hands on the railing, bleary, bloodshot eyes watching the Jeep in spite of the glare. He was aware that he must look like a refugee from the Bowery. *Thank God there's still some truth in advertising—that's what I feel like.*

Then the man in the passenger seat turned his head and saw Gard. The man was so huge that he looked like a creature from a fairy-tale. He was wearing sunglasses, so Gardener couldn't tell for sure if their eyes actually met or not. He thought they did; it felt that way. Either way, it didn't matter. He knew the look. As a veteran of half a hundred picket lines, he knew it well. He also knew it as a drunk who had awakened in the tank on more than one occasion.

The Dallas Police have arrived at last, he thought. The thought carried feelings of anger and regret . . . but what he felt mostly was relief. At least, for the moment.

He's a cop . . . but what's he doing in a Jeep? God, the size of his face . . . he's as big as a fucking house! Must be a dream. Must *be.*

The Jeep didn't stop; it rolled up the driveway and out of sight. Now Gardener could only hear its roaring motor.

Headed out back. Going up there in the woods. They knew, all right. Oh Christ, if the government gets it—

All of his earlier dismay rose in him like bile; his dazed relief blew away like smoke. He saw Ted the Power Man throwing his jacket over the littered remains of the levitation machine and saying, *What gadget?*

Dismay was replaced by the old, sick fury.

HEY BOBBI GET YOUR ASS OUT HERE! he shrieked in his mind as loudly and clearly as he could.

Fresh blood burst from his nose and he staggered weakly back, grimacing in disgust and groping for his handkerchief. *What does it matter, anyway? Let them have it. It's the devil on either hand, and you know it. So what if the Dallas Police get it? It's turning Bobbi and everyone in town into the Dallas Police. Particularly her company. The ones she brings out late at night, when she thinks I'm asleep. The ones she takes into the shed.*

This had happened twice, both times around three in the morning. Bobbi thought Gardener was sleeping heavily—a combination of hard work, too much booze, and Valium. The level of pills in the Valium bottle was going steadily down, that was true, but not because Gardener was swallowing them. Each night's pill was actually going down the toilet.

Why this stealth? He didn't know, any more than he knew why he had lied to Bobbi about what he had seen on Sunday afternoon. Flushing a Valium tablet every night wasn't really *lying,* because Bobbi hadn't asked him outright if he was taking them; she had simply looked at the decreasing level of the tablets and drawn an erroneous conclusion Gardener hadn't bothered to correct.

Just as he had not bothered to correct her idea that he was sleeping heavily. In fact, he had been plagued by insomnia. No amount of drink seemed to put him under for long. The result was a kind of constant, muddled consciousness across which thin gray veils of sleep were sometimes drawn, like unwashed stockings.

The first time he had seen lights splash across the wall of the guestroom in the early hours of the morning, he had looked out to see a large Cadillac pulling into the driveway. He had looked at his watch and thought: *Must be the Mafia . . . who else would show up at a farm way out in the woods in a Caddy at three in the morning?*

But when the porch light went on, he had seen the vanity plate, KYLE-1, and doubted if even the Mafia went for vanity plates.

Bobbi had joined the four men and one woman who had gotten out. Bobbi was dressed but barefoot. Gardener knew two of the men—Dick Allison, head of the local volunteer fire department, and Kyle Archinbourg, a local realtor who drove a fat-ass Cadillac. The two others were vaguely familiar. The woman was Hazel McCready.

After a few moments Bobbi had led them to her back shed. The one with the big Kreig lock on the door.

Gardener thought: *Maybe I ought to go out there. See what's going on.* Instead, he'd lain down again. He didn't want to go *near* the shed. He was afraid of it. Of what might be in there.

He had dozed off again.

The next morning there had been no Caddy, no sign of Bobbi's company. Bobbi had in fact seemed more cheerful, more her old self on that morning than at any time since Gardener had returned. He had convinced himself it was a dream, or perhaps something—not the DTs, exactly, but close—that had crawled out of a bottle. Then, not four nights ago, KYLE-1 had arrived again. Those same people had gotten out, met with Bobbi, and gone around to the shed.

Gard collapsed into Bobbi's rocking chair and felt for the bottle of Scotch he had brought out here this morning. The bottle was there. Gardener raised it slowly, drank, and felt liquid fire hit his belly and spread. The sound of the Jeep was fading now, like something in a dream. Perhaps that was all it had been. Everything seemed that way now. What was that line in the Paul Simon song? *Michigan seems like a dream to me now.* Yes, sir. Michigan, weird ships buried in the ground, Jeep Cherokees, and Cadillacs in the middle of the night. Drink enough and it all faded into a dream.

Except it's no dream. They're the take-charge people, those people who come in the Cadillac with the KYLE-1 plates. Just like the Dallas Police. Just like good old Ted, with his reactors. What kind of shot are you giving them, Bobbi? How are you souping them up even more than the rest of the resident geniuses? The old Bobbi wouldn't have pulled that kind of shit but the New Improved Bobbi does, and what's the answer to all of this? Is there one?

"Devils on every side!" Gardener cried out grandly. He slugged back the last of the Scotch and threw the bottle over the porch railing and into the bushes. "Devils on every side!" he repeated, and passed out.

16

"That guy saw us," Butch said as the Jeep bulled across Anderson's garden on a diagonal, knocking over huge cornstalks and sunflowers that towered high over the Cherokee's roof.

"I don't care," Ev said, wrestling the wheel. They emerged from the garden on the far side. The Cherokee's wheels rolled over a number of pumpkins that were coming to full growth amazingly early. Their hides were strangely pale, and when they burst they disclosed unpleasant fleshy-pink interiors. "If they don't know we're in town by now, then I'm wrong about everything . . . Look! Didn't I tell you?"

A wide, rutted track wound into the woods. Ev bounced onto it.

"There was blood on his face." Dugan swallowed. It was hard. His head ached very badly now, and all the fillings in his teeth seemed to be vibrating very fast. His guts were churning again. "And his shirt. Looked like somebody popped him one in the n—

"Pull over, I'm going to be sick again."

Ev jammed on the brakes. Dugan opened his door and leaned out, vomited a thin yellow stream onto the dirt, and then closed his eyes for a moment. The world was swooping and turning.

Voices rustled in his head. A great many voices.

(Gard saw them he's yelling for help)

(how many)

(two two in a Cherokee they were headed)

"Look," Butch heard himself say, as if from a great distance, "I don't want to spoil the party, but I'm sick. *Seriously* sick."

"Thought you might be." Hillman's voice came down a long, echoing hall. Somehow Butch managed to haul himself up again in the passenger seat, but he didn't even have strength enough to pull the door closed. He felt as weak as a new kitten. "You ain't had time to build up any resistance, and we're right where it's strongest. Hold on. I got something that'll fix you up. Least I think I do."

Ev pushed the switch that lowered the Cherokee's electric rear window, got out, lowered the tailgate, and pulled out the gunnysack. He dragged it back to the Jeep and then hoisted it onto the seat. He glanced at Dugan, and didn't like what he saw. The trooper's face was the color of candlewax. His eyes were shut, the lids purplish. His mouth was half-open and he was breathing in quick, shallow gasps. Ev found a moment to wonder how whatever-it-was could be doing that to Dugan when he himself felt nothing, absolutely nothing.

"Hang on, friend," he said, and used his pocketknife to cut the rope holding the neck of the bag.

". . . sick . . ." Dugan wheezed, and retched brownish fluid. Ev saw that there were three teeth in the mess.

He got out a light plastic oxygen-supply tank—what the clerk at Maine Med Supplies had called a flat-pack. He stripped the gold-foil circle from the end of the hose leading out of the flat-pack, revealing a stainless-steel female connector. Now he brought out a gold-colored plastic cup—the sort jet airliners come equipped with. A segmented white plastic tube was attached to this, and at the end there was a white plastic male connector—a valve.

If this don't work the way that guy said it would, I do believe this big fella's going to die on me.

He slammed the male connector of the mask into the female connector on the oxygen supply—violent intercourse which he hoped would result in keeping Dugan going. He heard oxygen sighing gently inside the gold cup. All right. So far, so good.

He leaned over and put the cup over Dugan's mouth and nose, using the elastic straps. Then he waited anxiously to see what would happen. If Dugan didn't come out of his tailspin in thirty or forty seconds, he would haul ass. David was missing and Hilly was sick, but neither thing gave him the right to murder Dugan, who hadn't known what sort of mess he was getting into.

Twenty seconds passed. Then thirty.

Ev dropped the Cherokee into reverse, meaning to turn around on the edge of Anderson's garden, when Dugan gasped, jerked, and opened his eyes. They looked very wide and blue and bewildered above the rim of the gold cup. Some color had come back into his cheeks.

"What the hell—" His hands groped for the cup.

"Leave it on," Ev said, putting one of his big arthritis-warped old hands over one of Butch's. "It was the outside air poisoning you. You in a hurry for another dose?"

Butch stopped reaching for the cup. It bobbed on his face as he said, "How long will this stuff last?"

"Twenty-five minutes or so, the guy said. It's a demand valve, though. Every now and then you can pull it down. When you start feeling woozy again, put it back on. I want to go on in, if you think you can. It can't be far, and . . . and I feel like I got to know."

Butch Dugan nodded.

The Cherokee lurched forward again. Dugan stared

out at the woods around them. Silent. No birds. No animals. No nothing. This was very wrong. Very bad and very damned *wrong*.

Faintly, far back in his mind, he could hear thoughts like a whisper of shortwave transmissions.

He looked at Ev. "What the blue fuck is going on here, anyway?"

"That's to find out." Without taking his eyes off the rough track, Ev rummaged in the sack. Dugan winced as the Cherokee's undercarriage screamed over a stump sawed off a little higher than the others.

Ev brought out a big .45. It looked old enough for its original owner to have carried it in World War I.

"Yours?" Dugan asked. It was amazing how fast the oxygen was bringing him around.

"Yeah. They teach you to use these things, don't they?"

"Yes." Although the one Hillman had looked like an antique.

"You might have to use it today," Ev said, and handed it over.

"What—"

"Have a care. It's loaded."

Up ahead, the land suddenly sloped downward. Through the trees came a giant reflection: sunshine bouncing off a huge metal object.

Ev stamped the brake, suddenly terrified to the depths of his heart.

"What the hell?" he heard Dugan mutter beside him.

Ev opened the door and got out. As his feet touched the ground, he became aware that the earth was criss-crossed with small dusty cracks and that it was vibrating very rapidly. At the next moment music so loud that it was deafening blew through his head at gale force. It went on for perhaps thirty seconds, but the pain was excruciating and it seemed forever. At last, it simply winked out.

He saw Dugan standing in front of the Cherokee, the cup now hooked under his chin. He held the flat-pack by the strap in one hand, the .45 in the other. He was looking at Ev apprehensively.

"I'm all right," Ev said.

"Yeah? Your nose is bleeding. Just like that guy back at the farm we passed."

Ev wiped his nose with his finger and looked at the

smear of blood. He wiped his finger on his pants and nodded toward Dugan. "Remember to put the mask back on when you start to feel woozy."

"Oh, don't worry."

Ev leaned back into the Cherokee and rummaged in his bag of tricks again. He brought out a Kodak disk camera and something that looked like a cross between a pistol and a blow-dryer.

"Your flare-gun?" Dugan asked, smiling a little.

"Ayuh. Get on the gas again, Trooper. Your losin y'color."

Dugan pulled it up, and the two men started toward that glittering thing in the woods. Fifty feet from the Cherokee, Ev stopped. It was more than huge; it was titanic, a thing that would perhaps be large enough to dwarf an ocean liner when completely uncovered.

"Gimme your hand," he said roughly to Dugan.

Dugan did as he asked, but wanted to know why.

"Because I'm scared shitless," Ev said. Dugan squeezed his hand. Ev's arthritis flared, but he squeezed back anyway. After a moment, the two men started forward again.

17

Bobbi and Jud got the guns from the hardware store and put them in the back of the pickup. The side trip hadn't taken long but Dick and the others had gotten a good start and Bobbi pushed the pickup as fast as she dared to catch up. The truck's shadow, shortening as the day approached noon, ran beside them.

Bobbi suddenly stiffened a little behind the wheel. "Did you hear it?"

"Heard something," Jud said. "It was your friend, wasn't it?"

Bobbi nodded. "Gard saw them. He's yelling for help."

"How many?"

"Two. In a Jeep. They were headed out to where the ship is."

Jud brought a fist down on one leg. "The fuckers! The dirty snooping fuckers!"

"We'll catch them," Bobbi said. "Don't worry."

They were at the farm fifteen minutes later. Bobbi pulled her truck in behind Allison's Nova and Archinbourg's Cadillac. She looked at the group of men and thought how much like the nights they had met out here this was . . . the ones who were to be made

(to "become" first)

especially strong. But Hazel wasn't here and Beach was; Joe Summerfield and Adley McKeen had never been inside the shed either.

"Get the guns," she told Jud. "Joe, you help. Remember—no shooting unless you have to, and don't shoot the cop, no matter what."

She looked toward the porch and saw Gard lying there on his back. Gard's mouth was open and he was breathing in slow, rusty snores. Bobbi's eyes softened. There were plenty of people in Haven—Dick Allison and Newt Berringer probably chief among them—who thought she should long since have gotten rid of Gard. Nothing had been said out loud, but in Haven you no longer *had* to say things out loud. Bobbi knew if she put a bullet through Gard's head, there would be a whole platoon of willing workers out here an hour later to help bury him. They didn't like Gard because the plate in his head made him immune to the "becoming." And it made him hard to read. But he was her brake. And even that was crap. The truth was simpler yet: she still loved him. She was still human enough for that.

And they would all have to admit that, drunk or not, when they had needed a warning, Gard had given it.

Jud and Joe Summerfield came back with the rifles. There were six of them, varied calibers. Bobbi saw that five went to people she could trust completely. She gave the sixth, a .22, to Beach, who would complain if he didn't get a shooting iron.

Occupied with the ritual of guns, none of them saw that Gardener had half-opened his bloodshot eyes and was looking at them. No one heard his thoughts; he had learned how to seal them off.

"Let's go," Bobbi said. "And remember: I want that cop."

They moved out in a group.

18

Ev and Butch stood well back from the edge of what was now a ragged slash running better than three hundred yards from right to left and yawning sixty feet across at its widest point. Anderson's old mongrel of a truck stood off to one side, looking tired and used. Next to it was the souped-up payloader with its giant screwdriver snout. There were other tools in a lean-to of peeled logs. Ev saw a chainfall on one side, a chipper on the other. There was a big pile of sodden sawdust below the mouth of the chipper's exhaust vent. There were cans of gasoline in the lean-to, and a black drum labeled DIESEL. When Ev had first heard those noises in the woods, he had thought New England Paper must be doing some logging, but this was no logging operation. This was an excavation.

That dish. That monstrous dish glittering in the sun.

The eye could not stay away; it was drawn back again and again. Gardener and Bobbi had removed a lot more hillside. Ninety feet of polished silver-gray metal now jutted out of the earth and into the green-gold sunlight. If they had looked into the slash, they would have seen another forty feet or better.

Neither of them went close enough to look.

"Holy Jesus," Dugan said. The gold cup bobbed on his face, and above its rim his blue eyes bulged. "Holy Jesus, it's a spaceship. Is it ours or is it Russian, do you think? Holy Jesus *Christ,* it's as big as the *Queen Mary,* that ain't Russian, that ain't . . . ain't . . ."

He fell silent again. In spite of the oxygen, his headache was coming back.

Ev raised the disk camera and clicked off seven shots as fast as his finger could push the camera's button. Then he moved twenty feet to the left and took another five, standing by the chipper.

"Move to the right!" he said to Dugan.

"Huh?"

"Your right! I want you in these last three, for perspective."

"Forget it, Pop!" Even muffled by the cup, there was a shrill note in Dugan's voice.

"You don't have to. Four steps will do it."

Dugan moved four very small steps to the right. Ev

raised the disk camera again—a Father's Day present from Bryant and Marie—and clicked off the final three shots. Dugan was a very big man, but the ship in the earth reduced him to the size of a pygmy.

"Okay," Ev said. Dugan stepped quickly back to where he had been. He walked with mincing, tentative steps, looking at the great round object as he went.

Ev wondered if the pictures would turn out. His hands had been shaking. And the ship—for it certainly was some sort of spaceship—might be putting out radiation that would fog the film.

Even if it does come out, who's gonna believe it? Who, in a world where kids go off to the movies every damn Saturday and see things like Star Wars?

"I want to get out of here," Dugan said.

Ev looked at the ship a moment longer, wondering if David was in there, imprisoned, wandering through unknowable corridors or passing through doorways cut for no human shape, starving in the darkness. *No . . . if he was in there, he would have starved a long time ago. Starved, or died of thirst.*

Then he slipped the small camera in his pants pocket, walked back to Dugan, and picked up the flare gun. "Ayuh. I guess—"

He broke off, looking in the direction of the Cherokee. There was a line of men—and one woman—standing in the trees, some armed. Ev recognized all of them . . . and none of them.

19

Bobbi started down the slope toward the two men. The others followed.

"Hello, Ev," Bobbi said pleasantly enough.

Dugan raised the .45, wishing bitterly for the familiar feel of his service .357. "Stop," he said. He didn't like the way the gold cup muffled the word, robbed it of authority. He pulled the air mask down. "*All* of you. Those of you with rifles, put them down. You're all under arrest."

"You're outgunned, Butch," Newt Berringer said pleasantly.

"Damned tooting!" Beach growled. Dick Allison frowned at him.

"You better put y'mask on again, Butch," Adley McKeen said with a lazy, mocking smile. "I think you're losing it."

Butch had begun to feel woozy as soon as he pulled the mask off. Hearing the steady whisper of their thoughts made it worse. He pulled it up, wondering how much air could be left in the flat-pack.

"Put it down," Bobbi said. "And you put down the flare-gun, Ev. No one wants to hurt you two."

"Where's David?" Ev asked roughly. "I want him, you bitch."

"He's on Altair-4 with Robby the Robot and Dr. Mobius," Kyle Archinbourg said with a titter. "He's picnicking amid the Krell memory-banks."

"Shut up," Bobbi said. She suddenly felt confused, ashamed of herself, unsure. Bitch? Was that what the old man had called her? A bitch? She found herself wanting to tell him that he was confused—*she* wasn't a bitch. That was her sister Anne.

A sudden, confused image came to her—the old man's distress, Gard's distress, even her own, all mingled. She was distracted. While she was, Ev Hillman raised the flare-pistol and fired. If Dugan had done it, they would have read his intention before he could have acted, but the old man was different.

There was a hollow *fuddd!* and a whoosh. Beach Jernigan exploded into white flame and staggered backward, the .22 flying out of his hands. His eyes filmed, simmered, then burst as they filled with burning phosphorus. His cheeks began to run. He opened his mouth and began to claw at his chest as the superheated air he drew in expanded and ruptured his lungs. This all happened in a space of seconds.

The line of men wavered and lost coherency as they stumbled backward, their faces blank with terror. They were hearing Beach Jernigan die inside their heads.

"Come on!" Ev shrieked at Dugan, and ran for the Cherokee. Jud Tarkington moved sluggishly to stop him. Ev swept the hot barrel of the flaregun across his face, branding his cheek and breaking his nose. Jud went flailing backward, stumbled over his own feet, went sprawling.

Beach was burning on the muddy, churned ground. He

clawed weakly at his throat with one twisted, tallowy hand, shuddered, and then stilled.

Dugan got moving, running after the old man, who was clawing at the driver's-side door of the Cherokee.

Bobbi heard Beach's thoughts fade away, wink out, and turned to see that the old man and the cop were on the verge of getting away.

Jesus Christ you guys *stop* them!

That broke their paralysis, but Bobbi moved first. She got to Ev and slammed the butt of the shotgun she was carrying into the nape of the old man's neck. Ev's face whacked the top of the Jeep's door. Blood sprayed from his nose and he dropped to his knees, dazed. Bobbi raised the shotgun butt to hit him again, when Dugan, standing on the other side of the Cherokee, fired the old man's .45 through the passenger window.

Bobbi felt a large hot hammer suddenly slam her lower right shoulder. Her right arm was driven powerfully upward, and she lost her grip on the shotgun. The hammer numbed her flesh for a moment and then the heat was back, an expanding furnace glow that was baking her from the inside out.

She was thrown backward, her left hand going for the place the hammer had hit her, expecting to find blood, finding none—at least, not yet—only a hole in her shirt and in the flesh beneath. The hole had hard edges that felt hot and throbby. Blood was running down her back, a lot of it, but shock had numbed her and she felt little pain yet. Her left hand had found the small entrance wound; the exit wound was as big as a kid's fist.

She saw Dick Allison, his face white and slack with panic

this isn't going right Christ not right at all get him before he gets us oh you fucking snoop fucking snoop FUCKING SNOOP!

"Don't shoot him!" Bobbi screamed. Pain exploded through her. Blood flew from her mouth in a scrawny spray. The bullet had torn her right lung open.

Allison hesitated. Before Dugan could raise the gun again, Newt and Joe Summerfield had stepped in. Dugan turned toward them, and Newt clubbed the barrel of his rifle down on the hand holding the .45 as he did. Dugan's second shot went into the dirt.

"Hold it, Trooper, hold it or you're dead!" John Enders,

the grammar-school principal, screamed. *"Four guns on you right now!"*

Dugan looked around. He saw four men with rifles. And Allison, still walleyed and only one small step from unglued, looked ready to shoot the moment a squirrel farted.

They'll kill you anyway. Might as well go out like John Wayne. Shit, they're all crazy.

"No," Bobbi said. She was leaning against the Jeep's hood now. Blood trickled steadily from her mouth. The back of her shirt was soaking. "We're not crazy. We're not going to kill you. Check me."

Dugan probed clumsily toward Bobbi Anderson's mind and saw that she meant it . . . but there was a catch somewhere, something he might have caught on to if he hadn't been so new at this eerie mind-reading trick. It was like the fine print in some slick car salesman's contract. He would think about it later. These guys were amateurs, and there might still be a chance to get away clean. If . . .

Suddenly Adley McKeen ripped the gold mask off his face. Butch felt a wave of dizziness almost at once.

"I like you better this way," Adley said. "You won't think s'much about excapin with your goddam canned air turned off."

Butch fought the dizziness and looked back at Bobbi Anderson. *I think she's going to die.*

think what you want

He straightened and took a step backward as that unexpected thought filled his head. He looked at her more closely.

"What about the old man?" he asked flatly.

"Not—" Bobbi coughed, spraying more blood. Bubbles formed on her nostrils. Kyle and Newt started toward her. Bobbi waved them back. "Not your business. You and me are going to get in the front of the Jeep. You drive. There'll be three men with guns in the back, if you think of trying anything funny."

"I want to know what's going to happen to the old man," Butch repeated.

Bobbi raised her gun with a great effort. She brushed her sweaty hair away from her eyes with her left hand. Her right dangled uselessly by her side. It was as if she wanted Dugan to see her very clearly, to measure her. Butch did. The coldness he saw in her eyes was real.

"I don't want to kill you," she said softly. "You know that. But if you say one more word, I'll have these men execute you right here. We'll bury you next to Beach and take our chances."

Ev Hillman was struggling to his feet. He looked dazed, not sure where he was. He armed blood off his forehead like sweat.

Another wave of dizziness washed through Butch, and a thought of infinite comfort came to him: *This is a dream. All just a dream.*

Bobbi smiled without humor. "Think that if you want," she said. "Just get in the Jeep."

Butch got in and slid across behind the wheel. Bobbi started around to the passenger side. She began coughing again, spraying blood, and her knees buckled. Two of the others had to help her.

Never mind the "think." I know *she's going to die.*

Bobbi turned her head and looked at him. That clear mental voice

(think what you want)

filled his head again.

Archinbourg, Summerfield, and McKeen crammed into the back seat of the Cherokee.

"Drive," Bobbi whispered. "Slow."

Butch began to back up. He would see Everett Hillman once more but would not remember—later, most of Butch's mind would have been rubbed away like chalk from a blackboard. The old man stood there in the sunlight, that stupendous saucer-shape behind him. He was surrounded by big men, and five feet to his left, there was something on the ground that looked like a charred log.

You didn't do too bad, old man. In your day you must have been quite a high rider . . . and you sure as hell weren't crazy.

Hillman looked up and shrugged, as if to say: *Well, we tried.*

More dizziness. Butch's sight wavered.

"I'm not sure I can drive," he said, his voice seeming to boom into his ears from a great distance. "That thing . . . it makes me sick."

"Is there any air left in his little kit, Adley?" Bobbi

whispered. Her face was ashy pale. The blood on her lips seemed very red by comparison.

"Face mask's hissin a little."

"Put it on him."

A moment after it was jammed firmly over Butch's mouth and nose again, he began to improve.

"Enjoy it while you can," Bobbi whispered, and then passed out.

20

"Ashes to ashes . . . dust to dust. Thus we commit the body of our friend Ruth McCausland to the ground, and her soul to a loving God."

The mourners had moved on to the pretty little graveyard on the hill west of the village. They stood loosely gathered around an open grave. Ruth's casket was suspended over it on runners. There were far fewer mourners here than there had been in the church; many of the out-of-towners, either headachy and nauseated or glowing feverishly with strange new ideas, had taken the chance afforded by the intermission between acts to slip away.

The flowers at the head of the grave ruffled gently in a fresh summer breeze. As the Rev. Goohringer raised his head, he saw a bright yellow rose go twirling down the grassy hill. Beyond and below Homeland's weatherbeaten white fence, he could see the town-hall clock-tower. It wavered slightly in the bright air, like something seen through a heat-haze. Still, Goohringer thought, it was a damned good illusion. These strangers in town had seen the best magic-lantern slide in history and didn't even know it.

His eyes met Frank Spruce's for just an instant—he read relief clearly in Frank's eyes, and he supposed Frank could see it just as clearly in his own. Many of the outsiders would go back to wherever they came from and tell their friends that Ruth's death had rocked the little community to its foundations; they had hardly seemed to be there at all. What none of them knew, Goohringer reflected, was that they had been following the events near the ship with most of their attention. For a while things out there had gone very badly. Now they were under control again, but Bobbi Anderson might die if they couldn't get her back to the shed in time, and that was bad.

Still, things were under control. The "becoming" would continue. That was the only important consideration.

Goohringer held his Bible open in one hand. Its pages fluttered a little in the wind. Now he raised the other hand in the air. The mourners standing around Ruth's grave lowered their heads.

"May the Lord bless you and keep you; may the Lord lift up His face and make it shine upon you and give you peace. Amen."

The mourners raised their heads. Goohringer smiled. "There'll be refreshments in the library, for those of you who'd care to stop by for a while and remember Ruth," he said.

Act II was over.

21

Kyle reached gently into Bobbi's pants pocket and probed until he found her keyring. He worked it out, picked through the keys, and found the one that opened the padlock on the shed door. He inserted the key in the lock but didn't turn it.

Adley and Joe Summerfield were covering Dugan, who was still behind the wheel of the Jeep. Butch was finding it harder and harder to pull air from the mask. The needle on the supply dial had been in the red for five minutes now. Kyle rejoined them.

"Go check the drunk," Kyle said to Joe Summerfield. "Looks like he's still passed out, but I don't trust the fucker."

Joe crossed the side yard, climbed the porch, and examined Gardener carefully, wincing at his sour breath. This time there really was no sham; Gardener had gotten a fresh bottle of Scotch and had drunk himself into oblivion.

As the two other men stood waiting for Joe to come back, Kyle said: "Bobbi is most likely going to die. If she does, I'm going to get rid of that lush first thing."

Joe came back. "He's out."

Kyle nodded and turned the key in the shed's padlock as Joe joined Adley in keeping the cop covered. Kyle pulled the lock free and opened the door partway. Brilliant green light poured out—it was so bright it seemed to dim the sunlight. There was an odd liquid churning sound. It was almost (but not quite) the sound of machinery.

Kyle took an involuntary step backward, his face tightening momentarily into an expression of fright, revulsion, and awe. The smell alone—thick and fetid and organic—was damn near enough to knock a man over. Kyle understood—they all did—that the two-hearted nature of the Tommyknockers was now growing together. The dance of deception was nearly done.

Liquid churning sounds, that smell . . . and then another sound. Something like the feeble, bubbly yap of a drowning dog.

Kyle had been in the shed twice before, but remembered little about it. He knew, of course, that it was an important place, a fine place, and that it had speeded his own "becoming." But the human part of him was still almost superstitiously afraid of it.

He came back to Adley and Joe.

"We can't wait for the others. We've got to get Bobbi in there right now if there's going to be any chance of saving her at all."

The cop, he saw, had taken off the mask. It lay, used up, on the seat beside him. That was good. As Adley had said out in the woods, he would think less about escaping without his canned air.

"Keep your gun on the cop," Kyle said. "Joe, help me with Bobbi."

"Help you take her into the shed?"

"No, help me take her to the Rumford Zoo so she can see the fucking lion!" Kyle shouted. "Of course, the shed!"

"I don't . . . I don't think I want to go in there. Not just now." Joe looked from that green light back to Kyle, a shamed, slightly sickened smile on his lips.

"I'll help you," Adley said softly. "Bobbi's a good old sport. Be a shame if she croaked before we got to the end of it."

"All right," Kyle said. "Cover the cop," he said to Joe. "And if you screw up, I swear to God I'll kill you."

"I won't, Kyle," Joe said. That shamed grin still hung on his mouth, but there was no mistaking the relief in his eyes. "I sure won't. I'll watch him good."

"See that you do," Bobbi said feebly. It startled them all.

Kyle looked at her, then back to Joe. Joe flinched away from the naked contempt in Kyle's eyes . . . but he didn't look toward the shed, toward that light, those churning, squelching sounds.

"Come on, Adley," Kyle said at last. "Let's get Bobbi in there. Soonest started, soonest done."

Adley McKeen, fiftyish, balding, and stocky, flagged for only a moment. "Is it . . ." he licked his lips. "Kyle, is it bad? In there?"

"I don't really remember," Kyle said. "All I know is I felt wonderful when I came out. Like I knew more. Could *do* more."

"Oh," Adley said in an almost nonexistent voice.

"You'll be one of us, Adley," Bobbi said in that same feeble voice.

Adley's face, although still frightened, firmed up again. "All right," he said.

"Let's try not to hurt her," Kyle said.

They got Bobbi into the shed. Joe Summerfield turned his attention briefly away from Dugan to watch them disappear into that glow—and it seemed to him that they really did disappear rather than just step inside; it was like watching objects disappear into a dazzling corona.

His lapse was brief, but it was all the old Butch Dugan would have needed. Even now he saw the opportunity; he was simply unable to use it. No strength in his legs. Churning nausea in his stomach. His head thudded and pounded.

I don't want to go in there.

Nothing he could do about it if they decided to drag him in, though. He was as weak as a kitten.

He drifted.

After a while he heard voices and raised his head. It took an effort, because it seemed as if someone had poured cement into one of his ears until his head was full of it. The rest of the posse was pushing out of the tangle that was Bobbi Anderson's garden. They were shoving the old man roughly along. Hillman's feet tangled and he fell down. One of them—Tarkington—kicked him to his feet, and Butch got the run of Tarkington's thoughts clearly: he was outraged at what he thought of as the murder of Beach Jernigan.

Hillman stumbled on toward the Cherokee. The shed door opened then. Kyle Archinbourg and Adley McKeen came out. McKeen no longer looked frightened—his eyes were glowing and a big toothless grin stretched his lips. But that wasn't all. Something else . . .

Then Butch realized.

In the few minutes the two men had been inside there, a large portion of Adley McKeen's hair appeared to have disappeared.

"I'll go in anytime, Kyle," he was saying. "No problem."

There was more, but now everything wanted to drift away again. Butch let it.

The world dimmed out until there was nothing left but those churning sounds and the afterimage of green light on his eyelids.

22

Act III.

They sat in the town library—the name would be changed to the Ruth McCausland Memorial Library, all agreed. They drank coffee, iced tea, Coca-Cola, ginger ale. They drank nothing that was alcoholic. Not at *Ruth's* wake. They ate tiny triangular tuna-fish sandwiches, they ate similar ones containing a paste of cream cheese and olives, they ate sandwiches containing a paste of cream cheese and pimiento. They ate cold cuts and a Jell-O salad with shreds of carrot suspended in it like fossils in amber.

They talked a great deal, but the room was mostly silent—if it had been bugged, the listeners would have been disappointed. The tension that had drawn many faces tight in the church as the situation in the woods teetered on the dangerous verge of careening out of control had now smoothed out. Bobbi was in the shed. That nosey-parker of an old man had also been taken in. Last of all, the nosey-parker policeman had been taken into the shed.

The group mind lost track of these people as they went into the thick, corroded-brass glow of that green light.

They ate and drank and listened and talked and no one said a word and that was all right; the last of the outsiders had left town following Goohringer's graveside benediction, and they had Haven to themselves again.

(will it be all right now)

(yes they'll understand about Dugan)

(are you sure)

(yes they will understand; they will think *they understand)*

The tick of the Seth Thomas on the mantelpiece, donated by the grammar school after last year's spring bottle-and-can drive, was the loudest sound in the room. Occasionally there was the decorous clink of a china cup. Faintly, beyond the open screened windows, the sound of a faraway airplane.

No birdsong.

It was not missed.

They ate and drank, and when Dugan was escorted from Bobbi's shed around one-thirty that afternoon, they knew. People rose, and now talk, *real* talk, began all at once. Tupperware bowls were capped. Uneaten sandwiches were popped into Baggies. Claudette Ruvall, Ashley's mother, put a piece of aluminum foil over the remains of the casserole she had brought. They all went outside and headed toward their homes, smiling and chatting.

Act III was over.

23

Gardener came to around sundown with a hangover headache and a feeling that things had happened which he could not quite remember.

Finally made it, Gard, he thought. *Finally had yourself another blackout. Satisfied?*

He managed to get off the porch and to walk shakily around the corner of the house, out of view of the road, before throwing up. He saw blood in the vomit, and wasn't surprised. This wasn't the first time, although there was more blood this time than ever before.

Dreams, Christ, he'd had some weird nightmares, blackout or no. People out here, coming and going, so many people that all they needed was a brass band and the Dallas

(Police, the Dallas Police were out here this morning and you got drunk so you wouldn't see them you fucking coward)

Cowgirls. Nightmares, that was all.

He turned away from the puddle of puke between his feet. The world was wavering in and out of focus with every beat of his heart, and Gardener suddenly knew that he had edged very close to death. He was committing suicide after all . . . just doing it slowly. He put his arm against the side of the house and his forehead on his arm.

"Mr. Gardener, are you all right?"

"Huh!" he cried, jerking upright. His heart slammed two violent beats, stopped for what seemed forever, and then began to beat so rapidly he could barely distinguish the individual pulses. His headache suddenly cranked up to overload. He whirled.

Bobby Tremain stood there, looking surprised, even a little amused . . . but not really sorry for the scare he had given Gardener.

"Gee, I didn't mean to creep up on you, Mr. Gardener—"

You fucking well did, and I fucking well know it.

The Tremain kid blinked rapidly several times. He had caught some of that, Gardener saw. He found he didn't give a shit.

"Where's Bobbi?" he asked.

"I'm—"

"I know who *you* are. I know *where* you are. Right in front of me. Where's *Bobbi?"*

"Well, I'll tell you," Bobby Tremain said. His face became very open, very wide-eyed, very honest, and Gardener was suddenly, forcibly reminded of his teaching days. This was how students who had spent a long winter weekend skiing, screwing, and drinking looked when they started to explain that they couldn't turn in their research papers today because their mothers had died on Saturday.

"Sure, tell me." Gardener leaned against the clapboard side of the house, looking at the teenager in the reddish glow of sunset. Over his shoulder he could see the shed, padlocked, its windows boarded up.

The shed had been in the dream, he remembered.

Dream? Or whatever it is you don't want to admit was real?

For a moment the kid looked genuinely disconcerted by Gardener's cynical expression.

"Miss Anderson had a sunstroke. Some of the men found her near the ship and took her to Derry Home Hospital. You were passed out."

Gardener straightened up quickly. "Is she all right?"

"I don't know. They're still with her. No one has called here. Not since three o'clock or so, anyway. That's when I got out here."

Gardener pushed away from the building and started around the house, head down, working against the hangover. He had believed the kid was going to lie, and perhaps he *had* lied about the *nature* of what had happened to Bobbi, but Gardener sensed a core of truth in what the kid said: Bobbi was sick, hurt, *something*. It explained those dreamlike comings and goings he remembered. He supposed Bobbi had called them with her mind. Sure. Called them with her mind, neatest trick of the week. Only in Haven, ladies and germs—

"Where are you going?" Tremain asked, his voice suddenly very sharp.

"Derry." Gardener had reached the head of the driveway. Bobbi's pickup was parked there. The Tremain kid's big yellow Dodge Challenger was pulled in next to it. Gardener turned back toward the kid. The sunset had painted harsh red highlights and black shadows on the boy's face, making him look like an Indian. Gardener took a closer look and realized he wasn't going anywhere. This kid with the fast car and the football-hero shoulders hadn't been put out here just to give Gard the bad news as soon as Gard managed to throw off enough of the booze to rejoin the living.

Am I supposed to believe Bobbi was out there in the woods, excavating away like a madwoman, and she keeled over with a sunstroke while her sometime partner was lying back on the porch drunk as a coot? That it? Well, that's a good trick, because she was supposed to be at the McCausland woman's funeral. She went into the village and I was out here alone and I started thinking about what I saw Sunday . . . I started thinking and then I started drinking, which is mostly the way it works with me. Of course Bobbi could *have gone to the funeral, come back here, changed, gone out in the woods to work, and then had a sunstroke . . . except that isn't what happened. The kid's lying. It's written all over his face, and all of a sudden I'm very fucking glad he can't read my thoughts.*

"I think Miss Anderson would rather have you stay here and keep on with the work," Bobby Tremain said evenly.

"*You* think?"

"That is, we *all* think." The kid looked momentarily more disconcerted than ever—wary, a bit rocky on his feet. *Didn't expect Bobbi's pet drunk to have any teeth or claws left, I guess.* That kicked off another, much queerer thought, and he looked at the kid more closely in the light which was now fading into orange and ashy pink. Football-hero shoulders, a handsome cleft-chinned face that might have been drawn by Alex Gordon or Berni Wrightson, deep chest, narrow waist. Bobby Tremain, All-American. No wonder the Colson girl was nuts over him. But that sunken, infirm-looking mouth went oddly with the rest, Gardener thought. *They* were the ones who kept losing teeth, not Gardener.

Okay—what's he here for?

To guard me. To make sure I stay put. No matter what.

"Well, all right," he said to Tremain in a softer, more conciliatory voice. "If that's what you all think."

Tremain relaxed a little. "It really is."

"Well, let's go in and put on the coffee. I could use some. My head aches. And we'll have to get going early in the morning . . ." He stopped and looked at Tremain. "You *are* going to help out, aren't you? That's part of it, isn't it?"

"Uh . . . yessir."

Gardener nodded. He looked at the shed for a moment, and in the fading light he could see brilliant green tattooed in the small spaces between the boards. For a moment his dream shimmered almost within his grasp—deadly shoemakers hammering away at unknown devices in that green glare. He had never seen the glow as bright as this before, and he noticed that when Tremain glanced in that direction, his eyes skittered away uneasily.

The lyric of an old song floated, not quite randomly, into Gardener's mind and then out again:

Don't know what they're doing, but they laugh a lot behind the green door . . . green door, what's that secret you're keepin'?

And there was a sound. Faint . . . rhythmic . . . not at all identifiable . . . but somehow unpleasant.

The two of them had faltered. Now Gardener moved on toward the house. Tremain followed him gratefully.

"Good," Gardener said, as if the conversation had never lagged. "I can use some help. Bobbi figured we'd get down to some sort of hatchway in about two weeks . . . that we'd be able to get inside."

"Yes, I know," Tremain said without hesitation.

"But that was with two of us working."

"Oh, there'll always be someone else with you," Tremain said, and smiled openly. A chill rippled up Gardener's back.

"Oh?"

"Yes! You bet!"

"Until Bobbi comes back."

"Until then," Tremain agreed.

Except he doesn't think Bobbi's going to be back. Ever.

"Come on," he said. "Coffee. Then maybe some chow."

"Sounds good to me."

They went inside, leaving the shed to churn and mutter to itself in the growing dark. As the sun disappeared, the stitching of green at the cracks grew brighter and brighter and brighter. A cricket hopped into the luminous pencil-mark one of these cracks printed onto the ground, and fell dead.

10.

A BOOK OF DAYS— THE TOWN, CONCLUDED

1

Thursday, July 28th:

Butch Dugan woke up in his own bed in Derry at exactly 3:05 A.M. He pushed back the covers and swung his feet out onto the floor. His eyes were wide and dazed, his face puffy with sleep. The clothes he had worn on his trip to Haven with the old man the day before were on the chair by his small desk. There was a pen in the breast pocket of the shirt. He wanted that pen. This seemed to be the only thought his mind would clearly admit.

He got up, went to the chair, took the pen, tossed the shirt on the floor, sat down, and then just sat for several moments looking out into the darkness, waiting for the next thought.

Butch had gone into Anderson's shed, but very little of him had come out. He seemed shrunken, lessened. He had no clear memories of anything. He could not have told a questioner his own middle name, and he did not at all remember being driven to the Haven-Troy town line in the Cherokee Hillman had rented, or sliding behind the wheel after Adley McKeen got out and walked back to Kyle Archinbourg's Cadillac. He likewise did not remember driving back to Derry. Yet all these things had happened.

He had parked the Cherokee in front of the old man's

apartment building, locked it, then got into his own car. Two blocks away, he had stopped long enough to drop the Jeep keys into a sewer.

He went directly to bed, and had slept until the alarm clock planted in his mind woke him up.

Now some new switch clicked over. Butch blinked once or twice, opened a drawer, and drew out a pad of paper. He wrote:

> *I told people Tues. night I couldn't go to her funeral because I was sick. That was true. But it was not my stomach. I was going to ask her to marry me but kept putting it off. Afraid she'd say no. If I hadn't been scared, she might be alive now. With her dead there doesn't seem to be anything to look forward to.*
>
> *I am sorry about this mess.*

He looked the note over for a moment and then signed his name at the bottom: *Anthony F. Dugan.*

He laid the pen and note aside and went back to sitting bolt upright and looking out the window.

At last another relay kicked over.

The last relay.

He got up and went to the closet. He ran the combination of the wall safe at the back and removed his .357 Mag. He put the belt over his shoulder, went back to the desk, and sat down.

He thought for a moment, frowning, then got up, turned off the light in the closet, shut the closet door, went back to the desk, sat down again, took the .357 from its holster, put the muzzle of the gun firmly against his left eyelid, and pulled the trigger. The chair toppled and hit the floor with a flat, undramatic wooden clap—the sound of a gallows trapdoor springing open.

2

Front page, Bangor Daily News, *Friday, July 29th:*

DERRY STATE POLICEMAN APPARENT SUICIDE
Was in Charge of Trooper Disappearance Investigation
by John Leandro

Cpt. Anthony "Butch" Dugan of the Derry state police barracks apparently shot himself with his service revolver early Thursday morning. His death hit the Derry barracks, which was rocked last week by the disappearance of two troopers, hard indeed . . .

3

Saturday, July 30th:

Gardener sat on a stump in the woods, his shirt off, eating a tuna-and-egg sandwich and drinking iced coffee laced with brandy. Across from him, sitting on another stump, was John Enders, the school principal. Enders was not built for hard work, and although it was only noon, he looked hot and tired and almost fagged out.

Gardener nodded toward him. "Not bad," he said. "Better than Tremain, anyway. Tremain'd burn water trying to boil it."

Enders smiled wanly. "Thank you."

Gardener looked beyond him to the great circular shape jutting from the ground. The ditch kept widening, and they had to keep using more and more of that silvery netting which somehow kept it from caving in (he had no idea how they made it, only knew that the large supply in the cellar had been almost depleted and then, yesterday, a couple of women from town had come out in a van with a fresh supply, neatly folded like freshly ironed curtains). They needed more because they kept taking away more and more of the hillside . . . and still the thing continued down. Bobbi's whole house could now have fit into its shadow.

He looked at Enders again. Enders was looking at it with an expression of adoring, religious awe—as if he were a rube druid and this was his first trip from the boonies to see Stonehenge.

Gardener got up, staggering slightly. "Come on," he said. "Let's do a little blasting."

He and Bobbi had reached a point weeks earlier where the ship was as tightly embedded in dour bedrock as a piece of steel in concrete. The bedrock hadn't hurt the ship; hadn't put so much as a scratch on its pearl-gray hull, let alone dented or crushed it. But it was tightly plugged. The plug had to be blasted away. It would have been a job for a construction crew who understood how to use dynamite—a *lot* of dynamite—under other circumstances.

But there was explosive available in Haven these days that made dynamite obsolete. Gardener still wasn't clear on what the explosion in Haven Village had been, and wasn't sure he ever wanted to be clear on it. It was a moot point anyway, because no one was talking. Whatever it had been, he was sure that some huge piece of brickwork had taken off like a rocket, and some of those New and Improved Explosives had been involved. There had been a time, he remembered, when he had actually wasted time speculating on whether or not the super brain-food Bobbi's artifact was putting into the air could produce weapons. That time now seemed incredibly distant, that Jim Gardener incredibly naive.

"Can you make it, Johnny?" he asked the school principal.

Enders got up, wincing, putting his hands in the small of his back. He looked desperately tired, but he managed a small smile just the same. Looking at the ship seemed to refresh him. Blood was trickling from the corner of one eye, however—a single red tear. Something in there had ruptured. *It's being this close to the ship,* Gard thought. On the first of the two days Bobby Tremain had spent "helping" him, he had spit out his last few teeth like machine-gun bullets almost as soon as they got here.

He thought of telling Enders that something behind his right eye was leaking, then decided to let him discover it on his own. The guy would be all right. Probably. Even if he wasn't, Gardener wasn't sure he cared . . . this more than anything else shocked him.

Why should it? Are you kidding yourself that these cats are human anymore? If you are, you better wise up, Gard ole Gard.

He headed down the slope, stopping at the last stump before rocky soil gave way to chipped and runneled bedrock. He picked up a cheap transistor radio made of yellow high-impact plastic. It looked like Snoopy. Attached to it was the board from a Sharp calculator. And, of course, batteries.

Humming, Gardener made his way down to the edge

of the trench. There the music dried up and he was quiet, only staring at the titanic gray flank of the ship. The view did not refresh him, but it did inspire a deep awe which had overtones of steadily darkening fear.

But you still hope, too. You'd be a liar if you said you didn't. The key could still be here . . . somewhere.

As the fear darkened, however, the hope did too. Soon he thought it would be gone.

The hillside excavation now made the ship's flank too far away to touch—not that he wanted to; he didn't enjoy the sensation of having his head turning into a very large speaker. It hurt. He rarely bled now when he did touch it (and touching it was sometimes inevitable), but the blast of radio always came, and on occasion his nose or ears could still spray a hell of a lot more blood than he cared to look at. Gardener wondered briefly just how much borrowed time he was now living on, but that question was also moot. From the morning he had awakened on that New Hampshire breakwater, it had all been borrowed time. He was a sick man and he knew it, but not too sick to appreciate the irony of the situation in which he found himself: after busting his hump to dig this fucker up with a variety of tools which looked as if they might have come out of the Hugo Gernsback Whole Universe Catalogue, after doing what the rest of them probably couldn't have done without working themselves to death in a kind of hypnotic trance, he might not be able to go inside when and if they came to the hatch Bobbi believed was there. But he meant to try. You could bet your watch and chain on that.

Now he set his boot into a rope stirrup, slid the knot tight, and put the Snoopy radio in his shirt. "Let me down easy, Johnny."

Enders began to turn a windlass and Gardener began to slide downward. Beside him the smooth gray hull slid up and up and up.

If they wanted to get rid of him, this would be as easy a way as any, he supposed. Just send a telepathic order to Enders: *Let go of the wheel, John. We're through with him.* And down he would plunge, forty feet to the solid bedrock at the bottom, slack rope trailing up behind him. Crunch.

But of course he was at their mercy anyhow . . . and he supposed they recognized his usefulness, however reluctantly. The Tremain kid was young, strong as a bull, but he had fagged out in two days. Enders was going to last out today—maybe—but Gardener would have bet his watch and chain *(what* watch and chain, ha-ha?) that there would be somebody else out here tomorrow to keep tabs on him.

Bobbi was okay.

Bullshit *she was—if you hadn't come back, she would've killed herself.*

But she hung in there better than Enders or the Tremain kid—

His mind returned inexorably: *Bobbi went into the shed with the others. Tremain and Enders never did . . . at least, not that you ever saw. Maybe that's the difference.*

So what's in there? Ten thousand angels dancing on the head of a pin? The ghost of James Dean? The Shroud of Turin? What?

He didn't know.

His foot touched down at the bottom.

"I'm down!" he yelled.

Enders' face, looking very small, appeared at the edge of the cut. Beyond, Gardener could see a tiny wedge of blue sky. *Too* tiny. Claustrophobia whispered in his ear—a voice as rough as sandpaper.

The space between the side of the ship and the wall covered with that silvery netting was very narrow down here. Gardener had to move with great care to avoid touching the ship's side and setting off one of those brainbursts.

The bedrock was very dark. He squatted and ran his fingers over it. They came away wet. They had come away a little wetter each day for the last week.

That morning he had cut a small square four inches on a side and a foot into the floor of the bedrock using a gadget that had once been a blowdryer. Now he opened his toolkit, removed a flashlight, and shone the light into it.

Water down there.

He got to his feet and screamed: "Send down the hose!"

". . . what? . . ." drifted down. Enders sounded apologetic. Gardener sighed, wondering just how much longer he himself could hold out against the steady drag of exhaustion. All this Hugo Gernsback Whole Universe

equipment, and no one thought to rig an intercom between up there and down here. Instead, they were screaming their throats out.

Oh, but none of their bright ideas run in that direction, and you know it. Why would they think about intercoms when they can read thoughts? You're the horse-and-buggy human here, not them.

"The hose!" he shrieked. *"Send down the motherfucking hose, tripehead!"*

". . . oh . . . kay . . ."

Gardener stood waiting for the hose to come down, wishing miserably that he was anywhere else in the world than here, wishing he could convince himself all of it was only a nightmare.

It was no good. The ship was madly exotic, but this reality was also too prosy to be a dream: the acrid smell of John Enders' sweat, the slightly boozy smell of his own, the dig of the rope loop into his instep as he went down into the cut, the feel of rough, moist bedrock under his fingers.

Where's Bobbi, Gard? Is she dead?

No. He didn't think she was dead, but he had become convinced that she *was* desperately ill. Something had happened to her on Wednesday. Something had happened to *all* of them on Wednesday. Gardener could not quite bring his memories into focus, but he knew there had been no real blackout or DT nightmare. It would have been better for him if there *had* been. There had been some sort of cover-up last Wednesday—a frantic cut-and-paste. And in the course of it, he believed that Bobbi had been hurt . . . taken ill . . . something.

But they're not talking about it.

Bobby Tremain: *Bobbi? Heck, Mr. Gardener, nothing wrong with Bobbi—just a li'l ole heatstroke. She'll be back in no time. She can use the rest! You know that better'n anyone, I guess!*

It sounded great. So great you'd almost think the Tremain kid believed it himself until you looked closely at his odd eyes.

He could see himself going to those he was coming to think of as the Shed People, *demanding* to know what had happened to her.

Newt Berringer: *Next thing you know, he'll be trying to tell us that* we're *the Dallas Police.*

And boy, they'd sure all start to laugh then, wouldn't they? *Them,* the Dallas Police? That was pretty funny. That was a scream.

Maybe, Gard thought, *that's why I feel so much like doing it. Screaming, I mean.*

Now he stood deep in this manmade crack in the earth, a crack that contained a titanic alien flying ship, waiting for the hose to come down. And suddenly the final, horrible passage of George Orwell's *Animal Farm* clanged in his head like a death-cry. It was strange, the things you discovered you'd gotten by heart. *"Clover's old eyes flitted from one face to another. And as the animals outside looked from pig to man, and man to pig, and pig to man again, it seemed that some strange thing was happening. It was impossible to say which was which."*

Jesus, Gard, cut it out!

Here came the hose at last, a seventy-footer from the volunteer fire department. It was of course meant to *spray* water, not suck it up, but a vacuum pump had neatly reversed its function.

Enders paid it out jerkily. The end swung back and forth, sometimes striking the hull of the ship. Each time this happened there was a cludding sound that was dull yet curiously penetrating. Gardener didn't like it and quickly came to anticipate each clud.

Christ, I wish he hadn't got that thing swinging.

Clud . . . clud . . . clud. Why can't it just clink? Why does it have to keep making that other sound, like dirt being shoveled on top of a coffin?

Clud . . . clud . . . clud.

Christ, I should have jumped when I had the chance. Just stepped off that fucking breakwater at Arcadia Beach. July 4th, wasn't it? Shit, I could have been a Yankee Doodle Deader.

Well, go on, then. When you go back to the house tonight, gobble all the Valium in the medicine cabinet. Kill yourself if you haven't got the guts to either see this thing through or put a stop to it. The good people of Haven will probably throw a party over your body. You think they want you here? If there wasn't some of the Old, Unimproved Bobbi still around, I think you'd be gone already. If she wasn't standing between you and them . . .

Clud . . . clud . . . clud.

Was Bobbi still standing between him and the rest of

Haven? Yeah. But if she died, how long would it be before he himself was scrubbed from the equation?

Not long, buddy. Not long at all. Like maybe fifteen minutes.

Clud . . . clud . . . cl—

Wincing, teeth set against the dull dead sound, Gard leapt up and caught the brass nozzle of the hose before it could rap against the side of the ship again. He pulled it down, knelt over the hole, and craned his head up at Enders' small face.

"Start the pump!" he yelled.

". . . what? . . ."

Jesus wept, Gardener thought.

"Start the motherfucking pump!" he shrieked, and this time he felt, actually *felt* his head fall apart. He closed his eyes.

". . . oh . . . kay . . ."

When he looked up, Enders was gone.

Gardener plunged the end of the hose into the glory-hole he had cut out from rock that morning. The water began to bubble slowly, almost contemplatively. It was frigid at first, but his hands quickly became numb. Although the trench he was in was only forty feet deep, they had removed a whole hillside in the process of cutting a base level, so that the place where Gardener now crouched had probably been, until late June, ninety feet under the earth. Measuring the freeboard surface of the ship would have given an exact figure, but Gardener didn't give a shit. The simple fact was that they seemed to have nearly reached the aquifer: spongy rock filled with water. Apparently the bottom half or two-thirds of the ship was floating in a large underground lake.

His hands were now so numb they had forgotten what they were.

"Come on, asshole," he muttered.

As if in answer, the hose began to vibrate and wriggle. He couldn't hear the pump's motor from here, but he didn't have to. As the water level in the glory-hole dropped, Gardener was able to see his reddened, dripping hands again. He watched as the water level continued to drop.

If we hit the aquifer, it's going to slow us down.

Yeah. We might lose a whole day while they figure out

some sort of super-pump. There might be a delay, but nothing's *going to stop them, Gard. Don't you know that?*

The hose began to emit the sound of a giant soda straw in a giant Coke glass. The glory-hole was empty.

"Turn it off!" he shouted. Enders just went on looking down at him. Gardener sighed and yanked hard on the hose. Enders looked startled, then made a thumb-and-forefinger circle at Gardener. He disappeared. A few seconds later the hose stopped vibrating. Then it began to rise as Enders wound it up.

Gardener made sure that the end of it was perfectly still and wouldn't pendulum before he let it go.

He now took the radio out of his shirt and turned it on. There was a built-in ten-minute delay. He put the radio on the bottom of the glory-hole, then covered it with loose chunks of rock. A lot of the explosion's force would be channeled upward anyway, but this was powerful stuff, whatever it was—enough would be left to tear perhaps three vertical feet of bedrock into chunks which they could quickly load into a sling and power-winch up. And the ship would not be hurt. Apparently *nothing* could do that.

Gardener slid his foot into the sling and shouted: *"Pull me up!"*

Nothing happened.

"PULL ME UP, JOHNNY"! he screamed. Once again there was that feeling that his head was splitting along some rotted midseam.

Still nothing.

His wrist-deep plunge into the icy water had dropped Gardener's body temperature perhaps two whole degrees. Nonetheless, a damp and slickly unpleasant sweat suddenly sprang out on his forehead. He looked at his wristwatch. Two minutes had passed since he had turned on the Snoopy radio. From his watch, his eyes moved to the loose pile of chunked granite in the glory-hole. Plenty of time to yank the rocks out and turn off the radio.

Except turning off the radio wouldn't stop whatever was going on *inside* the radio. He knew that somehow.

He looked up for Enders and Enders wasn't there.

This is how they're getting rid of you, Gard.

A drop of sweat ran into his eyes. He brushed it away with the back of his hand.

"ENDERS! HEY, JOHNNY!"

Shinny up the rope, Gard.

Forty feet? Dream on. Maybe in college. Maybe not even then.

He looked at his watch. Three minutes.

Yeah, this is how. Poof. All gone. A sacrifice to the Great Ship. A little something to propitiate the Tommy-knockers.

"*. . . start it going yet?*"

He looked up so quickly his neck popped, his growing fear turning immediately to rage.

"I started it almost five minutes ago you fucking shit-for-brains! Get me out of here before it goes off and blows me sky-high!"

Enders' mouth dropped into an O that was almost comical. He disappeared again and Gardener was left looking at his watch through what was becoming a blur of sweat.

Then the loop around his foot jerked and a moment later he began to rise. Gardener closed his eyes and clung to the rope. Apparently he wasn't quite as ready to sniff the pipe as he thought he was. Maybe that wasn't such a bad thing to know, either.

He reached the top of the cut, stepped out, loosened the loop around his foot, and walked over to where Enders stood.

"Sorry," Enders said, smiling fussily. "I thought we'd agreed that you'd give me a shout before—"

Gardener hit him. The thing was done and Enders was on the ground, his glasses hanging from one ear and his mouth bloody, before Gardener was even wholly aware of what he meant to do. And although he was not telepathic, he thought he could feel every head in Haven suddenly turn toward this place, alert and listening.

"You left me down there with that thing going, asshole," he said. "If you—or anyone else in this town—ever does it again, you better just leave me down there. Do you hear me?"

Rage dawned in Enders' eyes. He fixed his glasses back in place as well as he could and got to his feet. There was dirt on his bald head. "I don't think you know who you're talking to."

"I know more than you think," Gardener said. "Listen, Johnny. And the rest of you, if you're hearing this, and I think you are, you listen too. I want an intercom down there. I want some ordinary fucking consideration. I've played square with you; I'm the only one in this town that didn't have to have his brains scrambled to do it, either. *I want some fucking consideration.* Do you hear me?"

Enders looked at him, but Gardener thought he was listening too. Listening to other voices. Gardener waited for their decision. He was too angry to really care much.

"All right," Enders said softly, pressing the back of his hand against his bloody mouth. "You may have a point. We'll put in an intercom, and we'll see that you have a bit more . . . what did you call it?" A contemptuous flick of smile touched his lips. It was a smile with which Gardener was extremely familiar. It was the way the Arbergs and McCardles of the world smiled. It was the way the guys who ran the nukes smiled when they talked about atomic-power facilities.

"The word was 'consideration.' You want to remember it. But smart guys can learn, yeah, Johnny? There's a dictionary back at the house. You need it, asshole?" He took a step toward Enders and had the distinct satisfaction of seeing the man fall back two steps, the contemptuous little smile disappearing. It was replaced with a look of nervy apprehension. *"Consideration,* Johnny. You remember. All of you remember. If not for me, then for Bobbi."

They were standing by the equipment lean-to now, Enders' eyes small and nervous, Gardener's large and bloodshot and still angry.

And if Bobbi dies, your idea of consideration may extend all the way to a quick and painless death. That's about the size of it, am I right? Would you say that just about describes the topography of this situation, you bald-headed little fuck?

"I—*we*—appreciate your plain speaking," Enders said. His lips, with no teeth to back them up, pooched in and out nervously.

"I bet you do."

"Perhaps a little plain speaking of our own is in order." He took off his glasses, began to wipe them on the sweaty front of his shirt (an action which Gardener thought would only leave them more smeared than before), and Gardener saw a dirty, furious gleam in his eyes. "You don't want to . . . to strike out like that, Jim. I advise you—we *all* advise you—never do it again. There are . . . uh . . . changes . . . yes, *changes* . . . going on in Haven—"

"No shit."

"And some of these changes have made people . . . uh . . . short-tempered. So striking out like that could be . . . well, a bad mistake."

"Do sudden noises bother you?" Gardener inquired.

Enders looked wary. "I don't understand your p—"

"Because if the timer in that radio is jake, you're about to hear one."

He stepped behind the lean-to, not quite running, but by no means lingering. Enders threw a startled glance toward the ship and then ran after him. He tripped over a shovel and went sprawling in the dirt, grabbing at his shin and grimacing. A moment later a loud, crumping roar shook the earth. There was a series of those dull yet penetrating cludding sounds as chunks of rock flew against the ship's hull. Others sprayed into the air, then fell onto the edge of the cut or rattled back into it. Gardener saw one rebound from the ship's hull and bounce an amazing distance.

"You small-minded, practical-joking son of a *bitch!*" Enders shouted. He was still lying on the ground, still clutching his shin.

"Small-minded, hell," Gardener said. "You left me down there."

Enders glared at him.

Gardener stood where he was for a moment, then walked over to him and held out his hand. "Come on, Johnny. Time to let bygones be bygones. If Stalin and Roosevelt could cooperate long enough to fight Hitler, I guess we ought to be able to cooperate long enough to unglue this sucker from the ground. What do you say?"

Enders would say nothing, but after a moment he took Gardener's hand and got up. He brushed sullenly at his clothes, occasionally favoring Gardener with an almost catlike expression of dislike.

"Want to go see if we brought in our well yet?" Gardener asked. He felt better than he had in days—months, actually, maybe even years. Blowing up at Enders had done him a world of good.

"What do you mean?"

"Never mind," Gardener said, and went over to the

cut alone. He peered down, looking for water, listening for gurgles and splashes. He saw nothing, heard nothing. It seemed they had lucked out again.

It suddenly occurred to him that he was standing here with his hands planted on his upper thighs, bent over a forty-foot drop with a man somewhere behind him to whom he had just administered a punch in the mouth. *If Enders wanted, he could run up behind me and tumble me into this hole with one hard push, he thought, and heard Enders saying: Striking out like that could be a very bad mistake.*

But he didn't look around, and that sense of well-being, absurdly out of place or not, held. He was in a fix, and strapping a rearview mirror onto his head so he could see who was coming up behind him wasn't going to get him out of it.

When he turned around at last, Enders was still by the lean-to, looking at him with that sulky kicked-cat expression. Gardener suspected he had been on the party-line again with his fellow mutations.

"What do you say?" Gardener called over to him. There was an edged pleasantness in his voice. "There's a lot of broken rock down there. Do we go back to work, or do we air a few more grievances?"

Enders went into the shed, grabbed the levitation-pack they used to move the bigger rocks, and started toward Gardener with it. He held it out. Gardener shouldered the pack. He started back toward the sling, then looked back at Enders.

"Don't forget to hoist me up when I yell."

"I won't." Enders' eyes—or perhaps it was only the lenses of his spectacles—were murky. Gardener discovered he didn't really care which. He put his foot into the rope sling and tightened it as Enders went back to the winch.

"Remember, Johnny. Consideration. That's the word for today."

John Enders lowered him without saying anything.

4

Sunday, July 31st:

Henry Buck, known to his friends as Hank, committed the last act of outright irrational craziness to take place in Haven at a quarter past eleven on that Sunday morning.

People in Haven are short-tempered, Enders had told Gard. Ruth McCausland had seen evidences of this short temper during the search for David Brown; hot words, scuffles, a thrown punch or two. Ironically, it had always been Ruth herself—Ruth and the clear moral imperative she had always represented in these people's lives—who had prevented the search from turning into a free-for-all.

Short-tempered? "Crazy" was probably a better word.

In the shock of the "becoming," the town had been like a gas-filled room, waiting only for someone to light a match . . . or to do something even more accidental but just as deadly, as an explosion in a gas-filled room may be set off by an innocent delivery-boy pushing a doorbell and creating a spark.

That spark never came. Part of it was Ruth's doing. Part of it was Bobbi's doing. Then, after the visits to the shed, a group of half a dozen men and one woman began to work like the hippie LSD-trip-guides of the sixties, helping Haven through to the end of the first difficult stage of "becoming."

It was well for the people of Haven that the big bang never did come, well for the people of Maine, New England, perhaps for the whole continent or the whole planet. I would not be the one to tell you there are no planets anywhere in the universe that are not large dead cinders floating in space because a war over who was or was not hogging too many dryers in the local Laundromat escalated into Doomsville. No one ever really knows where things will end—or *if* they will. And there had been a time in late June when the entire world might well have awakened to discover a terrible, worldripping conflict was going on in an obscure Maine town—an exchange which had begun over something as deeply important as whose turn it had been to pick up the coffee-break check at the Haven Lunch.

Of course we may blow up our world someday with no outside help at all, for reasons which look every bit as trivial from a standpoint of light-years; from where we rotate far out on one spoke of the Milky Way in the Lesser Magellanic Cloud, whether or not the Russians invade the Iranian oilfields or whether NATO decides to install American-made Cruise missiles in West Germany may seem every bit as important as whose turn it is to pick up the tab for five coffees and a like number of

Danish. Maybe it all comes down to the same thing, when viewed from a galactic perspective.

However that may be, the tense period in Haven really ended with the month of July—by this time, almost everyone in town had lost his teeth, and a number of other, stranger mutations had begun. Those seven people who had visited Bobbi's shed, communing with what waited in the green glow, had begun to experience these mutations some ten days earlier, but had kept them secret.

Considering the nature of the changes, that was probably wise.

Because Hank Buck's revenge on Albert "Pits" Barfield was really the last act of outrageous craziness in Haven, and in that light it probably deserves a brief mention.

Hank and Pits Barfield were part of the Thursday-night poker circle to which Joe Paulson had also belonged. By July 31st the poker games had ended, and not because that bitch 'Becka Paulson had gone crazy and roasted her husband. They had stopped because you can't bluff at poker when all the players are telepaths.

Still, Hank held a grudge against Pits Barfield, and the more he thought about it, the more it grew in his mind. All these years, Pits had been bottom-dealing. Several of them suspected it—Hank could remember a night in the back room of Kyle Archinbourg's place, seven years ago it must have been, playing pool with Moss Harlingen, and Moss had said: "He's bottom-dealing just as sure as you're born, Hank. Six-ball in the side." *Whack!* The six-ball shot into the side pocket as if on a string. "Thing is, bastid's *good* at it. If he was just a little slower, I could catch him at it."

"If that's what you think, y'ought to get out'n the game."

"Shit! Everyone else in that game is as honest as the day is long. And the truth is, I can outplay most of 'em. Nine-ball. Corner." *Whap!* "Suckardly little prick is fast, and he never overuses it—just does a little if he really starts to go in the hole. You notice how he comes out every Thursday night? 'Bout even?"

Hank had. All the same, he had thought the whole thing was just a little buggyboo in Moss's head—Moss *was* a good poker player, and he resented anyone whose money he couldn't take. But others had voiced a similar suspicion over the intervening years, and more than a few of them—some of them damned nice fellows, too, fellows Hank had really enjoyed pulling a few beers and dealing a few hands with—had dropped out of the game. They did this quietly, with no fuss or bother, and the possibility that Pits Barfield might be responsible was never hinted at. It was that they had finally gotten into the Monday-night bowling league up to Bangor and their wives didn't want them out late two nights a week. It was that their work schedules had changed and they couldn't take that late night anymore. It was that winter was coming (even if it was only May) and they had to do a little work on their snowmobiles.

So they dropped out, leaving the little core of three or four that had been there all along, and somehow that made it worse, knowing those outsiders had either picked it up or smelled it as clearly as you could smell the jungle-juice aroma which arose from Barfield's unwashed body most of the time. *They* got it. Him and Kyle and Joe had been snookered. All these years they had been snookered.

After the "becoming" got rolling really well, Hank discovered the truth once and for all. Not only had Pits been doing a little basement dealing, he had also, from time to time, indulged in a little discreet card-marking. He had picked these skills up in the long, monotonous hours of duty at a Berlin repple-depple in the months after the end of World War II. Some of those hot, muggy July nights Hank would lie awake in bed, head aching, and imagine Pits sitting in a nice warm farmhouse, shirt and shoes off, stinking to high heaven and grinning a great big shit-eating grin as he practiced cheating and dreamed of the suckers he would fleece when he got back home.

Hank endured these dreams and headaches for two weeks . . . and then, one night, the answer came. He would just send old Pits back to the repple-depple, that's what he would do. *Some* repple-depple, anyway. A repple-depple maybe fifty light-years away, or maybe five hundred, or five million. A repple-depple in the Phantom Zone. And Hank knew just how to do it. He sat bolt-upright in bed, grinning a huge grin. His headache was gone at last.

"Just what the hell *is* a repple-depple, anyway?" he muttered, and then decided that was the least of his problems. He got out of bed and set to work right then, at three in the morning.

He caught up to Pits a week after the idea had struck him. Pits was sitting in front of Cooder's market, tipped back in a chair and looking at the pictures in a *Gallery* magazine. Looking at pictures of naked women, bottom-dealing, and stinking up repple-depples—these were the specialties of Pits Barfield, Hank decided.

It was Sunday, overcast and hot. People saw Hank walking toward where Albert "Pits" Barfield sat tipped back in his chair, workboots curled around the front rungs, checking out all those Girls Next Door; they felt-heard the one thought beating steadily

(reppledepplereppledepplereppledepple)

in Hank's mind, they saw the great big ghetto-blaster radio he was carrying by the handle, saw the pistol jammed into the front of his pants, and they stepped away quickly.

Pits was deeply absorbed in the *Gallery* gatefold. It showed a great deal of a girl named Candi (whose hobbies, the magazine said, included "sailing and men with hands both strong and gentle"), and he looked up far too late to do anything constructive on his own behalf. Considering the size of the pistol Hank was carrying, people opined (usually without even opening their mouths, except to shovel in more food) over supper that night, it had probably been too late for poor old Pits when he got up that Sunday morning.

Pits's chair came down with a bang.

"Hey, Hank! What—"

Hank pulled the gun—it was a souvenir of his own Army service. He had done *his* time in Korea, and not in any repple-depple, either.

"You just want to sit right there," Hank said, "or they're gonna be washing your guts off that store window, you cheating son of a bitch."

"Hank . . . Hank . . . what . . ."

Hank reached inside his shirt and brought out a small pair of Borg earphones. He jacked them into the big radio, turned it on, and tossed the phones toward Pits.

"Put em on, Pits. Let's see you deal your way out of *this* one."

"Hank . . . please . . ."

"I ain't going to treat with you on this, Pits," Hank said with great sincerity. "I'll give you a five-count to put on those earphones, and then I'm gonna give you a sinus operation."

"Christ, Hank, it was a fucking quarter-limit poker game!" Pits screamed. Sweat poured down his face, stained his khaki shirt. The smell of him was large, vinegary, and amazingly repugnant.

"One . . . two . . ."

Pits looked around wildly. There was no one there. The street had cleared magically. There wasn't so much as a car to be seen moving on Main Street, although there were plenty slant-parked in front of the market. Complete silence had fallen. In it, both he and Hank could hear the music coming from the earphones—Los Lobos wondering if the wolf would survive.

"It was a lousy three-raise quarter-limit poker game and I hardly ever did it anyway!" Pits shrieked. *"Somebody for Chrissake put a halter over this guy!"*

" . . . three . . ."

And with a final ludicrous defiance, Pits screamed: *"And he's a sore fucking loser!"*

"Four," Hank said, and raised his service pistol.

Pits, his entire shirt now stained nearly black with sweat, his eyes rolling, smelling like a manure pile which had just been napalmed, gave in. *"Okay! Okay! Okay!"* he screamed, and picked up the earphones. "I'm doin' it, see? I'm doin' it!"

He put the phones on. Still holding the pistol on him, Hank bent over the ghetto-blaster, which could play cassette tapes as well as receive AM and FM stations. The Play button below the cassette holder had been taped over. Written on the tape was this one rather ominous word: Send.

Hank pushed it.

Pits started to scream. Then the screams began to fade, as if someone inside were turning down his volume. At the same time someone seemed to be turning down his vividness, his physical coherence . . . his *there-ness*. Pits Barfield faded like a photograph. Now his mouth was moving soundlessly, his skin was milk.

A little piece of reality—a piece of reality roughly the size of a Dutch door's lower half—seemed to open behind him. There was a feeling that reality—Haven reality—had rotated on some unknowable axis, like a trick bookcase in a haunted-house spoof. Behind Pits now was an eerie purple-black landscape.

Hank's hair began to flutter about his ears; his collar stuttered with a sound like a silenced automatic weapon; the litter on the asphalt—candy wrappers, flattened cigarette packages, a couple of Humpty Dumpty potato-chip bags—zoomed across the pavement and into that hole. They were drawn on the river of air which flowed into that nearly airless other place. Some of that litter went between Pits's legs. And some, Hank thought, seemed to pass right *through* them.

Then, suddenly, as if he himself had become as light as the litter which had been on the market's paved apron, Pits was vacuumed into that hole. His *Gallery* magazine went after him, pages flapping like batwings. *Good for you, fuckface,* Hank thought, *now you got something to read in the repple-depple.* Pits's chair toppled over, scraped across the asphalt, and lodged half-in, half-out of that opening. A wind-tunnel of air was now rushing around Hank. He bent over his radio, finger coming to rest on the Stop button.

Just before he pushed it, he heard a high, thin cry coming from that other place. He looked up, thinking: *That ain't Pits.*

It came again.

"*. . . hilly . . .*"

Hank frowned. It was a kid's voice. A *kid's* voice, and there was something familiar about it. Something—

"*. . . over yet? I want to come ho-oome . . .*"

There was a bright, toneless jingle as the window in Cooder's market, which had blown inward in the town-hall explosion the previous Sunday, was now sucked outward. A glass-storm flew all around Hank, leaving him miraculously untouched.

"*. . . please, it's hard to breeeeeeathe . . .*"

Now the B&M beans on special which had been pyramided in the market's front window began to fly around Hank as they were sucked through the doorway in reality he had somehow opened. Five-pound bags of lawn food and ten-pound bags of charcoal slithered across the pavement with dry, papery sounds.

Gotta shut the sucker up, Hank thought, and as if to confirm this judgment, a can of beans slammed into the back of his head, bounced high in the air, then zoomed into that purple-black bruise.

"Hilleeeeee—"

Hank hit the Stop button. The doorway disappeared at once. There was a woody crunch as the chair lodged in the opening was cut in two, on an almost perfect diagonal. Half of the chair lay on the asphalt. The other half was nowhere to be seen.

Randy Kroger, the German who had owned Cooder's since the late fifties, grabbed Hank and turned him around. "You're payin' for that display window, Buck," he said.

"Sure, Randy, whatever you say," Hank agreed, dazedly rubbing the lump that was rising on the back of his head.

Kroger pointed at the strange slanting half-chair lying on the asphalt. "You're paying for the chair too," he announced, and strode back inside.

That was how July ended.

5

Monday, August 1st:

John Leandro finished talking, knocked back the rest of his beer, and asked David Bright: "So what do you think he'll say?"

Bright thought for a moment. He and Leandro were in the Bounty Tavern, a wildly overdecorated Bangor pub with only two real marks in its favor—it was almost directly across the street from the editorial offices of the Bangor *Daily News,* and on Mondays you could get Heineken for a buck a bottle.

"I think he'll start by telling you to hurry over to Derry and finish getting the rest of the Community Calendar," Bright said. "Then I think he might ask you if you've thought about psychiatric help."

Leandro looked absurdly crushed. He was only twenty-four, and the last two stories he had covered—the disappearance (read: presumed murder) of the two state troopers and the suicide of a third—had whetted his appetite for the high-voltage stuff. When stacked up against being in on a grim midnight hunt for the bodies of two state troopers, reporting on the Derry Amvets' covered-dish supper wasn't much. He didn't want the heavy stuff to end. Bright felt almost sorry for the little twerp—trouble was, that was what Leandro was. Being a twerp at twenty-four was acceptable. He was pretty sure, however, that Johnny Leandro was still going to be a twerp at forty-four . . . sixty-four . . . at eighty-four, if he lived that long.

A twerp of eighty-four was a slightly awesome and wholly frightening idea. Bright decided to order another beer after all.

"I was just joking," Bright said.

"Then you think he *will* let me follow it up?"

"No."

"But you just said—"

"I was joking about the psychiatric-help part," Bright said patiently. *"That's* what I was joking about."

"He" was Peter Reynault, the city editor. Bright had learned a good many years ago that city editors had one thing in common with God Himself, and he suspected that Johnny Leandro was about to learn it himself very soon now. Reporters might propose, but it was city editors like Peter Reynault who eventually disposed.

"But—"

"You have nothing to follow up," Bright said.

If Haven's inner circle—those who had made the trip into Bobbi Anderson's shed—could have heard what Leandro said next, his life expectancy might well have sunk to days . . . maybe mere hours.

"I've got *Haven* to follow up," was what he said, and quaffed the rest of his Heineken Dark in three long swallows. "Everything starts there. The kid disappears in Haven, the woman dies in Haven, Rhodes and Gabbons are coming back from Haven. Dugan commits suicide. Why? Because he loved the McCausland woman, he says. The McCausland woman from Haven."

"Don't forget lovable old Gramps," Bright said. "He's running around saying his grandson's disappearance was a conspiracy. I kept expecting him to start whispering about Fu Manchu and white slavery."

"So what is it?" Leandro asked dramatically. *"What's going on in Haven?"*

"It *is* the insidious doctor," Bright said. His beer arrived. He no longer wanted it. He only wanted to get out of here. Bringing up lovable old Gramps had been a mistake. Thinking about lovable old Gramps made him feel a trifle uneasy. Gramps was obviously off his rocker, but there had been something about his eyes . . .

"What?"

"Dr. Fu Manchu. If you see Nayland Smith hanging around, I think you've got the story of the century." Bright leaned forward and whispered hoarsely: "White slavery. Remember who you heard it from when you get the call from the New York *Times.*"

"I don't think that's very funny, David."

An eighty-four-year-old twerp, Bright thought again. *Imagine it.*

"Or, here's one," Bright said. "Little green men. The invasion of earth is already under way, see, only no one knows it. And—TA-DA! *No One Will Believe This Heroic Young News-Hawk! Robert Redford Stars as John Leandro in This Nail-Biting Saga of—*"

The bartender wandered down and said, "You want to turn it down?"

Leandro got up, his face stiff. He dropped three dollar bills on the bar. "Your sense of humor is adolescent, David."

"Or try this," Bright said dreamily. "It's *both* Fu Manchu *and* green men from space. An alliance formed in hell. And no one knows but you, Johnny. *Klaatu barada nictu!*"

"Well, I don't care if Reynault lets me follow it up or not," Leandro said, and Bright saw that he might have twanged Johnny's strings just a little too hard; the twerp was furious. "My vacation starts next Friday. I may just go down to Haven. Follow it up on my own time."

"Sure," Bright said, excited. He knew he should let up—pretty soon Leandro was probably going to try to punch him in the mouth—but the guy just kept giving him openings. "Sure, that's gotta be part of it! Redford wouldn't take the part unless he could go it alone. The Lone Wolf! *Klaatu barada nictu!* Wow! Just remember to wear your special watch when you go down there."

"What watch?" Leandro asked, his face still angry. Oh, he was pissed, all right, but he kept leading with his chin just the same.

"You know, the one that sends out an ultrasonic signal that only Superman can hear when you pull out the stem," Bright said, demonstrating with his own watch (and spilling a fair amount of beer into his crotch). "It goes *zeeeeeeeee—*"

"I don't care what Peter Reynault thinks, and I don't care how many stupid jokes you make," Leandro said. "You both just might get a big surprise."

He started out, then turned back.

"And for the record, I think you're a cynical shithead with no imagination."

Having delivered this valedictory, Johnny Leandro turned on his heel and stalked grandly out.

Bright lifted his glass and tipped it toward the bartender. "Let's drink to the cynical shitheads of the world," he said. "We have no imagination, but we're remarkably resistant to twerpism."

"Whatever you say," the bartender said. He believed he had seen it all before . . . but then, he had never tended bar in Haven.

6

Tuesday, August 2nd:

There were six of them who met late that afternoon in Newt Berringer's office. It was going on five P.M., but the clock in the tower—a tower that looked real but which a bird could easily have flown through, if there had been any birds left in Haven Village—still read five past three. All six had spent some time in Bobbi's shed; Adley McKeen was the most recent addition to their number. The others included Newt, Dick Allison, Kyle, Hazel, and Frank Spruce.

They discussed the few things they had to discuss without talking aloud.

Frank Spruce asked how Bobbi was.

Still alive, Newt responded; no one knew any more. She might come out of the shed again. More likely she would not. Either way, they would know when it happened.

Discussion turned briefly to what Hank Buck had done the day before, and what Hank said he'd heard coming from that other world. None of them were much concerned with the late and not-so-great Pits Barfield. Perhaps the punishment had suited the crime; perhaps it had been a little too extreme. It didn't matter. It was over. Nothing had happened to Hank as a result of what he had done; he had given Randy Kroger a personal check for the broken display window and the goods that had been sucked through the hole Hank had spiked into reality. Kroger called Northern National in Bangor to verify the check. He found it was good, and that was all *he* cared about.

There was little they could have done about Hank even if they'd had a mind to; the town's one jail cell was in the town hall's basement, a converted storeroom where Ruth had jugged a few weekend drunks, and it might hold Hank Buck for all of ten minutes. A strong fourteen-year-old could have broken out of it. And they couldn't very well have sent Hank up to county jail. The charge would have looked pretty *odd.* The alternatives available to them were simple—let him alone or pack him off to Altair-4. Luckily, they were able to look closely into Hank's mind and motivations. They saw that his anger and confusion were subsiding, as they were all over town. He was not apt to do anything radical again, so they took away his converted radio, asked him not to make another, and moved on to what concerned them a bit more . . . the voice he claimed to have heard.

It was David Brown, all right, Frank Spruce said now. Anybody doubt it?

No one did.

David Brown was on Altair-4.

No one knew exactly where Altair-4 *was,* or *what* it was, and they didn't much care. The words themselves came from some old movie and meant no more than the name Tommyknockers, which came from some old rhyme. What mattered (and even this didn't, much) was that Altair-4 was a kind of cosmic warehouse, a place where all sorts of things were stored. Hank had sent Pits there, but first he had put the smelly old son of a bitch through some half-assed sort of disintegration process.

This had apparently not been the case with David Brown.

Long, thoughtful silence.

(yes probably yes)

This last was not ascribable to any one person; it was group-think, hivelike, and complete in itself.

(but why why bother)

They looked at each other with no emotion. They could *feel* emotion, but not over such a minor matter as this.

Bring him back, Hazel said indifferently. It'll please Bryant and Marie. And Ruth. She would have wanted it. And we all did love her, you know. Her thought had the tone of a woman suggesting that a friend buy her son a soft drink as a treat for being good.

No, Adley said, and they all looked toward him. It was the first time he had entered their conversation. He looked embarrassed but pushed on anyway. Every paper and TV station in the state'd be down here to get a story on the "miracle return." They think he must be dead, only four and gone over two weeks now. If he shows up, it'll make too much whoop-de-doo.

They were nodding now.

And what would *he* say? Newt put in. When they asked him where he'd been, what would *he* say?

We could blank his memories, Hazel said. That would be no problem at all, and the press people would accept amnesia as perfectly natural. Under the circumstances.

(yes but that's not the problem)

It was the many voices again, as one voice. They came together in a strange combination of words and images. The problem was that things had now gone too far to allow *anyone* in town except for the most transient through-travelers . . . and even most of them could be discouraged with fake road construction and detour signs. The last people they wanted in Haven were a bunch of reporters and TV camera crews. And the clock-tower wouldn't show up on film; it was a mind-slide, really no more than a hallucination. No, David Brown was best left alone, all things considered. He would be all right for yet a while. They knew little about Altair-4, but they did know that time ran at a different speed there—on Altair-4, less than a year had passed since earth had been flung out of the sun. So David Brown had in fact just gotten there. Of course he still might die; strange microbes might invade his system, some strange Altair-4 warehouse-rat might gobble him up, or he might die of simple shock. But he probably wouldn't, and if he did, it really wasn't very important.

I've a feeling the boy might come in handy, Kyle said.

(how)

As a diversion.

(what do you mean)

Kyle didn't *know* exactly what he meant. It was only a

feeling that if a spotlight were to be trained on Haven again—the way Ruth had tried to train one on the town with her damned exploding dolls, which had worked *ever* so much better than they were supposed to work—perhaps they could bring David Brown back and set him down somewhere else. If that was done in the right way, they might gain a little more time here. Time was always a problem. Time to "become."

Kyle expressed these ideas in no coherent way, but the others nodded at the drift of his thoughts. It would be well to keep David Brown waiting in the wings, so to speak, awhile longer.

(don't let Marie know—she hasn't gone far enough in the "becoming"—you must hide this from Marie yet awhile)

All six looked around, eyes widening. That voice, weak but clear, belonged to none of them. It had come from Bobbi Anderson.

Bobbi! Hazel cried, half-rising from her seat. Bobbi, are you all right? How you doing?

No answer.

Bobbi was gone—there was not even a feel of her left in the air. They looked at each other cautiously, testing each other's impressions of that thought, confirming that it *had* been Bobbi. Each knew that if he or she had been alone, with no confirmation available, he or she would have dismissed it as an incredibly powerful hallucination.

How are we going to keep it from Marie? Dick Allison asked, almost angrily. We can't hide nothing from *anybody* else!

Yes, Newt returned. *We* can. Not good enough yet, maybe, but we can dim out our thoughts a little. Make them hard to see. Because—

(because we've been)

(been out there)

(been in the shed)

(Bobbi's shed)

(we wore the headphones in Bobbi's shed)

(and ate ate to "become")

(take ye eat do this in remembrance of me)

A sigh ran gently through them.

We'll have to go back, Adley McKeen said. Won't we?

"Yes," Kyle said. "We will." It was the only time anyone spoke aloud during the entire meeting, and it marked its end.

7

Wednesday, August 3rd:

Andy Bozeman, who had been Haven's only realtor up until three weeks ago, when he simply closed his office, had discovered that mind-reading was something a fellow got used to very quickly. He didn't realize *how* quickly, or how much he had come to depend on it, until it was his turn to go on out to Bobbi's place to help and to keep an eye on the drunk.

Part of his problem—he knew it was going to be a problem after talking to Enders and the Tremain lad—was being this close to the ship. It was like standing next to the biggest power generator in the world; constant eddies and flows of its weird force ran over his skin like skirling sand-devils in the desert. Sometimes large ideas would float dreamily into his mind, making it impossible to concentrate on what he was doing. Sometimes the exact opposite would occur: thought would break up completely, like a microwave transmission interrupted by a burst of ultraviolet rays. But most of it was just the physical *fact* of the ship, looming there like something out of a dream. It was exhilarating, awe-inspiring, frightening, wonderful. Bozeman thought he now understood how the Israelites must have felt carrying the Ark of the Covenant through the desert. In one of his sermons, the Rev. Goohringer said that some fellow had ventured to stick his head in there, just to see what all the shouting was about, and he had dropped dead on the spot.

Because it had been God in there.

There might be a kind of God in that ship, too, Andy thought. And even if that God had fled, It had left some residue . . . some of Itself . . . and thinking about it made it hard to keep your mind on the business at hand.

Then there was Gardener's unsettling blankness. You kept running into it like a closed door that should have been open. You'd yell at him to hand you something, and he would go right on with what he was doing.

Just . . . no response. Or you'd go to tune in on him—just sort of fall into the run of his thoughts, like picking up a telephone on a party line to see who was talking, and there would be no one there. No one at all. Nothing but a dead line.

There was a buzz from the intercom nailed to the inside wall of the lean-to. Its wire ran across the muddy, churned ground and into the trench from which the ship jutted.

Bozeman flipped the toggle over to Talk. "I'm here."

"The charge is set," Gardener said. "Haul me up." He sounded very, very tired. He had thrown himself a pretty fair country drunk last night, Bozeman thought, judging by the sound of the puking he had heard from the back porch around midnight. And when he glanced into Gardener's room this morning, he had seen blood on his pillow.

"Right away." The episode with Enders had taught them all that when Gardener asked to be brought up, you didn't waste time.

He went to the windlass and began to crank. It was a pain in the ass, having to do this by hand, but there was a temporary shortage of batteries again. Give them another week and everything out here would be running like clockwork . . . except Bozeman doubted if he would be here to see it. Being near the ship was exhausting. Being near *Gardener* was exhausting in a different way—it was like being near a loaded gun that had a hair trigger. The way he had sucker-punched poor John Enders, now—the only reason John hadn't known it was coming was because Gardener was such an *infuriating* blank. Every now and then a bubble of thought—partial or complete—would rise to the surface of his mind, as readable as a newspaper headline, but that was all. Maybe Enders had it coming—Bozeman knew that *he* wouldn't be too nuts about being stuck at the bottom of a trench with one of those explosive radios. But that wasn't the *point.* The point was that Johnny hadn't been able to see it coming. Gardener could do anything, at any time, and no one could stop him, because *no* one could see it coming.

Andy Bozeman almost wished Bobbi would die so they could get rid of him. It would be tougher with just Havenites working on the project, true, it would slow them down, but it would almost be worth it.

The way he could come out of left field at you was so *fucking* unsettling.

This morning, for instance. Coffee break. Bozeman

sitting on a stump eating some of those little peanut-butter-and-cracker sandwiches and drinking iced coffee from his thermos. He had always preferred hot coffee to cold even in warm weather, but since he'd lost his teeth, really hot drinks seemed to bother him.

Gardener had been sitting cross-legged like one of those Yoga masters on a dirty swatch of tarpaulin, eating an apple and drinking a beer. Bozeman didn't see how *anyone* could eat an apple and drink a beer at the same time, especially in the *morning,* but Gardener was doing it. From here, Bozeman could see the scar an inch or so above Gardener's left eyebrow. The steel plate would be under that scar. It—

Gardener had turned his head and caught Bozeman looking at him. Bozeman flushed, wondering if Gardener was going to start to yell and rant. If maybe he was going to come over here and try to sucker-punch him the way he had Johnny Enders. If he tries *that,* Bozeman thought, curling his hands into fists, he's going to find that I'm no sucker.

Instead, Gard had begun to speak in a clear, carrying voice—there was a small, cynical smile on his mouth as he did it. After a moment, Bozeman realized he wasn't just *speaking,* he was *reciting.* The man was sitting out here in the woods cross-legged on a dirty tarp, hung-over out of his mind, the glittering body of the ship in the earth casting moving ripples of reflection on his cheek, and reciting like a schoolboy—the man was un-fucking-stable, Bozeman would tell the world. He sincerely wanted Gardener dead.

" 'Tom gave up the brush with reluctance in his face, but alacrity in his heart,' " Gardener said, eyes half-closed, face turned up toward the warm morning sun. That little smile never left his lips. " 'And while the late steamer *Big Missouri* worked and sweated in the sun, the retired artist sat on a barrel in the shade close by, dangled his legs, munched his apple, and planned the slaughter of more innocents.' "

"What—" Andy began, but Gardener, his smile now spreading into a genuine—if nonetheless cynical—grin, overrode him.

" 'There was no lack of material; boys happened along every little while; they came to jeer, but they remained to whitewash. By the time Ben was fagged out, Tom had traded the next chance to Billy Fisher for a kite, in good repair; and when *he* played out, Johnny Miller bought in for a dead rat, and a string to swing it with . . .' "

Gardener drank the rest of his beer, belched, and stretched.

"You never brought me a dead rat and a string to swing it with, but I got an intercom, Bozie, and I guess that's a start, huh?"

"I don't know what you're talking about," Bozeman said slowly. He had only gotten two years of college, business admin, before having to drop out and go to work. His father had a heart condition and chronic high blood pressure. High-flown fellows like this made him nervous and angry. Lording it over ordinary folks, as if being able to quote from something written by someone who had died a long time ago made their shit smell sweeter than other people's.

Gardener said, "That's okay. It's from chapter two of *Tom Sawyer*. When Bobbi was a kid back in Utica, seventh grade, they had this thing called Junior Exhibition. It was a recitation competition. She didn't want to be in it, but her sister Anne decided she ought to be, that it would be good for her, or something, and when sister Anne decided something, brother, it was *decided*. Anne was a real tartar then, Bozie, and she's a real tartar now. At least I guess she is. I haven't seen her in a long time, and that's the way, oh-ho, uh-huh, I like it. But I think it's fair to say she's still the same. People like her very rarely change."

"Don't call me Bozie," Andy said, hoping he sounded more dangerous than he felt. "I don't like it."

"When I had Bobbi in freshman comp, she wrote once about how she froze trying to recite *Tom Sawyer*. I just about cracked up." Gardener got to his feet and started walking toward Andy, a development the ex-realtor viewed with active alarm. "I saw her after class the next day and asked her if she still remembered how 'Whitewashing the Fence' went. She did. I wasn't surprised. There are some things you never forget, like when your sister or your mother bulldozed you into some horror-show like Junior Ex. You may forget the piece when you're standing up there in front of all those people. Otherwise, you could recite it on your deathbed."

"Look," Andy said, "we ought to get back to work—"

"I let her get about four sentences in, then I joined her. Her jaw dropped almost down to her knees. Then she started grinning, and we went through it together, word for word. It wasn't so strange. We were both shy kids, Bobbi and I. Her sister was the dragon in front of her cave, my mother was the dragon in front of mine. People like that often get this very weird idea that the way to cure a shy kid is to put him into the sort of situation he dreads the most—something like Junior Ex. It wasn't even much of a coincidence that we'd both gotten that whitewashing thing by heart. The only one more popular for recitation is 'The Tell-Tale Heart.' "

Gardener drew in breath and screamed:

"Stop, fiends! Dissemble no more! Tear up the floor-boards! Here! Here! 'Tis the beating of his hideous heart!"

Andy had uttered a small shriek. He dropped his thermos, and half a cup of cold coffee stained the crotch of his pants.

"Uh-oh, Bozie," Gardener said conversationally. "Never get that out of those polyester slacks.

"Only difference between the two of us was that *I* didn't freeze," Gardener said. "In fact, I won a second-prize ribbon. But it didn't cure my fear of talking in front of crowds . . . only made it worse. Whenever I stand up in front of a group to read poetry, I look at all those hungry eyes . . . I think of 'Whitewashing the Fence.' Also, I think about Bobbi. Sometimes that's enough to get me through. Anyway, it made us friends."

"I don't see what any of that has to do with getting this *work* done!" Andy cried in a hectoring voice utterly unlike him. But his heart had been beating too fast. For a moment there, when Gardener had shrieked, he really had believed the man had gone insane.

"You don't see what this has to do with whitewashing the fence?" Gardener asked, and laughed. "Then you must be blind, Bozie."

He pointed to the ship leaning skyward at its perfect forty-five-degree angle, rising out of the wide trench.

"We're digging it up instead of whitewashing it, but that doesn't change the principle a bit. I have fagged out Bobby Tremain and John Enders, and if you're back tomorrow I'll eat your Hush Puppies. Thing is, I never seem to get any *prizes* for it. You tell whoever comes out tomorrow I want a dead rat and a string to swing it by,

Bozie . . . or a bully taw, at the very least." Gardener had stopped halfway to the trench. He looked around at Andy. Andy's failure to read this big man with the sloping shoulders and the indistinct, oddly broken face had never made Bozeman more uncomfortable than it did then.

"Better still, Bozie," Gardener had said in a voice so soft Andy could hardly hear it, "get Bobbi out here tomorrow. I'd like to find out if the New Improved Bobbi still remembers how to recite 'Whitewashing the Fence' from *Tom Sawyer.*"

Then, without another word, he had gone to the sling and waited for Andy to lower him down.

If *that* whole thing hadn't been left-field, Andy didn't know what was. And, he added to himself as he turned the winch, that had only been Gardener's first beer of the day. *He'll put away another five or six at lunch and* really *get wild and crazy.*

Gardener now came swaying to the top of the trench, and Andy had an urge to let go of the windlass crank. Solve the problem.

Except he couldn't—Gardener belonged to Bobbi Anderson, and until Bobbi either died or came out of the shed, things had to go on pretty much as they were.

"Come on, Bozie. Some of those rocks fly a long way." He started toward the lean-to. Andy fell in beside him, hurrying to keep up.

"I told you I don't like you calling me Bozie," he said.

Gardener spared him a curiously flat glance. "I know," he said.

They went around the lean-to. About three minutes later another of those loud, crumping roars shuddered out of the trench. A spray of rocks rose into the sky and came down, rattling off the hull of the ship with dull clangs and clongs.

"Well, let's—" Bozeman began.

Gardener grabbed his arm. His head was tilted, his face alert, his eyes dark and lively. *"Shhh!"*

Andy wrenched his arm away. "What in the hell's wrong with you?"

"Don't you hear it?"

"I don't h—"

Then he did. A hissing sound, like a giant teakettle, was coming from the trench. It was growing. A mad excitement suddenly seized Andy. There was more than a little terror in it.

"It's them!" he whispered, and turned toward Gard. His eyes were the size of doorknobs. His lips, shiny with loose spittle, were trembling. "They weren't dead, we woke them up . . . *they're coming out!*"

"Jesus is coming and is He pissed," Gardener remarked, unimpressed.

The hissing grew louder. Now there was another crunching thud—this wasn't an explosion; it was the sound of something heavy collapsing. A moment later something else collapsed: Andy. The strength ran out of his legs and he fell to his knees.

"It's them, it's them, it's them!" he slobbered.

Gardener hooked a hand into the man's armpit, wincing a little at the hot, jungly dampness there, and pulled him to his feet.

"That's not the Tommyknockers," he said. "It's water."

"Huh?" Bozeman looked at him with dazed incomprehension.

"Water!" Gardener cried, giving Bozeman a brisk little shake. "We just brought in our swimming pool, Bozie!"

"Wh—"

The hiss suddenly exploded into a soft, steady roar. Water jetted out of the trench and into the sky in a widening sheet. This was no column of water; it was as if a giant child had just pressed his finger over a giant faucet to watch the water spray everywhere. At the bottom of the trench, water was driving up through a number of fissures in just that way.

"Water?" Andy asked weakly. He couldn't get it right in his mind.

Gardener didn't reply. Rainbows danced in the water; it ran down the sleek hull of the ship in rivulets, leaving beads behind . . . and as he watched, he saw those drops begin to skitter, the way water flicked into hot fat on a griddle will skitter and hop. Only this was not random. The drops were lining up in obedience to lines of force which ran down the hull of the ship like lines of longitude on a globe.

I can see *it,* Gardener thought. *I can* see *the force radiating from the ship's skin in those drops. My* God—

There was another crunch. Gardener seemed to feel the earth actually *drop* a bit under his feet. At the bottom of the trench, water pressure was finishing the work the blasting had begun—widening fissures and holes, pulling the friable rock apart. More water began to escape, and more easily. The sheets of spray fell back. A last diffuse rainbow wavered in the air and disappeared.

Gardener saw the ship shift as the rock weld which had prisoned it so long let go. It moved so slightly it might have been imagination, but it wasn't. In that brief movement he could see how it would look coming out of the ground—he could see its shadow rippling slowly over the ground as it came up and out, could hear the unearthly wailing of its hull scraping over the bones of bedrock, could sense everyone in Haven looking this way as it rose into the sky, hot and glittering, a monstrous silver coin slowly heeling over to the horizontal for the first time in millennia, floating soundlessly in the sky, floating free . . .

He wanted that. God! Right or wrong, he wanted that so *bad.*

Gardener gave his head a brisk shake, as if to clear it. "Come on," he said. "Let's take a look."

Without waiting, Gardener walked across to the trench and looked in. He could hear rushing water, but it was hard to see. He attached one of the big kliegs they used for night-work to the stirrup of the sling and lowered it about ten feet. That was plenty; if he had lowered it another ten, it would have been underwater. It had been a lake they had broken into, all right; no joke. The trench was filling rapidly.

After a moment, Andy joined him. His face was wretched. "All that work!" he cried.

"Did you bring your diving board, Bozie? Are we going to have Free Swim on Thursdays or Fr—"

"Shut up!" Andy Bozeman screamed at him. "Shut up, I hate you!"

Wild hysteria washed over Gardener. He staggered away to a stump and sat down, wondering if the goddam thing had stayed watertight all these years, wondering what the fair market price was for a flying saucer with water damage. He began to laugh. Even when Andy Bozeman came over and hit him upside the face and knocked him onto the ground, Jim Gardener couldn't stop laughing.

8

Thursday, August 4th:

When it got to be a quarter to nine and still no one had shown up, Gardener began to wonder if maybe they were quitting. He toyed with the idea as he sat in Bobbi's rocker on the porch, fingering the big puffy bruise on the side of his face where Bozeman had clouted him.

A bunch of them had been out in Archinbourg's Cadillac again, after midnight. Mostly the same bunch. Another Midnight Shed Party. Gardener had hiked himself up on one elbow and watched them through the guestroom window, wondering who brought the chips and dip to these soirees. They were just shadows grouped around the long front end of the Coupe DeVille. They stood there for a moment, then went to the shed. When they opened the door, that viciously brilliant light poured out in a flood that lit the entire yard and the guestroom itself with a sick radium-dial glow. They went inside. The glow faded down to a thick vertical bar but didn't go out entirely. They had left the door ajar. The folks in this little jerkwater Maine town were now the brightest people on earth, but apparently not even they had been able to figure out how to padlock a door from the outside, and they hadn't thought to put one on the inside.

Now, sitting on the porch and looking toward the village, Gardener thought: *Maybe when they get inside there, they get too exalted to think of mundane things like padlocks.*

He shaded his eyes with one hand. A truck was coming. A big old pulp truck that was vaguely familiar. There was a tarpaulin over something in the back. It flapped casually in the wind. Gardener knew it was going to turn in. Of course they hadn't given up.

Woke up last night in the guestroom bed, saw the folks going into the Tommyknockers' shed. Could have looked in, but I didn't quite dare; don't want to know what goes on in there.

He didn't think, somehow, that the judges of the Yale Younger Poets competition would think much of it. *But,* Gardener thought, *This Is Where Jim Gardener Is Now, as they say. Maybe later on they'll call it my Tommyknocker Phase. Or my Shed Period. Or—*

The truck changed to a lower gear and came groaning into Bobbi's dooryard. The engine died with a wheeze. The man in the strap-style T-shirt who got out was the man who had given Gard his ride to the Haven town line on July 4th. He recognized the man at once. *Coffee,* he thought. *You gave me coffee with a lot of sugar in it. Tasted good.* He looked like an extra from the James Dickey novel about those city boys and their weekend canoe trip down the Cahoolawassee. Gardener didn't think the man was from Haven, though—hadn't he said Albion?

Stuff's spreading, he thought. *Well, why not? It's fallout, isn't it? And Albion's downwind.*

" 'Lo there," the truck driver said. "Guess you don't 'member me." His tone added: Don't fuck with me, Fred.

"Guess I do," Gard said, and the name rose magically in his mind, even after all this—a single month that seemed more like ten years, with all these strange events. "Freeman Moss. Gave me a ride. I was coming to check on Bobbi. But I guess you know that."

"Ayuh."

Moss went to the back of the truck and began pulling slipknots and yanking rope. "Want to give me a help with this?"

Gardener started down the steps, then stopped, smiling a little. First Tremain, then Enders, then Bozeman with his somehow pitiful pale yellow polyester pants.

"Sure," he said. "Just tell me one thing."

"Ayuh?" Moss left off pulling the ropes. He flipped back the tarpaulin, and Gardener saw about what he had expected: a weird conglomeration of equipment: tanks, hoses, three car batteries nailed to a board. A New and Improved Pump. "Will if I can."

Gardener grinned without much humor. "Did you bring me a dead rat and a string to swing it with?"

9

Friday, August 5th:

No air traffic had overflown Haven on a regular basis since the late 1960s when Dow Air Force Base in Bangor had closed down. If someone had uncovered the ship in the earth back in those days, there might have been trouble; there had been Air Force fighter planes zooming overhead four and five times a day, rattling windows and sometimes breaking them with sonic booms. The pilots weren't supposed to boom over the continental United States unless absolutely necessary, but the hotshots who flew the F-4s, most of them with adolescent acne still fading from their cheeks and foreheads, sometimes got a little exuberant. The jets made the Mustangs and Chargers these overgrown boys had been driving only a year before look mighty tame. When Dow closed there were still a few Air National Guard flights, but the patterns were shifted north, toward Loring in Limestone.

After some dithering, the base was turned into a commercial airfield, named Bangor International Airport. Some thought the name rather grand for an airport that serviced a few wheezy Northeast Airlines flights to Boston each day and a handful of puddle jumper Pipers bound for Augusta and Portland. But the air traffic eventually grew, and by 1983 BIA had become a thriving air terminal. Besides serving two commercial airlines, it was also a refueling point for many international carriers, and so it finally earned its grand name.

For a while, some commercial airliners did overfly Haven—this was in the early seventies. But pilots and navigators regularly reported radar problems in the area coded Quadrant G-3, a square which took in most of Haven, all of Albion, and the China Lakes region. This cloudy interference, known as "popcorn," or "echo-haze," or, even more colorfully, as "ghost-turds," is also reported regularly over the Bermuda Triangle. Compasses went wacky. Sometimes there were funny cuckoo electrical glitches in the equipment.

In 1973 a Delta jet southbound from BIA to Boston nearly collided with a TWA jet bound from London to Chicago. Drinks on both planes were spilled; a TWA stewardess was scalded by hot coffee. No one but the flight crews knew how close it had been. The copilot on the Delta plane ran a hot special-delivery into his pants, laughed hysterically all the way to Boston, and quit flying forever two days later.

In 1974 a Big Sky charter jet loaded with happy gamblers bound for Las Vegas from Bangor and the Canadian

Maritimes lost power in one engine over Haven and had to return to Bangor. When the engine was restarted on the ground, it ran fine.

There was another near-miss in 1975. By 1979, all commercial air traffic had been routed out of the area. If you had asked an FAA controller about it, he only would have shrugged and called it a dragon. It was a word they used. There were such places here and there; no one knew why. It was easier to route planes away and forget it.

By 1982, private air traffic was also being routinely vectored away from G-3 by controllers in Augusta, Waterville, and Bangor. So no pilot had seen the great shiny object winking up from the exact center of map-square G-3 on FAA Map ECUS-2.

Not until Peter Bailey saw it on the afternoon of August 5th.

Bailey was a private pilot with two hundred hours on his own in the air. He flew a Cessna Hawk XP, and he would have been the first to tell you that it had cost him a few banana-skins. This was Peter Bailey's phrase for money. He found it hilarious. The Hawk cruised at a hundred and fifty miles an hour and had good sky capability; 17,000 feet without breathing hard. The Cessna nav-pack made it hard to get lost (the optional nav antenna had also cost a few banana-skins). In other words it was a good plane, one that could damn near fly itself—only it didn't have to with a good pilot like him driving.

If Peter Bailey had a bitch, it was the goddam insurance. It was highway robbery, and he had bored his golfing partners to tears with the outrage the insurance companies had foisted on him.

He had friends who flew, he assured them grimly, plenty of them. A lot with less hours on their licenses than he had were forking over fewer banana-skins to the insurance heathens than he was. Some were guys he wouldn't have flown with, he said, if they owned the last plane on earth and his wife was in Denver dying of a brain hemorrhage. And the *amount* wasn't the greatest humiliation of all. The greatest humiliation of all was that *he*, Peter Bailey, *he,* a respected neurosurgeon who made well over three hundred thousand banana-skins a year, had to accept *pool coverage* if he wanted to fly. Well, he told his captive audiences (who often wished fervently that they had only played the front nine, or, better, had stayed in the bar and soaked up a few Bloody Marys), *pool coverage* was *assigned-risk coverage,* the sort teenagers and convicted drunks had to carry on their cars. Shit! If that wasn't goddam discrimination he didn't know what was. If he wasn't such a busy man he'd slap the bastards with a class action suit and he'd *win*, too.

Many of Bailey's golf companions were lawyers, and most knew it wouldn't wash. Risk coverage was made on the basis of actuarial tables, and the fact was, Peter Bailey wasn't just a neurosurgeon; he was a *doctor*, and doctors have the worst record as private pilots of any professional group in the world.

After escaping one of these foursomes, one of the players remarked as Bailey headed toward the clubhouse, still fuming: "I wouldn't even *drive* to Denver with the long-winded son of a bitch if my wife was dying of a brain hemorrhage."

Peter Bailey was exactly the sort of flier for whom the tables had been invented. There were undoubtedly doctors all over America who were exemplary pilots. Bailey wasn't one of them. Quick and decisive in the operating theater when a patient lay before him with a window of skull cut away to reveal the pinkish-gray brain tissue, as delicate as a dancer with scalpel and laser knife, he was a ham-fisted pilot who constantly violated assigned altitudes, FAA safety rules, and his own flight patterns. He was a bold pilot, but with only two hundred hours on his license, he could by no stretch of the imagination be called an *old* pilot. His status as an assigned risk only confirmed the old saw: a pilot may be one or the other, but no pilot is both.

He was flying alone that day from Teterboro outside New York to Bangor. At Bangor he would rent a car and drive to Derry Home Hospital. He had been asked to consult in the case of young Hillman Brown. Because the case was interesting and the price right (and because he had heard good things about the golf course in Orono), he had agreed.

The weather had been clear the whole way, the air smooth. Bailey had enjoyed the trip tremendously. As usual, his logbook was botched, he had missed one VOR beacon entirely and had decided another must be on the blink (he had hit the frequency dial with his elbow), he had wandered from his assigned altitude of 11,000 feet as high as 15,000 and as low as 6,000, and had once again avoided killing anyone . . . a blessing he was unfortunately too stupid to count.

He also wandered well off his flight-path, and so happened to overfly Haven, where a great blink of light suddenly flicked into his eye; it was as if someone had just flashed the lid of the world's biggest Crisco can up at him.

"*What* in the Sam *Hill*—"

He looked down and saw a tantalizing glimmer of that brightness. He might have dismissed it, might have gone on and survived to fight yet another day (or perhaps to collide with a fully loaded airliner), but he was early and intrigued. He banked the Hawk and went back.

"Now where—"

It flashed again, bright enough to dazzle a blue crescent of afterimage onto his eyes. Ripples of light ran across the top of the pilot's cabin.

"Jee-*zus!*"

There, below him in a clearing in the gray-green woods, was a huge silver object. He could tell little about it before it was gone again under the port wing.

At 6,000 feet for the second time that day, Bailey banked back again. His head had begun to ache—he noticed this and dismissed it as excitement. His first thought had been that it was a water-tower, but no one would locate a water-tower that big in the woods.

He overflew the object again, this time at 4,000. He had the Hawk throttled back as far as he dared (which was a good deal further than a more experienced pilot would have dared do, but the Hawk was a good plane and it forgave him).

Artifact, he thought this time, almost sick with excitement. A great dish-shaped artifact in the earth . . . or some government thing? But if it was government, how come it wasn't covered with a camouflage net? And the ground around it had been *excavated*—from up here, the trench cut into the earth was perfectly clear.

Bailey determined to overfly it again—hell, he'd buzz it!—and then his eye fell on his gauges and his heart took an unsteady leap. His compass was winding itself around in big stupid circles, the tank indicators were flashing red. The altimeter suddenly ran up to 22,000 feet, stopped briefly, and then dropped back to dead zero.

The Hawk's husky 195-horsepower motor gave a terrifying hitch. The nose dipped. Bailey's heart did the same. His head throbbed. In front of his bulging eyes needles were whirling, lights flashed from green to red like pygmy traffic signals, and the altitude warning beeper, which was supposed to tell a bemused pilot *Wake up, dummy, you are about to run into a large immovable object called Mother Earth*, began to sound, even though it wasn't supposed to go off until the plane passed through five hundred and Bailey's own eyes told him the Hawk was still at four thousand feet, perhaps a bit more. He looked at the digital thermometer which recorded the outside air temperature. It blinked from 47 to 58, then to 5. It paused there for a moment, then showed 999. The red numerals held there, pulsing distractedly, and then the thermometer shorted out.

"What in Christ's name is going on here?" Bailey screamed, and was stupidly amazed to see one of his front teeth fly out of his mouth, bounce off his airspeed indicator, and fall on the floor.

The engine hitched again.

"Fuck," he whispered. He was now sick with fright. Blood from the socket where his tooth had been trickled down his chin. A drop splashed on his Lacoste shirt.

The gleaming thing in the earth passed under his wings again.

The Hawk's engine ran choppily and stalled. It began to lose altitude. Forgetting all his training, Bailey hauled up on the wheel as hard as he could, but the silent plane didn't, couldn't, answer. Bailey's head pounded and thudded. The Cessna dropped to 4,000 feet . . . 3,500 . . . 3,000. Bailey groped out with one hand like a blind man and thumbed the button marked EMERGENCY RESTART. Hi-test av-gas boomed hollowly in the Hawk's carbs. The propeller jerked, then stopped again. Now the Cessna had slid down to 2,500 feet. It passed over the Old Derry Road close enough for Bailey to be able to see the service board in front of the Methodist church.

"Motherfuck," he whispered. "I'm gonna die."

He pulled the choke all the way out and hit the restart button again. The engine coughed, ran for a while, then began to stutter.

"No!" Bailey screamed. One eye ruptured and filled up with blood. The blood sheeted thinly down his left cheek. In his panicky, terrorized state, he didn't even notice. He slammed the choke in again. *"No, don't you stall, you ratshit plane!"*

The engine roared; the propeller blurred into invisibility with a wedge of reflected sunshine in it. Bailey hauled up on the wheel. The overburdened Hawk began to lug again.

"Ratshit plane! Ratshit plane! Ratshit plane!" he screamed. His left eye was now full of blood and he was on some level aware that the world seemed to have taken on a strange pinkish aspect, but if he'd had the time or inclination to think about this at all, he would have thought it no more than rage at this idiotic situation.

He let off on the wheel; the Hawk, allowed to climb at an angle which was almost sane, began to buckle down to its job again. Haven Village passed beneath it, and Bailey was aware of people looking up at him. He was low enough so someone could take his number if they thought of it. *Go ahead!* he thought grimly. *Go ahead, take it, because when I finish with Cessna Corporation, every goddam stockholder they have is gonna be standing in his underwear! I'm going to sue those negligent sons of bitches for every banana-skin they've got!*

The Hawk was rising smoothly now, its engine smooth and sweet. Bailey's head was trying to tear itself right off his shoulders, but an idea suddenly came to him—an idea of such stupefying simplicity and staggering ramifications that everything else was driven from his mind. He understood nothing less than the physiological basis of bicamerality in the human brain. This led to an instant understanding of race memory, not as a hazy Jungian concept but as a function of recombinant DNA and biological imprinting. And with this came an understanding of what the increased millierg generating capacity of the *corpus callosum* during periods of increased ductless-gland activity, which had puzzled students of the human brain for thirty years, actually meant.

Peter Bailey suddenly understood that time travel—actual *time travel*—was in his grasp.

At the same instant, a large portion of his own brain exploded.

White light flashed in his head—white light exactly like

the reflection that had winked at him from that object in the woods.

If he had collapsed forward, pushing the wheel in, the people of Haven would have had another mess on their hands. But instead he fell backward, head lolling on his neck, blood running from his ears. He stared up at the ceiling of the pilot's compartment with an expression of stupendous, terminal surprise printed on his face.

If the Cessna's autopilot had been engaged, it would almost certainly have flown serenely on until it ran out of fuel. Weather conditions were optimum, and such things have happened before. As it was, it flew along almost dead level at 5,500 feet for five minutes anyway. The radio squawked at the dead neurosurgeon, telling him to get his ass up to his assigned altitude right now.

Over Derry a wind current threw the plane into a gentle bank. It flew in a long, looping arc toward Newport. The bank grew steeper, turned into a spiral. The spiral became a spin. A kid fishing off a bridge on Route 7 looked up and saw a plane falling out of the sky, and whirling like a screw-auger as it did. He stared open-mouthed as it crashed in Ezra Dockery's north field and exploded in a pillar of flame.

"Holy *jeezum!*" the kid yelled. He dropped his fishing-pole and ran for the Newport Mobil up the road to call the fire department. Shortly after he left, a bass snatched his worm and pulled his pole into the water. The kid never found the pole, but in the excitement of fighting the grass-fire in Dockery's field and pulling the crispy pilot out of the remains of the Cessna, he barely noticed.

10

Saturday, August 6th:

Newt and Dick were sitting in the Haven Lunch. The newspaper was between them. The lead story was another outbreak of hostilities in the Mideast; the story that concerned them that morning was below the fold. NEUROSURGEON KILLED IN LIGHT PLANE CRASH, the headline read. There was a photo of the plane. Nothing recognizable remained of the once beautiful Cessna Hawk except its tail.

Their breakfasts were pushed to one side, mostly untouched. Molly Fenderson, Beach's niece, was cooking now that Beach was dead. Molly was a helluva nice girl, but her fried eggs looked like broiled assholes. Dick thought they tasted that way, too, although he'd never actually *eaten* an asshole, broiled or any other way.

Might have, Newt said.

Dick looked at him, eyebrows raised.

They put damn near *anything* in hot dogs. Least, that's what I read once.

Dick's gut rolled over. He told Newt to shut his fucking gob.

Newt paused, then said: Must have been twenty, thirty people seen that ijit come low acrost the village.

All from town? Dick asked.

Yes.

Then we have no problem, do we?

No, I don't think so, Newt replied, sipping coffee. At least, not unless it happens again.

Dick shook his head. Shouldn't do. Paper says he was off-course.

Yeah. So it said. You ready?

Sure.

They left without paying. Money had ceased to hold much interest to the residents of Haven. There were several large cardboard cartons of cash in Dick Allison's basement, carelessly tucked into the old coal-hold—twenties, tens, and ones, mostly. Haven was a small town. When people needed cash for something, they came and got some. The house was unlocked. Besides telepathic typewriters and water heaters that ran on the power of collapsing molecules, Haven had discovered a nearly perfect form of collectivism.

On the sidewalk in front of the Lunch, they stared toward the town hall. The brick clock-tower was flickering uneasily. One moment it was there, as solid as the Taj Mahal, if not so beautiful. The next, there was only blue sky above the jagged ruin of the tower's base. Then it would come back. Its long morning shadow fluttered like the shadow of a window-shade blown by an intermittent wind. Newt found the fact that sometimes the *shadow* of the clock-tower was there when the tower itself was not, particularly disturbing.

Christ! If I looked at that sucker too long, I'd go batshit, Dick said.

Newt asked if someone was taking care of the deterioration.

Tommy Jacklin and Hester Brookline have had to go up to Derry, Dick said. They're supposed to go to about five different service stations, plus both auto-parts stores. I sent damn near seven hundred bucks with them, told them to come back with as many as twenty car batteries, if they could. But they're supposed to spread the buy around. There's people in some of the towns around here that think folks have gone battery-crazy in Haven.

Tommy Jacklin and Hester Brookline? Newt asked dubiously. Christ, they're just kids! Has Tommy got a driver's license, Dick?

No, Dick said reluctantly. But he's fifteen and he's got a permit and he drives real safe. Besides, he's big. Looks older than he really is. They'll be okay.

Christ, it's so fucking risky!

It is, but—

They communed in thoughts that were more images than words; this was happening more and more in Haven, as the people in town learned this strange new thought-language. For all of his misgivings, Newt understood the basic problem that had caused Dick to send a couple of underage kids to Derry in the Fannins' pickup truck. They needed batteries, *needed* them, but it was getting harder and harder for the people who *lived* in Haven to *leave* Haven. If a codger like Dave Rutledge or an old coot like John Harley tried it, he would be dead—and probably rotting—before he got to the Derry city line. It would take younger men like Newt and Dick a slightly longer time, but they would also go . . . and probably in agony, because of the physical changes that had begun in Bobbi's shed. It didn't surprise either man that Hilly Brown was in a coma, and he had left when things were just starting to really roll. Tommy Jacklin was fifteen, Hester Brookline a well-developed thirteen. They at least had youth on their side, and could hope to leave and come back alive without the equivalent of NASA spacesuits to protect them from what was now an alien and inimical atmosphere. Such equipment would have been out of the question even if they'd had it. They probably could have cobbled something together, but if a couple of folks showed up at the Napa auto-parts store in Derry wearing moonsuits, there might be a few questions. Or more than a few.

I don't like it, Newt said at last.

Hell, I don't either, Dick replied. I'm not going to have a minute's peace until they get back, and I've got ole Doc Warwick parked out by the Haven-Troy line to take care of em just as soon as they do—

If they do.

Ayuh . . . *if*. I think they will, but they'll be hurting.

What kind of problems do you expect?

Dick shook his head. He didn't know, and Doc Warwick refused to even guess . . . except to ask Dick in a cross mental voice what he, Dick, thought would happen to a salmon if it decided to ride a bike upstream to the spawning grounds instead of swimming.

Well . . . Newt said doubtfully.

Well, nothing, Dick returned. We can't leave that thing—he nodded toward the oscillating clock-tower—the way it is.

Newt returned: We're almost down to the hatchway now. I think we could leave it.

Maybe. Maybe not. But we need batteries for other things, and you know it. And we need to keep being careful. You know *that*, too.

Don't teach your grammy to suck eggs, Dick.

(Fu)

Fuck *that*, asshole, was what Newt had been about to say, but he squashed it, although he found more to dislike about Dick Allison with every passing day. The truth was, Haven *ran* on batteries now, just like a kid's toy car from FAO Schwarz. And they kept needing more, and bigger ones, and mail-order was not only too slow, it was the sort of thing that might send up a warning flag to someone somewhere. You could never tell.

All in all, Newt Berringer was a troubled man. They had survived the plane-crash; if something happened to Tommy and Hester, could they survive that?

He didn't know. He only knew he wouldn't have much peace until the kids were back in Haven, where they belonged.

11

Sunday, August 7th:

Gardener was at the ship, looking at it, trying to decide—again—if any good could come of this mess . . . and if not, if there was any way out. He had heard the light plane two days before, although he had been in the house and had come out a moment too late to see it on its third pass. Three passes was just about two too many; he had been pretty sure the pilot had spotted the ship and the excavation. The thought had afforded Gardener a strange, bitter relief. Then, yesterday, he had seen the story in the paper. You didn't have to be a college graduate to see the connection. Poor old Dr. Bailey had wandered off-course, and that leftover from the space armada of Ming the Merciless had stripped his gears.

Did that make him, Jim Gardener, an accessory to murder? It might, and, wifeshooter or not, Gard didn't care for the thought.

Freeman Moss, the dour woodsman from Albion, hadn't shown up this morning—Gard supposed the ship had blown his fuses as it had those of the others before him. Gard was alone for the first time since Bobbi had disappeared. On the surface, that seemed to open things up. But when you looked deeper, the same old conundrums remained.

The story of the dead neurosurgeon and the crashed plane had been bad, but to Gard's mind, the story above the fold—the one Newt and Dick had ignored—was worse. The Mideast was getting ready to explode again, and if there was shooting this time, some of it might be nuclear. The Union of Concerned Scientists, those happy folks who kept the Black Clock, had advanced the hands to two minutes to nuclear midnight yesterday, the paper reported. Happy days were here again, all right. The ship could maybe pull the pin on all that . . . but was that what Freeman Moss, Kyle Archinbourg, Bozie, and all the rest of them wanted? Sometimes Gard felt a sickening surety that cooling out the powderkeg the planet was sitting on was the *last* thing the New and Improved Haven was concerned with. And so?

He didn't know. Sometimes being a telepathic zero was a pain in the ass.

His eye moved to the pumping machinery squashed into the mud at the edge of the trench. Working at the ship had previously been a matter of dust and dirt and rocks and stumps that wouldn't come up until you were just about half-crazy with frustration. Now it was wet work—very wet work indeed. The last couple of nights he had gone home with wet clay in his hair, between his toes, and in the crack of his ass. Mud was bad, but clay was worse. Clay *stuck*.

The pumping equipment was the strangest, ugliest conglomeration yet, but it worked. It also weighed tons, but the mostly silent Freeman Moss had transported it from Bobbi's dooryard all by himself . . . it had taken him most of Thursday and about five hundred batteries to do it, but he *had* done it, something which would have taken an ordinary construction crew a week or more to accomplish.

Moss had used a gadget like a metal-detector to guide each component to its final resting-place—first off the truck, then through the garden, then out along the well-worn path to the dig. The components floated serenely through the warm summer air, their shadows pooled beneath them. Moss carried the thing which had once been a metal-detector in one hand, and something which looked like a walkie-talkie handset in the other. When he raised the curved stainless-steel antenna on the end of the walkie-talkie gadget and moved the dish at the end of the detector, the motor or pump would rise. When he moved them to the left, the piece of equipment went left. Gard, watching this with the bemusement of a veteran drunk (and surely no one sees as many strange things as one of those), thought that Moss looked like a scrofulous animal trainer leading mechanical elephants through the woods to the site of some unimaginable circus.

Gardener had seen the laborious moving of enough heavy equipment to know that this device could revolutionize construction techniques. Such things were outside his practical knowledge, but he guessed that a single gadget such as the one Moss had used on Thursday with such absent ease could cut the cost of a project the size of the Aswan Dam by twenty-five percent or more.

In at least one respect, however, it was like the illusion being maintained at the town hall—it required a lot of juice.

"Here," Moss said, handing Gard a heavy packsack. "Put this on."

Gard winced shouldering the straps. Moss saw it and smiled a little. "It'll get lighter as the day goes along. Don't you worry about *that.*" He plugged the jack of a transistor earphone into the side of the radio-controller and pushed the phone into his ear.

"What's in the pack?" Gardener asked.

"Batteries. Let's go."

Moss had switched the gadget on, seemed to listen, nodded, then pointed the curved antenna at the first motor. It rose in the air and hung there. Holding the controller in one hand and the customized metal-detector in the other, Moss walked toward the motor. For every step he took, the motor retreated a similar distance. Gard brought up the rear.

Moss walked the motor between the house and the shed, urging it around the Tomcat, and then ahead of him through Bobbi's garden. A wide path had been worn through this, but on both sides of it the plants continued to grow in rampant splendor. Some of the sunflowers were now twelve feet high. They reminded Gardener of *The Day of the Triffids.* One night about a week ago he had awakened from a terrible nightmare. In it, the sunflowers in the garden had uprooted themselves and begun to walk, eldritch light shining from their centers and onto the ground like the beams of flashlights with green lenses.

There were summer squashes in the garden as big as U-boat torpedoes. Tomatoes the size of basketballs. Some of the corn was nearly as high as the sunflowers. Curious, Gardener had picked one of the ears; it was easily two feet long. A single ear, had it been good, would have fed two hungry men. But Gard had spat out the single mouthful of butter-and-sugar kernels he had bitten off, grimacing and wiping his mouth. The taste had been meaty and hideous. Bobbi was growing a garden full of huge plants, but the vegetables were inedible . . . perhaps even poisonous.

The motor had cruised serenely ahead of them along the path, cornstalks rustling and bending on either side as it pushed its way through. Gardener saw smears and swatches of grease and engine oil on some of the militantly green, swordlike leaves. On the far side of the garden, the motor began to sag. Moss had lowered the antenna, and the motor settled to the earth with a gentle thump.

"What's up?" Gardener had asked.

Moss only grunted and produced a dime. He stuck it in the base of his controller, twisted it, and pulled six double-A Duracells out of the battery compartment. He tossed them indifferently on the ground. "Gimme some more," he said.

Gardener unshouldered the knapsack, undid the straps, opened the flap, and saw what looked at first glance like a billion double-A's; it was as if someone had hit the Grand Jackpot at Atlantic City and the machine had paid off in batteries instead of bucks.

"Jesus!"

"I ain't Him," Moss said. "Gimme half a dozen of those suckers."

For once Gardener didn't seem to have a wisecrack left in him. He handed six batteries over and watched Moss fit them into the compartment. Then Moss replaced the battery hatch, turned it on, refitted the earplug in his ear, and said, "Let's go."

Forty yards into the woods there was another battery change; sixty yards later, another. Floating the motor sucked less juice when it was going downhill, but by the time Moss had finally settled the big motor-block on the edge of the trench, they had gone through forty-two batteries.

Back and forth, back and forth; one by one they brought the pieces of pumping machinery from Freeman Moss's truck to the edge of the trench. The knapsack on Gardener's back grew steadily lighter.

On the fourth trip, Gard had asked Moss if he could try. A large industrial pump, whose *raison d'être* before this odd little side-trip had probably been pumping sewage from clogged septic tanks, was sitting on a tilted angle about a hundred yards from the trench. Moss was once more changing batteries. Dead double-A's lay all along the path now, reminding Gard with odd poignance of the kid at Arcadia Beach. The kid with the firecrackers. The kid whose mother had given up drinking . . . and everything else. The kid who had known about the Tommyknockers.

"Well, you can give her a try." Moss handed over the

gadget. "I could use a smidge of help, and I don't mind sayin so. Wears a man out, liftin all that." He saw Gardener's look and said: "Oh, ayuh, I'm doin part of it m'self; that's what the plug's for. You can try it, but I don't think you'll have much luck. You ain't like us."

"I noticed. I'm the one that isn't going to have to buy a set of teeth from Sears and Roebuck when all this is over."

Moss looked at him sourly and said nothing.

Gard used his handkerchief to wipe off the brown coating of wax Moss had left on the earplug, then stuck it in his ear. He heard a distant sound like the one you heard when you held a conch shell to your ear. He pointed the antenna at the pump as he had seen Moss do, then cautiously flickered the antenna upward. The quality of the dim seashore rumble in his ear changed. The pump moved the tiniest bit—he was sure it wasn't just his imagination. But an instant later, two other things happened. He felt warm blood coursing down his face from his nose, and his head was filled with a blaring voice. "CARPET YOUR DEN OR YOUR WHOLE HOME FOR LESS!" screamed some radio announcer, who was suddenly sitting right in the middle of Gardener's head and apparently yelling into an electric bullhorn. "AND YES WE DO HAVE A NEW SHIPMENT OF THROW-RUGS! THE LAST ONE SOLD OUT FAST, SO BE SURE—"

"Owww, Jesus, shut up!" Gardener had cried. He dropped the handset and reached for his head. The earphone was dragged out of his ear, and the blaring announcer cut out. He had been left with a nosebleed and a head that was ringing like a bell.

Freeman Moss, startled out of his taciturnity, stared at Gardener with wide eyes. "What in Christ's name was that?" he asked.

"That," Gardener said weakly, "was WZON, Where It's Only Rock and Roll Because That's the Way You Like It. You mind if I sit down for a minute, Moss? Think I just pissed myself."

"Your nose is bleedin, too."

"No shit, Sherlock," Gardener said.

"Think maybe you better let me use the lifter after this." Gard had been more than happy to abide by that. It took them the rest of the day to get all the equipment out to the trench, and Moss was so tired when the last piece arrived that Gardener had to practically carry the man back to his truck.

"Feel like I just chopped two cord of wood and shit m'brains out while I was doin it," the older man gasped.

After that, Gard hadn't really expected the man to come back. But Moss had shown up promptly at seven the next day. He had been driving a beat-up split-grille Pontiac instead of his truck. He got out of the Pontiac banging a dinner bucket against his leg.

"Come on. Let's get to it."

Gardener respected Moss more than the other three "helpers" put together . . . in fact, he liked him.

Moss glanced at him as they walked out to the ship with the morning dew of that Friday morning wetting down the cuffs of their pants. "Caught that one," he grunted. "You're okay too, I guess."

That was about all Mr. Freeman Moss had to say to him that day.

They sank a nest of hoses into the trench and rigged more hoses—outflow hoses, this time—to direct the water they pumped out downhill, on a slope that ran a bit southeast of Bobbi's place. These "dumper hoses," as Moss called them, were big wide-bore rolls of canvas that Gard supposed had been scavenged from the VFD.

"Ayuh, got a few there, got a few other places," Moss said, and would offer no more on that subject.

Before starting the pumps, he had Gardener pound a number of U-shaped clamps over the dumper hoses. "Else they'll go whippin around, sprayin water everywhere. If you've ever seen a fireman's hose outta control, you know someone c'n get hurt. And we ain't got enough men to stand around holdin a bunch of pissin hoses all day."

"Not that there'd be any volunteers standing in line. Right?"

Freeman Moss had looked at him silently, saying nothing for a moment. Then he grunted: "Pound those clamps in good. We'll still have to stop pretty often to pound 'em back in. They'll loosen up."

"Can't you control the outflow so you don't have to bother with all this clamping shit?" Gardener asked.

Moss rolled his eyes impatiently at his ignorance. "Sure,"

he said, "but there's one fuck of a lot of water down in that hole, and I'd like to get it out before doomsday, if it's all the same to you."

Gardener held out his hands, half-laughing. "Hey, I was just asking," he said. "Peace."

The man had only grunted in his inimitable Freeman Moss style.

By nine-thirty, water was pouring downhill and away from the ship at a great rate. It was cold and clear and as sweet as water can be—which is sweet indeed, as anyone with a good well could attest. By noon they had created a brand-new stream. It was six feet wide, shallow, but brawling right along, carrying pine needles, loamy black topsoil, and small shrubs away. There was not much for the men to do but to sit around and make sure none of the plump, straining dumper hoses came free and started to fly around spraying water like bombed-out fire hydrants. Moss shut the pumps down regularly, in sequence, so that they could pound in loose clamps or switch them to a new place if the ground was getting loose where they had been.

By three o'clock, the stream was rolling larger bushes downstream, and just before five o'clock, Gardener heard the rending rumble of a biggish tree going over. He got up and craned his neck, but it had happened too far down the new stream's course to see.

"Sounded like a pine," Moss said.

It was Gardener's turn to look at Moss and say nothing.

"Might have been a spruce," Moss said, and although the man's face remained perfectly straight, Gardener believed Moss might just have made a joke. A very small one, but a joke, just the same.

"Is this water reaching the road, do you think?"

"Oh, ayuh, I sh'd suspect."

"It'll wash it out, won't it?"

"Nope. Town crew's already puttin in a new culve't. Large bore. S'pose they'll have to detour traffic couple of days while they tear up the tarvy, but they ain't's much traffic out here as there used to be, anyway."

"I noticed," Gardener said.

"Damn good thing, if you ask me. Summer people're always a pain in the ass. Looka here, Gardener—I'm gonna cut the outflow on these pumps way down, but they'll still pump fifteen, maybe seventeen gallons a minute overnight. With four pumps workin, that's thirty-eight hundred gallons an hour, all night long. Not bad for runnin on automatic. Come on, let's go. Yon ship's lovely, but it makes my blood pressure jumpy. I'll drink one of your beers before I head home to the missus, if you'll let it be so."

Moss had shown up again yesterday, Saturday, in his old Pontiac, and had promptly run the pumps up to capacity—thirty-five gallons per minute each, eighty-four hundred gallons an hour.

This morning, no Freeman Moss. He had finally played out like the others, leaving Gardener to consider the same old options.

First option: Business as usual.

Second option: Run like hell. He had already come to the conclusion that if Bobbi died, he would suffer a fatal accident soon afterward. It might take as long as half an hour for him to have it. If he decided to run, would they know in advance? Gardener didn't think so. He and the rest of Haven still played poker the old-fashioned way: with all the cards dealt facedown. Oh, and by the way, gang—how *far* would he have to run to get out of the reach of them and their Buck Rogers gadgetry?

Actually, Gard didn't think it would be that far. Derry, Bangor, even Augusta . . . all those might be too close. Portland? Maybe. *Probably.* Because of what he thought of as the Cigarette Analogy.

When a kid started to smoke, he was lucky if he could get through half a butt without puking his guts out or almost fainting. After six months' experience, he might be able to get through five or ten butts a day. Give a kid three years and you had yourself a two-and-a-half-pack-a-day candidate for lung cancer.

Then turn it over. Tell a kid who has just finished his first butt and who is wandering around green-faced and gagging that he has to quit smoking, and he'll probably fall down and kiss your ass. Catch him when he's doing five or ten smokes a day and you've got a kid who probably doesn't care much one way or another . . . although a kid habituated even at that level may find himself eating too many sweets and wishing for a smoke when he's bored or nervous.

Ah, Gardener thought, but take your smoking vet. Tell him he's got to quit the coffin-nails and he clutches his chest like a man who's having a heart attack . . . only he's just protecting the smokes in the breast pocket of his shirt. Smoking, Gardener knew from his own mostly successful efforts to either quit the habit or at least damp it down to a less lethal vice, is a physical addiction. In the first week off cigarettes, smokers suffer from jitters, headaches, muscle spasms. Doctors may prescribe B_{12} to quiet the worst of these symptoms. They know, however, that there are no pills to combat the ex-smoker's feelings of loss and depression during the six months which begin the instant the smoker crushes out his last butt and starts his or her lonely voyage out of addiction.

And Haven, Gardener thought now, running the pumps up to full power, *is like a smoke-filled room. They were sick here at first . . . they were like a bunch of kids learning to smoke cornshucks out behind the barn. But now they* like *the air in the room, and why not? They're the ultimate chainsmokers. It's in the air they breathe, and God knows what kinds of physiological changes are going on in their brains and bodies. Lung sections show formation of oat cells in the lung tissue of people who have been smoking for only eighteen months. There's a high incidence of brain tumors in towns where there are high-pollution milling operations or, God save us, nuclear reactors. So what is this doing to* them?

He didn't know—he had seen no surface, observable changes except for the loss of teeth and the increased shortness of temper. But he didn't think they'd chase him very far if he split. They might begin by lighting out after him with the fervor of a posse in a Republic western, but he somehow thought they would lose interest very quickly . . . as soon as the withdrawal symptoms set in.

He got all four pumps running at top speed, swelling the creek into a wide stream almost at once. Then he began the day's work of checking the U-clamps which held the hoses still.

If he got away, his choices were two: keep his mouth shut or blow the whistle. He knew that, for a variety of reasons, he would probably keep quiet. Which meant simply dealing himself out—writing off the last month of back-breaking labor, writing off any chance to change the suicidal course of world politics at a stroke, most of all writing off his good friend and erstwhile lover Bobbi Anderson, who had been *in absentia* for the best part of two weeks now.

Third option: Get rid of it. Blow it up. Destroy it. Make it no more than another vague rumor, like the supposed aliens in Hangar 18.

In spite of his dull fury at the insanity of nuclear power and the energy-swilling technocratic pigs who had created it and underwritten it and refused to see its dangers even in the wake of Chernobyl, in spite of his depression at the AP Wirephoto of the scientists advancing the Black Clock to two minutes before midnight, he fully recognized the possibility that destroying the ship might be the best thing he could possibly do. The oxidation of whatever had been impregnated in the surface of its hull (deliberately, he had no doubt) had created a cornucopia of mind-blowing gadgets out here; God alone knew what wonderful things might be waiting inside. But there was the other stuff, wasn't there? The neurosurgeon in the crashed plane, that old man and the big state cop, maybe the lady constable, Mrs. McCausland, maybe the two other state cops who had disappeared, maybe even the Brown kid . . . how much of this could be laid at the door of this thing he was staring at, which was jutting out of the ground like the breeching snout of the greatest white whale ever dreamed of? Some? All? None of the above?

Gardener was sure of one thing—it wasn't the last.

That the ship in the earth was a font of creation was undeniable . . . but it was also the wrecked craft of an unknowable species from somewhere far out in the blackness—creatures whose minds might be as different from those of human beings as human minds were from the minds of spiders. It was a marvelous, improbable artifact shining in the hazy sunlight of this Sunday morning . . . but it was also a haunted house where demons might still walk between the walls and in the hollow places. There were times when he would look at it and feel his throat fill up with strangeness, as at the sight of flat eyes staring up at him from the earth.

But get rid of it *how?* Blow it up *how?* Even supposing he wanted to, how would he do it? The packet charges they had used to chop up the bedrock holding the ship fast were more powerful than dynamite, but they didn't even scratch the hull of the thing. Was he supposed to trot off to Limestone Air Force Base, steal an A-bomb, moving with the silky, unbelievable smoothness of Dirk Pitt in a Clive Cussler novel? And wouldn't it be funny, wouldn't it really be the last laugh, if he actually did manage to get a nuke and set it off, only to discover that all he'd really managed to do was to set the ship, still uncannily unharmed and unscratched, free at a stroke?

Those were his options, the third of which was not an option at all . . . and apparently his hands had known more than his brain, for while he went on turning them over in his mind for the umptieth time, he had gone calmly about the morning's work—driving the pumps up to full blast and making sure that the dumper hoses were solidly planted. Now he was back at the trench checking the sucker hoses, and the level of the water. He was happy to find he needed a powerful flashlight to see the water—it was falling rapidly. He guessed that blasting and excavation could begin again by Wednesday, Thursday at the latest . . . and once they got going again, the work would go fast. The rock of an aquifer was spongy and large-pored. They wouldn't need to waste time digging glory-holes for explosives, because there would be enough natural spots for not just exploding radios but satchel charges. The next phase would be like moving from a dense, gluey batter to a freshly risen dough.

Gard stood bent over the cut in the earth for some time, shining the big light into the black depths. Then he clicked it off, meaning to inspect the clamps again. Here it was, only eight-thirty in the morning, and already he wanted a drink.

He turned around.

Bobbi was standing there.

Gardener's mouth dropped open. He closed it with a snap after a moment and started toward her, fully expecting this hallucination to grow transparent, then be gone. But Bobbi stayed solid, and Gard saw that she had lost a great deal of hair—her brow, a pale and shining white, extended back nearly to the middle of her skull, leaving the world's biggest widow's peak in the center. Nor were these newly exposed sections of skull the only pale things about her; she looked like someone who had been through a terrible debilitating illness. Her right arm was in a sling. And—

—and she's wearing makeup. Pan-Cake makeup. I'm pretty sure that's what it is—she's laid it on heavy the way a lady does when she wants to cover up a bruise. But it's her . . . Bobbi . . . no dream . . .

His eyes suddenly filled with tears. Bobbi doubled, then trebled. It wasn't until then—that moment—that he realized just how scared he had been. And how lonely.

"Bobbi?" he asked hoarsely. "Is it really you?"

Bobbi smiled, that old sweet smile he loved so well, the one that had saved him from his own idiot self so often. It was Bobbi. It was Bobbi and he loved her.

He went to her, put his arms around her, laid his tired face against her neck. He had done this before, too.

"Hello, Gard," she said, and began to cry.

He was crying too. He kissed her. Kissed her. Kissed her.

His hands were suddenly all over her; her free one was on him.

No, he said, still kissing her. No, you can't—

Shh. I have to. It's my last chance, Gard. *Our* last chance.

Kissed. They kissed. Oh they kissed and now her shirt was unbuttoned and this was not the body of a sex goddess, it was white and sickish, the muscles flabby, the breasts saggy, but he loved it and he kissed her and kissed her and their tears were all over each other's faces.

Gard my dear, my dear, always my

shhhh

Oh please I love you

Bobbi I love

love

kiss me

kiss

yes

Pine needles under them. Sweetness. Her tears. His tears. They kissed, kissed, kissed. And as he entered her, Gard realized two things at once: how much he had missed her, and that not a single bird was singing. The woods were dead.

Kissed.

12

Gard used his shirt, not very clean anyway, to wipe swatches of brown makeup from his naked body. It hadn't just been on her face. Had she come out here expecting to make love to him? Something it might be just as well not to think about. Now, anyway.

Although they both should have been Thanksgiving dinner for the noseeums and moose-flies, spouting sweat as they had been doing, he hadn't a single bite. He didn't think Bobbi had any, either. *It's not only an IQ booster,* he thought, looking at the ship, *it's got every insect repellent on the market beat hollow.*

He tossed his shirt aside and touched Bobbi's face, running a finger down her cheek, picking up a little more of the makeup. Most of it, however, had either been sweated off . . . or washed away by her tears.

"I hurt you," he said.

You loved me, she answered.

"What?"

You hear me, Gard. I know you do.

"Are you angry?" he asked, aware that the barriers were going up again, aware that he was acting again, aware that it was over, all the things they'd had were finally over. These were sorry things to be aware of. "Is that why you won't talk to me?" He paused. "I wouldn't blame you. You've put up with a lot of shit from me over the years, woman."

"I *was* talking to you," she said, and, sorry as he was to be lying to her after loving her, he was glad to sense her doubt. "With my *mind*."

"I didn't hear."

"You did before. You heard . . . and you answered. We *talked*, Gard."

"We were closer to . . . that." He flagged an arm at the ship.

She smiled wanly up at him and put her cheek against his shoulder. With most of the makeup scrubbed away, her flesh had an unsettling translucence.

"Did I? Hurt you?"

"No. Yes. A little." She smiled. It was that old Bobbi Anderson go-to-hell grin, but a final tear ran slowly down her cheek nonetheless. "It was worth it. We saved the best for last, Gard."

He kissed her gently, but now her lips were different. The lips of the New and Improved Roberta Anderson.

"First, last, or in the middle, I didn't have any business making love to you, and you don't have any business out here."

"I look tired, I know," Bobbi said, "and I'm wearing a lot of goop, as you already found out. You were right—I let myself get overtired and I had something like a complete physical breakdown."

Bullshit, Gardener thought, but he covered this thought with white noise so Bobbi couldn't read it—he did this with barely a conscious thought. Such hiding was becoming second nature to him now.

"The treatment was . . . radical. It's resulted in some superficial skin problems and some hair loss. But it'll all grow back."

"Oh," Gardener said, thinking: *You still can't lie for shit, Bobbi.* "Well, I'm glad you're all right. But you maybe ought to take a couple of days off, put your feet up—"

"No," Bobbi said quietly. "This is the time for the final push, Gard. We're almost there. We started this, you and me—"

"No," Gardener said. *"You* started it, Bobbi. You literally stumbled over it. Back when Peter was alive. Remember?"

Gard saw pain in Bobbi's eyes at the mention of Peter. Then it was gone. She shrugged Gard's qualification off. "You were here soon enough. You saved my life. I wouldn't be here without you. So let's do it together, Gard. I bet it's no more than another twenty-five feet down to that hatchway."

Gardener had a strong hunch she was right, but he suddenly didn't feel like admitting it. There was a spike turning and turning in his heart, and the pain was worse than any hangover headache he'd ever had.

"If you think so, I'll take your word for it."

"What do you say, Gard? One more mile. You and me."

He sat thoughtfully, looking at Bobbi, noticing again how still, how almost malignant the woods seemed with no birdsong in them.

This is how it would be—this is how it will *be—if one of their asshole power plants ever does melt down. The people will have smarts enough to get out—if they're warned in time, that is, and if the power plant in question and the NRC have balls enough to tell them—but you can't tell an owl or woodpecker to clear the area. You can't tell a scarlet tanager not to look at the fireball. So their eyes will melt and they'll just go flapping around, blind as bats, running into trees and the sides of buildings until they starve to death or break their necks. Is this a spaceship, Bobbi? Or is it a great big containment housing that's already leaking? It has, hasn't it? That's why these woods are so quiet, and that's why the Polyester-Clad Neurologist Bird fell out of the sky on Friday, isn't it?*

"What do you say, Gard? One more mile?"

So where's the good solution? Where's peace with honor? Do you run? Do you turn it over to the American Dallas Police so they can use it on the Soviet Dallas Police? What? What? Any new ideas, Gard?

And suddenly he *did* have an idea . . . or the glimmer of one.

But a glimmer was better than nothing.

He hugged Bobbi with a lying arm. "Okay. One more mile."

Bobbi's grin started to widen . . . and then it became a look of curious surprise. "How much did he leave you, Gard?"

"How much did who leave me?"

"The Tooth Fairy," Bobbi said. "You finally lost one. Right there in the front."

Startled and a little afraid, Gard raised his hand to his mouth. Sure enough, there was a gap where one of his incisors had been yesterday.

It had started, then. After a month working in the shadow of this thing, he had foolishly assumed immunity, but it wasn't so. It had started; he was on his way to becoming New and Improved.

On his way to "becoming."

He forced an answering smile. "I hadn't noticed," he said.

"Do you feel any different?"

"No," Gard said truthfully. "Not yet, anyway. What do you say, you want to do some work?"

"I'll do what I can," Bobbi said. "With this arm—"

"You can check the hoses and tell me if any of them are starting to come loose. And talk to me." He looked at Bobbi with an awkward smile. "None of those other guys knew how to talk, man. I mean, they were sincere, but . . ." He shrugged. "You know?"

Bobbi smiled back, and Gardener saw another brilliant, unalloyed flash of the old Bobbi, the woman he had loved. He remembered the safe dark harbor of her neck and that screw in his heart turned again. "I think I do," she said, "and I'll talk your ear off, if that's what you want. I've been lonely, too."

They stood together, smiling at each other, and it was almost the same, but the woods were silent with no birdsong to fill them up.

The love's over, he thought. *Now it's the same old poker game, except the Tooth Fairy came last night and I guess the bastard will be back tonight. Probably along with his cousin and his brother-in-law. And when they start seeing my cards, maybe exposing that glimmer of an idea like an ace in the hole, it'll be all over. In a way, it's funny. We always assumed the aliens would have to at least be* alive *to invade. Not even H. G. Wells expected an invasion of ghosts.*

"I want to have a look into the trench," Bobbi said.

"Okay. You'll like the way it's draining, I think."

Together they walked into the shadow cast by the ship.

13

Monday, August 8th:

The heat was back.

The temperature outside of Newt Berringer's kitchen window was seventy-nine at a quarter past seven that Monday morning, but Newt wasn't in the kitchen to read it; he was standing in the bathroom in his pajama bottoms, inexpertly applying his late wife's makeup to his face and cursing the way the sweat made the Pan-Cake clump up. He had always thought makeup a lot of harmless ladies' foofraw, but now, trying to use it according to its original purpose—not to accent the good but to conceal the bad (or, at least, the startling)—he was discovering that putting on makeup was like giving someone a haircut. It was a fuck of a lot harder than it looked.

He was trying to cover up the fact that, over the last week or so, the skin of his cheeks and forehead had begun to fade. He knew, of course, that it had something to do with the trips he and the others had made into Bobbi's shed—trips he could not remember afterward; only that they had been frightening but even more exhilarating, and that he had come out all three times feeling ten feet tall and ready to have sex in the mud with a platoon of lady wrestlers. He knew enough to associate what was happening with the shed, but at first he had thought it was simply a matter of losing his usual summer tan. In the years before an icy winter afternoon and a skidding bread truck had taken her, his wife Elinor liked to joke that all you needed to do was to put Newt under one ray of sun after the first of May and he turned as brown as an Indian.

By last Friday afternoon, however, he was no longer able to fool himself about what was going on. He could see the veins, arteries, and capillaries in his cheeks, exactly as you could see them in that model he'd gotten his nephew Michael two Christmases ago—the Amazing Visible Man, it was called. It was damned unsettling. It wasn't just being able to see into himself, either; when he pressed his fingers against his cheeks, the cheekbones felt definitely squashy. It was as if they were . . . well . . . *dissolving*.

I can't go out like this, he thought. *Jesus, no.*

But on Saturday, when he had looked in the mirror and realized after some thought and a lot of squinting that the gray shadow he was seeing through the side of his face was his own tongue, he had almost flown over to Dick Allison's.

Dick answered the door looking so normal that for a few terrible moments Newt believed this was happening to him and him alone. Then Dick's firm, clear thought filled his head, making him weak with relief: Christ, you can't go around looking like that, Newt. You'll scare people. Come in here. I'm going to call Hazel.

(The phone, of course, was really not necessary, but old habits died hard.)

In Dick's kitchen, under the fluorescent ring in the ceiling, Newt had seen clearly enough that Dick was wearing makeup—Hazel, Dick said, had shown him how to put it on. Yes, it had happened to all the others except Adley, who had gone into the shed for the first time only two weeks ago.

Where does it all end, Dick? Newt had asked uneasily. The mirror in Dick's hallway drew him like a magnet and he stared at himself, seeing his tongue behind and through his pallid lips, seeing a tangled undergrowth of small pulsing capillaries in his forehead. He pressed the tips of his fingers against the shelf of bone over his eyebrows and saw faint finger indentations when he took them away. They were like fingermarks in hard wax, right down to the discernible loops and sworls of his fingertips sunk into the livid skin. Looking at that had made him feel sick.

I don't know, Dick had answered. He was talking on the phone with Hazel at the same time. But it doesn't really matter. It's going to happen to everyone eventually. Like everything else. *You* know what I mean.

He knew, all right. The first changes, Newt thought, looking into the mirror on this hot Monday morning, had in many ways been even worse, more shocking, because they had been so . . . well, intimate.

But he had gone a ways toward getting used to it, which only went to show, he supposed, that a person could get used to anything, given world enough and time.

Now he stood by the mirror, dimly hearing the deejay on the radio informing his listening audience that an influx of hot southern air coming into the area meant they could look forward to at least three days and maybe a week of muggy weather and temps in the upper eighties and low nineties. Newt cursed the coming humid weather—it would make his hemorrhoids itch and burn, it always did—and went on trying to cover his increasingly transparent cheeks, forehead, nose, and neck with Elinor's Max Factor Pan-Cake. He finished cursing the weather and went fluently on to the makeup with never a break in his monologue, having no idea that makeup grew old and cakey after a long period of time (and this particular lot had been in the back of a bathroom drawer since long before Elinor's death in February 1984).

But he supposed he would get used to putting the crap on . . . until such time as it was no longer necessary, anyhow. A person could get used to damn near anything. A tentacle, white at its tip, then shading to rose and finally to a dark blood-red as it thickened toward its unseen base, fell out through the fly of his pajama bottoms. Almost as if to prove his thesis, Newt Berringer only tucked it absently back in and went on trying to get his dead wife's makeup to spread evenly on his disappearing face.

14

Tuesday, August 9th:

Old Doc Warwick slowly pulled the sheet up over Tommy Jacklin and let it drop. It billowed slightly, then settled. The shape of Tommy's nose was clearly defined. He'd been a handsome kid, but he'd had a big nose, just like his dad.

His dad, Bobbi Anderson thought sickly. *Someone's going to have to tell his dad, and guess who's going to be elected?* Such things shouldn't bother her anymore, she knew—things like the Jacklin boy's death, things like knowing she would have to get rid of Gard when they reached the ship's hatchway—but they sometimes still did.

She supposed that would burn away in time.

A few more trips to the shed. That was all it would take.

She brushed aimlessly at her shirt and sneezed.

Except for the sound of the sneeze and the stertorous breathing of Hester Brookline in the other bed of the makeshift little clinic the Doc had set up in his sitting-*cum*-examination room, there was only shocked silence for a moment.

Kyle: He's really *dead*?

No, I just like to cover em up that way sometimes for a joke, Warwick said crossly. Shit, man! I knew he was going at four o'clock. That's why I called you all here. After all, you're the town fathers now, ain't you?

His eyes fixed for a moment on Hazel and Bobbi.

Excuse me. And two town mothers.

Bobbi smiled with no humor. Soon there was going to be only one sex in Haven. No mothers; no fathers. Just another Burma-Shave sign, you might say, on the Great Road of "Becoming."

She looked from Kyle to Dick to Newt to Hazel and saw that the others looked as shocked as she felt. Thank God she was not alone, then. Tommy and Hester had gotten back all right—ahead of schedule, actually, because when Tommy started to feel really ill only three hours after they had driven out of the Haven-Troy area, he had begun to push it, moving as fast as he could.

The damn kid was really a hero, Bobbi thought. *I guess the best we can do for him is a plot in Homeland, but he was still a hero.*

She looked toward where Hester lay, pallid as a wax cameo, breathing dryly, eyes closed. They could have—maybe should have—come back when they felt the headaches coming on, when their gums began to bleed, but they hadn't even discussed it. And it wasn't only their gums. Hester, who had been menstruating lightly all during the "becoming" (unlike older women, teenage girls didn't ever seem to stop . . . or hadn't yet, anyway), made Tommy stop at the Troy General Store so she could buy heavier sanitary napkins. She had begun to flow copiously. By the time they had bought three car batteries and a good used truck battery in the Newport-Derry Town Line Auto Supply on Route 7, she had soaked four Stayfree Maxi-Pads.

Their heads began to ache, Tommy's worse than Hester's. By the time they had gotten half a dozen Allstate batteries at the Sears store and well over a hundred C, D, and double- and triple-A cells at the Derry Tru-Value Hardware (which had just gotten a new shipment in), they both knew they had to get back . . . quick. Tommy had begun to hallucinate; as he drove up Wentworth Street, he thought he saw a clown grinning up at him from an open sewer manhole—a clown with shiny silver dollars for eyes and a clenched white glove filled with balloons.

Eight miles or so out of Derry, headed back toward Haven on Route 9, Tommy's rectum began to bleed.

He pulled over, and, face flaming with embarrassment,

asked Hester if he could have some of her pads. He was able to explain why when she asked, but not to look at her while he did so. She gave him a handful and he went into the bushes for a minute. He came back to the car weaving like a drunk, one hand outstretched.

"You got to drive, Hester," he said. "I'm not seeing so hot."

By the time they got back to the town line, the front seat of the car was splashed with gore and Tommy was unconscious. By then Hester herself was able to see only through a dark curtain; she knew it was four of a bright summer's afternoon, but Doc Warwick seemed to come to her out of a thundery purple twilight. She knew he was opening the door, touching her hands, saying: *It's all right, my darling, you are back, you can let go of the wheel now, you are back in Haven.* She was able to give a more or less coherent account of their afternoon as she lay in the protective circle of Hazel McCready's arms, but she had joined Tommy in unconsciousness long before they got to the Doc's, even though Doc was doing an unheard-of sixty-five, his white hair flying in the wind.

Adley McKeen whispered: What about the girl?

Well, her blood pressure's dropping, Warwick said. The bleeding's stopped. She is young and tough. Good country stock. I knew her parents and her grandparents. She'll pull through. He looked around at them grimly, his watery old blue eyes not deceived by their makeup, which in this light made them look like half a dozen ghastly suntanned clowns.

But I don't think she'll ever regain her sight.

There was a numb silence. Bobbi broke it:

That's not so.

Doc Warwick turned to look at her.

She'll see again, Bobbi said. When the "becoming" is finished, she'll see. We'll all see with one eye then.

Warwick met her gaze for a moment, and then his own eyes dropped. Yes, he said. I guess. But it's a damned shame, anyway.

Bobbi agreed without heat. Bad for her. Worse for Tommy. No bed of roses for their folks. I have to go see them. I could use company.

She looked at them, but their eyes dropped away from hers a pair at a time and their thoughts dulled into a smooth hum.

All right, Bobbi said. I'll manage. I guess.

Adley McKeen spoke up humbly. I guess I'll come with you if you want, Bobbi. Keep you company.

Bobbi gave him a tired yet somehow brilliant smile and squeezed his shoulder. Thank you, Ad. For the second time, thank you.

The two of them went out. The others watched them, and when they heard Bobbi's truck start, they turned toward where Hester Brookline lay unconscious, hooked up to a sophisticated life-support machine whose component parts had come from two radios, a turntable record-changer, the auto-tuning device from Doc's new Sony TV . . .

. . . and, of course, lots of batteries.

15

Wednesday, August 10th:

In spite of his tiredness, his confusion, his inability to stop playing Hamlet, and—worst of all—the persistent feeling that things in Haven were going wronger all the time, Jim Gardener had managed the booze pretty well since the day Bobbi had come back and they had lain together on the fragrant pine needles. Part of the reason was pure self-interest. Too many bloody noses, too many headaches. Some of this was undoubtedly the influence of the ship, he thought—he hadn't forgotten that he'd had one after Bobbi had repeatedly urged him to touch her find, and he had seized the leading edge of the ship and felt that rapid, numbing vibration—but he was wise enough to know that his steady drinking was doing its part, as well. There had been no blackouts *per se,* but there had been days when his nose had bled three and four times. He had always tended toward hypertension, and he had been told more than once that steady drinking could worsen what was a borderline condition.

So he was doing fairly well until he heard Bobbi sneezing.

That sound, so terribly familiar, called up a set of memories and a sudden terrible idea exploded in his mind like a bomb.

He went into the kitchen, opened the hamper, and looked at a dress—the one she'd been wearing yesterday evening. Bobbi did not see this inspection; she was asleep. She had sneezed in her sleep.

Bobbi had gone out the previous evening with no explanation—she had seemed nervous and upset to Gardener, and although both of them had worked hard all day, Bobbi had eaten almost no supper. Then, near sundown, she had bathed, changed into the dress, and driven off into the hot, still, muggy evening. Gardener had heard her come back around midnight, had seen the brilliant flare of light as Bobbi went into the shed. He thought she came back in around first light, but wasn't sure.

All day today she had been morose, speaking only when spoken to, and only then in monosyllables. Gardener's clumsy efforts to cheer her up met with no success. Bobbi skipped supper again tonight, and just shook her head when Gardener suggested a few cribbage hands on the porch, just like in the old days.

Bobbi's eyes, looking out of that weird coating of flesh-colored makeup, had looked somber and wet. Even as Gardener noticed this, Bobbi yanked a handful of Kleenex from the table behind her and sneezed into them two or three times, rapidly.

"Summer cold, I guess. I'm going to hit the rack, Gard. I'm sorry to be such a party-pooper, but I'm whipped."

"Okay," Gard said.

Something—some remembered familiarity—had been gnawing at him, and now he stood here with her dress in his hands, a light sleeveless summer cotton. In the old days it would have been washed this morning, hung on the line out back to dry, ironed after supper, and back in the closet again long before bed. But these weren't the old days, these were the New and Improved Days, and they washed clothes only when they absolutely had to; after all, there were more important things to do, weren't there?

As if to confirm his idea, Bobbi sneezed twice in her sleep.

"No," Gard whispered. "Please." He dropped the dress back into the hamper, no longer wanting to touch it. He slammed the lid and then stood stiffly, waiting to see if the sound would wake Bobbi.

She took the truck. Went to do something she didn't want to do. Something that upset her. Something formal enough to need a dress. She came back late and went into the shed. Didn't come into the house to change. Went in like she needed *to go in. Right away.* Why?

But the answer, coupled with the sneezes and what he had found on her dress, seemed inevitable.

Comfort.

And when Bobbi, who lived alone, needed comfort, who had always been there to give it? Gard? Don't make me laugh, folks. Gard only showed up to *take* comfort, not give it.

He wanted to be drunk. He wanted that more than at any time since this crazy business had begun.

Forget it. As he turned to leave the kitchen, where Bobbi kept the alcoholic staples as well as the clothes hamper, something clitter-clicked to the boards.

He bent over, picked it up, examined it, bounced it thoughtfully on his hand. It was a tooth, of course. Big Number Two. He put a finger into his mouth, felt the new socket, looked at the smear of blood on his fingerpad. He went to the kitchen doorway and listened. Bobbi was snoring gustily in her bedroom. Sounded as if her sinuses were closed up as tight as timelocks.

A summer cold, she said. Maybe so. Maybe that's what it is.

But he remembered the way Peter would sometimes leap up into her lap when Bobbi sat in her old rocker by the windows to read, or when she sat out on the porch. Bobbi said Peter was most apt to make one of his boob-destroying leaps when the weather was unsettled, just as he was more apt to bring on one of her allergy attacks when the weather was hot and unsettled. *It's like he knows,* she'd said once, and ruffled the beagle's ears. *DO you, Pete? Do you know? Do you LIKE to make me sneeze? Misery loves company, is that it?* And Pete had seemed to laugh up at her in that way of his.

Gardener remembered, when Bobbi's return had briefly wakened him last night (Bobbi's return and that flare of green light), hearing distant and meaningless heat-wave thunder.

Now he remembered that sometimes *Pete* needed a little comfort too.

Especially when it thundered. Pete was deathly afraid of that sound. The sound of thunder.

Dear Christ, has she got Peter out in that shed? And if she does, in God's name WHY?

There had been smears of some funny green goo on Bobbi's dress.

And hairs.

Very familiar short brown and white hairs. Peter was in the shed, and had been all this time. Bobbi *had* lied about Peter being dead. God alone knew how many other things she had lied about . . . but why this?

Why?

Gardener didn't know.

He changed direction, went to the cupboard to the right and beneath the sink, bent, pulled out a fresh bottle of Scotch, and broke the seal. He held the bottle up and said, "To man's best friend." He drank from the neck, gargled viciously, and swallowed.

First swallow.

Peter. What the fuck did you do to Peter, Bobbi?

He meant to get drunk.

Very drunk.

Fast.

BOOK III

The Tommy-knockers

Meet the new boss. Same as the old boss.

—THE WHO,
"Won't Get Fooled Again"

Over on the mountain:
thunder, magic foam,
let the people know my wisdom,
fill the land with smoke.
Run through the jungle . . .
Don't look back to see.

—CREEDENCE CLEARWATER REVIVAL,
"Run Through the Jungle"

I slept and I dreamed the dream. This time there was no disguise anywhere. I was the malicious male-female dwarf figure, the principle of joy-in-destruction; and Saul was my counterpart, male-female, my brother and my sister, and we were dancing in some open place, under enormous white buildings, which were filled with hideous, menacing, black machinery which held destruction. But in the dream, he and I, or she and I, were friendly, we were not hostile, we were together in spiteful malice. There was a terrible yearning nostalgia in the dream, the longing for death. We came together and kissed, in love. It was terrible, and even in the dream I knew it. Because I recognised in the dream those other dreams we all have, when the essence of love, of tenderness, is concentrated into a kiss or a caress, but now it was the caress of two half-human creatures, celebrating destruction.

—Doris Lessing,
The Golden Notebook

1.

SISSY

1

"I hope you enjoyed the flight," the stewardess by the hatch told the fortyish woman who left Delta's flight 230 with a trickle of other passengers who had stuck it out all the way to Bangor, 230's terminating point.

Bobbi Anderson's sister Anne, who was forty but who *thought* fifty as well as *looking* it (Bobbi would say—during those infrequent times she was in her cups—that sister Anne had thought like a woman of fifty since she was thirteen or so), halted and fixed the stew with a gaze that might have stopped a clock.

"Well, I'll tell you, babe," she said. "I'm hot. My pits stink because the plane was late leaving La Garbage and even later leaving Logan. The air was bumpy and I hate to fly. The trainee they sent back to Livestock Class spilled someone's screwdriver all over me and I've got orange juice drying to a fine crack-glaze all over my arm. My panties are sticking in the crack of my ass and this little town looks like a pimple on the cock of New England. Other questions?"

"No," the stew managed. Her eyes had gone glassy, and she felt as if she had suddenly gone about three quick rounds with Boom-Boom Mancini on a day when Mancini was pissed at the world. This was an effect Anne Anderson often had on people.

"Good for you, dear." Anne marched past the attendant and up the jetway, swinging a large, screamingly purple totebag in one hand. The attendant never even had time to wish her a pleasant stay in the Bangor area. She decided it would have been a wasted effort anyway. The lady looked as if she had never had a pleasant stay anywhere. She walked straight, but she looked like a woman who did it in spite of pain somewhere—like the little mermaid, who went on walking even though every step was like knives in her feet.

Only, the flight attendant thought, *if that babe has got a True Love stashed anywhere, I hope to God he knows about the mating habits of the trapdoor spider.*

2

The Avis clerk told Anne she had no cars to rent; that if Anne hadn't made a reservation in advance, she was out of luck, so sorry. It was summer in Maine, and rental cars were at a premium.

This was a mistake on the part of the clerk. A bad one.

Anne smiled grimly, mentally spat on her hands, and went to work. Situations like this were meat and drink to sister Anne, who had nursed her father until he had died a miserable death on the first of August, eight days ago. She had refused to have him removed to an I.C. facility, preferring instead to wash him, medicate his bedsores, change his incontinence pants, and give him his pills in the middle of the night, by herself. Of course she had driven him to the final stroke, worrying at him constantly about selling the house on Leighton Street (he didn't want to; she was determined that he would; the final monster stroke, which occurred after three smaller ones at two-year intervals, came three days after the house was put up for sale), but she would no more admit that she knew this than she would admit the fact that although she had attended St. Bart's in Utica ever since earliest childhood and was one of the leading laywomen in that fine church, she believed the concept of God was a crock of shit. By the time Anne was eighteen she had bent her mother to her will, and now she had destroyed her father and watched dirt shoveled over his coffin. No slip of an Avis clerk could stand against Sissy. It took her about ten minutes to break the clerk down, but she brushed aside the offer of the compact car which Avis held in reserve for the occasional—*very* occasional—celebrity passing through Bangor and pressed on, scenting the young clerk's increasing fear of her as clearly as a hungry carnivore scents blood. Twenty minutes after the offer of the compact, Anne drove serenely away from Bangor International behind the wheel of a Cutlass Supreme reserved for a businessman scheduled to deplane at 6:15 P.M. By that time the clerk would be off-duty—and besides, she had been so unnerved by Anne's steady flailing that she wouldn't have cared if the Cutlass had been earmarked for the President of the United States. She went tremblingly into the inner office, shut the door, locked it, put a chair under the knob, and smoked a joint one of the mechanics had laid on her. Then she burst into tears.

Anne Anderson had a similar effect on many people.

3

By the time the clerk had been eaten, it was going on three o'clock. Anne could have driven straight to Haven—the map she'd picked up at the Avis counter put the mileage at less than fifty—but she wanted to be absolutely fresh for her confrontation with Roberta.

There was a cop at the X-shaped intersection of Hammond and Union streets—a streetlight was out, which she thought typical of this little running sore of a town—and she stopped halfway across to ask him for directions to the best hotel or motel in town. The cop intended to remonstrate with her for holding up traffic in order to ask for directions, and then, at the look in her eyes—the warm look of a fire in the brain which has been well-banked and might flare at any time—decided it might be less trouble to give her the directions and get rid of her. This lady looked like a dog the cop had known when he was a kid, a dog who had thought it fine fun to tear the seats from the pants of kids passing on the way to school. That kind of hassle on a day when both the temperature and his ulcer were too hot, he didn't need. He directed her to Cityscape Hotel out on Route 7 and was glad to see the ass end of her, going away.

4

Cityscape Hotel was full.

That was no trouble for sister Anne.

She got herself a double, then bullied the harried manager into giving her another because the air conditioner in the first rattled and because the color on the TV was so bad, she said, that all the actors looked like they had just eaten shit and would soon die.

She unpacked, masturbated to a grim-and-cheerless climax with a vibrator nearly the size of one of the mutant carrots in Bobbi's garden (the only climaxes she had were of the grim-and-cheerless type; she'd never been with a man in bed and never intended to), showered, napped, then went to dinner. She scanned the menu with a darkening frown, then bared her teeth in a spitless grin at the waiter who came to take her order.

"Bring me a bunch of vegetables. Raw, leafy vegetables."

"Madame wants a sal—"

"Madame wants a bunch of raw, leafy vegetables. I don't give a shit what you call them. Just wash them first to get the bugpiss off. And bring me a sombrero right now."

"Yes, madame," the waiter said, licking his lips. People were looking at them. A few smiled . . . but those who got a look at Anne Anderson's eyes soon stopped. The waiter started away and she called him back, her voice loud and even and undeniable.

"A sombrero," she said, "has Kahlua and cream in it. *Cream.* If you bring me a sombrero with milk in it, chum, you're going to be shampooing with the motherfucker."

The waiter's Adam's apple went up and down like a monkey on a stick. He tried to summon the sort of aristocratic, pitying smile which is a good waiter's chief weapon against vulgar customers. To do him full credit, he got a pretty good start on that smile—then Anne's lips curved up in a grin that froze it dead. There was no good nature in that grin. There was something like murder in it.

"I mean it, chum," sister Anne said softly. The waiter believed her.

5

She was back in her room at seven-thirty. She undressed, put on a robe, and sat looking out the fourth-story window. In spite of its name, Cityscape Hotel was actually far out on Bangor's outskirts. The view Anne looked out on was, except for the lights in the small parking lot, one of almost unalloyed darkness. That was exactly the sort of view she liked.

There were amphetamine capsules in her purse. Anne took one of them out, opened it, poured the white powder onto the mirror of her compact, made a line with one sensibly short nail, and snorted half of it. Her heart immediately began to jackrabbit in her narrow chest. A flush of color bloomed in her pallid face. She left the rest for the morning. She had begun to use yellowjackets this way shortly after her father's first stroke. Now she found she could not sleep without a snort of this stuff, which was the diametric opposite of a sedative. When she had been a little girl—a *very* little girl—her mother had once cried at Anne in utter exasperation, "You're so contrary cheese'd physic ya!"

Anne supposed it had been true then, and that it was true now . . . not that her mother would ever dare say it now, of course.

Anne glanced at the phone and then away. Just looking at it made her think of Bobbi, of the way she had refused to come to Father's funeral—not in words but in a cowardly way that was typical of her, by simply refusing to respond to Anne's increasingly urgent efforts to communicate with her. She had called twice during the twenty-four hours following the old bastard's stroke, when it became obvious he was going to snuff it. The phone had not been answered either time.

She called again after her father died—this time at 1:04 on the morning of August 2nd. Some drunk had answered the telephone.

"I'd like Roberta Anderson, please," Anne said. She stood stiffly at the pay phone in the lobby of Utica Soldiers' Hospital. Her mother sat in a nearby plastic chair, surrounded by endless brothers and endless sisters with their endless Irish-potato faces, weeping and weeping and weeping. "Right now."

"Bobbi?" the drunk voice at the other end said. "You want the old boss or the New and Improved Boss?"

"Spare me the bullshit, Gardener. Her father has—"

"Can't talk to Bobbi now," the drunk—it was Gardener, all right, she recognized the voice now—broke in. Anne closed her eyes. There was only one piece of phone-related bad manners she hated worse than being broken in upon. "She's out in the shed with the Dallas Police. They're all getting even Newer and *more* Improved."

"You tell her her sister Anne—"

Click!

Dry rage turned the sides of her throat to heated flannel. She held the telephone handset away from her and looked at it the way a woman might look at a snake that has bitten her. Her fingernails were white-going-on-purple.

The piece of phone manners she hated *most* was being hung up on.

6

She had dialed back at once, but this time, after a long pause, the telephone began to make a weird sirening noise in her ear. She hung up and went over to her weeping mother and her harp relatives.

"Did you get her, Sissy?" her mother asked Anne.

"Yes."

"What did she say?" Her eyes begged Anne for good news. "Did she say she'd come home for his funeral?"

"I couldn't get a commitment one way or another," Anne said, and suddenly all of her fury at Roberta—Roberta, who had had the temerity to try to escape—suddenly burst out of her heart, but not in shrillness. Anne would never be still *or* shrill. That sharklike grin surfaced on her face. The murmuring relatives grew silent and looked at Anne uneasily. Two of the old ladies gripped their rosaries. "She *did* say that she was glad the old bastard was dead. Then she laughed. Then she hung up."

There was a moment of stunned silence. Then Paula Anderson clapped her hands to her ears and began to shriek.

7

Anne had had no doubt—at least at first—that Bobbi would be at the funeral. *Anne* meant for her to be there, and so she would be. Anne always got what she wanted; that made the world nice for her, and that was the way things should be. When Roberta did come, she would be confronted with the lie Anne had told—probably not by their mother, who would be too pathetically glad to see her to mention it (or probably even to remember it), but surely by one of the harp uncles. Bobbi would deny it, so the harp uncle would probably let it go—unless the harp uncle happened to be very drunk, which was always a good possibility with Mama's brothers—but they would all remember Anne's statement, not Bobbi's denial.

That was good. Fine, in fact. But not enough. It was time—overtime—that Roberta came home. Not just for the funeral; for good.

She would see to it. Leave it to Sissy.

8

Sleep did not come easily to Anne that night in the Cityscape. Part of it was being in a strange bed; part of it was the dim gabble of TVs from other rooms and the sense of being surrounded by other people, just another bee trying to sleep in just another chamber of this hive where the chambers were square instead of hexagonal; part of it was knowing that tomorrow would be an extremely busy day; most of it, however, was her continuing dull fury at being balked. It was the thing which she hated above all others—it reduced such annoyances to minor piffles. *Bobbi* had balked her. So far she had balked her utterly and completely, necessitating this stupid trip during what the weather forecasters were calling the worst heatwave to hit New England since 1974.

An hour after her lie about Bobbi to her mother and the harp aunts and uncles, she had tried to phone again, this time from the undertaker's (her mother had long since tottered home, where Anne supposed she would be sitting up with her cunt of a sister Betty, the two of them drinking that shitty claret they liked, wailing over the dead man while they got slopped). She got nothing but that sirening sound again. She called the operator and reported trouble on the line.

"I want you to check it, locate the trouble, and see that it's corrected," Anne said. "There's been a death in the family, and I need to reach my sister as soon as possible."

"Yes, ma'am. If you'll give me the number you're calling from—"

"I'm calling from the undertaker's," Anne said. "I'm going to pick out a coffin for my father and then go to bed. I'll call in the morning. Just make sure my call goes through then, honey."

She hung up and turned to the undertaker.

"Pine box," she said. "Cheapest one you've got."

"But, Ms. Anderson, I'm sure you'll want to think about—"

"I don't want to think about *anything,*" Anne barked. She could feel the warning pulses which signaled the onset of one of her frequent migraine headaches. "Just sell me the cheapest pine box you've got so I can get the fuck out of here. It smells dead."

"But . . ." The undertaker was flabbergasted. "But won't you want to see . . ."

"I'll see it when he's wearing it," Anne said, drawing her checkbook out of her purse. "How much?"

9

The next morning Bobbi's telephone was working, but there was no answer. There continued to be no answer all day. Anne grew steadily more angry. Around four P.M., with the wake in the next room going full-blast, she had called Maine directory assistance and told the operator she wanted the number of the Haven Police Department.

"Well . . . there's no *police* department, exactly, but I have a listing for the Haven constable. Will that—"

"Yeah. Give it to me."

The directory-assistance operator did. Anne called. The phone rang . . . rang . . . rang. The tone of the ring was exactly the same as the tone she got when she dialed the house where her spineless sister had been hiding out for the last thirteen years or so. A person could almost believe they were ringing into the same receiver.

She actually toyed with the idea for a moment before brushing it aside. But giving such a paranoid thought even a moment's house-room was unlike her, and it made her angrier. The rings sounded alike because the same little dipshit backwoods phone company sold and serviced all the phone equipment in town, that was all.

"Did you get her?" Paula asked timidly, coming to the door.

"No. *She* doesn't answer, the town *constable* doesn't answer, I think the whole fucking town went to Bermuda. Jesus!" She blew a lock of hair off her sweaty forehead.

"Perhaps if you called one of her friends—"

"What friends? The loony she's shacked up with?"

"Sissy! You don't know—"

"I know who answered the phone the one time I did get through," she returned grimly. "After living in this family, it's easier for me to tell when a man's drunk by his voice."

Her mother said nothing; she had been reduced to wet-eyed, trembling silence, one hand hovering at the collar of her black dress, and that was just how Anne liked her.

"No, he's there, and they both know I'm trying to get through and why, and they're going to be sorry they fucked with me."

"Sissy, I do so wish you wouldn't use that lang—"

"Shut up!" Anne screamed at her, and of course her mother did.

Anne picked up the telephone again. This time when she dialed directory assistance, she asked for the number of the Haven mayor. They didn't have one of those either. There was something called a town manager, whatever the fuck that was.

Muffled little clicks, like rats' claws on glass, as the operator looked things up on her computer screen. Her mother had fled. From the other room came the theatrically overblown sobs and wails of Irish grief. Like a V-2 rocket, Anne thought, an Irish wake was powered by liquid fuel, and in both cases the liquid was the same. Anne closed her eyes. Her head thumped. She ground her teeth together—it produced a bitter, metallic taste. She closed her eyes and imagined how good, how wonderful it would be to perform a little surgery on Bobbi's face with her fingernails.

"Are you still there, honey," she asked without opening her eyes, "or did you suddenly run off to the W.C.?"

"Yes, I have a l—"

"Give it to me."

The operator was gone. A robot recited a number in odd, herky-jerky cadences. Anne dialed it. She fully expected no answer, but the phone was picked up promptly. "Selectmen's. Newt Berringer here."

"Well, it's good to know *someone's* there. My name's Anne Anderson. I'm calling from Utica, New York. I tried to call your constable, but apparently he's gone fishing."

Berringer's voice was even. "He's a she, Miss Anderson. She died unexpectedly last month. The office hasn't been filled. Probably won't be until next town meeting."

This stopped Anne for only an instant. She focused instead on something which interested her more.

"*Miss* Anderson? How did you know I was a Miss, Berringer?"

There was no pause. Berringer said, "Ain't you Bobbi's sister? If you are, and if you were married, you wouldn't be Anderson, would you?"

"You know Bobbi then, do you?"

"Everyone in Haven knows Bobbi, Miss Anderson. She's our resident celebrity. We're real proud of her."

It went through the meat of Anne's brain like a sliver of glass. *Our resident celebrity. Oh dear bleeding Christ.*

"Good job, Sherlock. I've been trying to reach her on whatever passes for phones up there in Moosepaw County to tell her her father died yesterday and he's going to be buried tomorrow."

She had expected some conventional sentiment from this faceless official—after all, he knew Bobbi—but there was none. "Been some trouble with the phones out her way," was all Berringer said.

Anne was again put momentarily off-pace (*very* momentarily; Anne was never put off-pace for very long). The conversation was not going as she had expected. The man's responses were a little strange, too reserved even for a Yankee. She tried to picture him and couldn't. There was something very odd in his voice.

"Could you have her call me? Her mother is crying her eyes out in the other room, she's near collapse, and if Roberta doesn't get here in time for the funeral, I think she *will* collapse."

"Well, I can't *make* her call you, Miss Anderson, can I?" Berringer returned with infuriating, drawly slowness. "She's a grown woman. But I'll surely pass the message along."

"Maybe I'd better give you the number," Anne said through clenched teeth. "I mean, we're still here at the same old stand, but she calls so seldom these days, she might have forgotten it. It's—"

"No need," Berringer interrupted. "If she don't remember, or have it written down, there's always d'rect'ry assistance, ain't there? I guess that's how you must have gotten this'un."

Anne hated the telephone because it allowed only a fraction of the full, relentless force of her personality to come through. She thought she had never hated it so much as she did at this moment. "Listen!" she cried. "I don't think you understand—"

"Think I do," Berringer said. This was the second interruption, and the conversation was not three minutes old. "I'll go out 'fore I have m'dinner and pass it on. Thanks for calling, Miss Anderson."

"Listen—"

Before she could finish, he did the thing she hated the *most.*

Anne hung up, thinking she could cheerfully stand by and watch as the jag-off to whom she'd just been speaking was eaten alive by wild dogs.

She had been grinding her teeth together madly.

10

Bobbi didn't return her call that afternoon. Nor that early evening, as the V-2 of the wake entered the boozosphere. Nor that late evening as it went into orbit. Nor in the two hours past midnight as the last of the wakers stumbled blearily out to their cars, with which they would menace other drivers on their way home.

Anne lay sleepless and ramrod straight in her bed most of the night, wired up on speed like a suitcase bomb, alternately grinding her teeth and digging her nails into her palms, planning revenge.

You'll come back, Bobbi, oh yes you will. And when you do—

When she still hadn't called the next day, Anne put the funeral off in spite of her mother's weak wailings that it wasn't fitting. Finally Anne whirled on her and snarled, "I'll say what's fitting and what isn't. What's fitting is that that little whore should be here and she hasn't even bothered to call. Now leave me alone!"

Her mother slunk away.

That night she tried first Bobbi's number, then the selectmen's office. At the first number the sirening sound continued. At the second, she got a recorded message. She waited patiently until the beep and then said, "It's Bobbi's sis again, Mr. Berringer, cordially hoping that you'll be afflicted with syphilis that won't be diagnosed until your nose falls off and your balls turn black."

She called directory assistance back and asked for three Haven numbers—the number of Newt Berringer, a Smith ("*Any* Smith, dear, in Haven they're all related"), and a Brown (the number she received in response to this last request was, by virtue of alphabetical order, Bryant's). She got the same siren howl at each number.

"Shit!" Anne yelled, and threw the phone at the wall.

Upstairs in bed, her mother cringed and hoped Bobbi would not come home . . . at least not until Anne was in a better mood.

11

She had put the funeral and interment off yet another day.

The relatives began to rumble, but Anne was more than equal to *them*, thank you. The funeral director took one look at her and decided the old mick could rot in his pine box before he got involved. Anne, who spent the whole day on the phone, would have congratulated him on making a wise decision. Her fury was rapidly passing all previous bounds. Now *all* the phones into Haven seemed out of service.

She could not delay the funeral another day longer and she knew it. Bobbi had won this battle; all right, so be it. But not the war. Oh no. If she thought that, the bitch had several more things coming—and all of them would be painful.

Anne bought her plane tickets angrily but confidently—one from upstate New York to Bangor . . . and two returns.

12

She would have flown to Bangor the following day—that was when the ticket was for—but her idiotic mother fell down the back stairs and broke her hip. Sean O'Casey had once said that when you lived with the Irish you marched in a fool's parade, and oh how right he had been. Her mother's screams brought Anne in from the back yard, where she had been lying on a chaise longue soaking up some sun and going over her strategy for keeping Bobbi in Utica once she had gotten her here. Her mother was sprawled at the bottom of the narrow staircase, bent at a hideous angle, and Anne's first thought was that for a row of pins she would gladly have left the stupid old bitch there until the anesthetic effects of the claret began to wear off. The new widow smelled like a winery.

In that angry, dismayed moment Anne knew that all of her plans would have to be changed, and she thought that their mother might actually have done it on purpose—

gotten drunk to nerve herself up and then not just fallen but *jumped* downstairs. Why? To keep her from Bobbi, of course.

But you won't, she had thought, going to the phone. *You won't; if I want a thing to be, if I* mean *a thing to be, that thing* will *be; I am going to Haven and I am going to cut a wide swath there. I'm going to bring Bobbi back, and they're going to remember me for a long time. Especially the hayseed dork who hung up on me.*

She picked up the phone and punched the Medix number—it had been pasted to the phone ever since her father's first stroke—with quick, angry stabs of her forefinger. She was grinding her teeth.

13

Thus it was the ninth of August before she could finally get away. In the caesura, there was no call from Bobbi, and Anne didn't try to get her again, or the hick town manager, or Bobbi's drunk fuck in Troy. He had apparently moved in so he could poke her full-time. Okay. Let them both fall into a lull. That would be very fine.

Now she was here, in Bangor's Cityscape Hotel, sleeping badly . . . and grinding her teeth.

She had always ground her teeth. Sometimes it was so loud it awoke her mother in the night . . . on a few occasions even her father, who slept like a brick. Her mother mentioned it to the family doctor when Anne was three. That fellow, a venerable upstate New York G.P. whom Doc Warwick would have felt right at home with, looked surprised. He considered a moment, then said: "I think you must be imagining that, Mrs. Anderson."

"If I am, it must be catching," Paula had said. "My husband's heard it too."

They looked toward Anne, who was building a shaky tower of blocks, one on top of the other. She worked with grim, unsmiling concentration. As she added a sixth block, the tower fell down . . . and as she started to rebuild it, they both heard the grim, skeletal sound of Anne grinding her baby teeth together.

"She also does that in her *sleep*?" the doctor asked.

Paula Anderson nodded.

"Well, it'll probably go away," the doctor said. "It's harmless." But of course it didn't go away and it wasn't harmless; it was bruxism, a malady which, along with heart attacks, strokes, and ulcers, often afflicts driven, self-assertive people. The first of Anne's baby teeth to fall out was noticeably eroded. Her parents commented on it . . . then forgot it. By then Anne's personality had begun to assert itself in more gaudy and startling ways. By six and a half she was already ruling the Anderson family in some strange way you could never quite put your finger on. And they had all gotten used to the thin, slightly gruesome whisper of Anne's teeth grinding together in the night.

The family dentist had noticed the problem wasn't going away but getting worse by the time Anne was nine, but it wasn't treated until she was fifteen, when it began to cause her actual pain. By then she had worn her teeth down to the live nerves. The dentist fitted her with a rubber mouth-splint taken from a mold of her teeth, then an acrylic one. She wore these appliances, which are called "night-guards," to bed every night. At eighteen she was fitted with all-metal crowns on most of her top and bottom teeth. The Andersons couldn't afford it, but Anne insisted. They had allowed the problem to slide, and she was not going to allow her skinflint father to turn around when she was twenty-one and say, "You're a grownup now, Anne; it's *your* problem. If you want crowns, *you* pay the bill."

She had wanted gold, but that really was beyond their means.

For several years thereafter, Anne's infrequent smiles had a glittery, mechanized look that was extremely startling. People often actually recoiled from that grin. She took a grim enjoyment from these reactions, and when she had seen the villain Jaws in one of the later James Bond movies, she had laughed until she thought her sides would split—this unaccustomed burst of amusement had left her feeling dizzy and ill. But she had understood exactly why, when that huge man first bared his stainless-steel teeth in a sharklike grin, people had recoiled from her, and she almost wished she hadn't finally had porcelain fused over the metal. Yet, she thought, it was perhaps better not to show oneself so clearly—it could be as unwise to wear your personality on your sleeve as it was to wear your heart there. Maybe you didn't have to *look* as though you could chew your way through a door made of oak planks to get what you wanted as long as you knew you *could*.

Bruxism aside, Anne also had had a lot of cavities both as a child and as an adult, in spite of Utica's fluoridated water and her own strictly observed regimen of oral hygiene (she often flossed her teeth until her gums bled). This was also due in large part to her personality rather than her physiology. Drive and the urge to dominate afflict both the softest parts of the human body—stomach and vitals—and the hardest, the teeth. Anne had a chronic case of dry-mouth. Her tongue was nearly white. Her teeth were dry little islands. Without a steady flow of saliva to wash away crumbs of food, cavities began quickly. By this night when she lay sleeping uneasily in Bangor, Anne had better than twelve ounces of silver-amalgam fillings in her mouth—on infrequent occasions she had set off airport metal detectors.

In the last two years she had begun to lose teeth in spite of her fanatic efforts to save them: two on the top right, three on the bottom left. In both cases she had opted for the most expensive dental bridgework available—she had to travel to New York City to have the work done. The dental surgeon removed the rotting husks, flayed her gums to the dull white of the jawbone, and implanted tiny titanium screws. The gums were sewn back together and healed nicely—some people reject metal implants in the bone, but Anne Anderson had no trouble at all accepting them—leaving two little titanium posts sticking out of the flesh. The bridgework was placed over the metal anchors after the flesh around them had healed.

She didn't have as much metal in her head as Gard did (Gard's plate *always* set off airport metal detectors), but she had a lot.

So she slept without knowing that she was a member of an extremely exclusive club: those people who could enter Haven as it was now with a bare chance of surviving.

14

She left for Haven in her rental car at eight the following morning. She made one wrong turn, but still arrived at the Troy-Haven town line by nine-thirty.

She had awakened feeling as nervous and randy-dandy as a thoroughbred dancing her way into the starting gate. But somewhere, in the last fifteen or twenty miles before she reached the Haven town line—the land around her nearly empty, dreamingly ripe in the breathless summer heat-hush—that fine feeling of anticipation and wire-thin nervy readiness had bled away. Her head began to ache. At first it was just a minor throb, but it quickly escalated into the familiar pounding of one of her near-migraines.

She drove past the town line into Haven.

By the time she got to Haven Village, she was hanging on to herself by force of will and not much more. The headache came and went in sickish waves. Once she thought she had heard a burst of hideously distorted music coming out of her mouth, but that must have been imagination, something brought on by the headache. She was faintly aware of people on the streets in the little village, but not of the way they all turned to look at her . . . her, then each other.

She could hear machinery throbbing in the woods somewhere—the sound was distant and dreamlike.

The Cutlass began to weave back and forth on the deserted road. Images doubled, trebled, came reluctantly back together, then began doubling and trebling again.

Blood trickled from the corners of her mouth unnoticed.

She held hard to one thought: *It's on this road, Route 9, and her name will be on the mailbox. It's on this road, Route 9, and her name will be on the mailbox. It's on this road—*

The road was mercifully deserted. Haven slept in the morning sun. Ninety percent of out-of-town traffic had been rerouted now, and this was a good thing for Anne, whose car pitched and yawed wildly, left-hand wheels now spuming dust from one shoulder, right-hand wheels spuming dust from the other a few moments later. She knocked down a turn sign without being aware of it.

Young Ashley Ruvall saw her coming and pulled his

bike a prudent distance off the road and stood astride it in Justin Hurd's north pasture until she was gone.

(a lady there's a lady and I can't hear her except her pain)

A hundred voices answered him, soothing him.

(we know Ashley it's all right . . . shhh . . . shhh)

Ashley grinned, exposing his pink, baby-smooth gums.

15

Her stomach revolted.

Somehow she was able to pull over and shut off the engine before her breakfast bolted up and out a moment after she managed to claw the driver's door open. For a moment she just hung there with her forearms propped on the open window of the half-open door, bent awkwardly outward, consciousness no more than a single spark which she maintained by her determination that it should not go out. At last she was able to straighten up and pull the door closed.

She thought in a dim and confused way that it must have been breakfast—headaches she was used to, but she almost never threw up. Breakfast in the restaurant of that fleabag that was supposed to be Bangor's best hotel. The bastards had poisoned her.

I may be dying . . . oh God yes, it really feels as if I might be dying. But if I'm not, I am going to sue them from here to the steps of the U.S. Supreme Court. If I live, I'll make them wish their mothers never met their fathers.

Perhaps it was the bracing quality of this thought which made Anne feel strong enough to get the car moving again. She crept along at thirty-five, looking for a mailbox with ANDERSON written on it. A terrible idea came to her. Suppose Bobbi had painted out her name on the mailbox? It wasn't so crazy when you really thought about it. She might well suspect Sissy would turn up, and the spineless little twat had always been afraid of her. She was in no shape to stop at every farm along the way, inquiring after Bobbi (not that she'd get much help from Bobbi's hayseed neighbors if the donkey she'd spoken to on the phone was any indication), and—

But there it was: R. ANDERSON. And behind it, a place

she had seen only in photographs. Uncle Frank's place. The old Garrick farm. There was a blue truck parked in the driveway. The *place* was right, yes, but the *light* was wrong. She realized this clearly for the first time as she approached the driveway. Instead of feeling the triumph she had expected at this moment—the triumph of a predator that has finally succeeded in running its prey to earth—she felt confusion, uncertainty, and, although she did not even really realize it for what it was because it was so unfamiliar, the first faint trickle of fear.

The *light.*

The *light* was wrong.

This realization brought others in quick succession. Her stiff neck. The circles of sweat darkening her dress under her arms. And—

Her hand flew to her crotch. There was a faint dampness there, drying now, and she isolated a dim ammoniac smell in the car. It had been there for some time, but her conscious mind had just now tumbled to it.

I pissed myself, I pissed myself and I've been in this fucking car almost long enough for it to dry—

(and the light, Anne)

The *light* was wrong. It was sunset light.

Oh no—it's nine-thirty in the—

But it *was* sunset light. There was no denying it. She had felt better after vomiting, yes . . . and she suddenly understood why. The knowledge had been there all along, really, just waiting to be noticed, like the patches of sweat under the arms of her dress, or that faint smell of drying urine. She had felt better because the period between closing the door and actually starting the car again hadn't been seconds or minutes, but *hours*—she had spent all that brutally hot summer day in the oven of the car. She had lain in a deathlike stupor, and if she had been using the Cutlass's air-conditioning with all the windows rolled up when she stopped the car, she would have cooked like a Thanksgiving turkey. But her sinuses were nearly as bad as her teeth, and the canned air manufactured by automobile air conditioners irritated them. This physical problem, she realized suddenly, staring at the old farm with wide, bloodshot eyes, had probably saved her life. She had been running with all four windows open. Otherwise—

This led to another thought. She had spent the day in a

deathlike stupor, parked by the side of the road, *and no one had stopped to check on her.* That no one had come along a main road like Route 9 in all those hours since nine-thirty was something she just couldn't accept. Not even out in the sticks. And when they did see you in trouble in Sticksville, they didn't just put the pedal to the metal and keep on going, like New Yorkers stepping over a wino.

What kind of town is this, anyway?

That unaccustomed trickle again, like hot acid in her stomach.

This time she recognized the feeling as fear, seized it, wrung its neck . . . and killed it. Its brother might show up later on, and if so, she would kill it too, and all the sibs that might follow.

She drove into the yard.

16

Anne had met Jim Gardener only twice before, but she never forgot a face. Even so, she barely recognized the Great Poet, although she believed she could have *smelled* him at forty yards if she had been downwind on even a moderately breezy day. He was sitting on the porch in a strappy T-shirt and a pair of blue jeans, an open bottle of Scotch in one hand. He had a three- or four-day beard-stubble, much of it gray. His eyes were bloodshot. Although Anne didn't know this—and wouldn't have cared—Gardener had been in this state, more or less, for the last two days. All his noble resolves had gone by the boards since finding the dog hairs on Bobbi's jacket.

He watched the car pull into the dooryard (missing the mailbox by bare inches) with a drunk's bleary lack of surprise. He watched the woman get out, stagger, and hold on to the open door for a minute.

Oh wow, Gardener thought. *It's a bird, it's a plane, it's Superbitch. Faster than a speeding hate-letter, able to leap cringing family members at a single bound.*

Anne shoved the car door closed. She stood there for a moment, throwing a long shadow, and Gardener felt an eerie sense of familiarity. She looked like Ron Cummings when Ron had a skinful and was trying to decide if he could walk across the room.

Anne made her way across the dooryard, trailing a steadying hand along the side of Bobbi's truck. When she had passed the truck, she reached at once for the porch railing. She looked up, and in the slanting light of seven o'clock, Gardener thought the woman looked both aged and ageless. She also looked evil, he thought—jaundiced and yellowish-black with a heavy freight of evil that was simultaneously wearing her out and eating her up.

He raised the Scotch, drank, gagged on the rank burn. Then he tipped the neck of it at her. "Hello, Sissy. Welcome to Haven. Having said that much, I now urge you to leave as fast as you can."

17

She got up the first two steps okay, then stumbled and went to one knee. Gardener held out a hand. She ignored it.

"Where's Bobbi?"

"You don't look so good," Gard said. "Haven has that effect on people these days."

"I'm fine," she said, at last gaining the porch. She stood over him, panting. "Where is she?"

Gardener inclined his head toward the house. The steady hiss of water came from one of the open windows. "Shower. We've been working in the woods all day and it was esh . . . *ex*tremely hot. Bobbi believes in showering to remove dirt." Gardener raised the bottle again. "I believe in simply disinfecting. Shorter and pleasanter."

"You smell like a dead pig," Anne remarked, and started past him toward the house.

"While my own nose is undoubtedly not as keen as your own, dear heart, you have a delicate but noticeable odor of your own," Gard said. "What do the French call that particular perfume? *Eau de Piss?*"

She turned on him, startled into a snarl. People—people in Utica, at least—didn't speak to her that way. *Never.* But of course, they knew her. The Great Poet had undoubtedly judged her on the basis of his jizz receptacle: Haven's resident celebrity. And he was drunk.

"Well," Gardener said, amused but also a trifle uneasy under her smoking gaze, "it was you who brought up the subject of aroma."

"So I did," she said slowly.

"Maybe we ought to start again," he said with drunken courtesy.

"Start *what* again? You're the Great Poet. You're the drunk who shot his wife. I have nothing to say to you. I came for Bobbi."

Good shot, the thing about the wife. She saw his face freeze, saw his hand tighten on the neck of the bottle. He stood there as if he had at least temporarily forgotten where he was. She offered him a sweet smile. That smart-ass crack about *Eau de Piss* had gotten through, but sick or not, she thought she was still ahead on points.

Inside, the shower shut off. And—perhaps it was only a hunch—Gardener had a clear sense of Bobbi listening.

"You always did like to operate without anesthetic. I guess I never got anything but exploratory surgery before this, huh?"

"Maybe."

"Why now? After all these years, why did you have to pick *now*?"

"None of your business."

"*Bobbi's* my business."

They faced each other. She drilled him with her gaze. She waited for his eyes to drop. They didn't. It suddenly occurred to her that if she started into the house without saying more, he might attempt to restrain her. It wouldn't do him any good, but it might be simpler to answer his question. What difference did it make?

"I've come to take her home."

Silence again.

There are no crickets.

"Let me give you a piece of advice, sister Anne."

"Spare me. No candy from strangers, no advice from drunks."

"Do exactly what I told you when you got out of the car. Leave. Now. Just *go*. This is not a good place to be right now."

There was something in his eyes, something desperately honest, that brought on a recurrence of her earlier chill and that unaccustomed confusion. She had been left all day in her car at the side of the road as she lay in a swoon. What sort of people did that?

Then every bit of her Anne-ness rose up and crushed these little doubts. If she *wanted* a thing to be, if she *meant* a thing to be, that thing *would* be; so it had been, was, and ever would be, alleluia, amen.

"Okay, Chumly," she said. "You gave me yours, I'll give you mine. I'm going inside that shack, and about two minutes later a very large chunk of shit is going to hit the fan. I suggest you go for a walk if you don't want to get splattered. Sit on a rock somewhere and watch the sun go down and jerk off or think up rhymes or do whatever it is Great Poets do when they watch the sunset. But you want to keep out of what goes on in the house, no matter what. It's between Bobbi and me. If you get in my way, I'll rip you up."

"In Haven, you're more likely to be theripp*ee* than the ripp*er*."

"Well, that's something I'll have to see for myself, even though I'm *not* from Missouri," Anne said, and started for the door.

Gardener tried once more.

"Anne . . . Sissy . . . Bobbi's not the same. She . . ."

"Take a walk, little man," Anne said, and went inside.

18

The windows were open but for some reason the shades were drawn. Every now and then a puff of faint breeze would stir, sucking the shades into the openings a little way. When it happened, they looked like the sails of a becalmed ship doing their best and failing. Anne sniffed and wrinkled her nose. Bluh. The place smelled like a monkey-house. From the Great Poet she would have expected it, but her sister had been raised better. This place was a pigsty.

"Hello, Sissy."

She turned. For a moment Bobbi was just a shadow, and Anne felt her heart go into her throat because there was something odd about that shape, something all *wrong*—

Then she saw the white blur of her sister's robe, heard

the patter of water, and understood that Bobbi had just come from the shower. She was all but naked. Good. But her pleasure was not as great as it should have been. Her unease remained, her feeling that there was something *wrong* about the shape in the dooorway.

This is not a good place to be right now.

"Daddy's dead," she said, straining her eyes to see better. For all her straining, Bobbi remained only a dim figure in the door which communicated between living room and—she assumed—bathroom.

"I know. Newt Berringer called and told me."

Something about her voice. Something even more basically different in the vague suggestiveness of her shape. Then it came to her. The realization brought a nasty shock and stronger fear. She didn't sound afraid. For the first time in her life, Bobbi didn't sound afraid of her.

"We buried him without you. Your mother died a little when you didn't come home, Bobbi."

She waited for Bobbi to defend herself. There was only silence.

For Christ's sake, come out where I can see you, you little coward!

Anne . . . Bobbi's not the same . . .

"She fell downstairs four days ago and broke her hip."

"Did she?" Bobbi asked indifferently.

"You're coming home with me, Bobbi." She meant to convey force and was appalled by the weak shrillness of her voice.

"It was your teeth that let you get in," Bobbi said. "Of course! I should have thought of that!"

"Bobbi, get out here where I can see you!"

"Do you want me to?" Her voice had taken on a strange teasing lilt. "I wonder if you do."

"Stop fucking with me, Bobbi!" Her voice rose unevenly.

"Oh, listen!" Bobbi said. "I never thought I'd hear anything like that from *you,* Anne. After all the years you fucked with me . . . with *all* of us. But okay. If you insist. If you insist, that's fine. Just fine."

She didn't want to see. Suddenly Anne didn't want anything but to run, and keep running until she was far from this shadowy place and this town where they left you fainting all day at the side of the road. But it was too late. She saw the blurred movement of her younger sister's hand, and the lights went on at the same moment the robe dropped with a soft rustle.

The shower had washed off the makeup. Bobbi's entire head and neck were transparent and jellylike. Her breasts had swelled bulbously outward and seemed to be merging into one single nippleless outcropping of flesh. Anne could see dim organs in Bobbi's stomach that looked nothing at all like human organs—there was fluid circulating in there but it looked green.

Behind Bobbi's forehead she could see the quivering sac of mind.

Bobbi grinned toothlessly.

"Welcome to Haven, Anne," she said.

She felt herself stepping backward in a spongy dream. She was trying to scream but there was no air.

At Bobbi's crotch, a grotesque thatch of tentacles like sea-grass wavered from her vagina . . . the place where her vagina had been, anyway. Anne had no idea if it was still there or not, and didn't care. The sunken valley which had replaced her crotch was enough. That . . . and the way the tentacles seemed to be pointing toward her . . . *reaching* for her.

Naked, Bobbi began walking toward her. Anne tried to back away and stumbled over a footstool.

"No," she whispered, trying to crawl away. "No . . . Bobbi . . . no . . ."

"Good to have you here," Bobbi said, still smiling. "I hadn't counted on you . . . not at all . . . but I think we can find a job for you. Positions, as they say, are still open."

"Bobbi . . ." She managed this one final terrified whisper, and then she felt the tentacles moving lightly on her body. She jerked, tried to move away . . . and they slithered around her wrists. Bobbi's hips thrust out in a movement that was like an obscene parody of copulation.

2.

GARDENER TAKES A WALK

1

Gardener took Anne's advice and went for a walk. He went, in fact, all the way out to the ship in the woods. This was the first time he had been out here by himself, he realized, and it would soon be full dark. He felt vaguely afraid, as a child might passing near a haunted house. *Are there ghosts in there? The ghosts of Tommy-knockers past? Or are the real Tommyknockers themselves still in there, maybe in suspended animation, beings like freeze-dried coffee, waiting to be thawed out? And just what were they, anyhow?*

He sat on the ground by the lean-to, looking at the ship. After a while the moon rose and lit its surface an even more ghostly silver. It was strange and yet very beautiful.

What's going on around here?

I don't want to know.

What it is ain't exactly clear . . .

I don't want to know.

Hey, stop, what's that sound, everybody look what's going down . . .

He tipped the bottle up and drank deep. He put it aside, rolled over, and rested his throbbing head on his arms. He fell asleep that way, in the woods near the graceful circular jut of the ship.

He slept there all night.

In the morning there were two teeth on the ground.

It's what I get for sleeping so close to it, he thought dully, but there was at least one compensation—he had no headache at all, although he had put away nearly a fifth of Scotch. He had noticed before that, all its other attributes aside, the ship—or the change in the atmosphere the ship had generated—seemed, at very close range, to provide hangover protection.

He didn't want to leave his teeth just lying there. Heeding an obscure urge, he kicked dirt over them. As he did it he thought again: *Playing Hamlet is a luxury you can no longer afford, Gard. If you don't commit to one course or the other very soon—in the next day or so, I think—you're not going to be able to do anything but march along with the rest of them.*

He looked at the ship, thought of the deep ravine which extended down its smooth, unmarked side, and thought again: *We'll be down to the hatchway soon, if there* is *a hatchway. . . . What then?*

Rather than trying to answer, he struck off for home.

2

The Cutlass was gone.

"Where were you last night?" Bobbi asked Gardener.

"I slept in the woods."

"Did you get really drunk?" Bobbi asked with surprising gentleness. Her face was dark with makeup again. And Bobbi had been wearing shirts which seemed oddly loose and baggy the last few days; this morning he thought he could see why. Her chest was thickening. Her breasts had begun to look like a single unit instead of two separate things. It made Gardener think of guys who pumped iron.

"Not very. One or two nips and I passed out. No hangover this morning. And no bug bites." He raised his arms, darkly tanned on top, white and strangely vulnerable beneath. "Any other summer, you'd wake up the next morning so bug-bit you couldn't open your eyes. But now they're gone. Along with the birds. And the beasts. In fact, Roberta, it seems to repel everything but fools like us."

"Have you changed your mind, Gard?"

"You keep asking me that, have you noticed?"

Bobbi didn't reply.

"Did you hear the news on the radio yesterday?" He knew she hadn't. Bobbi didn't see, hear, or think about anything now but the ship. Her headshake was no surprise. "Troops massing in Libya. More fighting in Lebanon. American troop movements. The Russians getting louder and louder about SDI. We're all still sitting on the powderkeg. That hasn't changed a bit since 1945 or so. Then you discover a *deus ex machina* in your back yard, and now you keep wanting to know if I've changed my mind about using it."

"*Have* you?"

"No," Gardener said, not sure if he was lying or not—but he was *very* glad Bobbi couldn't read him.

Oh, can't she? I think she can. Not much, but more than she could a month ago . . . more and more each day. Because you're "becoming" now, too. Changed *your mind? That's a laugh; you can't fucking* make up *your mind!*

Bobbi dismissed it, or appeared to do so. She turned toward the pile of hand-tools stacked on the corner of the porch. She had missed making up a spot just below her right ear, Gardener saw—it was the same spot many men miss when they are shaving. He realized with a sickish lack of surprise that he could see *into* Bobbi—her skin had changed, had become kind of semi-transparent jelly. Bobbi had grown thicker, shorter over the last few days—and the changes were accelerating.

God, he thought, horrified and bitterly amused, *is that what happens when you turn into a Tommyknocker? You start looking like someone who got caught in a great big messy atomic meltdown?*

Bobbi, who had been bending over the tools and gathering them up in her arms, turned quickly to look at Gardener, her face wary.

"What?"

I said let's get moving, you lazy juggins, Gardener sent clearly, and that wary, puzzled expression became a reluctant smile.

"Okay. Help me with these, then."

No, of course victims of high-gamma radiation didn't turn transparent, like Claude Rains in *The Invisible Man*. They didn't start to lose inches as their bodies twisted and thickened. But, yes, they were apt to lose teeth, their hair was apt to fall out—in other words, there was a kind of physical "becoming" in both cases.

He thought again: *Meet the new boss. Same as the old boss.*

Bobbi was looking narrowly at him again.

I'm running out of maneuvering room, all right. And fast.

"*What* did you say, Gard?"

"I said, 'Let's go, boss.' "

After a long moment, Bobbi nodded. "Yeah," she said. "Daylight's wasting."

3

They rode out to the dig on the Tomcat. It did not fly the way the little boy's bike had flown in *E.T.*; Bobbi's tractor would never soar cinematically in front of the moon, hundreds of feet above the rooftops. But it did cruise silently and handily eighteen inches above the ground, large wheels spinning slowly like dying propellers. It smoothed the ride out a whole hell of a lot. Gard was driving, Bobbi standing behind him on the yoke.

"Your sister left?" Gard said. There was no need to yell. The Tomcat's engine was a faint, distant purr.

"That's right," Bobbi said. "She left."

You still can't lie worth shit, Bobbi. And I think—I really do—that I heard her scream. Just before I hit the patch going into the woods, I think I heard her scream. How much would it take to make a high-stepping, pure-d, ball-cutting bitch like Sissy let out a howl? How bad would it have to be?

The answer to that one was easy. Very bad.

"She was never the type to exit gracefully," Bobbi said. "Or to let anyone *be* graceful, if she could help it. She came to bring me home, you know . . . watch that stump, Gard, it's a high one."

Gardener shoved the gear lever all the way up. The Tomcat rose another three inches, skimming over the top of the high stump. Once past, he relaxed his hand and the Tomcat sank back to its previous altitude, eighteen inches above the ground.

"Yes, she just came up with her bit and her hackamore,"

Bobbi said, sounding faintly amazed. "There was a time when she might have taken me, too. As things are now, she never had a chance."

Gardener felt cold. There were a lot of ways a person could interpret a remark like that, weren't there?

"I'm still surprised that it took you only one evening to convince her," Gardener said. "I thought Patricia McCardle was bad, but your sister made ole Patty look like Annette Funicello."

"I just wiped off some of this makeup. When she saw what was underneath, she screamed and left so fast you would have thought there were rockets in her heels. It was actually pretty funny."

It was plausible. It was so plausible that the temptation to believe it was almost insuperable. Unless you ignored the simple fact that the lady under discussion couldn't have gone *anywhere* in a hurry without help. The lady could barely *walk* without help.

No, Gardener thought. *She never left. The only question is whether you killed her or if she's out in the goddam shed with Peter.*

"How long do the physical changes go on, Bobbi?" Gardener asked.

"Not much longer," Bobbi said, and Gardener thought again that Bobbi had never been able to lie worth shit. "Here we are. Park it over by the lean-to."

4

The following evening they knocked off early—the heat was still holding, and neither of them felt capable of going on until the last light died. They returned to the house, pushed food around on their plates, even ate some of it. With the dishes washed, Gardener said he thought he would go for a walk.

"Oh?" Bobbi was looking at him with that wary expression which had become one of her main stocks in trade. "I would have thought you'd gotten enough exercise today for anyone."

"Sun's down now," Gard said easily. "It's cooler. No bugs. And . . ." He looked clear-eyed at Bobbi. "If I go out on the porch, I'm going to take a bottle. If I take a bottle, I'm going to get drunk. If I go for a long walk and come back tired, maybe I can fall into bed sober for one night."

All of this was true enough . . . but there was another truth nested inside it, like one Chinese box inside another. Gardener looked at Bobbi and waited to see if she would go hunting for that inner box.

She didn't.

"All right," she said, "but you know I don't care how much you drink, Gard. I'm your friend, not your wife."

No, you don't care how much I drink—you've made it very easy for me to drink all I want. Because it neutralizes me.

He walked along Route 9 past Justin Hurd's place, and when he struck the Nista Road he turned left and moved along at a good pace, his arms swinging easily. The last month's labor had toughened him more than he would have believed—not so long ago even a two-mile walk such as this would have left him rubber-legged and winded.

Still, it was eerie. No whippoorwills greeted the encroaching twilight; no dog barked at him. Most of the houses were dark. No TVs flickered inside the few lighted windows he passed.

Who needs Barney Miller *reruns when you can "become" instead?* Gardener thought.

By the time he reached the sign reading ROAD ENDS 200 YARDS, it was almost full dark, but the moon was rising and the night was very bright. At the end of the road he reached a heavy chain strung between two posts. A rusty, bullet-holed NO TRESPASSING sign hung from it. Gard stepped over the chain, kept walking, and was soon standing in an abandoned gravel pit. The moonlight on its weedy sides was white as bone. The silence made Gardener's scalp prickle.

What had brought him here? His own "becoming," he supposed—something he had picked out of Bobbi's mind without even knowing he'd done it. It must have been that, because whatever had brought him out here had been a lot stronger than just a hunch.

To the left there was a thick triangular scar against the whiteness of the undisturbed gravel. *This* stuff had been moved around. Gardener walked over, shoes crunching. He dug into the fresher gravel, found nothing, moved, dug another hole, found nothing, moved, dug a third, found nothing—

Oh, hey, wait a minute.

His fingers skimmed across something much too smooth to be a stone. He leaned over, heart thudding, but could see nothing. He wished he had brought a flashlight, but that probably would have made Bobbi even more suspicious. He dug wider, letting the dirt run and rattle down the inclined slope.

He saw he had uncovered a car headlight.

Gardener looked at it, filled with an eerie, skeletal amusement. THIS *is what it's like to find something in the earth,* he thought. *To find some strange artifact. Only I didn't have to stumble over it, did I? I knew where to look.*

He dug faster, climbing the slope and throwing dirt back between his legs like a mutt digging for a bone, ignoring his pounding head, ignoring his hands, which first scraped, then chafed, then began to bleed.

He was able to clear a level place on the Cutlass's hood just above the right-side headlights where he could stand, and then the work went faster. Bobbi and her buddies had done a casual burial job at best. Gardener pulled loose gravel down by the armload, then kicked it off the car. Pebbles shrieked and squealed on the metalwork. His mouth was dry. He was working his way up to the windshield, and he honestly didn't know which would be better—to see something, or nothing.

His fingers brushed slick smoothness again. Without allowing himself to stop and think—the silent creepiness of the place might have gotten to him then; he might have just turned and run—he dug a clear place on the windshield and peered in, cupping his hands to the glass to cut the glare from the moon.

Nothing.

Anne Anderson's rented Cutlass was empty.

They could have put her in the trunk. The fact is, you still don't know anything for sure.

He thought he did, however. Logic told him that Anne's body wasn't in the trunk. Why would they bother? Anyone who found a brand-new car buried out here in a deserted gravel pit was going to find it suspicious enough to investigate the trunk . . . or to call the police, who would do it.

No one in Haven would give a rip one way or another. They have concerns more pressing than cars buried in gravel pits right now. And if someone from town did happen to find it, calling the police is the last thing they'd do. That would mean outsiders, and we don't want any outsiders in Haven this summer, do we? Perish the thought!

So she wasn't in the trunk. Simple logic. QED.

Maybe the people who did this didn't have your sterling powers of logic, Gard.

That was a crock of shit, too. If he could see a thing from three angles, the Haven Quiz Kids could see it from *twenty*-three. They didn't miss a trick.

Gardener backed to the edge of the hood on his knees and jumped down. Now he was aware of his scraped, burning hands. He would have to take a couple of aspirin when he got back and try to conceal the damage from Bobbi in the morning—work-gloves were going to be the order of the day. *All* day.

Anne wasn't in the car. Where was Anne? In the shed, of course; in the shed. Gardener suddenly understood why he had come out here—not just to confirm a thought he had plucked from Bobbi's head (if that was what he had done; his subconscious mind might simply have fixed on this as the handiest place to get rid of a big car quick), but because he had needed to make sure it was the shed. *Needed* to. Because he had a decision to make, and he knew now that not even seeing Bobbi change into something which was not human was enough to force him into that decision—so much of him still wanted to dig the ship out, dig it out and put it to use—so much, so very much.

Before he could make the decision, he had to see what was in Bobbi's shed.

5

Halfway back he stopped in the cold, slippery moonlight, struck by a question—why had they bothered to hide the car? Because the rental people would report it missing and more police would turn up in Haven? No. The Hertz or Avis people might not even *know* it was missing for days, and it would be longer still before the cops traced

Anne's family connection here. At least a week, more like two. And Gardener thought by then Haven would be done worrying about outside interference, one way or another, for good.

So who had the car been hidden from?

From you, Gard. They hid it from you. They still don't want you to know what they're capable of when it comes to protecting themselves. They hid it and Bobbi told you Anne went away.

He went back with this dangerous secret turning in his mind like a jewel.

3.

THE HATCH

1

It happened two days later, as Haven lay sprawled and sunstruck under the August heat. Dog-days had come, except of course there were no dogs left in Haven—unless maybe there was one in Bobbi Anderson's shed.

Gard and Bobbi were at the bottom of a cut which was now a hundred and seventy feet deep—the hull of the ship formed one side of this excavation, and the other side, behind the silvery mesh crisscrossing it, showed a cutaway view of thin soil, clay, schist, granite, and spongy aquifer. A geologist would have loved it. They were wearing jeans and sweatshirts. It was stiflingly hot on the surface, but down here it was chilly—Gardener felt like a bug crawling on the side of a water cooler. On his head he wore a hardhat with a flashlight attached to it by silver utility tape. Bobbi had cautioned him to use the light as sparingly as possible—batteries were in limited supply. Both of his ears were stuffed with cotton. He was using a pneumatic drill to shag up big chunks of rock. Bobbi was at the other end of the cut, doing the same thing.

Gardener had asked her that morning why they had to drill. "I liked the radio-explosives better, Bobbi old kid," he said. "Less pain and strain on the American brain, know what I mean?"

Bobbi didn't smile. Bobbi seemed to be losing her sense of humor along with her hair.

"We're too close now," Bobbi said. "Using an explosive might damage something we don't want to damage."

"The hatch?"

"The hatch."

Gardener's shoulders were aching, and the plate in his head was aching as well—that was probably mental, steel couldn't ache, but it always *seemed* to when he was down here—and he hoped Bobbi would signal soon that it was time for them to knock off for lunch.

He let the drill chatter and bite its way toward the ship again, not bothering too much about grazing that dull silver surface. You had to be careful not to let the tip of the drill walk onto it too hard, he had discovered; it was apt to rebound and tear off your foot if you weren't careful. The ship itself was as invulnerable to the rough kiss of the drill as it had been to the explosives he and his parade of helpers had used. There was at least no danger of damaging the goods.

The drill touched the ship's surface—and suddenly its steady machine-gun thunder turned to a high-pitched squeal. He thought he saw smoke squirt from the pulsing blur of the drill's tip. There was a snap. Something flew past his head. All this happened in less than a second. He shut the drill off and saw the drill-bit was almost entirely gone. All that remained was a jagged stub.

Gardener turned around and saw the part that had gone winging past his face embedded in the rock of the cut. It had sheared a strand of the meshwork neatly in two. Delayed shock hit, making his knees want to come unlocked and spill him to the ground.

Missed me by a whore's hair. No more, no less. Mother!

He tried to pull it out of the rock, and thought at first it wasn't going to come. Then he began to wiggle it back and forth. *Like pulling a tooth out of a gum,* he thought, and a hysterical titter escaped him.

The chunk of drill-bit came free. It was the size of a .45 slug, maybe a little bigger.

Suddenly he was on the verge of passing out. He put an arm on the mesh-covered wall of the cut and rested his head on it. He closed his eyes and waited for the world to either go away or come back. He was dimly aware that Bobbi's drill had also cut out.

The world began to come back . . . and Bobbi was shaking him.

"Gard? Gard, what's wrong?"

There was real concern in her voice. Hearing it made Gardener feel absurdly like weeping. Of course, he was very tired.

"I almost got shot in the head by a forty-five-caliber drill-bit," Gardener said. "On second thought, make that a .357 Magnum."

"What are you talking about?"

Gardener handed her the fragment he had worked out of the wall. Bobbi looked at it and whistled. "Jesus!"

"I think He and I just missed connections. That's the second time I've almost gotten killed down in this shithole. The first was when your friend Enders almost forgot to send down the sling after I'd set one of those radio explosives."

"He's no friend of mine," Bobbi said absently. "I think he's a dork. . . . Gard, what did you hit? What made it happen?"

"What do you mean? A rock! What else is there down here to hit?"

"Were you near the ship?" All of a sudden Bobbi looked excited. No; more than that. Nearly feverish.

"Yes, but I've grazed the ship with the drill before. It just bounces b—"

But Bobbi wasn't listening anymore. She was at the ship, down on her knees, digging into the rubble with her fingers.

It looked like it was steaming, Gardener thought. *It—*

It's here, Gard! Finally here!

He had joined her before he realized that she hadn't spoken the conclusion of her thoughts aloud; Gardener had heard her in his head.

2

Something, all right, Gardener thought.

Pulling aside the rock Gardener's drill had chunked up just before it exploded, Bobbi had revealed, finally, a line in the ship's surface—one single line in all of that huge featureless expanse. Looking at it, Gardener understood Bobbi's excitement. He stretched out his hand to touch it.

"Better not," she said sharply. "Remember what happened before."

"Leave me alone," Gardener said. He pushed Bobbi's hand aside and touched that groove. There was music in his head, but it was muffled, and quickly faded. He thought he could feel his teeth vibrating rapidly in their sockets and suspected he would lose more of them tonight. Didn't matter. He wanted to touch it; he *would* touch it. This was the way in; this was the closest they had been to the Tommyknockers and their secrets, their first real sign that this ridiculous thing wasn't just solid through and through (the thought *had* occurred to him; what a cosmic joke *that* would have been). Touching it was like touching starlight made solid.

"It's the hatch," Bobbi said. "I *knew* it was here!"

Gardener grinned at her. "We did it, Bobbi."

"Yeah, we did it. Thank God you came back, Gard!"

Bobbi hugged him . . . and when Gardener felt the jellylike movement of her breasts and torso, he felt sick revulsion rise in him. Starlight? Maybe the stars were touching *him*, right now.

It was a thought he was quick to conceal, and he thought that he *did* conceal it, that Bobbi got none of it.

That's one for me, he thought. "How big do you think it is?"

"I'm not sure. I think we might be able to clear it today. It's best if we do. Time's gotten short, Gard."

"How do you mean?"

"The air over Haven has changed. This did it." Bobbi rapped her knuckles on the hull of the ship. There was a dim, bell-like note.

"I know."

"It makes people sick to come in. You saw the way Anne was."

"Yes."

"She was protected to some degree by her dental work. I know it sounds crazy, but it's true. Still, she left in a hell of a hurry."

Oh? Did she?

"If that was all—the air poisoning people who came into town—that would be bad enough. *But we can't leave anymore, Gard.*"

"Can't?"

"No. I think *you* could. You might feel sickish for a

few days, but you could leave. It would kill me, and very quickly. And something else: we've had a long siege of hot, still weather. If the weather changes—if the wind blows hard enough—it's going to blow our biosphere right out over the Atlantic Ocean. We'll be like a bunch of tropical fish just after someone pulled the plug on the tank and killed the rebreather. We'll die."

Gard shook his head. "The weather changed the day you went to that woman's funeral, Bobbi. I remember. It was clear and breezy. That was what was so weird about you catching a sunstroke after all that hot and muggy."

"Things have changed. The 'becoming' has speeded up."

Would *they all die?* Gardener wondered, *ALL of them? Or just you and your special pals, Bobbi? The ones that have to wear makeup now?*

"I hear doubt in your head, Gard," Bobbi said. She sounded half-exasperated, half-amused.

"What I doubt is that any of this can be happening at all," Gardener said. "Fuck it. Come on. Dig, babe."

3

They took turns with a pick. One of them would use it for fifteen minutes or so, and then both would clear away the rubble. By three that afternoon Gard saw a circular groove that looked about six feet in diameter. Like a manhole cover. And here, at last, was a symbol. He looked at it wonderingly, and at last he had to touch it. The blast of music in his head was louder this time, as if in weary protest, or in weary warning—a warning to get away from this thing before its protection lapsed entirely. But he needed to touch it, confirm it.

Running his fingers over this almost Chinese symbol, he thought: *A creature who lived under the glow of a different sun conceived this mark. What does it mean?* NO TRESPASSING? WE CAME IN PEACE? *Or is it maybe a plague symbol, an alien version of* ABANDON HOPE, ALL YE WHO ENTER IN HERE?

It was pressed into the metal of the ship like a bas-relief. Merely touching it brought on a species of superstitious dread he had never felt before; he would have laughed if, six weeks ago, someone had told him he might feel this way—like a caveman watching an eclipse of the sun or a medieval peasant watching the arrival of what would eventually become known as Halley's Comet.

A creature who lived under the glow of a different sun conceived this mark. I, James Eric Gardener, born in Portland, Maine, United States of America, Western Hemisphere of the World, am touching a symbol made and struck by God only knows what sort of being across a black distance of light-years. My God, my God, I am touching a different mind!

He had, of course, been touching different minds for some time now, but this was not the same . . . not the same at all.

Are we really going in? He was aware that his nose was bleeding again, but not even that could make him take his hand away from that symbol; he trailed the pads of his fingers restlessly back and forth across its smooth, unknowable surface.

More accurately, are you going to try *to go in there? Are you, even though you know it may—probably will—kill you? You get a jolt every time you touch the thing; what's going to happen if you're foolish enough to go inside? It will probably set up a harmonic vibration in that damned steel plate of yours that will blow your head apart like a stick of dynamite in a rotten turnip.*

Awfully concerned about your welfare for a man who was on the verge of suicide not very long ago, aren't you, goodbuddy? he thought, and had to grin in spite of himself. He drew his fingers away from the shape of the symbol, flicking them absently to get rid of the tingle, like a man trying to shake off a good-sized booger. *Go on and go for it. What the fuck, if you're gonna step out anyway, having your brains vibrated to death inside of a flying saucer is a more exotic way to go than most.*

Gard laughed aloud. It was a strange sound at the bottom of that deep slit in the ground.

"What's funny?" Bobbi asked quietly. "What's funny, Gard?"

Laughing harder, Gardener said: "Everything. This is . . . something else. I guess it's laugh or go crazy. You dig it?"

Bobbi looked at him, obviously not digging it, and Gardener thought: *Of course she doesn't. Bobbi got stuck with the other option. She can't laugh because she went crazy.*

Gardener roared until tears rolled down his cheeks, and some of these tears were bloody, but he did not notice this. Bobbi did, but Bobbi didn't bother to tell him.

4

It took them another two hours to completely clear the hatchway. When they were done, Bobbi stuck out a dirty, makeup-streaked hand in Gardener's direction.

"What?" Gardener asked, shaking it.

"That's it," Bobbi said. "We're finished with the dig. We're done, Gard."

"Yeah?"

"Yeah. Tomorrow we go inside, Gard."

Gard looked at her without saying anything. His mouth felt dry.

"Yes," Bobbi said, and nodded, as if Gard had questioned this. "Tomorrow we go in. Sometimes it seems like I started this about a million years ago. Sometimes like it was just yesterday. I stumbled over it, and I saw it, and I ran my fingers along it and blew off the dirt. That was the start. One finger dragged through the dirt. This is the end."

"That was a different Bobbi at the beginning," Gardener said.

"Yes," Bobbi said meditatively. She looked up, and there was a sunken gleam of humor in her eyes. "A different Gard, too."

"Yeah. Yeah, I guess you know, it'll probably kill me to go in there . . . but I'm going to give it a shot."

"It won't kill you," Bobbi said.

"No?"

"No. Now, let's get out of here. I've got a lot to do. I'll be out in the shed tonight."

Gardener looked at Bobbi sharply, but Bobbi was looking upward as the motorized sling trundled down on its cables.

"I've been building things out there," Bobbi said. Her voice was dreamy. "Me and a few others. Getting ready for tomorrow."

"They'll be joining you tonight," Gardener said. It was not a question.

"Yes. But first I need to bring them out here, to look at the hatch. They . . . they've been waiting for this day too, Gard."

"I'll bet they have," Gardener said.

The sling arrived. Bobbi turned to look at Gardener narrowly. "What's that supposed to mean, Gard?"

"Nothing. Nothing at all."

Their eyes met. Gardener could feel her clearly now, working at his mind, trying to dig into it, and he had again that sense of his secret knowledge and secret doubts turning and turning like a dangerous jewel.

He thought deliberately:

(get out of my head Bobbi you're not welcome here)

Bobbi recoiled as if slapped—but there was also faint shame on her face, as if Gard had caught her peeking where she had no business peeking. There was still some humanness left in her, then. That was comforting.

"Bring them out, by all means," Gard said. "But when it comes to opening it up, Bobbi, it's just you and me. We dug the fucker up, and we go in the fucker first. You agree?"

"Yes," Bobbi said. "We go in first. The two of us. No brass bands, no parades."

"And no Dallas Police."

Bobbi smiled faintly. "Not them either." She held out the sling. "You want to ride up first?"

"No, you go. It sounds like you got a schedule and a half still ahead of you."

"I do." Bobbi swung astride the sling, pressed a button, and started up. "Thanks again, Gard."

"Welcome," Gardener said, craning his neck to follow Bobbi's upward progress.

"And you'll feel better about all of this—"

(when you "become" when you finish your own "becoming")

Bobbi rose up and up and out of sight.

4.

THE SHED

1

It was August 14th. A quick calculation told Gardener that he had been with Bobbi for forty-one days—almost exactly a biblical period of confusion or unknown time, as in "he wandered in the desert for forty days and forty nights." It seemed longer. It seemed like his entire life.

He and Bobbi did no more than pick at the frozen pizza Gardener heated up for their supper.

"I think I'd like a beer," Bobbi said, going to the fridge. "How about you? Want one, Gard?"

"I'll pass, thanks."

Bobbi raised her eyebrows but said nothing. She got the beer, walked out on the porch, and Gardener heard the seat of her old rocker creak comfortably as she sat down. After a while he drew a cold glass of water from the tap, went out, and sat beside Bobbi. They sat there for what seemed a long time, not speaking, just looking out into the hazy stillness of early evening.

"Been a long time, Bobbi, you and me," he said.

"Yes. A long time. And a strange ending."

"Is that what it is?" Gardener asked, turning in his chair to look at Bobbi. "The end?"

Bobbi shrugged easily. Her eye slid away from Gardener's. "Well, you know. End of a phase. How's that? Any better?"

"If it's *le mot juste,* then it's not just better, not even the best—just the only *mot* that matters. Isn't that what I taught you?"

Bobbi laughed. "Yeah, it was. First damned class. Mad dogs, Englishmen . . . and English *teachers.*"

"Yeah."

"Yeah."

Bobbi sipped her beer and looked out at the Old Derry Road again. Impatient for them to arrive, Gardener supposed. If the two of them had really said everything there was left to say after all these years, he almost wished he had never heeded the impulse to come back at all, no matter what the reasons or eventual outcome. Such a weak ending to a relationship which had, in its time, encompassed love, sex, friendship, a period of tense *détente,* concern, and even fear, seemed to make mock of the whole thing—the pain, the hurt, the effort.

"I always loved you, Gard," Bobbi said softly and thoughtfully, not looking at him. "And no matter how this turns out, remember that I still do." Now she did look at Gardener, her face a strange parody of a face under the thick makeup—surely this was some hopeless eccentric who happened to resemble Bobbi a little. "And I hope you'll remember that I never asked to stumble over the goddam thing. Free will was not a factor here, as some wise-ass or other has surely said."

"But you chose to dig it up," Gardener said. His voice was as soft as Bobbi's but he felt a new terror steal into his heart. Was that crack about free will a roundabout apology for his own impending murder?

Stop it, Gard. Stop jumping at shadows.

Is the car buried out at the end of Nista Road a shadow? his mind returned at once.

Bobbi laughed softly. "Man, the idea that whether or not to dig something like that up could ever *be* a function of free will . . . you might be able to stick that to a kid in a high-school debate, but we out on de po'ch, Gard. You don't really think a person *chooses* something like that, do you? Do you think people can choose to put away *any* knowledge once they've seen the edge of it?"

"I had been picketing nuclear power plants on that assumption, yes," Gardener said slowly.

Bobbi waved it away. "Societies may choose not to *implement* ideas—actually I doubt even that, but for the sake of argument we'll say it's so—but ordinary people?

No, Gard, I'm sorry. When ordinary people see something sticking out of the ground, they got to dig on it. They got to dig on it because it might be treasure."

"And you didn't have the slightest inkling that there would be . . ." *Fallout* was the word that came to mind. He didn't think it was a word Bobbi would like. ". . . consequences?"

Bobbi smiled openly. "Not a hint in the world."

"But Peter didn't like it."

"No. Peter didn't like it. But it didn't kill him, Gard."

I'm quite sure it didn't.

"Peter died of natural causes. He was *old.* That thing in the woods is a ship from another world. Not Pandora's box, not a divine apple tree. I heard no voice from heaven singing *Of this ship shalt thou not eat lest ye die.*"

Gard smiled a little. "But it *is* a ship of knowledge, isn't it?"

"Yes. I suppose."

Bobbi was looking toward the road again, obviously not wanting to pursue the topic further.

"When do you expect them?" Gardener asked.

Instead of answering, Bobbi nodded at the road. Kyle Archinbourg's Caddy was coming, followed by Adley McKeen's old Ford.

"Guess I'll go inside and catch some winks," Gardener said, getting up.

"If you want to go out to the ship with us, you're welcome to."

"With you, maybe. With them?" He cocked a thumb toward the approaching cars. "They think I'm crazy. Also, they hate my guts because they can't read my mind."

"If I say you go, you go."

"Well, I think I'll pass," Gardener said, getting up and stretching. "I don't like them, either. They make me nervous."

"I'm sorry."

"Don't be. Just . . . tomorrow. The two of us, Bobbi. Right?"

"Right."

"Give them my best. And remind them I helped, steel plate in my head or not."

"I will. Of course I will." But Bobbi's eyes slid away again, and Gardener didn't like that. He didn't like it at all.

2

He thought they might go in the shed first, but they didn't. They stood around outside for a while talking—Bobbi, Frank, Newt, Dick Allison, Hazel, the others—and then moved off toward the woods in a tight group. The light was shading down toward purple now, and most of them were carrying flashlights.

Watching, Gard felt that his last real moment with Bobbi had come and gone. There was nothing now but to go into the shed and see what was in there. Make up his mind once and for all.

Saw an eyeball peepin through a smoky cloud behind the green door . . .

He got up and went through the house to the kitchen in time to see them heading into Bobbi's rampant garden. He counted noses quickly, making sure that they were all there, then headed for the cellar. Bobbi kept a spare keyring down there.

He opened the cellar door and paused one final time.

Do you really want to do this?

No; no, he did not. But he *meant* to do it. And he discovered that, more than fear, he felt a great sense of loneliness. There was literally no one else he could turn to for help. He had been in the desert with Bobbi Anderson forty days and forty nights, and now he was in the desert on his own. God help him.

To hell with it, he thought. Like the old World War I platoon sergeant was supposed to have said: Come on, you guys, you want to live forever?

Gardener went downstairs to get Bobbi's keyring.

3

It was there, hanging on its nail with every key neatly labeled. The only catch was the shed key was gone. It *had* been here; he was quite sure of that. When had he last *seen* it here? Gard tried to remember and couldn't. Bobbi taking precautions? Maybe.

He stood in the New and Improved Workshop, sweat on his forehead and sweat on his balls. No key. That was great. So what was he supposed to do? Grab Bobbi's ax and make like Jack Nicholson in *The Shining?* He could see it. Smash, crash, bash: *Heeeeeere's GARDENER!* Except that might be a bit hard to cover up before the pilgrims came back from the Viewing of the Sacred Hatch.

He stood in Bobbi's workshop, feeling time slip away, feeling Old and Unimproved. How long *would* they be out there, anyway? No way of telling, was there? No way at all.

Okay, where do people put keys? Always assuming she really was just taking precautions and not just hiding it from you.

A thought struck him so hard he actually slapped his forehead. *Bobbi* hadn't taken the key. Nor had anyone been trying to hide it. The key had disappeared when Bobbi had supposedly been in Derry Home Hospital recovering from sunstroke. He was almost positive of that, and what memory would not or could not supply, logic did.

Bobbi hadn't been in Derry Home; she had been in the shed. Had one of the others taken the spare key, to tend her when Bobbi needed tending? Did they all have copies? Why bother? No one in Haven was into stealing these days; they were into "becoming." The only reason the shed was kept locked was to keep *him* out. So they could just—

Gardener remembered watching them arrive on one of the occasions after the "something" had happened to Bobbi . . . the "something" that had been a lot more serious than heat prostration.

He closed his eyes and saw the Caddy. KYLE-1. They get out and . . .

. . . and Archinbourg splits off from the rest for a moment or two. You're up on one elbow, looking out the window at them, and if you think of it at all, you think he must have stepped around there to tap a kidney. But he didn't. He went around to get the key. Sure, that's what he did. Went around to get the key.

It wasn't much, but it was enough to get him moving. He ran back up the cellar stairs, headed for the door, then doubled back. In the bathroom there was an ancient pair of Foster Grant sunglasses on top of the medicine cabinet—they had come to rest up there with the finality that trivial objects manage to obtain only in a single man or woman's quarters (like the makeup which had belonged to Newt Berringer's wife). Gardener took the sunglasses down, blew a thick coating of dust from the lenses, wiped them carefully, then folded the bows and put them in his breast pocket.

He went out to the shed.

4

He stood by the padlocked plank door for a moment, looking out along the path which led to the dig. Dusk had advanced far enough now so that the woods beyond the garden were a massy blue-gray with no detail to them. He saw no bobbing line of returning flashlights.

But they could turn up. At any time at all, they could turn up and catch you with your arm all the way down in the jam-jar.

I think they'll spend a pretty good while out there mooning over it. They've got the klieg lights.

But you don't know for sure.

No. Not for sure.

Gardener shifted his gaze back to the plank door. Between the planks he could see that green light, and he could hear a dim, unpleasant noise, like an old-fashioned washing machine with a gutful of clothes and thick suds.

No—not just *one* washing machine; more like a whole line of them, not quite in sync.

That light was pulsing in time to the low slurping sound.

I don't want to go in there.

There was a smell. Even that, Gardener thought, was slightly sudsy, bland with a faint hint of rancidity. Old soap. Cakey soap.

But it's no bunch of washing machines. That sound's alive. *It's not telepathic typewriters inside there, not New and Improved water heaters, it's something* alive, *and I don't want to go in there.*

But he was going to. After all, hadn't he come back

from the dead just to look inside Bobbi's shed and catch the Tommyknockers at their strange little benches? He supposed he had.

Gard went around to the far side of the shed. There, hanging on a rusty nail under the eave, was the key. He reached up with a hand that trembled and took it down. He tried to swallow. At first he couldn't. His throat felt as if it had been coated with dry, heated flannel.

A drink. Just one drink. I'll go into the house long enough to get just one, a short peg. Then I'll be ready.

Fine. Sounded great. Except he wasn't going to do it, and he knew he wasn't. The drinking part was done. So was the delaying part. Holding the key tightly in his damp hand, Gardener went around to the door. He thought: *Don't want to go in. Don't even know if I can. Because I'm so afraid—*

Stop it. Let that part be over, too. Your Tommyknocker Phase.

He looked around again, almost hoping to see the line of flashlights coming out of the woods, or to hear their voices.

But you wouldn't, because they talk in their heads.

No flashlights. No movements. No crickets. No birdsong. The only sound was the sound of washing machines, the sound of amplified, leaky heartbeats: *slisshh-slisshhh-slissshhh* . . .

Gardener looked at the pulsing green light fingering its way through the cracks between the boards. He reached into his pocket, took out the old sunglasses, and put them on.

It had been a long time since he had prayed, but he prayed now. It was short, but a prayer for all that.

"God, please," Jim Gardener said into the dim summer dusk, and slid the key into the padlock.

5

He expected a blast of head-radio, but none came. Until it didn't, he hadn't realized that his stomach was tight and sucked in, like a man expecting an electric shock.

He licked his lips and turned the key.

A small noise, barely audible over the low slooching noises from the shed:—*click!*—

The hasp sprang up a little from the body of the lock. He reached for it with an arm that felt like lead. He pulled it free, clicked the hasp down, and put it into his left front pocket with the key still sticking out. He felt like a man in a dream. It was not a good one to be having.

The air in there had to be okay—well, perhaps not *okay*; perhaps none of the air in Haven was exactly *okay* anymore. But it was about the same as the air outside, Gard thought, because the shed was a sieve of cracks. If there was such a thing as a pure Tommyknocker biosphere, this couldn't be it. At least, he didn't *think* so.

All the same, he would take as few risks as possible. He took a deep breath, held it, and told himself to count his steps: *Three. You go in no more than three steps. Just in case. One good look around and then out. In one big hurry.*

You hope.

Yes, I hope.

He took a final look along the path, saw nothing, turned back to the shed, and opened the door.

The green glow, brilliant even through the dark glasses, washed over him like corrupt sunlight.

6

At first he could see nothing at all. The light was too bright. He knew it had been brighter than this on other occasions, but he had never been so close to it before. Close? God, he was *in* it. Someone standing just outside the open door looking for him now would hardly be able to see him.

He slitted his eyes against that brilliant greenness and shuffled forward a step . . . then another step . . . then a third. His hands were held out in front of him like those of a groping blind man. Which he was; shit, he even had the dark glasses to prove it.

The noise was louder. *Slissh-slissshh-slisshhh* . . . off to the left. He turned in that direction but didn't go any further. He was afraid to go any further, afraid of what he might touch.

Now his eyes began to adjust. He saw dark shapes in

the green. A bench . . . but no Tommyknockers at it; it had simply been shoved back against the wall, out of the way. And . . .

My God, it is *a washing machine! It really is!*

It was, all right, one of the old-fashioned kind with wringer-roller at the top, but it wasn't making that weird noise. It had also been pushed back against the wall. It was in the process of being modified somehow; someone was working on it in the best Tommyknocker tradition, but it wasn't running now.

Next to it was an Electrolux vacuum cleaner . . . one of the old long ones that ran on wheels, low to the ground, like a mechanical dachshund. A chainsaw mounted on wheels. Stacks of smoke-detectors from Radio Shack, most still in their boxes. A number of kerosene drums, also on wheels, with hoses attached to them, and things like arms . . .

Arms, of course they are, they're robots, fucking robots in the making, and none of them looks exactly like the white dove of peace, does it, Gard? And—

Slishh-slishh-slishhh.

Further left. The source of the glow was here.

Gard heard a funny, hurt noise escape him. The breath he had been holding ran weakly out like air from a pricked balloon. The strength ran out of his legs in exactly the same way. He reached out blindly, his hand found the bench, and he did not sit but simply plopped down on it. He was unable to take his eyes from the left-rear corner of the shed, where Ev Hillman, Anne Anderson, and Bobbi's good old beagle Peter had somehow been hung up on posts in two old galvanized steel shower cabinets with their doors removed. They hung there like slabs of beef on meathooks. But they were alive, Gard saw . . . somehow, some way still alive.

A thick black cord which looked like a high-voltage line or a very big coaxial cable ran out of the center of Anne Anderson's forehead. A similar cable ran out of the old man's right eye. And the entire top of the dog's skull had been peeled away; dozens of smaller cords ran out of Peter's exposed and pulsing brain.

Peter's eyes, free of cataracts, turned toward Gard. He whined.

Jesus . . . oh my Jesus . . . oh my Jesus Christ.

He tried to get up from the bench. He couldn't.

Portions of the old man's skull and Anne's skull had also been removed, he saw. The doors had been torn off the shower stalls but they were still full of some clear liquid—it was being contained in the same way that tiny sun was contained in Bobbi's water heater, he supposed. If he tried to get into one of those stalls, he would feel a tough springiness. Plenty of give . . . but no access.

Want to get in? *I only want to get* out!

Then his mind returned to its former scripture:

Jesus . . . dear Jesus . . . oh my Jesus look *at them . . . I don't* want *to look at them.*

No. But he couldn't tear his eyes away.

The liquid was clear but emerald green. It was moving—making that low, thick sudsy sound. For all its clarity, Gardener thought that liquid must be very gluey indeed, perhaps the consistency of dish detergent.

How can they breathe in there? How can they be alive? Maybe they're not; maybe it's only the movement of the liquid that makes you think they are. Maybe it's just an illusion, please Jesus let it be an illusion.

Peter . . . you heard him whine—

Nope. Part of the illusion. That's all. He's hanging on a hook in a shower-stall filled with the interstellar equivalent of Joy dish-detergent, he couldn't whine in that, it would come out all soap-bubbles, and you're just freaking out. That's what it is, just a little visit from King Freakout.

Except he wasn't just freaking, and he knew it. Just as he knew he hadn't heard Peter whine with his *ears.*

That hurt, helpless whining sound had come from the same place the radio music came from: the center of his brain.

Anne Anderson opened her eyes.

Get me out of here! she screamed. *Get me out of here, I'll leave her alone, only I can't feel anything except when they make it hurt make it hurt make it hurrrrtt . . .*

Gardener tried again to get up. He was very faintly aware that he was making a sound. Just some old sound. The sound he was making was probably a lot like the sound a woodchuck run over in the road might make, he thought.

The greenish, moving liquid gave Sissy's face a gassy, ghastly corpse-hue. The blue of her eyes had bleached out. Her tongue floated like some fleshy undersea plant. Her fingers, wrinkled and pruney, drifted.

I can't feel anything except when they make it hurrrrrttttt! Anne wailed, and he couldn't shut her voice out, couldn't stick his fingers in his ears to make it go away, because that voice was coming from inside his head.

Slisshhh-slishhh-slisshhh.

Copper tubing running into the tops of the shower stalls, making them look like a hilarious combination of Buck Rogers suspended-animation chambers and Li'l Abner moonshine stills.

Peter's fur had fallen out in patches. His hindquarters appeared to be collapsing in on themselves. His legs moved through the liquid in long lazy sweeps, as if in his dreams he was running away.

When they make it hurrrrrrt!

The old man opened his one eye.

The boy.

This thought was utterly clear; unquestionable. Gardener found himself responding to it.

What boy?

The answer was immediate, startling for a moment, then unquestionable.

David. David Brown.

That one eye stared at him, a ceaseless sapphire with emerald tints.

Save the boy.

The boy. David. David Brown. Was he a part of this somehow, the boy they had hunted for so many exhausting hot days? Of course he was. Maybe not directly, but a part of it.

Where is he? Gardener thought at the old man who floated in his pale green solution.

Slishhh-slishhh-slishhh.

Altair-4, the old man returned finally. *David's on Altair-4. Save him . . . and then kill us. This is . . . it's bad. Real bad. Can't die. I've tried. We all have. Even*

(bitchbitch)

her. This is being in hell. Use the transformer to save David. Then pull the plugs. Cut the wires. Burn the place. Do you hear?

For the third time Gardener tried to get up and fell bonelessly back onto the bench. He became aware that thick electrical cords were scattered all over the floor, and that brought back a ghostly memory of the band that had picked him up on the turnpike when he was coming back from New Hampshire. He puzzled at this, and then got the connection. The floor looked like a concert stage just before a rock group started to play. That, or a big-city TV studio. The cables snaked into a huge crate filled with circuit boards and a stack of VCRs. They were wired together. He looked for a DC current converter, saw none, and then thought: *Of course not, idiot. Batteries* are *DC.*

The cassette recorders had been plugged into a mix of home computers—Ataris, Apple II's and III's, TRS-80s, Commodores. Blinking on and off on the one lit screen was the word

PROGRAM?

Behind the modified computers were more circuit boards—hundreds of them. The whole thing was uttering a low sleepy hum—a sound he associated with—

(use the transformer)

big electrical equipment.

Light spilled out of the crate and the computers placed haphazardly next to it in a green flood—but the light was not quite steady. It was cycling. The pulse of the light and its relation to the sudsing sounds coming from the shower cabinets was very clear.

That's the center, he thought with an invalid's weak excitement. *That's the annex to the ship. They come in the shed to use that. It's a transformer, and they draw their power from there.*

Use the transformer to save David.

Might as well ask me to fly Air Force One. *Ask me something easy, Pop. If I could bring him back from wherever he was by reciting Mark Twain—Poe, even—I'd take a shot. But that thing? It looks like an explosion in an electronics warehouse.*

But—the boy.

How old? Four? Five?

And where in God's name had they put him? The sky was, literally, the limit.

Save the boy . . . use the transformer.

There was, of course, not even any time to look closely at the damned mess. The others would be coming back. Still, he stared at the one lighted video terminal with hypnotic intensity.

PROGRAM?

What if I typed Altair-4 *on the keyboard?* he wondered, and saw there *was* no keyboard; at the same second the letters on the screen changed.

ALTAIR-4

it now read.

No! his mind screamed, full of intruder's guilt. *No, Jesus, no!*

The letters rippled.

NO JESUS NO

Sweating, Gardener thought: *Cancel! Cancel!*

CANCEL CANCEL

These letters blinked on and off . . . on and off. Gardener stared at them, horrified. Then:

PROGRAM?

He made an effort to shield his thoughts and tried again to get to his feet. This time he made it. Other wires came out of the transformer. These were thinner. There were . . . He counted. Yes. Eight of them. Ending in earplugs.

Earplugs. Freeman Moss. The animal trainer leading mechanical elephants. Here were more earplugs. In a crazy way it reminded him of a high-school language lab.

Are they learning another language in here?

Yes. No. They're learning to "become." The machine is teaching them. But where are *the batteries? I don't see any. There should be ten or twelve big old Delcos hooked up to that thing. Just a maintenance charge running through it. There should be—*

Stunned, he raised his eyes to the shower stalls again.

He looked at the coaxial cable coming out of the woman's forehead, the old man's eye. He watched Peter's legs moving in those big dreamy strides and wondered just how Bobbi had gotten the dog hairs on her dress—had she been giving Peter the equivalent of an interstellar oil change? Had she been perhaps overcome by a simple human emotion? Love? Remorse? Guilt? Had she perhaps hugged her dog before filling that cabinet up with liquid again?

There *are the batteries. Organic Delcos and Evereadys, you might say. They're sucking them dry. Sucking them like vampires.*

A new emotion crept through his fear and bewilderment and revulsion. It was fury, and Gardener welcomed it.

They make it hurrrt . . . make it hurrrt . . . make it hurrrrrr—

Her voice cut off abruptly. The dull hum of the transformer changed pitch; cycled down even lower. The light coming out of the crate faded a little. He thought she had fallen unconscious, thereby lowering the machine's total output by x number of . . . what? Volts? Dynes? Ohms? Who the fuck knew?

End it, son. Save my grandson and then end it.

For a moment the old man's voice filled his head, perfectly clear and perfectly lucid. Then it was gone. The old man's eye slipped closed.

The green light from the machine grew paler yet.

They woke up when I came in, he thought feverishly. The anger still pounded and drilled at his mind. He spat out a tooth almost without realizing he had done so. *Even Peter woke up a little. Now they've gone back to whatever state they were in . . . before. Sleeping?* No. Not sleeping. Something else. Organic cold storage.

Do batteries dream of electric sheep? he thought, and uttered a cracked cackle.

He moved backward, away from the transformer,

(what exactly is it transforming how why)

away from the shower stalls, the cables. His eyes turned toward the array of gadgets ranged against the far wall. The wringer washer had something mounted on top of it, something that looked like the boomerang TV antennas you sometimes saw on the backs of big limos. Behind the washer and to its left was an old-fashioned treadle sewing machine with a glass funnel mounted on its sidewheel. Kerosene drums with hoses and steel arms . . . a butcher knife, he saw, had been welded to the end of one of those arms.

Christ, what is all this? What is it for?

A voice whispered: *Maybe it's protection, Gard. In*

case the Dallas Police show up early. It's the Tommyknocker Yard-Sale Army—old washing machines with cellular antennas. Electrolux vacuums, chainsaws on wheels. Name it and claim it, baby.

He felt his sanity tottering. His eyes were drawn relentlessly back to Peter, Peter with most of his skull peeled away, Peter with a bunch of wires plugged into what remained of his head. His brain looked like a pallid veal roast with a bunch of temperature probes stuck into it.

Peter with his legs racing dreamily through that liquid, as if running away.

Bobbi, he thought in despair and fury, *how could you do it to Peter? Christ!* The people were bad, awful—but Peter was somehow worse. It was a curse piled on top of an obscenity. Peter, his legs loping and loping, as if running away in his dreams.

Batteries. Living batteries.

He backed into something. There was a dull metallic thump. He turned around and saw another shower cabinet, little blossoms of rust on its sides, its front door gone. Holes had been punched in the back. Wires had been threaded through these; they now hung limply down, large-bore steel plugs at their tips.

For you, Gard! his brain yammered. *This plug's for you, like the beer commercials say! They'll open up the back of your skull, maybe short out your motor-control centers first so you can't move, and then they'll drill—drill for the place where they get their power. This plug's for you, for all you do . . . all ready and waiting! Wow! Neato-keeno!*

He snatched for his thoughts, which were tightening into a hysterical spiral, and brought them under control. *Not* for him; at least, not originally. This had already been used. There was that faint smell, bland and sudsy. Streaks of dried gunk on the inner walls—the last traces of that thick green liquid. *It looks like the Wizard of Oz's semen,* he thought.

Do you mean Bobbi's got her sister floating in a big sperm bank?

That weird cackle escaped him again. He pressed the heel of his hand against his mouth, pressed hard, to stifle it.

He looked down and saw a pair of tan shoes tossed

beside the shower cabinet. He picked one up, saw splashes of dried blood on it.

Bobbi's. Her one pair of good shoes. Her "going-out" shoes. She was wearing them when she left for the funeral that day.

The other shoe was also bloody.

Gard looked behind the shower cabinet and saw the rest of the clothing Bobbi had been wearing that day.

The blood, all that blood.

He didn't want to touch the blouse, but the shape under it was too clear. He pinched as small a piece of it as he could between his fingers and peeled it up from Bobbi's good charcoal-colored skirt.

Underneath the shirt was a gun. It was the biggest, oldest-looking gun Gardener had ever seen except for pictures in a book. After a moment he picked the gun up and rolled the cylinder. There were still four rounds in it. Two gone. Gardener was willing to bet that one of those rounds had gone into Bobbi.

He pushed the cylinder back into place and stuck it in his belt. At once a voice spoke up in his mind. *Shot your wife . . . good fucking deal.*

Never mind. The gun might come in handy.

When they see it's gone, it's you they'll come looking for, Gard. I thought you already came to that conclusion.

No; that was one thing he didn't think he had to worry about. They would have noticed the changed words on the computer screen, but these clothes hadn't been touched since Bobbi took them off (or since they took them off her, which was probably more likely).

They must be too exalted when they get in here to bother much about housekeeping, he thought. *Damn good thing there's no flies.*

He touched the gun again. This time the voice in his head was silent. It had decided, perhaps, that there were no wives here to worry about.

If you have to shoot Bobbi, will you be able to?

That was a question he couldn't answer.

Slishhh-slishhh-slishhh.

How long had Bobbi and her company been gone? He didn't know; hadn't the slightest idea. Time had no meaning in here; the old man was right. This was hell. And did Peter still respond to his strange master's caress when she came in here?

His stomach was on the edge of revolt.

He had to get out—get out right now. He felt like a creature in a fairy-tale, Bluebeard's wife in the secret room, Jack grubbing in the giant's pile of gold. He felt ripe for discovery. But he held the stiff, bloody garment in front of him as if frozen. Not as if; he *was* frozen.

Where's Bobbi?

She had a sunstroke.

Hell of a strange sunstroke that had soaked her blouse with blood. Gardener had retained a morbid, sickish interest in guns and the damage they could do to the human body. If she had been shot with the big old gun now in his own belt, he guessed Bobbi had no right to be alive—even if she had been taken quickly to a hospital which specialized in the emergency treatment of gunshot wounds, she probably would have died.

They brought me in here when I was blown apart, but the Tommyknockers fixed me up right smart.

Not for him. The old shower stall was not for him. Gardener had a feeling that he would be put out of the way with more finality. The shower stall had been for Bobbi.

They had brought her in here, and . . . what?

Why, hooked her up to their batteries, of course. Not Anne, she had not been here then. But to Peter . . . and Hillman.

He dropped the blouse . . . then forced himself to pick it up again and put it back on top of the skirt. He didn't know how much of the real world they noticed when they got in here (not much, he guessed) but he didn't want to take any extra chances.

He looked at the holes in the back of the cabinet, the dangling cords with the steel plugs at their tips.

The green light had begun to pulse brighter and more rapidly again. He turned around. Anne's eyes were open again. Her short hair floated around her head. He could still see that unending hate in her eyes, now mixed with horror and growing strangeness.

Now there were bubbles.

They floated up from her mouth in a brief, thick stream.

Thought/sound exploded in his head.

She was screaming.

Gardener fled.

7

Real terror is the most physically debilitating of all emotions. It saps the endocrines, dumps muscle-tightening organic drugs into the bloodstream, races the heart, exhausts the mind. Jim Gardener staggered away from Bobbi Anderson's shed on rubber legs, his eyes bugging, his mouth hanging stupidly open (the tongue lolled in one corner like a dead thing), his bowels hot and full, his stomach cramped.

It was hard to think beyond the crude, powerful images which stuttered on and off in his mind like barroom neon: those bodies hung up on hooks, like bugs impaled on pins by cruel, bored children; Peter's relentlessly moving legs; the bloody blouse with the bullet-hole in it; the plugs; the old-fashioned washing machine topped with the boomerang antenna. Strongest of all was the image of that short, thick stream of bubbles emerging from Anne Anderson's mouth as she screamed inside his head.

He got into the house, rushed into the bathroom, and knelt in front of the toilet bowl, only to discover he couldn't puke. He *wanted* to puke. He thought of maggoty hot-dogs, moldy pizza, pink lemonade with hairballs floating in it; finally he rammed two fingers down his throat. He was able to trip a simple gag reaction by this last, but no more. He couldn't sick it up. Simple as that.

If I can't, I'll go crazy.

Fine, go crazy if you have to. But first do what you have to do. Keep it together that long. And just by the way, Gard, do you have any more questions about what you should do?

Not anymore he didn't. Peter's relentlessly moving legs had convinced him. That stream of bubbles had convinced him. He wondered how he could have hesitated so long in the face of a power that was so obviously corrupting, so obviously dark.

Because you were mad, he answered himself. Gard nodded. That was it. No more explanation was needed. He had been mad—and not just for the last month or so. It was late to wake up, oh yes, very late, but late was better than never.

The sound. *Slishh-slishhh-slishhh.*

The smell. Bland yet meaty. A smell his mind insisted on associating with raw veal slowly spoiling in milk.

His stomach lurched. A burning, acidic burp scorched his throat. Gardener moaned.

The idea—that glimmer—returned to him, and he clutched at it. It might be possible either to abort all of this . . . or at least to put it on hold for a long, long time. It just might.

You got to let the world go to hell in its own way, Gard, two minutes to midnight or not.

He thought of Ted the Power Man again, thought of mad military organizations trading ever-more-sophisticated weapons with each other, and that angry, inarticulate, obsessed part of his mind tried to shout down sanity one final time.

Shut up, Gardener told it.

He went into the guest bedroom and pulled off his shirt. He looked out the window and now he could see sparks of light coming out of the woods. Dark had come. They were returning. They would go into the shed and maybe have a little séance. A meeting of minds around the shower cabinets. Fellowship in the homey green glow of raped minds.

Enjoy it, Gardener thought. He put the .45 under the foot of the mattress, then unbuckled his belt. *It may be the last time, so—*

He looked down at his shirt. Sticking out of the pocket was a bow of metal. It was the padlock, of course. The padlock which belonged on the shed door.

8

For a moment which probably seemed much longer than it actually was, Gardener was unable to move at all. That feeling of unreal fairy-tale terror stole back into his tired heart. He was reduced to a horrified spectator watching those lights move steadily along the path. Soon they would reach the overgrown garden. They would cut through. They would cross the dooryard. They would reach the shed. They would see the missing padlock. Then they would come into the house and either kill Jim

Gardener or send his discorporated atoms to Altair-4, wherever that was.

His first coherent thought was simple panic yelling at the top of its voice: *Run! Get out of here!*

His second thought was the shaky resurfacing of reason. *Guard your thoughts. If you ever guarded them before, guard them now.*

He stood with his shirt off, his unbuckled and unzipped jeans sagging around his hips, staring at the padlock in his shirt pocket.

Get out there right now and put it back. Right NOW!

No . . . no time . . . Christ, there's no time. They're at the garden.

There might be. There might be just enough if you quit playing pocket-pool and get moving!

He broke the paralysis with a final harsh effort of will, bent, snatched up the lock with the key still sticking out of the bottom, and ran, zipping his pants as he went. He slipped out the back door, paused for just a moment as the last two flashlights slipped into the garden and disappeared, then ran for the shed.

Faintly, vaguely, he could hear their voices in his mind—full of awe, wonder, jubilation.

He closed them out.

Green light fanning out from the shed door, which stood ajar.

Christ, Gard, how could you have been so stupid? his cornered mind raved, but he knew how. It was easy to forget such mundane things as relocking doors when you had seen a couple of people hung up on posts with coaxial cables coming out of their heads.

He could hear them in the garden now—could hear the rustle of the useless giant cornstalks.

As he reached toward the hasp, lock in hand, he remembered closing it before dropping it into his pocket. His hand jerked at the thought and he dropped the goddam thing. It thumped to the ground. He looked for it, and at first couldn't see it at all.

No . . . there it was, there just beyond the narrow fan of pulsing green light. There was the lock, yes, but the key wasn't in it anymore. The key had fallen out when the lock thumped to the ground.

God my God my God, his mind sobbed. His body was

now covered with oozing sweat. His hair hung in his eyes. He thought he must smell like a rancid monkey.

He could hear cornstalks and leaves rustling louder. Someone laughed quietly—the sound was shockingly near. They would be out of the garden in seconds—he could feel those seconds bustling by, like self-important businessmen with potbellies and attaché cases. He went down on his knees, snatched up the lock, and began to sweep his hand back and forth in the dirt, trying to find the key.

Oh you bastard where are you? Oh you bastard where are you? Oh you bastard *where* are *you?*

Aware that even now, in this panic, he had thrown a screen around his thoughts. Was it working? He didn't know. And if he couldn't find the key, it didn't matter, did it?

Oh you bastard where are you?

He saw a dull glint of silver beyond where he was sweeping his hand—the key had gone much further than he would have believed. His seeing it was only dumb luck . . . like Bobbi stumbling over that little rim of protruding metal in the earth two months before, he supposed.

Gardener snatched it and bolted to his feet. He would be hidden from them by the angle of the house for just a moment longer, but that was all he had left. One more screw-up—even a little one—would finish him, and there might not be enough time left even if he performed each of the mundane little operations involved in padlocking a door perfectly.

The fate of the world may now depend on whether a man can lock a shed door on the first try, he thought dazedly. *Modern life is* SO *challenging.*

For a moment he didn't think he was even going to be able to slot the key in the lock. It chattered all the way around the slit without going in, a prisoner of his shaking hand. Then, when he thought it really was all over, it slid home. He turned it. The lock opened. He closed the door, slipped the arm of the padlock through the hasp, and then clicked it shut. He pulled the key out and folded it into his sweating hand. He slid around the corner of the shed like oil. At the exact moment he did, the men and women who had gone out to the ship emerged into the dooryard, moving in single file.

Gardener reached up to hang the key on the nail where he had found it. For one nightmare moment he thought he was going to drop it again and have to hunt for it in the high weeds growing on this side of the shed. When it slipped onto the nail he let out his breath in a shuddering sigh.

Part of him wanted not to move, to just freeze here. Then he decided he'd better not take the risk. After all, he didn't *know* that Bobbi had her key.

He continued slipping along the side of the shed. His left ankle struck the haft of an old harrow that had been left to rust in the weeds, and he had to clamp his teeth over a cry of pain. He stepped over it and slipped around another corner. Now he was behind the shed.

That sudsing sound was maddeningly loud back here.

I'm right behind those goddam showers, he thought. *They're floating inches from me . . . literally* inches.

A rustle of weeds. A minute scrape of metal. Gardener felt simultaneously like laughing and screeching. They *hadn't* had Bobbi's key. Someone had just come around to the side of the shed and taken the key Gardener had hung up again only seconds before—probably Bobbi herself.

Still warm from my hand, Bobbi, did you notice?

He stood in back of the shed, pressed against the rough wood, arms slightly spread, palms tight on the boards.

Did you notice? And do you hear me? Do any of you hear me? Is someone—Allison or Archinbourg or Berringer—going to suddenly pop his head around here and yell out "Peekaboo, Gard, we seeee *you"? Is the shield still working?*

He stood there and waited for them to take him.

They didn't. On an ordinary summer night he probably would not have been able to hear the metallic rattle as the door was unlocked—it would have been masked by the loud *ree-ree-ree* of the crickets. But now there were no crickets. He heard the unlocking; heard the creak of the hinges as the door was opened; heard the hinges creak again as the door was pushed shut. They were inside.

Almost at once the pulses of light falling through the cracks began to speed up and become brighter, and his mind was split by an agonized scream:

Hurts! It hurrrrr—

He moved away from the shed and went back to the house.

9

He lay awake a long time, waiting for them to come out again, waiting to see if he had been discovered.

All right, I can try to put a stop to the "becoming," he thought. *But it won't work unless I actually can go inside the ship. Can I do that?*

He didn't know. Bobbi seemed to have no worries, but Bobbi and the others were different now. Oh, he himself was also "becoming"; the lost teeth proved that; the ability to hear thoughts did too. He had changed the words on the computer screen just by thinking them. But there was no use kidding himself: he was far behind the competition. If Bobbi survived the entry into the ship and her old buddy Gard dropped dead, would any of them, even Bobbi herself, spare a tear? He didn't think so.

Maybe that's what they all want. Bobbi included. For you to go into the ship and just fall over with your brains exploding in one big harmonic radio transmission. It would save Bobbi the moral pain of taking care of you herself, for one thing. Murder without tears.

That they intended to get rid of him, he no longer doubted. But he thought that maybe Bobbi—the old Bobbi—would let him live long enough to see the interior of the strange thing they had worked so long to dig up. That at least *felt* right. And in the end, it didn't matter. If murder was what Bobbi was planning, there was no real defense, was there? He *had* to go into the ship. Unless he did that, his idea, crazy as it undoubtedly was, had no chance to work at all.

Have to try, Gard.

He had intended to try as soon as they were inside, and that would probably be tomorrow morning. Now he thought that maybe he ought to press his luck a little further. If he went according to the rag and a bone he supposed he had to call his "original plan," there would be no way he could do anything about that little boy. The kid would have to come first.

Gard, he's probably dead anyway.

Maybe. But the old man didn't think so; the old man thought there was still a little boy left to save.

One kid doesn't matter—not in the face of all this. You know it, too—Haven is like a great big nuclear reactor that's ready to go red-line. The containment is melting. To coin a phrase.

It was logical, but it was a croupier's logic. Ultimately, killer logic. Ted the Power Man logic. If he wanted to play the game that way, why even bother?

The kid matters or nothing matters.

And maybe this way he could even save Bobbi. He didn't think so; he thought Bobbi had gone too far for salvation. But he could try.

Long odds, Gard ole Gard.

Sure. The clock's at a minute to midnight . . . we're down to counting seconds.

Thinking that, he slipped into the blankness of sleep. This was followed by nightmares where he floated in a clear green bath, tethered by thick coaxial cables. He was trying to scream but he couldn't, because the cables were coming out of his mouth.

5.

THE SCOOP

1

Entombed in the overdecorated confines of the Bounty Tavern—drinking buck-a-bottle Heinekens and laughed at by David Bright, who had sunk to vulgar depths of humor, who had even ended up comparing John Leandro to Superman's pal Jimmy Olsen—Leandro had wavered. No use telling himself otherwise. He *had,* indeed, wavered. But men of vision have always had to endure barbs of ridicule, and not a few have been burned or crucified or had their height artificially extended by five or six inches on the Inquisitorial rack of pain for their visions. Having David Bright ask him over beers in the Bounty if his Secret Wristwatch was in good working order was hardly the worst thing that could have befallen him.

But oh shit it hurt.

John Leandro determined that David Bright, and anyone else to whom Bright had related Crazy Johnny's ideas that Something Big Was Going on in Haven, would end up laughing on the other side of his or her face. Because something big *was* going on there. He felt it in every bone in his body. There were days, when the wind was blowing from the southeast, that he almost imagined he could *smell* it.

His vacation had begun the previous Friday. He had hoped to go down to Haven that very day. But he lived with his widowed mother, and she had been counting *so* on him running her up to Nova Scotia to see her sister, she said, but if John had commitments, why, she understood; after all, she was old and probably not much fun anymore; just someone to cook his meals and wash his underwear, and that was fine, you go on, Johnny, go on and hunt up your *scoop,* I'll just call Megan on the telephone, maybe in a week or two your cousin Alfie will bring *her* down here to see *me,* Alfie's so good to his mother, *et cetera, et cetera, ibid., ibid., ad infinitum, ad infinitum.*

On Friday, Leandro took his mother to Nova Scotia. Of course they stayed over, and by the time they got back to Bangor, Saturday was shot. Sunday was a bad day to begin anything, what with his Sunday-school class of first- and second-graders at nine, full worship services at ten, and Young Men for Christ in the Methodist rectory at five P.M. At the YMC meeting, a special speaker gave them a slide show on Armageddon. As he explained to them how unrepenting sinners would be inflicted with boils and running sores and ailments of the bowels and the intestines, Georgina Leandro and the other members of the Ladies' Aid passed out paper cups of Za-Rex and oatmeal cookies. And during the evening there was always a songfest for Christ in the church basement.

Sundays always left him feeling exalted. And exhausted.

2

So it was Monday, the fifteenth of August, before Leandro finally tossed his yellow legal pads, his Sony tape recorder, his Nikon, and a gadget-bag filled with film and various lenses into the front seat of his used Dodge and prepared to set out for Haven . . . and what he hoped would be journalistic glory. He would not have been appalled if he had known he was approaching ground-zero of what was shortly to become the biggest story since the crucifixion of Jesus Christ.

The day was calm and blue and mellow—very warm but not so savagely hot and humid as the last few days had been. It was a day everyone on earth would mark forever in his memory. Johnny Leandro had wanted a story, but he had never heard the old proverb that goes, "God says take what you want . . . and pay for it."

He only knew that he had stumbled onto the edge of something, and when he tried to wiggle it, it remained firm . . . which meant it was maybe bigger than one might at first think. There was no way he was going to walk away from this; he intended to excavate. All the David Brights in the world with their smart cracks about Jimmy Olsen wristwatches and Fu Manchu could not stop him.

He put the Dodge in drive and began to roll away from the curb.

"Don't forget your lunch, Johnny!" his mother called. She came puffing down the walk with a brown-paper sack in one hand. Large grease spots were already forming on the brown paper; since grade school, Leandro's favorite sandwich had been bologna, slices of Bermuda onion, and Wesson Oil.

"Thanks, Mom," he said, leaning over to take the bag and put it down on the floor. "You didn't have to do that, though. I could have picked up a hamburger—"

"If I've told you once I've told you a thousand times," she said, "you have no business going into those roadside luncheonettes, Johnny. You never know if the kitchen's dirty or clean.

"Microbes," she said ominously, leaning forward.

"Ma, I got to g—"

"You can't see *microbes* at all," Mrs. Leandro went on. She was not to be turned from her subject until she had had her say on it.

"Yes, Mom," Leandro said, resigned.

"Some of those places are just havens for *microbes*," she said. "The cooks may not be clean, you know. They may not wash their hands after leaving the lavatory. They may have dirt or even excrement under their nails. This isn't anything I want to discuss, you understand, but sometimes a mother has to instruct her son. Food in places like that can make a person very, very sick."

"Mom—"

She uttered a long-suffering laugh and dabbed momentarily at the corner of one eye with her apron. "Oh, I know, your mother is silly, just a silly old woman with a lot of funny old ideas, and she probably ought to just learn to shut up."

Leandro recognized this for the manipulative trick it

was, but it still always made him feel squirmy, guilty, about eight years old.

"No, Mom," he said. "I don't think that at all."

"I mean, you are the big newsman, I just sit home and make your bed and wash your clothes and air out your bedroom if you get the farts from drinking too much beer."

Leandro bent his head, said nothing, and waited to be released.

"But do this for me. Stay out of roadside luncheonettes, Johnny, because you can get sick. From *microbes.*"

"I promise, Mom."

Satisfied that she had extracted a promise from him, she was now willing to let him go.

"You'll be home for supper?"

"Yes," Leandro said, not knowing any better.

"At six?" she persisted.

"Yes! Yes!"

"I know, I know, I'm just a silly old—"

"Bye, Mom!" he said hastily, and pulled away from the curb.

He looked in the rearview mirror and saw her standing at the end of the walk, waving. He waved back, then dropped his hand, hoping she would go back into the house . . . and knowing better. When he made a right turn two blocks down and his mother was finally gone, Leandro felt a faint but unmistakable lightening of his heart. Rightly or wrongly, he always felt this way when his mom finally dropped out of sight.

3

In Haven, Bobbi Anderson was showing Jim Gardener some modified breathing apparatus. Ev Hillman would have recognized it; the respirators looked very similar to the one he had picked up for the cop, Butch Dugan. But that one had been to protect Dugan from the Haven air; the respirators Bobbi was demonstrating drew on reserves of just that—Haven air was what they were used to, and Haven air was what the two of them would breathe if they got inside the Tommyknockers' ship. It was nine-thirty.

At that same time, in Derry, John Leandro had pulled

over to the side of the road not far from the place where the gutted deer and the cruiser requisitioned to officers Rhodes and Gabbons had been found. He thumbed open the glove compartment to check on the Smith & Wesson .38 he had picked up in Bangor the week before. He took it out for a moment, not putting his forefinger anywhere near the trigger even though he knew it was unloaded. He liked the compact way the gun fitted his palm, its weight, the feeling of simple power it somehow conveyed. But it also made him feel a trifle skittery, as if he might have torn off a chunk of something that was far too big for the likes of him to chew.

A chunk of what?

He wasn't quite sure. Some sort of strange meat.

Microbes, his mother's voice spoke up in his mind. *Food in places like that can make a person very, very sick.*

He checked to make sure the carton of bullets was still in the glove compartment, then put the gun back. He guessed that transporting a handgun in the glove compartment of a motor vehicle was probably against the law (he thought again of his mother, this time without even realizing he was doing so). He could imagine a cop pulling him over for something routine, asking to see his registration, and getting a glimpse of the .38 when Leandro opened the glove compartment. That was the way the murderers always got caught on *Alfred Hitchcock Presents,* which he and his mother watched every Saturday night on the cable station that showed it. It would *also* be a scoop of a different sort: BANGOR "DAILY NEWS" REPORTER ARRESTED ON ILLEGAL-WEAPONS CHARGE.

Well then, take your registration out of the glove compartment and put it in your wallet, if you're so worried.

But he wouldn't do that. The idea made perfect sense, but it also seemed like buying trouble . . . and that voice of reason sounded altogether too much like the voice of his mother warning him about *microbes* or instructing him (as she had when he was a boy) on the horrors which might result if he forgot to put paper all over the ring of a public toilet before sitting on it.

Leandro drove on instead, aware that his heart was beating a little too fast, and that he felt just a little sweatier than the heat of the day could explain.

Something big . . . some days I can almost smell it.

Yes. Something was out there, all right. The death of

the McCausland woman (a furnace explosion in July? oh *really?*); the disappearance of the investigating troopers; the suicide of the cop who had supposedly been in love with her. And before any of those things, there had been the disappearance of the little boy. David Bright had said David Brown's grandfather had been spouting a lot of crazy nonsense about telepathy and magic tricks that really worked.

I only wish you'd come to me instead of Bright, Mr. Hillman, Leandro thought for perhaps the fiftieth time.

Except now *Hillman* had disappeared. Hadn't been back to his rooming house in over two weeks. Hadn't been back to Derry Home Hospital to visit his grandson, although the nurses had had to boot him out nights before. The official state-police line was that Ev Hillman *hadn't* disappeared, but that was catch-22, because a legal adult *couldn't* disappear in the eyes of the law until *another* legal adult so reported that person, filling out the proper forms in consequence. So all was jake in the eyes of the law. All was *far* from jake in the eyes of John Leandro. Hillman's landlady told him that the old man had stiffed her for sixty bucks—as far as Leandro had been able to find out, it was the first unpaid bill the old guy had left in his life.

Something big . . . strange meat.

Nor was that all of the weirdness emanating out of Haven these days. A fire, also in July, had killed a couple on the Nista Road. This month a doctor piloting a small plane had crashed and burned. That had happened in Newport, true, but the FAA controller at BIA had confirmed that the unfortunate doc had overflown Haven, and at an illegally low altitude. Phone service in Haven had begun to get oddly glitchy. Sometimes people could get through, sometimes they couldn't. He had sent to the Augusta Bureau of Taxation for a list of Haven voters (paying the required fee of six dollars to get the nine computer sheets) and had managed to trace relatives of nearly sixty of these Havenites—relatives living in Bangor, Derry, and surrounding areas—in his spare time.

He couldn't find one—*not one*—who had seen his or her Haven relations since July 10th or so . . . over a month before. *Not one.*

Of course, a lot of those he interviewed didn't find this strange at all. Some of them weren't on good terms with their Haven relations and couldn't care less if they didn't hear from or see them in the next six months . . . or six years. Others seemed first surprised, then thoughtful when Leandro pointed out the length of time they were talking about. Of course, summer was an active season for most people. Time passed with a light easiness that winter knew nothing about. And, of course, they had spoken to Aunt Mary or Brother Bill a time or two on the phone—sometimes you couldn't get through, but mostly you could.

There were other suspicious similarities in the testimony of the people Leandro interviewed, similarities that had made his nose flare with the smell of something decidedly off:

Ricky Berringer was a house-painter in Bangor. His older brother, Newt, was a carpenter-contractor who also happened to be a Haven selectman. "We invited Newt up for dinner near the end of July," Ricky said, "but he said he had the flu."

Don Blue was a Derry realtor. His Aunt Sylvia, who lived in Haven, had been in the habit of coming up to take dinner with Don and his wife every Sunday or so. The last three Sundays she had begged off—once with the flu *(flu seems to be going around in Haven,* Leandro thought, *nowhere else, you understand—just in Haven),* and the other times because it was so hot she just didn't feel like traveling. After further questioning Blue realized it had been more like *five* Sundays since his aunt had favored them—and maybe as many as six.

Bill Spruce kept a herd of dairy cows in Cleaves Mills. His brother Frank kept a herd in Haven. They usually got together every week or two, merging two extremely large families for a few hours—the clan Spruce would eat tons of barbecue, drink gallons of beer and Pepsi-Cola, and Frank and Bill would sit either at the picnic table in Frank's back yard or on the front porch of Bill's house and compare notes about what they simply called the Business. Bill admitted it had been a month or more since he'd seen Frank—there had been some problem first with his feed supplier, Frank had told him, then with the milk inspectors. Bill, meanwhile, had had a few problems of his own. Half a dozen of his holsteins had died during this last hot-spell. And, he added as an afterthought, his wife had had a heart attack. He and his brother just hadn't had time to visit much this summer

. . . but the man had still expressed unfeigned surprise when Leandro dragged out his wallet calendar and the two of them figured out just how long it had been: the two brothers hadn't gotten together since June 30th. Spruce whistled and tilted his cap back on his head. "Gorry, that *is* a long time," he had said. "Guess I'll have to take a ride down Haven and see Frank, now that my Evelyn's on the mend."

Leandro said nothing, but some of the other testimony he had gathered over the last couple of weeks made him think that Bill Spruce might find a trip like that hazardous to his health.

"Felt like I was dine," Alvin Rutledge told Leandro. Rutledge was a long-haul trucker, currently unemployed, who lived in Bangor. His grandfather was Dave Rutledge, a lifelong Haven resident.

"What exactly do you mean?" Leandro asked.

Alvin Rutledge looked at the young reporter shrewdly. "Another beer'd go down good just about now," he said. They were sitting in Nan's Tavern in Bangor. "Talkin's amazin dusty work, chummy."

"Isn't it," Leandro said, and told the waitress to draw two.

Rutledge took a deep swallow when it came, wiped foam from his upper lip with the heel of his hand, and said: "Heart beatin too fast. Headache. Felt like I was gonna puke my guts out. I *did* puke, as a matter of fact. Just 'fore I turned around. Rolled down the window and just let her fly into the slipstream, I did."

"Wow," Leandro said, since some remark seemed called for. The image of Rutledge "letting her fly into the slipstream" flapped in his mind. He dismissed it. At least, he tried.

"And looka here."

He rolled back his upper lip, revealing the remains of his teeth.

"Ooo see a ho in funt?" Rutledge asked. Leandro saw a good many holes in front, but thought it might not be politic to say so. He simply agreed. Rutledge nodded and let his lip fall back into place. It was something of a relief.

"Teeth never have been much good," Rutledge said indifferently. "When I get workin again and can afford me a good set of dentures, I'm gonna have all of em jerked. Fuck em. Point is, I had my two front teeth there on top before I headed up to Haven week before last to check on Gramp. Hell, they wasn't even *loose*."

"They fell out when you started to get close to Haven?"

"Didn't *fall* out." Rutledge finished his beer. "I *puked* em out."

"Oh," Leandro had replied faintly.

"You know, another brew'd go down good. Talkin's—"

"Thirsty work, I know," Leandro said, signaling the waitress. He was over his limit, but he found he could use another one himself.

4

Alvin Rutledge wasn't the only person who had tried to visit a friend or relative in Haven during July, nor the only one to become ill and turn back. Using the voting lists and area phone-books as a starting point, Leandro turned up three people who told stories similar to Rutledge's. He uncovered a fourth incident through pure coincidence—or almost pure. His mother knew he was "following up" some aspect of his "big story," and happened to mention that her friend Eileen Pulsifer had a friend who lived down in Haven.

Eileen was fifteen years older than Leandro's mother, which put her close to seventy. Over tea and cloyingly sweet gingersnaps, she told Leandro a story similar to those he had already heard.

Mrs. Pulsifer's friend was Mary Jacklin (whose grandson was Tommy Jacklin). They had visited back and forth for more than forty years, and often played in local bridge tournaments. This summer she hadn't seen Mary at all. Not even *once*. She'd spoken to her on the phone, and she seemed fine; her excuses always sounded believable . . . but all the same, something about them—a bad headache, too much baking to do, the family had decided on the spur of the moment to go down to Kennebunk and visit the Trolley Museum—wasn't quite *right*.

"They were fine by the one-by-one, but they seemed odd by the bunch, if you see what I mean." She offered the cookies. "More 'snaps?"

"No thank you," Leandro said.

"Oh, go ahead! I know you boys! Your mother taught you to be polite, but no boy ever born could turn down a gingersnap! Now, you just go on and take what you hanker for!"

Smiling dutifully, Leandro took another gingersnap.

Settling back and folding her hands on her tight round belly, Mrs. Pulsifer went on: "I begun to think something might be wrong . . . I *still* think that maybe something's wrong, truth to tell. First thing to cross my mind was that maybe Mary didn't want to be my friend anymore . . . that maybe I did or said something to offend her. But no, says I to myself, if I'd done something, I guess she'd tell me. After forty years of friendship I guess she would. Besides, she didn't really sound *cool* to me, you know—"

"But she *did* sound different."

Eileen Pulsifer nodded decisively. "Ayuh. And that got me thinking that maybe she was sick, that maybe, God save us, her doctor had found a cancer of something inside her, and she didn't want any of her old friends to know. So I called up Vera and I said, 'We're going to go down to Haven, Vera, and see Mary. We ain't going to tell her we're coming, and that way she can't call us off. You get ready, Vera,' I says, 'because I'm coming by your house at ten o'clock, and if you ain't ready, I'm going to go without you.' "

"Vera is—"

"Vera Anderson, in Derry. Just about my best friend in the whole world, John, except for Mary and your mother. And your mother was down in Monmouth, visiting her sister that week."

Leandro remembered it well: a week of such peace and quiet was a week to be treasured.

"So the two of you headed down."

"Ayuh."

"And you got sick."

"*Sick!* I thought I was dying. My *heart!*" She clapped a hand dramatically over one breast. "It was beating so *fast!* My head started to ache, I got a nosebleed, and Vera got scared. She says, 'Turn around, Eileen, right now, you got to get to the hospital right away!'

"Well, I turned around somehow—I don't hardly remember how, the world was spinning so—and by then my mouth was bleeding, and two of my teeth fell out. Right out of my head! You ever hear the beat of it?"

"No," he lied, thinking of Alvin Rutledge. "Where did it happen?"

"Why, I told you—we were going to see Mary Jacklin—"

"Yes, but were you actually in Haven when you got sick? And which way did you come in?"

"Oh, *I* see! No, we weren't. We were on Old Derry Road. In Troy."

"*Close* to Haven, then."

"Oh, 'bout a mile from the town line. I'd been feeling sick for a little time—whoopsy, you know—but I didn't want to say so to Vera. I kept hoping that I would feel better."

Vera Anderson hadn't gotten sick, and this troubled Leandro. It didn't fit. Vera hadn't gotten a bloody nose, nor lost any teeth.

"No, she didn't get sick at all," Mrs. Pulsifer said. "Except with terror. I guess she was sick with that. For me . . . and for herself too, I imagine."

"How do you mean?"

"Well, that road's awful empty. She thought I was going to pass out. I almost did. It might have been fifteen, twenty minutes before someone came along."

"She couldn't have driven you?"

"God bless you, John, Vera's had muscular dystrophy for years. She wears great big metal braces on her legs—cruel-looking things, they are, like something you'd expect to see in a torture chamber. It just about makes me cry sometimes to see her."

5

At a quarter to ten on the morning of August 15th, Leandro crossed into the town of Troy. His stomach was tight with anticipation and—let's face it, folks—a tingle of fear. His skin felt cold.

I may get sick. I may get sick, and if I do, I'm going to leave about ninety feet of rubber reversing out of the area. Got that?

I got it, boss, he answered himself. *I got it, I got it.*

You may lose some teeth too, he cautioned himself, but the loss of a few teeth seemed a small price to pay for a story which might win him a Pulitzer Prize . . . and, just as important, one which would surely turn David Bright green with envy.

He passed through Troy Village, where everything seemed fine . . . if a little slower than usual. The first jag in the normal run of things came about a mile further south, and from a direction he wouldn't have expected. He had been listening to WZON out of Bangor. Now the normally strong AM signal began to waver and flutter. Leandro could hear one . . . no, two . . . no, three . . . other stations mixed in with its signal. He frowned. That sometimes happened at night, when radiant cooling thinned the atmosphere and allowed radio signals to travel further, but he had never heard of it happening on an AM bank in the morning, not even during those periods of optimum radio-transmission conditions which ham operators call "the skip."

He ran the tuner on the Dodge's radio, and was amazed as a flood of conflicting transmissions poured out of the speakers—rock-and-roll, country-and-western, and classical music stepped all over each other. Somewhere in the background he could hear Paul Harvey extolling Amway. He turned the dial further and caught a clear transmission so surprising he pulled over. He sat staring at the radio with big eyes.

It was speaking in Japanese.

He sat and waited for the inevitable clarification—"This lesson in Beginners' Japanese has been brought to you by your local Kyanize Paint dealer," something like that. The announcer finished. Then came the Beach Boys' "Be True to Your School." In Japanese.

Leandro continued to tune down the kHz band with a hand that shook. It was much the same all the way. As it did at night, the tangle of voices and music got worse as he tuned toward the higher frequencies. At last the tangle grew so severe it began to frighten him—it was the auditory equivalent of a squirming mass of snakes. He turned the radio off and sat behind the wheel, eyes wide, body thrumming slightly, like a man on low-grade speed.

What is *this?*

Foolish to speculate when the answer lay no more than six miles up ahead . . . always assuming he could uncover it, of course.

Oh, I think you'll uncover it. You may not like it when

you do, but yeah, I think you'll uncover it with no trouble at all.

Leandro looked around. The hay in the field on his right was long and shaggy. *Too* long and shaggy for August. There hadn't been any first cutting in early July. Somehow he didn't think there was going to be any August cutting, either. He looked left and saw a tumble-down barn surrounded by rusty auto parts. The corpse of a '57 Studebaker was decaying in the barn's maw. The windows seemed to stare at Leandro. There were no *people* to stare, at least not that he could see.

A very quiet, very polite little voice spoke up inside him, the voice of a child at a tea party that has become decidedly scary:

I would like to go home, please.

Yes. Home to Mother. Home in time to watch the afternoon soaps with her. She would be glad to see him back with his scoop, maybe even more glad to see him back without it. They'd sit and eat cookies and drink coffee. They would talk. *She* would talk, rather, and he would listen. That was how it always was, and it really wasn't that bad. She could be an irritating thing sometimes, but she was . . .

Safe.

Safe, yeah. That was it. Safe. And whatever was going on south of Troy on this dozy summer afternoon, it wasn't at all safe.

I would like to go home, please.

Right. There had probably been times when Woodward and Bernstein felt that way when Nixon's boys were really putting the squeeze on. Bernard Fall had probably felt that way when he got off the plane in Saigon for the last time. When you saw the TV news correspondents in trouble spots like Lebanon and Tehran, they only *looked* cool, calm, and collected. Viewers never had a chance to inspect their shorts.

The story is out there, and I'm going to get it, and when I collect my Pulitzer Prize, I can say I owe it all to David Bright . . . and my secret Superman wristwatch.

He put the Dodge in gear again and drove on toward Haven.

6

He hadn't gone a mile before he began to feel ill. He thought this must be a physical symptom of his fear and ignored it. Then, when he began to feel worse, he asked himself (as one is apt to do when he realizes that the nausea sitting in his stomach like a small dark cloud is not going away) what he had eaten. There was no blame to be laid in that direction. He hadn't been afraid when he got up that morning, but he *had* been feeling a lot of anticipation and high-spirited tension; as a result he had refused the usual bacon and scrambled eggs and settled for tea and dry toast. That was all.

I would like to go home! The voice was now more shrill.

Leandro pushed on, teeth clamped grimly together. The scoop was in Haven. If he couldn't get into Haven, there would *be* no scoop. You couldn't hit 'em if you couldn't see 'em. QED.

Less than a mile from the town line—the day was eerily, utterly dead—a series of beeping, booping, and buzzing noises began to come from the back seat, startling him so badly that he cried out and pulled over to the side of the road again.

He looked in back and at first was unable to credit what he was seeing. It had to be, he thought, a hallucination brought on by his increasing nausea.

When he and his mother had been in Halifax this past weekend, he had taken his nephew Tony out for a Dairy Queen. Tony (whom Leandro privately thought was an ill-mannered little snot) had sat in the back playing with a plastic toy that looked a bit like the handset of a Princess phone. This toy was called Merlin, and it ran on a computer chip. It played four or five simple games which called for simple feats of memory or the ability to identify a simple mathematical series. Leandro remembered it had also played tic-tac-toe.

Anyway, Tony must have forgotten it, and now it was going crazy in the back seat, its red lights flashing on and off in random patterns (but *were* they? or just a little too fast for him to catch?), making its simple series of sounds again and again and again. It was running by itself.

No . . . no. I hit a pothole or something. That's all. Jogged its switch. Got it going.

But he could *see* the small black switch on the side. It was pushed to Off. But Merlin went on booping and beeping and buzzing. It reminded him of a Vegas slot-machine paying off a big jackpot.

The thing's plastic case began to smoke. The plastic itself was sinking . . . drooling . . . running like tallow. The lights flashed faster . . . faster. Suddenly they all went on at once, bright red, and the gadget emitted a strangled buzzing sound. The case cracked open. There was a brittle shower of plastic shards. The seat-cover started to smolder underneath it.

Ignoring his stomach, Leandro got up on his knees and knocked it onto the floor. There was a charred spot on the seat where Merlin had lain.

What is *this?*

The answer, irrelevant, nearly a scream:

I WOULD LIKE TO GO HOME NOW PLEASE!

"The ability to isolate a simple mathematical series." Did I think that? The John Leandro that flunked general math in high school? Do you mean it?

Never mind that, just bug OUT!

No.

He put the Dodge in gear and drove on again. He had gone less than twenty yards when he thought suddenly, with crazy exhilaration:

The ability to isolate a simple mathematical series indicates the existence of a general case, doesn't it? You could express it this way, come to think of it:

$ax[2] + bxy = cy[2] + dx + ey + f - 0.$

Yup. It'll work as long as a, b, c, d, and f are constants. I think. Yeah. You bet. But you couldn't let a, b, or c be 0—that'd fuck it for sure! Let f take care of itself! Ha!

Leandro felt like puking, but he still uttered a shrill, triumphant laugh. All at once he felt as if his brain had lifted off, right through the top of his skull. Although he didn't know it (having pretty much dozed through that part of Nerd Math), he had reinvented the general quadratic equation in two variables, which can indeed be used to isolate components in a simple mathematical series. It blew his mind.

A moment later, blood burst from his nose in an amazing flood.

That was the end of John Leandro's first effort to get into Haven. He threw the gearshift into reverse and backed unsteadily up the road, weaving from side to side, right arm hooked over the front seat, blood pouring onto the shoulder of his shirt as he stared out through the back window with watering eyes.

He backed up for almost a mile, then turned around in a driveway. He looked down at himself. His shirt was drenched with blood. But he felt better. A *little* better, he amended. Still, he didn't linger; he drove back to Troy Village and parked in front of the general store.

He walked in, expecting the usual gathering of old men to stare at his bloody shirt with silent Yankee surprise. But only the shopkeeper was there, and he didn't look surprised at all—not at the blood, not at Leandro's question about any shirts he might have in stock.

"Look like your nose might've bled a tetch," the storekeeper said mildly, and showed Leandro a selection of T-shirts. An inordinately large selection for such a small store as this, Leandro thought—he was slowly getting hold of himself, although his head still ached and his stomach still felt sour and unsteady. The flow of blood from his nose had scared him very badly.

"You could say that," Leandro said. He allowed the old man to thumb through the shirts for him, because there was tacky blood still drying on his own hands. They were sized S, M, L, and XL. WHERE TH' HELL IS TROY, MAINE? some said. On others there was a lobster and the slogan I GOT THE BEST PIECE OF TAIL I EVER HAD IN TROY, MAINE. On others there was a large blackfly which looked like a monster from outer space. THE MAINE STATE BIRD, these proclaimed.

"You sure do have lots of shirts," Leandro said, pointing to a WHERE TH' HELL in an M size. He thought the lobster shirt was amusing, but thought his mother would be less than wild about the innuendo.

"Ayuh," the storekeeper said. "*Have* to have a lot. *Sell* a lot."

"Tourists?" Leandro's mind was already racing ahead, trying to figure out what came next. He had thought he was onto something big; now he believed it was one hell of a lot bigger than even *he* had believed.

"Some," the storekeeper said, "but there ain't been

many down this way this summer. Mostly I sell em to folks like you."

"Like me?"

"Ayuh. Folks with bloody noses."

Leandro gaped at the storekeeper.

"Their noses bleed, they wreck their shirts," the storekeeper said. "Same way you wrecked yours. They want a new one, and if they're just locals—like I 'spect you are—they ain't got no luggitch and no changes. So they stop first place they come to and buy a new one. I don't blame em. Drivin' around in a shirt all over blood like yours'd make me puke. Why, I've had ladies in here this summer—*nice*-looking ladies, too, dressed to the nines—who smelled like guts in a hogshead."

The storekeeper cackled, showing a mouth that was perfectly toothless.

Leandro said slowly: "Let me get this straight. *Other* people come back from Haven with bloody noses? It's not just me?"

"Just you? Hell, no! Shittagoddam! The day they buried Ruth McCausland, I sold fifteen shirts! That one day! I was thinkin about retirin on the proceeds and movin to Florida."

The storekeeper cackled again.

"They was all out-of-towners." He said this as if it explained everything—and perhaps in his mind, it did. "Couple of em was still spoutin when they come in here. Noses like fountains! Ears too, sometimes. Shittagoddam!"

"And nobody *knows* about this?"

The old man looked at Leandro from wise eyes.

"*You* do, sonny," he said.

6.

INSIDE THE SHIP

1

"You ready, Gard?"

Gardener was sitting on the front porch, looking out at Route 9. The voice came from behind him, and it was easy—too easy—for him not to flash on a hundred sleazy prison movies, where the warden arrives to escort the condemned man along the Last Mile. Such scenes always beginning, of course, with the warden growling, *Are you ready, Rocky?*

Ready for this? You got to be kidding.

He got up, turned around, saw the equipment in Bobbi's arms, then the little smile on Bobbi's face. There was something knowing in that smile that he didn't like.

"See something funny?" he asked.

"Heard it. Heard *you,* Gard. You were thinking about old prison movies," Bobbi said. "And then you thought, 'Ready for this? You got to be kidding.' I caught all of that one, and that's very rare . . . unless you're deliberately sending. That's why I was smiling."

"You were peeking."

"Yes. And it's getting easier to do," Bobbi said, still smiling.

From behind his decaying mental shield, Gardener thought: *I have a gun now, Bobbi. It's under my bed. I got it in the First Reformed Church of the Tommyknockers.* It was dangerous . . . but it would be more dangerous not to know just how deep Bobbi's ability to "peek" now went.

Bobbi's smile faltered a little. "What was that one?" she asked.

"You tell me," he said, and when her smile began to change to a look of narrow suspicion he added easily, "Come on, Bobbi, I was just pulling your string a little. I was only wondering what you got there."

Bobbi brought the equipment over. There were two rubber snorkel mouthpieces attached to tanks and home-made regulators.

"We wear these," she said. "When we go inside."

Inside.

Just the word lit a hot spark in his belly and triggered all sorts of conflicting emotions—awe, terror, anticipation, curiosity, tension. Part of him felt like a superstitious native preparing to walk on taboo ground; the rest felt like a kid on Christmas morning.

"The air inside *is* different, then," Gardener said.

"Not so different." Bobbi had put her makeup on indifferently this morning, perhaps having decided there was no longer any need to hide the accelerating physical changes from Gardener. Gard realized he could see Bobbi's tongue moving inside her head as she spoke . . . only it didn't look precisely like a tongue anymore. And the pupils of Bobbi's eyes looked bigger, but somehow uneven and wavering, as if they were peering up at him from underwater. Water with a slight greenish tinge. He felt his stomach turn over.

"Not so different," she said. "Just . . . rotten."

"Rotten?"

"The ship's been sealed for over twenty-five thousand centuries," Bobbi said patiently. "*Totally* sealed. We'd be killed by the outrush of bad air as soon as we opened the hatch. So we wear these."

"What's in them?"

"Nothing but good old Haven air. The tanks are small—forty, maybe fifty minutes of air. You clip it to your belt like this, see?"

"Yes."

Bobbi offered him one of the rigs. Gard attached the tank to his belt. He had to raise his T-shirt to do it, and he was very glad he'd decided to leave the .45 under the bed for now.

"Start using the canned air just before I open it up," Bobbi said. "Almost forgot. Here. Just in case *you* forget." She handed Gardener a pair of noseplugs. Gard stuffed them into a jeans pocket.

"Well!" Bobbi said briskly. "*Are* you ready, then?"

"We're really going in there?"

"We really are," Bobbi said almost tenderly.

Gardener laughed shakily. His hands and feet were cold. "I'm pretty fucking excited," he said.

Bobbi smiled. "I am too."

"Also, I'm scared."

In that same tender voice Bobbi said, "No need to be, Gard. Everything will be all right."

Something in that tone made Gardener feel more scared than ever.

2

They took the Tomcat and cruised silently through the dead woods, the only sound the minute hum of batteries. Neither of them talked.

Bobbi parked the Tomcat by the lean-to and they stood for a moment looking at the silver dish rising out of the trench. The morning sun shone on it in a pure, widening wedge of light.

Inside, Gardener thought again.

"Are you ready?" Bobbi asked again. Come on, Rocky—just one big jolt, you'll never feel a thing.

"Yeah, fine," Gardener said. His voice was a trifle hoarse.

Bobbi was looking at him inscrutably with her changing eyes—those floating, widening pupils. Gardener seemed to feel mental fingers fluttering over his thoughts, trying to pull them open.

"Going in there *could* kill you, you know," Bobbi said at last. "Not the air—we've got that licked." She smiled. "It's funny, you know. Five minutes on one of those mouthpieces would knock someone from the outside unconscious, and half an hour of it would kill him. But it'll keep us alive. Does that tickle you, Gard?"

"Yes," Gard said, looking at the ship and wondering the things he always wondered: *Where did you come from? And how long did you have to cruise the night to get here?* "It tickles me."

"I *think* you'll be okay, but you know—" Bobbi shrugged. "Your head . . . that steel plate interacts somehow with the—"

"I know the risk."

"As long as you do."

Bobbi turned and walked toward the trench. Gardener stood where he was for a moment, watching her go.

I know the risk from the plate. *What I'm less clear on is the risk from* you, *Bobbi. Is it Haven air I'm going to get when I have to use that mask, or something like Raid?*

But it didn't matter, did it? He had thrown the dice. And *nothing* was going to keep him from seeing inside that ship, if he could—not David Brown, not the whole world.

Bobbi reached the trench. She turned and looked back, her made-up face a dull mask in the morning light angling through the old pines and spruces which surrounded this place. "Coming?"

"Yeah," Gardener said, and walked over to the ship.

3

Getting down proved to be unexpectedly tricky. Ironically, getting up was the easy part. The button at the bottom was right there, in fact no more than the 0 on a remote telephone handset. At the top, the button was a conventional electrical switch set on one of the posts which supported the lean-to. This was fifty feet from the edge of the trench. For the first time Gardener realized how all those car recalls could happen; until now, neither of them had bothered with the fact that their arms were somewhat less than fifty feet long.

They had been using the sling to go up and down for a long time now, long enough to take it for granted. Standing at the edge of the trench, they realized that they had never both gone down together. What both also realized but neither said was that they could have gone down one at a time; with someone to run the buttons at the bottom, all would have been well. Neither said it because it was understood between them that this time, and only this time, they must go down together, perfectly together, both with one foot in the single stirrup, arms around each other's waists, like lovers in a descending swing. It was stupid; just stupid, just stupid enough to be the only right way.

They looked at each other without saying a word—but two thoughts flew, and crossed in the air.

(here we are a couple of college graduates)

(Bobbi where'd I leave my left-handed monkey wrench)

Bobbi's strange new mouth quivered. She turned around and snorted. Gard felt a moment of the old warmth touch his heart then. It was the last time he really ever saw the Old and Unimproved Bobbi Anderson.

"Well, can you rig a portable unit to run the sling?"

"I can, but it's not worth taking the time. I've got another idea." Her eyes touched Gardener's face for a moment, thoughtful and calculating. It was a look Gardener could not quite interpret. Then Bobbi walked away to the lean-to.

Gardener followed her partway and saw Bobbi swing open a large green metal box that had been mounted on a pole. She pawed through the tools and general junk inside, and then came back with a transistor radio. It was smaller than the ones his helpers had turned into New and Improved satchel charges while Bobbi was recuperating. Gard had never seen this particular radio, before. It was very small.

One of them brought it out last night, he thought.

Bobbi pulled up its stubby antenna, inserted a jack in its plastic case and the plug in her ear. Gard was instantly reminded of Freeman Moss, moving the pumping equipment like an elephant trainer moving the big guys around the center ring.

"This won't take long." Bobbi pointed the antenna back toward the farm. Gardener seemed to hear a heavy, powerful hum—not on the air but *inside* the air, somehow. For just a moment his mind muttered with music and there was a headachy pain in the middle of his forehead, as if he had drunk too much cold water too fast.

"Now what?"

"We wait," Bobbi said, and repeated: "It won't take long."

Her speculative gaze passed over Gardener's face again, and this time Gardener thought he understood that look. *It's something she wants me to see. And this chance came up to show me.*

He sat down near the trench and discovered a very old pack of cigarettes in his breast pocket. Two were left. One was broken, the other bent but whole. He lit it and smoked reflectively, not really sorry about this delay. It gave him a chance to go over his plans again. Of course, if he dropped dead as soon as he went through that round hatch, it would put something of a crimp in those plans.

"Ah, here we go!" Bobbi said, getting up.

Gard also got up. He looked around, but at first saw nothing.

"Over there, Gard. The path." Bobbi spoke with the pride of a kid showing off her first soapbox racer. Gardener finally saw it, and began to laugh. He didn't really want to laugh, but he couldn't help it. He kept thinking he was getting used to the brave new world of Haven's jury-rigged superscience, and then some odd new combination would tumble him right back down the rabbit-hole. Like now.

Bobbi was smiling, but faintly, vaguely, as if Gardener's laughter meant nothing one way or the other.

"It *does* look a little strange, but it will do the trick. Take my word for it."

It was the Electrolux he had seen in the shed. It was not running on the ground but just above it, its little white wheels turning. Its shadow ran placidly off to one side, like a dachshund on a leash. From the back, where the vacuum-hose attachments would have gone in a sane world, two filament-thin wires protruded in a V shape. *Its antenna,* Gardener thought.

Now it landed, if you could call a touchdown from three inches a landing, and trundled over the beaten earth of the excavation area to the lean-to, leaving narrow tracks behind it. It stopped below the switchbox which controlled the sling.

"Watch this," Bobbi said in that same pleased showing-off-my-soapbox-racer voice.

There was a click. A hum. Now a thin black rope began to rise out of the vacuum cleaner's side, like a rope rising out of a wicker basket in the Indian rope trick. Only it wasn't a rope, Gardener saw; it was a length of coaxial cable.

It rose in the air . . . up . . . up . . . up. It touched the side of the switchbox and slid around to the front. Gardener felt a crawl of revulsion. It was like watching something like a bat—a blind thing which had some sort of radar. A blind thing that could . . . could *seek.*

The end of the cable found the buttons—the black one which started the sling going down or up, the red one which stopped it. The end of the cable touched the black one—and suddenly went rigid. The black button popped neatly in. The motor behind the lean-to started up, and the sling started to slip into the trench.

The tension went out of the cable. It slipped down to the red Stop button, stiffened, pushed it. When the motor had died—leaning over, Gardener could see the sling dangling against the side of the cut about twelve feet down—the cable rose and pushed the black button again. The motor started once more. The sling came back up. When it reached the top of the trench, the motor died automatically.

Bobbi turned to him. She was smiling, but her eyes were watchful. "There," she said. "Works fine."

"It's incredible," Gardener said. His eyes had moved steadily back and forth between Bobbi and the Electrolux as the cable ran the buttons. Bobbi had not been gesturing with the radio, as Freeman Moss had with his walkie-talkie, but Gardener had seen the little frown of concentration, and the way her eyes had dropped just an instant before the coaxial cable slipped down from the black button to the red one.

It looks like a mechanical dachshund, something out of one of those terminally cute Kelly Freas SF paintings. That's what it looks like, but it's not a robot, not really. It has no brain. Bobbi's *its brain . . . and she wants me to know it.*

And there had been a *lot* of those customized appliances in the shed, lined up against the wall. The one his mind kept trying to fix on was the washing machine with the boomerang antenna mounted on it.

The shed. That raised a hell of an interesting question. Gard opened his mouth to ask it . . . then closed it again, trying at the same time to thicken the shield over his thoughts as much as he could. He felt like a man who has nearly strolled over the lip of a chasm a thousand feet deep while looking at the pretty sunset.

No one back home—at least that I know of—and the shed's padlocked on the outside. So just how did Fido the Vacuum Cleaner get out?

He had really been only an instant from asking that question when he realized Bobbi hadn't mentioned *where* the Electrolux had come from. Gard could suddenly smell his own sweat, sour and evil.

He looked at Bobbi and saw Bobbi looking at him with that small irritated smile that meant she knew Gardener was thinking . . . but not what.

"Where did that thing come from, anyway?" Gardener asked.

"Oh . . . it was around." Bobbi waved her hand vaguely. "The important thing is that it works. So much for the unexpected delay. Want to get going?"

"Fine. I just hope that thing's batteries don't go flat while we're down there."

"*I'm* its battery," she said. "As long as I'm all right, you'll get up again, Gard. Okay?"

Your insurance policy. Yes, I think I get it.

"Okay," he said.

They went to the trench. Bobbi rode the sling down first while the cable rising from the side of the Electrolux ran the buttons. The sling came back up and Gardener stepped into it, holding the rope as it began to go down again.

He took a final look at the battered old Electrolux and thought again: *How the hell did it get out?*

Then he was sliding into the dimness of the trench and the dank mineral smell of wet rocks, the smooth surface of the ship rising up and up on his left, like the side of a skyscraper without windows.

4

Gard stepped off the sling. He and Bobbi stood shoulder to shoulder in front of the circular groove of the hatch, which had the shape of a large porthole. Gardener found it almost impossible to take his eyes from the symbol etched upon it. He found himself remembering something from earliest childhood. There had been an outbreak of diphtheria in the Portland suburb where he'd been raised. Two kids had died, and the public-health office had imposed a quarantine. He remembered walking to the library, his hand safely caught up in his mother's, and passing houses where signs had been stapled to the front doors, the same word in heavy black letters heading each. He asked her what it meant, and she said it meant there was sickness in the house. It was a good word, she said, because it warned people not to go in. If they did, she said, they might catch the disease and spread it.

"*Are* you ready?" Bobbi asked, breaking in on his thoughts.

"What does that mean?" He pointed at the symbol on the hatch.

"Burma-Shave." Bobbi was unsmiling. "*Are* you?"

"No . . . but I guess I'm as close as I'll ever get."

He looked at the tank clipped to his belt and wondered again if he was going to draw some poison that would explode his lungs at the first breath. He didn't think so. This was supposed to be his reward. One visit inside the Holy Temple before he was erased, once and for all, from the equation.

"All right," Bobbi said. "I'm going to open it—"

"You're going to *think* it open," Gardener said, looking at the plug in Bobbi's ear.

"Yes," Bobbi replied dismissively, as if to say *What else?* "It's going to iris open. There'll be an explosive outrush of bad air . . . and when I say bad, I mean *really* bad. How are your hands?"

"What do you mean?"

"Cuts?"

"Nothing that isn't scabbed over." He held his hands out like a little boy submitting to his mother's predinner inspection.

"Okay." Bobbi took a pair of cotton work-gloves from her back pocket and drew them on. To Gard's inquiring look she said, "Hangnails on two fingers. It might not be enough—but it might. When you see the hatch start to iris open, Gard, close your eyes. Breathe from the tank. If you whiff on what comes out of the ship, it's going to kill you as quick as a Dran-O cocktail."

"I," Gardener said, "am convinced." He slipped the snorkel mouthpiece into his mouth and used the nose-plugs. Bobbi did the same. Gardener could hear/feel his pulse in his temples, moving very fast, like someone tapping rapidly on a muffled drum with one finger.

This is it . . . this is finally it.

"Ready?" Bobbi asked one last time. Muffled by the mouthpiece, it came out sounding like Elmer Fudd: *Weady?*

Gardener nodded.

"Remember?" *Wememboo?*

Gardener nodded again.

For Christ's sake, Bobbi, let's go!

Bobbi nodded.

Okay. Be ready.

Before he could ask her for what, that symbol suddenly broke apart in curves, and Gardener realized with a deep, almost sickening excitement that the hatch was opening. There was a high thin screaming sound, as if something rusted shut for a long time was now moving again . . . but with great reluctance.

He saw Bobbi turn the valve on the tank clipped to her belt. He did the same, then closed his eyes. A moment later, a soft wind pushed against his face, shoving his shaggy hair back from his brow. Gardener thought: *Death. That's death. Death rushing past me, filling this trench like chlorine gas. Every microbe on my skin is dying right now.*

His heart was pounding much too fast, and he had actually begun to wonder if the outrush of gas *(like the rush of gas out of a coffin,* his skittish mind chattered) wasn't killing him somehow after all, when he realized he had been holding his breath.

He pulled a breath in through the mouthpiece. He waited to see if it *would* kill him. It didn't. It had a dry, stale taste, but it was perfectly breathable.

Forty, maybe fifty minutes of air.

Slow down, Gard. Take it slow. Make it last. No panting.

He slowed down.

Tried, at least.

Then that high, screaming noise quit. The outrush of air grew softer against his face, then stopped entirely. Then Gardener spent an eternity in the dark, facing the open hatch with his eyes shut. The only sounds were the muffled drum of his heart and the sigh of air through the tank's demand regulator. His mouth already tasted of rubber, and his teeth were locked much too hard on the rubber pins inside the snorkel mouthpiece. He forced himself to get cool and ease up.

At last, eternity ended. Bobbi's clear thought filled his mind:

Okay . . . should be okay . . . you can open those baby blues, Gard.

Like a kid at a surprise party, Jim Gardener did just that.

5

He was looking along a corridor.

It was perfectly round except for a flat ledge of walkway halfway up one side. The position looked all wrong. For a wild moment he visualized the Tommyknockers as grisly intelligent flies crawling along that walkway with sticky feet. Then logic reasserted itself. The walkway was canted, *everything* was canted, because the ship was at an angle.

Soft light glowed out of the round, featureless walls.

No dead batteries here, Gardener thought. *These are* really *long-life jobbies.* He looked into the corridor beyond the hatch with a deep and profound sense of wonder. *It* is *alive. Even after all these years. Still alive.*

I'm going in, Gard. Are you coming?

Gonna try, Bobbi.

She stepped in, ducking her head so as not to bump it on the upper curve of the hatch. Gardener hesitated a moment, biting down on the rubber pins inside the mask again, and followed.

6

There was a moment of transcendent agony—he felt rather than heard radio transmissions fill his head. Not just one; it was as if every radio broadcast in the world momentarily shrieked inside his brain.

Then it was gone—simply gone. He thought of the way that radio transmissions faded when you went into a tunnel. He had entered the ship, and all outside transmissions had been damped down to nothing. Nor was it only outside transmissions, he discovered a moment later. Bobbi was looking at him, obviously sending a thought—*Are you all right?* was Gardener's best guess, but a guess was all it was. But he could no longer hear Bobbi in his head at all.

Curious, he sent back: *I am fine, go on!*

Bobbi's questioning expression didn't change—she was much better at this than Gardener, but she wasn't getting anything either. Gard gestured for her to go on. After a moment, she nodded, and did.

7

They walked twenty paces up the corridor. Bobbi moved with no hesitation, nor did she hesitate when they came to a round interior hatch set into the surface of the flat walkway on their left. This hatch, about three feet in diameter, was open. Without looking back at Gardener, Bobbi climbed into it.

Gardener paused, looking back along the softly lit corridor. The hatchway to the outside was back there, a round porthole giving onto the darkness of the trench. Then he followed.

There was a ladder bolted to the new corridor, which was almost small enough in diameter to be called a tunnel. Gard and Bobbi did not need the ladder; the ship's position had rendered the corridor almost horizontal. They went on their hands and knees with the ladder sometimes scraping their backs.

The ladder made Gardener uneasy. The rungs were spaced almost four feet apart, that was one thing. A man—even a very long-legged one—would have had difficulty using it. The other thing about the rungs was more unsettling: a pronounced semicircular dip, almost a notch, in the center of each.

So the Tommyknockers had really bad fallen arches, he thought, listening to the rasp of his own respiration. *Big deal, Gard.*

But the picture that came to him was not of flat feet or fallen arches; the picture which stole into his mind, softly and yet with a simple undeniable power, was of some not-quite-seen creature climbing that ladder, a creature with a single thick claw on each foot, a claw which fit neatly into each of those dips as it climbed. . . .

Suddenly the round, dimly lit walls seemed to be pressing in on him, and he had to grapple with a terrible bout of claustrophobia. The Tommyknockers were here, all right, and still alive. At any moment he might feel a thick, inhuman hand close about his ankle. . . .

Sweat ran into his eye, stinging.

He whipped his head around, looking back over one shoulder.

Nothing. Nothing, Gard. Get yourself under control!

But they *were* here. Perhaps dead—but somehow alive just the same. In Bobbi, for one thing. But . . .

But you have to see, Gard. Now GO!

He started crawling again. He was leaving faint sweaty handprints on the metal, he saw. Human handprints inside this thing which had come from God knew where.

Bobbi reached the mouth of the passage, turned on her stomach, and dropped out of sight. Gard followed, stopping at the mouth of the passageway to look out. Here was a large open space, hexagonal in shape, like a large chamber in a beehive. It was also canted at a crazy funhouse angle as a result of the crash. The walls glowed with soft colorless light. A thick cable came out of a gasket on the floor; this split into half a dozen thinner cords, and each ended in a set of things which looked like headphones with bulging centers.

Bobbi wasn't looking at these. She was looking into the corner. Gardener followed her gaze and felt his stomach gain weight. His head swam dizzily; his heart faltered.

They had been gathered around their telepathic steering wheel or whatever the hell it was when the ship hit. They had perhaps been trying to pull out of their dive to the very last, but it hadn't worked. And here they were, two or three of them, at least, slung into a far corner. It was hard to tell what they looked like—they were too tangled together. The ship had hit, and they had been thrown to that end of this room. There they still lay.

Interstellar car crash, Gardener thought sickly. *Is that all there is, Alfie?*

Bobbi did not go toward those brown husks piled in the lowest angle of this strange bare room. She only stared, her hands clenching and unclenching. Gardener tried to understand what she was thinking and feeling and could not. He turned and carefully lowered himself over the edge of the passageway. He joined her, walking carefully on the canted floor. Bobbi looked at him with her strange new eyes—*What do I look like to her through those new eyes?* Gard wondered—and then back toward the tangled remains in the corner. Her hands continued to open and snap closed.

Gardener started toward them. Bobbi clutched at his arm. Gardener shook her grip off without even thinking. He had to look at them. He felt like a child drawn toward an open grave, full of fear but compelled to go on anyway. He had to *see.*

Gardener, who had grown up in southern Maine, crossed what he believed to be—for all its starkness—the control room of an interstellar spacecraft. The floor under his feet looked as smooth as glass, but his sneakers held their grip easily. He heard no sound but his own harsh breathing, smelled only dusty Haven air. He walked down the slanted floor to the bodies and looked at them.

These are the Tommyknockers, he thought. *Bobbi and the others aren't going to look exactly like them when they're done "becoming," maybe because of the environment or maybe because the original physiological makeup of the—what would you call it? target group?—results in a slightly different look each time this happens. But there's a kissin-cousin resemblance, all right. Maybe these aren't the originals . . . but they're close enough. Ugly fuckers.*

He felt awe . . . horror . . . and a revulsion that ran blood-deep.

Late last night and the night before, a wavering voice sang in his mind. *Tommyknockers, Tommyknockers, knocking at the door.*

At first he thought there were five, but there were only four—one was in two pieces. None of them looked as if he—she—it—had died easily or with any serenity. Their faces were ugly and long-snouted. Their eyes were filmed over to the whiteness of cataracts. Their lips were drawn back in uniform snarls.

Their skins were scaly but transparent—he could see frozen muscles laid in crisscross patterns around jaws, temples, and necks.

They had no teeth.

8

Bobbi joined him. Gard saw awe on her face—but no revulsion.

These are her gods now, and one is rarely if ever revolted by one's own gods, Gardener thought. *These are her gods now, and why not? They made her what she is today.*

He pointed to each one of them in turn, deliberately, like an instructor. They were naked, and their wounds were clear. Interstellar car-crash, yes. But he didn't believe there had been any mechanical failure. Those weird scaly bodies were slashed, scored with ragged cuts. One six-fingered hand was still wrapped around the haft of something that looked like a knife with a circular blade.

Look at them, Bobbi, he thought, even though he knew Bobbi couldn't read him in here even if he opened up all the way. He pointed here, to a grinning mouth buried in another creature's throat; there, to a wide wound gaping in a thick, inhuman chest; there, to a knife still clutched in one hand.

Look at them, Bobbi. You don't have to be Sherlock Holmes to see they were fighting. Having a good old knock-down-drag-out here in the old control room. None of this "Come-let-us-reason-together" shit for your *gods. They were whipping some heavy numbers on each other. Maybe it started as an argument about whether or not to land here, or maybe it was about whether or not they should have hooked a left at Alpha Centauri. Anyway, the results are the same. Remember how we always assumed a technologically advanced race of beings would be, if one ever made contact with us? We thought they'd be smart like Mr. Wizard and wise like Robert Young on* Father Knows Best. *Well, here's the truth, Bobbi. The ship crashed because they were having a fight. And where are the blasters? The phasers? The transporter room? I see one knife. The rest they must have done with mirrors . . . or their bare hands . . . or those big claws.*

Bobbi looked away, frowning strenuously—a pupil who didn't want to learn the lesson, a pupil who was in fact determined *not* to learn it. She started to move off. Gardener caught her by the arm and pulled her back. Pointed at the feet.

If Bruce Lee had had a foot like that, he would have killed a thousand people a week, Bobbi.

The Tommyknockers' legs were grotesquely long—they made Gardener think of those guys who don stilts and Uncle Sam suits and march in Fourth of July parades. The muscles below the semitransparent skins were long, ropy, gray. The feet were narrow, and not precisely toed. Instead, each foot sloped into that one thick, chitinous claw, like a bird's talon. Something like a giant vulture's.

Gardener thought of the dips in the ladder rungs. He shuddered.

Look, Bobbi. See how dark *the claws are. That's blood,*

or whatever they had inside them. It's on the claws because they did most of the damage. This place sure as shit didn't look like the bridge of the starship Enterprise *before it crashed. Just before it hit, it probably looked more like a free-for-all cockfight out behind some redneck's barn. This is progress, Bobbi? Next to these guys, Ted the Power Man looks like Gandhi.*

Frowning, Bobbi pulled away. *Leave me alone,* her eyes said.

Bobbi, can't you see—

Bobbi turned away. She wasn't into *seeing.*

Gardener stood by the desiccated bodies, watching her climb the deck like a woman climbing a steep smooth hill. She didn't slip at all. She turned toward a far wall where there was another round opening and boosted herself in. For a moment Gardener could see her legs and the dirty soles of her tennis shoes, and then she was gone.

Gard walked up the slope and stood for a moment near the center of the room, looking at the single thick cord coming out of the floor, at the earphones that split off from it. The similarity to the setup in Bobbi's shed was perfectly clear. Otherwise . . .

He looked around. Hexagonal room. Barren. No chairs. No pictures of Niagara Falls—or Cygnus-B Falls, for that matter. No astrogation charts, no Mad Labs equipment. All the big-time science-fiction producers and special-effects men would have been disgusted by this emptiness, Gardener thought. Nothing but some earphones lying tangled on the floor, and the bodies, perfectly preserved but probably as light as autumn leaves by now. Earphones and remains like husks piled in that far corner, where gravity had tossed them. Nothing very interesting about it. Nothing very smart. That fit. Because the Havenites were doing lots of stuff, but none of it was very smart, when you got right down to where the short hairs grew.

It wasn't disappointment he felt so much as stupid correctness. Not rightness—God knew there was nothing right about this—but correctness, as if part of him had always known it would be this way when and if they got in. No Disneyland razzmatazz; only a dreary species of blankness. He found himself remembering W. H. Auden's poem about running away: sooner or later you always ended up in one room, under a naked light bulb, playing solitaire at three in the morning. Tomorrowland, it seemed, ended up being an empty place where people smart enough to capture the stars got mad and tore each other to shreds with the claws on their feet.

So much for Robert Heinlein, Gard thought, and followed Bobbi.

9

He trekked uphill, realizing he had entirely lost track of what his position was in relation to the world outside. It was easier not to think about it. He used the ladder to help himself along as he went. He came to a rectangular porthole and looked through it into something that might have been an engine room—big metal blocks, square on one end, rounded on the other, marched off in a double row. Pipes, thick and dull silver in color, protruded from the square ends of these blocks and moved off at strange, crooked angles.

Like straight-pipes coming out of a kid's jalopy, Gard thought. He became aware of liquid warmth on the skin above his mouth. It divided in two and ran down his chin. His nose was bleeding again . . . slowly, but as if it meant to keep it up for a while.

Is the light brighter in here now?

He stopped and looked around.

Yes. And could he hear a faint humming, or was that imagination?

He cocked his head. No; not imagination. Machinery. Something had started up.

It didn't just start, and you know it. We *started it up. We're kicking it over.*

He bit down hard on the mouthpiece. He wanted out of here. Wanted to get *Bobbi* out. The ship was alive; in a weird way he supposed it was the Ultimate Tommyknocker. It was a howl. It was also the most horrible thing of all. Sentient creature . . . What? Woke it up, of course. Gard wanted it asleep. All of a sudden he felt too much like Jack nosing around the castle while the giant slept. They had to get out. He began to crawl faster. Then a new thought struck him, stopping him dead.

What if it won't let *you out?*

He pushed the idea away and kept going.

10

The corridor branched into a Y, left arm continuing to angle up, the right turning steeply downward. He listened and heard Bobbi crawling to the left. He moved that way and came to another hatch. She was standing below it. She glanced briefly up at Gardener with eyes that were wide and frightened. Then she looked back again.

He got one leg over the lip of the hatch and paused. No way he was going in there.

The room was lozenge-shaped. It was full of hammocks suspended in metal frames—there were hundreds of them. All were canted drunkenly upward and to the left; the room looked like a snapshot of a sailing ship's bunkroom taken just as the ship rolled in the trough of a swell. All the hammocks were full, their occupants strapped in. Transparent skins; doglike snouts; milky, dead eyes.

A cable ran from each scaled triangular head.

Not just strapped, Gardener thought. CHAINED. *They were the ship's drive, weren't they, Bobbi? If this is the future, it's time to eat the gun. These are dead galley slaves.*

They were snarling, but Gardener saw that some of the snarls were half-obliterated, because some of their heads seemed to have exploded—as if, when the ship crashed, there had been a gigantic backflow of energy that had literally blown their brains out.

All dead. Strapped forever in their hammocks, heads lolling, snouts frozen in eternal snarls. All dead in this tilted room.

Close by, another engine started up—chopping rustily at first, then smoothing out. A moment later fans whirred into life—he supposed the newly started engine was driving them. Air blew against his face—whether or not it was fresh was something he didn't intend to personally check on.

Maybe opening the outer hatch started this stuff up, but I don't believe it. It was us. What starts up next, Bobbi?

Suppose *they* started up next—the Tommyknockers

themselves? Suppose their grayish-transparent six-fingered hands started to clench and unclench, as Bobbi's hands had been doing as she stared at the corpses in the barren control room? What if those taloned feet began to twitch? Or suppose those heads began to turn, and those milky eyes looked at them?

I want out. The ghosts here are very lively and I want out.

He touched Bobbi's shoulder. She jumped. Gardener glanced at his wrist, but there was no watch there—only a fading white shape on his otherwise tanned wrist. It had been a Timex, a tough old baby that had gone on a lot of toots with him and come out alive. But two days of working on the excavation had killed it. THERE'S *one John Cameron Swayze never tried in those old TV ads,* he thought.

Bobbi took the point. She pointed at the air bottle clipped to her belt and raised her eyebrows at Gardener. *How long has it been?*

Gardener didn't know and didn't care. He wanted out before the whole damned ship woke up and did God-knew-what.

He pointed back down the passageway. *Long enough. Let's bug out.*

A thick, oily chuckling noise began in the wall next to Gardener. He shrank from it. Drops of blood from his slowly bleeding nose splattered the wall. His heart was beating madly.

Stop it, it's just some sort of pump—

The oily noise began to smooth out . . . and then something went wrong. There was a screech of grinding metal and a quick, thudding series of explosions. Gardener felt the wall vibrate, and for a moment the light seemed to flicker and dim.

Could we find our way out of here in the dark if the lights went out? You make thee joke I theenk, señor.

The pump tried to start again. There was a long metallic scream that set Gardener's teeth biting at the rubber plugs in his mouthpiece. It died away at last. There was a long loud rattle, like a straw in an empty glass. Then nothing.

Not everything lasted all that time with no damage, Gardener thought, and found this idea actually relieving.

Bobbi was pointing: *Go, Gard.*

Before he did, he saw Bobbi pause and look back once at the ranks of hammocked dead. That frightened look was back on her face.

Then Gard was crawling back the way he came, trying to keep an even, steady pace as the claustrophobia wrapped itself around him.

11

In the control room, one of the walls had turned into a gigantic picture window fifty feet long and twenty feet high.

Gardener stood gape-jawed looking at the blue Maine sky and the fringe of pines and spruces and maples around the trench. In the lower-right-hand corner he could see the rooftree of their equipment lean-to. He stared at this for several seconds—long enough to see big white summer clouds drifting across the blue sky—before realizing it couldn't be a window. They were somewhere toward the middle of the ship, and deep in the ground as well. A window in that wall should show only more ship. Even if they had been near the hull, which they weren't, it would have given on a vista of mesh-covered rock wall, with maybe a squib of blue sky at the very top.

It's a TV picture of some kind. Something *like a TV picture, anyway.*

But there were no lines. The illusion was perfect.

Forgetting, in this powerful new fascination, his claustrophobic need to get out, Gardener walked slowly toward the wall. The angle gave him a perverse sensation of flying—the effect was like slipping behind the controls of an airline trainer and pulling the mock controls up into a steep climb. The sky was so bright he had to squint. He kept looking for the wall, the way you might expect to see a movie screen through the picture as you got closer to it, but the wall just didn't seem to be there. The pines were a true, clear green; only the fact that he couldn't feel any breeze or smell the woods worked against the persuasive illusion.

He walked closer, still looking for the wall.

It's a camera, got to be—mounted on the outer rim of the ship, maybe even the part Bobbi stumbled over. The angle confirms that. But, Jesus! It's so fucking real! *If the people at Kodak or Polaroid saw this, they'd go out of their gou—*

His arm was grabbed—grabbed hard—and terror leapt up in him. He turned, expecting to see one of *them,* a grinning thing with a dog's head, holding a cable with a plug tip in one hand: *Just bend down, Mr. Gardener; this won't hurt a bit.*

It was Bobbi. She pointed to the wall. Held out her hands and arms and jittered them rapidly in some kind of charade. Then pointed at the window-wall again. After a moment, Gardener got it. In a grisly way it was almost funny. Bobbi had been miming electrocution, telling him that touching the window-wall would probably be a lot like touching the third rail of a subway.

Gardener nodded, then pointed toward the wider companionway through which they had entered. Bobbi nodded back and led the way.

As Gardener boosted himself up, he thought he heard a leaf-dry rattle and turned back, feeling a child's dreamy terror tug at his mind. He felt that it must be them, those corpses in the corner; them, rising slowly to their taloned feet like zombies.

But they still lay in their tangled drift of strange arms and legs. The wide, clear view of the sky and the trees on the wall (or *through* the wall) was dimming, losing reality and definition.

Gardener turned away and crawled after Bobbi as fast as he could.

7.

THE SCOOP, CONTINUED

1

You're crazy, you know, John Leandro told himself as he pulled into exactly the same parking slot Everett Hillman had used not three weeks ago. Leandro did not of course know this. That was probably just as well.

You're crazy, he told himself again. *You bled like a stuck pig, there's two teeth less in your head, and you're planning to go back there. You're crazy!*

Right, he thought, getting out of the old car. *I'm twenty-four, unmarried, getting bulgy around the middle, and if I'm crazy it's because I found this, I did,* me, *I tripped over it. It's big, and it's mine. My story. No, use the other word. It's old-fashioned, but who gives a fuck—it's the right word. My* scoop, *I'm not going to let it kill me, but I am going to ride it until it bucks me off.*

Leandro stood in the parking lot at a quarter past one on what was rapidly becoming the longest day of his life (it would also be the last, despite all his mental avowals to the contrary) and thought: *Good for you. Gonna ride it till it bucks you off. Probably Robert Capa, Ernie Pyle, thought the same thing from time to time.*

Sensible. Sarcastic, but sensible. That deeper part of his mind seemed to be beyond such sense, however. *My story,* it returned stubbornly. *My scoop.*

John Leandro, now clad in a T-shirt reading WHERE TH' HELL IS TROY, MAINE? (David Bright would probably have laughed himself into a hemorrhage over *that* one), crossed the small parking lot of Maine Med Supplies *("Specializing in Respiration Supplies and Respiration Therapy Since 1946")* and went inside.

2

"Thirty bucks is a stiff deposit for an air mask, don't you think?" Leandro asked the clerk, thumbing through his cash. He guessed he had the thirty, but it was going to leave him with about a buck and a half. "Wouldn't think they'd be a big black-market item."

"We never used to require one at all," the clerk said, "and we still don't if we know the individual or the organization, you know. But I lost one a couple, three weeks ago. Old man came in and told me he wanted some air. I figured he meant for diving, you know—he was old, but he looked tough enough for it—so I started telling him about Downeast ScubaDive in Bangor. But he said no, he was interested in ground portability. So I rented it to him. I never got it back. Brand-new Bell flat-pack. Two-hundred-dollar piece of equipment."

Leandro looked at the clerk, almost sick with excitement. He felt like a man following arrows deeper and deeper into a frightening but fabulous and totally unexplored cavern.

"You rented this mask? Personally?"

"Well, it was a flat-pack, actually, but yes. My dad and I run the place. He was delivering oxy bottles down to Augusta. I caught hell from him. I don't know if he'll like me renting another Bell, even, but with the deposit I guess it's okay."

"Can you describe the man?"

"Mister, do you feel okay? You look a little white around the—"

"I'm fine. Can you describe the man who rented the flat-pack?"

"Old. Had a tan. He was mostly bald. He was skinny . . . stringy, I guess you'd say. Like I say, he looked tough." The clerk thought. "He was driving a Valiant."

"Could you check the day he rented the flat-pack?"

"You a cop?"

"Reporter. Bangor *Daily News.*" Leandro showed the

clerk his press card. Now the clerk also began to look excited.

"He do somethin else? Besides rip off our flat-pack, I mean?"

"Could you look up the name and date for me?"

"Sure."

The clerk flipped back through his rental book. He found the entry and turned the book so Leandro could read it. The date was July 26th. The name was scrawled but still legible. Everett Hillman.

"You never reported the loss of the equipment to the police," Leandro said. It was not a question. If a complaint of theft had been lodged against the old geezer to complement his landlady's understandable unhappiness at being stiffed for two weeks' rent, the cops might have taken more interest in how or why Hillman had disappeared . . . or where he had disappeared *to*.

"No, Dad said not to bother. Our insurance doesn't cover the theft of rented equipment, see, and . . . well, that's why."

The clerk shrugged and smiled, but the shrug was slightly embarrassed, the smile slightly uneasy, and taken together they told Leandro a lot. He might be a terminal twerp, as David Bright feared, but he was not a stupid one. If they had reported the theft or disappearance of the flat-pack, the insurance company wouldn't cover the loss. But this fellow's father knew some other way they *could* stick it to the insurance company. But for now all that was very much a secondary consideration.

"Well, thank you for all your help," Leandro said, turning the book back around. "Now, if we could finish up here—"

"Sure, of course." The clerk was obviously happy to leave the subject of insurance behind. "And you won't put any of this in the paper until you check with my father, will you?"

"Absolutely not," Leandro said with a warm sincerity that P. T. Barnum himself would have admired. "Now, if I could just sign the agreement—"

"Right. I'll have to see some ID first, though. I didn't ask the old guy, and I also heard from Dad about *that,* I can tell you."

"I just showed you my press card."

"I know, but maybe I ought to see some *real* identification."

Sighing, Leandro pushed his driver's license across the counter.

3

"Slow down, Johnny," David Bright said. But Leandro was standing at an outdoor phone kiosk near the edge of a drive-in-restaurant parking lot. He heard the beginnings of excitement in Bright's voice. *He believes me. Son of a bitch, I think he finally believes me!*

As he had driven away from Maine Med Supplies and back toward Haven, Leandro's excitement and tension had grown until he thought he might explode if he didn't talk to someone else. And he *had* to; he recognized that as a responsibility that superseded his desire to get his scoop alone. He had to because he was going back, and something could easily happen to him, and if it did, he wanted to be sure somebody knew what he was onto. And Bright, as insufferable as he could be, was at least utterly honest; he wouldn't double-cross him.

Slow down, yeah, I got to.

He switched the phone to his other ear. The afternoon sun was hot on his neck, but it didn't feel bad at all. He started with the ride to Haven: the incredible jam-up of stations on the radio; the violent nausea; the bloody nose; the lost teeth. He told him about his conversation with the old man in the general store, how empty the place had been, how the whole area could have been wearing a big sign that said GONE FISHIN. He didn't mention his mathematical insights, because he could barely remember having them. *Something* had happened, but it was now all vague and diffuse in his mind.

Instead, he told Bright that he had gotten the idea that the air in Haven had been poisoned somehow—that there had been a chemical spill or something, or maybe the escape of some natural but deadly gas from inside the earth.

"A gas that improves radio transmissions, Johnny?"

Yes, he knew it was unlikely, he knew all the pieces didn't fit yet, but he had *been* there and he was sure it was the air that had made him sick. So he had decided to get some portable oxygen and go back.

He related his coincidental discovery that Everett Hillman, whom Bright himself had dismissed as a nutty old man, had been there before him, on exactly the same errand.

"So what do you think?" Leandro said finally.

There was a momentary lag, and then Bright said what Leandro believed to be the sweetest words he had ever heard in his life. "I think you were right all the time, Johnny. Something very weird is happening out there, and I advise you very strongly to stay away."

Leandro closed his eyes for a moment and leaned his head against the side of the telephone. He was smiling. It was a large and blissful smile. *Right. Right all the time.* Ah, they were good words; fine words; words of balm and beatitude. *Right all the time.*

"John? Johnny? Are you still there?"

Eyes still closed, still smiling, Leandro said: "I'm here." *Just relishing it, David, old man, because I think I have been waiting my entire life for someone to tell me I was right all the time. About something. About* anything.

"Stay away. Call the state cops."

"Would you?"

"Fuck, no!"

Leandro laughed. "Well, there you go. I'll be okay. I've got oxygen—"

"According to the guy at the medical-supply place, Hillman did too. He's just as gone."

"I'm going," Leandro repeated. "Whatever's going on in Haven, I'm going to be the first one to see it . . . and get pictures of it."

"I don't like it."

"What time is it?" Leandro's own watch had stopped. Which was funny; he was almost sure he'd wound it when he got up that morning.

"Almost two."

"Okay. I'll call in by four. Again at six. Et cetera, until I'm home and dry. If you or somebody there doesn't hear from me every two hours, call the cops."

"Johnny, you sound like a kid playing with matches telling his father if he catches on fire, Dad has permission to put him out."

"You're not my father," Leandro said sharply.

Bright sighed. "Look, Johnny. If it makes any difference, I'm sorry I called you fucking Jimmy Olsen. You were right, isn't that enough? Stay out of Haven."

"Two hours. I want two hours, David. I *deserve* two hours, goddammit." Leandro hung up the phone.

He started back to his car . . . then turned and marched defiantly back to the walk-up window and ordered two cheeseburgers with everything on them. It was the first time in his life he had ever ordered food from one of those places his mother called *roadside luncheonettes*—only when she said the words she made such places sound like the blackest pits of horror, as in *It Came from the Roadside Luncheonette,* or *Earth vs. the Microbe Monsters.*

When they came, the cheeseburgers were hot and wrapped in grease-spotted sheets of waxed paper with the marvelous words DERRY BURGER RANCH printed all over them. He had gobbled the first even before he got back to his Dodge.

"Wonderful," he said, the word muffled to something that sounded like *wunnel.* "Wonderful, wonderful."

Microbes, do your worst! he thought with almost drunken defiance as he pulled out onto Route 9. He was, of course, unaware that things were changing rapidly in Haven now, and had been ever since noon; the situation in Haven was, in nuclear parlance, critical. Haven had in fact become a separate country, and its borders were now policed.

Not knowing this, Leandro drove on, tearing into his second cheeseburger and regretting only that he hadn't ordered a vanilla shake to go with them.

4

By the time he passed the Troy general store, his euphoria had dissipated, and his former low nervousness had returned—the sky overhead was a clear blue in which a few wispy white clouds floated, but his nerves felt as if there were a thunderstorm on the way. He glanced at the flat-pack on the seat beside him, the gold cup covered with a round of cellophane which read SANI-SEALED FOR YOUR PROTECTION. *In other words,* Leandro thought, *microbes, keep out.*

No cars on the road. No tractors in the fields. No boys walking barefoot along the side of the road with fishing rods. Troy dreamed silent (and, Leandro guessed, toothless) under the August sun.

He kept the radio tuned to WZON, and as he passed the Baptist church, he began to lose the signal in a rising mutter of other voices. Not long after that, his cheeseburgers began to first walk around uneasily in his stomach, and then to jump up and down. He could imagine them squirting grease as they did so. He was very close to the place where he had pulled over on his first effort to get into Haven. He pulled over now without delay—he didn't want the symptoms to get any worse. Those cheeseburgers had been too damned good to lose.

5

With the oxygen mask in place, the queasiness went away at once. That sense of low, gnawing nervousness did not. He caught a glimpse of himself, gold cup bobbing on his mouth and nose, in the rearview mirror and felt a moment of fright—was that him? That man's eyes looked too serious, too intent . . . they looked like the eyes of a jet fighter pilot. Leandro didn't want people like David Bright to think he was a twerp, but he wasn't sure he wanted to look *that* serious.

Too late now. You're in it.

The radio babbled in a hundred voices, maybe a thousand. Leandro turned it off. And there, up ahead, was the Haven town line. Leandro, who knew nothing at all about invisible nylon stockings, drove up to the town-line marker . . . and then past it, into Haven, with no trouble at all.

Although the battery situation in Haven was approaching the critical point again, force-fields *could* have been set up along most of the roads leading into town. But in the frightened confusion over the developing events of the morning, Dick Allison and Newt had made one decision that came to directly affect John Leandro. They wanted Haven closed, but they didn't want anyone to strike an inexplicable barrier in the middle of what appeared to be thin air, turn around, and carry the tale back to the wrong people . . .

. . . . which was everyone else on earth just now.

I don't believe anyone could get that close, Newt said. He and Dick were in Dick's pickup truck, part of a procession of cars and trucks racing out to Bobbi Anderson's place.

I used to think so too, Dick replied. But that was before Hillman . . . and Bobbi's sister. No, someone *could* get in . . . but if they do, they'll never get out again.

All right, fine. You're Queen for a Day. Now, can't you drive this fucker any faster?

The texture of both men's thoughts—of the thoughts all around them—was dismayed and furious. At that moment the possible incursion of outsiders into Haven seemed the least of their worries.

"I *knew* we should have gotten rid of that goddam drunk!" Dick cried out loud, and slammed his fist down on the dashboard. He was wearing no makeup today. His skin, as well as becoming increasingly transparent, had begun to roughen. The center of his face—and Newt's face, and the faces of all of those who had spent time in Bobbi's shed—had begun to swell. To grow decidedly snoutlike.

6

John Leandro of course knew nothing of this—he knew only that the air around him was poisonous—more poisonous than even he would have believed. He had slipped the gold cup down long enough to take a single shallow breath, and the world had immediately begun to fade into dimness. He put the cup back quickly, heart racing, hands cold.

Some two hundred yards past the town-line marker, his Dodge simply died. Most Haven cars and trucks had been customized in such a way as to make them immune to the steadily increasing electromagnetic field thrown off by the ship in the earth over the last two months or so (much of this work was done at Elt Barker's Shell), but Leandro's car had undergone no such treatment.

He sat behind the wheel a moment, staring stupidly down at the red idiot lights. He threw the transmission into Park and turned the key. The motor didn't crank. Hell, the solenoid didn't even click.

Battery cable came off, maybe.

It wasn't a battery cable. If it had been, the OIL and AMP lights wouldn't be glowing. But that was minor. Mostly he knew it wasn't his battery cable just because he knew it.

There were trees along both sides of the road here. The sun through their moving leaves made dappled patterns on the asphalt and white dirt of the soft shoulders. Leandro suddenly felt that eyes were looking out at him from behind trees. This was silly, of course, but the idea was nonetheless very powerful.

Okay, now you have got to get out, and see if you can walk out of the poison belt before your air runs out. The odds get longer every second you sit here giving yourself the creeps.

He tried the ignition key once more. Still nothing.

He got his camera, hooked the strap over his shoulder, and got out. He stood looking uneasily at the woods on the right side of the road. He thought he heard something behind him—a shuffling sound—and whirled quickly, lips pulled up in a dry grin of fear.

Nothing . . . nothing he could *see.*

The woods are lovely, dark and deep . . .

Get moving. You're just standing here using up your air.

He opened the door again, leaned in, and got the gun out of the glove compartment. He loaded it, then tried to put it in his right front pocket. It was too big. He was afraid it would fall out and go off if he left it there. He pulled up his new T-shirt, stuck it in his belt, then pulled the shirt down over it.

He looked at the woods again, then bitterly at the car. He could take pictures, he supposed, but what would they show? Nothing but a deserted country road. You could see those all over the state, even at the height of the summer tourist season. The pictures wouldn't convey the lack of woods sounds; the pictures would not show that the air had been poisoned.

There goes your scoop, Johnny. Oh, you'll write plenty of stories about it, and I've got a feeling you'll be telling a lot of network-news filming crews which is your good side, but your picture on the cover of Newsweek? *The Pulitzer Prize? Forget it.*

Part of him—a more adult part—insisted that was dumb, that half a loaf was better than none, that most of the reporters in the world would kill to get just a slice from *this* loaf, whatever it turned out to be.

But John Leandro was a man younger than his twenty-four years. When David Bright believed he had seen a generous helping of twerp in Leandro, he hadn't been wrong. There were reasons, of course, but the reasons didn't change the fact. He felt like a rookie who gets a fat pitch during his first at-bat in the majors and hits an opposite-field triple. Not bad . . . but in his heart a voice cries out: *Hey, God, if you was gonna give me a fat one, why didn't You let me get it* all?

Haven Village was less than a mile away. He could walk it in fifteen minutes . . . but then he would never get out of the poison belt before the air in the flat-pack ran out, and he knew it.

If only I'd rented two of these goddam things.

Even if you'd thought of it, you didn't have cash enough to pay the frigging security deposit on two. The question is, Johnny, do you want to die for your scoop or not?

He didn't. If his picture was going to be on the cover of *Newsweek,* he didn't want there to be a black border around it.

He began to trudge back toward the Troy town line. He got five dozen steps before realizing he could hear engines—a lot of them, very faint.

Something going on over on the other side of town.

Might as well be something happening on the dark side of the moon. Forget it.

With another uneasy glance at the woods, he started walking again. Got another dozen steps and realized he could hear another sound: a low, approaching hum from behind him.

He turned. His jaw dropped. In Haven, most of July had been Municipal Gadget Month. As the "becoming" progressed, most Havenites had lost interest in such things . . . but the gadgets were still there, strange white elephants such as the ones Gardener had seen in Bobbi's shed. Many had been pressed into service as border guards. Hazel McCready sat in her townhall office before a bank of earphones, monitoring each briefly in turn. She was furious at being left behind to do this duty while the future of *everything* hung in the balance out at Bobbi's farm. But now . . . someone *had* entered town after all.

Glad of the diversion, Hazel moved to take care of the intruder.

7

It was the Coke machine which had been in front of Cooder's market. Leandro stood frozen with amazement, watching it approach: a jolly red-and-white rectangle six and a half feet high and four wide. It was slicing rapidly through the air toward him, its bottom about eighteen inches over the road.

I've fallen into an ad, Leandro thought. *Some kind of weird ad. In a second or two the door of that thing will open and O. J. Simpson is going to come flying out.*

It was a funny idea. Leandro started to laugh. Even as he was laughing, it occurred to him that here was the picture . . . oh God, here was the picture, here was a Coca-Cola vending machine floating up a rural stretch of two-lane blacktop!

He grabbed for the Nikon. The Coke machine, humming to itself, banked around Leandro's stalled car and came on. It looked like a madman's hallucination, but the front of the machine proclaimed that, however much one might want to believe the contrary, this was THE REAL THING.

Still giggling, Leandro realized it wasn't stopping—it was, in fact, speeding up. And what was a soda machine, really? A refrigerator with ads on it. And refrigerators were *heavy*. The Coke machine, a red-and-white guided missile, slid through the air at Leandro. The wind made a tiny hollow hooting noise in the coin return.

Leandro forgot the picture. He leapt to the left. The Coke machine struck his right shin and broke it. For a moment his leg was nothing but a bolt of pure white pain. He screamed into the gold cup as he landed on his stomach at the side of the road, tearing his shirt open. The Nikon flew to the end of its strap and hit the gravelly soft shoulder with a crunch.

Oh you son of a bitch that camera cost four hundred dollars!

He got to his knees and turned around, shirt torn open, chest bleeding, leg screaming.

The Coke machine banked back. It hung in the air for a moment, its front turning back and forth in small arcs that reminded Leandro of the sweeps of a radar dish. The sun flashed off its glass door. Leandro could see bottles of Coke and Fanta inside.

Suddenly it pointed at him—and accelerated toward him.

Found me, Christ—

He got up and tried to hop toward his car on his left foot. The soda machine bore down on him, coin return hooting dismally.

Shrieking, Leandro threw himself forward and rolled. The Coke machine missed him by perhaps four inches. He landed in the road. Pain bellowed up his broken leg. Leandro screamed.

The machine turned, paused, found him, and started back again.

Leandro groped for the pistol in his belt and brought it out. He fired four times, balanced on his knees. Each bullet went home. The third shattered the machine's glass door.

The last thing Leandro saw before the machine—which weighed just a bit over six hundred pounds—hit him was various soft drinks foaming and dripping from the broken necks of the bottles his bullets had shattered.

Broken bottle-necks coming at him at forty miles an hour.

Mama! Leandro's mind shrieked, and he threw his arms up in front of his face in a crisscross.

He didn't have to worry about jagged bottle-necks after all, or the microbes which might have been in the cheeseburgers from the Burger Ranch, for that matter. One of life's great truths is this: when one is about to be struck by a speeding six-hundred-pound Coke machine, one need worry about nothing else.

There was a thudding, crunching sound. The front of Leandro's skull shattered like a Ming vase hurled onto the floor. A split second later his spine snapped. For a moment the machine carried him along, plastered to it like a very large bug plastered to the windshield of a fast-moving car. His splayed legs dragged on the road, the white line unreeling between them. The heels of his loafers eroded to smoking rubber nodules. One fell off.

Then he slid down the front of the vending machine and flopped onto the road.

The Coke machine started back toward Haven Village. Its coin-holder had been jarred when the machine hit Leandro, and as it moved rapidly through the air, humming, a steady stream of quarters, nickels, and dimes spewed out of the coin return and went rolling about on the road.

8.

GARD AND BOBBI

1

Gardener knew that Bobbi would make her move soon—the old Bobbi had fulfilled what the New and Improved Bobbi saw as its last obligation to good old Jim Gardener, who had come to save his friend and who had stayed on to whitewash one hell of a strange fence.

He thought, in fact, that it would be the sling—that Bobbi would want to go up first, and, once up, would simply not send it back down. There he'd be, down by the hatch, and there he'd die, next to that strange symbol. Bobbi wouldn't even have to deal with the messy reality of murder. There would be no need to think about good old Gard dying slowly and miserably of starvation, either. Good old Gard would die of multiple hemorrhages very quickly.

But Bobbi insisted that Gard go up first, and the sardonic cut of her eyes told Gardener that Bobbi knew exactly what he had been thinking . . . and she hadn't had to read his mind to do it, either.

The sling rose in the air and Gardener clung tightly to the cable, fighting a need to vomit—that need, he thought, was quickly going to become impossible to deny, but Bobbi had sent him a thought which came through loud and clear as soon as they wriggled out through the hatch again: *Don't take the mask off until you get topside.* Were Bobbi's thoughts clearer, or was it his imagination? No. Not imagination. They had both gotten another boost inside the ship. His nose was still bleeding and his shirt was sopping with it; the air mask was filling up. It was by far the worst nosebleed he'd had since Bobbi first brought him out here.

Why not? he had sent back, trying to be very careful and send only that top thought—nothing below it.

Most of the machines we heard were air-exchangers. Breathing what's in the trench now would do you in just as quick as breathing what was in the ship when we first opened it. The two won't equalize for the rest of the day, maybe longer.

Not the sort of thinking one would usually suspect in a woman who wanted to kill you—but that look was still in Bobbi's eyes, and the *feel* of it colored all of Bobbi's thoughts.

Hanging on to the cable for dear life, biting at the rubber pegs, Gardener fought to hold on to his stomach.

The sling reached the top. He wandered away on legs that felt as if they were made of rubber bands and paper clips, barely seeing the Electrolux and the length of cable manipulating the buttons; *Count ten,* he thought. *Count ten, get as far from the trench as you can, then take off the mask and take what comes. I think I'd rather die than feel like this, anyway.*

He got as far as five and could hold back no longer. Crazy images danced before his eyes: dumping the drink down Patricia McCardle's dress, seeing Bobbi reeling off her porch to greet him when he finally arrived; the big man with the gold cup over his mouth and nose turning to look at him from the passenger window of a four-wheel-drive as Gardener lay drunk on the porch.

If I'd dug in a few different places out at that gravel pit, why, I just might have found that one too! he thought, and that was when his stomach finally rebelled.

He tore the mouthpiece off and threw up, groping for a pine tree at the edge of the clearing and clinging to it for support.

He did it again, and realized he had never experienced this sort of vomiting in his entire life. He had read about it, however. He was ejecting stuff—most of it bloody—in wads that flew like bullets. And bullets were almost what they were. He was having a seizure of projectile vomiting. This was not considered a sign of good health in medical circles.

Gray veils drifted over his sight. His knees buckled.

Oh fuck I'm dying, he thought, but the idea seemed to have no emotional gradient. It was dreary news, no more, no less. He felt his hand slipping down the rough bark of the pine. He felt tarry sap. Faintly he was aware that the air smelled foul and yellow and sulfuric—it was the way a paper mill smells after a week of still, overcast weather. He didn't care. Whether there were Elysian fields or just a big black nothing, there would not be that stink. So maybe he would come out a winner anyway. Best to just let go. To just—

No! No, you will not just let go! You came back to save Bobbi, and Bobbi was maybe already beyond saving, but that kid's around and he might not be. Please, Gard, at least try!

"Don't let it be for nothing," he said in a cracked, wavering voice. "Jesus Christ, please don't let it be for nothing."

The wavering gray mists cleared a little. The vomiting subsided. He raised a hand to his face and flung away a sheet of blood with it.

A hand touched the back of his neck as he did, and Gardener's flesh pebbled with goosebumps. A hand . . . Bobbi's hand . . . but not a *human* hand, not anymore.

Gard, are you all right?

"All right," he answered aloud, and managed to get to his feet.

The world wavered, then came back into focus. The first thing he saw in it was Bobbi. The look on Bobbi's face was one of cold, cheerless calculation. He saw no love there, not even a counterfeit of concern. Bobbi had become beyond such things.

"Let's go," Gardener said hoarsely. "You drive. I'm feeling . . ." He stumbled and had to grab at Bobbi's bunched, strange shoulder to keep from falling. ". . . a little under the weather."

2

By the time they got back to the farm, Gardener was better. The bleeding from his nose had subsided to a trickle. He had swallowed a fair amount of blood while wearing the mouthpiece, and a lot of the blood he had seen in his vomit must have been that. He hoped.

He had lost a total of nine teeth.

"I want to change my shirt," he told Bobbi.

Bobbi nodded without much interest. "Come on out in the kitchen after you do," she said. "We have to talk."

"Yes. I suppose we do."

In the guestroom, Gardener took off the T-shirt he had been wearing and put on a clean one. He let it hang down over his belt. He went to the foot of the bed, lifted the mattress, and got the .45. He tucked it into his pants. The T-shirt was too big; he had lost a lot of weight. The outline of the gun butt hardly showed at all if he sucked in his gut. He paused for a moment longer, wondering if he was ready for this. He supposed there was no way to tell such a thing in advance. A dull headache gnawed his temples, and the world seemed to move in and out of focus in slow, woozy cycles. His mouth hurt and his nose felt stuffed with drying blood.

This was it; as much a showdown as any Bobbi had ever written in her westerns. High noon in central Maine. Make yore play, pard.

A ghost of a smile touched his lips. All of those two-for-a-penny sophomore philosophers said life was a strange proposition, but really, this was outrageous.

He went out to the kitchen.

Bobbi was sitting at the kitchen table watching him. Strange, half-glimpsed green fluid circulated below the surface of her transparent face. Her eyes—larger, the pupils oddly misshapen—looked at Gardener somberly.

On the table was a boom-box radio. Dick Allison had brought it out to Bobbi's three days ago, at her request. It was the one Hank Buck had used to send Pits Barfield to that great repple-depple in the sky. It had taken Bobbi less than twenty minutes to connect its circuitry to the toy photon pistol she was pointing at Gardener.

On the table were two beers and a bottle of pills. Gardener recognized the bottle. Bobbi must have gone into the bathroom and gotten it while he was changing his shirt. It was his Valium.

"Sit down, Gard," Bobbi said.

3

Gardener had raised his mental shield as soon as he was out of the ship. The question now was how much of it still remained.

He walked slowly across the room and sat at the table. He felt the .45 digging into his stomach and groin; he also felt it digging into his mind, lying heavy against whatever was left of that shield.

"Are those for me?" he asked, pointing at the pills.

"I thought we'd have a beer or two together," Bobbi said evenly, "the way friends do? And you could take a few of those at a time while we talk. I thought it would be the kindest way."

"Kind," Gardener mused. He felt the first faint tug of anger. Won't get fooled again, the song said, but the habit must be awfully hard to break. He himself had been fooled plenty. *But then,* he thought, *maybe you're an exception to the rule, Gard ole Gard.*

"I get the pills and Peter got that weird seaquarium in the shed. Bobbi, your definition of kindness has undergone one *fuck* of a radical change since the days when you'd cry if Peter brought home a dead bird. Remember those days? We lived here together, we stood your sister off when she came, and never had to stick her in a shower stall to do it. We just kicked her ass the hell out." He looked at her somberly. "Remember, Bobbi? That was when we were lovers as well as friends. I thought you might have forgotten. I would have died for you, kiddo. And I would have died *without* you. Remember? Remember *us?"*

Bobbi looked down at her hands. Did he see tears in those strange eyes? Probably all he saw was wishful thinking.

"When were you in the shed?"

"Last night."

"What did you touch?"

"I used to touch *you,"* Gardener mused. "And you me. And neither of us minded. Remember?"

"What did you touch?" she screamed shrilly at him, and when she looked back up he didn't see Bobbi but only a furious monster.

"Nothing," Gardener said. "I touched nothing." The

contempt on his face must have been more convincing than any protest would have been, because Bobbi settled back. She sipped delicately at her beer.

"Doesn't matter. You couldn't have done anything out there anyway."

"How could you do it to Peter? That's how it keeps coming at me. The old man I didn't know, and Anne barged in. But I knew *Peter. He* would have died for you too. How could you do it? God's name!"

"He kept me alive when you weren't here," Bobbi said. There was just the faintest uneasy, defensive note in her voice. "When I was working around the clock. He was the only reason there was anything left for you to save when you got here."

"You fucking *vampire!"*

She looked at him, then away.

"Jesus *Christ,* you did something like that and *I went along with it.* Do you know how that hurts? *I went along!* I saw what was happening to you . . . to a lesser degree I saw what was happening to the others, but *I still went along with it.* Because I was crazy. But of course you knew that, didn't you? You used me the same way you used Peter, but I wasn't even as smart as an old beagle dog, I guess, because you didn't even have to put me in the shed and stick one of those *filthy stinking rotten* cables in my head to do it. You just kept me oiled. You handed me a shovel and said, 'Here you go, Gard, let's dig this baby up and stop the Dallas Police.' *Except* you're *the Dallas Police. And I went along with it."*

"Drink your beer," Bobbi said. Her face was cold again.

"And if I don't?"

"Then I'm going to turn on this radio," Bobbi said, "and open a hole in reality, and send you . . . somewhere."

"To Altair-4?" Gardener asked. He kept his voice casual and tightened his mental grip

(shield-shield-shield-shield)

on that barrier in his mind. A slight frown creased Bobbi's forehead again, and Gardener felt those mental fingers probing again, digging, trying to find out what he knew, how much . . . and how.

Distract her. Make her mad and distract her. How?

"You've been snooping a *lot,* haven't you?" Bobbi asked.

"Not until I realized how much you were lying to me." And suddenly knew. He had gotten it in the shed without even knowing it.

"Most of the lies you told to yourself, Gard."

"Oh? What about the kid that died? Or the one that's blind?"

"How do you kn—"

"The shed. That's where you go to get smart, isn't it?"

She said nothing.

"You sent them to get *batteries*. You killed one and blinded the other to get *batteries*. Jesus, Bobbi, how stupid could you get?"

"We're more intelligent than you could ever hope to—"

"Who's talking about *intelligence?*" he cried furiously. "I'm talking about *smarts!* Common-fucking-*sense!* The CMP power lines run right behind your *house!* Why didn't you tap them?"

"Sure." Bobbi smiled with her weird mouth. "A really intelligent—pardon me, *smart*—idea. And the first time some tech at the Augusta substation saw the power drain on his dials—"

"You're running almost everything on C, D, and double-A batteries," Gard said. "That's a *trickle*. A guy using house current to run a big band-saw would bang those needles harder."

She looked momentarily confused. Seemed to listen—not to anyone else, but to her own interior voice. "Batteries run on direct current, Gard. AC power lines wouldn't do us any g—"

He struck his temples with his fists and screamed: *"Haven't you ever seen a goddam DC converter?* You can get them at Radio Shack for three bucks! Are you seriously trying to tell me you couldn't have made a simple DC converter when you can make your tractor fly and your typewriter run on telepathy? Are you—"

"Nobody thought of it!" she screamed suddenly.

There was a moment of silence. She looked stunned, as if at the sound of her own voice.

"Nobody thought of it," he said. "Right. So you sent those two kids, all ready to do or die for good old Haven, and now one of them is dead and the other one's blind. It's shit, Bobbi. I don't care who or what has taken you over—part of you has to be inside *someplace*. Part of you has to realize that you people haven't been doing anything creative at all. Quite the opposite. You've been taking dumb-pills and congratulating each other on how wonderful it all is. *I* was the crazy one. I kept telling myself it would be okay even after I knew better. But it's the same old shit it always was. You can disintegrate people, you can teleport them to someplace for safekeeping, or burial, or whatever, but you're as dumb as a baby with a loaded pistol."

"I think you better shut up now, Gard."

"You didn't think of it," he said softly. "Jesus, Bobbi! How can you even look at yourself in the mirror? *Any* of you?"

"I said I think—"

"Idiot savant, you said once. It's worse. It's like watching a bunch of kids getting ready to blow up the world with Soapbox Derby plans. You guys aren't even evil. Dumb, but not evil."

"Gard—"

"You're just a bunch of dumbbells with screwdrivers." He laughed.

"Shut up!" she shrieked.

"Jesus," Gard said. "Did I really think Sissy was dead? *Did* I?"

She was trembling.

He nodded toward the photon gun. "So if I don't drink the beer and take the pills, you pack me off to Altair-4, right? I get to babysit David Brown until we both drop dead of asphyxiation or starvation or cosmic-ray poisoning."

She was viciously cold now, and it hurt—more than he ever would have believed—but at least she wasn't trying to read him. In her anger, she had forgotten.

The way they had forgotten how simple it was to plug a battery-driven tape recorder into a wall socket with a DC converter between the instrument and the power source.

"There really isn't an Altair-4, just as there aren't really any Tommyknockers. There *aren't* any nouns for some things—they just *are.* Somebody pastes one name on those things in one place, somebody pastes on another someplace else. It's never a very good name, but it doesn't matter. You came back from New Hampshire talking and thinking about Tommyknockers, so here that's what we are. We've been called other things in other places. Altair-4 has, too. It's just a place where things get stored. Usually not live things. Attics can be cold, dark places."

"Is that where you're from? Your people?"

Bobbi—or whatever this was that looked a bit like her—laughed almost gently. "We're not a 'people,' Gard. Not a 'race.' Not a 'species.' Klaatu is not going to appear and say 'Take us to your leader.' No, we're not from Altair-4."

She looked at him, still smiling faintly. She had recovered most of her equanimity . . . and seemed to have forgotten the pills for the time being.

"If you know about Altair-4, I wonder if you've found the existence of the ship a little strange."

Gardener only looked at her.

"I don't suppose you've had time enough to wonder why a race with access to teleportation technology"—Bobbi wiggled the plastic gun slightly—"would even *bother* zipping around in a physical ship."

Gardener raised his eyebrows. No, he *hadn't* considered that, but now that Bobbi brought it up, he remembered a college acquaintance once wondering aloud why Kirk, Spock, and company bothered with the starship *Enterprise* when it would have been so much simpler to just *beam* around the universe.

"More dumb-pills," he said.

"Not at all. It's like radio. There are wavelengths. But beyond that, we don't understand it very well. Which is true of us about most things, Gard. We're builders, not understanders.

"Anyway, we've isolated something like ninety thousand 'clear' wavelengths—that is, pro-linear settings which do two things: avoid the binomial paradox that prevents the reintegration of living tissue and unfixed matter, and actually seem to *go* somewhere. But in almost all cases, it isn't anywhere anyone would want to go."

"Like winning an all-expenses-paid trip to Utica, huh?"

"Much worse. There's a place which seems to be very much like the surface of Jupiter. If you open a door on *that* place, the difference in pressure is so extreme it starts a tornado in the doorway which quickly assumes an extremely high electrical charge which blows the door open wider and wider . . . like tearing a wound open. The gravity is so much higher that it starts sucking out the earth of the incursive world the way a corkscrew pulls a cork. If left on that particular 'station' for long, it would cause a gravonic fault in the planet's orbit, assuming the mass was similar to earth's. Or, depending on the planet's composition, it might just rip it to pieces."

"Did anything like that come close to happening *here?"* Gard's lips were numb. Such a possibility made Chernobyl seem as important as a fart in a phone-booth. *And you went along with it, Gard!* his mind screamed at him. *You helped dig it up!*

"No, although some people had to be dissuaded from doing too much tinkering along transmitter/transmatter lines." She smiled. "It happened somewhere else we visited, though."

"What happened?"

"They got the door shut before Shatterday, but a lot of people cooked when the orbit changed." She sounded bored with the subject.

"*All* of them?" Gardener whispered.

"Nope. There are still nine or ten thousand of them alive at one of the poles," Bobbi said. "I think."

"Jesus. Oh my Jesus, Bobbi."

"There are other channels which open on rock. Just rock. The inside of some place. Most open in deep space. We've never been able to chart a single one of those locations using our star-charts. Think of it, Gard! Every place has been a strange place to us . . . even to us, and we are great sky travelers."

She leaned forward and sipped a little more beer. The toy pistol which was no longer a toy did not waver from Gardener's chest.

"So that's teleportation. Some big deal, huh? A few rocks, a lot of holes, one cosmic attic. Maybe someday someone will open a wavelength into the heart of a sun and flash-fry a whole planet."

Bobbi laughed, as if this would be a particularly fine jest. The gun didn't waver from Gard's chest, however.

Growing serious again, Bobbi said: "But that's not *all,* Gard. When you turn on a radio, you think of tuning a station. But a band—megahertz, kilohertz, shortwave, whatever—isn't just *stations.* It's also all the blank space *between* stations. In fact, that's what some bands are mostly made up of. Do you follow?"

"Yes."

"This is my roundabout way of trying to convince you

to take the pills. I won't send you to the place you call Altair-4, Gard—there I know you'd die slowly and unpleasantly."

"The way David Brown is dying?"

"I had nothing to do with that," she said quickly. "It was his brother's doing entirely."

"It's like Nuremberg, isn't it? Nothing was really *anyone's* fault."

"You idiot," Bobbi said. "Don't you realize that sometimes that's the truth? Are you so gutless you can't accept the idea of random occurrence?"

"I can accept it. But I also believe in the ability of the individual to reverse irrational behavior," he said.

"Really? *You* never could."

Shot your wife, he heard the booger-picking deputy say. *Good fucking deal, uh?*

Maybe sometimes people start the old Atonement Boogie a little late, he thought, looking down at his hands.

Bobbi's eyes flicked sharply at his face. She had caught some of that. He tried to reinforce the shield—a tangled chain of disconnected thoughts like white noise.

"What are you thinking about, Gard?"

"Nothing I want you to know," he said, and smiled thinly. "Think of it as . . . well, let's say a padlock on a shed door."

Her lips drew back from her teeth for a moment . . . then relaxed into that strange gentle smile again. "It doesn't matter," she said. "I might not understand anyway. As I say, we've never been very good understanders. We're not a race of super-Einsteins. Thomas Edison in Space would be closer, I think. Never mind. I won't send you to a place where you'll die a slow, miserable death. I still love you in my way, Gard, and if I *have* to send you somewhere, I'll send you to . . . nowhere."

She shrugged.

"It's probably like taking ether . . . but it *might* be painful. Agony, even. Either way, the devil you know is always better than the devil you don't."

Gardener suddenly burst into tears.

"Bobbi, you could have saved me *yea* grief if you'd reminded me of that sooner."

"Take the pills, Gard. Deal with the devil you know. The way you are now, two hundred milligrams of Valium will take you off very quickly. Don't make me mail you like a letter addressed to nowhere."

"Tell me some more about the Tommyknockers," Gardener said, wiping at his face with his hands.

Bobbi smiled. "The pills, Gard. If you start taking the pills, I'll tell you anything you want to know. If you don't—" She raised the photon pistol.

Gardener unscrewed the top of the Valium bottle, shook out half a dozen of the blue pills with the heart shape in the middle *(Valentines from the Valley of Torpor,* he thought), tossed them into his mouth, cracked the beer, and swallowed them. There went sixty milligrams down the old chute. He could have hidden one under his tongue, maybe, but six? Come on, folks, be real. *Not much time now. I vomited my belly empty, I've lost a lot of blood, I haven't been taking this shit and so have no tolerance to it, I'm some thirty pounds lighter than I was when I picked up the first mandatory prescription. If I don't get rid of this shit quick, they'll hit me like a highballing semi.*

"Tell me about the Tommyknockers," he invited again. One hand dropped into his lap below the table and touched the butt

(shield-shield-shield-shield)

of the gun. How long before the stuff started to work? Twenty minutes? He couldn't remember. And nobody had ever told him about OD'ing on Valium.

Bobbi moved the gun a bit toward the pills. "Take some more, Gard. As Jacqueline Susann may have once said, six is not enough."

He shook out four more but left them on the oilcloth.

"You were scared shitless out there, weren't you?" Gardener asked. "I saw the way you looked, Bobbi. You looked like you thought they were all going to get up and walk. *Day of the Dead.*"

Bobbi's New and Improved eyes flickered . . . but her voice remained soft. "But we *are* walking and talking, Gard. We *are* back."

Gard picked up the four Valiums, bounced them in his palm. "I want you to tell me just one thing, and then I'll take these." Yes. Just that one thing would in some fashion answer all the other questions—the ones he was never going to get a chance to ask. Maybe that was why he hadn't tried Bobbi with the gun yet. Because this was what he really needed to know. This one thing.

"I want to know what you *are,*" Gardener said. "Tell me what you *are.*"

4

"I'll answer your question, or at least try to," Bobbi said, "if you'll take those pills you're bouncing in your hand right now. Otherwise, you're going bye-bye, Gard. There's something in your mind. I can't quite read it—it's like seeing a shape through gauze. But it makes me *extremely* nervous."

Gardener put the pills in his mouth and swallowed them.

"More."

Gardener shook out another four and took them. All the way up to 140 milligrams now. Shooting the moon. Bobbi seemed to relax.

"I said Thomas Edison was closer than Albert Einstein, and that's as good a way to put it as any," Bobbi said. "There are things here in Haven that would have made Albert boggle, I suppose, but Einstein knew what $E = mc^2$ *meant.* He *understood* relativity. *He* knew things. *We* . . . we make things. Fix things. We don't theorize. We build. We're handymen."

"You *improve* things," Gardener said. He swallowed. When Valium took hold of him, his throat began to feel dry. He remembered that much. When it started to happen, he would have to act. He thought maybe he had already taken a lethal dose, and there were at least a dozen pills left in the bottle.

Bobbi had brightened a little.

"*Improve!* That's right! That's what we do. The way they—we—improved Haven. You saw the potential as soon as you got back. No more having to suck the corporate tit! Eventually it's possible to convert totally to . . . uh . . . organic-storage-battery sources. They're renewable and long-lasting."

"You're talking about people."

"Not *just* people, although higher species *do* seem to produce longer-lasting power than the lower ones—it may be a function of spirituality rather than intelligence. The Latin word for it, *esse,* is probably the best. But even Peter has lasted a remarkably long time, produced a great deal of power, and he's only a *dog.*"

"Maybe because of his spirit," Gardener said. "Maybe because he loved you." He took the pistol out of his belt. He held it

(shield-shield-shield-shield)

against his inner left thigh.

"That's beside the point," Bobbi said, waving the subject of Peter's love or spirituality away. "You have decided for some reason that the morality of what we're doing is unacceptable—but then, the spectrum of what you think of as morally acceptable behavior is very narrow. It doesn't matter; you'll be going to sleep soon.

"We have no history, written or oral. When you say the ship crashed here because those in charge were, in effect, fighting over the steering wheel, I feel there's an element of truth in that . . . but I also feel that perhaps it was meant, fated, to happen. Telepaths are at least to some degree precognitives, Gard, and precognitives are more apt to let themselves be guided by the currents, both large and small, that run through the universe. 'God' is the name some people give those currents, but God's only a word, like Tommyknockers or Altair-4.

"What I mean is, we would almost certainly be long extinct if we hadn't trusted those currents, because we've always been short-tempered, ready to fight. But 'fight' is too general a word. We . . . we . . ." Bobbi's eyes suddenly glowed a deep, frightful green. Her lips spread in a toothless grin. Gardener's right hand clutched the gun with a sweaty palm.

"We *squabble!*" Bobbi said. "*Le mot juste,* Gard!"

"Good for you," Gardener said, and swallowed. He heard a click. That dryness hadn't just sneaked up—all at once it was just there.

"Yes, we squabble, we've always squabbled. Like kids, you could say." Bobbi smiled. "We're very childlike. That's our good side."

"Is it now?" A monstrous image suddenly filled Gardener's head: grammar-school kids heading off to school armed with books and Uzis and Smurf lunchboxes and M-16s and apples for the teachers they liked and fragmentation grenades for those they didn't. And, oh

Christ, every one of the girls looked like Patricia McCardle and every one of the boys looked like Ted the Power Man. Ted the Power Man with greeny-glowing eyes that explained the whole sorry fucking mess, from Crusades and crossbow to Reagan's missile-tipped satellites.

We squabble. Every now and then we even tussle a bit. We're grownups—I guess—but we still have bad tempers, like kids do, and we also still like to have fun, like kids do, so we satisfied both wants by building all these nifty nuclear slingshots, and every now and then we leave a few around for people to pick up, and do you know what? They always do. People like Ted, who are perfectly willing to kill so no woman in Braintree with the wherewithal to buy one shall want for electricity to run her hair dryer. People like you, Gard, who see only minimal drawbacks to the idea of killing for peace.

It would be such *a dull world without guns and squabbles, wouldn't it?*

Gardener realized he was getting sleepy.

"Childlike," she repeated. "We fight . . . but we can also be very generous. As we have here."

"Yes, you've been very generous to Haven," Gardener said, and his jaws abruptly cracked open in a huge, tendon-stretching yawn.

Bobbi smiled.

"Anyway, we might have crashed because it was 'crash-time,' according to those currents I mentioned. The ship wasn't hurt, of course. And when I started to uncover it, we . . . came back."

"Are there more of you out there?"

Bobbi shrugged. "I don't know." *And don't care,* the shrug said. *We're* here. *There are improvements to be made. That is enough.*

"That's really all you are?" He wanted to make sure; make sure there was no more to it. He was terribly afraid he was taking too long, much too long . . . but he *had* to know. "That's *all?*"

"What do you mean, *all?* Is it so little, what we are?"

"Frankly, yes," Gard said. "You see, I've been looking for the devil outside my life *all* my life because the one inside was so fucking hard to catch. It's hard to spend such a long time thinking you're . . . Homer . . ." He yawned again, hugely. His eyelids had bricks on them.

". . . and discover you were . . . Captain Ahab all the time."

And finally, for the last time, with a kind of desperation, he asked her:

"*Is* that all you are? Just people who fix things up?"

"I guess so," she said. "I'm sorry it's such a letdown for y—"

Gardener lifted the pistol under the table, and at the same moment felt the drug finally betray him: the shield slipped.

Bobbi's eyes glowed—no, this time they *glared.* Her voice, a mental scream, blasted through Gardener's head like a meat cleaver

(GUN HE'S GOT A GUN HE'S GOT A)

chopping through the rising fog.

She tried to move. At the same time, she tried to bring the photon pistol to bear on him. Gardener aimed the .45 at Bobbi under the table and pulled the trigger. There was only a dry click. The old slug had misfired.

9.

THE SCOOP, CONCLUDED

1

John Leandro died. The scoop did not.

David Bright had promised to give Leandro until four, and that was a promise he had intended to keep—because it was honorable, of course, but also because he was not sure this was anything he wanted to stick his hand into. It might turn out to be a threshing machine instead of a news story. Nonetheless, he never doubted Johnny Leandro had been telling the truth, or his perception of it, crazed as his story sounded. Johnny was a twerp, Johnny sometimes didn't just jump to conclusions but broad-jumped them completely, but he wasn't a liar (even if he had been, Bright didn't believe he was smart enough to fabricate something this woolly).

Around two-thirty that afternoon, Bright suddenly began to think of another Johnny—poor, damned Johnny Smith, who had sometimes touched objects and gotten "feelings" about them. That had been crazy, too, but Bright had believed Johnny Smith, had believed in what Smith said he could do. It was impossible to look into the man's haunted eyes and not believe. Bright was not touching anything which belonged to John Leandro, but he could see his desk across the room, the hood pulled neatly over his word-processor terminal, and he began to get a feeling . . . a very dismal one. He felt that Johnny Leandro might be dead.

He called himself an old woman, but the feeling didn't

go away. He thought of Leandro's voice, desperate and cracking with excitement. *This is my story, and I'm not going to give it up just like that.* Thought of Johnny Smith's dark eyes, his trick of constantly rubbing at the left side of his forehead. Bright's eyes were drawn again and again to Leandro's hooded word-cruncher.

He held out until three o'clock. By then the feeling had become sickening assurance. Leandro was dead. There was just no maybe in it. He might not ever have another genuine premonition in his life, but he was having one now. Not crazy, not wounded, not one of the missing. Dead.

Bright picked up the phone, and although the number he dialed had a Cleaves Mills exchange, both Bobbi and Gard would have known it was really long-distance: fifty-five days after Bobbi Anderson's stumble in the woods, someone was finally calling the Dallas Police.

2

The man Bright talked to at the Cleaves Mills state police barracks was Andy Torgeson. Bright had known him since college, and he could talk to him without feeling that he had the words NEWS SNOOP tattooed on his forehead in bright red letters. Torgeson listened patiently, saying little, as Bright told him everything, beginning with Leandro's assignment to the story of the missing cops.

"His nose bled, his teeth fell out, he got vomiting, and he was convinced that all of this was coming out of the air?"

"Yes," Bright said.

"Also, this whatever-it-is in the air improved the *shit* out of his radio reception."

"Right."

"And you think he might be in a lot of trouble."

"Right again."

"I think he might be in a lot of trouble too, Dave—it sounds like he's gone section-eight."

"I know how it *sounds*. I just don't think that's the way it *is*."

"David," Torgeson said in a tone of great patience, "it might be possible—at least in a movie—to take over a little town and poison it somehow. But there's a *highway* that runs through that little town. There's *people* in that little town. And *phones*. Do you think someone could poison a whole town or shut it off from the outside world with no one the wiser?"

"Old Derry Road isn't really a highway," Bright pointed out. "Not since they finished the stretch of I-95 between Bangor and Newport thirty years ago. Since then, the Old Derry Road has been more like this big deserted landing strip with a yellow line running down the middle of it."

"You're not trying to tell me *nobody's* tried to use it lately, are you?"

"No. I'm not trying to tell you much of anything . . . but Johnny *did* say he'd found some people who hadn't seen their relatives in Haven for a couple of months. And some people who tried to go in to check on them got sick and had to leave in a hurry. Most of them chalked it up to food poisoning or something. He also mentioned a store in Troy where this old crock is doing a booming business in T-shirts because people have been coming out of Haven with bloody noses . . . and that it's been going on for weeks."

"Pipe dreams," Torgeson said. Looking across the barracks ready-room, he saw the dispatcher sit up abruptly and switch the telephone he was holding to his left hand, so he could write. Something had happened somewhere, and from the goosed look on the dispatcher's face, it wasn't a fender-bender or purse-snatching. Of course, people being what they were, something always *did* happen. And, as little as he liked to admit it, something might be happening in Haven as well. The whole thing sounded as mad as the tea party in *Alice,* but David had never impressed him as a member of the fruits-and-nuts brigade. At least not a card-carrying one, he amended.

"Maybe they are," Bright was saying, "but their essential pipe-dreaminess can be proved or disproved by a quick trip out to Haven by one of your guys." He paused. "I'm asking as a friend. I'm not one of Johnny's biggest fans, but I'm worried about him."

Torgeson was still looking into the dispatcher's office, where Smokey Dawson was now ratchet-jawing away a mile a minute. Smokey looked up, saw Torgeson looking, and held up one hand, all the fingers splayed. *Wait,* the gesture said. *Something big.*

"I'll see that someone takes a ride out there before the end of the day," Torgeson said. "I'll go myself if I can, but—"

"If I was to come over to Derry, could you pick me up?"

"I'll have to call you," Torgeson said. "Something's happening here. Dawson looks like he's having a heart attack."

"I'll be here," Bright said. "I'm *seriously* worried, Andy."

"I know," Torgeson said—there had not even been a flicker of interest from Bright when Torgeson mentioned something big was apparently up, and that wasn't like him at all. "I'll call you."

Dawson came out of the dispatcher's office. It was high summer, and except for Torgeson, who was catching, the entire complement of troopers on duty was out on the roads. The two of them had the barracks to themselves.

"Jesus, Andy," Dawson said. "I dunno what to make of *this.*"

"Of what?" He felt the old tight excitement building in the center of his chest—Torgeson had his own intuitions from time to time, and they were accurate within the narrow band of his chosen profession. Something big, all right. Dawson looked as if someone had hit him with a brick. That old tight excitement—most of him hated it, but part of him was a junkie for it. And now that part of him made a sudden exhilarating connection—it was irrational but it was also irrefutable. This had something to do with what Bright had just called about. *Somebody get the Dormouse and the Mad Hatter, plop the Dormouse into the pot,* he thought. *I think the tea party's getting under way.*

"There's a forest-fire in Haven," Dawson said. "*Must* be a forest-fire. Report says it's probably in Big Injun Woods."

"*Probably?* What's this *probably* shit?"

"The report came from a fire-watch station in China Lakes," Dawson said. "They logged smoke over an hour ago. Around two o'clock. They called Derry Fire Alert and Ranger Station Three in Newport. Engines were sent from Newport, Unity, China, Woolwich—"

"Troy? Albion? What about *them?* Christ, they *border* the town!"

"Troy and Albion didn't report."

"Haven itself?"

"The phones are dead."

"Come on, Smokey, don't break my balls. *Which* phones?"

"*All* of them." He looked at Torgeson and swallowed. "Of course, I haven't verified that for myself. But that isn't the nuttiest part. I mean, it's pretty crazy, but—"

"Go on and spill it."

Dawson did. By the time he finished, Torgeson's mouth was dry.

Ranger Station Three was in charge of fire control in Penobscot County, at least as long as a fire in the woods didn't develop a really broad front. The first task was surveillance; the second was spotting; the third was locating. It sounded easy. It wasn't. In this case, the situation was even worse than usual, because the fire had been reported from twenty miles away. Station Three called for conventional fire engines because it was still technically possible that they might be of some use: they hadn't been able to reach anyone from Haven who could tell them one way or the other. As far as the fire wardens at Three knew, the fire could be in Frank Spruce's east pasture or a mile into the woods. They also sent out three two-man crews of their own in four-wheel-drive vehicles, armed with topographical maps, and a spotter plane. Dawson had called them Big Injun Woods, but Chief Wahwayvokah was long gone, and today the new, nonracist name on the topographical maps seemed more apt: Burning Woods.

The Unity fire engines arrived first . . . unfortunately for them. Three or four miles from the Haven town line, with the growing pall of smoke still at least eight miles distant, the men on the pumper began to feel ill. Not just one or two; the whole seven-man crew. The driver pressed on . . . until he suddenly lost consciousness behind the wheel. The pumper ran off Unity's Old Schoolhouse Road and crashed into the woods, still a mile and a half shy of Haven. Three men were killed in the crash; two bled to death. The two survivors had literally crawled out of the area on hands and knees, puking as they went.

"They said it was like being gassed," Dawson said.

"That was them on the phone?"

"Christ, no. The two still alive are on their way to Derry Home in an amb'lance. That was Station Three. They're trying to get things together, but right now it looks like there's a hell of a lot more going on in Haven than a forest-fire. But that's spreading out of control, the Weather Service says there's going to be an easterly wind by nightfall, and it don't seem like no one can get in there to put it out!"

"What else do they know?"

"Jack *shit!*" Smokey Dawson exclaimed, as if personally offended. "People who get close to Haven get sick. Closer you get, the sicker you are. That's all anyone knows, besides something's burning."

Not a single fire unit had gotten into Haven. Those from China and Woolwich had gotten closest. Torgeson went to the anemometer on the wall and thought he saw why. They'd been coming from upwind. If the air in and around Haven was poisoned, the wind was blowing it the other way.

Dear God, what if it's something radioactive?

If it was, it was like no kind of radiation Torgeson had ever heard of—the Woolwich units had reported one-hundred-percent engine failure as they approached the Haven town line. China had sent a pumper and a tanker. The pumper quit on them, but the tanker kept running and the driver had somehow managed to reverse it out of the danger zone with vomiting men stuffed into the cab, clinging to the bumpers, and spread-eagled on top of the tank. Most had nosebleeds; a few, ear-bleeds; one had a ruptured eye.

All of them had lost teeth.

What kind of fucking radiation is THAT?

Dawson glanced into the dispatcher's booth and saw that all of his incoming lines were lighted.

"Andy, the situation's still developing. I gotta—"

"I know," Torgeson said, "you've got to go talk to crazy people. I've got to call the attorney general's office in Augusta and talk to other crazy people. Jim Tierney's the best A.G. we've had in Maine since I put on this uniform, and do you know where *he* is this gay day, Smokey?"

"No."

"On *vacation,*" Torgeson said with a laugh that was

slightly wild "First one since he took the job. The only man in the administration that might be able to understand this nuttiness is camping with his family in Utah. Fucking *Utah!* Nice, huh?"

"Nice."

"What the fuck's going on?"

"I don't know."

"Any other casualties?"

"A forest ranger from Newport died," Dawson said reluctantly.

"Who?"

"Henry Amberson."

"What? Henry? *Christ!"*

Torgeson felt as if he had been hit hard in the pit of the stomach. He had known Henry Amberson for twenty years—the two of them hadn't been best friends, nothing like it, but they had played some cribbage together when times were slow, done a little fly-fishing. Their families had taken dinner together.

Henry, Jesus, Henry Amberson. And Tierney was in fucking *Utah.* "Was he in one of the Jeeps they sent out?"

"Yeah. He had a pacemaker, you know, and—"

"What? What?" Torgeson took a step toward Smokey as if to shake him. *"What?"*

"The guy driving the Jeep apparently radioed in to Three that it exploded in Amberson's chest."

"Oh my Jesus Christ!"

"It's not sure yet," Dawson said quickly. "Nothing is. The situation is still developing."

"How could a pacemaker *explode?"* Torgeson asked softly.

"I don't know."

"It's a joke," Torgeson said flatly. "Either some weird joke or something like that radio show that time. *War of the Worlds."*

Timidly Smokey said: "I don't think it's a joke . . . or a hoax."

"Neither do I," Torgeson said. He headed for his office and the telephone.

"Fucking *Utah,"* he said softly, and then left Smokey Dawson to try to keep up with the increasingly unbelievable information that was coming in from the area of which Bobbi Anderson's farm was the center.

3

Torgeson would have called the A.G.'s office first if Jim Tierney hadn't been in fucking Utah. Since he was, he put it off long enough to make a quick call to David Bright at the Bangor *Daily News.*

"David? It's Andy. Listen, I—"

"We've got reports there's a fire in Haven, Andy. Maybe a big one. Have you got that?"

"Yeah, we do. David, I can't take you over there. The information you gave me checks out, though. Fire crews and recon people can't get into town. They get sick. We've lost a forest ranger. A guy I knew. I heard . . ." He shook his head. "Forget what I heard. It's too goddam crazy to be true."

Bright's voice was excited. "What was it?"

"Forget it."

"But you say firemen and rescue crews are getting sick?"

"*Recon* people. We don't know yet if anyone needs rescuing or not. Then there's the shit about the fire trucks and Jeeps. Vehicles seem to stop running when they get close to or into Haven—"

"*What?*"

"You heard me."

"You mean it's like the pulse?"

"Pulse? What pulse?" He had a crazy idea that Bright was talking about Henry's pacemaker, that he had known all along.

"It's a phenomenon that's supposed to follow big nuclear bangs. Cars stop dead."

"Christ. What about radios?"

"Them too."

"But your friends said—"

"All over the band, yes. Hundreds. Can I at least quote you on the sick firemen and rescue people? The vehicles stopping?"

"Yeah. As Mr. Source. Mr. Informed Source."

"When did you first hear—"

"I don't have time to do the *Playboy* interview, David. Your Leandro went to Maine Med Supplies for air?"

"Yes."

"*He* thought it was the air," Torgeson said, more to himself than to Bright. "That's what *he* thought."

"Andy . . . you know what else stops cars dead, according to the reports we get from time to time?"

"What?"

"UFOs. Don't laugh; it's true. People who sight flying saucers at close range when they're in their cars or planes almost always say their motors just drop dead until the thing goes away." He paused. "Remember the doctor who crashed his plane in Newport a week or two ago?"

War of the Worlds, Torgeson thought again. *What a pile of crap.*

But Henry Amberson's pacemaker had . . . what? *Exploded?* Could that possibly be true?

He would make it his business to find out; *that* you could take to the bank.

"I'll be talking to you, Davey," Torgeson said, and hung up. It was 3:15. In Haven, the fire which had begun at the old Frank Garrick farm had been burning for over an hour, and was now spreading toward the ship in a widening crescent.

4

Torgeson called Augusta at 3:17 P.M. At that time, two sedans with a total of six investigators in them were already northbound on I-95; Fire Station Three had called the A.G.'s office at 2:26 P.M. and the Derry state police barracks at 2:49. The Derry report included the first jagged elements—the crash of the Unity pumper, the death of a forest ranger who appeared to have been shotgunned by his own pacemaker. At 1:30 P.M. mountain time, a Utah State Police cruiser stopped at the campground where Jim Tierney and his family were staying. The trooper informed him there was an emergency in his home state. What sort of emergency? That, the trooper had been told, was information obtainable strictly on a need-to-know basis. Tierney could have called Derry, but Torgeson in Cleaves Mills was a guy he knew and trusted. Right now he wanted more than anything else to talk to someone he trusted. He felt a slow, sinking dread in his gut, a feeling that it had to be Maine Yankee, had to be something with the state's only nuclear plant, had to be, only something that big could have caused this kind of extraordinary response almost a whole country away. The trooper patched him through. Torgeson was both delighted and relieved to hear Tierney's voice.

At 1:37 P.M. mountain time, Tierney climbed into the shotgun seat of the cruiser and said, "How fast does this go?"

"Sir! This vehicle will go one hundred and thirty miles an hour and I am a Mormon sir and I am not afraid to drive it at that speed sir because I am confident that I will avoid hell! Sir!"

"Prove it," Tierney said.

At 2:03 P.M. mountain time, Tierney was in a Learjet with no markings but the U.S. flag on its tail. It had been waiting for him at a small private airfield near Cottonwoods . . . the town of which Zane Grey wrote in *Riders of the Purple Sage,* the book which had been Roberta Anderson's favorite as a girl, the one which had perhaps set her course forever as a writer of westerns.

The pilot was in mufti.

"Are you Defense Department?" Tierney asked.

The pilot looked at him with expressionless dark glasses. "Shop." It was the only word he spoke before, during, or after the flight.

That was how the Dallas Police entered the game.

5

Haven had been nothing but a wide place in the road, dreaming its life away comfortably off the major Maine tourist tracks. Now it had been noticed. Now people headed there in droves. Since they knew nothing of the anomalies that were being reported in ever-increasing numbers, it was only the growing pall of smoke on the horizon which drew them at first like moths to candle flames. It would be almost seven o'clock that evening before the state police, with the help of the local National Guard unit, would be able to block off all the roads to the area—the minor ones as well as the major. By morning, the fire would become the greatest forest-fire in Maine history. The brisk easterly wind came up right on schedule, and once it did, there was no way the fire's running start could be overcome. The realization did not sink in all at once, but it *did* sink in: the fire might have burned unchecked even if the day had been dead calm. You couldn't do much about a fire you couldn't get to, and efforts to get near this one had unpleasant results.

The spotter plane had crashed.

A busload of National Guardsmen from Bangor ran off the road, struck a tree, and exploded when the driver's brain simply burst like a tomato loaded with a cherry-bomb. All seventy weekend warriors died, but maybe only half of them in the crash; the rest died in a fruitless effort to crawl out of the poison belt.

Unfortunately, the wind was blowing the wrong way . . . as Torgeson could have told them.

The forest-fire which had begun in Burning Woods had crisped half of Newport before fire-fighters could properly go to work . . . but by then they were strung too thin to do much good, because the fire line was nearly six miles long.

By seven that evening, hundreds of people—some self-appointed fire-fighters, most your common garden-variety *Homo rubberneckus*—had poured into the area. Most promptly poured right back out again, faces white, eyes bulging, noses and ears jetting blood. Some came clutching their lost teeth in their hands like pitted pearls. And not a few of them died . . . not to mention the hundred or so hapless residents of eastern Newport who got a sudden dose of Haven when the wind turned brisk. Most of those died in their houses. Those who came to gawk and stayed to asphyxiate on the rotten air were found in or beside various roads, curled in fetal positions, hands clutched over their stomachs. Most, one G.I. later told the Washington *Post* (under the strict condition that he not be identified), looked like bloody human commas.

Such was not the fate of Lester Moran, a textbook salesman who lived in a Boston suburb and spent most of his days on the highways of northern New England.

Lester was returning from his annual late-summer selling trip to the schools in the SADs (school administrative districts) of Aroostook County when he saw smoke—a lot of it—on the horizon. This was at about 4:15 P.M.

Lester diverted immediately. He was in no hurry to get back, being a bachelor and having no plans for the next two weeks or so, but he would have diverted even if the national sales conference had been slated to begin the next day with him as the principal speaker and his speech still unwritten. He couldn't have helped himself. Lester Moran was a fire-freak. He had been one since earliest childhood. In spite of having spent the last five days on the road, in spite of a fanny that felt like a board and kidneys that felt like bricks after the constant jolting his sprung car had taken on the shitty roads of townships so small they mostly had map coordinates for names, Lester never thought twice. His weariness fell away; his eyes glowed with that preternatural light which fire-chiefs from Manhattan to Moscow know and dread: the unholy excitement of the natural-born fire-freak.

They are the sort of people fire-chiefs will, however, put to use . . . if driven to the wall. Five minutes ago, Lester Moran, who had applied to the Boston Fire Department at the age of twenty-one and been turned down because of the steel plate in his skull, had felt like a whipped dog. Now he felt like a man highballing on amphetamines. Now he *was* a man who would happily don an Indian pump which weighed almost half as much as he did himself and lug it on his back all night, breathing smoke the way some men breathe the perfume on the nape of a beautiful woman's neck, fighting the flames until the skin of his cheeks was cracked and blistered and his eyebrows were burned clean off.

He exited the turnpike at Newport and burned up the road which led toward Haven.

The plate in his head was the result of a hideous accident which had occurred when Moran was twelve, and a junior-high patrol-boy. A car had struck him and thrown him thirty feet, where his flight had been interrupted by the obdurate brick wall of a furniture warehouse. He had been given last rites; his weeping parents had been told by the surgeon who operated on him that their son would likely die within six hours, or remain in a coma for several days or weeks before succumbing. Instead, the boy had been awake and asking for ice cream before the end of the day.

"I think it's a miracle," the boy's sobbing mother cried. "A miracle from God!"

"Me too," said the surgeon who had operated on Lester

Moran, and who had looked at the boy's brain through a gaping hole in the poor kid's shattered skull.

Now, closing in on all that delightful smoke, Lester began to feel a little sick to his stomach, but he chalked that up to excitement and then forgot all about it. The plate in his skull was, after all, nearly twice the size of the one in Jim Gardener's. The absence of police, fire, or Forestry Department vehicles in the thickening murk he found both extraordinary and oddly exhilarating. Then he rounded a sharp curve and saw a bronze-colored Plymouth lying upside-down in the left-hand ditch, its red dashboard flasher still pulsing. Written on the side was DERRY F.D.

Lester parked his old Ford wagon, got out, and trotted over to the wreck. There was blood on the steering wheel and the seat and driver's-side floormat. There were droplets of blood on the windshield.

All in all, quite a lot of blood. Lester stared at it, horrified, and then looked toward Haven. Dull red colored the base of the smoke now, and he realized he could actually *hear* the dull crackle of burning wood. It was like standing near the world's biggest open-hearth furnace . . . or as if the world's biggest open-hearth furnace had sprouted legs and was slowly approaching *him*.

Next to that sound, next to the sight of that dull yet titanic red glow, the overturned Derry fire-chief's car and the blood inside began to seem a good deal less important. Lester went back to his own car, fought a brief battle with his conscience, and won by promising himself he would stop at the first pay phone he came to and call the state police in Cleaves Mills . . . no, Derry. Like most good salesmen, Lester Moran carried a detailed map of his territory in his head, and after consulting it, he decided Derry was closer.

He had to resist the yammering urge to goose the wagon up to its top speed . . . which was about sixty these days. He expected at every turn of the road to come upon sawhorses blocking the road, a confusion of crazily parked vehicles, the sound of CB radios squealing out messages at top gain, shouting men in hard-hats, helmets, and rubber coats.

It didn't happen. Instead of sawhorses and a boiling nest of activity he came upon the overturned Unity pumper, cab broken off its body, the tank itself still spraying the last of its load. Lester, who was now breathing smoke as well as air that would have killed almost anyone else on earth, stood on the soft shoulder, mesmerized by the limp white arm he saw dangling from the window of the pumper's amputated cab. Rivulets of drying blood ran erratic courses down the arm's white and vulnerable underside.

Something wrong here. Something a lot more wrong than just a woods fire. You got to get out, Les.

But instead he turned toward the fire again and was lost.

The smoky taste in the air was stronger. The sound of burning was now not a crackle but a rolling thunder. The truth of it suddenly fell on him like a bucket of cement: *No one was fighting this fire. No one at all.* For some reason he couldn't understand, they either hadn't been able to get into the area or hadn't been *allowed* in. As a result, the fire was burning out of control, and with the freshening wind to help, it was growing like a radioactive monster in a horror movie.

The idea made him ill with terror . . . and excitement . . . and sick, dark joy. It was bad to feel a thing like that last, but it was there and it was impossible to deny. Nor was he the only one who had felt it. That dark joy had seemed to be a part of every fire-fighter he had ever bought a drink for (which was almost every fire-fighter he'd ever met since he flunked his own BFD physical).

He fumbled and stumbled back to his car, started it with some difficulty (assuming that in his excitement he had probably almost flooded the damned dinosaur), boosted the air conditioner all the way up, and headed toward Haven again. He was aware this was idiocy of the purest ray serene—he was, after all, not Superman but a forty-five-year-old textbook salesman who was going bald and who was still a bachelor because he was too shy to ask women for dates. He was not just behaving in an *idiotic* fashion, either. Harsh as that judgment was, it was still a rationalization. The truth was, he was behaving like a lunatic. And yet he could no more stop himself than a junkie can stop himself when he sees his fix cooking in the spoon.

He couldn't *fight* it . . .

. . . but he could still go *see* it.

And it would really be something to see, wouldn't it?

Lester thought. Sweat was already rolling down his face, as if in anticipation of the heat ahead. Something to see, oh yeah. A forest-fire that was for some reason being allowed to rage utterly out of control as they had millions of years ago, when men were little more than a small tribe of hairless monkeys cowering in the twin cradles of the Nile and the Euphrates and the great fires themselves were touched off by spontaneous combustion, strokes of lightning, or meteor-falls instead of drunk hunters who didn't give a shit what they did with their cigarette butts. It would be a bright orange furnace, a firewall ninety feet high in the woods; across the clearings and gardens and hayfields it would race like a Kansas prairie fire in the 1840s, gobbling houses so swiftly they would implode from the sudden change in air pressure, as houses and factories had done during the World War II firebombings. He would be able to see the road he was on, *this very road,* disappearing into that furnace, like a highway into hell.

The tar itself, he thought, would first begin to run in sticky little rivulets . . . and then to burn.

He stepped down harder on the gas, and thought: How could you not go on? When you had a chance—a once-in-a-lifetime chance—to see something like that, how could you not?

6

"I just don't know how I'm going to explain to my dad, is all," the Maine Med Supplies clerk said. He wished he had never argued four years ago for expanding their business to include rentals in the first place. His father had thrown that in his face after the old guy rented the flat-pack and never returned it, and now all hell was breaking loose in Haven—the radio said it was a forest-fire and then went on to hint that even weirder things might be happening there—and he was betting he'd never see the flat-pack he had rented that morning to the reporter with the thick glasses, either. Now here were two *more* fellows, state troopers no less, both big, and, most unsettling of all, one about as black as a fellow could be, demanding not just one flat-pack each, but *six* of them.

"You can tell your dad we requisitioned them," Torgeson said. "I mean, you *do* provide respiration gear for firemen, don't you?"

"Yes, but—"

"And there's a forest-fire in Haven, isn't there?"

"Yes, but—".

"Then get them out here. I don't have time to bullshit."

"My father is gonna kill me!" he wailed. "That's all we got!"

Torgeson had met Claudell Weems pulling into the parking lot of the barracks just as Torgeson himself was pulling out. Claudell Weems, Maine's only black state trooper, was tall—not as tall as the late Monster Dugan, but a very respectable six-four. Claudell Weems had one gold tooth in the front of his mouth, and when Claudell Weems moved very close to people—suspects, for instance, or reluctant clerks—and smiled, revealing that sparkling gold incisor, they became very nervous. Torgeson once asked Claudell Weems why this was, and Claudell Weems said he *b'leeved* it was dat ole black magic. And then laughed until the glass in the barracks windows seemed to tremble in its frames.

Weems now leaned very close to the clerk and employed dat ole black magic dat he wove so well.

When they left Maine Med with the flat-packs, the clerk was not really sure what had happened . . . except that the black fella had the biggest gold tooth he had ever seen in his life.

7

The toothless old man who had sold Leandro the T-shirt stood on his porch and watched expressionlessly as Torgeson's cruiser blasted by. When it was gone he went inside and made a phone call to a number most people wouldn't have been able to reach; they would have heard the sirening sound which had infuriated Anne Anderson instead. But there was a gadget on the back of the storekeeper's phone, and soon he was talking to an increasingly harried Hazel McCready.

8

"So!" Claudell Weems said cheerfully after craning his neck to look at the speedometer. "I see we are driving at just over ninety miles an hour! And since the consensus is that you're probably the shittiest motor-vehicle operator in the entire Maine State Police—"

"*What* fucking consensus?" Torgeson asked.

"*My* fucking consensus," Claudell Weems said. "Anyway, that leads to a deduction. The deduction is that I will die very soon. I don't know if you believe in that bullshit about granting a doomed man's last request, but if you do, maybe you'd tell me what this is all about. If you can before we receive our engine-block implants, that is."

Andy opened his mouth, then closed it again. "No," he said. "I can't. It's too nuts. Just this much. You may start to feel sick. If you do, put some of that canned air to you right away."

"Oh, Christ," Weems said. "The *air's* been poisoned in Haven?"

"I don't know. I think so."

"Oh Christ," Weems said again. "Who spilled what beans?"

Andy only shook his head.

"*That's* why no one's fighting the fire." The smoke boiled up from the horizon in a widening swath—mostly white so far, thank God.

"I don't know. I think so. Run one of the bands on the radio."

Weems blinked as if he thought Torgeson might be crazy. "*Which* band?"

"*Any* band."

So Weems began to run the police band, at first getting nothing but the confused, beginning-to-be-frightened babble of cops and firemen who wanted to fight a fire and somehow couldn't get to where it was. Then, further down, they heard a request for backup units at the scene of a liquor-store robbery. The address given was 117 Mystic Avenue, Medford.

Weems looked at Andy. "Jeepers-creepers, Andy, I didn't know there *was* any Mystic Avenue in Medford—in fact, I didn't think there was any avenues at *all* in Medford. Couple of pulproads, maybe."

"I think," Andy said, and his voice seemed to be coming to his own ears from very far away, "that particular squeal is coming from Medford, *Massachusetts.*"

9

Two hundred yards over the Haven town line, Lester Moran's motor died. It did not cough; it did not hitch; it did not backfire. It just died, quietly and without fanfare. He got out without bothering to switch off the key.

The steady crackle of the fire filled the whole world, it seemed. The air temperature had gone up at least twenty degrees. The wind was carrying the heavy smoke toward him but up, so the air was breathable. It still had a hot, acrid taste.

Here on the left and right were wide fields—Clarendon land on the right, Ruvall land on the left. It rose in a long, undulating slope toward the woods. In those woods, Lester could see steadily brightening winks of red and orange light; smoke poured up from them in a torrent which was steadily darkening. He could hear the thumping explosions of hollow trees imploding as the fire sucked the oxygen out of them like marrow from old bones. The wind was not straight into his face, but close enough; the fire was going to break out of the woods and into the field in minutes . . . seconds, maybe. Its rush down to where he stood, face red and running with sweat, might be lethally quick. He wanted to be back in his car before that happened—it would start, of course it would, old gal had never failed him yet—and piling up distance between himself and that red, oncoming beast.

Go, then! Go, for Chrissake! You've seen it, now GO!

Thing was, he really *hadn't* seen it. He'd felt its heat, seen it wink its eyes and fume smoke from its dragon's nostrils . . . but he really hadn't *seen* the fire.

But then he did.

It came out of Luther Ruvall's west field in a pounce. The main fire-front bore on into Big Injun Woods, but this side now broke free of the forest. The trees massed at the far end of the field were no match for the red animal. They seemed for a moment to grow blacker as the light behind them was turned up—yellow to orange, orange to glare-red. Then they simply swept into flame. It happened in an instant. For a moment Lester could see their tops, and then they were gone, too. It was like the act of some fabulcus prestidigitator, the sort of magician Hilly Brown had once wanted to be with all his heart and soul.

The fire-line was before him, eighty feet high and eating trees as Lester Moran stood mesmerized, mouth gaping, before it. Flames began to run down the slope of the field. Now the smoke began to rafter around him, thicker, choking. He began to cough.

Get out! For Christ's sake, get out!

Yes. Now he would; now he *could*. He had seen it and it was every bit as spectacular as he had expected it would be. But it *was* a beast. And what a right-thinking man did when confronted with a beast was run. Run just as fast and far as he could. All living things did it. All living things—

Lester backed halfway to his car and then stopped.

All living things.

Yes. All living things ran before a forest-fire. The old patterns were suspended. The coyote ran beside the rabbit. But there were no rabbits and no coyotes coming down that field; there were no birds in the gunmetal-colored sky.

No one here but him.

No birds or animals running from the fire meant there were none in the woods.

The overturned F.D. car, the blood everywhere.

The pumper wrecked in the woods. The bloody arm.

What's going on here? his mind screamed.

He didn't know . . . but he knew he was putting on those fabled boogie shoes. He pulled the door open—and then looked back one final time.

What he saw rising out of that great pillar of smoke jerked a scream from him. He drew in smoke, coughed on it, screamed again.

Something—some huge *something*—was rising out of the smoke like the greatest whale in creation slowly breaching.

Smoke-hazed sunlight gleamed mellowly on its side—and still it came up, came up, came up, and there was no sound except for the awkward thunder-crunch strides of the fire.

Up . . . and up . . . and up . . .

His neck craned to follow its slow, impossible progress, and so he never saw the small, queer thing which came out of the smoke and trundled smartly down the road toward him. It was a red wagon. It had belonged to little Billy Fannin at the beginning of the summer. In the center of the wagon was a platform. On the platform was a Bensohn brush-trimmer—little more than a power blade at the end of a long pole. The blade was controlled by a pistol-grip control. A sales tag reading CUT UP A STORM WITH YOUR BENSOHN! still fluttered from the top of the pole. It was on a moving gimbal, and looked a bit like the jutting prow of an absurd ship.

Lester was cringing against his car and staring up into the sky when the gadget's EEG sensor—which had begun life as a digital meat probe—triggered the brush-trimmer's electronic starter (a modification the Bensohn designers had never considered). The blade shrieked into life, the small gas motor howling like a hurt cat.

Lester turned and saw something like a fishing-pole with teeth coming at him. He cried out and ducked toward the rear of his car.

What's going on here? his mind screamed. *What's going on, what's going on, what's going on, what's—*

The brush-trimmer swung on its gimbal, seeking Lester, following his brain-waves, which it sensed as neat little pulses, not much different from radar blips. The brush-trimmer was not very bright (its brain came from a programmable toy called the Terrible Tracker Tank), but it was bright enough to stay homed in on the low electrical output of Lester Moran's own brain. His battery, one might say.

"Get *out!*" Lester screamed as Billy Fannin's wagon trundled toward him. "Get *away!* Get *awaaaay!*"

Instead, the wagon seemed to leap at him. Lester Moran, his heart hammering wildly in his chest, zigged. The brush-trimmer zigged with him. Lester Moran tried to zag—and then a huge, slowly moving shadow fell over him, and he looked up in spite of himself . . . he just couldn't help it. His feet tangled in each other and the brush-cutter pounced. Its whirling blade chewed into Lester's head. It was still working on him when the fire engulfed both it and its victim.

10

Torgeson and Weems saw the body in the road at the same time. They were both breathing canned air now; nausea had come on them quickly with frightening power, but with the masks in place, it disappeared completely. Leandro had been right. The air. Something in the air.

Claudell Weems had ceased asking questions after they'd picked up the police-band squeal from Massachusetts. After that he only sat with his hands in his lap, his eyes moving steadily and cautiously. Further down-tuning had brought them news of police doings in such interesting places as Friday, North Dakota; Arnette, Texas.

Torgeson stopped and the two men got out. Weems paused, then took the riot gun clipped under the dash. Torgeson nodded. Things were starting to come clear. Not *sane*, but *clear*. Gabbons and Rhodes had disappeared on their way back from this town. And Monster had been here the day before he committed suicide. What was that Phil Collins song, the one with the spooky drums? *I can feel it in the air tonight . . .*

It was in the air, all right.

Gently, Torgeson turned over the man he believed to be the one who had finally blown the whistle on this craziness.

He had cleaned up a lot of ugly messes on the highway, but he still drew in a harsh gasp and shied his face away.

"Christ, what hit him?" Weems asked. The mask muffled his words, but the tone of dismay came through loud and clear.

Torgeson didn't know. He had seen a man once who'd been hit by a snowplow. That guy had looked a little like this. That was the closest.

The guy was blood from the top of what had been his head all the way down to his waist. His belt buckle had been driven deep into his body.

"Christ, man, I'm sorry," he murmured, and laid the body down gently. He could go for the wallet, but he wanted nothing more to do with that smashed body. He headed for the car. Weems fell in beside him, riot gun held on a slant against his chest. In the distance, to the west, the smoke was growing thicker by the moment, but here there was only a faint woodsy tang.

"This is crazy shit," Weems said through his mask.

"Yes."

"I have a very bad feeling about being here."

"Yes."

"I believe we should vacate this area on the dou—"

There was a crackling sound from behind them, and for a moment Torgeson thought it must be the fire—it was far away, relatively speaking, but it could be over here too. Perfectly reasonable! When you were at the Mad Hatter's tea party, anything was. Turning, he realized that the sound was not burning branches but breaking ones.

"Holy *shit!*" Claudell Weems cried.

Torgeson's jaw dropped.

The Coke machine, stupid but reliable, moved in again. This time it came out of the brush at the side of the road. The glass display front was broken. The sides of the big rectangular box were scratched. And on the metal part of the machine's front, Torgeson saw a horridly suggestive shape driven in so deep it looked almost sculpted.

It looked like half a head.

The Coke machine moved out over the road and just hung there for a moment like a coffin painted in incongruously gay colors. They were gay, at least, until you noticed the blood which had dripped and run and was beginning to dry in maroon splotches.

Torgeson could hear a faint humming, and a clicking sound—*Like relays,* he thought. *Maybe it's been damaged. Maybe, but still—*

The Coke machine suddenly arrowed straight at them.

"MothaFUCKAH!" Weems shouted—there was dismay and terror in his voice, but a kind of crazed laughter as well.

"Shoot it, shoot it!" Torgeson cried, and leapt to the right.

Weems took a step back and promptly fell over Leandro's body. This was extremely stupid. It was also extremely lucky. The Coke machine missed him by inches. As it banked for another run, Weems sat up and pumped three quick shotgun blasts into it. Metal exploded inward in metal daisy shapes with black centers. The machine began to buzz. It stopped, jittering back and forth in the air like a man with Huntington's chorea.

Torgeson drew his service pistol and fired four rounds. The Coke machine started for him, but now it seemed lethargic, unable to get up any speed. It jerked to a stop, jerked forward, stopped, jerked forward again. It rocked drunkenly from side to side. The buzzing grew louder. Runnels of soda fell from the access door in sticky rivulets.

As it came at him, Torgeson pivoted easily away.

"Drop, Andy!" Weems yelled.

Torgeson dropped. Claudell Weems shot the Coke machine three more times, firing as fast as he could work the pump action. On the third shot, something inside it exploded. Black smoke and a brief belch of fire licked out one side of the machine.

Green fire, Torgeson saw. *Green.*

The Coke machine thumped to the road about twenty feet from Leandro's body. It tottered, then fell forward with a hollow bang. Broken glass jingled. There were three seconds of silence; then a long metallic croaking sound. It stopped. The Coca-Cola machine lay dead across the white line in the middle of Route 9. Its red-and-white hide was full of bullet-holes. Smoke poured from it.

"I have just drawn my weapon and killed a Coke machine, sir," Claudell Weems said hollowly inside his mask.

Andy Torgeson turned toward him. "And you never even ordered it to halt, or fired a warning shot. Probably draw a suspension, you dumb shit."

They stared at each other over the masks, and started to laugh. Claudell Weems laughed so hard he was nearly doubled over.

Green, Torgeson thought, and although he was still laughing, nothing felt very funny inside, where he lived. *The fire that came out of that fucker was* green.

"Never fired a warning shot," Weems cackled breathlessly. "No, I never did. Never did at all."

"Violated its fucking civil rights," Torgeson said.

"Have to be an investigation!" Weems laughed. "Yo, baby! I mean . . . mean . . ." He tottered on his feet, and there was a lot of Claudell Weems to totter. Torgeson suddenly realized he was dizzy himself. They were breathing pure oxygen . . . hyperventilating.

"*Stop laughing!*" he shouted, and his voice seemed to come from a long distance away. "Claudell, stop laughing!"

He somehow crossed the distance to where Weems was swaying woozily on his feet. The distance seemed very wide. When he was almost there, he stumbled. Weems somehow caught him and for a moment they stood swaying drunkenly, arms about each other, like Rocky Balboa and Apollo Creed at the end of the first fight.

"You pullin me down, asshole," Weems muttered.

"Fuck you, you started it." The world came into focus, wavered, steadied. *Slow breaths,* Torgeson told himself. *Big slow breaths, easy respiration. Be still, my beating heart.* That last made him giggle again, but he got hold of it.

The two of them wavered back toward the cruiser, arms about each other's waists.

"The body," Weems said.

"Leave it for now. He's dead. We're not. Yet."

"Look," Weems said as they passed Leandro's remains. "The bubs! They're out!"

The blue flashers, called bubbles or bubs by the troopers, on top of the cruiser were dead and dark. That wasn't supposed to be—leaving the flashers on at the scene of the accident was ingrained behavior.

"Did you—" Torgeson began, and then stopped.

Something in the landscape had changed. The day had darkened, as it does when a large cloud floats over the sun or when an eclipse begins. They looked at each other, then turned. Torgeson saw it first, a great silvery shape emerging from the boil of smoke. Its huge leading edge gleamed.

"Holy *Christ!*" Weems almost squealed. His large brown hand found Torgeson's arm and bore down upon it.

Torgeson barely felt it, although there would be bruises in the shape of Weems's hand the next day.

Up it came . . . and up . . . and up. Smoke-hazed sunlight glinted on its silvery-metallic surface. It rose on an angle of roughly forty degrees. It seemed to be wavering slightly, although that could have been an illusion or heat-haze.

Of course the whole thing was an illusion—*had* to be. No *way* it could be real, Torgeson thought; it was oxygen rapture.

But how can we both be having the same hallucination?

"Oh my dear God," Weems groaned, "it's a flyin saucer, Andy, it's a fuckin flyin saucer!"

But to Torgeson it did not look like a saucer. It looked like the underside of an Army mess-plate—the biggest damn plate in creation. Up it came and up it came; you thought it must end, that a hazy margin of sky must appear between it and the rafters of smoke, but still it came, dwarfing the trees, dwarfing all the landscape. It made the smoke of the forest-fire look like a couple of cigarette butts smoldering in an ashtray. It filled more and more of the sky, blotting out the horizon, rising, oh, something was rising out of Big Injun Woods, and it was deathly silent—there was no sound, no sound at all.

They stared at it, and then Weems clutched Torgeson and Torgeson clutched Weems, they hugged each other like children, and Torgeson thought: *Oh, if it falls on us—*

And still it came up from the smoke and the fire, and up, as if it would never end.

11

By nightfall, Haven had been cut off from the outside world by the National Guard. The Guardsmen surrounded it, those downwind wearing oxygen equipment.

Torgeson and Weems made it out—but not in their cruiser. That was as dead as John Wilkes Booth. They hoofed it. By the time they had used up the oxygen in the last flat-pack, swapping it back and forth, they were well into Troy and found themselves able to deal with the outside air—the wind left them lucky, Claudell Weems said later. They walked out of what would soon be referred to as "the zone of pollution" in top-secret government reports, and theirs was the first official word of what was going on in Haven, but by then there had been hundreds of unofficial reports on the lethal quality of the air in the area and *thousands* of reports of a gigantic UFO seen rising from the smoke in Big Injun Woods.

Weems made it out with a bloody nose. Torgeson lost half a dozen teeth. Both counted themselves lucky.

The initial perimeter, staffed with National Guardsmen from Bangor and Augusta, was thin. By nine P.M. it had been augmented by Guardsmen from Limestone and Presque Isle and Brunswick and Portland. By dawn a thousand more battle-equipped Guardsmen had been flown in from Eastern Corridor cities.

Between the hours of 7:00 P.M. and 1:00 A.M., NORAD stood at DEFCON-2. The President was circling the Midwest at sixty thousand feet in *Looking Glass* and chewing Tums five and six at a time.

The FBI was on the scene at 6:00 P.M., the CIA at 7:15 P.M. By 8:00 o'clock, they were yelling about jurisdiction. At 9:15 P.M. a frightened, infuriated CIA agent named Spacklin shot an FBI agent named Richardson. The incident was hushed up, but both Gardener and Bobbi Anderson would have understood perfectly—the Dallas Police were on the scene and in complete control of the situation.

10.

TOMMY-KNOCKERS, KNOCKING AT THE DOOR

1

There was a moment of paralyzed silence in Bobbi's kitchen following the misfire of Ev Hillman's old .45, a silence that was as much mental as it was physical. Gard's wide blue eyes stared into Bobbi's green ones.

"You tried—" Bobbi began, and her mind

(! tried to !)

produced an echo in Gardener's head. That moment seemed very long. And when it broke, it broke like glass.

Bobbi had dropped the photon pistol to her side in her surprise. Now she brought it up again. There was to be no second chance. In her agitation, her mind was completely open to Gardener, and he felt her shock at the chance she had given him. She intended that there should be no second chance.

There was nothing he could do with his right hand; it was under the table. Before she could aim the muzzle of the photon pistol at him, he put his left hand on the edge of the kitchen table and, without thinking, shoved as hard as he could. The table legs squealed harshly on the floor as the table moved. It struck Bobbi's lumped and misshapen chest. At the same instant, a beam of brilliant green light shot from the barrel of the toy gun hooked into Hank Buck's big radio/tape-player. Instead of hitting Gard's own chest, it jerked upward and passed over his shoulder—more than a foot above it, actually, but he could still feel the skin there tingle unpleasantly under the shirt, as if the surface molecules were dancing like drops of water on a hot skillet.

Gard twisted to the right and dropped down to get away from that beam of what looked like light. His ribs struck the table, struck it hard, and the table rammed Bobbi again, this time even harder. Bobbi's chair rocked backward on its rear legs, teetered, and then both it and she toppled over with a crash. The beam of green light swung upward, and Gardener was momentarily reminded of those guys who stand on airport tarmacs at night, using powerful flashlights to guide planes into their berths.

He heard a low crunching, crackling sound like splintering plywood from overhead, looked up, and saw the photon pistol had drawn a slit in the kitchen ceiling. Gardener staggered to his feet. Incredibly, his jaws cracked and wavered in another yawn. His head clanged and echoed with the grass-fire alarm of Bobbi's thoughts

(he's got a gun tried to shoot me bastard bastard gun he's got)

and he tried to shield himself before he went mad. He couldn't. Bobbi was screaming inside his head, and as she lay on the floor pinned for the moment between the table and overturned chair, she was trying to bring the gun to bear on him for another shot.

Gardener lifted his foot and shoved the table again, grimacing. It overturned, beers, pills, and boom-box radio all sliding off. Most of the stuff fell on Bobbi. Beer splashed in her face and ran, fizzing and foaming, over her New and Improved skin. The radio hit her neck, then the floor, landing in a shallow puddle of beer.

Flash, you fucker! Gardener screamed at it. *Explode! Self-destruct! Explode, goddammit, ex—*

The radio did more than that. It seemed to bulge, and then with a sound like rotten cloth ripping along a seam, it shattered outward in all directions, belching streaks of green fire like bottled lightning. Bobbi screamed. What he heard with his ears was bad; the sound inside his head was infinitely worse.

Gardener screamed with her, not hearing himself. He saw that Bobbi's shirt was burning.

He started for her, not thinking about what he was up to. He dropped the .45 as he did so, without even thinking. This time it *did* go off, sending a slug into Jim Gardener's ankle, shattering it. Pain blew through his mind like a hot wind. He screamed again. He took a shambling step forward, his head ringing with her horrid mental cries. They would send him mad in a moment. This thought was actually a relief. When he finally went mad, none of this shit would matter anymore.

Then, for one second, Gard saw *his* Bobbi for the last time.

He thought perhaps Bobbi was trying to smile.

Then the screaming began again. She screamed and tried to beat out the flames that were turning her torso to tallow, and that screaming was too much, far too much, too loud, far too loud; it was unbearable. For them both, he thought. He bent, found the triple-damned pistol on the floor, and picked it up. He needed to use both of his thumbs to get it cocked. The pain in his ankle was bad—he knew that—but for the moment it was lost to him, buried under Bobbi's shrieking agony. He pointed Hillman's pistol at her head.

Work, you goddam thing, oh please, please work—

But if it worked and he missed? There mightn't be another cartridge in the mag.

His motherfucking hands wouldn't stop shaking.

He fell to his knees like a man struck with a sudden violent need to pray. He crawled toward Bobbi, who lay shrieking and writhing and burning on the floor. He could smell her; could see black shards of plastic from the radio's case bubbling their way into her flesh. He almost overbalanced and fell on top of her. Then he pressed the.45 against the side of her neck and pulled the trigger.

Another click.

Bobbi, screaming and screaming. Screaming inside his head.

He tried to pull the slide back again. Almost got it. Then it slipped. *Snick.*

Please God, oh please let me be her friend this one last time!

This time he got the slide all the way back. He tried the trigger again. This time the gun went off.

The scream suddenly became a loud buzz in Gardener's head. He knew he was listening to the mental sound of mortal disconnect. He turned his head upward. A bright stripe of sunlight from the unzipped roof fell across his face, bisecting it. Gardener shrieked.

Suddenly the buzzing stopped and there was silence.

Bobbi Anderson—or whatever she had become—was as dead as the pile of autumn-leaf corpses in the control room of the ship, as dead as the galley slaves which had been the ship's drive.

She was dead and Gardener would have gladly died then, too . . . but it still wasn't over.

Not yet.

2

Kyle Archinbourg was having a Pepsi in Cooder's when the screams began in his head. The bottle dropped from his hand and shattered on the floor as his hands jerked up to his temples. Dave Rutledge, dozing outside Cooder's in a chair which he had caned himself, was tilted back against the building and dreaming weird dreams in alien colors. His eyes snapped open and he sat bolt upright as if someone had touched him with a live wire, scrawny tendons standing out on his throat. His chair slid out from under him, and when his head hit the wooden wall of the market, his neck shattered like glass. He was dead before he hit the asphalt. Hazel McCready was making herself a cup of tea. When the screams began, her hands jerked. The one holding the teapot spilled boiling water across the back of the one holding the cup, scalding it badly. She hurled the teapot across the room, screaming in pain and fear. Ashley Ruvall, riding his bike past the town hall, fell over into the street and lay there stunned. Dick Allison and Newt Berringer were playing cribbage at Newt's house, a pretty goddam stupid thing to be doing since each knew what the other held in his hand, but Newt didn't have a Parcheesi board, and besides, they were only passing time, waiting for the telephone to ring, waiting for Bobbi to tell them the drunk was dead and the next phase of the work could begin. Newt was dealing, and he sprayed cards all over the table and floor. Dick bolted to his feet, eyes wild, hair standing on end, and lurched for the door. He ran into the wall three feet to the right of it instead and went sprawling. Doc Warwick was in his study going over his old diaries. The scream hit him like a wall of cinderblocks being trundled along a set of tracks at brisk speed. His body dumped adrenaline into his heart in lethal quantities, and it blew like a tire. Ad McKeen was in his pickup truck, headed over to Newt's. He ran off the road and into Pooch Bailey's abandoned Hot Dog House. His face hit the steering wheel. He was momentarily stunned, but no more. He had been going slow. He looked around, dazed and terrified. Wendy Fannin was coming up from the cellar with two jars of peach preserves. Since her "becoming" had started, she ate little else. In the last four weeks she had eaten over ninety jars of peach preserves all by herself. She wailed and threw these two into the air like a spastic juggler. They came down, struck the stairs, shattered. Peaches and sticky juice ran and dripped. *Bobbi,* she thought numbly, *Bobbi Anderson's burning up!* Nancy Voss was standing blankly at the back window and thinking about Joe. She missed Joe, missed him a lot. She supposed that the "becoming" would eventually wipe that longing out—every day it seemed more and more distant—but although it hurt to miss Joe, she didn't want that hurt to stop. It made no sense, but there it was. Then the shrieks began in her head and she jerked forward so suddenly that she broke three of the windowpanes with her forehead.

3

Bobbi's screams blanketed Haven like an air-raid siren. Everything and everyone came to a complete stop . . . and then the changed people of Haven drifted into the streets of the village. Their looks were all one look: dismay, pain, and horror at first . . . then anger.

They knew who had caused those shrieks of agony.

While they went on, no other mental voice could be heard, and the only thing anyone could do was listen to them.

Then came the buzzing death-rattle, and a silence so complete it could only be death.

A few moments later there was the low pulse of Dick Allison's mind. It was emotionally shaken but clear enough in its command.

Her farm. Everyone. Stop him before he can do anything else.

Hazel's voice picked the thought up, strengthening it—the effect was like a second voice joining a first to make a duet.

Bobbi's farm. Go there. Everybody.

The beat of Kyle's mental voice made it a trio. The radius of the voice began to spread as it gained strength.

Everyone. Stop him—

Adley's voice. Newt Berringer's voice.

—before he can do anything else.

Those Gardener thought of as the Shed People had welded their voices into one voice of command, clear and beyond denial . . . not that anyone in Haven even *thought* of denying it.

Stop him before he can do anything to the ship. Stop him before he can do anything to the ship.

Rosalie Skehan left her kitchen sink without bothering to turn off the water running over the cod she had been freshening for supper. She joined her husband, who had been in the back yard chopping wood and who had barely missed amputating several of his toes when Bobbi's screams began. Without a word they went to their car, got in, and started for Bobbi's farm, four miles away. Turning out of their driveway, they nearly struck Elt Barker, who had taken off from his gas station on his old Harley. Freeman Moss was wheeling his pulp-truck. He felt a vague regret—he had sort of liked Gardener. He had what Freeman's pop had called "sand"—but that wouldn't stop him from tearing the bastard's gizzard out. Andy Bozeman was driving his Oldsmobile Delta 88, his wife sitting beside him with her hands folded neatly on her purse. In it was a molecule-exciter which could raise the spot heat of anything two inches in diameter roughly one thousand degrees in fifteen seconds. She was hoping to boil Gardener like a lobster. *Just let me get within five feet,* she kept thinking. *Just five feet, that's all I ask.* Beyond that distance, the gadget became unreliable. She knew she could have improved its effectiveness up to half a mile, and now wished she had done so, but if Andy didn't have at least six fresh shirts in the closet, he was like a bear. Bozeman himself wore a frozen sneer of rage, lips skinned back from his few remaining teeth in a dry, spitless grin. *I'll whitewash* your *fence when I get hold of you, fuckface,* he thought, and pushed the Olds up to ninety, passing a line of slower-moving cars, all headed for Bobbi's place. They all picked up the Command Voice, which was now a hammering litany: STOP HIM BEFORE HE CAN DO ANYTHING TO THE SHIP, STOP HIM BEFORE HE CAN DO ANYTHING TO THE SHIP, STOP HIM, STOP HIM, STOP HIM!

4

Gard stood over Bobbi's corpse, half-mad with pain and grief and shock . . . and abruptly his jaws snapped open in another wide, tendon-stretching yawn. He reeled to the sink, trying to hop but doing a bad job of it because of the load of dope he'd taken on. Each time he came down on the bad ankle, it felt as if there was a metal claw inside him, relentlessly digging. The dryness in his throat was much worse now. His limbs felt heavy. His thoughts were losing their former acuteness; they seemed to be . . . *spreading,* like broken egg yolks. As he reached the sink he yawned again and deliberately took a step on the shattered ankle. The pain slashed through the fog like a sharply honed meat cleaver.

He barely cracked the tap marked H and got a glass of warm—almost hot—water. Fumbled in the overhead cabinet, knocking a box of cereal and a bottle of maple syrup onto the floor. His hand closed around the carton of salt with the picture of the little girl on the front. *When it rains it pours,* he thought soupily. *That is very true.* He fumbled at the pour-spout for what seemed like at least a year and then spilled enough salt into the glass to turn the water cloudy. Stirred it with a finger. Chugged it. The taste was like drowning.

He retched, bringing up salt water dyed blue. He saw undissolved chunks of blue pills in the vomitus, as well. Some looked more or less intact. *How many did she get me to take?*

Then he threw up again . . . again . . . again. It was an encore performance of the projectile vomiting in the woods—some overworked circuit in his brain persistently triggering the gag reflex, a deadly hiccuping that could kill.

At last it slowed, then stopped.

Pills in the sink. Bluish water in the sink.

Blood in the sink. A lot.

He staggered backward, came down on the bad ankle, screamed, fell on the floor. He found himself looking into one of Bobbi's glazed eyes across the lumpy terrain of the linoleum, and closed his own. Immediately his mind began to drift away . . . but in that blackness there were voices. No—many voices blended into one. He recognized it. It was the voice of the Shed People.

They were coming for him, as he supposed he had always known they would . . . in time.

Stop him . . . stop him . . . stop him!

Get moving or they won't have *to stop you. They'll shoot you or disintegrate you or whatever they want to do to you while you're snoozing on the floor.*

He got to his knees, then managed to get to his feet with the help of the counter. He thought there was a box of No-Doz in the bathroom cabinet, but doubted if his stomach would hold them down after the latest insult he had dealt it. Under other circumstances it might have been worth the experiment, but Gardener was afraid that if the projectile vomiting started again, it might not stop.

Just keep moving. If it gets really bad, take a few steps on that ankle. That'll sharpen you up in a hurry.

Would it? He didn't know. All he knew was he had to move fast right now and wasn't sure he would be able to move for long at all.

He hop-staggered to the kitchen door and looked back one final time. Bobbi, who had rescued Gardener from his demons time after time, was little more than a hulk now. Her shirt was still smoking. In the end he hadn't been able to save her from hers. Just put her out of their reach.

Shot your best friend. Good fucking deal, uh?

He put the back of his hand against his mouth. His stomach grunted. He shut his eyes and forced the vomiting down before it could start.

He turned, opened them again, and started across the living room. The idea was to look for something solid, hop to it, and then hold on to it. His mind kept wanting to be that silver Puffer balloon it became just before he was carried away by the big black twister. He fought it as well as he could and marked things and hopped to them.

If there was a God, and if He was good, perhaps they all would bear his weight and he would make it across this seemingly endless room like Moses and his troops had the desert.

He knew that the Shed People would arrive soon. He knew that if he was still here when they did, his goose wasn't just cooked; it was nuked. They were afraid he might do something to the ship. Well, yes. Now that you mentioned it, that was part of what he had in mind, and he knew he would be safest there.

He also knew he couldn't *go* there. Not yet.

He had business in the shed first.

He made it out onto the porch where he and Bobbi had sat up late on so many summer evenings, Peter asleep on the boards between them. Just sitting here, drinking beers, the Red Sox playing their nightly nine at Fenway, or Comiskey Park, or some damn place, but playing mostly inside Bobbi's radio; tiny baseball men dodging between tubes and circuits. Sitting here with cans of beer in a bucket of cold well water. Talking about life, death, God, politics, love, literature. Maybe even once or twice about the possibility of life on other planets. Gardener seemed to remember such a conversation or two, but perhaps that was only his tired mind goofing with him. They had been happy here. It seemed a very long time ago.

It was Peter his tired mind fixed on. Peter was really the first goal, the first piece of furniture he had to hop to. This wasn't exactly true—the attempted rescue of David Brown had to come prior to ending Peter's torment, but David Brown did not offer him the emotional pulse-point he required; he had never seen David Brown in his life. Peter was different.

"Good old Peter," he remarked to the still hot afternoon (was it yet afternoon? By God it was). He reached the porch steps and then disaster struck. His balance suddenly deserted him. His weight came down on the bad ankle. This time he could almost see the splintered ends of the bones digging into each other. Gardener uttered a high, mewling shriek—not the scream of a woman but of a very young girl in desperate trouble. He grabbed for the porch railing as he collapsed sideways.

During her frantic early July, Bobbi had fixed the railing between the kitchen and the cellar, but had never bothered with the one between the porch and the dooryard. It had been rickety for years, and when Gard put his weight on it, both of the rotted uprights snapped. Ancient wood-dust puffed out into the summer sunlight . . . along with the heads of a few startled termites. Gard pitched sideways off the porch, yelling miserably, and fell into the dooryard with a solid meat thump. He tried to get up, then wondered why he was trying. The world was swaying in front of his eyes. He saw first two mailboxes, then three. He decided to forget the whole thing and go to sleep. He closed his eyes.

5

In this long, strange, and painful dream he was having, Ev Hillman felt/saw Gardener fall, and heard Gardener's thought

(forget the whole thing go to sleep)

clearly. Then the dream began to break up and that seemed good; it was hard to dream. It made him hurt all over, made him ache. And it hurt to combat the green light. If sunlight was too bright

(he remembered it a little sunlight)

you could close your eyes but the green light was inside, *always* inside*—a third eye that saw and a green light that burned. There were other minds here. One belonged to* THE WOMAN, *the other to* THE LESS-MIND *which had once been Peter. Now* THE LESS-MIND *could only howl. It howled sometimes for* BOBBI *to come and let it free from the green light . . . but mostly it only howled as it burned in the torment of the draining.* THE WOMAN *also screamed for release, but sometimes her thoughts cycled into appalling images of hate that Ev could barely stand. So: yes. Better*

(better)

to go to sleep

(easier)

and let it all go . . .

. . . but there was David.

David was dying. Already his thoughts—which Ev had received clearly at first—were falling into a deepening spiral that would end first in unconsciousness and then, swiftly, in death.

So Ev fought the dark.

Fought it and began to call:

"Get up! Get up! You out there in sunlight! I remember sunlight! David Brown deserves his time of sunlight. So get up! *Get up! Get up!* GET

6

UP GET UP GET UP!

The thought was a steady beat in Gardener's head. No; not a beat. It was something like a car, only the wheels were glass, they were cutting into his brain as the car motored slowly across it.

deserves his time of sunlight David Brown GET UP David GET David UP David Brown! GET UP! DAVID BROWN! GET UP! GET UP, DAMMIT!

"All *right!*" Gardener muttered through a mouth that was full of blood. "All *right,* I hear you, leave me alone!"

He managed to get to his knees. He tried to get to his feet. The world grayed out. No good. At least the rasping, cutting voice in his head had let up a little . . . he sensed its owner was somehow looking out of his eyes, using them like dirty windows,

(dreaming through them)

seeing some of what he saw.

He tried to get to his feet again and was again unable.

"My asshole quotient is still very high," Gardener croaked. He spat out two teeth and began to crawl through the dirt of the dooryard toward the shed.

7

Haven came after Jim Gardener.

They came in cars. They came in pickup trucks. They came on tractors. They came on motorcycles. Mrs. Eileen Crenshaw, the Avon lady who had been so bored at Hilly Brown's SECOND GALA MAGIC SHOW, came driving her son Galen's dune-buggy. The Reverend Goohringer rode behind her, the remaining strands of his graying hair blowing back from his sunburned pate. Vern Jernigan came in a hearse he had been trying to convert into a camper before the "becoming" got into high gear. They filled the roads. Ashley Ruvall wove between those on foot like a slalom racer, pedaling his bike like a madman. He had returned home long enough to get something he called a Zap Gun. This spring it had only been an outgrown toy, gathering dust in the attic. Now, equipped with a nine-volt battery and the circuit-board from his little brother's Speak 'n Spell, it was a weapon the Pentagon would have found interesting. It blew holes in things. *Big* holes. This was strapped onto the carrier of his bike, where he had once carried newspapers for delivery. They came in a ripping hurry and there were some accidents. Two people were killed when Early Hutchinson's VW collided with the Fannins' station wagon, but such minor things stopped no one. Their mental chant filled the hollow spaces in the air with a steady, rhythmic cry: *Before he can do anything to the ship! Before he can do anything to the ship!* It was a fine summer's day, a fine day for a killing, and if anyone needed killing it was James Eric Gardener, and so they came, well over five hundred of them in all, good country people who had learned some new tricks. They came. And they brought their new weapons with them.

8

By the time Gardener got halfway to the shed, he began to feel better—perhaps he was getting a second wind. More likely, he supposed, was the possibility that he really *had* gotten rid of almost all the Valium and was now starting to get on top of the rest.

Or maybe the old man was somehow feeding him strength.

Whatever it was, it was enough to get him on his feet again and hopping toward the shed. He clutched at the door for a moment, heart galloping wildly in his chest. He happened to glance down, and saw a hole in the door. It was round. The edges stuck out in a jagged bracelet of white splinters. It had a *chewed* look, that hole.

The vacuum cleaner that ran the buttons. This is how it

got out. It had a New and Improved cutting attachment. Christ, these people really are *crazy.*

He worked his way around the building and a cold certainty came to him: the key would be gone.

Oh Christ, Gard, give it a rest! Why would it—

But it *was.* It *was* gone. The nail where it had hung was empty.

Gardener leaned against the side of the shed, exhausted and trembling, his body sheened with sweat. He looked down and the sun gleamed off something on the ground—the key. The nail slanted down a bit. He had put the key back in a hurry and had probably pulled the nail down a bit in the soft wood himself. It had simply slid off.

He bent painfully, picked it up, and began to shamble around to the front again. He was exquisitely aware of how fast time was passing. They would arrive soon; how could he possibly get his business done in the shed and then get out to the ship before they did? Since it was impossible, it was probably best to ignore it.

By the time he got back to the shed door, he could hear the faint sound of motors. He stabbed the key at the lock and missed the keyway. The sun was bright, his shadow little more than a puddle hanging from his heels. Again. This time the key socked home. He turned it, shoved the door open, and lurched into the shed.

Green light enfolded him.

It was strong—stronger than it had been the last time he was here. That big piece of cobbled-together equipment

(the transformer)

was glowing brightly. It was cycling, as it had been before, but the cycles were faster now. Thin green fire ran across the silvery road maps of circuit-boards.

He looked around. The old man, floating in his green bath, was looking back at Gardener with his one good eye. That gaze was tortured . . . but sane.

Use the transformer to save David

"Old man, they are coming for me," Gardener croaked. "I'm out of time."

Corner, far corner

He looked and saw something that looked a bit like a television antenna, a bit like a large coat-hanger mobile, and a bit like those back-yard devices on which women hang clothes, turning them to do so.

"That?"

Take it out into the dooryard

Gardener didn't question. There was no time. The thing stood on a small square platform. Gardener supposed its circuits and batteries were in that. Close-up, he saw that the things which looked like the bent arms of a TV antenna were really narrow steel tubes. He seized the central pole. The thing wasn't heavy, but it was awkward. He was going to have to put some weight on his shattered ankle, like it or not.

He looked back at the tank in which Ev Hillman floated.

You sure about this, old-timer?

But it was the woman who answered. Her eyes opened. Looking into them was like looking into the witches' caldron in *Macbeth*. For a moment Gard forgot all his pain and weariness and sickness. He was held in thrall by that poisoned gaze. In that instant he understood all the truth and all the power of the fearsome woman Bobbi had called Sissy, and the reason Bobbi had fled from her, as from a fiend. She *was* a fiend. She *was* a witch. And even now, in her fearful agony, her hate held.

Take it, you stupid man! *I'll* run it!

Gardener put his hurt foot down and screamed as a savage hand reached all the way up from his ankle to seize the soft double sac of his testicles.

The old man:

wait wait

It rose on its own. Not far; only an inch or two. The green swamplight brightened even more.

You'll have to guide it, son

This he was able to manage. It wavered across the green shed like the skeleton of a crazy beach umbrella, nodding and dipping, casting weird elongated shadows on the walls and floor. Gardener hopped clumsily after it, not wanting, not *daring,* to look back into that insane woman's eyes. Over and over his mind played a single thought: *Bobbi Anderson's sister was a witch . . . a witch . . . a witch . . .*

He guided the bobbing umbrella out into the sunlight.

9

Freeman Moss arrived first. He swung the pulp-truck in which Gard had once hitched a ride into Bobbi's dooryard and was out almost before the laboring, farting engine had died. And by Christ, chummy, if the cocksucker wasn't right there, front and center, holding onto something that looked like a woman's clothes whirligig. Man looked like a winded runner. He was holding one of his feet—the left—up, like a dog with a thorn in its paw. That sneaker was bright red, dripping blood.

Looks like Bobbi put at least one good one into you, you snake.

Her murdering pal apparently heard the thought. He looked up and smiled wearily. He was still holding onto the whirligig with the platform stand on the bottom. He was supporting himself on it.

Freeman walked toward him, leaving the driver's door of the old truck hanging open. There was something childlike and winning in the man's grin, and in a moment Freeman understood what it was: with his missing teeth, it was the Halloween punkin grin of a little boy.

Jesus, I sorta liked you—why'd you have to be such a fuckup?

"What you doing out here, Freeman?" Gardener asked. "You should have stuck home. Watched the Red Sox. The fence is all whitewashed."

You sonofawhore!

Moss was wearing a down-filled vest but no shirt beneath; the vest was simply the first thing to come to hand as he rushed out of the house. Now he brushed it aside, revealing not a gimmick or a gadget but a Colt Woodsman. He pulled it out. Gardener stood looking at him, holding the whirligig's post, foot up.

Close your eyes. I'll make it quick. I can do that, at least.

10

(GET DOWN ASSHOLE GET DOWN OR YOU'LL LOSE YOUR HEAD WHEN HE LOSES HIS I DON'T GIVE A TIN SHIT WHO GOES SO GET DOWN IF YOU WANT TO LIVE)

In the tank, Anne Anderson's eyes blazed with stricken hate and fury; her teeth were gone but her bare gums ground together ground together ground together and a trail of small bubbles floated up.

The light pulsed faster and faster, like a carousel speeding up. It became strobelike. The hum rose to a low electric moan, and there was a rich smell of ozone in the shed's air.

On the one lit VDT screen the word

PROGRAM?

was replaced with

DESTROY

It began to flash rapidly, over and over again.

(GET DOWN ASSHOLE OR STAY UP I DON'T CARE WHICH)

11

Gardener ducked. His bad foot hit the ground. Pain leapt up his leg again. He dropped into the dust on his hands and knees.

Over his head, the whirligig began to spin, slowly at first. Moss stared at it, the gun sagging slightly for a moment in his hand. Realization crossed his face during the last instant he still *had* one. Then the slender pipes spilled green fire into the dooryard. For a moment the beach-umbrella illusion was perfect and complete. It looked exactly like a big green one that has been partially lowered so that its circular hem touches the ground. But this umbrella was made of fire, and Gard crouched below it, eyes squinted, one hand in front of his face, grimacing as if from strong heat . . . but there *was* no heat, at least not here, underneath Sissy's poison toadstool.

Freeman Moss was at the edge of the parasol. His pants blazed up, then the down vest. For a moment the flames were green; then they flared yellow.

He screamed and staggered backward, dropping the gun. Over Gardener's head, the whirligig spun faster. The skeletal metal arms, which had drooped comically downward, were pulled more and more erect by centrifugal force. The parasol's fire-hem belled outward, and Moss's shoulders and face were enveloped in sheeting flame as he backed away. In Gard's head, that hideous mental wailing began again. He tried to block it out, but there was no way—simply no way. He caught a wavery glimpse of a face running like warm chocolate, then covered his face like a kid at a scary movie.

The flames spun around Bobbi's dooryard in a widening gyre, making a black spiral of dooryard dirt fuse into a gritty sort of glass. Moss's pulp-truck and Bobbi's blue pickup were both in the thing's final circumference; the shed was barely beyond it, although its shape danced like a demon in the heat haze. It was *very* hot at the edge of the circle, if not where Gard crouched; no doubt of that.

The paint on the hood of Moss's truck and on the sides of the pickup first bubbled, then blackened, then burst into flame, burning down to clean white steel. The litter of bark, sawdust, and wood-chips in the back of Moss's truck blazed up like dry kindling in a woodstove. The two big trash-barrels in Bobbi's pickup, made of heavy pressed gypsum, also caught fire and burned like sconces. The dark circle at the edge of the fire-parasol's range became a brand in the shape of a saucer. The army blanket covering the torn seat in the cab of Moss's truck sprang alight, then the seat-covers beneath, then the tindery stuffing; now the entire cab was flickery furnace orange, with the skeletons of springs peering up through the glare.

Freeman Moss staggered backward, twisting and turning, looking like a movie stuntman who has forgotten his flame-suit. He collapsed.

12

Even overmastering Moss's dying screams, Anne Anderson's mental cry:

Eat shit and die! Eat shit and d—

Then, suddenly, something let go in whatever remained of her—there was a final brilliant flare of green light, a sustained pulse that lasted nearly two seconds. The heavy hum of the transformer rose a notch, and every board in the shed picked it up and rattled in sympathetic vibration.

Then the hum dropped back to its former sleepy drone; Anne's head slumped forward in the liquid, her hair trailing like that of a drowned woman. On the computer screen,

DESTROY

winked out like a blown candle and became

PROGRAM?

again.

13

The fiery parasol wavered, then disappeared. The whirligig, which had been spinning at a mad rate, began to slow, squeaking rhythmically, like an unlatched gate in a mild breeze. The pipes sank back to their former angle. It squeaked once more, then stopped.

The gas-tank of Bobbi's truck suddenly exploded. More yellow flames spouted at the sky. Gard felt a piece of metal whiz by him.

He raised his head and stared stupidly at the blazing truck, thinking: *Bobbi and I used to go to the Starlite Drive-In over in Derry in that truck sometimes. I think we even got laid there once during some stupid Ryan O'Neal picture. What happened? Lord, what happened?*

In his mind, the old man's voice, almost exhausted, but somehow imperative:

Quick! I can power the transformer when the rest come, but you got to be quick! The boy! David! Quick, man!

Not much time, Gardener thought wearily. *Jesus, there never is.*

He started back toward the open door of the shed, sweating, cheeks waxy-pale. He paused at that dark burned ring in the dirt, and then hopped clumsily over it. He somehow didn't want to touch it. He tottered on the edge of balance and then managed to hop on. As he made his way back inside the shed, the twin gas tanks of Moss's truck went up with a furious roar. The cab tore free of the body. The truck flipped over on its side like a tiddlywink. Burning chunks of seat-cover and seat-stuffing began to float out of the open passenger window and floated upward like blazing feathers. Most fell back into the dooryard and went out. A few, however, wafted their way over to the porch, and three or four actually floated through the open door on the first faint puff of the easterly wind which would soon come up. One of these burning cotton puffs alighted on a paperback novel which Gardener had left on the table just inside the door a week ago. The cover caught on fire.

In the living room, another burning fragment of seat-stuffing lit up a rag rug which Mrs. Anderson had made in her bedroom and sent surreptitiously to Bobbi one day when Anne was gone.

When Jim Gardener came out of the shed again, the entire house was on fire.

14

The light in the shed was at its lowest level ever—a dim and watery green the color of stagnant pond water.

Gardener looked cautiously toward Anne, afraid of those blazing eyes. But there was nothing to be afraid of. She only floated, head bent forward as if in deep thought, her hair trailing upward.

She's dead, son. If you're going to get the boy, it has to be now. I don't know how long I can provide the power. And I can't be divided, with half of myself looking out for *them* and half running the transformer.

He stared out at Gardener, and Gard felt deep pity . . . and admiration for the old bastard's brute courage. Could he have done half as much, gone half as far, if their positions had been reversed? He doubted it.

You're in a lot of pain, aren't you?

I ain't exactly feeling in the pink, son, if that's what you mean. But I'll get through it . . . if you get going, that is.

Get going. Yes. He had dilly-dallied too long, far too long.

His mouth popped open in another wrenching yawn, and then he stepped toward the equipment in and around that orange crate—what the old man called the transformer.

PROGRAM?

the keyless computer screen beckoned.

Hillman could have told Gardener what to do, but Gardener didn't need to be told. He knew. He also remembered the nosebleed and the blast of sound he'd taken as a result of his single experiment with Moss's levitation gadget. This made that thing look like a box of Lincoln Logs. Still, he had gone quite a ways down the path to becoming himself since then, like it or not. He would just have to hope it was enou—

Oh shit, son, hold the phone, we got company.

Then a louder voice overrode Hillman's, a voice Gard vaguely recognized but could not put a name to.

(BACK OFF BACK OFF HOLD ON ALL OF YOU)

Just I think just one or maybe two

That was the old man's exhausted mental voice again. Gardener felt his concentration go out to the whirligig in the dooryard. In the shed, the light began to grow bright once more, and the killing pulses began.

15

Dick Allison and Newt Berringer were still two miles from Bobbi's place when Freeman Moss's mental shrieks began. Moments before, they had swerved past Elt Barker. Now Dick looked up into the rearview mirror and saw Elt's Harley swerve across the road and go leaping through the air. For a moment Elt looked like Evel Knievel, white hair or no. Then he separated from the bike and landed in the scrub.

Newt hit the brakes with both feet and his truck screamed to a stop in the middle of the road. He looked at Dick with large eyes that were both frightened and furious.

Son of a bitch has got a gadget!

Yeah. Fire. Some kind of

Abruptly Dick raised his mental voice to a shout. Newt picked it up, amplified it. From Kyle Archinbourg's Cadillac, Kyle and Hazel McCready joined in.

(BACK OFF BACK OFF HOLD ON ALL OF YOU)

They stopped, holding their positions. They were not great takers of orders as a rule, these Tommyknockers, but Moss's hideous screams, fading now, were great persuaders. All stopped, that was, except for a blue Oldsmobile Delta 88 with a bumper sticker on the back reading REALTORS SELL IT BY THE ACRE.

When the command came to back off and hold position, Andy Bozeman was already in sight of the Anderson place. His hate had grown exponentially—Gardener lying bleeding and dead was all he could think of. He came slewing into Bobbi's driveway in a wild power turn. The Olds's rear end broke free when Bozeman stamped the brake; the big car nearly tipped over.

I'll whitewash *your* fence, you fucking asshole. I'll give *you* a dead rat and a string to swing it on, oh you bastard.

His wife pulled the molecule-exciter out of her purse. It looked like a Buck Rogers blaster which had been created by a fairly bright lunatic. Its frame had once been part of a garden tool marketed under the trade name of Weed Eater. She leaned out the car window and pulled the trigger utterly at random. The east end of Bobbi's farmhouse exploded into a caldron of fire. Ida Bozeman grinned a cheerful, reptilian grin.

As the Bozemans began to get out of the Olds, the whirligig started to spin. A moment later the green parasol of flame began to form. Ida Bozeman tried to aim what she called her "molecule disco" at it, but too late. If her first shot had hit the whirligig instead of the house, everything might have been different . . . but it didn't.

The two of them went up like firetrees. A moment later the Olds exploded with three payments still due on it.

16

Now, with the screams of Freeman Moss just beginning to fade from their minds, the screams of Andy and Ida Bozeman took their place. Newt and Dick waited them out, grimacing.

At last they faded.

Ahead, Dick Allison could see other vehicles parked on both sides of Route 9, and in the middle. Frank Spruce was leaning out of the cab of his big tanker truck, looking toward Newt and Dick urgently. He/they sensed the others—all the others—on this road, on other roads; some were standing in the fields they had been cutting across. All of them waiting for something—some decision.

Dick turned toward Newt.

Fire.

Yes. Fire.

Can we put it out?

There was a short mental silence as Newt thought about it; Dick could sense him wanting to simply push it aside and go on to where Gardener was. What Dick wanted wasn't complicated: he wanted to rip out Jim Gardener's gizzard. But that wasn't the answer and they both knew it—all the Shed People, even Adley, knew it. The stakes were higher now. And Dick was confident Jim Gardener was going to lose his gizzard anyway, in one fashion or another.

Crossing the Tommyknockers was a bad idea. It made them mad. This was a truth many races on other worlds had found out long before today's festivities in Haven.

He and Newt both looked out toward the tree-bordered field where Elt Barker had crashed. The grasses and the plumes of the trees were blowing—not hard, but clearly blowing in a wind which blew from east to west. Not even enough breeze to qualify as a cap o' wind . . . but Dick thought it showed signs of brisking.

Yes we can put out the fire, Newt replied at last.

Stop the fire and the drunk too? Can we be sure of that?

Another long, thinking pause, and then Newt came to the answer that Dick had already suspected.

I don't know if we can do both. I know one or the other but I don't know if we can do both.

Then we'll let the fire burn for now we'll
let it burn yes all right
The ship will be all right the ship
will not be hurt and the wind the way the wind's blowing

They looked at each other, grinning, as their thoughts came together in a moment of utter, chiming harmony—one voice, one mind.

The fire will be between him and the ship. He won't be able to get to the ship!

On the roads and in the fields, the people listening in on this party-line all relaxed slightly. *He won't be able to get to the ship.*

Is he still in the shed?

Yes.

Newt turned his puzzled, troubled face to Dick.

What the fuck's he *doing* in there? Does he have something making something? Something to hurt the ship?

There was a pause; and then Dick's voice, not just to Newt Berringer but to all the Shed People, clear and imperative:

NET YOUR MINDS. NET YOUR MINDS WITH OURS. ALL WHO CAN, NET YOUR MINDS WITH OURS AND LISTEN. LISTEN FOR GARDENER. LISTEN.

They listened. In the hot summer silence of the early afternoon, they listened. Two or three ridges over, the first smudges of smoke rose into the sky.

17

Gardener *felt* them listening. There was a horrid crawling sensation over the surfaces of his brain. It was ridiculous, but it was *happening*. He thought: *Now I know how a streetlight must feel with a lot of moths fluttering around it.*

The old man moved in his tank, trying to catch Gardener's eye. He missed his eye but caught his mind. Gardener looked up.

Never mind, son—they want to know what you're up to, but forget them. Won't hurt if they find out. Might even help. Slow 'em down. Relieve their minds. They don't care about David, only about their goddam ship. Go on, son! Go on!

Gardener was standing by the transformer and holding one of the earplugs in his hand. He didn't want to put it in. He felt like a man who's gotten a hefty shock from one particular switch-plate who is compelled to touch that same switch-plate again.

Do I really have to wear this fucker? I changed the screen just by thinking before.

Yes and that's all you *can* do. You got to wear it, son. I'm sorry.

Incredibly, Gardener's eyelids were growing heavy again. He had to force them up.

I'm afraid it will kill me, he thought at the old man, and then waited, hoping the old man would contradict him. But there was nothing—only the pained eye looking at him, and the dim *slisshh-slishhh-slissshhh* of the equipment.

Yeah, it may kill me, and he knows it, too.

Outside, dimly, he could hear the crackle of fire.

The fluttering feeling along the surfaces of his mind stopped. The moths had flown away.

Reluctantly Gardener put the plug in his ear.

18

Kyle and Hazel relaxed. They looked at each other. There was an identical—and very human—expression in their eyes. The expression of people discovering something just too good to be true.

David Brown? Kyle thought unbelieving at Hazel. Is that what you

pick up yes he's trying to save the kid, to

to bring him back

back from Altair-4

Then, for a moment overriding the net, came Dick Allison's voice, excited and full of sour triumph:

Hot DAMN! I KNEW that kid would come in handy!

19

For a moment Gardener felt nothing at all. He began to relax, on the edge of a doze again. Then pain hit him in a single awful crunch, a destructive battering ram that would tear his head apart.

"No!" he screamed. His hands went to his temples; beat against them. *"No, God no, it hurts too much, Jesus, no!"*

Ride with it, son, try to ride with it!

"*I can't I can't* OH CHRIST MAKE IT STOP!"

This made his shattered ankle feel like a mosquito bite. He was dimly aware that his nose was bleeding and that his mouth was filled with blood.

RIDE WITH IT, SON!

The pain backed off a little. It was replaced with another feeling. This new sensation was horrible, horrible and terrifying.

Once, while in college, he had participated in something called the Great McDonald's Eat-Out. Five frats had fielded "champion eaters." Gard had been Delta Tau Delta's "champ." He had been on his sixth Big Mac—not even close to the contest winner's eventual total—and had become suddenly aware that he was very close to total physical overload. He had never felt anything like it in his life. In a gross way it was almost interesting. His midsection felt thundery with food. He did not feel like vomiting; nausea did not exactly describe what it had been like. He saw his stomach as a huge, still dirigible lying bloated in still air at his center. He thought he could sense red lights going on in some mental Mission Control Center as various systems tried to deal with this insane load of meat, bread, and sauce. He didn't vomit. He walked it off. Very slowly, he walked it off. For hours he had felt like those drawings of Tweedledum and Tweedledee, his stomach stretched and smooth and terribly close to bursting.

Now it was his *mind* that felt like that, and Jim Gardener understood as coldly and rationally as a trapeze performer who works with no net that he was on the knife-edge of death. But there was another sensation, one which was unrelatable to anything, and for the first time he understood what the Tommyknockers were all about—what moved them; what propelled them onward.

In spite of the pain, which had only retreated, not left, and in spite of that dreadful smooth feeling of being as stuffed as a python which has swallowed a kid, part of him was *enjoying* this. It was like a drug—an incredibly powerful drug. His brain felt like the engine in the biggest fucking Chrysler ever built, idling on fat gas, waiting for him to drop the car into gear and peel out.

Peel out to where?

Anywhere.

The stars, if he wanted.

Son I'm losing you

That was the old man, sounding more exhausted than ever, and Gardener pulled himself back to the job at hand—the next piece of furniture he had to hop to. Oh, this feeling was drunkenly wonderful, but it was stolen. He forced himself to think again of those leaf-brown shapes locked in all those hammocks. Galley slaves. The old man was powering him; he was drinking the old man like a vampire drinking blood. How long until he was a vampire himself? Like *them?*

He thought at Hillman: I am with you, old horse.

Ev Hillman close his one good eye in silent relief. Gard turned to the monitor screen, absently holding the plug in his ear like a newsman on a live remote listening to a question from the anchor back in the studio.

In the closed space of Bobbi's shed, the light began to cycle up again.

20

listen

They all listened; they were all on a party-line which covered all of Haven, radiating out from a center about two miles from that still-faint smudge of smoke. They were all on the net and they all listened. They accepted no absolute common; Tommyknockers was a name they accepted as casually as any, but they were really interstellar gypsies with no king. Yet in this moment of crisis during the period of regeneration—a period when they were so vulnerable—they were willing to accept the voices of those Gardener called the Shed People. They were, after all, the clearest distillation of them all.

the time has come to close the borders

There was a universal sigh of agreement—a mental sound Ruth McCausland would have recognized: a sound like autumn leaves blown before a November wind.

For the time being, at least, the Shed People had lost all contact with Gardener. They were only content that he was occupied elsewhere. If he meant to go to their ship, the fire would soon be in his way.

The unified voice quickly explained the rota that was to be followed—some of these plans had been made, vaguely, weeks ago—these plans had become more concrete as the Shed People "became."

Gadgets had been made—haphazardly, it had seemed. But birds flying south as winter approaches may seem haphazard; their migration may even seem so to themselves—just something which felt like as good a way as any to spend the winter months. Want to go to North Carolina, dear? Of course, my love; what a wonderful idea.

So they had built, and sometimes they had killed each other with their new toys, and sometimes they had finished gadgets, looked at them doubtfully, and packed them away somewhere out of sight, since they were no obvious help in their daily round. But some they had toted out to Haven's borders, usually in the trunks of cars or in the backs of trucks, under tarps. One of these gadgets had been the Coke machine which had murdered John Leandro; it had been customized by the late Dave Rutledge, who had once serviced such machines for a living. One had been the Bensohn brush-trimmer which had cut up a storm on Lester Moran. There were duded-up televisions which shot fire; there were smoke-detectors (Gardener had seen some but not all of these on his first visit to the shed) which flew through the air like Frisbees, emitting killing waves of ultrasonic sound; at several locations there were force-barriers. Almost all of these gadgets could be mentally activated with the help of simple electronic devices which were casually dubbed "Callers," not much different from the device Freeman Moss had used to float the drainage machinery into the woods.

No one thought more about why these gadgets should be placed in a rough perimeter around the town than a bird thinks about flying south or a caterpillar thinks about weaving a cocoon. But of course, this time always came—the time when the borders had to be sealed. This time had come early . . . but, it seemed, not *too* early.

The Shed People also suggested that a number of Tommyknockers go back to the village. Hazel McCready was designated to go with them—she would be the representative of the more advanced Tommyknockers. The stuff protecting the borders would run pretty much without supervision until the batteries were dead. In the village there were more discretionary gadgets which could be sent into the woods to form a protective net around the ship, in case the drunk made a break for it.

And there was one other very important gadget which needed guarding on the off-chance that anyone—anyone at all—should break through. This gadget sat in Hazel McCready's backyard like a one-ring circus under a large five-man tent. It was the safety net. It would do many of the things the transformer in the shed could do, but this thing, which had once been a furnace, was vitally different from the transformer in the shed in two respects. The galvanized aluminum pipes which had once led to the ventilators in the various rooms of the McCready house now all pointed skyward. Hooked up to this New and Improved furnace, on two plywood ramps protected from the elements by more of the silvery netting which lined the trench in which the ship lay, were twenty-four truck batteries. When this gadget was turned on, it would make air.

Tommyknocker air.

Once this small atmosphere-manufacturing factory was in operation, they would no longer be at the mercy of winds and weather—even in the event of a hurricane, the air-exchanger, which had been surrounded by force-shields, would protect most of them if they gathered in the village.

The suggestion that the borders should be closed came as Gardener was putting one of the transformer earphones into his own ear. Five minutes later, Hazel and about forty others had dropped out of the net and were headed back to town—some to the town hall to oversee the borders and protect the ship with other gadgets; some to make sure the atmosphere factory was protected, in case of accident . . . or in case the reaction from the outside world was quicker, more informed, and better organized than they expected. All these things had happened before, at other times, on other worlds, and affairs were usually concluded in a satisfactory fashion . . . but the "becoming" did not *always* have a happy ending.

During the ten minutes between the command to close the borders and the departure of Hazel's party, the size and shape of the smoke rising into the sky did not change appreciably. The wind was not rising much . . . at least, not yet. This was good because the attention of the outside world would be slower in turning toward *them.* It was bad because Gardener would not be cut off from the ship so soon.

Still—Newt/Dick/Adley/Kyle thought Gardener's goose was just about cooked. They held the remaining Tommyknockers in place for five minutes, waiting for mental notice that the gadgets along the borders were waking up, getting ready to do their jobs.

This came as an awakening hum.

Newt looked at Dick. Dick nodded. The two of them dropped out of the net, and turned their attention back to the shed. Gardener, who had once been impossible for even Bobbi to pick up, was still a tough nut to crack. But they should have been able to read the transformer with no trouble at all; its steady, heavy pulses of energy should have been as easy for them to "hear" as RF interference on a TV or radio from the small motor in an electric mixer.

But the transformer was barely a whisper—no more than the dim sound of the ocean in a conch shell.

Newt looked at Dick again, frightened.

jesus he's gone motherfucker's

Dick smiled. He did not believe that Gardener, who could still barely thought-read or -send at all, could have accomplished his purpose so quickly . . . if it had ever been possible for him to accomplish at all. The man's presence here and Bobbi's perverse affection for him had been a nuisance . . . one which Dick now believed at an end.

He winked one of his strange eyes at Newt. This odd mixture of human and alien was both hideous and hilarious at the same time.

Not gone, Newt. The asshole's DEAD.

Newt looked at Dick thoughtfully for a moment, then began to smile.

They moved in, all of them together, drawing in toward Bobbi's house like a tightening noose.

21

Carrying a heavy head.

The phrase chimed constantly in the back of Gard's mind as he turned toward the monitor screen—it seemed to have been there for a long time. Once, and for a Jim Gardener that no longer existed, his poems had formed around such lines, like pearls around chips of grit.

Carrying a heavy head now, boss.

Was it from some chain-gang movie, like *Cool Hand Luke?* A song? Yeah. Some song. Something which seemed oddly mixed in his mind, something from the West Coast sixties, a waif-faced psychedelic flower-child wearing a Hell's Angels jacket and carrying a bike chain wrapped around one thin white violinist's hand . . .

Your mind, Gard, something happening to your mind—

Yeah, you're fucking-A, big daddy, I'm carrying a heavy head, that's what, I was born to be wild, I been caught in the crosstown traffic, and if they say I never loved you, you know they are a liar. Carrying a heavy head. I can feel every vein, artery, and capillary in it swelling up, getting plump, standing out the way the veins on our hands used to when we were kids and wrapped a dozen rubber bands around our wrists and left them there to see what would happen. Carrying a heavy head. If I looked into a mirror right now, I know what I'd see—green light spilling out of my pupils like the pencil-beams of flashlights. Heavy head—and if you joggle it, it will burst. Yes. So be careful, Gard. Be

careful, son

Yeah old man yeah.

David

Yeah.

That feeling of dipping and swaying out over the drop. He remembered the news film of Karl Wallenda, that grand old man of the aerialists, falling from the wire in Puerto Rico—gripping for the line, finding it, holding for a minute—then, gone.

Gardener dismissed it from his mind. He tried to dismiss everything from his mind and prepared to be a hero. Or die trying.

22

PROGRAM?

Gard pushed the earphone deep into his ear and frowned at the screen. Drove the heavy ram of his thoughts toward it. Felt pain flare; felt the balloon of his brain swell a little more. The pain faded; the feeling of increased swelling remained. He stared at the screen.

ALTAIR-4

Okay . . . what next? He listened for the old man to tell him, but there was nothing. Either his mental link to the transformer had excluded the old man or the old man didn't know. Did it really matter which? Nope.

He looked at the screen.

CROSS-FILE WITH—

The screen suddenly filled up with 9s, from top to bottom and side to side. Gardener stared at this with consternation, thinking: *Oh Jesus Christ, I broke it!*

The 9s disappeared. For just a moment

OH JESUS CHRIST I BROKE IT

glimmered on the screen like a ghost. Then the screen showed:

CROSS-FILE READY

He relaxed a little. The machine was okay. But his brain really was stretched to capacity, and he knew it. If this machine, which was being powered by the old man and whatever was left of Peter, could bring the boy back, he might actually be able to walk away . . . or hop, considering his ankle. But if it was going to try to draw from *him* as well, his brain would pop like a party noisemaker.

But this really wasn't the time to think of that, was it?

Licking his lips with his numb tongue, he looked at the screen.

CROSS-FILE WITH DAVID BROWN

9s across the screen.
9s for eternity.

CROSS-FILE SUCCESSFUL

Okay. Good. What next? Gardener shrugged. He knew what he was trying to do; why dance?

BRING DAVID BROWN BACK FROM ALTAIR-4

9s across the screen. *Two* eternities this time. Then a message appeared which was so simple, so logical, and yet so loony that Gard would have screamed laughter if he hadn't known to do so would be to blow every working circuit he had left.

WHERE DO YOU WANT TO PUT HIM?

The urge to laugh passed. The question had to be answered. Where indeed? Home plate at Yankee Stadium? Piccadilly Circus? On the breakwater jutting out from the beach in front of the Alhambra Hotel? None of those places; of course not—but not here in Haven. Christ, no. Even if the air didn't kill him, which it probably would, his parents were turning into monsters.

So, where?

He looked up at the old man, and the old man was looking back at him urgently, and suddenly it came to him—there was really only one place *to* put him, wasn't there?

He told the machine.

He waited for it to ask for further clarification, or to say it couldn't be done, or to suggest a system of commands he would be unable to execute. Instead, there were more 9s. This time they stayed forever. The green pulsing from the transformer became almost too bright to look at.

Gard closed his eyes and in the greenish deep-sea darkness behind his lids he thought he could hear, faintly, the old man screaming.

Then the power that had filled his mind left. Bingo! It was gone. Just like that. Gardener staggered backward, the earphone popping free and hitting the floor. His nose was still bleeding and he had soaked a fresh shirt. How many pints of blood were in the human body? And what had happened? There had been no

TRANSFER SUCCESSFUL

or

TRANSFER UNSUCCESSFUL

or even

A TALL DARK TOMMYKNOCKER WILL ENTER YOUR LIFE.

What had it all been *for?* He realized miserably that he was never going to know. Two lines of Edwin Arlington Robinson came to him: *So on we worked, and waited for the light,/And went without the meat, and cursed the bread . . .*

No light, boss; no light. If you wait for it they'll burn you in your tracks, and here's a fence ain't even half whitewashed yet.

No light; just a dull blank screen. He looked toward the old man and the old man was lolling forward, head down, exhausted.

Gardener was crying a little. His tears were mixed with blood. Dull pain radiated from the plate in his head, but that stuffed, near-to-bursting feeling was gone. So was the sense of power. He missed the latter, he discovered. Part of him longed for it to come back, no matter what the consequences.

Get moving, Gard.

Yes, okay. He had done what he could for David Brown. Maybe something had happened; maybe nothing. Maybe he had killed the kid; maybe David Brown, who had probably played with Star Wars action figures and wished he could meet an E.T. like Elliot had in the movie, was now just a cloud of dissipating atoms somewhere in deep space between Altair-4 and here. It was not for him to know. But he had reached this piece of furniture and held it long enough—too long, maybe. He knew it was time to move on.

The old man raised his head.

Old man, do you know?

If he's safe? No. But, son, you did your best. I thank you. Now please please, son please

Fading . . . the old man's mental voice was fading

please let me out of this

down a long hallway and

look on one of those shelves back there

Now Gardener had to strain to hear.

pleas oh PLEA

Faint, a whisper; the old man's head lolling forward, remains of thin white hair floating in green brew.

Peter's legs moved dreamily as he chased rabbits in his dim sleep . . . or looked for Bobbi, his darling.

Gard hopped over to the back shelves. They were dark, dusty, greasy. Here were old forgotten Buss fuses and a Maxwell House can full of bolts and washers and hinges and keys with locks whose location and purpose had long since been forgotten.

On one of these shelves was a Transco Sonic Space Blaster. Another kid's toy. On the side was a switch. He supposed the child who had received this for his birthday used it to make the gun ululate at different frequencies.

What did it do now?

Who gives a fuck? Gardener thought wearily. *All this shit has become one big dumb bore.*

Bore or not, he put the gun in his belt and hopped back across the shed. At the door, he looked back at the old man.

Thanks, guy.

Faint, fainter, faintest—a dry rustle of leaves:

out of this son

Yes. You and Peter both. You bet

He hopped outside and looked around. No one else had come yet. That was good—but his luck couldn't hold much longer. They were there; his mind touched theirs, like a couple waltzing with the care of strangers. He sensed them linked in a

(net)

single consciousness. They were not hearing him . . . feeling him . . . *whatever* they did. Either using the transformer or just being in the shed had cut his mind off from theirs. But they'd soon know that, like Elvis, fat, flailing, but game and blindly bopping just the same, he had made a comeback.

The sunshine was dazzling. The air was hot, full of a burning stink. Bobbi's farmhouse was blazing like a heap of dry kindling in a fireplace. As he watched, half the roof fell in. Sparks, nearly colorless in the bright declining day, rushed up to the sky in a flume. Dick, Newt, and the others had not observed much smoke because the fire was burning hot and colorless. Most of the smoke they'd seen had come from the burning vehicles in the dooryard.

Gard stood for a moment on his good leg in the shed doorway and then hopped for the whirligig. He made it about halfway and then sprawled full-length in the dust. As he came down, he thought of the Sonic Space Blaster in his belt. A kid's toy. No safety on a kid's toy. If the trigger was depressed, the essential Gardener might suddenly be drastically reduced. The Tommyknocker Weight-Loss Plan. He took the toy gun out of his belt, handling it as if it were a live mine. He crawled the rest of the way to the whirligig on his hands and knees, then pulled himself up.

Forty feet away, the other half of Bobbi's roof collapsed. Hot sparks whirled toward the garden and the woods beyond. Gard turned toward the shed and thought again, as hard as he could: *Thank you, my friend.*

He thought there was an answer—some weary, faint answer.

Gardener pointed the toy at the shed and pulled its trigger. A green ray no thicker than a pencil-lead shot out of its muzzle. There was a sound like bacon frying in a skillet. For a moment the green beam splashed from the side of the shed like water from a hose, and then the boards burst into flame. *More hot work,* Gardener thought wearily. *Smokey the Bear wouldn't dig me at all.*

He began to hop toward the back of the house, the Sonic Space Blaster in his hand. Sweat and bloody tears ran down his face. *Winston Churchill would have loved me,* he thought, and began to laugh. He saw the Tomcat . . . and then his jaws spread in another big yawn. It occurred to him that possibly Bobbi had saved his life without even knowing it. In fact, it was more than possible;

it was likely. The Valium could have protected him from the full force of the unimaginable power load that transformer carried. It might well have been the Valium which—

Something inside the burning house—one of Bobbi's gadgets—exploded with an artillery-shell bang. Gard ducked his head instinctively. Half of the house seemed to suddenly lift off. The far side of it, fortunately for Gardener. He looked up into the sky, and a second yawn turned into a large stupid gape.

There goes Bobbi's Underwood.

It flew up and up, a typewriter in the sky, whirling and turning.

Gard hopped on. He reached the Tomcat. The key was in the ignition. That was good. He'd had enough troubles with keys to last him the rest of his life—what little might remain.

He pulled himself up onto the seat. Behind him, vehicles approached and turned into the dooryard. He didn't turn around to look. The Tomcat was parked too close to the house. If he didn't get moving right now, he was going to bake like an apple.

He turned on the key. The Tomcat's motor made no sound, but that didn't bother him. It was vibrating faintly. Something else exploded inside the house. Sparks drifted down and prickled his skin. More vehicles turning into the yard. The minds of the arriving Tommyknockers were turned toward the shed, and they thought

baked apple he's
baked inside the shed
dead in the shed right yes

Good. Let them think that. The New and Improved Tomcat wouldn't clue them in. It was as noisy as a Ninja. And he had to go; the garden was already on fire, the giant sunflowers and huge cornstalks with their giant inedible ears of corn blazing. But the path down through the middle of the garden was still passable.

Hey! Hey! HEY, HE'S BEHIND THE HOUSE! HE'S ALIVE! HE'S STILL—

Gardener looked to his right, dismayed, and saw Nancy Voss roaring across the stony field which lay between Bobbi's place and the stone wall at the edge of the Hurd property. The Voss woman was on a Yamaha trail bike. Her hair was tied in braids which flew out behind her.

Her face was a harridan's glare . . . although she still looked like Rebecca of Sunnybrook Farm next to Sissy, Gard thought.

HEY! BACK HERE! BACK HERE!

Oh, you bitch, Gardener thought, and raised the Sonic Space Blaster.

23

Twenty or thirty of them had entered the yard. Adley and Kyle were among them; so were Frank Spruce, the Goldens, Rosalie Skehan, and Pop Cooder. Newt and Dick were back by the road, keeping all in order.

All of them turned toward

HERE! BACK HERE! ALIVE! THE SON OF A BITCH IS STILL

Nancy Voss's screams. They all saw her charging across the field on the bike, looking like a jockey riding a hard-charging horse as the Yamaha's tough suspension system bounced her up and down. They all saw the green pencil-beam shoot out from behind the burning house and envelop her.

None of them saw the whirligig as it started to turn again.

24

One whole side of the shed was in flames. Part of the roof fell in. Sparks swirled in a fat spiral. One landed in a pile of greasy rags and they bloomed with fire-roses.

Deliverance, Ev Hillman thought. *Last thing of all. Last thing—*

The transformer began to pulse a brilliant green for the last time, for a moment or two rivaling the fire.

25

Dick Allison heard the creak of the whirligig. His mind was filled with a furious, feral cry of rage as he realized Gardener was still alive. All of it happened fast; very fast. Nancy Voss was a flaming rag-doll in the field to the right of Bobbi's house. Her Yamaha ran on for twenty yards, struck a rock, and turned a backover flip.

Dick saw the burned hulks of Bobbi's truck, Moss's truck, the Bozemans' Olds—and then he saw the whirligig.

GET AWAY FROM THAT THING! GET AWAY! GET

But there was no chance. Dick had fallen out of the net and he couldn't get past the two thoughts it beat out like a primitive rock-and-roll backbeat:

Still alive. Behind the house. Still alive. Behind the house.

More people were arriving. They were moving across the dooryard in a tidal flow, ignoring the blazing house, the blazing shed, the guttering, blackened vehicles.

NO! FUCKING DAMN FOOLS! NO! GET DOWN! GET AWAY!

Mesmerized, Newt was staring at the inferno of the house, ignoring the whirligig, spinning faster and faster, and in that moment Dick could cheerfully have killed him. But he still needed him, and so he contented himself with pushing Newt rudely to the ground and falling on top of him.

A moment later, the green parasol spread its delicate web over the yard again.

26

Gard heard the screams—a multitude of them this time—and shut them out as best he could. They didn't matter. Nothing mattered except getting to the last stop on the line.

No sense trying to fly the Tomcat. He threw it into first gear and drove into Bobbi's monstrous useless burning garden.

There came a moment when he began to believe he wasn't going to make it; the fire had caught hold faster in the weeds and overgrown crops than he had believed possible. The heat was baking, tremendous. Soon his lungs would boil.

He heard dull thudding noises, like fat knots of pine exploding in a fireplace, looked, saw pumpkins and gourds exploding like pine knots in a fireplace. The Tomcat's wheel was blistering his hands.

Heat on his head. Gardener reached up. His hair was on fire.

27

The entire inside of the shed was ablaze now. In the middle of it the transformer waxed and waned, waxed and waned, a pulsating cat's-eye in the middle of an inferno.

Peter lay on his side, his legs stilled at last. Ev Hillman was looking at the transformer with exhausted concentration. The fluid encasing him was becoming very, very hot. That was all right; there was no pain, not in the physical sense. The insulation on the main cable connecting him to the transformer was now beginning to melt and fuse. But the connection still held. For the moment, in the burning shed, it held, and Ev Hillman thought:

The last thing. Give him a chance to get away. The last thing—

LAST THING

the computer screen flashed.

LAST THING LAST THING LAST THING

then filled up with 9s.

28

The destruction in Bobbi Anderson's dooryard was incredible.

Dick and Newt watched it, fascinated, almost unbelieving. As in the woods that day with the old man and the cop, Dick found himself wondering how things could *possibly* go so wrong. The two of them—they and all the others who hadn't arrived yet—were well outside the parasol's deadly perimeter, but still Dick didn't get up. He wasn't sure he *could*.

People were burning in the yard like dry scarecrows. Some ran, flapping and cawing and screeching with their voices and their minds. A few—a fortunate few—managed to back away in time. Frank Spruce walked slowly past where Dick and Newt lay, half of his face burned away so his jaw showed on that side in a half-grin. There were flash-explosions as the weapons some of them carried fused and self-destructed.

Dick's eyes met Newt's.

Send them around! Flank him! Got to

Yes I see but oh Christ there must be ten or twenty of us burning

STOP FUCKING WHINING!

Newt recoiled, lips bared in a toothless snarl. Dick ignored him. The mind-net had fallen apart. Now he could make himself heard.

Go around! Go around! Get him! Get the drunk! Go around!

They began to move, slowly at first, their faces dazed, and then with quickening purpose.

29

The computer screen imploded. There was a coughing explosion, like a giant clearing a throat thick with phlegm, and thick green fluid poured from the shower cabinet in which Ev Hillman had been kept prisoner. It met the fire and produced a deadly green steam. Ev, mercifully dead at last, washed out like a fish from a burst aquarium. A moment later, Peter followed. Anne Anderson came last, her dead hands still hooked into claws.

30

The fire-parasol died. Now there was no sound but the screams of the dying and Dick's insistent voice. The summer day was an inferno. Bobbi's dooryard was a dirt pond filled with islands of fire. But the Tommyknockers always brought fire in the end, and they got used to it quickly.

Newt joined his voice with Dick's. Kyle was dead, Adley badly burned. Nevertheless, Ad joined his own mortally wounded voice with theirs:

Get him before he can get to the ship! He's still alive! Get him before he can get to the ship! Before he can get to the ship!

The Tommyknockers had taken a mauling. That fifteen of them had been flash-fried in Bobbi's yard was not very important. But Bobbi was dead; Kyle was dead; Adley soon would be; the transformer had been destroyed just when the border closing had rendered their need for it critical. And Gardener was still alive. Incredibly, Gardener was still alive.

Perhaps worst of all, the wind was freshening.

31

Get him, and get him quick.

On the net; the Tommyknockers were on the net.

They came across the fields; came toward the spreading fire.

QUICK!

Dick Allison turned toward town and the net turned with him like a radar dish. He sensed Hazel's dumb amazement at the turn of events.

He

(the net)

brushed that aside.

Whatever you got out that way, Hazel: send it at him.

Dick turned toward Newt.

You didn't have to push me so effing hard, Newt said sulkily, and wiped a drip of blood from his chin.

"Fuck you," Dick said deliberately. "Let's get that sonofawhore."

32

The whirligig, dead now, had started a fire that was spreading out from Bobbi's house in a shape which resembled a lady's fan—a fire-fan. Bobbi's house, now only black bones shimmering in a red pillar of fire, was at its point of origination. The wings were spreading through the obscenely overgrown garden, and as the mutated plants burned, the fire glowed green.

Passing between the flames was Jim Gardener, crowned with burning hair. His shirt was smoldering; one of the sleeves squirted smoke and then burst into flames. He slapped them out. He wanted to scream but he seemed too tired, too woozy.

I have been badly used, Gardener thought, *and it is no one's fault but my own.*

He reached the far edge of the garden. The Tomcat lurched and waddled down a mild slope and into the woods. The low, scrubby bushes on the sides of the trail were on fire, and low runners of flame were already spreading into Big Injun Woods. Gard cared little for them. The feeling that he was going to be microwaved was passing. He whacked repeatedly at his head. His hair smelled dreadful—like food fried by a child.

Green fire sizzled over his right shoulder as the Tomcat entered the woods.

Gard flinched to the left and ducked. He looked back and there was Hank Buck, with his own Zap Gun. Hank had ridden a motorcycle out to the farm, had dumped it in the same field where Nancy Voss had come to ruin, had picked himself up and started to run.

Gardener turned around, held the Sonic Space Blaster out straight in his right hand, and gripped his right wrist with his left hand. He pulled the trigger. The pencil-beam stabbed out, and more by good luck than any sort of shooting skill, he struck Hank high up on the left side of the chest. There was the sound of frying bacon. Green death splashed up onto Hank's face and he fell over.

Gardener turned forward again and saw the Tomcat moving toward a large burning spruce at a complacent five miles an hour. He hauled on the wheel with both blistered hands, barely avoiding a head-on collision. One of the Tomcat's pillow tires scraped the trunk of the tree, and for a moment Gardener found himself shoving away blazing, fragrant spruce boughs like a man fighting his way through burning curtains. The little tractor tilted sickeningly, tottered . . . then thumped back down again. Gardener pushed the throttle-lever as far as it would go and hung on as the Tomcat made its way up the path into the woods.

33

They came. The Tommyknockers came. They came along the widening wings of that fiery lady's fan, and Dick Allison began to feel a kind of furious desperation, because they weren't going to catch him. Gardener had been able to use the path; that had made all the difference. Three minutes later—maybe even one—and Gardener really *would* have been cooked. Four of the Tommyknockers (Mrs. Eileen Crenshaw and the Reverend Goohringer among them) tried to follow him that way and were burned alive. Two of the gigantic flaming corn plants toppled onto the Crenshaw woman, who shrieked and let go of the dune-buggy's steering bar. The dune-buggy promptly drove itself into the depths of the flaming garden. Its tires exploded like bombs. Bare seconds later, fire choked the whole path.

Dick's frustration went deeper than the bone. The "becoming" had been thwarted and choked off before—not often, but it *had* happened—but always as the result of some natural intervention . . . as a whole generation of mosquito larvae breeding in a quiet, stagnant pond may be killed by a stroke of lightning from a summer storm. But this was no thunderstorm, no natural happening; this was *one man,* a man they had all regarded with the kind of wary contempt reserved for a stupid dog which may bite, this was *one man* who had spent most of his time with Bobbi in a drunken stupor, *one man* who had somehow tricked Bobbi and killed her and who refused to die no matter what they did.

We will not be stopped by one man, Dick thought frenziedly. *We will* NOT! But was there any real way to stop just that from happening? The fire front was now spreading too fast for them to catch him. Gardener had managed to shoot down the center of an alley of fire, but he would be the only one. Hank Buck had had a shot . . . but somehow the fucking son of a bitch had managed to shoot Hank dead.

Dick was in a perfect ecstasy of fury (Newt sensed it and kept his distance—Dick was twenty pounds heavier and ten years younger), but at the center of his rage was terror, like a cold curdle of rancid cream in the middle of a poisoned chocolate.

The Tommyknockers, Bobbi had told Gardener, were great sky travelers. This was true. But never, anywhere, had they met anyone quite like this *one man,* who kept going, even with his shattered ankle, his great loss of blood, and his ingestion of a drug that should have rendered him unconscious fifteen minutes ago, in spite of the great lot he had vomited up.

Impossible—but happening.

Somehow the fire that was supposed to keep Gardener from the ship had become Gardener's shield.

Now there were only the automated monitors—the gadgets.

"They'll get him," Dick whispered. He and Newt were standing on a knoll to the right of the house like a pair of generals, watching people stream into the woods . . . but doing so on a pair of infuriatingly oblique angles. Dick's hands opened; snapped closed; opened; closed. Green blood beat in his neck. "They'll get him, they'll stop him, he's not going to get to the ship, he's not, he's *not.*"

Newt Berringer kept prudently silent.

34

The smoke-detector, very like a flying saucer itself, whickered silently through the woods with the red sensor light on its underside pulsing erratically. Hazel McCready was controlling this baby herself. She had caught Dick Allison's wave of anger, despair, and fear, and had determined to take care of Gardener herself—by remote control, as it were. First she had put Pauline Goudge, whom she felt most trustworthy, to work on one other matter, and then Hazel had gone down to her office, closed the door, and locked it.

From the bottom drawer of her filing cabinet she brought out a ghetto-blaster a little smaller than the late Hank Buck's disposal unit. She put it on her desk, turned it on, took an earphone from the Out basket of her desk-minder, and put the plug in her ear.

Now she sat with her eyes closed, but she could see trees rush past on either side of the smoke-detector as it whizzed through the woods about six feet above the ground. Gardener would have been forcibly reminded of the sequence in *The Return of the Jedi,* when the good guys chase the bad guys through a seemingly endless forest at brain-numbing speeds on what appear to be air motorcycles.

Hazel, however, had no time for metaphors—nor ever would, if they got out of this; Tommyknockers weren't much into metaphors either.

Part of her—the smoke-detector part on the machine side of the cyborg interface she'd made—wanted to fulfill its original function and buzz, because the woods were full of smoke. It was similar to the feeling one has when a sneeze impends like a rainshower.

The smoke-detector banked easily from side to side, slaloming around trees, popping up over knolls, and then zooming back down them like the world's smallest crop-duster.

Hazel sat bent forward at her desk, earplug pushed firmly into her ear, concentrating fiercely. She was pushing the little smoke-detector through the woods faster than was safe, but it had been at the Haven-Newport border, fully five miles from the ship. She had to get to Gardener, and time was short.

The smoke-detector flipped onto its side and missed a small pine tree by inches. A close call, that. But . . . there he was, and there was the ship, throwing back its echoes of light, tattooing its dancing sun-dapples on the trees.

The smoke-detector hovered motionless above the thick mat of fallen needles on the floor of the forest for a moment . . . and then it arrowed directly at Gardener. Hazel prepared to turn on the ultrasound attachment that would turn Gardener's bones to smashed fragments in his body.

35

Hey, Gard! On your left!

The voice was unbelievable. It was also unmistakable. It was Bobbi Anderson's voice. The old, unimproved Bobbi. But Gardener had no time to think about that. He looked left and saw something slashing out of the woods at him. It was tan. There was a red light flashing on its underside. That was all he had time to see.

He brought the Sonic Space Blaster up, wondering how he could ever in the world hope to hit *that* thing, and at the same moment a wild thin shriek, like every mosquito in the world whining in perfect harmony, filled his ears . . . his head . . . his *body*. Yes, it was *inside* him; everything inside him was beginning to vibrate.

Then it felt as if hands seized his wrist—first seized it, then turned it. He fired. Green fire shot across the daylight. The smoke-detector exploded. Several jagged chunks of plastic flew near Gardener's head, barely missing him.

36

Hazel screamed and bolted upright in her old swivel chair. A tremendous backflow of energy surged through the earplug. She clawed at it—and missed. The plug was in her left ear. From her right one came a sudden squirt of greenish, soupy liquid. It looked like radioactive oatmeal. For a moment her brains continued to hose out of her head through her ear, and then the pressure became too great. The right side of her skull pushed open like a strange flower and her brains hit her Currier & Ives wall calendar with a liquid smack.

Hazel fell forward limply onto her desk, her hands outstretched, her glazing eyes staring unbelievingly at nothing.

The ghetto-blaster radio buzzed for a while and then stopped.

37

Bobbi? Gardener thought, looking around wildly.

Fuck you, old hoss, an amused voice returned. *That's all the help you get—after all, I'm dead, remember?*

I remember, Bobbi.

One piece of advice: watch out for rabid vacuum cleaners.

Then she was gone, if she had ever been there. From behind him came the rending, grinding crash of a tree falling over. The woods between here and the farm had begun to sound like a big open-hearth fireplace. Now he could hear voices from behind him, both mental and shouted aloud. Tommyknocker voices.

But Bobbi was gone.

You imagined it, Gard. The part of you that wants Bobbi—that NEEDS *Bobbi—is trying to reinvent her, that's all.*

Yeah, and what about the hand? The hand over my hand? Did I make that up? I couldn't have hit that thing all by myself. Annie Oakley couldn't have hit that thing without help.

But the voices—those in the air and those inside his head—were getting closer. So was the fire. Gardener drew in a throatful of smoke, put the Tomcat in gear again, and got going. There was no time for debate right now.

Gard headed for the ship. Five minutes later he came out in the clearing.

38

"Hazel?" Newt cried in a kind of religious terror. "Hazel? Hazel?"

Yes, Hazel! Dick Allison shouted back at him furiously, and could restrain himself no longer. He threw himself upon Newt. *Stupid bastard!*

Whoreboy! Newt spat back, and the two of them rolled about on the ground, green eyes glaring, grabbing for each other's throats. This was not at all logical under the circumstances, but any resemblance between the Tommyknockers and the likes of Mr. Spock was purely coincidental.

Dick's hands found the wattled folds of Newt's throat and began to squeeze. His fingers punched through the flesh and green blood bubbled up over Dick's fingers. He began to raise Newt up and slam him back down. Newt's struggles lessened . . . lessened . . . lessened. Dick choked him until he was quite dead.

With that done, Dick discovered that he felt a little better.

39

Gard dismounted the Tomcat, staggered, lost his balance, fell down. At that same instant, a buzzing, snarling projectile blasted through the air where he had been a moment before. Gardener stared stupidly at the Electrolux vacuum cleaner which had nearly torn his head off.

It bulleted across the clearing like a torpedo, banked, and came back at him. There was something on one end that distorted the air into a silvery ripple—something like a propeller.

Gardener thought of that round, chewed hole in the bottom of the shed door and all the spittle in his mouth dried up.

Watch out for—

It dive-bombed him, the cutter attachment whining and buzzing like the motor of a kid's gas-powered fighter plane. The little wheels, which were supposed to make the weary housewife's work easier as she trundled her faithful vacuum cleaner along behind her from room to room, spun lazily in the air. The hole where one was supposed to clip various attachment hoses gaped like an open mouth.

Gardener made as if to dive to the right, then held position a moment longer—if he jumped too soon, the vacuum cleaner would jog with him and chew through his guts as easily as it had chewed through the shed door when Bobbi called it.

He waited, feinted left this time, then threw himself to the right at the last moment. He thudded painfully into the dirt. The bones in his shattered ankle ground together. Gardener screamed miserably.

The Electrolux crashed. The propeller ate dirt. Then it bounced, like a plane rising into the air again after touching down too hard on a runway. It whistled off toward the great canted dish of the ship and then banked around for another run at Gardener. Now the cable it had used to run the buttons was emerging from the hose-attachment hole. The cable whistled in the air—a dry, snakelike sound that Gardener could just hear under the rumble-roar of the fire. The cable whickered, and for a moment Gardener was reminded of a Wild West rodeo his mother had taken him to once (in that rootin, tootin trail-drive town of Portland, Maine). There had been a cowboy in a tall white hat who had done rope-tricks. In one of the tricks, he had floated a big lasso at ankle height, dancing in and out of its circle while playing "My Gal Sal" on a harmonica. The cable whirling out from the attachment hole looked like that rope.

Fucker'll cut your head off just as slick as shit through a goose, if you let it, Gard ole Gard.

The Electrolux whistled at him, shadow tracking beneath.

On his knees, Gardener held out the Sonic Space Blaster and fired. The vacuum cleaner sheared off as he aimed, but Gardener winged it just the same. A chunk of chrome above a rear wheel blew off. The cable drew a wavering line through the dirt.

get him

yes get him before

before he can hurt the ship

Closer. The voices were closer. He had to end this.

The vacuum cleaner skirted a tree and circled back. It tilted upward, climbed, then dropped in a kamikaze power dive, its chopping blade turning faster and faster.

Gardener steadied himself by thinking of Ted the Power Man.

You oughta take a look at this shit, Teddy-boy, he thought crazily. *You'd go ape for it! Better living through electricity!*

He pulled the trigger on the toy gun, saw the green pencil-beam splash off the vacuum cleaner's snout, and then shoved himself forward, digging with both feet, and never mind the shattered ankle. The Electrolux struck the ground beside the Tomcat and buried itself three feet deep in the dirt. Black smoke jetted from the protruding end in a tight, compact little cloud. It made a thick farting noise and died.

Gardener got to his feet, holding onto the Tomcat for support, the Sonic Space Blaster dangling from his right hand. The plastic barrel, he saw, was partially melted. It wasn't going to be any good much longer. The same was undoubtedly true of himself.

The vacuum cleaner was dead—dead and sticking out of the ground like a dud bomb. But there were plenty of other gadgets on their way, some flying, some trundling enthusiastically through the woods on makeshift wheels. He couldn't wait around.

What was it the old man had been thinking at the end? *The last thing* . . . and . . . *Deliverance.*

"Good word," Gardener said hoarsely. "Dee-liverance. Great word."

Also, he realized, the name of a novel. A novel by a poet. James Dickey. A novel about city men who had to get slugged, mugged, and buggered before discovering they were good ole boys after all. But there was a line in that book . . . one of the men looking at one of the others and telling him calmly, "Machines are gonna fail, Lewis."

Gardener certainly *hoped* so.

He hopped over to the lean-to, then pushed the button which started the sling's descent. He was going to have to go down the cable hand over hand. It was stupid, but that was Tommyknocker technology for you. The motor began to whine. The cable began to descend. Gardener hopped over to the cut and stared down. If he could actually work his way down there, he would be safe.

Safe among the Tommyknocker dead.

The motor stopped. He could faintly see the useless sling at the bottom. The voices were closer, the fire was closer, and he sensed a rogue's gallery of gadgets closing in. Didn't matter. He had shot the chutes, climbed the ladders, and somehow got to the finish line before the others.

Congratulations, Mr. Gardener! You've won a flying saucer! Do you want to quit or go for the all-expenses-paid vacation in deep space?

"Fuck," Gardener croaked, tossing the half-melted toy gun aside. "Let's do it."

That also had reverberations.

He seized the cable and swung out over the cut. As he did, it came to him. Sure. Gary Gilmore. It was what Gary Gilmore said just before stepping in front of the firing squad in Utah.

40

He was halfway down when he realized the last of his physical strength had run out. If he didn't do something quick, he would fall.

He began to descend more quickly, cursing their thoughtless decision to put the motor controls so far from the trench. Hot, stinging sweat ran into his eyes. His muscles jumped and fluttered. His stomach was beginning to do long, lazy flips again. His hands slipped . . . held . . . slipped again. Then, suddenly, the cable was running through his hands like hot butter. He squeezed it, screaming in pain as the friction built. A steel thread which had popped up from one of the cable's steel pigtails punched through his palm.

"God!" Gardener screamed. *"Oh dear God!"*

He thudded neatly into the sling on his bad foot. Pain roared up his leg, through his stomach, through his neck. It seemed to rip off the top of his head. His knee buckled and struck the side of the ship. The kneecap popped like a bottlecap.

Gardener felt himself graying out and fought it. He saw the hatch. It was still open. The air-exchangers still droning.

His left leg was a frozen wall of pain. He looked down at it and saw it had become magically shorter than his right leg. And it looked . . . well, it looked *croggled,* like an old stogie that has been carried around too long in someone's pocket.

"Christ, I'm falling apart," he whispered, and then, amazing himself, he laughed. It *did* have this to recommend it: it was a *hell* of a lot more interesting than just stepping off a breakwater with a hangover would have been.

There was a high, sweet buzzing sound from overhead.

Something else had arrived. Gardener didn't wait to see what it was. Instead, he pushed himself into the hatch and began to crawl up the round corridor. The light from the walls glowed softly on the planes of his haggard face, and that light—white, not green—was kind. Someone seeing Gardener in that light might almost have believed he was not dying. Almost.

41

Late last night and the night before,
(over the river and through the woods)
Tommyknockers, Tommyknockers, knocking at the door.
(to grandmother's house we go)
They look so quiet, but they ain't quite dead,
(the horse knows the way to carry the sleigh)
You get that Tommyknocker flu inside your head!
(over the frozen fields of snow)

Doggerel chiming in his head, Gardener crawled up the corridor, pausing once to turn his head and vomit. The air in here was still pretty fucking rank. He thought a miner's canary would already be lying at the bottom of its cage, alive but only by an inch or so.

But the machinery, Gard . . . do you hear it? Do you hear how much louder *it's gotten just since you came in?*

Yes. Louder, more confident. Nor was it just the air-exchangers. Deeper in the ship, other machinery was humming into life. The lights were brightening. The ship was feeding off whatever was left of him. Let it.

He reached the first interior hatchway. He looked back. Frowned at the hatch giving on the trench. They would be arriving in the clearing very soon now; perhaps already had. They might try to follow him in. Judging by the awed reactions of his "helpers" (even hardheaded Freeman Moss hadn't been completely immune), he didn't think they would . . . but it wouldn't do to forget how desperate they were. He wanted to be sure the loonies were out of his life once and for all. God knew he hadn't much left; he didn't need those assholes fucking up what little there was.

Fresh pain blossomed in his head, making his eyes water, tugging at his brain like a fishhook. Bad, but nothing compared to the pain in his ankle and leg. He was not surprised to see the main hatchway had irised closed. Could he open it again, if he wanted to? He somehow doubted it. He was locked in now . . . locked in with the dead Tommyknockers.

Dead? Are you sure they're dead?

No; to the contrary. He was sure they were *not.* They had been lively enough to start it all up again. Lively enough to turn Haven into one weird munitions factory. Dead?

"Un-fucking-*likely,*" Gardener croaked, and pulled himself through another hatchway and into the corridor beyond. Machinery pounded and hummed in the guts of the ship; when he touched the glowing curved wall, he could feel the vibration.

Dead? Oh, no. You're crawling around inside the oldest haunted house in the universe, Gard ole Gard.

He thought he heard a noise and turned around quickly, heart speeding up, saliva glands squirting bitter juice into his mouth. Nothing there, of course. Except there *was. I had a perfectly good reason to raise this fuss; I met the Tommyknockers, and they were us.*

"Help me, God," Gardener said. He flicked his stinking hair out of his eyes. Over him was the spidery-thin ladder with its wide-spaced rungs . . . each with that deep, disquieting dip in the middle. That ladder would rotate to the vertical when . . . if . . . the ship ever heeled over to its proper horizontal flight position.

There's a smell in here now. Air exchangers or not, a smell, it's the smell of death, I think. Long death. And insanity.

"Please help me, God, just a little help, okay? Just a few breaks for the kid is all I'm asking for, 'kay?"

Still conversing with God, Gardener pressed onward. Shortly he reached the control room and lowered himself into it.

42

The Tommyknockers stood at the edge of the clearing, looking at Dick. More arrived each minute. They arrived—then just stopped, like simple computer devices whose few programmed operations had all been performed.

They stood looking from the canted plane of the ship . . . to Dick . . . back to the ship . . . to Dick again. They were like a crowd of sleepwalkers at a tennis match. Dick could sense the others, who had gone back to the village to run the border defenses, also simply waiting . . . looking through the eyes of those who were actually here.

Behind them, growing closer, gaining strength, came the fire. Already the clearing had begun to fill with tendrils of smoke. A few people coughed . . . but no one moved.

Dick looked back at them, puzzled—what, exactly, did they want from him? Then he understood. He was the last of the Shed People. The rest of them were gone, and directly or indirectly, the death of each had been Gardener's fault. It was really inexplicable, and more than a little frightening. Dick became more and more convinced that nothing quite like this had happened in all of the Tommyknockers' long, long experience.

They're looking at me because I'm the last, I'm supposed to tell them what to do next.

But there was nothing they *could* do. There had been a race, and Gardener should have lost, but somehow he hadn't, and now there was nothing to do but wait. Watch and wait and hope that the ship would kill him somehow before he could do anything. Before—

A large hand suddenly reached into Dick Allison's head and squeezed the meat of his brain. His hands flew up to his temples, the fingers splayed into stiff, galvanic spider shapes. He tried to scream but was unable. Below him, in the clearing, he was vaguely aware that people were falling to their knees in ranks, like pilgrims witnessing a miracle or a divine visitation.

The ship had begun to vibrate—the sound filled the air with a thick, subaural hum.

Dick was aware of this . . . and then, as his eyes blew out of his head like half-congealed chunks of moldy jelly, he knew no more. Then, or ever.

43

Little help, God, we got a deal?

He sat in the middle of the canted hexagonal room, his twisted, broken leg stuck out in front of him *(croggled,* that word wouldn't go away, his leg had been *croggled),* near where the thick master cable came out of the gasket in the floor.

Little help for the kid. I know I'm not much, shot my wife, good fucking deal, shot my best friend, another *good fucking deal, a New and Improved Good Fucking Deal, you might say, but please, God, I need an assist right now.*

That was no exaggeration, either. He needed more than just a *little.* The thick cable split off into eight thinner ones, each ending not in an earplug but in a set of headphones. If he had been playing Russian roulette back in Bobbi's shed, this was like sticking his head into a cannon and asking someone to pull the lanyard.

But it had to be done.

He picked up one set of phones, noticing again how the centers bulged inward, and then looked toward the tangle of brown, sere bodies in the far corner of the room.

Tommyknockers? Hey-nonny-nonny nonsense name or not, it was still too good for them. Cavemen from space, that was all they had been. Long claws operating machinery they made but didn't even try to understand. Toes like the spurs on fighting cocks. This thing was a malignant tumor that needed quick removal.

Please, God, let my little idea be right.

Could he tap *all of them?* That was really the $64,000 question, wasn't it? If the "becoming" was a closed system—something on the skin of the ship simply bio-degrading into the atmosphere—the answer was probably no. But Gardener had come to think—or perhaps only to hope—that it was more, that it was an open system where the ship fed the humans, causing them to "become," and the humans fed the ship so it could . . . what? Come again, of course. Could one use the word "resurrection"? Sorry, no. Too noble. If he was right, this was a kind of freak-show parthenogenesis whose proper place was under tawdry carnival lights and in cheap tabloids, not in undying myths or religious creeds. An open system . . . a slave system . . . quite literally a go-fuck-yourself system.

Please, God. Little help right now.

Gardener donned the headphones.

It happened instantaneously. No sensation of pain this time, only a great white radiance. The lights in the control room flashed up to full bright. One of the walls turned into a window again, showing the smoky sky and the fringe of trees. And then another of the room's eight walls went transparent . . . another . . . another. In a space of seconds Gard seemed to be sitting in an open space with the sky above him and the trench with its silvery netting on either side. The ship seemed to have disappeared. He had a 360-degree view.

Motors kicked in one by one and cycled up to full running pitch.

A bell was ringing somewhere. Huge thudding relays kicked over one by one, making the metal deck shiver under him.

The feeling of power was incredible; he felt as though the Mississippi was running through his head at flood level. He sensed it was killing him, but that was okay.

I've tapped them all, Gardener thought faintly. *Oh God, thank you God I've tapped them all! It worked!*

The ship began to tremble. To vibrate. The vibration became spasms of racking shudders. The time had come.

Baring the last few of his teeth, Gardener prepared to reach down and grasp his own bootstraps.

44

He had tapped all of them, but it was Dick Allison, because of his greater evolution, and Hazel's forty or so border-watchers back in town who bore the brunt of the ship's powering-up process—these latter were all tied together neatly in one unified web, and the ship simply reached out for it.

They slumped over, blood trickling from their eyes and noses, and died as the ship sucked their brains up.

The ship drew from the Tommyknockers in the woods as well, and several of the older ones died; most, however, felt only an excruciating pain in their heads as they either knelt or lay, half-fainting, around the perimeter of the clearing. A few understood that the fire was very close now. As the wind freshened, that burning lady's fan spread . . . and spread. Smoke ran across the clearing in thick grayish-white clouds. The fire crackled and thundered.

45

Now, Gardener thought.

He felt something in his mind slip, catch, slip . . . and catch firmly. It was like a gearshift. There was pain, but it was bearable.

THEY'RE *feeling most of the pain,* he thought faintly.

The sides of the trench appeared to move. At first just a little. Then a little more. There was a grinding, squealing sound.

Gardener bore down, his brow locked in a tremendous frown, his eyes squeezed into slits.

The silvery mesh began to slip past, slowly but steadily. Not that it was moving at all, of course; it was the *ship* that was moving; that grinding noise was the sound of it pulling itself free of the bedrock which had held it so long.

Going up, he thought incoherently. *Ladies' lingerie, hosiery, notions, and be sure to visit our pet department—*

It was gaining speed, the trench walls passing more quickly to either side. The sky widened out ahead—it was a dull gunmetal color. Sparks twisted by like formations of tiny burning birds.

He brimmed with exaltation.

Gardener thought of looking out of a subway window as the train left the station, slowly at first, then beginning to speed up—how the tile walls seemed to unroll backward like the strip of paper in a player piano, how you could read the ads as they passed from left to right—*Annie, A Chorus Line, These Times Demand the* Times, *Touch the Velvet.* Then into the darkness where there was only movement and a vague sensation of black walls rushing past.

A Klaxon went off three times, nearly deafening him, making him shriek; fresh blood spattered into his lap.

The ship shuddered and rumbled and squealed and dragged itself out of the earth's crypt; it rose into thickening bands of smoke and hazy sunlight, its polished flank coming out of the trench, out and out and up and up, a moving metal wall. One standing right next to this insane sight might have been tempted to believe that the earth was creating a stainless-steel mountain or injecting a titanium wall into the air.

As the arc of the edge grew broader and broader, it reached the edges of the trench Bobbi and Gardener had dug steadily wider—ripping at the earth with their smart-stupid tools like half-wits trying to perform a cesarean section.

Up and out and out and up. Rocks squealed. The earth moaned. Dust and the smoke of friction fumed from the trench. Up close the illusion of an emerging mountain or wall held, but even from such a short distance away as the edge of the clearing, the thing's circular shape was revealed—the titanic shape of the saucer, now emerging from the earth like a great engine. *It* was silent, but the clearing was filled with the coarse thunder of breaking rock. Up and out it came, cutting the trench wider and wider, its shadow gradually covering the whole clearing and burning woods.

Its leading edge—the one Bobbi had stumbled over—sheared off the top of the tallest spruce in the forest and sent it tumbling and crashing to the ground. And still the ship birthed itself from the womb which had held it so long; continued until it covered the whole sky and was reborn.

Then it stopped cutting the trench wider; a moment later there was actually a gap between the edges of the trench and the edge of the emerging ship. Its center had at last been reached and passed.

The ship rumbled out of the smoky trench, emerging into the smoky sunshine, and at last the squealing, rumbling sounds ceased, and there was daylight between the ground and the ship.

It was out.

It rose on a slanted, canted angle and then came to the horizontal, crushing trees with its unknown, unknowable weight, bursting their trunks open. Sap sprayed the air with thin amber veils.

It moved with slow, ponderous elegance through the

burning day, cutting a swath along the tops of the trees like a clipper trimming a hedge. Then it hovered, as if waiting for something.

46

Now the floor below Gardener was also transparent; he seemed to be sitting in thin air, looking down at the billowing reefs of smoke coming from the edge of the woods and filling the air.

The ship was fully alive now—but he was fading fast.

His hands crept up to the earphones.

Scotty, he thought, *gimme warp-speed. We're blowing this disco.*

He bore down hard inside his mind, and this time the pain was thick and fibrous and sickening.

Meltdown, he thought dimly, *this is what meltdown feels like.*

There was a sensation of tremendous speed. A hand knocked him sprawling to the deck, although there was no sensation of multi-g force; the Tommyknockers had apparently found a way to beat that.

The ship didn't tilt; it simply rose straight up into the air.

Instead of blotting out the whole sky, it blotted out only three-quarters, then half. It grew indistinct in the smoke, its hard-edged metal-alloy reality growing fuzzy, and thus dreamy.

Then it was gone in the smoke, leaving only the dazed, drained Tommyknockers to try to find their feet before the fire could overtake them. It left the Tommyknockers, and the clearing, the lean-to . . . and the trench, like a black socket from which some poisonous fang had been drawn.

47

Gard lay on the floor of the control room, staring up. As he watched, the smoky, chromed look of the sky disappeared. It became blue again—the brightest, clearest blue he had ever seen.

Gorgeous, he tried to say, but no word came out—not even a croak. He swallowed blood and coughed, his eyes never leaving that brilliant sky.

Its blue deepened to indigo . . . then to purple.

Please don't let it stop now, please—

Purple to black.

And now in that blackness he saw the first hard chips of stars.

The Klaxon blared again. He felt fresh pain as the ship drew from him, and there was a sensation of increasing speed as it slipped into a higher gear.

Where are we going? Gardener thought incoherently, and then the blackness overtook him as the ship fled up and out, escaping the envelope of the earth's atmosphere as easily as it had escaped the ground which had held it for so long. *Where are we—?*

Up and up, out and out—the ship rose, and Jim Gardener, born in Portland, Maine, went with it.

He drifted down through black levels of unconsciousness, and shortly before the final vomiting began—a vomiting of which he was never even aware—he had a dream. A dream so real that he smiled as he lay in the middle of blackness, surrounded by space and with the earth below him like a giant blue-gray croaker marble.

He had gotten through it—somehow gotten through it. Patricia McCardle had tried to break him, but she had never quite been able to do it. Now he was back in Haven, and there was Bobbi coming down the porch steps and across the dooryard to meet him, and Peter was barking and wagging his tail, and Gard grabbed Bobbi and hugged her, because it was good to be with your friends, good to be where you belonged . . . good to have some safe haven to come to.

Lying on the transparent floor of the control room, already better than seventy thousand miles out in space, Jim Gardener lay in a widening pool of his own blood . . . and smiled.

Epilogue

Curl up, baby! Curl up tight!
Curl up, baby! Keep it all outta sight!
Undercover
Keep it all outta sight,
Under cover of the night.

—THE ROLLING STONES,
"Undercover"

O every night and every day
A little piece of you is falling away . . .
Toe your line and play their game
Let the anaesthetic cover it all
Till one day they call your name:
You're only waiting for the hammer to fall.

—QUEEN,
"Hammer to Fall"

1

Most of them died in the fire.

Not all; a hundred or more never reached the clearing at all before the ship pulled itself out of the ground and disappeared into the sky. Some, like Elt Barker, who had gone flying off his motorcycle, did not reach it because they had been wounded or killed on the way . . . fortunes of war. Others, like Ashley Ruvall and old Miss Timms, who was the town librarian on Tuesdays and Thursdays, were simply too late or too slow.

Nor were all of those who did reach the clearing killed. The ship had gone into the sky and the awful, draining power which had seized them dwindled away to nothing before the fire reached the clearing (although by then sparks were drifting down and many of the smaller trees at the eastern edge were blazing). Some of them managed to stumble and limp further into the woods ahead of that spreading fiery fan. Of course, going straight west was no good to these few (Rosalie Skehan was among them, as were Frank Spruce and Rudy Barfield, brother of the late and mostly unlamented Pits), because eventually they would run out of breathable air, in spite of the prevailing winds. So it was necessary to first go west, and then turn either south or north in an effort to buttonhook around the fire-front . . . a desperation play where the penalty for failure was not losing the ball but being roasted to cinders in Big Injun Woods. A few—not all, but a few—actually did make it.

Most, however, died in the clearing where Bobbi Anderson and Jim Gardener had worked so long and hard—died within feet of that empty socket where something had been buried and then pulled.

They had been used roughly by a power which was much greater than the early, tentative state of their "becoming" could cope with. The ship had reached out to the net of their minds, seized it, and used it to obey the Controller's weak but unmistakable command, which had been expressed as WARP SPEED to the ship's organic-cybernetic circuits. The words WARP SPEED were not in the ship's vocabulary, but the concept was clear.

The living lay on the ground, most unconscious, some deeply dazed. A few sat up, holding their heads and moaning, oblivious of the sparks drifting down around them. Some, mindful of the danger coming from the east, tried to get up and fell back.

One of those who did not fall back was Chip McCausland, who lived on Dugout Road with his common-law wife and about ten kids; two months and a million years ago, Bobbi Anderson had gone to Chip for more egg cartons to hold her expanding collection of batteries. Chip shambled halfway across the clearing like an old drunk and fell into the empty trench. He tumbled, shrieking, all the way to the bottom, where he died of a broken neck and a shattered skull.

Others who understood the danger of the fire and who could possibly have gotten away elected not to do so. The "becoming" was at an end. It had ended with the departure of the ship. The purpose of their lives had been canceled. So they only sat and waited for the fire to take care of what remained of them.

2

By nightfall, there were less than two hundred people left alive in Haven. Most of the township's heavily wooded western half had burned or was burning flat. The wind grew stronger yet. The air began to change, and the remaining Tommyknockers, gasping and whey-faced, gathered in Hazel McCready's yard. Phil Golden and Bryant Brown got the big air-exchanger going. The survivors gathered around it as homesteaders might once have gathered around a stove on a bitter night. Their tortured breathing gradually eased.

Bryant looked over at Phil.

Weather for tomorrow?

Clear skies, diminishing winds.

Marie was standing nearby, and Bryant saw her relax.

Good that's good.

And so it was . . . for the time being. But the winds were not going to remain calm for the rest of their lives. And with the ship gone, there was only this gadget and twenty-four truck batteries between them and eventual strangulation.

How long? Bryant asked, and no one answered. There was only the flat shine of their frightened, inhuman eyes in the fireshot night.

3

The following morning there were twenty less. During the night John Leandro's story had broken worldwide, with all the force of a hammerfall. State and Defense departments denied everything, but dozens of people had taken photographs as the ship rose. These photographs were persuasive . . . and no one could stop the flood of leaks from such "informed sources" as frightened residents of the surrounding towns and the first arriving National Guardsmen.

The Haven border-barriers held, at least for the time being. The fire-front had advanced into Newport, where the flames were finally being brought under control.

Several Tommyknockers blew their brains out in the night.

Poley Andrews swallowed Dran-O.

Phil Golden awoke to discover that Queenie, his wife of twenty years, had jumped into Hazel McCready's dry well.

That day there were only four suicides, but the nights . . . the nights were worse.

By the time the Army finally broke into Haven, like

inept burglars into a strong safe, later that week, there were less than eighty Tommyknockers left.

Justin Hurd shot a fat Army sergeant with a kid's Daisy air rifle that squirted green fire. The fat sergeant exploded. A scared E-4 in the APC just then roaring past Cooder's market turned the .50-caliber he was sitting behind on Justin Hurd, who was standing in front of the hardware store, wearing only a yellowing pair of Hanes underpants and his orange work-shoes.

"Fixed them woodchucks!" Justin was screaming. *"Fixed them all, you're fucking-A, you're—*

Then he was hit by some twenty .50-caliber slugs. Justin nearly exploded, too.

The E-4 puked into his gas mask and nearly choked on the stuff before someone could get a fresh one over his face.

"Someone get that popgun!" a major shouted through an electric bullhorn. His mask muffled his words but did not destroy them. "Get it, but be careful! Pick it up by the barrel! I repeat, be extremely careful! Don't point it at anyone!"

Pointing it at someone, Gard would have said, always comes later.

4

More than a dozen were shot down on the first day of the invasion by scared, trigger-happy soldiers, kids, most of them, who pursued the Tommyknockers from house to house. After a while, some of the invaders' fear began to rub off. By afternoon they were actually having fun—they were like men driving rabbits through wheat. Two dozen more were killed before the Army doctors and Pentagon brain-trusters realized that the air outside of Haven was lethal to these freak-show mutations who had once been American tax payers. The fact that the invaders could not breathe the air *inside* Haven would have seemed to have made the converse self-evident, but in all the excitement, no one was really thinking very well (Gard wouldn't have found this very surprising).

Now there were only forty or so. Most were insane; those who weren't wouldn't talk. A makeshift stockade was built in the area which passed for a town square in Haven Village—just below and to the right of the towerless town hall. They were kept there for another week, and during that period another fourteen died.

The changed air was analyzed; the machine which manufactured it was carefully studied; the failing batteries were replaced. As Bobbi had suggested, it didn't take the braintrusters long to understand the mechanics of the device, and the underlying principles were already being studied at MIT, Cal Tech, Bell Labs, and the Shop in Virginia by scientists who were nearly vomiting with excitement.

The remaining twenty-six Tommyknockers, looking like the weary, pox-raddled remnants of the final Apache tribe in existence, were flown in the controlled-environment cargo-bay of a C-140 Starlifter to a government installation in Virginia. This installation, which had once been burned to the ground by a child, was the Shop. There they were studied . . . and there they died, one by one by one.

The last survivor was Alice Kimball, the schoolteacher who was a lesbian (a fact 'Becka Paulson had learned from Jesus one hot day in July). She died on October 31st . . . Halloween.

5

At about the same time Queenie Golden was standing on the edge of Hazel's dry well and preparing to jump in, a nurse stepped into Hilly Brown's room to check on the boy, who had shown some faint signs of returning consciousness over the last couple of days.

She looked at the bed, and frowned. She couldn't be seeing what she was seeing—it was an illusion of some kind, a double shadow thrown onto the wall by the light from the corridor—

She flipped the wall switch and took a step closer. Her mouth dropped open. It hadn't been an illusion. There were two shadows on the wall because there were two boys in the bed. They slept with their arms wrapped around each other.

"What—?"

She took another step, her hand going unconsciously to the crucifix she wore around her neck.

One of them, of course, was Hilly Brown, his face thin and wasted, his arms seemingly no thicker than sticks, his skin nearly as white as his hospital johnny.

She didn't know the other boy, who was very young. He was wearing blue shorts and a T-shirt which read THEY CALL ME DR. LOVE. His feet were black with dirt . . . and something about that dirt seemed unnatural to her.

"What—?" she whispered again, and the younger boy stirred and wrapped his arms more tightly around Hilly's neck. His cheek rested against Hilly's shoulder, and she saw with something like terror that the boys looked very much alike.

She decided she had to tell Dr. Greenleaf about this. Right now. She turned to leave, heart beating fast, one hand still clutching at her crucifix . . . and saw something that was quite impossible.

"What—?" she whispered for the third and last time. Her eyes were very wide.

More of that strange black dirt. On the floor. Tracks on the floor. Leading to the bed. The little boy had crossed to the bed and gotten in. The two boys' facial resemblance suggested that this was Hilly's missing—and long since presumed dead—brother.

The tracks didn't come from the hall. They started in the middle of the floor.

As if the little boy had come from nowhere.

The nurse bolted from the room, screaming for Dr. Greenleaf.

6

Hilly Brown opened his eyes.

"David?"

"Shut up, Hilly, I'm sleepun."

Hilly smiled, not sure where he was, not sure *when* he was, sure only that many things had been wrong—just what those things had been no longer mattered, because everything was okay now. David was here, warm and solid against him.

"Me too," Hilly said. "We got to trade G.I. Joes tomorrow."

"Why?"

"I dunno. But we got to. I promised."

"When?"

"I dunno."

"As long as I get Crystal Ball," David said, settling himself more firmly into the crook of Hilly's arm.

"Well . . . okay."

Silence . . . there was a dim commotion at the nurses' station down the hall, but here there was silence, and the sweet warmth of boys.

"Hilly?"

"What?" Hilly muttered.

"It was cold where I was."

"Was it?"

"Yes."

"Better now?"

"Better. I love you, Hilly."

"I love you too, David. I'm sorry."

"For what?"

"I dunno."

"Oh."

David's hand groped for the blanket, found it, and pulled it up. Ninety-three million miles from the sun and a hundred parsecs from the axis-pole of the galaxy, Hilly and David Brown slept in each other's arms.

August 19th, 1982
May 19th, 1987